P9-CAM-759

A
CHRISTINE
FEEHAN
*Holiday
Treasury*

A
CHRISTINE
FEEHAN
Holiday
Treasury

POCKET BOOKS
New York   London   Toronto   Sydney

POCKET BOOKS, a division of Simon & Schuster, Inc.
1230 Avenue of the Americas, New York, NY 10020

This book is a work of fiction. Names, characters, places and
incidents are products of the author's imagination or are used
fictitiously. Any resemblance to actual events or locales or persons,
living or dead, is entirely coincidental.

After the Music copyright © 2001 by Christine Feehan
The Twilight Before Christmas copyright © 2003 by Christine Feehan
Rocky Mountain Miracle copyright © 2004 by Christine Feehan

After the Music was originally published by Pocket Books in *A Very Gothic Christmas*.
The Twilight Before Christmas was originally published individually by Pocket Books.
Rocky Mountain Miracle was originally published by Pocket Star Books in *The Shadows
of Christmas Past.*

All rights reserved, including the right to reproduce
this book or portions thereof in any form whatsoever.
For information address Pocket Books, 1230 Avenue of the
Americas, New York, NY 10020

ISBN-13: 978-1-4165-3760-1
ISBN-10:   1-4165-3760-0

First Pocket Books hardcover edtion November 2006

10 9 8 7 6 5 4

POCKET and colophon are registered trademarks of
Simon & Schuster, Inc.

Manufactured in the United States of America

For information regarding special discounts for bulk purchases,
please contact Simon & Schuster Special Sales at 1-800-456-6798
or business@simonandschuster.com.

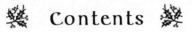

Contents

AFTER THE MUSIC

❧ Dedication ❧

For Manda and Christina, may you always be survivors.
Much love.

1

JESSICA FITZPATRICK WOKE UP screaming, her heart pounding out a rhythm of terror. Fear was a living, breathing entity in the darkness of her room. The weight of it crushed her, held her helpless; she was unable to move. She could taste it in her mouth, and feel it coursing through her bloodstream. Around her, the air seemed so thick that her lungs burned for oxygen. She knew something monstrous was stirring deep in the bowels of the earth. For a moment she lay frozen, her ears straining to hear the murmur of voices rising and falling, chanting words in an ancient tongue that should never be spoken. Red, glowing eyes searched through the darkness, summoning her, beckoning her closer. She felt the power of those eyes as they neared, focused on her, and came ever closer. Her own eyes flew open; the need to flee was paramount in her mind.

The entire room lurched, flinging her from the narrow bunk to the floor. At once the cold air brought her out of her nightmare and into the realization that they were not safe in their beds at home, but in the cabin of a wildly pitching boat in the middle of a ferocious storm. The craft, tossed from wave to powerful wave, was taking a pounding.

Jessica scrambled to her feet, gripping the edge of the bunk as she dragged herself toward the two children, Tara and Trevor Wentworth, who clung together, their faces pale and frightened. Tara screamed, her terrified gaze locked on Jessica.

Jessica managed to make it halfway to the twins before the next wild bucking sent her to the floor again.

"Trevor, get your life jacket back on this minute!" She reached them by crawling on her hands and knees, and then curled a supporting arm around each of them. "Don't be afraid, we'll be fine."

The boat rose on a wave, teetered and slid fast, tossing the three of them in all directions. Salt water poured in a torrent onto the deck and raced down the steps into the cabin, covering the floor with an inch of ice-cold water. Tara screamed, and clutched at her brother's arm, desperately trying to help him buckle his life jacket. "It's him. He's doing this, he's trying to kill us."

Jessica gasped, horrified. "Tara! Nobody controls the weather. It's a storm. Plain and simple, just a storm. Captain Long will get us safely to the island."

"He's hideous. A monster. And I don't want to go." Tara covered her face with her hands and sobbed. "I want to go home. Please take me home, Jessie."

Jessica tested Trevor's life jacket to make certain he was safe. "Don't talk that way, Tara. Trev, stay here with Tara while I go see what I can do to help." She had to shout to make herself heard in the howling wind and booming sea.

Tara flung herself into Jessica's arms. "Don't leave me—we'll die. I just know it—we're all going to die just like Mama Rita did."

Trevor wrapped his arms around his twin sister. "No, we're not, sis, don't cry. Captain Long has been in terrible storms before, lots of them," he assured. He looked up at Jessica with his piercing blue eyes. "Right, Jessie?"

"You're exactly right, Trevor," she agreed. Jessica had a firm hold on the banister and began to make her way up the stairs to the deck.

Rain fell in sheets; black clouds churned and boiled in the sky. The wind rose to an eerie shriek. Jessica held her breath, watched as Long struggled to navigate the boat through the heavier waves, taking them ever closer to the island. It seemed the age-old struggle between man and nature. Slowly, through the sheets of rain, the solid mass of the island began to take shape. Salt water sprayed and foamed off the rocks but the sea was calmer as they approached the shore. She knew it was only the captain's knowledge of the region and his expertise that allowed him to guide the craft to the dock in the terrible storm.

The rain was pouring from the sky. The clouds were so black and heavy overhead that the night seemed unrelentingly dark. Yet Jessica caught glimpses of the moon, an eerie sight with the swirling black of the clouds veiling its light.

"Let's go, Jessie," Captain Long yelled. "Bring up the kids and your luggage. I want you off this boat now." The words were nearly lost in the ferocity of the storm, but his frantic beckoning was plain.

She hurried, tossing Trevor most of the packs while she helped Tara up the stairs and across the slippery deck. Captain Long lifted Tara to the dock before aiding Trevor to shore. He caught Jessica's arm in a tight grip and pulled her close so he could be heard. "I don't like this—Jess, I hope he's expecting you. Once I leave you, you're stuck. You know he isn't the most pleasant man."

"Don't worry." She patted his arm, her stomach churning. "I'll call if we need you. Are you certain you don't want to stay overnight?"

"I'll feel safer out there," he gestured toward the water.

Jessica waved him off and turned to look up at the island while she waited to get her land legs back. It had been seven years since she'd last been to the island. Her memories of it were the things of nightmares. Looking up toward the ridge, she half expected to see a fiery inferno, with red and orange flames towering to the skies, but there was only the black night and the rain. The house that once had sat at the top of the cliff overlooking the ocean was long gone, reduced to a pile of ashes.

In the dark, the vegetation was daunting, a foreboding sight. The weak rays of light from the cloud-covered moon were mottled as they fell across the ground, creating a strange, unnatural pattern. The island was wild with heavy timber and thick with brush; the wind set the trees and bushes dancing in a macabre fashion. Naked branches bowed and scraped together with a grating sound. Heavy evergreens whirled madly, sending sharp needles flying through the air.

Resolutely, Jessica took a deep breath and picked up her pack, handing Trevor a flashlight to lead the way. "Come on, kids, let's go see your father."

The rain slashed down at them, drenching them, drops piercing like sharp icicles right through their clothes to their skin. Heads down, they began to trudge their way up the steep stone steps leading away from the sea toward the interior of the island where Dillon Wentworth hid from the world.

Returning to the island brought back a flood of memories of the good times—her mother, Rita Fitzpatrick, landing the job as housekeeper and nanny to the famous Dillon Wentworth. Jessica had been so thrilled. She had been nearly thirteen, already old enough to appreciate the rising star, a musician who would take his place among the greatest recording legends. Dillon spent a great deal of his time on the road, touring, or in the studio, recording, but when he was home, he was usually with his children or hanging out in the kitchen with Rita and Jessica. She had known Dillon in the good times, during five years of incredible magic.

"Jessie?" Trevor's young voice interrupted her reflection. "Does he know we're coming?"

Jessica met the boy's steady gaze. At thirteen, Trevor had to be well aware that if they had been expected, they wouldn't be walking by themselves in the dead of night in the middle of a storm. Someone would have met them by car on the road at the boathouse.

"He's your father, Trevor, and it's coming up on Christmas. He spends far too much time alone." Jessica slicked back her rain-wet hair and squared her shoulders. "It isn't good for him." And Dillon Wentworth had a responsibility to his children. He needed to look after them, to protect them.

The twins didn't remember their father the way she did. He had been so alive. So handsome. So everything. His life had been magical. His good looks, his talent, his ready laugh and famous blue eyes. Everyone had wanted him. Dillon had lived his life in the spotlight, a white-hot glare of tabloids and television. Of stadiums and clubs. The energy, the power of Dillon Wentworth were astonishing, indescribable, when he was performing. He burned hot and bright on stage, a man with a poet's heart and a devil's talent when he played his guitar and sang with his edgy, smoky voice.

But at home . . . Jessica also remembered Vivian Wentworth with her brittle laugh and red, talon-tipped fingers. The glaze in her eyes when she was cloudy with drugs, when she was staggering under the effects of alcohol, when she flew into a rage and smashed glass and ripped pictures out of frames. The slow, terrible descent into the madness of drugs and the occult. Jessica would never forget Vivian's friends who visited when Dillon wasn't there. The candles, the orgies, the chanting, always the chanting. And men. Lots of men in the Wentworth bed.

Without warning, Tara screamed, turning to fling herself at Jessica, nearly knocking her off the stairs. Jessica caught her firmly, wrapping her arms around the girl and holding her close. They were both so cold they were shivering uncontrollably. "What is it, honey?" Jessica whispered into the child's ear, soothing her, rocking her, there on the steep stairs with the wind slashing them to ribbons.

"I saw something, eyes glowing, staring at us. They were red eyes, Jess. Red, like a monster . . . or a devil." The girl shuddered and gripped Jessica harder.

"Where, Tara?" Jessica sounded calm even though her stomach was knotted with tension. Red eyes. She had seen those eyes.

"There." Tara pointed without looking, keeping her face hidden against Jessica. "Through the trees, something was staring at us."

"There are animals on the island, honey," Jessica soothed, but she was straining to see into the darkness. Trevor valiantly tried to shine the small circle of light toward the spot his twin had indicated, but the light couldn't penetrate the pouring rain.

"It wasn't a dog, it wasn't, Jessie, it was some kind of demon. Please take me home, I don't want to be here. I'm so afraid of him. He's so hideous."

Jessica took a deep breath and let it out slowly, hoping to stay calm when she suddenly wanted to turn and run herself. There were too many memories here, crowding in, reaching for her with greedy claws. "He was scarred terribly in a fire, Tara, you know that." It took effort to keep her voice steady.

"I know he hates us. He hates us so much he doesn't ever want to see us. And I don't want to see him. He *murdered* people." Tara flung the bitter accusation at Jessica. The howling wind caught the words and took them out over the island, spreading them like a disease.

Jessica tightened her grip on Tara, gave her a short, impatient shake. "I *never* want to hear you say such a terrible thing again, not *ever*, do you understand me? Do you know why your father went into the house that night? Tara, you're too intelligent to listen to gossip and anonymous phone callers."

"I saw the papers. It was in all the papers!" Tara wailed.

Jessica was furious. *Furious.* Why would someone suddenly, after seven years, send old newspapers and tabloids to the twins? Tara had innocently opened the package wrapped in a plain brown paper. The tabloids had been brutal, filled with accusations of drugs, jealousy, and the occult. The speculation that Dillon had caught his wife in bed with another man, that there had been an orgy of sex, drugs, devil worship, and murder, had been far too titillating for the scandal sheets not to play it up long before the actual facts could come out. Jessica had found Tara sobbing pitifully in her room. Whoever had seen fit to enlighten the twins about their father's past had called the house repeatedly whispering horrible things to Trevor and Tara, insisting their father had murdered several people including their mother.

"Your father went into a burning house to save you kids. He

thought you were both inside. Everyone who had gotten out tried to stop him, but he fought them, got away, and went into a burning inferno for you. That isn't hate, Tara. That's love. I remember that day, every detail." She pressed her fingers to her pounding temples. "I can't ever forget it no matter how much I try."

And she had tried. She had tried desperately to drown out the sounds of chanting. The vision of the black lights and candles. The scent of the incense. She remembered the shouting, the raised voices, the sound of the gun. And the flames. The terrible greedy flames. The blanket of smoke, so thick one couldn't see. And the smells never went away. Sometimes she still woke up to the smell of burning flesh.

Trevor put his arm around her. "Don't cry, Jessica. We're already here, we're all freezing, let's just go. Let's have Christmas with Dad, make a new beginning, try to get along with him this time."

Jessica smiled at him through the rain and the tears. Trevor. So much like his father and he didn't even realize it. "We're going to have a wonderful Christmas, Tara, you wait and see."

They continued up the stairs until the ground leveled out and Jessica found the familiar path winding through the thick timber to the estate. As islands went, in the surrounding sea between Washington and Canada, it was small and remote, no ferry even traveled to it. That was the way Dillon had preferred it, wanting privacy for his family on his own personal island. In the old days, there had been guards and dogs. Now there were shadows and haunting memories that tore at her soul.

In the old days the island had been alive with people, bustling with activities; now it was silent, only a caretaker lived somewhere on the island in one of the smaller houses. Jessica's mother had told her that Dillon tolerated only one older man on his island on a regular basis. Even in the wind and rain, Jessica couldn't help noticing the boathouse was ill-kept and the road leading around and up toward the house was overgrown, showing little use. Where there had always been several boats docked at the pier, none were in sight, although Dillon must still have had one in the boathouse.

The path led through the thick trees. The wind was whipping branches so that overhead the canopy of trees swayed precariously. The rain had a much more difficult time penetrating through the treetops to reach them, but drops hitting the pathway plopped loudly. Small animals rustled in the bushes as they passed.

"I don't think we're in Kansas anymore," Trevor quipped, with a shaky smile.

Jessica immediately hugged him to her. "Lions and tigers and bears, oh, my," she quoted just to watch the grin spread across his face.

"I can't believe he lives here." Tara sniffed.

"It's beautiful during the day," Jessica insisted, "give it a chance. It's such a wonderful place. The island's small, but it has everything."

They followed a bend, stumbling a little over the uneven ground. Trevor's flashlight cast a meager circle of light on the ground in front of them, which only served to make the forest darker and more frightening as it surrounded them. "Are you certain you know the way, Jess? You haven't been here in years," he said.

"I know this path with my eyes closed," Jessica assured him. Which wasn't exactly the truth. In the old days, the path had been well manicured and had veered off toward the cliff. This one was overgrown and led through the thick part of the forest toward the interior of the island, rising steadily uphill. "If you listen, you can hear the water rushing off to our left. The stream is large right now, but in the summer it isn't so strong or deep. There are ferns all along the bank." She wanted to keep talking, hoping it would keep fear at bay.

All three of them were breathing hard from the climb, and they paused to catch their breath under a particularly large tree that helped to shelter them from the driving rain. Trevor shined the light up the massive tree trunk and into the canopy, making light patterns to amuse Tara. As he whirled the light back down the trunk, the small circle illuminated the ground a few feet beyond where they were standing.

Jessica stiffened, jammed a fist in her mouth to keep from screaming, and yanked the flashlight from Trevor to shine it back to the spot he had accidentally lit up. For one terrible moment she could hardly breathe. She was certain she had seen someone staring at them. Someone in a heavily hooded long black cloak that swirled around the shadowy figure as if he were a vampire from one of the movies the twins were always watching. Whoever it was had been staring malevolently at them. He had been holding something in his hands that glinted in the flash of light.

Her hand was shaking badly but she managed to find the place where he had been with the flashlight's small circle of light. It was empty. There was nothing, no humans, no vampires in hooded cloaks. She continued to search through the trees, but there was nothing.

Trevor reached out and caught her wrist, pulling her hand gently to him, taking the flashlight. "What did you see, Jess?" He sounded very calm.

She looked at them then, ashamed of showing such naked fear, ashamed the island could reduce her to that terrified teenager she once had been. She had hoped for so much: to bring them all together, to find a way to bring Dillon back to the world. But instead she was hallucinating. That shadowy figure belonged in her nightmares, not in the middle of a terrible rainstorm.

The twins were staring up at her for direction. Jessica shook her head. "I don't know, a shadow maybe. Let's just get to the house." She pushed them ahead of her, trying to guard their backs, trying to see in front of them, on both sides.

With every step she took, she was more convinced she hadn't seen a shadow. She hadn't been hallucinating. She was certain something, *someone* had been watching them. "Hurry, Trevor, I'm cold," she urged.

As they topped the rise, the sight of the house took her breath away. It was huge, rambling, several stories high with round turrets and great chimneys. The original house had been completely destroyed in the fire and here, at the top of the rise, surrounded by timber, Dillon had built the house of his boyhood dreams. He had loved the Gothic architecture, the lines and carvings, the vaulted ceilings, and intricate passageways. She remembered him talking with such enthusiasm, spreading pictures on the counter in the kitchen for her and her mother to admire. Jessica had teased him unmercifully about being a frustrated architect and he had always laughed and replied he belonged in a castle or a palace, or that he was a Renaissance man. He would chase her around with an imaginary sword and talk of terrible traps in secret passageways.

Rita Fitzpatrick had cried over this house, telling Jessica how Dillon had clung to his dreams of music and how he had claimed that having the house built was symbolic of his rise from the ashes. But at some point during Dillon's months at the hospital, after he'd endured the pain and agony of such terrible burns and after he realized that his life would never return to normal, the house had become for him, and all who knew him, a symbol of the darkness that had crept into his soul. Looking at it, Jessica felt fear welling inside her, a foreboding that Dillon was a very changed man.

They stared at the great hulk, half expecting to see a ghost push open one of the shutters and warn them off. The house was dark with the exception of two windows on the third story facing them, giving the effect of two eyes staring back at them. Winged creatures seemed to be swarming up its sides. The mottled light from the moon lent the stone carvings a certain animation.

"I don't want to go in there," Tara said, backing away. "It looks . . ." she trailed off, slipping her hand into her brother's.

"Evil," Trevor supplied. "It does, Jess, like one of those haunted houses in the old movies. It looks like it's staring at us."

Jessica bit at her lower lip, glancing behind them, her gaze searching, wary. "You two have seen too many scary movies. No more for either of you." The house looked far worse than anything she had ever seen in a movie. It looked like a brooding hulk, waiting silently for unsuspecting prey. Gargoyles crouched in the eaves, staring with blank eyes at them. She shook her head to clear the image. "No more movies, you're making me see it that way." She forced a small, uneasy laugh. "Mass hallucination."

"We're a small mass, but it works for me." There was a trace of humor in Trevor's voice. "I'm freezing; we may as well go inside."

No one moved. They continued to stare up at the house in silence, at the strange animating effect of the wind and the moon on the carvings. Only the sound of the relentless rain filled the night. Jessica could feel her heart slamming hard in her chest. They couldn't go back. There was something in the woods. There was no boat to go back to, only the wind and piercing rain. But the house seemed to stare at them with that same malevolence as the figure in the woods.

Dillon had no inkling they were near. She thought it would be a relief to reach him, that she would feel safe, but instead, she was frightened of his anger. Frightened of what he would say in front of the twins. He wouldn't be pleased that she hadn't warned him of their arrival, but if she had called, he would have told her not to come. He always told her not to come. Although she tried to console herself with the fact that his last few letters had been more cheerful and more interested in the twins, she couldn't deceive herself into believing he would welcome them.

Trevor was the first to move, patting Jessica on the back in reassurance as he took a step around her toward the house. Tara followed him, and Jessica brought up the rear. At some point the area around the house had been landscaped, the bushes shaped, and beds of flowers planted, but it looked as though it hadn't been tended in quite a while. A large sculpture of leaping dolphins rose up out of a pond on the far side of the front yard. There were statues of fierce jungle cats strewn about the wild edges of the yard, peering out of the heavier brush.

Tara moved closer to Jessica, a small sound of alarm escaping her as they gained the slate walkway. All of them were violently shivering, their teeth were chattering, and Jessica told herself it was the rain and cold. They made it to within yards of the wraparound porch with its long thick columns when they heard it. A low, fierce growl welled up. It came out of the wind and rain, impossible to pinpoint but swelling in volume.

Tara's fingers dug into Jessica's arms. "What do we do?" she whimpered.

Jessica could feel the child shivering convulsively. "We keep walking. Trevor, have your flashlight handy—you may need it to hit the thing over the head if it attacks us." She continued walking toward the house, taking the twins with her, moving slowly but steadily, not wanting to trigger a guard dog's aggressive behavior by running.

The growl rose to a roar of warning. Lights unexpectedly flooded the lawn and porch, revealing the large German shepherd, head down, teeth bared, snarling at them. He stood in the thick brush just off the porch, his gaze focused on them as they gained the steps. The dog took a step toward them just as the front door was flung open.

Tara burst into tears. Jessica couldn't tell if they were tears of relief or fear. She embraced the girl protectively.

"What the hell?" A slender man with shaggy blond hair greeted them from the doorway. "Shut up, Toby," he commanded the dog.

"Get them the hell off my property," another voice roared from inside the house.

Jessica stared at the man in the doorway. "Paul?" There was utter relief in her voice. Her shoulders sagged and suddenly tears burned in her own eyes. "Thank God you're here! I need to get the kids into a hot shower and warm them up immediately. We're freezing."

Paul Ritter, a former band member and long-time friend of

Dillon Wentworth, gaped at her and the twins. "My God, Jess, it's you, all grown up. And these are Dillon's children?" He hastily stepped back to allow them entrance. "Dillon, we have more company. We need heat, hot showers, and hot chocolate!" As wet as she was, Paul gathered Jessica in his arms. "I can't believe you three are here. It's so good to see you. Dillon didn't say a word to me that you were coming. I would have met you at the dock." He shut the door on the wind and rain. The sudden stillness silenced him.

Jessica stared up at the shadowy figure on the staircase. For a moment she stopped breathing. Dillon always had that effect on her. He lounged against the wall, looking elegant and lazy, classic Dillon. The light spilled across his face, his angel's face. Thick blue-black hair fell in waves to his shoulders, as shiny as a raven's wing. His sculptured face, masculine and strong, had that hint of five o'clock shadow along his jaw. His mouth was so sensual, his teeth amazingly white. But it was his eyes, vivid blue, stunningly blue, burning with intensity that always mesmerized everyone, including Jessica.

Jessica felt Tara stir beside her, staring up in awe at her father. Trevor made a soft sound, almost of distress. The blue eyes stared down at the three of them. She saw joy, a welcoming expression of surprise dawning on Dillon's face. He stepped forward and gripped the banister with both hands, a heart-stopping grin on his face. He was wearing a short-sleeved shirt and his bare hands and arms were starkly revealed as if the spotlight had picked up and magnified every detail. Webs of scarred flesh covered his arms, wrists, and hands. His fingers were also scarred and misshapen. The contrast between his face and his body was so great it was shocking. That angel's face and the twisted, ridged arms and hands.

Tara shuddered visibly and flung herself into Jessica's arms. At once Dillon slipped back into the shadows, the welcoming smile fading as if it had never been. The burning blue eyes had gone from joyful to ice-cold instantly. His gaze raked Jessica's upturned face, slid over the twins, and came back to her. His sensual mouth tightened ominously. "They're freezing, Paul; explanations can wait. Please show them to the bathrooms so they can get out of those wet clothes. You'll need to prepare a couple more bedrooms." He started up the darkened stairway, taking care to stay well in the shadows. "And send Jess up to me the minute she's warm enough." His voice was still that perfect blend of smoke and edginess, a lethal combination that could brush over her skin like the touch of fingers.

Her heart beating in her throat, Jessica stared after him. She turned to look at Paul. "Why didn't you tell me? He can't play, can he? My God, he can't play his music." She knew what music meant to Dillon. It was his life. His soul. "I didn't know. My mother never brought me back. She came the one time with the twins, but I was ill. When I tried to see him on my own, he refused."

"I'm sorry." Tara was crying again. "I didn't mean to do that. I couldn't stop looking at his hands. They didn't look human. It was *repulsive*. I didn't mean to do that, I didn't. I'm sorry, Jessie."

Jessica knew the child needed comfort badly. Tara felt guilty and was tired, frightened, and very cold. Shaken by what she had discovered, Jessica had to fight back her own tears. "It's all right, honey, we'll find a way to fix this. You need a hot shower and a bed. Everything will be better in the morning." She looked at Trevor. He was staring up the stairway after his father as if mesmerized. "Trev? You okay?"

He nodded, clearing his throat. "I'm fine, but I don't think he is."

"That's why we're here," she pointed out. Jessica looked at Paul over Tara's bent head. She didn't believe for a minute that they'd find a way to fix the damage Tara had done, and looking at Paul's face, she guessed, neither did he. She forced a smile. "Tara, you might not remember him, you were just a little girl, but this is Paul Ritter. He was one of the original members of the *HereAfter* band, right from the very beginning. He's a very good friend of your family."

Paul grinned at the girl. "The last time I saw you, you were five years old with a mop of curly black hair." He held out his hand to Trevor. "You had the same mop and the same curls."

"Still do," Trevor said, grinning back.

2

THICK STEAM CURLED through the bathroom, filling every corner like an unnatural fog. The tiled bathroom was large and beautiful with its deep bathtub and hanging plants. After her long, hot shower, Jessica was feeling more human, but it was impossible to see much with the steam so thick. She toweldried the mirror, staring at the reflection of her pale face. She was exhausted, wanting only to sleep.

The last thing she wanted to do was face Dillon Wentworth looking like a frightened child. Her green eyes were too big for her face, her mouth too generous, her hair too red. She had always wished for the sophisticated, elegant look, but instead, she got the girl-next-door look. She peered closer at her reflection, hoping she seemed more mature. Without make-up she appeared younger than her twenty-five years. Jessica sighed, and shook her head in exasperation. She was no longer a child of eighteen, but a grown woman who had helped to raise Tara and Trevor. She wanted Dillon to take her seriously, to listen to what she had to say and not dismiss her as he might a teenager.

"Don't be dramatic, Jess," she cautioned aloud, "don't use words like 'life and death.' Just be matter-of-fact." She was trembling as she pulled on a dry pair of jeans, her hands shaking in spite of the hot shower. "Don't give him a chance to call you hysterical or imaginative." She hated those words. The police had used them freely when she'd consulted them after the twins had been sent the old tabloids and the phone calls had started. She was certain the police thought her a publicity-seeker.

Before she did anything else, she needed to assure herself the twins were being taken care of. Paul had shown her to a room on the second floor, a large suite with a bathroom and sitting room much like in a hotel. Jessica knew why Dillon had his private home built that way. In the beginning, he would have clung to the idea that he would play again. He would compose and record, and his home would be filled with guests. She ached for him, ached for the talent, the musical genius in him that must tear at his soul night and day. She couldn't imagine Dillon without his music.

She wandered down the wide hallway to the curving staircase. The stairs led up another story or down to the main floor. Jessica was certain she would find the twins in the kitchen and Dillon up on the third floor so she went downstairs, delaying the inevitable. The house was beautiful, all wood and high ceilings and stained glass. It had endless rooms that invited her to explore, but the sound of Tara's laughter caught at her and she hurried into the kitchen.

Paul grinned at her in greeting. "Did you follow the smell of chocolate?" He was still as she remembered him, too thin, too bleached, with a quick, engaging smile that always made her want to smile with him.

"No, the sound of laughter." Jessica kissed Tara and ruffled her hair. "I love to hear you laugh. Are you feeling better, honey?" She looked better, not so pale and cold.

Tara nodded. "Much. Chocolate always helps, doesn't it?"

"They're both chocolate freaks," Trevor informed Paul. "You have no idea how scary it gets if there's no chocolate in the house."

"Don't listen to him, Mr. Ritter," Tara scoffed. "He loves chocolate, too."

Paul burst out laughing. "I haven't had anyone call me Mr. Ritter in years, Tara. Call me Paul." He leaned companionably against the counter next to Jessica. "I had the distinct feeling Dillon had no idea you were coming. What brought you?"

"Christmas, of course," Jessica said brightly. "We wanted a family Christmas."

Paul smiled, but it didn't chase the shadows from his dark eyes. He glanced at the twins and bit off what he might have said. "We have more company now than we've had in years. The house is full, sort of old home week. Everyone must have had the same idea. Christmas, huh?" He rubbed his jaw and winked at Tara. "You want a tree and decorations and the works?"

Tara nodded solemnly. "I want a big tree and all of us decorating it like we did when Mama Rita was alive."

Jessica looked around the large kitchen, closer to tears than she would have liked. "It looks the same in here, Paul. It's the same kitchen that was in the old house." She smiled at the twins. "Do you remember?" The thought that Dillon had had her mother's domain reproduced exactly warmed her heart. They had spent five happy years in the kitchen. Vivian had never once entered it. They had often joked that she probably didn't even know the way. But Tara, Trevor, and Jessica had spent most of their time in or near that sanctuary. It was a place of safety, of peace. A refuge when Dillon was on the road and the house was no longer a home.

Trevor nodded. "Tara and I were just talking about it with Paul. It feels like home in here. I expected to find the cupboard I scratched my name into."

Paul caught Jessica's elbow, indicating with a jerk of his head to follow him out of the room. "You don't want to keep him waiting too long, Jessie."

With a falsely cheery wave at the twins, she went with him reluctantly, somersaults beginning in the pit of her stomach. Dillon. She was going to face him after all this time. "What did you mean, old home week? Who's here, Paul?"

"The band. Even though Dillon can't play the way he used to, he still composes. You know how he is with his music. Someone got the idea to record a few songs in his studio. He has an awesome studio, of course. The sound is perfect in it, all the latest equipment, and who could resist a Dillon Wentworth song?"

"He's composing again?" Joy surged through her. "That's wonderful, just what he needs. He's been alone far too long."

Paul matched her shorter strides on the stairs. "He's having a difficult time being around anyone. He doesn't like to be seen. And his temper . . . He's used to having his own way, Jessica. He isn't the Dillon you remember."

She heard something in his voice, something that sent alarm bells ringing in her head. She looked sideways at him. "I don't expect him to be. I know you're warning me off, trying to protect him, but Trevor and Tara need a father. He may have gone through a lot, but so did they. They lost their home and parents. Vivian might not have counted, they barely knew her and what they remember isn't pleasant, but he abandoned them. Add it up any way you like, he retreated and left them behind."

Paul stopped on the second floor landing, looking up the staircase. "He went through hell. Over a year in the hospital, so they could do what they could for his burns, all those surgeries, the skin grafts, and through it all, the reporters hounding him. And, of course, the trial. He went to court covered in bandages like a damned mummy. It was a media circus. Television cameras in his face, people staring at him like he was some freak. They wanted to believe he murdered Vivian and her lover. They wanted him to be guilty. Vivian wasn't the only one who died that night. Seven people died in that fire. They made him out to be a monster."

"I was here," Jessica reminded him softly, her stomach revolting at the memories. "I crawled through the house on my hands and knees with two five-year-olds, Paul. I pushed them out a window and followed them. Tara rolled down the side of the cliff and nearly drowned in the ocean. I didn't get her out of the sea and make my way around to the other side of the house in time to let Dillon know we were safe." She had been so exhausted after battling to save Tara who could barely stay afloat. She had wasted precious time lying on the shore with the children, her heart racing and her lungs burning. While she'd been lying there, Dillon had fought past the others and run back into the burning house to save the children. She pressed a hand to her head. "You think I don't think of it every day of my life? What I should have done? I can't change it, I can't go back and do it over." Guilt washed over her, through her, so that she felt sick with it.

"Jessica." Dillon's voice floated down the stairs. No one had a voice like Dillon Wentworth's. The way he said her name conjured up night fantasies, vivid impressions of black velvet brushing over exposed skin. He could weave spells with that voice, mesmerize, hold thousands of people enthralled. His voice was a potent weapon and she had always been very susceptible.

Jessica grasped the banister and went up to him. He waited at the top of the stairs. It saddened her to see that he had changed and was wearing a long-sleeved white shirt that concealed his scarred arms. A pair of thin black leather gloves covered his hands. He was thinner than in the old days, but still gave the impression of immense power that she remembered so vividly. He moved with grace, a sense of rhythm. His body didn't just walk across a stage, it flowed. He was only nine years older than she, but lines of suffering were etched into his face, and his eyes reflected a deep inner pain.

"Dillon." She said his name. There was so much more, so many words, so many emotions rising up out of the ashes of their past. She wanted to hold him close, gather him into her arms. She wanted him to reach for her, but she knew he wouldn't touch her. Jessica smiled instead, hoping he would see how she felt. "I'm so glad to see you again."

There was no answering smile on his face. "What in the

world are you doing here, Jessica? What were you thinking, bringing the children here?"

His face was a mask she couldn't penetrate. Paul was right. Dillon wasn't the same man any longer. This man was a stranger to her. He looked like Dillon, he even moved like Dillon, but there was a cruel edge to his mouth where before there had been a ready smile and a certain sensuality. His blue eyes had always burned with his intensity, his drive, his wild passions, his joy of life. Now they burned a piercing ice-blue.

"Are you taking a good look?" He had a way of twisting his words right at the end, a different accent that was all his own. His words were bitter but his voice was even, cool. "Look your fill, Jess, get it out of your system."

"I'm looking, Dillon. Why not? I haven't seen you in seven years. Not since the accident." She kept her voice strictly neutral when a part of her wanted to weep for him. Not for the scars on his body, but the ones far worse, the ones on his soul. And he was looking at her, his gaze like a rapier as it moved over her, taking in every detail. Jessica would not allow him to rattle her. This was too important for all of them. Tara and Trevor had no one else to fight for them, for their rights. For their protection. And neither, it seemed, did Dillon.

"Is that what you believe, Jessica? That it was an accident?" A small, humorless smile softened the edge of his mouth but made his eyes glitter like icy crystals. He turned away from her and led the way to his study. Dillon stepped back, gestured for her to precede him. "You're much more naive than I ever gave you credit for being."

Jessica's body brushed up against his as she stepped past him to enter his private domain. At once she became aware of him as a man, her every nerve ending leaping to life. Electricity seemed to arc between them. He drew in his breath sharply and his eyes went smoky before he turned away from her.

She looked around his study, away from him and his virility, and found it to be comforting. It was more like the Dillon she remembered. All warm leather, golds and browns, warm colors. Books were in floor-to-ceiling shelves, glass doors guarding treasures. "The fire was an accident," she ventured, feeling her way carefully with him.

The ground seemed to be shifting out from under her feet. This house was different, and yet the same as the one she remembered. There were places of comfort that could quickly disappear. Dillon was a stranger, and there was something threatening in his glittering gaze. He watched her with the same unblinking menace of a predator. Uneasily, Jessica seated herself across from him with the huge mahogany desk between them, feeling she was facing a foe, not a friend.

"That's the official verdict, isn't it? Funny word, official. You can make almost anything official if you write it up on paper and repeat it often enough."

Jessica was uncertain how to reply. She had no idea what he was implying. She twisted her fingers together, her green eyes watching him intently. "What are you saying, Dillon? Do you think Vivian started the fire on purpose?"

"Poor neglected Vivian." He sighed. "You bring back too many memories, Jess, ones I can do without."

In her lap, her fingers twisted together tightly. "I'm sorry for that, Dillon. Most of my memories of you are wonderful and I cherish them."

He leaned back in his chair, carefully positioned to keep his body in the deeper shadows. "Tell me about yourself. What have you been doing lately?"

Her green gaze met his blue one squarely. "I have a degree in music and I work at Eternity Studios as a sound engineer. But I think you know that."

He nodded. "They say you're brilliant at it, Jess." He watched her mouth curve and his body tightened in reaction. Actually hardened, in a heavy, throbbing ache. He was fascinated by her mouth and his fascination disgusted him. It brought up too many sins he didn't want to think about. Jessica Fitzpatrick should never have walked back into his life.

"You moved the house away from the cliffs," she said.

"I never liked it there. It wasn't safe." His blue eyes slid over her figure, deliberately appraising. Almost insulting. "Tell me about the men in your life. I presume you have one or two? Did you come here to tell me you've found someone and you're dumping the kids?" The idea of it enraged him. A volcanic heat that erupted into his bloodstream to swirl thick and hot and dangerous.

There was an edge to him, one she couldn't quite nail down. As soon as she focused on something, he shifted and moved so that she was thrown off balance. Their conversation seemed more like one of the chess matches they'd often played in her mother's kitchen so many years earlier. She was no match for him in sparring and she knew it. Dillon could cut the heart out of someone with a smile on his face. She'd seen him do it, charming, edgy, saying the one thing that would shatter his opponent like glass.

"Are we at war, Dillon?" Jessica asked. "Because if we are, you should lay out the rules for me. We came here to spend Christmas with you."

"Christmas?" He nearly spat the word. "I don't do Christmas."

"Well, we do Christmas, your children, your family, Dillon. You remember family, don't you? We haven't seen you in years; I thought you might be pleased."

His eyebrow shot up. "Pleased, Jess? You thought I'd be pleased? You didn't think that for a minute. Let's have a little honesty between us."

Her temper was beginning a slow smolder. "I doubt if you know the meaning of honesty, Dillon. You lie to yourself so much it's become a habit." She was appalled at her own lack of control. The accusation slipped out before she could censor it.

He leaned back in his leather chair, his body sprawled out, lazy and amused, still in the shadows. "I wondered when your temper would start to surface. I remember the old days when you would go up in flames if someone pushed you hard enough. It's still there, hidden deep, but you burn, don't you, Jess?"

Dillon remembered it all too vividly. He'd been a grown man, for God's sake, nearly twenty-seven with two children and an insane drug addict for a wife. And he'd been obsessed with an eighteen-year-old girl. It was sick, disgusting. Beyond his every understanding. Jessica had always been so alive, so passionate about life. She was intelligent; she had a mind that was like a hungry sponge. She shared his love of music, old buildings, and nature. She loved his children. He'd never touched her, never allowed himself to think of her sexually, but he had noticed every detail about her and he detested himself for that weakness.

"Are you purposely goading me to see what I'll do?" She tried not to sound hurt, but was afraid it showed on her face. He always noticed the smallest detail about everyone.

"Damn right I am," he suddenly admitted, his blue eyes glittering at her, his lazy, indolent manner gone in a flash. "Why the hell did you bring my children all this way, scaring the hell out of them, risking their lives . . ." He wanted to strangle her. Wrap his hands around her slender neck and strangle her for wreaking havoc with his life again. He couldn't afford to have Jessica around. Not now. Not ever.

"I did not risk their lives." Her green eyes glared at him as she denied the charge.

"You risked them in that kind of weather. You didn't even call me first."

Jessica took a deep breath and let it out slowly. "No, I didn't call. You would have said not to come. They belong here, Dillon."

"Jessica, all grown up. It's hard to stop thinking of you as a wild teen and accept that you're a grown woman." His tone was sheer insult.

Her chin lifted. "Really, Dillon, I would have thought you would have preferred to think of me as a much older woman. You certainly were willing to leave Trevor and Tara with me after Mama's death, no matter what my age."

He rose from his chair, moving quickly across the room,

putting distance between them. "Is that what this is about? You want more money?"

Jessica remained silent, simply watching him. It took a great deal of self-control not to get up and walk out. She allowed the silence to stretch out between them, a taut, tension-filled moment. Dillon finally turned to look at her.

"That was beneath even you, Dillon," she said softly. "Someone should have slapped your face a long time ago. Are you expecting me to feel sorry for you? Is that what you're looking for from me? Pity? Sympathy? You're going to have a long wait."

He leaned against the bookcase, his blue eyes fixed on her face. "I suppose I deserved that." His gloved fingers slid along the spine of a book. Back and forth. Whispered over the leather. "Money has never held much allure for you or your mother. I was sorry to hear of her death."

"Were you? How kind of you, Dillon, to be sorry to hear. She was my mother and the mother of your children, whether you want to acknowledge that or not. My mother took care of Tara and Trevor almost from the day they were born. They never knew any other mother. They were devastated at losing her. I was devastated. Your kind gesture of flowers and seeing to all the arrangements . . . lacked something."

He straightened, pulled himself up to his full height, his blue eyes ice-cold. "My God, you're reprimanding me, questioning my actions."

"What actions, Dillon? You made a few phone calls. I doubt that took more than a few minutes of your precious time. More likely you asked Paul to make the phone calls for you."

His dark brow shot up. "What did you expect me to do, Jessica? Show up at the funeral? Cause another media circus? Do you really think the press would have left it alone? The unsolved *murders* and the fire were a high profile case."

"It wasn't about you, Dillon, was it? Not everything is about you. All that mattered to you was that your life didn't change. It's been eleven months since my mother's death and it didn't change, did it? Not at all. You made certain of that. I just stepped right into my mother's shoes, didn't I? You knew I'd never give them up or let them go into foster care. The minute you suggested hiring a stranger, maybe breaking them up, you knew I'd keep them together."

He shrugged, in no way remorseful. "They belonged with you. They've been with you their entire life. Who better than you, Jessica? I already knew you loved them, that you would risk your life for them. Tell me why I was wrong not to want the best for my children?"

"They belong with you, Dillon. Here, with you. They need a father."

His laughter was bitter, without a trace of humor. "A father? Is that what I'm supposed to be, Jessica? I seem to recall my earlier parenting skills. I left them with their mother in a house on an island with no fire department. Do you remember that as vividly as I do? Because, believe me, it's etched in my brain. I left them with a mother who I knew was out of her mind. I knew she was flying on drugs, that she was unstable and violent. I knew she brought her friends here. And worse, I knew she was fooling around with people who were occultists. I let them into my home with my children, with you." He raked gloved fingers through his black hair, tousling the unruly curls so that his hair fell in waves around the perfection of his face.

He pushed away from the bookcase, a quicksilver movement of impatience, then stalked across the floor with all the grace of a ballet dancer and all the stealth of a leopard. When had his obsession started? He only remembered longing to get home, to sit in the kitchen and watch the expressions chasing across Jessica's face. He wrote his songs about her. Found peace in her presence. Jessica had a gift for silences, for laughter. He watched her all the time, and yet, in the end, he had failed her, too.

"Dillon, you're being way too hard on yourself," Jessica said softly. "You were so young back then, and everything came at once—the fame and fortune. The world was upside down. You used to say you didn't know reality, what was up or what was down. And you were working, making it all come together for everyone. You had so many others who needed the money you generated. Everyone depended on you. Why should you expect that you would have handled everything so perfectly? You weren't responsible for Vivian's decisions to use drugs nor were you responsible for any of the things she did."

"Really? She was clearly ill, Jess. Whose responsibility was she if not mine?"

"You put her in countless rehabs. We all heard her threaten to commit suicide if you left her. She threatened to take the kids." She threatened a lot more than that. More than once Vivian had rushed to the nursery, shouting she would throw the twins in the foaming sea. Jessica pressed a hand to her mouth as the memory rose up to haunt her. He had tried to get her committed, to put her in a psychiatric hospital, but Vivian was adept at fooling the doctors, and they believed her tales of a philandering husband who wanted her out of the way while he did drugs and slept with groupies. The tabloids certainly supported her accusations.

"I took the easy way out. I left. I went on the road and I left my children, and you, and Rita, to her insanity."

"The tour had been booked for a long time," Jessica pointed out. "Dillon, it's all water under the bridge. We can't change the things that happened, we can only go forward. Tara and Trevor need you now. I'm not saying they should live with you, but they should have a relationship with you. You're missing so much by not knowing them, and they're missing so much by not knowing you."

"You don't even know who I am anymore, Jess," Dillon said quietly.

"Exactly my point. We're staying through Christmas. That's nearly three weeks and it should give us plenty of time to get to know each other again."

"Tara finds me repulsive to look at. Do you think I would subject a child of mine to my own nightmare?" He paced across the hardwood floor, a quick restless movement, graceful and fluid, so reminiscent of the old Dillon. There was so much passion in him, so much emotion, he could never contain it. It flowed out of him, warmed those around him so that they wanted to bask in his presence.

Jessica was sensitive to his every emotion, she always had been. She could practically see his soul bleeding, cut so deeply the gash was nearly impossible to heal. But agreeing with his twisted logic wouldn't help him. Dillon had given up on life. He had locked his heart from the world and was determined to keep it that way. "Tara is only thirteen years old, Dillon. You're doing her an injustice. It was a shock to her, but it's unfair to keep her out of your life because she had a childish reaction to your scars."

"It will be better for her if you take her away from here."

Jessica shook her head. "It'll be better for you, you mean. You aren't thinking of her at all. You've become selfish, Dillon, living here, feeling sorry for yourself."

He whipped around, taking her breath away with his speed. He was on her before she had a chance to run, catching her arm, his fingers wrapping around it so tightly she could feel the thick ridges of his scars against her skin, despite the leather of his glove. He dragged her close to him, right up against his chest, pulled her tight so that every soft curve of her body was pressed relentlessly against him. "How dare you say that to me." His blue eyes glared at her, icy cold, *burning* with cold.

Jessica refused to flinch. She locked her gaze with his. "Someone should have said it a long time ago, Dillon. I don't know what you're doing here all alone in this big house, on your wild island, but it certainly isn't living. You dropped out and you don't have the right to do that. You *chose* to have children. You brought them into this world and you are responsible for them."

His eyes blazed down into hers, his mouth hardened into a cruel line. She felt the change in him. The male aggression. The savage hostility. His hand tangled in the wealth of hair at the nape of her neck, hauled her head back. He fastened his mouth to hers hungrily. Angrily. Greedily. It was supposed to frighten her, to punish her. To drive her away. He used a bruising force, demanded submission, in a primitive retaliation designed to send her running from him.

Jessica tasted the hot anger, the fierce need to conquer and control, but she also tasted dark passion, as elemental as time. She felt the passion flood his body, harden his every muscle to iron, soften his lips when they would have been brutal. Jessica remained passive beneath the onslaught, her heart racing, her body coming alive. She didn't fight him, she didn't resist, but she didn't participate either.

Dillon lifted his head abruptly, swore foully, dropped his hands as if she had burned him. "Get out of here, Jessica. Get out before I take what I want. I'm damned selfish enough to do it. Get out and take the kids with you, I won't have them here. Sleep here tonight and stay the hell out of my way, then go when the storm passes. I'll have Paul take you home."

She stood there, one hand pressed to her swollen lips, shocked at the way her body throbbed and clenched in reaction to his. "You don't have a choice in the matter, Dillon. You are perfectly within your rights to send me away, but not Tara and Trevor. Someone is trying to kill them."

3

"WHAT THE HELL are you talking about?" All at once Dillon looked so menacing, that Jessica actually stepped back.

She held up her hand, more frightened of him than she had

ever conceived she could be. There was something merciless in his eyes. Something terrifying. And for the first time, she recognized him as a dangerous man. That had never been a part of Dillon's makeup, but events had twisted him, shaped him, just as they had shaped her. She had to stop persisting in seeing him as the man she had loved so much. He was different. She could feel the explosive violence in him swirling close to the surface.

Had she made a terrible mistake in coming to Dillon? In bringing the children to him? Her first duty was to Trevor and Tara. She loved them as a mother would, or, at the very least, an older sister.

"What the hell are you up to?" he snapped.

"What am I . . ." Her voice broke off in astonishment. Fear gave way to a sudden wave of fury. She stopped backing away and even took a step toward him, her fingers curling into fists. "You think I'm making up a story, Dillon? Do you think I dragged the children out of a home they're familiar with, away from their friends, in secret, in the dead of night, to see a man they have no reason to love, who *obviously* doesn't want them here, on a whim? Because I felt like it? For what? Your stupid, pitiful money?" She sneered it at him, throwing his anger right back in his face. "It always comes back to that, doesn't it?"

"If I *obviously* don't want to have them here, why would you bring them?" His blue eyes burned with a matching fury, her words obviously stinging.

"You're right, we shouldn't have come here, it was stupid to think you had enough humanity left in you to care about your own children."

Their gazes were locked, two combatants, two strong, passionate personalities. There was a silence while Jessica's heart hammered out her fury and her eyes blazed at him. Dillon regarded her for a long time. He moved first, sighing audibly, breaking the tension, walking back to his desk with his easy, flowing grace. "I see you have a high opinion of me, Jessica."

"You're the one accusing me of being a greedy, grasping, money-hungry witch," she pointed out. "I'd say you were the one with a pretty poor opinion of me." Her chin jutted at him, her face stiff with pride. "I must say, while you're throwing out accusations, you didn't even have the courtesy to answer my letter suggesting the children come live with you after my mother died."

"There was no letter."

"There was a letter, Dillon. You ignored it like you ignored us. If I'm so money-hungry, why did you leave your children with me for all these months? Mom was dead, you knew that, yet you made no attempt to bring the children back here with you and you didn't respond to my letter."

"You might remember when you're stating things you know nothing about that you are in my home. I didn't turn you out, despite the fact that you didn't have the courtesy to phone ahead."

Her eyebrow shot up. "Is that a threat? What? You're going to kick me out into the storm or even better, send me to the boathouse or the caretaker's cottage? Give me a break, Dillon. I know you better than that!"

"I'm not that man you once knew, Jess, I never will be again." He fell silent for a moment watching the expressions chase across her face. When she stirred, as if to speak, he held up his hand. "Did you know your mother came to see me just two days before she died?" His voice was very quiet.

A chill went down her spine as she realized what he was saying. Her mother had gone to see Dillon and two days later she was dead in what certainly wasn't an accident. Jessica didn't move. She couldn't move as she assimilated the information. She knew the two incidents had to be connected. She could feel his eyes on her, but there was a strange roaring in her ears. Her legs were all at once rubbery and the room tilted crazily. *She had brought Trevor and Tara to him.*

"Jessica!" he said her name sharply. "Don't faint on me. What's wrong?" He dragged a chair out and forced her into it, pushing her head down, the leather covering his palm feeling strange on the nape of her neck. "Breathe. Just breathe."

She inhaled deeply, taking in great gulps of air, fighting off dizziness. "I'm just tired, Dillon, I'm all right, really I am." She sounded unconvincing even to her own ears.

"Something about your mother's coming here upset you, Jess. Why should that bother you? She often wrote or called to update me on the progress of the kids."

"Why would she come here?" Jessica forced air into her lungs and waited for the dizziness to subside completely. Dillon's hand was strong on her nape; he wasn't going to allow her to sit up unless she was fully recovered. "I'm fine, really." She pushed at his arm, not wanting the contact with him. He was too close. Too charismatic. And he had too many dark secrets.

Dillon abruptly let her go, almost as if he could read her thoughts. He moved away from her, back around the desk, back into the shadows, and hid his gloved hands below the desk, out of her sight. Jessica was certain his hands had been trembling.

"Why should it upset you that your mother came to see me? And why would you think someone might want to harm the twins?" The anger between them had dissipated as if it had never been, leaving his voice soft again, persuasive, so gentle it turned her heart over. "Does it hurt to talk about her? Is it too soon?"

Jessica gritted her teeth against his effect on her. They had been so close at one time. He had filled her life with his presence, his laughter, and warmth. He had made the entire household feel safe when he was home. It was difficult to sit across from him, thrown back to those days of camaraderie by his smoky voice, when she knew he was a different person now.

"My mother's car had been tampered with." Jessica blurted it out in a rush. She held up her hand to stop his inevitable protest. "Just hear me out before you tell me I'm crazy. I know what the police report said. Her brakes failed. She went over a cliff." She was choosing her words carefully. "I accepted that it was an accident but then other accidents started happening. Little disturbing things at first, things like the fan on a motor ripping loose and tearing through the hood and windshield of *my* car."

"What?" He sat up straight. "Was anyone hurt?"

She shook her head. "Tara had just gotten into the backseat. Trevor wasn't in the car. I had a few scratches, nothing serious. A mechanic explained the entire thing away, but it worried me. And then there was the horse. Trevor and Tara ride every Thursday at a local stable. Same time, every week. Trev's horse went crazy, bucking, spinning, squealing, it was awful. The horse nearly fell over backward. They discovered a drug in the horse's system." She looked straight at him. "I also found this in the horse's stall, sticking out of the straw." Watching his face she handed him the guitar pick with the distinctive design made for Dillon Wentworth as a gift so many years ago. "Trevor admitted that it might have been in his pocket and fallen out. That and other things were sent anonymously to the kids."

"I see." He sounded grim.

"The stable owners believe it was a prank on the horse, that it happens sometimes. The police thought Trevor did it, and grilled him until I called an attorney. Trevor would never do such a thing. But it felt wrong to me, two accidents so close together and only a few months after my mother's car went out of control." Jessica tapped her fingernail on the edge of his desk, a nervous habit when she was worried. "I might have accepted the accidents had that been the end of it, but it wasn't." She watched him very, very closely, trying to see past the impassive expression on his face. "Of course, the incidents didn't happen one on top of the other, a couple of weeks elapsed between them." She wanted desperately to read his blue eyes, but she saw only ice.

Jessica shivered again, experiencing a frisson of fear at being alone in the shadowy room with a man who wore a mask and guarded the darkness in his soul as if it were treasure.

"What is it, Jess?" He asked the question quietly.

What could she say? He was a stranger she no longer trusted completely. "Why did my mother come here and when?"

"Two days before her death. I asked her to come."

Her throat tightened. "In seven years you never asked us here. Why would you suddenly ask my mother to travel all the way out here to see you?"

One dark brow shot up. "Obviously because I couldn't go to see her."

The alarm bells were ringing in her mind again. He was sidestepping the question, not wanting to answer her. It was too much of a coincidence, her mother's visiting Dillon at his island home and two days later her brakes mysteriously failing. The two events had to be connected. She remained silent, suspicion finding its way into her heart.

"What else has happened? There must be more."

"Three days ago the brakes on my car failed, too. It was a miracle we all lived through it. The car was totaled. Someone also has been phoning the house and sent old newspaper accounts of the fire to the children. That's when the guitar pick was sent. The phone calls were frightening. That, along with the other incidents over the last few months, made me decide to bring them here to you. I knew they would be safe here." She injected a note of confidence into her voice which she no longer felt. Her instincts were on alert. "Christmas was a natural, a perfect excuse should anyone question why we decided to visit you." She had been so certain he would be softer at Christmastime, more vulnerable and much more likely to let them into his life again. She had run to him for protection, for healing, and she was very much afraid she had made an enormous mistake.

Dillon leaned toward her, his blue eyes vivid and sharp. "Tell me about these phone calls."

"The voice was recorded like a robot's voice. Whoever was calling must have prerecorded it and then played it when one of the twins answered. They said terrible things about you, accused you of murdering Vivian and her lover. Of locking everyone inside the room and starting the fire. Once he said you might kill them, too." She could hear her own heart beating as she confessed. "I stopped allowing the twins to answer the phone and I made plans to come here."

"Have you told anyone else about this?"

"Only the police," she admitted. She looked away from him, afraid of seeing something she couldn't face. "The minute they realized Trevor and Tara were your children, they seemed to think I was looking to grab headlines. They asked if I was planning to sell my story to the tabloids. The incidents, other than the car, were minor things easily explained away. In the end they said they would look into it, and they took a report, but I think they thought I was either a publicity-seeker or the hysterical type."

"I'm sorry, Jess, that must have been painful for you." There was a quiet sincerity in the pure sensuality of his voice. "I've known you all of your life. You've never been one to panic."

The moment he said the words aloud, her heart slammed hard in her chest. Both of them froze, completely still while the disturbing memories invaded, crowding in, filling the room like insidious demons crawling along the floor and the walls. A sneak attack, uninvited, unexpected, but all-invasive. The air seemed to thicken with the heavy weight of memory. Evil had come with the mere mention of a single word and both of them felt its presence.

Jessica did indeed know panic intimately. She knew complete and utter hysteria. She knew the feeling of being so helpless, so vulnerable, so stripped of power she had wanted to scream until her throat was raw. Humiliation brought color sweeping up her face and her green gaze skittered away from Dillon's. No one else knew. No one. Not even her mother. She had never told her mother the entire truth. The nightmare was too real, too ugly, and she couldn't look at it.

"I'm sorry, Jess, I didn't mean to bring it up." His voice was ultra soft, soothing.

She managed to get her shaky legs under her, managed to keep from trembling visibly, although her insides were jelly as she pushed away from his desk. "I don't think about it." But she dreamt about it. Night after night, she dreamt about it. Her stomach lurched crazily. She needed air, needed to get away from him, away from the intensity of his burning, all-seeing eyes. For a moment she detested him, detested that he saw her so naked and vulnerable.

"Jessica." He said her name. Breathed her name.

She backed away from him, raw and exposed. "I *never* think about it." Jessica took the coward's way out and retreated, whirling around and fleeing the room. Tears welled up, swimming in her eyes, blurring her vision, but somehow, she made her way down the stairs.

She could feel Dillon's eyes on her, knew he followed her descent down the stairs but she didn't turn around, didn't look at him. She kept moving, her head high, counting in her head to keep the echo of the long ago voices, of the ancient, hideous chanting from stealing its way into her mind.

When she reached her room, Jessica shut the door firmly, and threw herself, face down, onto the bed, breathing deeply, fighting for control. She was no child, but a grown woman. She had responsibilities. She had confidence in herself. She would not, *could* not let anything or anyone shake her. She knew she should get up, check on Tara and Trevor, make certain they were comfortable in the rooms Paul had provided for them, on either side of her room, but she was too tired, too drained to move. She lay there, not altogether asleep, not altogether awake, but drifting, somewhere in between.

And the memories came to take her back in time.

There was always the chanting when Vivian and her friends were together. Jessica forced herself to walk down the hallway, hating to go near them, but needing to find Tara's favorite blanket. Tara would never go to sleep otherwise. Her heart was pounding, her mouth dry. Vivian's friends frightened her with their sly, leering smiles, their black candles, and wild orgies. Jessica knew they pretended to worship Satan, they talked continually of pleasures and religious practices, but none of them really knew what they were talking about. They made it up as they went along, doing whatever they pleased, each trying to outdo the other in whatever outrageous perverted sexual ritual they could envision.

As Jessica moved past the living room, she glanced inside. Black heavy drapes darkened the windows, candles were lit in every conceivable space. Vivian looked up from where she sat on the couch, naked from the waist up, sipping her wine while a man lapped greedily at her breasts. Another woman was naked while several men surrounded her, touching and grunting eagerly. The sight sickened and embarrassed Jessica and she looked away quickly.

"Jessica!" Vivian's voice was imperious, that of a queen speaking to a peasant. "Come in here."

Jessica could see the madness on Vivian's flushed face, in her hard, over-bright eyes, and hear it in her loud, brittle laugh. She made herself smile vaguely. "I'm sorry, Mrs. Wentworth, I have to get back to Tara immediately." She kept moving.

A hard hand fell on her shoulder, another hand clapped over her mouth hard enough to sting. Jessica was dragged into the living room. She couldn't see her captor, but he was big and very strong. She struggled wildly, but he held her, laughing, calling out to Vivian to lock the door.

Hot breath hit her ear. "Are you the sweet little virgin Vivian is always teasing us with? Is this your little prize, Viv?"

Vivian's giggle was high-pitched, insane. "Dillon's little princess." Her words slurred and she circled Jessica and her captor several times. "Do you think he's had her yet?" A long-tipped fingernail traced a path down Jessica's cheek. "You're going to have such fun with us, little Jessica." She made a ceremony of lighting more candles and incense, taking her time, humming softly. "Tape her mouth, she'll scream if you don't." She gave the order and resumed her humming, stopping to kiss one of the men who was staring at Jessica with hot, greedy eyes. Jessica fought, biting at the hand covering her mouth, a terrified cry welling up. She could hear herself, screaming in her head, over and over, but no sound emerged.

She struggled, rolled over, the sound of ugly laughter fading into terrified weeping. She woke completely, sobbing wildly. She pushed the pillow harder against her face, muffling the sound, relieved it was a nightmare, relieved she had managed to wake herself up.

Very slowly she sat up and looked around the large, pleasant room. It was very cold, surprisingly so when Paul had turned on the heater to take the chill off. Pushing at her long hair, she sat on the edge of the bed with tears running down her face and the taste of terror in her mouth. She hadn't come back to the island with the sole purpose of keeping the children safe. She had come back in the hopes of healing herself, Dillon, and the children, of finding peace for all of them. Jessica rubbed her hand over her face, resolutely wiping the tears away. Instead the nightmares were getting worse. Dillon wasn't the same man she had known seven years ago. She wasn't the same hero-worshipping girl.

She had to think clearly, think everything through. Tara and Trevor were her greatest concern. Jessica flicked on the lamp beside the bed. She couldn't bear to sit in the dark when her memories were so raw. The curtains fluttered, danced gently, gracefully in the breeze. She stared at the window. It was wide open, fog and rain and wind creeping into her room. The window had been closed when she'd left the room. She was absolutely certain of it. A chill crept down her spine, unease prickling her skin.

Jessica looked quickly around the room, her gaze seeking the corners, peeking beneath the bed. She couldn't stop herself from looking in the closet, the bathroom, and the shower. It would be difficult for anyone to enter her room through the open window, especially in a rainstorm, because it was on the second floor. She tried to convince herself one of the twins must have come into her room to say goodnight and opened the window to let in some air. She couldn't imagine why, it didn't make any sense, but she preferred this explanation to the alternative.

She crossed the room to the window, stared out into the forest, and watched the wind as it played roughly in the trees. There was something elemental, powerful about storms that fascinated her. She watched the rain for a while, allowing a certain peace to settle back over her. Then, abruptly, she closed the window and went to check on Tara.

The bedside lamp was on in Tara's room, spilling a soft circle of light across it. To Jessica's surprise, Trevor lay on the floor wrapped in a heap of blankets, while Tara lay on the bed beneath a thick quilt. They were talking in low tones and neither looked at all astonished to see her.

"We thought you'd never come," Tara greeted, moving over, obviously expecting Jessica to share her bed.

"I thought I was going to have to go rescue you," Trevor added. "We were just discussing how to go about it since we didn't exactly know which room you were in."

Warmth drove out the cold in her soul, pushing away her nameless fears and the disturbing remnants of old horrors. She smiled at them and rushed to the bed, jumping beneath the covers and snuggling into the pillow. "Were you really worried?"

"Of course we were," Tara confirmed. She reached for Jessica's hand. "Did he yell at you?"

Trevor snorted. "We didn't see any fireworks, did we? If he yelled at her we would have seen the Fourth of July."

"Hey, now," Jessica objected. "I'm not that bad."

Trevor made a rude noise. "Flames fly off you, Jess, if someone gets you angry enough. I can't see you being all mealy-mouthed if our own father didn't want us for Christmas. You'd read him the riot act, probably knock him on his butt and march us out of his house. You'd make us swim back to the nearest city."

Tara giggled, nodding her head. "We call you Mama Tiger behind your back."

"What?" Jessica found herself laughing. "Total exaggeration. Total!"

"You're worse. You grow fangs and claws if someone is mean to us," Trevor pointed out complacently. "Justice for the children." He grinned at her. "Unless you're the one getting after us."

Jessica threw her pillow at him with perfect aim. "You little punk, I never get after you. What are you doing awake, it's four-thirty in the morning."

The twins erupted into laughter, pointing at her and mimicking her question. "That's called getting after us, Jess," Tara said. "You're worse than Mama Rita was."

"She spoiled you rotten," Jessica told them haughtily, laughter brimming over in her green eyes. "All right, fine, but nobody in their right mind is up at four-thirty in the morning. It's silly. *And* it was a perfectly *reasonable* question."

"Yeah, because we're not in some spooky old house with total strangers and a man who might want to throw us out on our butts or anything like that," Trevor said.

"Taking you off upstairs to do some dastardly deed we've never heard of," Tara said, adding her two cents.

"When did you two become such smart alecks?" Jessica wanted to know.

"We talked to Paul for a while downstairs," Trevor said when the laughter had subsided. "He's really nice. He said he knew us when we were little."

Jessica was aware of both pairs of eyes on her. She caught the pillow Trevor tossed to her and slipped it behind her back as she sat up, drawing up her knees. "He and your father were best friends long before the band was put together. Paul actually was the original singer for their band. Dillon wrote most of the songs and played lead guitar. He could play almost any instrument. Paul played bass guitar, but he sang the songs when they first started out. Brian Phillips was the drummer and I think it was his idea to form the band. They started out in a garage and played all the clubs and made the rounds. Eventually they became very famous."

"There were a couple of other band members, Robert something," Trevor interrupted. "He was on keyboard and for some reason I thought Don Ford was the bass player. He's on all the CD covers and in the old magazine articles written on *HereAfter*." There was a note of pride when he said the band's name.

Jessica nodded. "Robert Berg. Robert's awesome on the keyboard. And yes, Don was brought in to play bass. Somewhere along the line, Paul picked up a big drug habit."

Tara wrinkled her nose. "He seemed so nice."

Jessica pushed back her hair. "He is nice, Tara. People make mistakes, they get into things without thinking and then it's too late to get out. Paul told me he began using all the time and couldn't remember the lyrics to the songs during their live performances. Your father would step up and sing. Paul said the crowds went wild. Paul was on a downward spiral and eventually the band members wanted him out. He was doing crazy things, tearing places up, not showing up for scheduled events, that sort of thing, and they said enough."

"Just like you read in the tabloids," Trevor pointed out.

There was a small silence while both children looked at her. "Yes, that's true. But it doesn't make the things they wrote about your father true. Remember, this was all a long time ago. Sometimes when people become famous too fast, have too much money, they have a hard time handling it all. I think Paul was one of those people. It overwhelmed him. Girls were throwing themselves at him all the time, there was just too much of everything. Anyway, Dillon wouldn't give up on him. He made him go into rehab and helped him recover."

"Is that when they picked up another bass player?" Trevor guessed.

Jessica nodded. "The band really took off while Paul was cleaning himself up and they had to have another bass player, so Don was brought in. Dillon's voice rocketed them into stardom. But he wouldn't leave Paul behind. Your father gave Paul a job working in the studio and eventually made a place for him in the band. And when Dillon needed him most, Paul came through."

"Did Paul know Vivian?" Tara's question was hesitant.

Jessica realized Vivian still managed to bring tension into a room years after her death. "Yes he did, honey," she confirmed gently. "All of the members of the band knew Vivian. Paul didn't do all the tours with them so he often stayed here, seeing to things at home. He knew her better than most." And despised her. Jessica remembered the terrible arguments and Vivian's endless tirades. Paul had tried to keep her under control, tried to help Rita and Jessica keep the twins safe when she brought her friends in.

"Does he think my father murdered Vivian and that man she was with, like the newspaper said?"

Jessica swung her head around, her temper rising until she saw Tara's bent head. Slowly she let her breath out. How else was Tara going to learn the truth about her father if she couldn't ask questions? "Honey, you know most of those tabloids don't tell the truth, right? They sensationalize things, write misleading headlines and articles to grab people's attention. It wasn't any different when your father was at the height of his career. The tabloids twisted all the facts, made it sound as if Dillon found your mother in bed with another man. They made it sound like he shot them both and then burned down his own house to cover the murders. It didn't happen like that at all." Jessica curved her arm around Tara's shoulders and pulled her close, hugging her. "Your father was acquitted at the trial. He had nothing to do with the shooting or the fire. He wasn't even in the house when it all happened."

"What did happen, Jess?" Trevor asked, his piercing blue gaze meeting hers steadily. "Why wouldn't you ever tell us?"

"We're not babies," Tara pointed out, but she cuddled closer to Jessica's warmth, clearly for comfort.

Jessica shook her head. "I would prefer your father tell you about that night, not me."

"We'll believe you, Jess," Trevor said. "You turn beet red if you try to lie. We don't know our father. We don't know Paul. Mama Rita wouldn't say a word about it. You know it's time you told us the truth if someone is sending us newspapers filled with lies and calling us on the phone telling more lies."

"It's the three of us, Jessie," Tara added. "It's always been the three of us. We're a family. We want you to tell us."

Jessica was proud of them, proud of the way they were attempting to handle a volatile and frightening situation. And she heard the love in their voices, felt the answering emotion welling up in her. They weren't babies anymore, and they were right, they deserved to know the truth. She didn't know if Dillon would ever tell them.

Jessica took a deep breath, then she began. "There was a party at the house that night. Your father had been gone for months on a world tour and Vivian often invited her friends over. I didn't know her very well." The fact was, Jessica had never understood Dillon's relationship with his wife. Vivian had left the twins with Rita from almost the moment they were born so she could tour with the band. She rarely returned home the first three years of their lives. Yet during the last year of her life she had stayed home, the band's manager refusing to allow her to travel with them due to her violent mood swings and psychotic behavior.

"You've gone quiet again, Jessica," Trevor prompted.

"The fact is, Vivian drank too much and partied very heavily. Your father knew about her drinking, but she threatened him with you. She said she'd leave him, take you with her, and get a restraining order so he couldn't see you. She knew people who would take money in return for testimony against Dillon. He was often on the road, and bands, especially successful ones, always have reputations."

"You're saying he was afraid to risk a court fight," Trevor said, summing it up.

Jessica smiled at him. "Exactly. He was afraid the court would say you had to live with Vivian and he wouldn't be able to control what was happening to you if he didn't have custody. By staying with her, he hoped he could keep her contained. It worked for a while." Vivian didn't want to be home, she preferred the nightlife and the clubs of the cities. It was only during the last year, when the twins were five, that Vivian had returned home, unable to keep up appearances.

"That night, Jess," Trevor prompted.

Jessica sighed. There was no getting around telling them what they wanted to know. The twins were very persistent. "There was a party going on." She chose her words very carefully. "Your father came home early. There was a terrible fight between him and your mother, and he left the house to cool off. He made up his mind that he would leave Vivian and she knew it. There were candles everywhere. The fire inspector said the drapes caught fire and it spread fast, because there was alcohol on the furniture and the walls. The party was very wild. No one knows for certain where the gun came from or who shot whom first. But witnesses, including me, testified that Dillon had left the house. He ran back when he saw the flames and he rushed inside because he couldn't find you."

Jessica looked down at her hands. "I had taken you out a window on the cliff side of the house and he didn't know. He thought you were still inside so he went into the burning house."

Tara gasped, one hand covering her mouth to stop any sound but her eyes were glistening with tears.

"How did he get out?" Trevor asked, a lump in his throat. He couldn't get the sight of his father's terrible scars out of his mind. "And how could he make himself go into a burning house?"

Jessica leaned close to them. "Because that's how courageous your father is, how absolutely dependable, and that's how much he loves both of you."

"Did the house fall down on him?" Tara asked.

"They said he came out on fire, that Paul and Brian tackled him and put out the flames with their own hands. There were people on the island then, guards and groundskeepers who had all come to help. The helicopters had arrived I think. I just remember it being so loud, so angry . . ." her voice trailed off.

Trevor reached up and caught her hand. "I hate that sad look you get sometimes, Jess. You're always there for us. You always have been."

Tara kissed her cheek. "Me, too, I feel the same way."

"So no one really knows who shot our mother and her friends," Trevor concluded. "It's still a big mystery. But you saved our lives, Jess. And our father was willing to risk his life to save us. Did you see him after he came out of the house?"

Jessica closed her eyes, turned her head away from them. "Yes, I saw him." Her voice was barely audible.

The twins exchanged a long look. Tara took the initiative, wanting to wipe away the sorrow Jessica was so clearly feeling. "Now, tell us the story of the Christmas miracle. The one Mama Rita always told us. I love that story."

"Me, too. You said we were coming here for our miracle, Jess," Trevor said, "tell us the story so we can believe."

"We're all going to be too tired to get up tomorrow," Jessica pointed out. She slipped beneath the covers and flicked off the light. "You already believe in miracles, I helped raise you right. It's your father who doesn't know what can happen at Christmas, but we're going to teach him a lesson. I'll tell the story another time, when I'm not so darned sleepy. Goodnight you two."

Trevor laughed softly. "Cluck cluck. Jessica hates it when we get sappy."

The pillow found him even in the dark.

4

B RIAN PHILLIPS WAS FLIPPING pancakes in the kitchen when Jessica entered the room with Tara and Trevor early the next evening. She grinned at him in greeting. "Brian! How wonderful to see you again!"

Brian spun around, and missed a pancake as it came flying down to splat on the counter. "Jessica!" He swooped her up, hugged her hard. He was a big man, the drummer for *Here-After*. She had forgotten how strong he was until he nearly broke her ribs with his hard, good-natured squeeze. With his reddish hair and stocky body, he always had reminded Jessica of a boxer fresh from Ireland. At times she even heard the lilt in his voice. "My God, girl, you look beautiful. How long has it been?" There was a moment of silence as both of them remembered the last time they had seen one another.

Jessica resolutely forced a smile. "Brian, you must remember Tara and Trevor, Dillon's children. We were so exhausted we slept the day away. I see you're serving breakfast for dinner." She was still in the circle of Brian's arms as she turned to include the twins in the greeting. Her smile faltered as she met a pair of ice-cold eyes over the heads of the children.

Dillon lounged in the doorway, his body posture deceptively lazy and casual. His eyes were intent, watchful, focused on her, and there was a hint of something dangerous to the edge of his mouth. Jessica's green gaze locked with his. Her breathing was instantly impaired, her breath catching in her lungs. He had that effect on her. Dillon was wearing faded blue jeans, a long-sleeved turtleneck shirt, and thin leather gloves. He looked unmercifully handsome. His hair was damp from his shower and he was barefoot. She had forgotten that about him, how he liked to be without shoes in the house. Butterfly wings fluttered in the pit of her stomach. "Dillon."

Jessica ripped out his heart, whatever heart he had left, with her mere presence in his home. Dillon could hardly bear to look at her, to see her beauty, to see the woman she had become. Her hair was a blend of red and gold silk, falling around her face. A man could lose himself in her eyes. And her mouth . . . If Brian didn't take his hands off of her very, very soon Dillon feared he might give in to the terrible violence that always seemed to be swirling so close to the surface. Her green eyes met his across the room and she murmured his name again. Softly. Barely audible, yet the way she whispered his name tightened every muscle in his body.

The twins whirled around, Tara reaching out to take Trevor's arm for support as she faced her father.

Dillon's gaze reluctantly left Jessica's face to move brood-

ingly over the twins. He didn't smile, didn't change expression.
"Trevor and Tara, you've certainly grown." A muscle jerked
along his jaw but otherwise he gave no indication of the emotions he was feeling. He wasn't certain he could do this, look at
them, see the look in their eyes, face up to his past failures,
face the utter and total revulsion that he had seen in Tara's eyes
the night before.

Trevor's gaze flickered uncertainly toward Jessica before he
stepped forward, thrusting out his hand toward his father. "It's
good to see you, sir."

Jessica watched Dillon closely, willing him to pull his son
into a hug. To at least smile at the boy. Instead, he shook
hands briefly. "It's good to see you, too. I understand you're
here to celebrate Christmas with me." Dillon glanced at Tara.
"I guess that means you'll be wanting a tree."

Tara smiled shyly. "It's sort of an accepted practice."

He nodded. "I can't remember the last time I celebrated
Christmas. I'm a little rusty when it comes to holiday festivities." His gaze had strayed back to Jessica and he silently
damned himself for his lack of control.

"Tara will make sure you remember every little detail about
Christmas," Trevor said with a laugh, nudging his sister. "It's
her favorite holiday."

"I'll count on you, then, Tara," Dillon said with his custom-
ary charm, still watching Jessica intently. A smile slipped out.
Menacing. Threatening. "If you can manage to take your
hands off Jess, Brian, maybe we can all share those pancakes."
There was a distinct edge to his voice. "We keep strange hours
here, especially now that we're recording. I prefer to work at
night and sleep during the day."

Tara glanced at her brother and mouthed, "Vampire."

Trevor grinned at her, covering for his twin with a diversion.
"I take it we get pancakes for dinner."

"You'll grow to love them," Brian assured. He laughed
heartily and squeezed Jessica's shoulders quickly before dropping his arms. "She's turned into a real beauty, Dillon." He

leered at Jessica. "I don't know if I mentioned to you or not, that I'm recently divorced."

"Ever the lady's man." Jessica patted his cheek, determined not to let Dillon shake her confidence. "What was that, your third or fourth wife?"

"Oh, the pain of the arrows you sling, Jessica girl." Brian clutched his heart and winked at Trevor. "She never lets anything slip by, I'll bet."

Trevor grinned at him, wide and engaging, that famous Wentworth smile that Jessica knew so well. "Not a single thing, so be careful around her," he cautioned. "I'm a fairly good cook. I can help you with the pancakes. Don't let Jessie, even if she offers. The mere thought of her cooking anything is scary." He shuddered dramatically.

Jessica rolled her eyes. "He should be in acting." She was aware of Tara inching closer to her for comfort, aware of the tension in the room despite the banter. Trying to ignore Dillon, she drew the child to her and hugged her encouragingly as her father should have done. "Trevor turns traitor when he's in the company of other men, have you noticed?"

"I'm stating a fact," Trevor denied. "She sets the popcorn on fire in the microwave whenever we let her pop it."

"It's not my fault the popcorn behaves unpredictably when it's my turn to pop it," Jessica pointed out.

She stole a glance at Dillon. He was watching her intently, just as she suspected he was. When she inhaled, she took his clean, masculine scent into her lungs. He dominated the room simply by standing there, wrapped in his silence. Awareness spread through her body, an unfamiliar heat that thickened her blood and left her strangely restless.

"Can anyone join in the fun?"

The blood drained out of Jessica's face. She felt it, felt herself go pale as she turned slowly to face that strident voice. Vivian's voice. The woman was tall and model thin. Platinum blond hair was swept up onto her head and she wore scarlet lipstick. Jessica noticed her long nails were polished the exact same shade. Jessica swallowed the sudden lump in her throat and looked to Dillon for help.

"Brenda." Dillon said the woman's name deliberately, needing to wipe the fear out of Jessica's eyes. "Jess, I don't believe you ever had the chance to meet Vivian's sister. Brenda, this is Jessica Fitzpatrick and these are my children, Trevor and Tara."

The twins looked at one another and then at Jessica. Trevor put his arm around Tara. "We have an aunt, Jessie?"

"Apparently," Jessica said, her gaze on Dillon. She had never seen Brenda in her life. She had a vague recollection of someone mentioning her, but Brenda certainly had never come to see the children.

"Of course I'm your aunt," Brenda announced, waving her hand airily. "But I travel quite a bit and just haven't gotten around to visiting. No pancakes for me, Brian, just coffee." She walked across the kitchen and threw herself into a chair as if she were exhausted. "I had no idea the little darlings were coming, Dillon." She blew him a kiss. "You should have told me. They certainly take after you, don't they?"

"Must have been a lot of traveling," Trevor muttered, leaning into Jessica. He quirked an eyebrow at her, half amused, half annoyed, in a way that was very reminiscent of his father.

Jessica felt Tara tremble and immediately brushed the top of her head with a kiss. "It isn't quite dark yet, honey, would you like to go for a short walk? The storm's passed over us and it would be fun to show you how beautiful the island is."

"Don't leave on my account," Brenda said, "I don't get along with kiddies. I make no apologies for it. I need coffee, for heaven's sake, can't one of you manage to bring me a cup?" Her voice rose, a familiar pitch that was etched for all time in Jessica's memory. "Robert, the lazy slug, is still in bed." She yawned and leveled her gaze at Dillon. "You've turned us all around so we don't know whether it's morning or night anymore. My poor husband can't get out of bed."

"Are you here for Christmas?" Trevor ventured, uncertain

what to say, but instinctively wanting to find a way to smooth out the situation.

"Christmas?" It was Brian who answered derisively. "Brenda doesn't know what Christmas is, besides a day she expects to be showered with gifts. She's here for more money, aren't you, my dear? She's gone through Robert's money and the insurance money, so she dropped by with her hand out."

"So true." Brenda shrugged her shoulders, unconcerned with Brian's harsh assessment of her. "Money is the bane of all existence."

"She has an insurance policy on everyone, don't you, Brenda," Brian accused. "Me, Dillon," he indicated the twins with his jaw, his eyes glittering at her, "the kids. Poor Robert is probably worth far more dead than alive. What do you have on him, a cool million?"

Brenda raised one eyebrow, blew another kiss at him. "Of course, darling, it's just good sense. I figured you'd go first with your horrendous driving abilities, but, alas, no luck so far."

Brian glared at her. "You're a cold woman, Brenda."

"You didn't used to think so, babe."

Jessica stared at her. *Insurance policy on the kids. On Dillon.* She didn't dare look at Dillon; he would know exactly the suspicion going through her mind.

Brenda gave a tinkling laugh. "Don't look so shocked, Jessica, dear. Brian and I are old friends. It ended badly and he can't forgive me." She inspected her long nails. "He actually adores me and still wants me. I adore him, but choosing Robert was a good decision. He balances me." She lifted her head, moaning pathetically, her eyes pleading. "I could *kill* for a cup of coffee."

Jessica turned over the information in her mind. Insurance money. It had never occurred to her that someone other than Dillon or the children might have profited monetarily from Vivian's death. She remembered her mother talking about it with Dillon's lawyer after the fire. The lawyer had said it was good that Dillon didn't have a policy on his wife because an insurance policy was often considered a reason for murder.

Reason for murder. Could an insurance policy on Tara's and Trevor's lives be the motive behind the accidents? Jessica looked at Brenda, trying to see past her perfect makeup to the woman beneath.

"How could you have an insurance policy on Vivian, Brenda?" Jessica asked curiously. "Or on Brian or Dillon or the twins? That's not legal."

"Oh please." Brenda waved her hand. "I'm dying for coffee and you want to talk legalities. Fine, a little lesson, kiddies, in grown-up reality. Viv and I went together to get insurance on each other years ago. With consent it can be done. Dillon gave his consent," she blew him another kiss, "because we're family. Brian gave consent when we were together and Robert's my husband, so *of course* I have insurance on him."

"And you're so good at persuading people to let you have those policies, aren't you, Brenda," Brian snapped.

"Of course I am." Brenda smiled at him, in no way perturbed by his accusations. "You're becoming so tedious with your jealousy. Really, darling, you need help."

"You're going broke paying your insurance premiums," Brian sniped.

Brenda shrugged and waved airily. "I just call Dillon and he pays them for me. Now, stop being so mean, Brian, and bring me coffee; it won't hurt you to be nice for a change," Brenda wheedled, slumping dramatically over the table.

"Yes, it would," he said stubbornly. "Doing anything for you is bad karma."

"But how would you manage to take out a policy on the twins?" The very idea of it repulsed Jessica.

Brenda didn't lift her head from the tabletop. "My sister and Dillon gave me permission of course. I'm not talking anymore, without coffee! I'm fading here, people."

Jessica glared accusingly at Dillon across the room. He flashed a heart-stopping, rather sheepish smile and shrugged his broad shoulders. Brenda groaned loudly. Jessica gave in. It was clear that Brian wasn't going to get Vivian a cup of coffee and Dillon looked unconcerned. She found the mugs in a cupboard and did the honors. "Cream or sugar?"

"You don't have to do that, Jess," Dillon snapped suddenly, his mouth tightening ominously. "Brenda, get your own damn coffee."

"It's no big deal." Jessica handed the cup to Brenda.

"Thank you, my dear, you are a true lifesaver." Her eyes wandered over Jessica's figure, an indifferent, blasé appraisal, then she turned her attention to Tara. "You look nothing like your mother, but fortunately you inherited Dillon's good looks. It should take you far in life."

"Tara is at the top of her class," Jessica informed the woman, "her brains are going to take her far in life."

Trevor wolfed down a pancake without syrup. "Watch yourself now, Jessica's got that militant look in her eye." His voice changed, a perfect mimic of Jessica's. "'School is important and if you mess around thinking you can get by on good looks or charm, or think you're going to make it big in the arts, think again buddy, you're going nowhere if you don't have a decent education.'" He grinned at them. "Word for word, I swear, you opened a can of worms."

"Looks have gotten me what I want in life," Brenda muttered into her coffee cup.

"Maybe you weren't aspiring high enough," Jessica said, looking Brenda in the eye.

Brenda shuddered, surrendering. "I don't have the energy for this conversation. I told you I wasn't good with kiddies or animals."

"Tara," Jessica said, as she handed the girl a plate of pancakes, "you are the kiddie and that brother of yours is the animal."

Trevor grinned at her. "Too true, and all the girls know it."

Dillon watched them bantering back and forth so easily. *His* children. *His* Jessica. They were a family, basking in each other's love. He was the outsider. The circle was tight, the bond strong between the three of them. He watched the expressions chasing across Jessica's face as she snapped a tea towel at Trevor, laughing at him, teasing him. The way it should have been. The way it was supposed to be.

Jessica was aware of Dillon every moment that they stayed in the same room. Her wayward gaze kept straying to him. Her pulse raced and he affected her breathing. It was aggravating and made her feel like a teenager with a crush. "We want to go for that walk before it gets dark, don't we, Tara?" Now *she* wanted to escape. Needed to escape. She couldn't stay in the same room with him much longer.

"The grounds haven't been kept up, Jess," Dillon informed her. "It might be better if you amuse yourselves inside while we work."

Her eyebrow shot up. "Amuse ourselves?" She ignored Trevor's little warning nudge. "What did you have in mind? Playing hopscotch in the hall?"

Dillon looked at his son's face, the quick, appreciative grin the boy couldn't hide fast enough. Something warm stirred in him that he didn't want to think about or examine too closely. "Hopscotch is fine, Jess, as long as you draw the boxes with something we can erase easily." He said it blandly, watching the boy's reaction.

Trevor threw his head back and laughed. Brian joined in. Even Brenda managed a faint smile, more, Jessica suspected, because Trevor's laugh was infectious than because Brenda found anything humorous in Dillon's reply.

Jessica didn't want to look up and see Dillon smiling but she couldn't stop herself. She didn't want to notice the way his face lit up, or that his eyes were so blue. Or that his mouth was perfectly sculpted. Kissable. She nearly groaned, blushing faintly at the wild thought. The memory of his lips, velvet soft, yet firm, pressing against hers was all too vivid in her mind.

She had to say something, the twins would expect her to hold her own in a verbal sparring match, but she couldn't think, not when his blue eyes were laughing at her. Really laughing at her. For one brief moment, he looked happy, the terrible weight off his shoulders. Jessica glanced at the twins. They were observing her hopefully. She took a deep breath and deliberately leaned close to Dillon, close enough that she could feel electricity arcing between them. She put her mouth against Dillon's ear so that he could feel the softness of her lips as she spoke. "You cheat, Dillon." She whispered the three words, allowing her warm breath to play over his neck, heat his skin. To make him as aware of her as she was of him.

It was a silly, dangerous thing to do, and the moment she did it, she knew she'd made a mistake. The air stilled, the world receded until there was only the two of them. Desire flared in the depths of his eyes, burning hot, immediate. He shifted, a subtle movement but it brought his body in contact with hers. Hunger pulsed between them, deep, elemental, so strong it was nearly tangible. He bent his dark head to hers.

No one breathed. No one moved. Jessica stared into the deep blue of his eyes, mesmerized, held captive there, his perfect mouth only a scant inch from hers. "I play to win," he murmured softly, for her ears alone.

The sound of a creaking chair, as someone shifted restlessly, broke the enchantment. Jessica blinked, came out of her trance, and hastily stepped away from the beckoning heat of Dillon's body, from the magnetic pull of his sexual web. She didn't dare look at either of the children. Her heart was doing strange somersaults and the butterflies were having a field day in the pit of her stomach.

Dillon ran his gloved hand down the length of her hair in a gentle caress. "Were you and the children comfortable last night?"

Tara and Trevor looked at each other, then at Jessica. "Very comfortable," they said in unison.

Jessica was too wrapped up in the sound of his voice to answer. There was that smoky quality to it, the black velvet that was so sexy, but it was so much more. Sometimes the gentleness, the tenderness that came out of nowhere threw her completely off balance. Dillon was a mixture of old and new to her, and she was desperately trying to feel her way with him.

"That's good. If you need anything, don't hesitate to say so." Dillon poured the rest of his coffee down the sink and rinsed the cup out. "We're all pitching in with the chores as the house-keeping staff is gone on vacation this month. So I'll expect you kids to do the same. Just clean up after yourselves. You can have the run of the house with the exception of the rooms where the others are staying, my private rooms, and the studio. That's invitation only." He leaned his back against the sink and pinned the twins with his brilliant gaze. "We keep odd hours and if you get up before late afternoon, please keep quiet because most of us will be sleeping. The band is here to try recording some music, just to see what we can come up with. If it works, we hope to have a product to pitch again to one of the labels. It requires a great deal of time and effort on our part. We're *working,* not playing."

Trevor nodded. "We understand, we won't get in the way."

"If you're interested, you can watch later, after we've worked out a few kinks. I'm heading to the studio now, so if you need anything, say so now."

"We'll be fine," Trevor said. "Getting up at four or five o'clock in the afternoon and staying up all night is an experience in itself!" His white teeth flashed, an engaging smile, showing all the promise of his father's charisma. "Don't worry about us, Jess will keep us in line."

Dillon's blue gaze flicked to Jessica. Drank her in. She made his kitchen seem a home. He had forgotten that feeling. For-gotten what it was like to wake up and look forward to getting out of bed. He heard the murmur of voices around him, heard Robert Berg and Don Ford laughing in the hall as they made their way together to the kitchen. It was all so familiar yet completely different.

"Well, we have a houseful." Robert Berg, the keyboard player for the band, entered and crossed the kitchen to plant a kiss on the nape of Brenda's neck. Robert was short and compact with dark thinning hair and a small trim goatee gracing his chin. "This can't be the twins, they're all grown up."

Trevor nodded solemnly. "That happens to people. An unusual phenomenon. Time goes by and we just get older. I'm Trevor." He held out his hand.

"With the smart mouth," Jessica supplied, frowning at the boy as he shook hands with Robert. "Good to see you again, it has been a while." She dropped her hands onto Tara's shoulders. "This is Tara."

Robert smiled at the girl, saluted her as he snagged a plate and piled it high with pancakes. "Brian's been doing the cooking, Jessica, but maybe now that you're here we can have something besides pancakes."

Trevor choked, went into a coughing fit, and Tara burst out laughing. Dillon's heart turned over as he watched Jessica tug gently on Tara's hair, then mock strangle Trevor. The three of them were so easy with one another, playfully teasing, sharing a close camaraderie he had always wanted, but had never found. He had been so desperate for a home, for a family, and now when it was in front of him, when he knew what was important, what it was all about, it was too late for him.

"*Men* are the supreme chefs of the world," Jessica replied haughtily, "why would I want to infringe on their domain?"

"Here, here," Brenda applauded. "Well said."

"You coming, Brian." Dillon made it a command, not a question. "I'll expect the rest of you in ten minutes and someone get Paul up."

There was a small silence after Dillon left. It had always been that way, he dominated a room with his presence, the passion and energy in it had flowed from him. Now that he was gone there seemed to be a void.

Don Ford hurried in, his short brown hair spiked and tipped with blond and his clothes the latest fashion. "Had to get in my morning smoke. Dillon won't let us smoke in the house. Man, it's cold out there tonight." He shivered, rubbing his hands together for warmth as he looked around and caught sight of the twins and Jessica. He shoved small wire-rim glasses on his nose to peer at them. "Whoa! You weren't here when I went to bed or I'm giving up liquor for all time."

"We snuck in when you weren't looking," Jessica admitted with a smile. She accepted his kiss and made the introductions.

"Am I the last one up?"

"That would be Paul," Robert said, shoving cream and sugar across the counter toward Don.

Paul sauntered in, bent to kiss Jessica's cheek. "You're a sight for sore eyes," he greeted. "I'm here, I'm awake, you can cancel the firing squad." He winked at Tara. "Have you already made plans to go hunting for the perfect Christmas tree? We won't have time to go hunting one on the mainland so we'll have to do it the old-fashioned way and chop one down."

Brenda yawned. "I hate the sound of that. What a mess. There might be bugs, Paul. You aren't really going to get one from the wilds, are you?"

Tara looked alarmed. "We are going to have a Christmas tree, aren't we, Jessica?"

"*Jessica* doesn't have a say in the matter," Robert pointed out, "Dillon does. It's his house and we're here to work, not play. Brenda's right, a tree from out there," he said, gesturing toward the window, "would have bugs and it would be utterly unsanitary. Not to mention a fire hazard."

Tara flinched visibly. Trevor stood up, squared his shoulders, and walked straight over to Robert. "I don't think you needed to say that to my sister. And I don't like the way you said Jessica's name."

Jessica gently rested her hand on Trevor's shoulder. "Robert, that was uncalled for. None of us need reminders of the fire, we were all here when it happened." She tugged on Trevor's resistant body urging him away from Robert. "Tara, of course you'll have a tree. Your father has already agreed to one. We can't very well have Christmas without one."

Brenda sighed as she stood up. "As long as I'm not the one

dealing with all of those needles that will fall off it. You need such energy to cope with the kiddies. I'm glad it's you and not me, dear. I'm off to the studio. Robert, are you coming?"

Robert obediently followed her out without looking at any of them. Don drained his coffee cup, rinsed it carefully and waved to them. "Duty calls."

"I'm sorry about that, Jessie," Paul said. "Robert lives in his own little world. Brenda goes through money like water. Everything they had is gone. Dillon was the only one of us who was smart. He invested his share and tripled his money. The royalties on his songs keep pouring in. And because he had the kids he carried medical and fire insurance and all those grown-up things the rest of us didn't think about. The worst of it is, he tried to get us to do the same but we wouldn't listen to him. Robert needs this album to come about. If Dillon composes it and sings and produces it, you know it will go straight to the top. Robert is between a rock and a hard place. Without money, he can't keep Brenda, and he loves her." Paul shrugged and ruffled Tara's hair. "Don't let them ruin your Christmas, Tara."

"Whose idea was it to put the band back together?" Jessica asked. "I had the impression that Dillon wanted to do this, that it was his idea."

Paul shook his head. "Not a chance. He's always composing, music lives in him, he hears it in his head all the time, but up until last week, he hadn't worked with anyone but me since the fire. He can't play instruments anymore. Well, he plays, but not anything like he used to play. He doesn't have the dexterity, although he tries when he's alone. It's too painful for him. I think Robert talked to the others first and then they all came to me to see what I thought. I think they believed I could persuade him." His dark eyes held a hint of worry. "I hope I did the right thing. He's doing it for the others, you know, hoping to make them some money. That was the pitch I used and it worked. He wouldn't have done it for himself, but he's always felt responsible for the others. I thought it might be good for him but now, I don't know. If he fails . . ."

"He won't fail," Jessica said. "We'll clean up in here. You'd better go."

"Thanks, Jess." He bent and dropped a kiss on the top of her head. "I'm glad you're all here."

Trevor grinned at her the moment they were alone. "You're getting kissed a lot, Jess. I was thinking there for a few minutes when you were . . . er . . . *talking* with my dad, I might even get my first lesson in sex education." He took off running as Jessica madly snapped a tea towel at him. His taunting laughter floated back to her from up the stairs.

5

J ESSICA SLOWED MIDWAY up the staircase, the smile fading from her face. It was the smell. She would never forget the smell of that particular incense. Cedarwood and alum. She inhaled and knew there was no mistake. The odor seeped from beneath the door to her room and crept out into the hallway. Jessica paused for just a moment, allowing herself to feel the edginess creep back into her mind. It seemed to be there whenever she was alone, a warning shimmering in her brain, settling in the pit of her stomach.

"Jess?" Trevor stood at the top of the stairs, puzzlement on his face. "What is it?"

She shook her head as she walked past him to stand in front of the door to her room. Very carefully she pushed it open. Ice-cold air rushed out at her, and with it, the overpowering odor of incense. Jessica stood in the doorway of her room, unmoving, her gaze going immediately to the window. The curtains fluttered, floating on the breeze as if they were white, papery thin ghosts. For one moment there was vapor, a thick white fog permeating her room. She blinked and it seemed to dissolve, or merge with the heavy fog outside the house.

"It's freezing in here, why did you open the window?" Trevor hurried across the room to slam it closed. "What is that disgusting smell?"

Jessica had remained motionless in the doorway, but when she saw his shoulders stiffen, it galvanized her into action. She hurried to his side. "Trev?"

"What is that?" Trevor pointed to the symbol ground into the throw rug near the window.

Jessica took a deep breath. "Some people believe that they can invoke the aid of spirits, Trevor, by using certain ceremonies. What you're looking at is a crude magician's ring." She stared, mesmerized, at the two circles, one within the other, made from the ash of several sticks of incense.

"What does it mean?"

"Nothing at this point, there's nothing in it." Jessica's teeth tugged at her bottom lip. Two circles meant nothing. It was simply a starting point. "Some people believe that you can't make contact with spirits without a magic circle drawn and consecrated. The symbols invoking the spirit and also for protection would be inside." She sighed softly. "Let's check Tara's room and then yours, just to be on the safe side."

"You're shaking," Trevor pointed out.

"Am I?" Jessica rubbed her hands up and down her arms, determined not to scream. "It must be the cold." She wanted to run to Dillon, to have him hold her, to comfort her, but she knew the minute he saw that symbol he would throw each and every one of the band members out. And he would never try to make his music again.

"I want to go get Dad," Trevor said, as they entered Tara's room. "I don't like this at all."

Jessica shook her head. "Neither do I, but we can't tell your father just yet. You don't know him the way I do. He has an incredible sense of responsibility." She took his arm as they entered Tara's room. "Don't shake your head—he does. He didn't leave you alone because he didn't love you. He left you alone because he believed it was the right thing to do for you."

"Baloney!" Trevor poked around the room, making certain the window was securely closed and that no one had disturbed his sister's things. "How could he believe that leaving was the right thing to do, Jessie?"

"After the fire he spent a year in the hospital, and then he had over a year of physical therapy. You have no idea how painful it is to recover from the type of burns your father suffered. The kinds of things he had to endure. And then the trial dragged on for nearly two years. Not the actual trial, but the entire legal process. No one actually found the murderer so Dillon wasn't freed from suspicion. You had to know him. He took responsibility for everyone. He took the blame for everything that happened. He's his own worst enemy. In his mind he failed Vivian, the band, you kids, even my mother and me. I don't want to take a chance that he might quit his music. Someone wants us to go away and they know what frightens me. But they directed this prank at me, not at you."

"I knew you thought someone was trying to hurt us." Trevor shook his head as they walked into his room. "You should have told me. That's why you brought us to him."

She nodded. "He would never allow anything to happen to you. Never."

They finished the examination of Trevor's room. It was immaculate; he hadn't even pretended to be using it. "What was all that business about insurance money? Does Brenda really have a policy on us? Can she do that? It freaks me out."

"Unfortunately, it sounds as if she has. I intend to talk to your father about it at the earliest opportunity." Jessica sighed again. "I don't understand any of this. Why would someone want us gone enough to try to scare us with a magic circle?

They all know Dillon, they must realize he'd throw off the island whoever is trying to scare me. If the music is so important to them, why risk it?"

"I think it's Brenda," Trevor said. "Robert doesn't have any more money and she's looking at my dad. You come along and Dad's looking at you. Jealousy rears its ugly head. Case solved. It's the cold-hearted woman looking for the cash every time."

"Thank you, Sherlock, blame it on the woman, why don't you. Let's go back downstairs and find Tara. She's probably already cleaned the kitchen."

"Why do you think I'm stalling up here?"

Jessica was glad the tea towel was still in her hand. She snapped it at him as she followed him downstairs.

To Trevor's delight, Tara had tidied the kitchen so the three of them spent the next couple of hours exploring the house. It was fun discovering the various rooms. Dillon had antique and brand-new musical instruments of all kinds. There was a game room consisting of all the latest video and DVD equipment. Jessica had to drag Trevor out of a poolroom. The weight room caught her interest, but the twins dragged her out. Eventually they settled in the library, curled up together on the deep couch surrounded by books and antiques. Jessica found the Dickens Christmas classic and began to read it aloud to the twins.

"Jess! Damn it, Jess, where are you?" The voice came roaring out of the basement. Clipped. Angry. Frustrated.

Jessica slowly put the book aside as Dillon called for her a second time.

Tara looked frightened and reached for Jessica's hand. Trevor burst out laughing. "You're being yelled at, Jessie. I've never heard anyone yell at you before."

Jessica rolled her eyes heavenward. "I guess I'd better go answer the royal command."

"We'll just go along with you," Trevor decided, striving to sound casual as Dillon roared for her again.

Jessica hid her smile. Trevor was determined to protect her.

She loved him all the more for it. "Let's go then, before he has a stroke."

"What did you do to make him so angry?" Tara asked.

"I certainly didn't do anything," Jessica replied indignantly. "How could I possibly make him angry?"

Trevor flicked her red-gold hair. "You could make the Pope angry, Jessie. And you bait him."

"I do not!" Jessica chased him along the hall leading to the stairs. "Punky boy. An alien took you over in your sleep one night. You were good and sweet until then."

Trevor was running backward, dancing just out of her reach, laughing as he neared the top of the stairway. "I'm still good and sweet, Jessie, you just can't take hearing the truth."

"I'll show you truth," Jessica warned, making a playful grab for him.

Trevor stepped backward onto the first stair and unexpectedly slipped, his foot going out from under him. For a moment he teetered precariously, his hands flailing wildly as he tried to catch the banister. Jessica could see the fear on his young face and lunged forward to grab him, choking on stark, mind-numbing terror. Her fingers skimmed the material of his shirt, but missed. Tara, holding out both hands to her twin, screamed loudly as Trevor fell away from them.

Dillon rushed up the stairs, taking two at a time, furious that Jessica hadn't answered him when he knew *damn* well she'd heard him. Strangling her might not be a bad idea *after* she explained to that idiot Don what he was looking for. What was so difficult about hearing the right beat? The right pause? As Tara's scream registered, he glanced up to see Trevor falling backward. For one moment time stood still, his heart lodged in his throat. The boy hit him hard, squarely in the chest, driving the air out of his lungs in one blast. Protectively he wrapped his arms around his son as they both tumbled down the stairs to land heavily on the basement floor.

Jessica started down the stairs, Tara in her wake. The moment her foot touched the first stair, she felt herself slide.

Clutching the banister, she caught Tara. "Careful, baby, there's something slippery on the stair." They both clung to the banister as they rushed down.

"Are they dead?" Tara asked fearfully.

Jessica could hear muffled swearing and Trevor's yelp of pain as Dillon ran his hands none too gently over his son to check for damage. "Doesn't sound like it," she observed. She knelt beside Trevor, her fingers pushing his hair from his forehead tenderly. "Are you all right, honey?"

"I don't know." Trevor managed a wry grin, still lying on top of his father.

Dillon caught Jessica's hand, his thumb sliding over her inner wrist, feeling her frantic heartbeat. "He's fine, he fell on top of me. I'm the one with all the bruises." Fear, mixed with anger, pulsed through his body. He hadn't experienced such panic and dread in years. The sight of Trevor falling from the top of the stairs was utterly terrifying. "I can't breathe, the kid weighs a ton." Dillon didn't know whether to hug Trevor or to shake him until his teeth rattled.

Jessica pushed back the unruly waves of hair falling into the center of Dillon's forehead. "You're breathing. Thanks for catching him."

Her touch shook him. Dillon's blue gaze burned over her face hungrily. It was painful to be jealous of his son, of the tender looks she gave him, the way she loved him. The way she was so at ease with him. Dillon wanted to drag her to him right there in front of everybody and kiss her. Devour her. Consume her. She was wreaking havoc with his body, breaking his heart and reopening every gaping laceration in his soul. She was making him feel things again, forcing him to live when it was so much better to be numb.

"And it was a great catch," Trevor agreed.

Dillon shoved the boy to one side, glaring at him, furious that he had been so terrified, furious that his life was being turned upside down. "Stop fooling around, kid, you could have really been hurt. You're too old to be playing so carelessly on the stairway. Roughhousing belongs outside, that way you don't break things that don't belong to you or injure innocent parties with your stupidity."

The smile faded from Trevor's face and color crept up his neck into his face. Tara gasped, outraged. "Trevor didn't hurt your stupid staircase."

"And you need to learn how to speak to adults, young lady," Dillon concluded, switching his glare to her furious little face.

Jessica stood up, drawing Tara up with her. She reached down to help Trevor to his feet. "Trevor slipped on something on the stairs, just as I did, Dillon," she informed him icily. "Perhaps, instead of jumping to conclusions about Trevor's behavior, you should ask your other guests to be more careful and not spill things on the stairs that will send people flying."

Dillon climbed to his feet slowly, his face an expressionless mask. "What's on the stairs?"

"I didn't stop and check," Jessica answered.

"Well, let's go see." He started up the stairs with Jessica following him closely.

The top stair was shiny, a clear, oily substance covering it. Dillon hunkered down and studied it. "Looks like cooking oil, right out of the kitchen." He glanced down at the twins who were waiting at the bottom of the stairs as if suspecting them.

"They didn't spill oil here. They were with me," Jessica snapped. She reached past him, touched the oil with a fingertip, and brought it to her mouth. "Vegetable oil. Someone must have poured this oil onto the stair." Oil was used in magical ceremonies to invoke spirits. She remembered that piece of information all too well.

"Or accidentally spilled some and didn't realize it." Dillon's blue gaze slid over her. "And I wasn't accusing the kids, it didn't occur to me they did this. Don't jump to conclusions, Jess."

"Let's go ask the others," she challenged him.

He sighed. "You're angry with me." He held out his leather-covered hand to her, an instinctive gesture. The moment he realized what he'd done, he dropped his hand to his side.

"Of course I'm angry with you, Dillon, what did you expect?" Jessica tilted her head to look up at him. "Don't treat me like a child, and don't use that infuriating patronizing voice on me either. I told you the accidents that have been happening at home could easily be explained away. I'll guarantee you, no one in this house is going to admit to spilling cooking oil on the stairs."

He shrugged. "So what if they don't? This wasn't directed at Trevor and Tara—how could it be? We're recording down there. Why would anyone think the kids would come down? No one could possibly have predicted that I would be calling for you."

"I disagree. I love music and I'm a sound engineer, and everyone here knows it. And you mentioned earlier in the kitchen that the twins could come down later and watch."

He raised his eyebrow at her. "Everyone, including Brenda, is in the studio. How do you explain that?"

"The twins were with me the entire time, Dillon," Jessica countered, her green eyes beginning to smolder, "how do you explain that? And speaking of Brenda, why in the world would you give your consent to allow that woman to hold an insurance policy on you and your children?"

"She's family, Jessie, it's harmless enough, although costly," he shrugged carelessly, "and it makes her feel a part of something."

"It makes me feel like a vulture is circling overhead," Jessica muttered. She followed him back down the stairs to where the twins waited expectantly.

"Hey, we're wasting time," Brian called. "Are you two going to come and work or are you going to discuss the positive versus the negative flow of the universe around us? What's going on out there?"

"We fell down the stairs," Dillon said grimly. "We'll be right there." He leaned close to Jessica. "Take a breath, Mama Tiger, don't rip my head off," Dillon teased, searching for a way to ease the tension between them. "Pull in the claws."

Her instant, fierce defense of his children amused and pleased him.

Jessica glared at the twins. Both backed away innocently, shaking their heads in unison, awed that their father knew their secret pet name for Jessica. "I didn't tell him. Honest," Trevor added, when she kept glaring. "And he didn't mention fangs."

"Does she have fangs?" Dillon asked his son, his eyebrow shooting up. He was so relieved the boy hadn't hurt himself in the fall.

"Oh, yeah," Trevor answered, "absolutely. In a heartbeat. Fear for your life if you mess with us."

Dillon grinned suddenly, his face lighting up, mischief flickering for a brief moment in the deep blue of his eyes. "Believe me, son, I would."

Trevor stood absolutely still, shaken at the emotion pouring into him at his father's words. Jessica's hand briefly touched his shoulder in silent understanding.

"Come on, Jessica, we could use a little help." Dillon caught her arm and marched her down the hall as if she were his prisoner. He leaned close to her as they walked, his breath warm against her ear. "And I am *not* volatile." He glanced back at the twins, beckoning to them. "If you two can keep quiet, you can come and watch. Brenda! I have a job for you."

Jessica made a face at Trevor behind Dillon's back that set the children laughing as Dillon dragged her into the sound room.

"A job?" Brenda stretched languidly as she stood up. "Surely not, Dillon. I haven't actually worked in years. The idea is a bit on the daunting side."

"I think you'll find it easy enough. There's oil on the stairway, a large amount of it. It makes the stairs dangerous and it needs to be cleaned up. My household staff is gone, we're all pitching in, so this is your task for the day."

Brenda widened her eyes in shocked dismay. "You can't possibly be serious, Dillon. It was a terrible decision to allow your staff to leave. What were you thinking to do such a crazy thing?"

"That it was Christmastime and they might want to be with their families," Dillon lied. The truth was he hadn't wanted anyone to witness him falling flat on his face while he worked with the band. It was terrifying to think of the enormity of what he was doing. "You knew there was no staff, that we would be working. You agreed to help with the everyday chores if I allowed you to come."

"Well, chores, of course. Fluffing the towels in the bathroom, not cleaning up a mess on the stairs. You," she pointed to Tara, "surely you could do this little job."

Before Tara could reply Dillon shook his head. "You, Brenda, get to it. Tara and Trevor, sit over there. Jessica, take a look at my notations and listen to the tracks and see if it makes any sense to you. I'm ready to pull out my hair here." He pulled Jessica over to a chair, pressing down on her shoulders until she sat. "It's a nightmare."

Jessica waited until he was safely in the studio before muttering her reply. "It is now. Working with Dillon Wentworth is going to be pure hell." She winked at the twins. "Wait until you see him. He's all passion and energy. Quicksilver. And he yells when he doesn't get *exactly* what he wants."

"Big surprise there," Trevor said drolly.

Brenda threw a pencil onto the floor, a small rebellion. "That man is an overbearing, dominating madman when he's working. I don't know where he gets the mistaken idea he can boss me around."

"True, but he's a musical genius and he makes lots and lots of money for everyone," Jessica reminded, frowning down at the sheets of music. It was obvious Dillon's smaller motor skills were lacking, his musical notations were barely legible scratches.

Brenda sighed. "Fine then, it's true, we need our wonderful cash machine, so I'll do my part to make him happy. One of you kiddies should take a picture of me scrubbing the stairs like Cinderella. It might be worth a fortune." She gave her tinkling laugh. "I know Robert would certainly love to see such a thing, but then, it would ruin his image of me and I can't let him think I'm capable of working." She winked at Trevor. "I'm trusting you not to say a word to him. If you both want to come with me, I'll even pass on smoking, which the master has decreed I can't do in his house."

"Well, you shouldn't smoke. It's not good for you," Tara pointed out judiciously.

Brenda made a face at her. "Fine, stay here and listen to your father yell at everyone, but it won't be nearly as entertaining as watching me." Her high heels tapped out her annoyance as she left.

Jessica spent an hour deciphering Dillon's musical notations then listening through the tracks he had already recorded, trying to find the mix Dillon was looking for. The problem was, the band members weren't hearing the same thing in their heads that Dillon was hearing. Don was no lead guitarist; his gift lay in his skill with the bass. It was apparent to Jessica that the band needed a lead, but she wasn't altogether certain who could play Dillon's music the way he wanted it to be played. Most musicians had egos. No one was going to allow Dillon to tell him how to play.

She saw that the band had once more ground to a halt. Brian grimaced at her through the glass. Paul shook his head at her, worry plain on his face. She leaned over to flip the switch to flood the room with sound. Dillon paced back and forth, energy pouring out of him, filling the studio, flashes of brilliance, of pure genius mixed with building frustration and impatience.

"Why can't any of you hear it?" Dillon smacked his palm to his head, stormed over to the guitar leaning against the wall. "What's so difficult about anticipating the beat? Slow the melody down, you're rushing the riff. It isn't to show what an awesome player you are alone, it's a harmony, a blending so that it smokes." He cradled the guitar, held it lovingly, almost tenderly. The need to play what he heard in his head was so strong his body trembled.

Watching him through the glass, Jessica felt her heart shatter. She could read him, and his need to bring the music to life, so easily. Dillon had always been exacting, a perfectionist when it came to his music. His passion came through in his composing, in his lyrics, in his playing. It was what had shot the band to the top and all of them knew it. They wanted it again, and they were banking on him to find it for them.

Dillon glared at Don. "Try again and this time get it right."

Visibly sweating, Don glanced uneasily at the others. "I'm not going to play it any differently than I did the last time, Dillon. I'm not you. I'll never be you. I can't hear what you want me to hear just by you telling me about blending and smoke and strings. I'm not you."

Dillon swore, his blue eyes burning with such intensity Don stepped away from him and held up his hand. "I want this, I do. I'm telling you, we need to find someone else to play lead guitar because it's not going to be me. And no matter who we get, Dillon, it still won't be you. You aren't ever going to be satisfied."

Dillon winced as if Don had struck him. The two men stared at one another for a long moment and then Dillon turned and abruptly stalked out of the room. He stood in the sound room, head down, breathing deeply, trying to push down despair. He never should have tried, never should have thought he could do it. Aloud, he cursed his hands, cursed his scarred, useless body, cursed his passion for music.

Tears swam in Tara's eyes and she buried her face against her brother's shoulder. Trevor put his arm around his sister and looked at Jessica.

The movement snapped Dillon back to reality. Jessica was fiddling with a row of keys, concentrating intently, not looking at him. "Jess!" The sight of her was inspiring, a gift! He stalked across the room like a prowling panther, caught her arm, and pulled her to him. "You do it, Jess, I know you hear what I hear. It's there inside of you, it's always been there. We've always shared that connection. Get in there and play that song the way it's meant to be played." He was dragging her toward the door. "You've been playing guitar since you were five."

"What are you thinking? I can't play with your band!" Jessica was appalled. "Don will get it right, stop yelling at him and give him time."

"He'll never get it right, he doesn't love the melody. You have to love it, Jessica. Remember all those nights we sat up playing in the kitchen? The music's in you, you live it and breathe it. It's alive to you the same way it is for me."

"But that was different, it was just the two of us."

"I know you play guitar brilliantly, I've heard you. I know you would never give up playing, you hear it the same way I hear it." He was shoving her, actually pushing her as she mulishly tried to dig in her heels.

Jessica looked to the twins for support but they were wearing identical grins. "She plays every day, sometimes for hours," Tara volunteered helpfully.

"Little traitor," Jessica hissed, "you've been hanging around with your brother too long. Both of you have dish duty for the next week."

Both of us?" Trevor squeaked. "I'm innocent in this. Come on, Tara, let's leave them to it. We can explore that game room a little more."

"Deserters," Jessica added. "Rats off the sinking ship. I'll remember this." She was holding the door to the studio closed with her foot.

"Actually, I think it will be fun to catch Aunt Brenda cleaning the goop off the stairs," Tara said mischievously. She flounced out with a little wave and Trevor sauntered after her, grinning from ear to ear.

"It's obvious that you raised them," Dillon said, his lips against her ear, his arm hard around her waist. "They both have smart mouths on them."

"Stop making such a spectacle! You have the entire band grinning at us like apes!" Jessica pushed away from him, made a show of straightening her clothes and smoothing her hair. Her chin went up. "I'll do this, Dillon. I think I have an idea of what you're looking for, but it will take some time to pull it out of my head. Don't yell at me while I'm working. Not once, do you understand? Do not raise your voice to me or I will walk out of that room so fast you won't know what hit you."

"I'd like to get away with saying that," Brian observed.

"You all can take a break. Jessica is going to save the day for us."

"I am *not.*" She glared at Dillon. "I'm just going to see if I can figure it out and if I can get it, I'll play it for you. Do you mind, Don?"

"I'm grateful, Jess." Don smiled for the first time since entering the studio. "Yell very loud if you need help and we'll all come running."

"Great, the place is soundproof." Jessica picked up the guitar and idly began to play a blues riff, allowing her fingers to wander over the strings, her ear tuning itself to the tones of the instrument, familiarizing herself with the feel of it. "You're leaving me with Dillon, just remember that."

<h1 style="text-align:center">6</h1>

J ESSICA CLOSED HER EYES as she played, allowing the music to move through her body. Her heart and soul. It wasn't right, there was something missing, something she wasn't quite hitting. It was so close, so very close, but she couldn't quite reach it. She shook her head, listening with her heart. "It's not quite what it should be. It's almost there, but it isn't perfect."

There was frustration in her voice, enough that Dillon checked what he would have said and waited a heartbeat so that his own frustration wouldn't betray him. She didn't need him raging at her. What she needed was complete harmony between them. Unlike Don, Jessica was aware of what he wanted, she heard a similar sound in her own head, but it wasn't coming through her fingers. "Let's try something else, Jess. Pull it back a bit. Hold the notes longer, let the music breathe."

She nodded without looking at him, intense concentration on her face as her fingers lovingly moved over the strings. She listened to the flow, the pitch, a moody, introspective score, opening slowly, building, until the pain and heartbreak swelled, spilled over, filling the room until her heart was breaking and there were tears in her eyes. Her fingers stopped moving abruptly. "It's not the guitar, Dillon. The sound is there, haunting and vivid, the emotions pouring out of the music. Listen, right here, it's right here." She played the notes once, twice, her fingers lingering, drawing out the sounds. "This isn't a piece where we can just lay a track and have bass and drums doing their thing. It isn't ever going to be enough."

He snapped his fingers, indicating for her to play again, his head cocked to one side, his eyes closed. "A saxophone? Something soft and melancholy? Right there, cutting into that passage, lonely, something lonely."

Jessica nodded and she smiled, her entire face lighting up. "Exactly, that's it exactly. The sax has to cut in right there and take the spotlight for just a few bars, the guitar fading a bit into the background. This melody is too much for just bass and drums. We just aren't looking at the entire picture. When we mix it, we can try a few things, but I'd like to hear what it would sound like with Robert giving us synthesized orchestra sounds on the keyboard. This song should have more texture to it. The vocal will add the depth we need."

Dillon paced across the room, once, twice, then stopped in front of her. "I can hear the saxophone perfectly. It has to come in right on the beat in the middle of the buildup."

She nodded. "I'm excited—I think it will work. I've got the ideas for mixing. Don can come in and play it . . ."

"No!" He nearly bit her head off, his blue eyes burning at her. He looked moody, dark. Intriguing. Jessica nearly groaned. She looked away from him, wishing she didn't find him so attractive. Wishing it was only chemistry sizzling between them and not so many other things.

"Don will never have your passion, Jess. He knows that, he as much as said so. He told me to find another lead."

She leaned the guitar very carefully against the wall. "Well, it isn't going to be me. I can't play the way you want—I don't have enough experience. And even if I did, this is a men's club. Very few musicians want to admit that a woman can handle a guitar."

"You'll have the experience when we need it. I'll help you," he promised. "And the band wants this to work. They'll try anything to keep it going forward."

She shook her head, backing away from him as if he were stalking her.

Dillon's grin transformed his face. He looked boyish, charming, altogether irresistible. "Want to go for a walk with me?"

It was late, already dark outside. She had been away from the twins for a long while but the temptation of spending more time alone with him was too much to resist. She nodded her head.

"There's a door over here." He picked up one of the sweaters he'd thrown aside days earlier and dragged it over her head. Shrugging into his jacket, Dillon opened the door and stepped back to allow her to go first. He whistled softly and the German shepherd who had greeted Jessica and the twins so rudely when they had arrived, came running to them, a blur of dark fur.

The night was crisp, cold, the air coming off the ocean, misty with salt and tendrils of fog. They found a narrow path winding through the trees and took it, side by side, their hands occasionally brushing. Jessica didn't know how it happened but somehow her hand ended up snugly in his.

She glanced up at him, drawing in her breath, her heart fluttering, racing. Happy. But it was now or never. She either cleared the air between them or he would be lost to her. "How did you happen to end up with Vivian? She didn't seem to fit you."

For a long moment she thought he wouldn't answer her. They walked in silence for several yards and then he let out his breath in a long, slow exhale.

"Vivian." Dillon swept his free hand through his black hair and glanced down at her. "Why did I marry Vivian? That's a good question, Jess, and one I've asked myself hundreds of times."

They walked together beneath the canopy of trees, surrounded by thick forest and heavy brush. The wind rustled through the leaves gently, softly, a light breeze that seemed to follow them as they followed a deer path through the timber. "Dillon, I never understood how you chose her, you two were so different."

"I knew Vivian all of my life, we grew up in the same trailer park. We had nothing. None of us did, not Brian, or Robert, or Paul. Certainly not Viv. We all hung out together, playing our music and dreaming big dreams. She had a hard life, she and Brenda both. Their mother was a drunk with a new man every week. You can imagine what life was like for two little girls living unprotected in that environment."

"You felt sorry for her." Jessica made it a statement.

Dillon winced. "No, that would make me appear noble. I'm not noble in this, Jess, no matter how much you want me to be. I cared a great deal for her, I thought I loved her. Hell, I was eighteen when we got together. I certainly wanted to protect her, to take care of her. I knew she didn't want kids. She and Brenda were terrified of losing their figures and being left behind. Their mother drilled it into them that it was their fault the men always left because they had ruined her figure. She even told them, when her boyfriends came on to them, that it was their fault, that of course the men preferred them to her." He raked his hand through his hair again, a quick, impatient gesture. "I'd heard it from the time we were kids. I heard Vivian say she would never have a baby, but I guess I didn't listen."

They continued along the deer path for several more minutes in silence. Jessica realized they were moving toward the cliffs almost by mutual consent. "So many old ghosts," she observed, "and neither one of us has managed to lay them to rest."

Dillon brought her hand to the warmth of his chest, right over his heart. "You didn't have the kind of life we lived, Jess, you can't understand. She never had a childhood. I was all Vivian had—me and the band and Brenda, when she wasn't fighting her own demons. When Vivian found out she was pregnant, she freaked. Totally freaked. Couldn't handle it. She begged me to give her permission to get rid of them, but I wanted a family. I thought she'd come around after they were born. I married her and promised we'd hire a nanny to take care of the kids while we worked the band."

Dillon led the way out of the timberline onto the bare cliffs overlooking the sea. At once the wind whipped his hair across his face. Instinctively he turned so that his larger body sheltered hers. "I hired Rita to take care of the children and we left. We just left." He stared down at her, his blue eyes brooding as he brought her hand to the warmth of his mouth. His teeth scraped gently, his tongue swirled over her skin.

Jessica shivered in response, her body clenching, molten fire suddenly pooling low in her belly. She could hear the guilt in his voice, the regret, and she forced herself to stay focused. "The band was making it big."

"Not right away, but we were on the upswing." He reached out, because he couldn't stop himself, and crushed strands of bright red-gold hair in his fist. "I wanted it so bad, Jess, the money, the good life. I never wanted to have to worry about a roof over our heads or where the next meal was coming from. We worked hard over the next three years. When we would go home, Vivian would bring the twins bags of presents but she would never touch them, or talk to them." He allowed the silky strands to slide through his fingers. "By the time the twins were four, the band was a wild success but we were all falling apart." Abruptly he let go of her.

"I remember her coming in with gifts," Jessica acknowledged, shivering a little as the wind blew in from the sea. All at once she felt alone. Bereft. "Vivian stayed away from us, away from the twins. She didn't come home very often." Dillon had visited without her, but Vivian had preferred to stay in the city most of the time with the other band members.

A peculiar fog was drifting in on the wind from the sea. It was heavy, almost oppressive. The dog looked out toward the pounding waves and a growl rumbled low in his throat. The sound sent a chill down Jessica's spine but Dillon snapped his fingers and the animal fell silent.

"No, she didn't." Dillon shrugged out of his jacket and helped her into it. "She was always so fragile, so susceptible to fanatical thinking. I knew she was drinking. Hell, we were all drinking. Partying was a way of life back then. Brian was into some strange practices, not devil worship, but calling on spirits and gods and mother earth. You know how he can be, he runs a line of bull all the time. The problem was, he had Vivian believing all of it. I didn't pay attention, I just laughed at them. I didn't realize then that she was seriously ill. Later, the doctors told me she was bipolar, but at the time, I just thought it was all part of the business we were in. The drinking, even the drugs, I thought she'd tame down when she got it out of her system. I didn't realize she was self-medicating. But I should have, Jess, I should have seen it. She had the signs, the intense mood swings, the highs and lows and the abrupt changes in her thinking and behavior. I should have known."

His hands suddenly framed her face, holding her still. "I laughed, Jess, and while I was laughing about their silly ceremonies, she was going downhill, straight into madness. The drugs pushed her over the edge and she had a schizophrenic break. By the time I realized just how bad she really was, it was too late and she tried to hurt you."

"You put her in rehabs—how could you have known what bipolar even was?" She remembered that clearly. "No one told you that last year while you were on the world tour just how bad she'd gotten. You were in Europe. I heard them all discussing it; the decision was made not to say anything to you because you would have thrown it all away. The band knew. Paul, Robert, especially Brian, he called several times to talk to her. Your manager, Eddie Malone, was adamant that everyone stay quiet. He arranged for her to stay here, on the island. He thought with all the security she would be safe."

Dillon let go of her again, his blue gaze sliding out to sea. "I knew, Jess. I knew she had slipped past sanity, but I was so wrapped up in the tour, in the music, in myself, I didn't check on her. I left it to Eddie. When I'd talk to her on the phone she was always so hysterical, so demanding. She'd sob and threaten me. I was a thousand miles away and feeling so much pressure, and I was tired of her tantrums. At the time I listened to everyone telling me she would pull out of it. I let her down. My God, she trusted me to take care of her and I let her down."

"You were barely twenty-seven, Dillon—cut yourself some slack."

He laughed softly, bitterly. "You always persist in thinking the best of me. Do you think she started out the way she ended up? She was far too fragile for the life I took her into. I wanted everything. The family. The success. My music. It was all about what I wanted, not what she needed." He shook his head. "I did try to understand her at first, but she was so needy and my time was stretched so thin. And the kids. I blamed her for not wanting them, not wanting to be with them."

"That's natural, Dillon," Jessica said softly. She tucked her hand into the crook of his arm, wanting to connect herself to him, wanting the terrible pain, the utter loneliness etched so deeply into his face, to be gone.

The fog thickened, a heavy blanket that carried within it the whisper of something moving, of muffled sounds and veiled memories. It bothered her that the dog stared at the fog as if it held an enemy within its midst. She tried to ignore the animal's occasional growl. Dillon, too engrossed in their conversation, didn't appear to notice.

"Is it natural, Jess?" His eyebrow shot up as he looked down into her wide green eyes. "You're so willing to forgive my mistakes. I left the kids. I put my career first, my own needs first, what I wanted, first. Why was it okay for me, but unforgivable for her? She was ill. She knew she had something wrong with her; she was terrified of hurting the kids. She didn't need rehab, she needed help with mental illness." He rubbed his hand over his face, his breath coming in hard gasps. "I didn't come home much that year because of you, Jessica. Because I was feeling things for you I shouldn't have been feeling. Rita knew, God help me. I talked to her about it and we agreed the best thing to do was for me to stay away from you. It wasn't sex, Jess, I swear to you, it was never about sex."

There was so much pain in his voice her heart was breaking. She looked up at him and saw tears shimmering in his eyes. At once she put her arms around his waist, laid her head on his chest, holding him to her without words, seeking to comfort him. He had never touched her, never said a word that might be deemed improper to her, nor had she to him. But it was true they'd sought each other's company, talked endlessly, *needed* to be close. She could feel his body tremble, with emotion rising like a long dormant volcano come to life.

Dillon was all about responsibility; he always had been. She had always known that. His failure was eating him from the inside out. Jessica felt helpless to stop it. She drew back cautiously, putting a step between them so she could look up at his face. "Did you know she was into séances and calling up demons?" She had to ask him and her heart pounded in time to the rhythm of the sea as she waited for his answer.

"She and Brian would burn candles to spirits but there had been nothing remotely like devil worship, sacrifices, or the occult. I didn't know she had hooked up with some lunatic who preached orgies and drugs and demon gods. I had no idea until I walked into that room and saw you." He closed his eyes, his fist clenching.

"You got me out of there, Dillon," she reminded gently.

Rage. He tasted it again, just as it had swirled up in him that night, a violence he hadn't known himself capable of. He had wanted to destroy them all. Every single person in that room. He had beat Vivian's lover to a bloody pulp, satisfying some of his rage in that direction. He had vented on Vivian, his wrath nearly out of control, calling her every name he could think of, allowing her to see his disgust, ordering her out of his home. He had sworn she would never see the children, never be allowed into his life again. Vivian had stood there, naked, sobbing, and hanging on him, the musty smell of other men clinging to her as she begged him not to send her away.

Dillon looked down to meet Jessica's vivid gaze. They both recalled the scene clearly. How could they not remember every detail? The heavy fog carried a strange phosphorescence within, a shimmering of color that floated inland.

Dillon looked away from the innocence on Jessica's face. Staring at the white breakers he made his confession. "I wanted to kill her. I didn't feel pity, Jessica. I wanted to break her neck. And I wanted to kill her friends. Every last one of them."

There was honesty in his voice. Truth. She heard the echo of rage in his voice, and the memories washed over her, shook her. He had learned there was a demon hidden deep within him and Jessica had certainly witnessed it.

"You didn't kill them, Dillon." She said it with complete conviction.

"How do you know, Jess? How can you be so certain I didn't go back into that room after I carried you upstairs? How can you be so certain, after I laid you on the bed with your heart torn out, after I knew that she had encouraged some lecherous pervert to put his hands on you, to write symbols of evil all over your body? When I saw you like that, so frightened—"

His fist clenched tightly. "You were everything good and innocent that they weren't. They wanted to destroy you. Why
would you believe that I didn't walk back up the stairs, shoot
both of them, lock them all in that room, start the fire, and
leave the house?"

"Because I know you. Because the twins, the band members, my mother, and I were all in that house."

"Everyone is capable of murder, Jess, and believe me, I
wanted them dead." He sighed heavily. "You need to know the
truth. I did go back into the house that night."

A silence fell between them, stretching out endlessly while
the wind rose on a moan and shrieked eerily out to sea. Jessica
stood on the cliffs and stared down into the dark foaming
waves. So beautiful, so deadly. She remembered vividly the
feeling of the water closing over her head as she went after Tara
who had tumbled down the steep embankment. She felt exactly the same way now, as if she were being submersed in ice-
cold water and dragged down to the very bottom of the sea.
Jessica looked up at the moon. The clouds, heavy with moisture, were sliding through the sky to streak the silver orb with
shades of gray. The fog formed tendrils, long thin arms that
stretched out as greedily as the waves leapt and crashed against
the rocky shore.

"Everyone knows you went back. The house was on fire and
you ran in." Her voice was very low. There was sudden awareness, a knowledge growing inside of her.

Dillon caught her chin, looked into her eyes, forcing her to
meet his gaze, to see the truth. "After I left your room I went outside. Everyone saw me. Everyone knew I was furious at Vivian. I
was crying, Jess, after seeing you like that, knowing what you'd
been through. I couldn't stop ranting, couldn't hide the tears.
The band thought I'd caught Viv with a lover. I stalked out, huddled in the forest, walked around the house a couple of times.
But then I went to find your mother. I felt she ought to know
what Vivian, her friends, and that madman had done to you."

"She never said a word to me."

"I told her what happened. All of it. How I found you with them. What they were doing. I was crazy that night," he admitted. "Rita was the only person I could talk to and I knew you wouldn't tell her about it, you kept begging me not to, you couldn't bear for her to know." He raked a hand through his hair again in agitation, the memories choking him. "Rita blamed herself. She knew what Vivian was doing, had known for some time. I yelled at her when she admitted it, I was so angry, so out of control, wanting vengeance for what had happened to you. Looking back, I can see that it was my fault, all of it. I blamed everyone else for what happened to you, and I hated them and wanted them dead, but I was the one that allowed it to happen."

Dillon studied her face as she stared up at him with her wide eyes. He reached out, brushed her face with his gloved hand, his touch lingering long after he dropped his hand. "I went back into the house, angry and determined to avenge you. Rita knew I went back. Your mother believed I murdered Vivian and her lover. She thought the fire was an accident, caused by the candles being knocked over while we were fighting. She knew I went back into the house and she believed I shot them but she never told anyone."

Jessica's green gaze jumped to his face. "She didn't believe you killed them." She shook her head adamantly. "Mom would never believe that of you."

"She knew my state of mind. There was so much rage in me that night. I didn't even recognize myself. I had no idea I was capable of such violence. It consumed me. I couldn't even think straight."

Jessica shook her head. "I won't listen to this. I won't believe you." She turned away from him, away from the pounding sea and the heartache, away from the thick, beckoning fog, back toward the safety of the house.

Dillon caught her arms, held her still, his blue eyes raking her face. "You have to know the truth. You have to know why I stayed away all those years. Why your mother came to see me."

"I don't care what you say to me, Dillon, I'm not going to believe this. Seven people died in that fire. *Seven.* My mother may have kept quiet to save you because of what Vivian did to me, but she would never stay quiet if she thought you'd killed seven people."

"But then, if the fire was an accident, it wouldn't have been murder, and those seven people who died were having an orgy upstairs in my home, using Rita's daughter as the virginal sacrifice for their priests to enjoy." He said it harshly, his face a mask of anger. "Believe me, honey, she understood hatred and rage. She felt it herself."

Jessica stared up at him for a long while. "Dillon." She reached up to lay her hand along his shadowed jaw. "You will never get me to believe you shot Vivian. Never. I know your soul. I've always known it. You can't hide who you are from me. It's there each time you write a song." Her arms slid around his neck, her fingers twining in the silk of his hair. "You were different enough at first that I was afraid of who you had become, but you can't hide yourself from me when you compose music."

Dillon's arms stole around her. It was amazing to him, a miracle that she could believe in him the way she did. He held her tightly, burying his face in her soft hair, stealing moments of pleasure and comfort that didn't belong to him.

"My mother never said a word to me, Dillon, about what happened to me that night. Why didn't she talk to me about it all those years? The nightmares. I wanted someone to talk to." She had wanted him.

"She told me she waited for you to come to her, but you never did."

Jessica sighed softly as she pulled away from him. "I could never bring myself to tell her what happened. I felt guilty. I still go over every move I made, wondering what I should have done differently to avoid the situation." Her hand rubbed up and down his arms. She felt the raised ridges of his scars beneath her palm, the evidence of his heroism. A badge of love and honor he hid from the world. "How could Mom have thought you were guilty?"

"I told her what went on and the entire time I was breaking things, threatening them, swearing like a madman. She was sobbing; she sat on the floor in the kitchen with her hands over her face, sobbing. I went back upstairs. I didn't know what I was going to do. I think I was going to physically throw Vivian and her friends out of the house, one by one, into the ocean. Your mother saw me go up the stairs. I stood on the landing and could hear Vivian weeping, shrieking to the others to get out, and I knew I couldn't look at her again. I just couldn't. I went back downstairs and out through the courtyard. I didn't want to face your mother, or the band. I needed to be alone. I walked into the forest and sat down and cried."

She could breathe again. Really breathe again. He wasn't going to do anything silly such as try to convince her that he had actually shot Vivian. "I've always known you were innocent, Dillon. And I still don't think my mother believed you killed them."

"Oh, she believed it, Jessica. She stayed silent at the trial, but she made it abundantly clear that I wasn't to go near you or the children. I owed her that much. For what happened to you, I owed her my life if she asked for it."

Jessica felt as if he'd knocked her legs out from under her. "She never said anything but good things about you, Dillon."

"She knew I wanted you, Jess. There was no way I would ever be able to be around you and not make you mine." He admitted it without looking at her.

His tone was so casual, so matter-of-fact, she wasn't certain she heard him correctly. He was looking out to sea, into the thick veil of mist, not at her.

"And I would have let you." She confessed it in the same casual tone, following his example, looking out at the crashing waves.

His throat worked convulsively; a muscle jerked along his jaw at her honest admission. He waited a heartbeat. Two. Struggled for control of his emotions. "Someone has been attempting to blackmail me. They sent a threatening letter, telling me that they knew I had gone back into the house that night and that if I didn't give them ten thousand dollars a month, they would go to the police. I was supposed to transfer the money to a Swiss account on a certain day each month. They used words cut out of a newspaper and pasted onto paper. To my knowledge Rita was the only person who saw me go back into the house that night before the shots were fired. That was the reason I asked her to come here, to discuss the matter with me."

"You thought my mother was blackmailing you?" Jessica was shocked.

"No, of course not, but I thought she may have seen someone else that night, someone who saw me go back into the house."

"You mean one of the security people? The staff? One of the groundskeepers? There were so many people around back then. Do you think it was one of them?"

"It had to be someone familiar with the inside of the house, Jessie." He raked a hand through his hair, his gloved fingers tunneling deep, tousling the strands in his wake.

Jessica glanced back toward the house. "Then it has to be one of them. A member of the band. They lived there on and off. They all survived the fire. Robert? He and Brenda need the cash and it's a plan she's capable of coming up with. I doubt if blackmailing someone would bother her in the least."

Dillon had to laugh. "That's true—Brenda would think she was perfectly within her rights." His smile faded, leaving his blue eyes bleak. "But they all need money, every last one of them."

"Then it's possible one of the band members killed my mother. She must have seen someone, maybe she confronted them about it."

Dillon shook his head. "That's just not possible. I thought

about it until I thought I'd go out of my mind—it just isn't possible. I've known them all, with the exception of Don, all of my life. We were babies together, went through school, went through hard times together. We were family, more than family."

Her hand went to her throat, a curiously vulnerable gesture. "I can't imagine someone we know killing Mom."

"Maybe it really was an accident, Jessie," he said softly.

She just stood there looking up at him with that look of utter fragility on her face, tugging at his heartstrings. Unable to stop himself, Dillon reached out, pulled her to him, and bent his dark head to hers. There was time for a single heartbeat before his lips drifted over hers. Tasting. Coaxing. Tempting. Kissing Jessica seemed as natural to him as breathing. The moment he touched her, he was lost.

Dillon drew her into his arms and she fit perfectly, her body molding to his. Soft. Pliant. Made for him. His tongue skimmed gently along the seam of her lips, asking for entrance. His teeth tugged at her lower lip, a teasing nip, causing her to gasp. At once he took possession, sweeping inside, claiming her, exploring the heated magic of her. Where she might have wanted to be cautious, with him she was all passion, a sweet eruption of hunger that built with his insistence.

Her mouth was addicting and he fed there while the wind whipped their hair around them and tugged at their clothing. The sea breeze cooled the heat of their skin as the temperature rose. His body was full, heavy, and painful. The hunger raged through his body for her, a dark craving he dared not satisfy. Abruptly he lifted his head, a soft curse escaping him.

"You don't have an ounce of self-preservation in you," he snapped at her, his blue eyes hot with an emotion she dared not name.

Jessica stared up at his beloved face. "And you have too much of it," she told him softly, her mouth curving into a teasing smile.

He swore again. She looked bemused, her eyes cloudy, sensual, her mouth sexy, provocative. Kissable. Dillon shook his head, determined to break free of her spell. She was so beautiful to him. So innocent of the vicious things people were capable of doing to one another. "Never, Jess. I'm not doing this with you. If you have some crazy idea of saving the pitiful musician, you can think again." He sounded fierce, angry even.

Jessica lifted her chin. "Do I look the type of woman who would feel pity for a man who has so much? You don't need pity, Dillon, you never have. I didn't run away from life, you did. You had a choice. No matter what my mother said to you about staying away from me and the children, you still had a choice to come back to us." She couldn't quite keep the hurt out of her voice.

His expression hardened perceptibly. "It was my choices that brought us all to this point, Jess. My wants. My needs. That isn't going to happen again. Have you forgotten what they did to you? Because if you haven't, I can tell you in vivid detail. I remember everything. It's etched into my memories, burned into my soul. When I close my eyes at night I see you lying there helpless and frightened. Damn it, we aren't doing this!" Abruptly he turned his back on her, turned away from the turbulent sea and stalked back toward the house.

Jessica stared after him, her heart pounding in rhythm with the foaming waves, the memories crowding so close that for a moment madness swirled up to consume her. The fog slid between them, thick and dangerous, obscuring her vision of Dillon. She swayed, heard chanting carried on the ocean breeze. Beside her, the German shepherd snarled, his growl rumbling low and ominous as he stared at the moving vapor.

"Jess!" Dillon's impatient tone cut through the strange illusion, dispelling it instantly. "Hurry up, I'm not leaving you out here alone."

Jessica found herself smiling. He sounded gruff, but she heard the inadvertent tenderness he tried so hard to keep from her, to keep from himself. She went to him without a word, the dog racing with her. There was time. It wasn't Christmas yet and miracles always happened on Christmas.

7

"COME ON, JESSIE," Trevor wheedled, stuffing a third pancake in his mouth. "We've been here a week. Nothing's happened to us. There's no weird stuff happening and we haven't even had a chance to explore the island."

Jessica shook her head adamantly. "If you two want to explore, I'll go with you. It's dangerous."

"What's dangerous?" Trevor glared at her as he picked up a huge glass of orange juice. "If Tara and I are in any danger, it's of being sucked into one of those video games we're playing so much. Come on, you and the others have been locked in the studio and we're always alone. We can only watch so many movies and play so many games. We're living like zombies, sleeping all day and staying up all night."

"No." Jessica didn't dare look at the band members. She knew they thought she was overly protective when it came to the twins.

Brenda snickered. "It's none of my business but if you ask me, they're old enough to go outside all by themselves."

"I have to agree with her," Brian seconded, "and that's plain scary. Trevor's a responsible kid, he's not going to do anything silly."

Tara glared at Brian. "I am *very* responsible. I said we'd *look* for a Christmas tree. Trevor wants to find one and chop it down."

Jessica paled visibly. "*Trevor!* Chopping involves an axe. You certainly aren't going to go chopping down trees." The thought was truly frightening.

"They aren't babies." Brenda sounded bored with the entire

conversation. "Why shouldn't they go outside to play? All that fresh air is supposed to be good for kiddies, isn't it?"

Jessica glared at the twins' aunt as she sipped her morning coffee. "Stop calling them kiddies, Brenda," she snapped irritably. "They have names and like it or not you are related to them."

Brenda slowly lowered her coffee mug and peered intently at Jessica. "Do us all a favor, hon, just have sex with him. Get it over with and out of your system so we can all live in peace around here. Dillon's walking around like a bear with a sore tooth and you're so edgy you exhaust me."

Trevor spewed orange juice across the counter, nearly choking. Tara gasped audibly, spinning around to glare accusingly at Jessica.

"Oh dear," Brenda sighed dramatically. "Another huge gaffe. I suppose I shouldn't have said 'sex' in front of them. One must learn to censor oneself around kid . . ." she paused, rolled her eyes, and continued. *"Children."*

"Don't worry, Brenda," Trevor said good-naturedly, "we *kiddies* learn all about sex at an early age nowadays. I think we were a little more shocked at your mentioning Jessica and our dad doing the . . ." he glanced at his sister.

"Dastardly deed," Tara supplied without missing a beat.

Brian mopped up the orange juice with a wet cloth, winking at Jessica. "It would be dastardly if you decided to hop in the sack with Dillon. All his wonderful angst and creativity might evaporate in a single night."

"Shut up," Jessica snapped, placing her hands on her hips. "This conversation is not appropriate and it never will be. And we aren't doing anything, dastardly or otherwise, not that it's any of your business."

Tara tugged at the pocket of Jessica's jeans. "You're blushing, Jessie, is that why you're irritable all the time?"

"I am certainly *not* irritable." Jessica was outraged at the suggestion. "I've been working my you-know-what off with a madman perfectionist and his group of comedy club wannabes. If I've been a teensy little bit *edgy*, that would be the reason."

"Teensy?" Brenda sniffed disdainfully. "That doesn't begin to describe you, dear. Robert, rub my shoulders. Having to watch my every word is making me tense."

Robert obediently massaged his wife's shoulders while Brian circled around Jessica completely, peering at her with discerning eyes. "Your you-know-what is definitely intact and looking delicious, Jess, no need to worry about that."

"Thank you very much, you pervert," Jessica replied, trying not to laugh.

Dillon paused in the doorway to watch her with hungry eyes. To drink in the sight of her. The sound of her laughter and her natural warmth drew him like a magnet.

He had spent the last week avoiding brushing up against her soft skin, avoiding looking at her, but he couldn't avoid the scent of her or the sound of her voice. He couldn't avoid the way his blood surged hotly and little jackhammers pounded fiercely in his head when she was in the same room with him. He couldn't stop the urgent demands of his body. The relentless craving. She haunted his dreams and when he was awake she became an obsession he had no way to combat.

Thoughtfully, Dillon leaned one hip against the door. The intensity of his sexual hunger surprised him. He had always felt that Jessica was a part of him, even in the old days when it was simply companionship he had sought from her. They merged minds. Her voice blended perfectly with his. Her quick wit always brought him out of his brooding introspections and pulled him into passionate battles in every aspect of music. Jessica was well versed in music history and had strong opinions about composers and musicians. His conversations with her inspired him, animated him.

There was so much more. He felt alive again after a long interminable prison sentence. It wasn't at all comfortable, but along with bringing him to life, Jessica was putting the soul back into his music. He swore to himself, each time the moment he opened his eyes that he wouldn't give in to the whispers of temptation, but it seemed to him that he had gone from a barren, frozen existence straight into the fires of hell.

He couldn't help loving his children, being proud of them. He couldn't help seeing the way Jessica loved them and the way they loved her back. And he couldn't help the desperate longing to be part of that bond, that intense love. Dillon had no idea how much longer he could keep his hands to himself, how much longer he could resist the lure of a family. Or even if he wanted to resist. Did he have the right to allow them into his world? He had failed once and it had changed the course of so many people's lives. Death and destruction had followed him. Did he dare reach out again, risk harming the ones he loved? He swept a hand through his thick hair and Jessica immediately turned, her vivid eyes meeting his.

Jessica could feel her heart thundering at the sight of him. A faint blush stole into her face as she wondered if he had overheard the conversation. She could only imagine what he must be thinking. Looking at him nearly took her breath away. There had always been such a casual masculine beauty to Dillon. Now, it seemed more careless, a sensual allure against which she had no resistance. One look from his smoldering eyes sent her body into meltdown. He was looking at her now, his blue eyes burning over her, intense, hungry, beyond her ability to resist.

Jessica tilted her chin at him in challenge. She had no reason to resist the strong pull between them. She wanted him to belong to her, body and soul. She saw no reason to deny it. As if knowing her thoughts, he lowered his gaze which drifted over her body, nearly a physical touch that left her aching and restless and all too aware of his presence.

"Dad?" Tara's voice instantly stopped all conversation in the room. It was the first time she had addressed Dillon that way. "Trevor and I want to go looking for a Christmas tree." She glared at Jessica. "We aren't going to chop one down, only look for one."

Dillon smiled unexpectedly, looking like a mischievous,

charming boy, so much like Trevor. "Is Mama Tiger showing her fangs?"

"Her claws anyway," Brenda muttered into her coffee mug.

"The weather's good, so we'll be perfectly safe," Trevor added, a glimmer of hope in his eyes. "Someone has to get this Christmas thing off the ground. We have less than two weeks to go. You're busy, we don't have that much time left, so Tara and I can handle the decorations while you work."

Dillon didn't look at Jessica. He *couldn't* look at her. The boy's face was hopeful and eager and trusting. Tara had called him 'Dad.' It tugged at his heartstrings as nothing else could have. His gaze shifted to his daughter's face. She wore an expression identical to her brother's. Trust was a delicate thing. It was the first time he'd come close to believing in miracles, that there might be second chances given out in life, even when he didn't deserve it. "You think you can find the perfect tree? Do you know how to choose one?"

Jessica blinked, her teeth sinking into her lower lip to keep from protesting. Dillon's tone had been casual, but there was nothing casual in the vivid blue of his eyes, or the set of his mouth. His gloved hand rubbed along his denim-clad thigh, betraying his uncharacteristic show of nerves. The gesture disarmed her, stole her heart. She wanted to put her arms around him, hold him close, protectively, to her.

Tara nodded eagerly. She grinned at Trevor. "I have a long list of requirements. I know exactly what we want."

Don had been sitting quietly in a chair by the window but he turned with a quick frown. "You don't just arbitrarily chop down trees because you want a momentary pleasure. In case you're not aware of it, when you chop the tree down, it dies." The frown deepened into a fierce scowl when Dillon turned to face him. "Hey, it's just my opinion, but then that doesn't count for much around here, does it?"

"I'm well aware of your environmentalist concerns, Don," Dillon said gently. "I share your views, but there's no harm in topping a tree or taking one that's growing too close to another and has no chance of survival."

"We're supposed to be working here, Dillon, not celebrating some commercialized holiday so the privileged little rich kids can get a bunch of presents from their rich daddy." There was unexpected venom in Don's voice.

Tara slid close to Jessica for comfort. Immediately Jessica pulled the girl into her arms, stroking the dark, wavy hair with gentle fingers. Beside her, Trevor shifted, but Jessica caught his wrist in a silent signal and he remained silent. His arms went around both Jessica and Tara, holding them close to him. The silence stretched to apprehension.

Dillon stirred then, straightening from where he had been leaning lazily against the doorframe. Dillon walked over to stand in front of his children. Very gently he caught Tara's chin in the palm of his gloved hand and lifted her face so that her blue eyes met his. "I'm looking forward to Christmas this year, Tara, it's been far too long for me without laughter and fun. Thank you for giving the holiday back to me." He bent his head and kissed her forehead. "I apologize for my friend's rudeness. He's obviously forgotten, in his old age, how fun holidays can be."

He touched his son then, his hand on the boy's shoulder. "I would greatly appreciate it if you and your sister would go out this evening before it gets too dark and find us the best tree you can. If we weren't in the middle of working this song I'd go with you. You find it and we'll go together to get it tomorrow evening." His fingers tightened momentarily as his heart leapt with joy. His son. His daughter. The terrible darkness that had consumed him for so long was slowly receding. His body actually trembled with the intensity of his emotions. He had never dared to dream of the two beloved faces staring up at him with such confidence and faith. "I'm trusting you to take care of your sister, Trevor."

Trevor swelled visibly. He glanced at Jessica, a tremor running through him, his hands tightening until his fingers dug into Jessica's arm. She smiled up at him with reassurance. With understanding. She could not allow her fears to take the pleasure from all of them. Especially when she didn't even know if her fears were grounded in reality. When she looked back at Dillon her feelings were naked on her face.

Dillon's breath caught in his chest. There was raw love on Jessica's face, in her eyes. She looked up at him as no other in his life ever had. Complete confidence, unconditional love. There was never a hidden agenda with Jessica. She loved his children completely, fiercely, protectively. And she was beginning to love him the same way. "You and Tara go now before it gets dark. I have some business matters to discuss."

Trevor nodded his understanding, grinning triumphantly at Don. He led Tara out of the room, urging her to hurry to get her jacket so they wouldn't lose the light they needed.

Dillon reached down and took Jessica's hand, raised it to the warmth of his mouth. His blue gaze burned into her green one. Mesmerizing her. Holding her captive with his sensual spell, in front of all the band members, he slowly pressed a kiss into the exact center of her palm, blatantly branding her. Staking his claim.

Jessica could feel hot tears burning behind her eyes, clogging her throat. Dillon. Her Dillon. He was coming back to life. The miracle of Christmas. The story her mother had so often told her at night. There was a special power at Christmas, a shimmering, translucent, positive, force that flowed steadily, that was there for the taking. One had only to believe in it, to reach for it. Jessica reached with both hands, with her heart and soul. Dillon needed her, needed his children. He had only to open his heart again and believe with her.

Dillon tugged on her hand, drew her to him so that her soft curves fit against the hard strength of his body. Then he turned his head above hers toward Don, pinning the man with a gaze of icy cold fury. "Don't you ever speak that way to my children again. Not ever, Don. If you have a gripe with me, feel free to tear into me, but never try to get to me through my children." There was a promise of swift and brutal retaliation in his voice.

Jessica looked up into his face and shivered. Dillon was different now, no matter how many glimpses she caught of the person she had once known.

"You want me out, don't you, Wentworth? You've always wanted me out. It's always been about 'Precious Paul' with you. You're loyal to him no matter what he does," Don snarled. "I worked hard, but I never got the recognition. You've always resented me being in the band. Paul," he gestured toward the man sitting ramrod stiff in the chair by the window. "He can do anything and you forgive him."

"You're not so innocent, Don." Brenda yawned and lazily waved a dismissing hand. "You musicians are so dramatic. Who cares who loves whom best? At least Paul didn't use his lover to get him into the band."

Dillon's head snapped up, his eyes glittering. "What the hell are you talking about, Brenda?"

Jessica glanced around the room. Everyone had gone still, looking nervous, guilty, even Paul. Don flushed a dull red. His eyes shifted away from Dillon.

Brenda winced. "Ouch. How was I to know you were kept in the dark?" Dillon's relentless blue gaze continued to bore into her. "Fine, blame me, I'm always in trouble. I thought you knew; everyone else certainly knew."

Dillon's fingers tightened around Jessica's hand. She could feel the tension running through his body. He was trembling slightly. She shifted closer to him, silently offering support.

"Tell me now, Brenda."

For the first time, Jessica saw Brenda hesitate. For a moment she looked uncertain and vulnerable. Then her expression changed and she shrugged her shoulders carelessly, her tinkling laugh a little forced. "Oh for heaven's sake, what's the big deal? It was a million years ago. It's not as if you thought Vivian had been faithful."

Jessica felt him take the blow in his heart. It was a gut-wrenching jolt that shook him, turned his stomach so that for a moment he had to fight to breathe, to keep from being sick. She felt his struggle as clearly as if she were experiencing it herself. Dillon's face never changed expression, he didn't so much as blink. He could have been carved from stone, but Jessica felt the turmoil raging in him.

"So Viv had an affair with Don, no big deal." Brenda shrugged again. "She got him into the band. You needed a bass player—it all worked out."

"Viv and I weren't having problems when Don joined the band," Dillon said. His voice held no expression and he didn't look at Don.

Brenda inspected her long nails. "You know Viv, she had problems, she always had to be with someone. You were working on songs for the band, trying to help Paul. If you weren't with her every minute, she felt neglected."

Dillon waited a heartbeat of time. A second. A third. He was aware of Jessica, of her hand, of her body, but there was a strange roaring in his head. His gaze shifted, settled on Don. "You were sleeping with my wife and playing in my band, allowing me to believe you were my friend?" He remembered how hard he had tried to make Don feel a part of the band.

Don's mouth tightened perceptibly. "You knew, everyone knew. It was no secret Viv liked to pick up a man now and then. And you got what you wanted. A bass player to kick around, someone to put up with your wife's tantrums when you didn't have the time or inclination to put up with her yourself. I won't even mention the extra money you saved because she was always wanting me to buy her things. I'd say we were more than even."

Dillon remained silent, only a muscle jerked along his jaw, betraying his inner turmoil.

"She was a bloodsucker," Don continued, looking around the room for support.

"She was ill," Dillon corrected softly.

"She had no loyalty and she was as cold as ice," Don insisted. "Damn it, Dillon, you had to have known about us."

When Dillon continued to look at him, Don dropped his gaze again. "I thought that was why you didn't want me in the band."

"Your own guilt made you think I didn't want you in the band." Dillon's voice was very soft, yet deep inside he was screaming at Jessica to help him. To stop him from saying or doing anything crazy. To save him. There had been such a surge of hope in him. A spreading warmth, a belief that he might reclaim his life. In a blink it was gone. He felt ice-cold inside. Emotionless. His heart and soul had been torn out. Everything he had built or cared about had been destroyed. He thought it had all been taken from him, but there was more, gouging old wounds to deepen them, to reopen them. He was shattering, crumbling, piece by piece until there was nothing left of who he had been.

"Damn it, Dillon, you had to have known," Don was almost pleading.

Dillon shook his head slowly. "I can't discuss this right now. No, I didn't know, I had no idea. I always thought of you as my friend. I did my best to understand you. I trusted you. I thought our friendship was genuine."

Jessica reached up and touched his face. Gently. Lovingly. "Take me out of here, Dillon. Right now. I want to be away from here." More than anything she wanted to get him away from treachery and betrayal. He had just begun to emerge into the sun after a long, bleak, cold winter. She could feel hands pulling him away from her, back into the deeper shadows. She kept her voice soft, persuasive. Her hands stroked his jaw, the pad of her thumb caressed his lips, a brush of a caress that centered his attention on her. His vivid blue gaze met hers. She saw the dangerous emotions swirling in the depths of his eyes.

Jessica tugged at him, forced him to move away from the others, out of the kitchen. She guided him through the house up to his private floor. He went with her willingly enough, but she could still feel the edge of violence in him, roiling and swirling all too close to the surface.

"I learned a lot of things about myself when I was at the burn center," Dillon said, as he pushed open the door to his study and stepped back to allow her to precede him. "There's so much pain, Jess, unbelievable pain. You think you can't bear any more, but there's always more. Every minute, every second, it's a matter of endurance. You have no choice but to endure it because it never goes away. There's no way to sleep through it, you have to persevere."

The room was dark with the shadows of the late afternoon but he didn't turn on the light. Outside, the wind set the tree branches in motion so that they brushed gently against the sides of the house, producing an eerie music. Inside the room the silence stretched between them as they faced one another. Jessica could feel the turbulence of his emotions, wild, chaotic, yet on the surface he was as still as a hunter. She knew his strength of will, knew why he had survived such a terrible injury. Dillon was a man of deep passions. He sounded as if he was describing his physical pain, but she knew he was telling her about the other kinds of pain he'd also endured. The emotional scars were every bit as painful and deep as the physical ones.

"Don't look at me like that, Jess, it's too dangerous." He warned her softly, even as he moved to close the distance between them. "I don't want to hurt you. You can't look at me with your beautiful eyes so damn trusting. I'm not the man you think I am and I never will be." Even as he uttered the words aloud, meaning every one of them, his hands, of their own volition, were framing her face.

Electricity arced and crackled, a sizzling whip dancing with white-hot heat through their blood. The heat from his body seeped into hers, warming her, drawing her like a magnet. His head was bending toward her, his dark silky hair spilling around his angel's face like a cloud. Jessica's breath caught in her lungs. There was no air to breathe, no life other than his perfectly sculpted lips. His mouth settled over hers, velvet soft and firm. The touch was tantalizing. She opened her mouth as his teeth tugged teasingly at her lips to give him entrance to her sweetness, to the dark secrets of passion and promise.

Dillon closed his eyes to savor the taste of her, the hot silk of her. There was sheer magic in Jessica's kiss. It was madness to indulge his craving for her, but he couldn't stop, taking his time, leisurely exploring, swept away from the gray bleakness of his nightmare world into one of vivid colorful fireworks, bursting around him, in him. The need was instantaneous and elemental, the hunger, voracious. His body was all at once savagely alive, thick and hard and pounding with an edgy, greedy lust that shook him to the foundations of his soul. He'd never experienced it before, but now, it surged through his body, primitive and hot, demanding that he make her his.

Jessica felt his mouth harden, change, felt the passion flare between them, hot and exciting, a rush that dazzled her every sense. Her body melted into his, pliant and soft and inviting. His mouth raged with hunger, devoured hers, dominating and persuasive and commanding her response. She gave herself up to the blazing world of sheer sensation, allowed him to take her far from reality.

The earth seemed to shift and move out from under her feet as his palms slid over her back, down to her bottom, where they settled to align her body more firmly with his. His touch was slow and languorous, at odds with his assaulting mouth. His tongue plundered, his hands coaxed. His mouth was aggressive, his hands gentle.

Dillon's body was a hard, painful ache, his jeans stretched tight, cutting into him. The feel of her, so soft and pliant, was driving him slowly out of his mind. There was a strange roaring in his head; his blood felt thick and molten like lava. She tasted hot and sweet. He couldn't get close enough to her, wanting her clothes gone so that he could press himself against her, skin to skin.

His mouth left hers to travel along her throat, with playful little kisses and bites, his tongue swirling to find shadows and hollows, to reach little trigger points of sheer pleasure. When he found them, she rewarded him with a little gasp of bliss. The sound was music to him, a soft note that drowned out his every sane thought. He didn't want sanity, he didn't want to know that what he was doing was wrong. He wanted to bury his body deep inside of her, to lose himself forever in a firestorm of mindless feeling.

His mouth found the hollow of her throat, the pulse beating so frantically there. He nudged aside the neckline of her blouse to find the swell of her breasts. She was soft, a miracle of satin skin. His hand closed over her breast, her taut nipple pushing into his palm through her blouse, through his glove. Beckoning. Urging him on. He bent his head to temptation.

The door to Dillon's study burst open and Tara stood there, her face white, her hair wildly disheveled. There was sheer panic on her face. "You have to come right now. *Right now!* Jessica! Hurry, oh, God, I think he's crushed under the logs and dirt. Hurry, you have to hurry!"

Panic sent adrenaline coursing through Jessica's body. She looked up at Dillon, sheer terror in her eyes. His eyes mirrored her fear. He circled Jessica's waist with one strong arm, pulling her tight against him so that, briefly, they leaned into one another, comforting them both.

"Take a deep breath, Tara, we need to know what happened." Dillon's voice was calm and authoritative. He pulled the child into the circle of his arms, up against Jessica where she felt safe.

Tara gulped back her tears, buried her face against Jessica's shoulder. "I don't know what happened. One minute we were walking along and then Trevor said something weird, it didn't make sense, something about a magic circle and he ran ahead of me. I heard him yell and then there was a huge noise. The side of a hill gave way, rocks and dirt and logs rolling down. His yell was cut off and when I got to where I thought he was, the air was all dirty and cloudy. I couldn't find him and when I called and called, he didn't answer me. I think he was buried under all of it. The dog started digging and barking and growling and I ran to get you."

"Show me, Tara," Dillon commanded. "Jessica, you'll have to find the others, tell Paul we'll need shovels just in case." He was already pushing his daughter ahead of him.

They ran down the stairs, Dillon calling for the band members. As he jerked open the front door and raced across the front verandah, he nearly knocked Brian back down the front steps. They steadied one another. "It's Trevor. It sounds bad, Brian, come with me," Dillon said.

Brian nodded. "Where are the others?"

"Jess is rounding them up," Dillon replied. Tara ran ahead of him, but he kept pace easily, swearing under his breath. Night was falling all too fast and it would be very dark in a matter of minutes. He prayed his daughter didn't get lost, that she could lead them straight to his son.

Tara ran fast, keeping to the main path, her heart pounding loudly in her ears, but terror had subsided now that her father was taking command. He seemed so calm, so completely in control, that she felt her panic fading. She was afraid she wouldn't be able to find the exact location in the dark so she ran as fast as she could in an attempt to outrun the nightfall. It was even more of a relief when the large German shepherd came bounding out of the timberline to pace beside her. He knew the way to Trevor.

Jessica took several deep breaths as she hurried through the large house calling for the others. She found Brenda outside the kitchen, in the courtyard, smoking. "What is it now? I swear there's no rest for the wicked around this place."

"Where are the others?" Jessica demanded. Brenda's chic hiking boots were covered in mud. Pine needles were stuck to the bottom and Brenda was trying to remove them without getting her fingernails dirty. "There's been an accident and we need everyone to help."

"Oh good heavens, it's those kids again, isn't it?" Brenda sounded annoyed. She backed up a step holding up a placating hand as Jessica advanced on her. "Really, darling, you wear me out with your agonizing over those *children*. See? I'm learning. Tell me what's wrong and I'll do my part to help, although I hope you send them both to their rooms and punish them suitably for disrupting my day."

"Where are the others?" Jessica spit each word out distinctly. "This is an emergency, Brenda. I think Trevor is trapped under a landslide, under dirt and rocks. We need to dig him out fast."

"Surely not!" Brenda's hand fluttered to her throat and she paled visibly. Her throat worked as if she was struggling to speak but no words would come. When they did, it was a choked whisper. "This place really is cursed, or maybe just Dillon is."

Jessica was surprised to see the woman was close to tears. "Brenda," she said desperately. "Help me!"

"I'm sorry, of course." Brenda straightened her shoulders. "I'll find Robert, he'll know what to do. Paul's around back playing horseshoes, at least he was when I walked up. I think Don was going to the beach, but I'm not certain. You get Paul and I'll find the others and send them to you. Which way did they go?"

"Thanks." Jessica put a hand on Brenda's arm, touching her to offer comfort. There was something very vulnerable on Brenda's face when her mask slipped. "I think they took the main trail heading into the forest."

"I just came back from that way," Brenda frowned. "I didn't see the kids."

Jessica didn't wait to hear any more; she raced around to the back of the house. Paul was idly tossing horseshoes. He paused in mid-swing when he spotted her. "What is it?" He tossed the horseshoe aside and hurried to her.

Feeling desperate, Jessica blurted out what she knew. Time seemed to be going by while she was getting nowhere. She wanted to race to Trevor, dig him out with her bare hands, not rely on the others.

"I'll get the lights," Paul told her, pulling open the door to a small shed. "There are shovels in here. I'll meet you around in the front." He was gone quickly.

Jessica pressed a hand to her churning stomach as she looked frantically through the potting shed for the shovels. All the larger tools were at the back of the shed. She felt sick, *sick* with fear for Trevor. How many minutes had gone by? Not many, her conversation with Brenda had taken only seconds, but it seemed an eternity. It was dark in the shed, the waning light insufficient to light the interior. She felt her way to the back, placing her hand on first a rake, a pry bar, and two sharper tools before she found the shovels. Triumphantly she caught up all three and rushed out of the small building.

Don was waiting impatiently for her. "Paul's gone on ahead." He grabbed the shovels from her, frowning as he did so. "What the hell did you do to your hand?"

Jessica blinked in surprise. Her palm was muddy and a single long slash in the center mingled blood with the dirt. A few stray pine needles stuck in the mixture as if it were artwork. "It doesn't matter," she muttered, and hurried past him to take the trail.

Darkness had fallen in the forest, the heavier canopy blocking out what little light remained. Jessica ran fast, uncaring of her burning lungs. She had to get to Trevor and Tara. To Dillon. It couldn't be that bad. She consoled herself with the thought that someone would have come for her if the news were the worst. She could hear Don running beside her, and was vaguely aware of her throbbing palm. She wiped it on her thigh as they spotted lights off to her left.

Tara threw herself at Jessica, nearly knocking her over. "He's under all those big rocks and dirt. That big log fell on him, too! Dad's been trying to dig him out with his bare hands and Robert's been helping."

"They'll get him out quickly," Jessica reassured, holding the little girl close, "the soil is soft enough for them to dig him out very fast."

"Take her up there, out of the way," Dillon directed. His gaze met Jessica's over Tara's head as he caught in midair the shovel that Don tossed to him. "It's going to be okay, baby, I promise. He's talking, so he's alive and conscious. He's got air to breathe, we just have to get him out to see the damage."

Jessica nodded. Hugging Tara closer to her, she bent down to the child's ear. "Let's move out of the way, honey. We'll go up there." She pointed to a small embankment off to the side but up above where the men were frantically digging.

The dog nudged her legs as she walked and Jessica absently patted his head. "Are you all right, Tara?" The girl was trembling.

Tara shook her head. "I shouldn't have insisted we keep looking. We found two trees we thought you and Dad might like, but I wanted to keep looking. Trevor said it was getting dark and wanted to go back to the house." She rubbed her face against Jessica's jacket. "I knew if I hadn't been with him he would have kept looking. I hate that, the way he always treats me like I'm a baby."

"Trevor looks out for you," Jessica corrected gently. "That's a good thing, Tara. He loves you very much. And this wasn't your fault." She stroked the girl's hair soothingly. "It just happened. Sometimes things just happen."

Tara shivered again. She looked up at Jessica, her eyes too large for her face. "I saw something," she whispered softly and looked around quickly. "I saw a shadow back in the trees, over there." She pointed toward the left in the deeper timber. "It looked like someone with a long cape and hood, very dark. I couldn't see the face, but he was watching us; he watched it all happen. I know he was there, it wasn't my imagination."

If it was possible, Jessica's heart began to pound even harder. "He was watching you while the rocks and dirt crumbled down on Trevor?" Jessica struggled to get the timing right. She believed Tara, she'd seen a cloaked figure in the woods the night they'd arrived, but she couldn't imagine any of the band members not rushing to aid the twins. Whoever had been in that cloak really might want to cause harm to one of them. Could someone other than the band members be on the island? The groundskeeper was an older, kindly man. The island was large enough that someone could hide out, camping, but surely the dog would have alerted the children to a stranger's presence. The twins had been spending time with the animal and she knew the German shepherd had guard instincts.

Tara nodded. "I yelled and yelled for help. I couldn't see Trev, he was buried under everything and when I looked back, the person was gone." She wiped her face, smearing dirt across her chin and cheek. "I'm telling the truth, Jessie."

Jessica brushed the top of the girl's head with a kiss. "I know you are, honey. I can't imagine why whoever it was didn't come to help you." She was determined to find out, though. She had been lulled into a false sense of security, but if the cloaked figure was a band member, and it had to be, then one of them was behind the accidents and the death of her mother. Which one? "Stay here, honey, away from the edge."

She couldn't stand still, pacing back and forth restlessly, her fist jammed in her mouth to keep from screaming at them to hurry. Don and Robert pried a rather large rock loose and it took all of the men to move it carefully away from the site.

Brenda joined Tara a little hesitantly. "He'll be all right, honey," she offered, placing her hand on her niece's shoulder in an attempt to offer comfort.

"He hasn't moved," Tara told her tearfully. "He hasn't moved at all."

"He's breathing though," Brenda encouraged. "Robert said Trevor told them he dove into a small space, a depression against the hillside."

"He was talking? Dillon said he spoke, but I haven't heard anything." And Jessica wanted the reassurance of the sound of his voice. She continued to pace, rubbing her arms as she did so, shivering in the night air. "Are you certain he spoke?"

"I'm pretty sure," Brenda answered.

Jessica stared up at the sky. She could hear the pounding of the sea in the distance. The wind rustling through the trees. The chink of the shovels against rock. Even the heavy breathing of the men as they worked. She could not hear Trevor's voice. She listened. She prayed. There was not even a murmur.

"He'll be all right." Brenda tried again to be reassuring. She tapped her foot, drawing Jessica's attention to the muddy ground strewn with pine needles and vegetation. A few fallen trees crisscrossed the area from the violent storm. Most had been there for some time but two smaller ones were fairly fresh.

She couldn't help the terrible suspicion that slid into her mind. Another accident. Could it have been rigged? Almost without even being aware of it, she examined the ground, the position of the logs, searching for clues, searching for anything that might provide an answer for what had happened. There was nothing she could see, nothing that would make Dillon listen to her that something wasn't quite right. Maybe she was paranoid, she didn't know, only that she had to find a way to make the children safe.

"I won't be able to take it if anything's happened to him," Jessica murmured to no one in particular. She meant it. Her heart was breaking. She was white-faced, sick to her stomach, and moving to keep from being sick in front of everyone. "I shouldn't have let him go off like that. I should have been with him."

"Jessica, you couldn't have prevented this," Brenda said firmly. "They'll get him out." Awkwardly she hugged Tara to her as a muffled sob escaped the child. "Neither one of you could have stopped this. After a storm, sometimes the land is soft and it just shifts. You both would have been hurt had you been with him."

Jessica crouched down, peering at the men as they frantically dug away the dirt and rocks to free Trevor. She could see
his legs and part of one shoe. "Dillon?" Her voice wavered.
Trevor wasn't moving. "Why is he so still?" She could barely
breathe, her lungs burning for air.

"Don't go getting all sappy," Trevor's disembodied voice
floated up to her. He sounded thin and reedy, but it was his
usual cocky humor. "You'll just be mad at me later if everyone
sees you all teary-eyed."

Jessica slowly attempted to stand, her body trembling with
relief. Her legs felt rubbery, and for a moment she was afraid
she might faint. Brenda shoved her head down, held her there
until the earth stopped spinning so crazily. Robert came up on
the other side of her, holding her arm as she swayed. Jessica bit
down hard on her fist to keep from crying as she straightened.
Tears glittered in her eyes, on her lashes. Her gaze met Dillon's
in complete understanding. For a moment there was no one
else, just the two of them and the sheer relief only a parent
could feel after such a frightening experience.

Tara hugged her, relief in the vivid blue of her eyes. Jessica
barely registered it. She couldn't remember ever being so shaky
but she managed a tentative smile at Brenda and Robert.
"Thanks for keeping me from landing on my face in the dirt."

Brenda shrugged with her casual eloquence. "I can't let anything happen to you. I'd be stuck with the kiddies." She
winked at Tara even as she went into her husband's arms. She
seemed to fit there, to belong.

Tara grinned back at her. "We grow on you."

"No they don't," Jessica replied firmly, "they take years off
your life. I think you have the right idea, Brenda, no kiddies or
animals." Her eyes remained on Trevor as they slowly freed him.
He was stretching his legs cautiously. She could hear him talking
with Dillon. His voice was still shaking, but he was holding his
own, laughing softly at something his father said to him.

"Brenda, would you mind taking Tara back to the house?
It's already so dark. She should take a hot bath, and when I

come in I'll fix hot chocolate. She's muddy and wet and shaking whether she knows it or not," Jessica said.

"So are you," Brenda pointed out with unexpected gentleness.

"I'll be right in," Jessica promised. She squeezed Tara's hand. "Thank you for getting everyone here so quickly, honey, you were wonderful."

"We'll get her to the house safely," Robert assured Jessica, and with an arm around Brenda and one around Tara, he started back toward the house.

Jessica had to touch Trevor, to make certain he had not suffered a single injury. She made her way down to the site and knelt beside Dillon next to Trevor. Dillon examined every inch of the boy, testing for broken bones, lacerations, even bruises. His hands were unbelievably gentle as he ran them over his son.

Trevor was filthy, but grinning at them. "It's a good thing I'm skinny," he quipped, patting Jessica's shoulder, knowing if he hugged her she'd burst into tears in front of everyone and then he'd really be in trouble.

"He's fine, a few bumps and bruises. Tomorrow he's going to be sore," Dillon announced to the others. "Thank you all for helping." He sat back, wiped his hand across his forehead, leaving behind a smear of dirt. His hand was trembling. "You took a couple of years off my life, son. I can't afford it."

Paul gathered up the shovels. "None of us can afford it."

"Don't feel alone," Trevor said. "It felt like the entire hillside came down on top of me. For a few minutes there, all I could think about was being buried alive. Not a pleasant thought."

Jessica stepped back to allow Paul room. Dillon and Paul lifted Trevor to his feet. The boy swayed slightly but stood upright, his familiar grin on his face. "Jess, I'm really okay, you know?"

Dillon watched her face crumble, her composure gone as she circled Trevor's neck with her slender arms and hugged him fiercely, protectively, to her. There was no awkwardness in the boy's manner as he tightened his arms around her and buried his face in her shoulder. They were easy, natural, loving with one another. Dillon felt a burning in his chest, behind his eyes, as he watched them. A terrible longing welled up, nearly blindsided him. The layers of insulation were being stripped away, exposing his heart, so that he was raw and vulnerable.

Part of him wanted to lash out at them like a wounded animal. Part of him wanted to embrace them, to hold them safely to him. *Safe.* The word shimmered bitterly in his mind. He tasted bitterness in his mouth. For a heartbeat of time he stared at them, his heart pounding, adrenaline surging. His blue eyes glittered with the violence that always seemed to be swirling just below the surface.

Before Dillon could turn away from them, Jessica lifted her head, her gaze colliding with his. At once he was lost in the joy on her face. Her smile was radiant, like a burst of sunshine. She held out her hand to him. An invitation to a place he couldn't go. He stared down at her hand. Delicate. Small. A bridge back to living.

He didn't move. Dillon later swore to himself he hadn't moved, but there he was, taking her hand in his. His gloves were filthy but she didn't seem to notice, her fingers tightening around his. Touching her, he was lost in her spell, a web of enchantment, losing all touch with reality, with sanity. He found himself drawn up against the soft invitation of her body. Her head nuzzled his chest, her silky hair catching in the shadow along his jaw.

Without thought, without hesitation, his hand circled her vulnerable throat, tipping her head back. Her green eyes were large, haunting, cloudy with emotion. He swore softly, a surrender, a defeat, as he bent his dark head to hers. Her mouth was perfection, velvet soft, yielding, hot and moist and filled with tenderness. With the taste of love. The smoldering ember buried deep in his gut flared to life, flooded his system with such craving he fed on her, devoured her, swept away by the addicting taste of her. By the rich promise of passion, of laughter, of life itself.

She found a way past his every barricade, past his every defense. She wrapped herself around his heart, his soul, until he couldn't breathe without her. The loneliness that had consumed him for so long, and the bleak endless existence, vanished when she was near him. Need slammed into his body, hard and urgent, a demand that threatened to steal his control. The sheer force of their chemistry alarmed him. His body trembled, his mouth hardened, his tongue thrusting and probing, a hot mating dance his body desperately needed to perform.

Trevor cleared his throat loudly, dragging Dillon back to reality. Startled, he lifted his head and blinked, slowly coming back into his own scarred body and soul.

Trevor grinned up at him. "Don't look so shell-shocked, Dad, it's kind of embarrassing when I had this image of you all suave with the ladies."

"Suave isn't the word for it," Don muttered acidly under his breath.

Dillon heard him and turned the weight of his stare in Don's direction. The others attacked from all directions, diverting him.

"Boyo," Brian let out his breath in a slow whistle. "What the hell was that?"

"I'd like to see that on rewind," Paul said, nudging Dillon with his elbow. "A little vicarious experience goes a long way around here."

Jessica hid her scarlet face against Dillon's shoulder. "All of you go away."

"We don't dare, Jessie girl, no telling what you might do to our beloved leader," Brian teased. "We want the boyo suffering angst and melancholy. Haven't you heard that makes for the best songs?"

"Frustration's good for that, too," Paul chimed in.

Jessica reached up to frame Dillon's face with her hand. "I don't think it matters what state he's in," she objected, "he manages to compose beautiful music."

Dillon caught her hand and turned up her palm, his eyes narrowing. "What the hell did you do to your hand? It's bleeding."

He sounded so accusatory Jessica couldn't help smiling. "I was feeling around in the tool shed for the shovels and cut my hand on something sharp." Now that he'd pointed it out, the wound was beginning to burn.

"We have to wash that. I don't want you picking up an infection." Dillon indicated the path, retaining possession of Jessica's hand. "Are you steady enough to walk back, Trevor?"

Trevor nodded, hiding his smile as he turned onto the trail, following Paul closely. Don and Brian gathered up the lights. Dillon brought Jessica's hand up for another, much closer inspection. "I don't like the look of this, honey—you clean it the moment you get to the house." He was fighting to breathe, to stay sane. What the hell was he doing? He raked a hand through his hair, breathing hard, feeling as if he'd run miles. Emotions were crowding in so fast, so overwhelming he couldn't sort them out.

Jessica couldn't suppress the small surge of joy rushing through her. Dillon sounded so worried about such a trivial cut. They walked close together, his hand holding hers. Above their heads the stars tried valiantly to shine for them despite the gray clouds stretching out into thin veils covering the tiny lights.

Dillon deliberately slowed his pace to allow the others to get ahead of them. "I'm sorry, Jess, I shouldn't have kissed you like that in front of the others."

"Because they're going to tease us? They've already been doing that," she pointed out. She tilted her chin at him, a clear challenge to deny what was between them.

He sighed. "Because I wanted to tear your clothes off and take you right there, right then. I think I made it damned obvious to the band. You aren't some groupie and I don't want them looking at you that way—to ever see you in that light. You always think the best of everyone. Has it occurred to you, that their seeing me kissing you like that, they might consider you fair game?"

Jessica shrugged her shoulders, feigning a casualness she didn't feel. A heat wave spread through her body at his words. The thought of Dillon so out of control left her breathless. She managed to keep her voice even. "I doubt that I'll faint if one of them makes an attempt. This might shock you, Dillon, but other men have actually found me attractive and some of them have even asked me out. Believe it or not, you're not the only man who has ever kissed me." She felt him stiffen, felt the sudden tension in him.

A hint of danger crept into the deep blue of his eyes. "I don't think now is the best time to talk to me about other men, Jess." His voice was rougher than she'd ever heard it, that smoky, edgy tone very much in evidence. He halted abruptly, dragging her into the deeper shelter of the trees. "Do you have any idea what you're doing to me? Any idea at all?" He pulled her uninjured hand between his legs, rubbed her palm along the front of his jeans where the material was stretched taut, where he was thick and hard and she could feel heat right through the fabric. "I haven't been with a woman in a very long time, honey, and if you keep this up, you're going to get a hell of a lot more than you bargained for. I'm not some teenager looking for a quick feel. You keep looking at me the way you've been doing and I'm going to take you up on the invitation."

For one moment Jessica thought about slapping his handsome face, outraged that he would try to reduce her to a teen with a crush. That he would try to frighten her, or that he would think that he ever could frighten her. If there was one man on earth she trusted implicitly with her body, it was Dillon Wentworth. It took a heartbeat to realize he had captured her uninjured palm, that he was still cradling her wounded hand against his chest. Carefully. Tenderly. The pad of his thumb was rubbing gently along the edge of her hand and he wasn't even aware of it. But she was.

Deliberately provocative, she rubbed the stretched material at the front of his jeans. "You aren't very well suited to the role of big bad wolf, Dillon, but if it's some fantasy you have, I guess I can play along." Her tone was seductive, an invitation. Her fingers danced and teased, stroking and caressing, feeling him respond, thicken more, harden more.

His eyes glittered down at her like two burning gemstones. "You don't have a clue about fantasies, Jessie."

"You're in the wrong century, Dillon." Her tongue slid provocatively along her lush bottom lip and, damn her, she was laughing at him. "I certainly wouldn't mind unzipping your jeans and wrapping my hand around you, feeling you, *watching* you grow even harder. And I did consider not wearing my bra so that the next time you kissed me and started working your way along my throat, you would feel my body is ready for you. The thought of your mouth on . . ."

"Damn it." A little desperately he bent his head and stopped her nonsense the only way he could think of. He took possession of her mouth and instantly was lost in her answering hunger. She was too sexy, too hot, too everything. Magic. Jessica was sheer magic. He caught her shoulders and resolutely set her away from him before he lost his mind completely.

She smiled up at him. "Are you ever going to kiss me without swearing first?"

"Are you ever going to learn self-preservation?" he countered.

"I don't have to learn," Jessica pointed out, "you watch out for me very nicely."

9

JESSICA TOOK HER TIME in the shower, allowing the hot water to soak into her skin. *Dillon.* He filled her thoughts and kept her mind from dwelling on the possibility that she could have lost Trevor. She had never experienced such a powerful attraction. They had always belonged together. Always. Best friends when it hadn't made sense. She had always found him magnetic, but it had never occurred to her that one day the sexual chemistry between them would be so explosive. She shook with her need for him.

She closed her eyes as she dried her body with a thick towel, the material sliding over her sensitive skin, heightening her awareness of unfamiliar sexual hunger. She didn't feel like herself at all around him. His blue gaze burned over her and made her feel a wanton seductress. Jessica shook her head as she dressed with care. She wanted to look her best to face him.

By the time she was back downstairs, everyone was already in the kitchen ahead of her. Dillon looked handsome in clean black jeans and a long-sleeved sweater. It bothered her that he still felt the need to wear gloves in front of his family and friends, in front of her. His hair was still damp from his shower, curling in unruly waves to his shoulders. As always he was barefoot, and for some strange reason, it made her blush. She found it amazingly sexy and intimate. He looked up the moment she appeared in the doorway as if he had built-in radar where she was concerned.

Dillon almost groaned when he turned his head. He knew she was there, how could he not know the moment she was close to him? She was so beautiful she took his breath away. Her jeans rode low on her hips showing a little too much skin for his liking. Her top was an inch too short, and the material lovingly hugged her full breasts the way his hands might. Her red-gold hair looked wine-red, still wet from her shower and pulled back away from her face, exposing the column of her neck. He blinked, looking closer. She damn well had better be wearing a bra under that thin almost nonexistent top. When she moved, he thought he saw the darker outline of her nipples, but then, he wasn't certain.

Just looking at her made him so hard he didn't want to take a step. "Did you put something on that cut?" His voice was harsh enough that even he winced at his tone.

Brian caught her wrist as she swept past him and turned up

her palm for his inspection, halting her before she could make her way to Dillon's side. "It's still bleeding a bit, Jessie girl," he observed. "She needs to cover it with a bandage, Dillon," he added helpfully, tugging until Jessica followed him around the counter.

Dillon grit his teeth together, watching them. Brian was a large bear of a man and Jessica looked small and delicate beside him. His scowl deepened as he watched the drummer span her waist and lift her onto the counter, wedging himself between her legs as he bent forward to examine her palm. His forehead nearly brushed her breasts. Brian said something that made Jessica laugh.

"What the hell are you doing?" Dillon burst out, stalking around the counter to jerk the bandage out of Brian's hand. "It doesn't take a rocket scientist to put a Band-Aid on her hand." He just managed to restrain himself from pushing Brian out of the way. Her thighs were open and she looked sexy as hell sitting there with her large green eyes silently reprimanding him. "Move," he said rudely.

Grinning broadly, Brian held his hands up in surrender and strode back around to the other side of the counter. "The man's like a bear with a sore tooth," he confided to Trevor in an overloud whisper.

"I noticed," Trevor replied in the same exaggerated whisper.

Dillon didn't care. He slipped into the spot Brian had vacated, nudging Jessica's thighs apart and moving close enough to catch that fresh elusive scent that stirred his senses. At once the heat of her body beckoned. And damn her, she wasn't wearing a bra, he was certain of it. He bent over her palm, examining the laceration.

The smile faded from Jessica's mouth. She nearly snatched her hand back. His breath was warm on the center of her palm sending tiny whips of lightning dancing up her arm. His hips were wedged tight between her legs. The smallest movement caused a heated friction along the inside of her thighs and spread fire to her deepest core. Her body clenched unexpectedly as he moved closer, his head brushing her breasts. She bit down on her lip to keep a small moan from escaping. Her breasts were achy and tender, so sensitive she could barely stand the lightest touch. He moved again, his forehead skimming against her blouse as he examined her palm. Right over her taut nipple. Tongues of fire lapped at her breasts, her body clenched again, throbbed and burned for release. All he had to do was turn his head slightly to pull her aching flesh into his hot, moist mouth. Her breath hitched in her throat.

His blue gaze found hers. Both of them stopped breathing.

"Well, is she going to live?" Paul asked, breaking the web of sexual tension between them. "Because if you don't finish up over there, the rest of us might not make it through the night."

"Holy cow, Jess," Trevor began.

"You don't need to say a word, young man," Jessica stopped him. She kept her eyes averted from Dillon; it was the only safe thing to do. She noticed it was awkward for him to manipulate the bandage into place. The brush of his fingers was like a caress against her skin, the glove stroked across her hand as he worked. Her body clenched more with each graze. She trembled. His hand tightened around hers, brought her injured palm to his chest, right over his heart.

"I think that should protect it, baby," he said gently. He caught her waist, only his gloves preventing him from touching her bare skin as he helped her to the floor. "It doesn't hurt, does it?"

She shook her head. "Thanks, Dillon, I appreciate it."

"How long is the darned thing going to take to heal?" Don demanded. "We need her to play. We're not nearly finished."

"I laid down several different guitar tracks earlier today, before you were up," Jessica said. "I wanted to try a few things, so at least you have something to work with." She moved cautiously around Dillon's large frame, careful not to touch his body with hers. She curled her fingers in Trevor's hair, needing to touch him, but not wanting to injure his boyish pride by making too big a fuss now that he was safe.

"What things?" Robert asked curiously, a hint of eagerness in his voice. "I thought bringing in the sax was a perfect touch. The orchestral background worked like magic. You have some great ideas, Jess."

Jessica gave him a quick grin of thanks. "I wanted to record a few different guitar sounds. I used the progression we started with yesterday but enhanced it with some melodic embellishments. I wanted an edgy sound to go with the lyrics so I used the *Les Paul* for rhythm. I still would like to do a little more layering. You should listen to it, Robert, and see what you think. I thought we might use the *Strat* for lead over the rhythm. The different sounds layered might really add to the piece."

"Or make it too busy," Don objected. "Dillon has a hell of a voice, we can't just blast over the top of him."

"But that's the beauty of it, Don," Jessica countered. "We're still sticking to basic sounds. Very simple. Layering allows us to do that."

Brenda slumped over the tabletop dramatically. "Just one night I'd like to talk about something other than music."

"I thought they were talking in a foreign language," Tara said. She pulled out the chair beside her aunt. "Boring."

Jessica laughed at her. "You just want that hot chocolate I promised you. I'll get it for you. Trevor? Anyone else?"

"You shouldn't be so careless, Jessie," Don reprimanded. "We only have a short time to get this together. You can't afford to damage your hands."

She paused in the act of removing mugs from the cupboard. "I don't honestly remember you being such a jerk, Don. Have you always been this way, or just recently?" If he took one more potshot at Dillon she was afraid she might throw a mug at his head. She didn't look at Dillon as she took the milk and chocolate from the refrigerator. There were wounds that went deep and Don seemed to want to rake at them. Jessica set everything very carefully on the counter and smiled sweetly, expectantly, at Don.

Trevor and Tara exchanged a long, amused glance. They'd heard Jessica use that tone before and it didn't bode well for Don. Tara nudged Brenda to include her, and was rewarded with a small smirk and a raised eyebrow.

"I didn't mean anything by it, Jess—everyone's too sensitive," Don replied defensively.

"I suppose we'll all overlook it this time but you need to work on your social skills. Some things are acceptable and some things aren't." Without turning her head she raised her voice. "You'd better not be mimicking me, Trev."

The twins exchanged another quick grin. Trevor had been mouthing the words, having heard them said numerous times. "Wouldn't think of it," he said cheekily.

"Dillon, would you like me to make you a cup of hot chocolate?" Jessica offered.

Dillon shook his head adamantly, shuddering at the mere thought of it. "I can't bear to look at the stuff. I had enough of that at the burn center."

"Why do you keep it then?" Jessica asked curiously.

"For Paul, of course." Dillon grinned boyishly at his friend. "He practically lives on the stuff. I think it's his one vice."

Jessica held up a mug. "How about you then, Paul?"

"Not tonight, I've had enough excitement. It might keep me up." He ruffled Tara's hair. "I figure we can share it until Christmas, then I expect it to be replaced by gift certificates and Hershey bonuses."

"I write lovely I.O.U.'s," Tara announced. "Just ask Trev."

"And you'll be old before you can cash them in," Trevor warned Paul. "But her handwriting is beautiful."

"So true, I'm vain about my handwriting. I need to be famous so I can sign autographs." Tara took a sip of the chocolate. "Why did you have too much chocolate at the burn center, Dad?"

There was a small silence. Brenda casually draped her arm around Tara. "Good question. What did they do, make you live on the stuff?"

"Actually, yes." Dillon looked across the room at Paul, a vulnerable, almost helpless look on his handsome face. It was so at odds with his usual commanding presence, his expression tugged at Jessica's heartstrings.

It was Paul who answered very matter-of-factly. "Burn patients need calories, Tara, lots and lots of calories. Where your father was, they made drinks using chocolate. You'd think they would taste good, but they didn't—the mixture was awful, and he was forced to drink them all the time."

"They ruined chocolate for you?" Tara was outraged. "That's terrible."

Dillon gave her his heart-stopping, lopsided grin. "I guess it was a small price to pay for surviving."

"Chocolate is my comfort drink," Tara admitted. "What's yours?"

"I never really thought about it," he admitted. His blue gaze was drawn to Jessica. There had been no comfort in his life since he'd lost his family, lost his music, lost everything that mattered to him. Until Jessica. He felt a sense of peace when he was with her. In spite of the overwhelming emotions, the explosive chemistry, in spite of all of it, when she was near him, he felt comforted. He could hardly say that to his thirteen-year-old daughter. If he didn't understand it, how could anyone else?

"I like that thought, Tara," Paul said, "I use chocolate for my comfort drink, too."

"Coffee, black as can be," Brenda chimed in. "Robert likes a martini." She smiled up at him. "I drive him to drink."

"You drive everyone to drink," Brian pointed out.

"You were swilling six-packs of beer long before I ever came on the scene," Brenda said, looking bored. "Your sins are all your own."

"We went to kindergarten together," Brian reminded everyone.

"And you were already beyond salvation."

"Give it a rest," Don begged.

Jessica thought it a perfect time to change the subject. "By the way, who owns the long, hooded cape?" she asked with feigned indifference. "It's quite dramatic."

"I have one," Dillon said. "I used it onstage years ago. I haven't thought of it in years. What in the world made you ask?"

"I've seen it a couple of times," Jessica said, her eyes meeting Tara's as they sipped their chocolate. "It was so different, I wanted to get a look at it up close."

"It has to be here somewhere," Dillon said, "I'll look around for it."

A chill seemed to creep into the room with her question. Jessica shivered. Once again the terrible suspicion found its way into her mind. Had someone deliberately lured Trevor to that exact spot? It wasn't possible. No one could actually predict a rockslide closely enough to set a trap. She was really becoming paranoid. Dillon couldn't have been the one wearing the cape when the rockslide had buried Trevor because Dillon had been with her. She glanced around the room surreptitiously, realizing she really knew very little about the other band members.

"I remember that cape!" Brenda sat up very straight with a wide smile. "Do you remember, Robert? Viv loved it. She was always swirling it around her and pretending to be a vampire. Dillon, we borrowed it from you for that Hollywood Halloween thing, Robert wore it, remember, hon?" She looked up at her husband, patting his hands as he gently massaged her shoulders.

"I remember it," Paul said. "It was hanging in your closet, Dillon, at least it was a month ago. I hung your shirts up when they came back from the laundry service. Viv thought vampire and you thought magician."

"I thought women," Brian said. "You know how many women wanted to see me in that cape and nothing else?" He puffed out his chest.

"Ugh." Tara wrinkled her nose. "That's totally gross."

"That's beyond gross, Brian," Brenda protested, "I'll never get the picture out of my mind." She covered her face with her hands.

"You loved it," Brian pounced immediately. "You begged me."

"Way too much information," Jessica cautioned.

"I did not, you idiot!" Brenda was outraged. "I may be many things, Brian, but I have taste. Seeing you prance around naked in a vampire cape is not my idea of sexy."

"You know, Brian," Robert said conversationally, "I actually like you. But I may have to shove your teeth down your throat if you aren't more careful in the way you choose to taunt my wife."

"Wow! That's so cool," Tara said, her blue eyes shining up at him. "He's pretty cool, after all, Brenda."

Brenda grinned at her in complete agreement. "He is, isn't he?"

Dillon leaned against Jessica, trapping her body between his large frame and the counter. "That cape might have possibilities," he whispered wickedly against her bare neck. His teeth skimmed very close to her pulse as if he might bite into her exposed skin.

"Not with knowing what Brian was doing in it," she whispered back. She pushed back against him, resting her bottom very casually against him. With the counter between their bodies and the rest of the room, no one could see her blatantly tempting him. She ached for him, her body heavy and needful. She wanted to turn into his arms, be held by him, and lie beside him, under him. She wanted to see his blue eyes blazing, burning for her alone.

Dillon savored the feel of her small, curved bottom pressed tightly against him. He was becoming used to walking around in a continual state of arousal. At least, he knew he was alive. She had the softest skin, and smelled so enticing he couldn't think of too much else when she was near. He cleared his throat, trying to pull his mind away from the thought of her body.

"Are you going to tell us about your Christmas trees?" Dillon wanted to find a way to connect with the children. They always seemed just out of his grasp. He reached around Jessica to remove the mug of chocolate from her hand. The smell was making him feel slightly sick and he wanted to inhale her delicate scent. To think about the possibility of a future, not remember the agony of where he had been. Jessica gave him such hope. His arms caged her, brought his chest in contact with the sweeping line of her back. She was the bridge between Dillon and the children. She was the bridge that led from merely existing to living life.

"We found two that might work," Trevor said, "but neither was perfect."

"Does a Christmas tree have to be perfect?" Don asked.

"Perfect for us," Trevor answered before Jessica could draw a breath and breathe fire. "We know what we're looking for, don't we, Tara?"

"Well, next time you'd better be a little more careful and stay on the trails," Dillon cautioned, using his most authoritative voice.

"There isn't going to be a next time," Jessica muttered rebelliously, "my heart couldn't stand it."

Trevor looked mutinous. "I knew you were going to be like that, Jess. It could have happened to anybody. You always get so crazy, even when we fall off a bike."

"Watch your tone." Dillon's mouth settled in an ominous line. "I think Jessica and the rest of us are entitled to feel protective. You were completely buried, Trevor, we didn't know if you were alive or dead or whether you were able to breathe or were broken into a million pieces." His arms tightened around Jessica, holding her close, feeling the tremor go through her body. His chin nuzzled the top of her head in sympathy. "Have the decency to let us be shaken up. But don't worry, we'll get a Christmas tree."

Jessica wanted to protest. She didn't want Trevor going anywhere outside, but Dillon was his father. There was no sense in dissenting, but she was *not* letting the twins go anywhere outside by themselves, father or no father.

Dillon felt her instant reaction, her body stiffening, but she remained silent. He pressed a quick kiss against the tempting nape of her neck. "Good girl." Her skin was so soft he wanted to rub his face against her. His palms itched to hold the soft weight of her breasts. His mind was becoming cloudy with erotic fantasies right there in the kitchen with everyone standing around.

"Sorry, Jessie," Trevor mumbled. "I saw that circle. The one with two rings, one inside of the other. The one you said was used to invoke spirits or something. It was drawn on a flat rock. It was really bright. I went off the trail to check it out."

There was a sudden silence in the room. Only the wind outside could be heard, a low mournful howl through the trees. A chill went down Jessica's spine. She felt the difference in Dillon immediately. His body was nearly blanketing hers as they both leaned against the counter, so it was impossible to miss the sudden tension in him. His body actually trembled with some sudden overwhelming emotion.

"Are you certain you saw a double circle, Trevor?" Dillon's face was an expressionless mask, but his eyes were blazing.

"Yes, sir," Trevor answered, "it was very distinct. I didn't get close enough to see what it was made out of before everything came down on me. It wasn't drawn or painted onto the rock. The circles were made of something and set on the rock. That's all I saw before I tripped on a log and everything crashed on top of me. I fit into the little opening against the hill so I wasn't crushed. I covered my mouth and nose and as soon as everything settled, I breathed shallowly, hoping you'd hurry. I knew Tara would get you fast."

Dillon continued to look at his son. "Brian, have you brought that filth into my home? Did you dare to do that after all that happened?"

No one moved. No one spoke. No one looked at the drummer. Brian sighed softly. "Dillon, I have my faith and I practice it, yes, wherever I am."

Dillon turned his head slowly to pin Brian with his steely glare. "You are practicing that garbage here? In my home?" He straightened up unhurriedly and there was something very dangerous, very lethal in his body posture as he rose to his full height.

Dillon was vaguely aware of Jessica laying a restraining hand very gently on his arm, but he didn't even glance down at her. The anger always simmering far too close to the surface rose in a vicious surge. The memories, dark and hideous, welled up to devour him. Screams. Chanting. The smell of incense mingled with the musty smell of sexual lust. Jessica's terror-stricken face. Her nude body painted with disgusting symbols. A man's hand violating her innocent curves while others crowded around her breathing heavily, obscenely. Watching. Stroking and pumping to bring their own bodies to a fever pitch of excitement while they urged their leader on.

Bile rose, threatening to choke him. Dillon suppressed the urge to coil his hands around Brian's throat and squeeze. Instead he held himself utterly still, curling his fingers into fists. "You dared to bring that abomination back to my home after all the damage that was done here?" His tone was soft, menacing, a spine-chilling threat.

"Trevor and Tara, go upstairs right now." Jessica stood up straight, too, very afraid of what might happen. "Go, right now and don't argue with me."

Jessica rarely used that particular tone of voice. The twins looked from their father to Brian and obediently left the room. Trevor glanced back once, worried about Jessica, but she wasn't looking at him and he had no choice but to go with Tara.

"I want you off this island, Brian, and don't ever come back," Dillon bit out each word distinctly.

"I'll go, Dillon," Brian's dark eyes betrayed his own rising anger, "but you're going to listen to me first. I do not now, nor have I ever had anything to do with the occult. I don't worship the devil. I never turned Viv on to that scene, someone else did. I did my best to talk to her, to influence her away from it."

Jessica rubbed her hand soothingly up and down Dillon's stiff arm, feeling the ridges of his skin, the raised scars, reminders of that horror-filled night that were forever etched into his flesh.

"Go on," Dillon said, his voice rough.

"My religion is old, yes, but it is the worshiping of things of the earth, spirits that live in harmony with the earth. I use the magic circles, but I don't invoke evil. That would be against everything I believe. I did my best with Viv to make her understand the difference. She was so vulnerable to anything destructive." Tears glittered in his eyes, his mouth trembled slightly. "You aren't the only one who loved her, we all did. And we all lost her. I watched her go downhill just like you did. I did my best to stop her, I really did, the minute I found out she was involved with that Satanic crowd."

Dillon raked a hand through his hair. "They weren't even the real thing," he said softly, sighing heavily.

"She went nuts when she hooked up with Phillip Trent," Brian said. "She listened to everything he said as if it was gospel. I swear to you, Dillon, I tried to stop her, but I couldn't counteract his influence." He looked as if he were breaking apart, his face crumbling under the memories.

Dillon felt his rage subsiding. He had known Brian nearly all of his life. He knew the truth when he heard it. "Trent dragged her down into a world of drugs and manic delusion so fast I don't think any of us could have stopped her. I had him investigated. He had his own little religious practices, looking for money, drugs, and sex, kicks maybe, but not based on anything he didn't make up."

Jessica stepped away from him, her lungs burning. She needed to be alone. Away from them all. Even Dillon. The memories were crowding far too close. None of the others knew what had happened to her and the discussion was skimming the edges of where she did not want to go.

"I'm sorry, Brian, I guess it just seems so much easier to blame someone else. I thought I'd gotten over that. I should have tried harder to put her into a hospital."

"I don't worship in your house," Brian said. "I know how

you feel. I know you keep battery-powered lights rather than candles in case your generator breaks down because you can't stand to see an open flame. I know you don't want incense or any reminders of the occult here and I don't blame you, so I take it outside away from your home. I'm sorry—I didn't mean to upset you, Dillon."

"I shouldn't have accused you. Next time, get rid of the circle so the kids don't get curious. I don't want to have to explain all that to them."

Brian looked confused. "I didn't set up for a ceremony anywhere near the trail, or that area." His protest was a low murmur.

Dillon's gaze and attention was on Jessica. She was very pale. Her hands were trembling and she put them behind her as she backed toward the door. "Jess." It was a protest.

She shook her head, her eyes begging him for understanding. "I'm turning in, I want to spend some time with the twins."

Dillon let her go, watched her take his heart with her as she hurried out of the room.

10

TARA HELD THE COVERS back to allow Jessica to leap beneath the quilt. Clad in her drawstring pajama bottoms and a spaghetti strap top, Jessica's hair spilled loosely down her back in preparation for bed. She hopped over Trevor's makeshift bed and slid in beside Tara. "Why is the room so cold?"

"Your mysterious window-opener has struck in Tara's room," Trevor said. "It was wide open and the curtains were wet from the rain. The room was all foggy, Jess." He deliberately didn't tell her about the magic circle made of incense ash on the floor beside the bed which both he and Tara had worked to clean. She would never let them out of her sight if she found out about it.

Jessica sighed. "How silly. Someone has a fetish for open windows. How about your room, Trev, anything out of place?"

"No, but then I set up the video camera in my room," he said with a cheeky grin. "I thought someone had come in and gone through my things so I wanted to catch them in the act if they came back." He wiggled his eyebrows at her.

"And just who did you suspect and what did you think they were looking for?" Jessica demanded.

"I figured I'd catch Brenda looking for the cash," he admitted.

"Brenda's nice now," Tara objected. "She's not going to go through your smelly old socks looking for the money everyone knows you stash in them."

"Only you know that." Trevor glared at her.

"Now I do," Jessica pointed out with an evil smirk.

Tara wrinkled her nose. "He puts the money in his dirtiest, smelliest pair."

"That is so disgusting, Trevor. Put your dirty socks in the clothes hamper," Jessica lectured, "they aren't a money bank."

"So are you going to tell us whether or not Dad killed Brian?" Trevor tried to sound very casual, but there was an underlying hint of worry in his voice. "The suspense is doing me in."

"Of course he didn't. Brian's religion is a very old one, the worshipping of the earth and deities that are in harmony with the earth. He does not worship the devil, nor is he into the occult." She hesitated, looked at the two identical faces. "Your mother followed his example for a while but during the last year of her life, when she became so ill, she met a man named Phillip Trent. He was truly evil." Just saying his name sickened her. She felt it then, that terrible coldness that could creep into a room. Unnatural. Unbidden. Beneath the covers she pressed her hand to her stomach, terrified she would be sick.

"What's wrong, Jess?" Trevor sat up very straight.

She shook her head. It was a long time ago. A different house. That evil man was dead and nothing that he had brought to life remained behind. It was impossible. Everything had burnt to the ground, reduced to a pile of ashes. It was only her imagination that the curtain stirred slightly on a cold air current when the window was closed. It was only her imagination that she felt eyes watching her. Listening. To think that if she spoke of that time, something evil would triumph, would be set free.

"Your father knows the difference. Brian explained that he worships outside, rather than in the house, out of respect for Dillon's feelings. I didn't ask him about the circle in my room because I want to ask him about it in private. Dillon is protective of all of us. They're good friends and they've talked it out." Jessica shivered again, her gaze darting around the room to the corners hidden in shadows. She felt uneasy. Memories were far too close to the surface. She knotted her fist in the quilt.

Tara leaned close to her, studying her face. She glanced at her brother, and then put her hand over Jessica's, rubbing lovingly. "Tell us the Christmas story, Jessie. It always makes us feel better."

Jessica slipped deeper into the bed, snuggling into the pillow, wanting to hide beneath the covers like a frightened child. "I'm not certain I remember it exactly."

Trevor snorted his disbelief but gamely opened the familiar tale. "Once upon a time there were two beautiful children. Twins, a boy and a girl. The boy was smart and handsome and everyone loved him, especially all the girls in the neighborhood, and the girl was a punky little thing but he generously tolerated her."

"The true story is just the opposite," Tara declared with a sniff.

"The true story is, they were both wonderful," Jessica corrected, falling in with their all too obvious ploy. "The children were good and kind and very loving, and they deserved much happiness. Alas, they both suffered broken hearts. They hid it well, but the evil, wicked Sorcerer had stolen their father. The Sorcerer had locked him away in a tower far from the children, in a bitter, cold land where there was no sun, where he never saw the light of day. He had no laughter, no love, and no music. His world was bleak and his suffering great. He missed his children and his one true love."

"You know, Jess," Trevor piped up, "that whole one true love thing used to make me gag when I was little, but I think I like it now."

"That's the best part," Tara objected, appalled at her brother's lack of romance. "If you can't see that, Trev, there's no hope you're ever going to get the girl."

He laughed softly. "It's all in the genes, little sister."

Tara rolled her eyes. "He's so weird, Jessie, is there hope for him? Don't answer, just tell us why the evil Sorcerer took him away and put him in the tower."

"He was a beautiful man with an angel's face and a poet's heart. He sang with a voice like a gift from the gods and wherever he went, people loved him. He was kind and good and did his best to help everyone. He brought joy to their hard lives with his music and his wonderful voice. The Sorcerer grew jealous because the people loved him so very much. The Sorcerer didn't want him to be happy. He wanted the father to be ugly and mean inside, to be cruel the way he was. So the Sorcerer took away everything that the father loved. His children. His music. His one true love. The Sorcerer wanted him to be bitter and to grow hateful and twisted. He had the father tortured, a painful, hideous cruelty in the dungeons of the tower. The Sorcerer's evil minions hurt him, disfigured him and then they threw him in the tower, sentenced to an eternity of darkness. He was left alone without anyone to talk to, to comfort him, and his heart wept."

There was a catch in Jessica's voice. They would never know completely what life had done to him, taken from him. The twins had been five at the time of the fire and they had only vague memories of Dillon as he was in the old days, the charismatic, joyful poet who brought such happiness to everyone with his very existence.

"The children, Jess," Trevor prompted, "tell us about them."

"They loved their father dearly, so much so that they cried so many tears the river swelled and flooded the banks. Their father's one true love comforted them and reminded them that he would want his children to be strong, to be examples of how he had always lived his life. Helping people. Loving people. Taking responsibility when others would not. And the children carried on his legacy of service to the people, of loyalty and love even as their hearts wept in tune with his.

"One night, when it was cold and the rain poured down, when it was dark and the stars couldn't shine, a white dove landed on their windowsill. It was tired and hungry. The children immediately fed it their bread and gave it their water. The father's one true love warmed the shivering bird in her hands. To their amazement the dove spoke to them saying that Christmas was near. That they should find the perfect tree and bring it into their home, and decorate it with small symbols of love. Because of their kindness, a miracle would be granted them. The dove said they could have riches untold, they could have life immortal. But the children and the father's one true love said they wanted only one thing. They wanted their father returned to them."

"The dove said he wouldn't be the same, that he would be different," Tara chimed in eagerly with the detail.

"Yes, that's true, but the children and the father's one true love didn't care, they wanted him back any way they could have him. They knew that what was in his heart would never be changed."

Outside Tara's room, Dillon leaned against the door, listening to the sound of Jessica's beautiful voice telling her Christmas tale. He had come looking for her, hating the sorrow he'd seen on her face, needing to remove the swirling nightmares from her eyes. He should have known she would be with the twins. His children. His family. They were on the other side of the door. Waiting for him. Waiting for a miracle. Tears burned in his eyes, ran down his cheeks unchecked, and clogged his throat, threatening to choke him as he listened to the story of his life.

"Did they find the perfect tree?" Tara prompted. There was such a hopeful note in her voice that Dillon closed his eyes against another fresh flood of tears. They were wrenched from the deepest gouge in his soul. Enough to overflow the banks of the mythical river.

"At first they thought the dove meant perfection, as in physical beauty." Jessica's voice was so low he had to strain to hear. "But eventually, as they looked through the forest, they realized it was something far different. They found a small, bushy tree in the shadow of much larger ones. The branches were straggly and there were gaps but they knew at once it was the perfect giving tree. Everyone else had overlooked it. They asked the tree if it would like to celebrate Christmas with them and the tree agreed. They made wonderful ornaments and carefully decorated the tree and the three of them sat up on Christmas Eve waiting for the miracle. They knew they had chosen the perfect tree when the dove settled happily in the branches."

There was a long silence. The bed creaked as someone turned over. "Jessie. Aren't you going to tell us the end of the story?" Trevor asked.

"I don't know the end of the story yet," Jessica answered. Was she crying? Dillon couldn't bear it if she were crying.

"Of course you do," Tara complained.

"Leave her alone, Tara," Trevor advised. "Let's just go to sleep."

"I'll tell you on Christmas morning," Jessica promised.

Dillon listened to the sound of silence in the next room. The tightness in his chest was agony. He stumbled away from the pain, back up the stairs, back into the darkness of his lonely tower.

Jessica lay listening to the sounds of the twins sleeping. It was comforting to hear the steady breathing. Outside the house, the wind was knocking at the windows like a giant hand, shaking the sills until the panes rattled alarmingly. The rain hit the glass with force, a steady rhythm that was soothing. She loved the rain, the fresh clean scent it brought, the way it cleared the air of any lingering smell of smoke. She inhaled, drifting, half in and half out of sleep. Fog poured into the room carrying with it an odor she recognized. She smelled incense and a frown flitted across her face. She tried to move. Her arms and legs were too heavy to lift. Alarmed, she fought to wake herself, recognizing she had moved beyond drifting, past dreams to her all too familiar nightmare.

She wouldn't look at them. Any of them. She had gone beyond terror to someplace numb. She tried not to breathe. She didn't want to smell them, or the incense, or hear the chanting, or to think about what was happening to her body. She felt the hand on her, deliberately rough, cruelly touching her while she lay helplessly under the assault. She had fought until she had no strength. Nothing would stop this demented behavior and she would endure it because she had no other choice.

The hand squeezed her hard, probed in tender, secret places. She would not feel, would not scream again. She couldn't stop the tears; they ran down her face and fell onto the floor. Without warning the door burst open, kicked in so that it splintered and hung at an angle from broken hinges. He looked like an avenging angel, his face twisted with fury, his blue eyes blazing with rage.

She cringed when he looked at her, when he saw the obscenity of what they were doing to her. She didn't want him to see her naked and painted with something evil touching her body. He moved so fast she wasn't certain he was real, ripping Phillip Trent away from her. There was the sound of fist meeting flesh, the spray of blood in the air. She was helpless, unable to move, unable to see what was happening. There were screams, grunts, a bone cracked. Shouted obscenities. The smell of alcohol. She was certain she would never be able to bear the odor again.

And then he was wrapping her in his shirt, loosening the ties that bound her hands and feet. He lifted her, with tears streaming down his face. "I'm sorry, baby, I'm sorry," he whispered against her neck as he carried her from the room. She caught glimpses of broken furniture, of glass and scattered objects. Bodies writhing and moaning on the floor as he carried her out. His hands were bloody but gentle as he placed her in her bed, rocked her gently while she cried and wept until both their hearts were broken. She begged him not to tell anyone how he found her.

She had no idea how much time passed. He was filled with fury, his rage was still lethal. He was arguing she needed her mother, stalking from her room to cool off outside where he couldn't hurt anyone. She scrubbed herself in the shower until her skin was raw, until there were no tears left. She was dressing, her hands shaking so badly she couldn't button her blouse, when she heard the volley of shots ring out. The sound of the gun was distinctive. The smell of smoke was overwhelming. It took a few moments to realize it wasn't steam from the bathroom that was making the room hazy, it was clouds of thick smoke. She had to crawl through the hall to the twins' room. They were crying, hiding under the bed. Flames ate greedily at the hall, up the curtains. There was no getting to the others.

She dragged the children to the large window, shoved them through, following, dropping to earth, skidding on the slick dirt. Tara crawled forward blindly, tears streaming from her swollen eyes that prevented her from seeing. She screamed as she slipped over the edge. Jessica lunged after her. They rolled, bounced, sliding all the way to the sea. Tara disappeared beneath the waves, Jessica hurtled after her. Down. Into darkness. The salt water stung. It was icy cold. Her fingers brushed the child's shirt, slipped off, she grabbed again, caught a handful of material and held on. Kicking strongly. Surfacing. Struggling through the pounding waves with her burden. They lay together on the rocks, gasping for breath, the child in her arms. Her world in ruins.

Black smoke. Noise. Orange flames reaching the clouds. Screams. Wearily she pulled Trevor into her arms when he joined them. Together they slowly made their way back up the path lead-ing to the front of the house. She saw Dillon lying there. He was motionless. His body was black, his arms outstretched. He was ut-terly silent but his eyes were screaming as he looked down in shock at the blackened ruin of his body. He looked up at her. Looked past her to the children. She understood then. Understood why he had entered a burning inferno. His gaze met hers as he stared helplessly up at her, in much the same way she must have stared up at him when he'd rescued her. As long as she lived, she would never forget the look on his face, the horror in his eyes. Jessica watched his blackened fingers turn to ash, watched the ash fall to the ground. She heard herself screaming in denial. Over and over. The sound was pure anguish.

"Jessie," Trevor called her name softly, his arm around Tara. They helplessly watched as Jessica pressed herself against the wall near the window and screamed and screamed, her face a mask of terror. Her eyes were open, but they knew she wasn't seeing them, but something else, something vivid and real to her, that they couldn't see. Night terrors were eerie. Jessica was caught up in the web of a nightmare and anything they did often made it worse.

The door to the bedroom was flung open and their father rushed in, still buttoning his jeans. He wore no shirt, he was barefoot. His hair was wild and disheveled, falling around his perfectly sculpted face like dark silk. His chest and arms were a mass of rigid scars and whorls of raised red skin. The scars streaked down his arms and spread down his chest to his belly fading into normal skin.

"What the hell is going on?" Dillon demanded but his fran-tic gaze had already found Jessica pressed against the wall. He glanced at his children. "Are you all right?"

Tara was staring at the mass of scars. She pulled her gaze up to his face with an effort. "Yes, she has nightmares. This is a bad one."

"I'm sorry, I forgot my shirt," Dillon told her softly before turning his attention back to Jessica. "Wake up, baby, it's over," he crooned softly. His voice was low and compelling, almost hypnotic. "It's me, sweetheart, you're safe here. I'm not going to let anyone hurt you."

Tara turned her head as more people crowded into the doorway of her room. She had to blink tears out of her eyes in order to focus on them. Trevor put his arm around her, offering comfort, and she took it.

"Good heavens," Brenda said, "what happened now?"

"Get them out of here, Trevor," Dillon ordered, "get out and close the door."

Trevor acted at once. He didn't want anyone staring at Jessica, seeing her in such a vulnerable state. And he didn't like the way they were staring at his father's body, either. He took Tara with him, pushing through the group, closing the door firmly and leaving Dillon alone with Jessica. "Show's over," he said gruffly, "you all might as well go back to bed."

Brenda glared at him. "I was actually trying to be helpful. If Jessie needs me, I don't mind sitting up with her."

To everyone's astonishment, Tara wrapped her arms around Brenda's waist and looked up at her. "I need you," she confided. "I hurt him again."

Trevor cleared his throat. "No you didn't, Tara." He was happy to see the band members dispersing, leaving only Brenda and Robert behind.

"Yes I did, I was staring at his scars and he noticed," Tara confessed, looking up at Brenda. "Even with Jessie screaming and how much he wanted to help her, he noticed. And he said he was sorry." Tears welled up and spilled over. "I didn't mean to stare at him, I should have looked away. It must have hurt him so much."

It was Robert who dropped his hand on her head in a clumsy effort to comfort her. "We couldn't stop him. The house was completely engulfed in flames. He was calling for you and your brother, for Jessica. He ran toward the house. I caught him, so did Paul. He knocked us both down." There was sorrow in his voice, guilt, a ragged edge. Robert paused, rubbed the bridge of his nose, frowning slightly.

Brenda put her hand on his arm. Casually. As if it didn't matter, but Trevor saw that it did. That it steadied Robert. Robert smiled down at Brenda's hand and leaned forward to kiss her fingertips. "He ran inside the house, right through a wall of flames. Paul tried to go in after him, but Brian and I tackled him and held him down. We should have done that to Dillon. We should have." He shook his head at the memories.

Trevor found himself reaching out to his uncle, touching him for the first time. "No one could have stopped him. If I know anything about my father, it's that no one could have stopped him from trying to get to us." He glanced back at the closed door. Jessica's screams had stopped. He could hear the soft murmur of Dillon's voice. "No one could have stopped him from trying to get to Jess."

Robert blinked and focused on Trevor. "You're so like him, like he was back in the old days. Tara, what I'm trying to say to you is, don't be afraid of looking at your father's scars. Don't ever be ashamed of the way he looks. Those scars are evidence of how much he loves you, what you mean to him. He's a great man, someone you should be proud of, and he'll always put you first. Few people have that and I think it's important for you to know that you do have it. I could never have entered that house, none of the rest of us could go in, even when we heard the screams."

"Don't, Robert," Brenda said sharply. "No one could have saved those people. You didn't even know they were up there."

"I know, I know." He rubbed a hand over his face, wiping away old horrors and determinedly forcing a smile to his face, needing to change the subject. "Anyone up for one of Brenda's silly board games? She's obsessed with them."

"I always win," Brenda pointed out smugly.

Trevor glanced at the closed door anxiously, then switched his attention back to his aunt. "I always win," he countered.

Tara slipped her hand into Robert's. "He does," she confided.

"Then it's all-out war," Brenda decided, leading the way back to her rooms. "I detest losing at *anything.*"

"Do you really have an insurance policy on us?" Trevor asked curiously as he followed her down the hall.

"Of course, silly, you're a boy, the odds are much higher that you'll do something stupid," Brenda remarked complacently. "All that lovely lollie," she added, grinning back at him over her shoulder.

Trevor shook his head. "I'm not buying your act anymore, *Auntie.* You're not the bad girl you want the world to believe you are."

Brenda flinched visibly. "Don't even say that, it's sacrilegious. And by the way, your cute little pranks aren't scaring me in the least, so you may as well stop."

"I don't pull cute little pranks," Trevor objected strenuously to her choice of words. "If I was pulling off a prank, it wouldn't be cute or little. And it would scare you. I'm a master at practical jokes."

Brenda pushed open the door to her room, raising one eyebrow artfully as he preceded her into the suite. "Oh, really? So what is with the hooded face appearing in the window, and the mysterious messages written on my makeup mirror? *Get out while there's still time.*" She rolled her eyes. "Really! Perfectly childish. And just how do you explain the water running in the bathtub with the stopper in the drain and the room always filled with steam? If I didn't know it was you, it would give me the creeps. The open window and Brian's magic circle is such a clever touch, throwing suspicion his way. We've all talked about it, we know it's you two. Even that motley dog is in cahoots with you, growling at the steam and staring at nothing just to scare us."

There was a small silence. Tara and Trevor exchanged a long look. "Is your window open when you come into your room?" Tara ventured, her voice tight. "And fog or steam all through the room?"

Robert looked at her sharply. "Are you saying you kids

haven't been pulling these pranks?" He poured them both a soda from the small ice chest they had stashed in their room.

Trevor shook his head, took a long grateful drink of the cold liquid, nearly draining the glass. He hadn't realized how thirsty he was. "No, sir, we haven't. And Jessica's window is open all the time." A chill crept into the room with his denial. "Tara's window was open this evening. And there was burned incense and one of those circles on the floor of both Jessie's and Tara's rooms. Jess didn't tell Dillon because she was afraid he would quit recording with everyone, and she thinks it's important for him and everyone else to make the music."

Robert and Brenda exchanged a long look. "If you kids have been playing tricks, it's all right to say so," Robert persisted. "We know kids do that sort of thing." He pulled a *Clue* game from the closet, carried it to the table.

"How perfectly apropos, a murder game on a dark and stormy night just when we're discussing mysterious occurrences," Brenda quipped as they spread the game board out on the small table.

"We didn't do any of those things," Trevor insisted. "I don't know who it is or why, but something wants us out of here."

"Why do you say that?" Robert asked sharply as he separated the cards.

Trevor noticed his clue sheet was filled and he crumpled it, looking around for a wastebasket. He couldn't toss it, practicing his technique, because the basket was filled with newspaper. With a sigh he got up and walked over to it. For some reason his stomach was beginning to cramp uncomfortably and his skin felt clammy. The conversation was bothering him a lot more than he realized. "I don't know, I always feel like something's watching us. We've been letting the dog in and sometimes we're in a room alone and it starts growling, looking at the door. All the hair rises up on its back. It's freaky. But when I go look, no one's there."

"I'd think you were making it up," Robert said, "but there

have been some strange things happening in here, too. We thought it was you kids, so we didn't say anything either, but I don't like the sound of that. Have you told Jessie?"

Trevor bent down to press the sheet of paper into the waste-basket. The newspaper caught his eye. It had tiny little holes in it where words were cut out. He glanced back at his aunt and uncle. They were putting the game pieces on the board. Tara looked pale, a frown on her face. She was holding her stomach as if she had cramps, too. Trevor lifted the newspaper slightly. It reminded him of movies where ransom notes had been concocted from printed words pasted on paper. The glass in front of Tara was empty. A frisson of fear went down his spine. Very slowly he straightened, moved casually away from the evidence in the wastebasket.

"No, I haven't told Jessie much at all. She's been busy with the recording and she's so darned overprotective." He looked directly at his aunt. "I'm feeling a little sick. It wasn't the soda, was it?"

"I'm not feeling very well either," Tara admitted.

Brenda bent over Tara solicitously. "Is it the flu?"

"You tell me," Trevor challenged. A wave of nausea hit him. "We need Jessie."

Brenda sniffed. "I think I'm quite capable of taking care of a couple of little kiddies with the flu."

"I hope so," Tara said, "because I'm going to throw up." She ran to the bathroom, holding her stomach.

Brenda looked harassed for a moment, then rushed after her.

11

"JESS, BABY, CAN YOU hear me now? Do you know who I am?" Dillon used his voice shamelessly, a velvet blend of heat and smoke. He didn't make the mistake of trying to approach her, knowing he could become part of her frightening world. Instead, he flicked on the light, bathing the room in a soft glow. He hunkered down across from her, his movements slow and graceful. "Honey, come back to me now. You don't need to be in that place, you don't belong there."

She was staring, focused on something beyond his shoulder. There was so much terror and horror in her eyes that he actually turned his head, expecting to see something. It was icy cold in the room. The window behind her was fully open, the curtains fluttering like twin white flags. It made him uneasy. She was pressed up against the wall, her hands restlessly searching the surface, seeking a place of refuge. His breath hitched in his throat when her fingers skimmed the windowsill and she inched toward it.

"Jess, it's Dillon. See me, baby, know I'm here with you." He slowly straightened, shifted to the balls of his feet. His heart was hammering out his own fright. Her screams had stopped but she was staring at something he couldn't see, couldn't fight.

With a small moan of terror, Jessica flung herself at the open window, crawling out as quickly as she could pull herself through. Dillon was on top of her in an instant, his hands wrapping securely around her waist, dragging her backward into the room. She fought like a wild thing, tearing at the windowsill, the curtains, her fingernails digging into wood as she desperately tried to make her escape.

"You're two stories up, Jess," Dillon said, twisting to avoid her scissoring legs. He managed to wrestle her to the floor without hurting her, holding her down, straddling her, pinning her there so she couldn't harm herself. "Wake up. Look at me."

Her gaze persisted in going beyond him, caught in a web he couldn't break through. When she stopped fighting, he pulled her onto his lap, his arms still holding her tightly there on the floor, and he sang softly to her. It had been her favorite song as long as he could remember. His voice filled the room with a warmth, a soothing comfort, a promise of love and commitment. He had written it in the days of hope and belief, when he believed in love and miracles. When he believed in himself.

Jessica blinked, looked around her, focused on Dillon's angel's face. It took a few moments to realize she was on his lap, his arms binding her tightly to him. She turned her head to search for the twins. The room was empty. She shivered, relaxed completely into Dillon, allowing his voice to drive away the remnants of terror.

"Are you back, baby?" His voice was a wealth of tenderness. "Look at me." He brought both of her hands to his mouth, kissed her fingers. "Tell me you know who I am. I swear I won't let anything happen to you." With Jessica on his lap, only thin cloth separated them, and the knowledge was awakening his body. Her breasts were spilling out of her thin top giving him a generous view of soft skin. The temptation to lean down and taste her was strong.

A small smile managed to find its way to her trembling mouth. "I know that, Dillon. I've always known that. Did I frighten Tara and Trevor?"

"Tara and Trevor?" he echoed, astonished. "You frightened *me.*" He brought her palm to his bare chest, straight over his pounding heart. "I can't take much more of this. I really can't." He traced her trembling lips with a scarred fingertip. The raised whorls rasped sensually over her soft mouth. "What in the hell am I supposed to do with you? If I had a heart left, I'd have to tell you, you're breaking it." He had been so afraid for her that he had left his room with his body uncovered. He had turned on the light to help dispel her dream world, not thinking what it would reveal of him. He held her in his lap, his scarred body exposed to her gaze when it was the last thing he ever intended.

"I'm sorry, Dillon." Tears shimmered in her vivid green eyes, threatened to spill over onto her long lashes. Her lips were still trembling, tearing at his heart even more. "I didn't mean for this to happen. I didn't know it would be like this."

He groaned, a sound of surrender. The last thing he wanted was for her to be sorry. He helped her from his lap, rose and hauled her up beside him, his arm curling around her waist, clamping her to his side. "Don't cry, Jess, I swear to God if you cry you'll destroy me."

She buried her face against his chest, against the scars of his past life. She didn't wince, she didn't even stare in utter disgust. His Jessica. His one light in the darkness. He could feel her tears wet against his skin. With an oath he lifted her, cradled her slight weight to him. There was only one place to take her, the only place she belonged. He took the stairs fast, climbing to the third story, his refuge, his sanctuary, the lair of the wounded beast. He kicked the door closed behind him.

"Are you afraid of me, Jess?" he asked softly. "Tell me if you're afraid of how I look." He strode to the large bed and laid her down on his sheets. "Tell me if you're afraid I went back into that house and did what most people think I did."

She rested her head on the pillow, met the hypnotic blue of his eyes, was lost instantly, drowning in the deep turbulent sea. "I've never been afraid of you, Dillon," she answered honestly. "You know I don't believe you shot anyone that night. I've never believed it. Knowing you went back into the house before the gun was fired doesn't change what I know about you." She reached up, framed his face with one hand while the other skimmed lightly over his chest. How could he ever think his scars would repulse her? He had gone into a burning inferno to save his children. The scars were as much a part of him now as his angel's face. Her fingertips traced a whorl of ridged flesh. His badge of courage, of love—she could never think of his scars any other way. "And you've always been beautiful to me. Always. You were the one who kept me away from you. I tried so many times to see you in the burn center and you wouldn't give your consent." There was hurt in her voice, pain in her eyes. "You cut yourself off from me and you left me struggling on my own. For so long I couldn't breathe without you. I couldn't talk to anyone. I didn't know how to go on."

"You deserve something better than this, Jess," he said grimly.

"What's better, Dillon? Being without you? The pain doesn't go away. Neither does the loneliness, not for me or the children."

"I always knew exactly what I was doing, what I was worth." Confusion slipped across his face. "My music was my measure of who I was, what I could offer. Now I don't know what I can give you. But you have to be certain being with me is what you really want. I can't have you and then lose you. I have to know it means the same thing to you as it does to me."

Jessica smiled at him as she stood up. Deliberately she moved in front of the large sliding glass door leading to the balcony. She wanted what light there was to fall on her, so there would be no mistake. For her answer, she simply caught the hem of her tank top and pulled it over her head.

Standing there, facing him with the glass framing her, she looked like an exotic beauty, ethereal, out of reach. Her skin gleamed at him, a satin sheen, beckoning his touch. Her breasts were full, firm, jutting toward him, so perfect he felt his heart slam hard in his chest and his mouth go dry. His body tightened painfully, his need so urgent his body was straining against the fabric of his jeans.

He reached out to the offering, his palm skimming along her soft skin. She felt exactly as she looked and the texture was mesmerizing. Jessica's breath hitched in her throat, her body trembled as he cupped her breasts in his hands. His thumbs found taut buds and stroked as he leaned into her to settle his mouth over hers.

Jessica was aware of so many sensations. Her breasts achingly alive, wanting his touch, his thumbs sending bolts of lightning whipping through her bloodstream until her lower body was heavy and needy. Every nerve ending was alive, so that his silken hair brushing her skin sent tiny darts of pleasure coursing through her. His mouth was hard and dominant, moving over and into hers with male expertise and hot, silken passion.

Outside the wind began to moan, shifting back from the sea, rattling at the glass doors as if seeking entrance. Dillon's mouth left hers to follow the line of her shoulder, the hollow of her throat, to close, hot and hungry, around her breast. Jessica's body jerked with reaction, her arms coming up to cradle his head. His mouth was fiery hot, suckling strongly, a starving man let loose on a feast. His hands skimmed her narrow rib cage, tugged impatiently at the drawstring of her pajamas.

Her body wound tighter and tighter, a spiral of heat she couldn't hope to control. The pajama bottoms dropped to the floor and she kicked them aside, reveling in the way his hands glided possessively over her.

"I've wanted you for so long," he breathed the words against her satin skin, moving to her other breast, his fingers stroking the curve of her bottom, finding every intriguing indentation, every shadow. "I can't believe you're really here with me."

"I can't believe it either," she admitted, closing her eyes, throwing back her head to arch more fully into his greedy mouth. She felt a wildness rising in him, skating the edge of his control. It gave her a sense of power that she might not have had otherwise. He wanted her with the same force of need as she did him, which allowed her a boldness she might never have managed. Her hands found the waistband of his jeans. She deliberately rubbed her palm over his bulging hardness, just as she'd done in the woods. She felt the breath slam out of his lungs. He lifted his head, his blue gaze burning into her like a brand.

Jessica smiled at him as she unfastened his jeans. "I've wanted to do this," she confided as he burst free. Thick and long and ready for her, pulsing with heat and life. Her fingers wrapped around the length of him, a proprietary gesture. Her thumb stroked the velvet head until he groaned aloud.

Very gently he exerted pressure on her, forcing her back toward the bed. "I don't want to wait any longer, I don't think I can."

Jessica knelt on the bed, still stroking him, leaning forward to kiss his sculpted mouth, loving the hunger in his gaze. He was more intimidating than she had expected so she took her time getting used to the feel and size of him. She fed on his mouth, trailed kisses over his scarred chest, experimentally swirled her tongue over the head of his shaft. He jumped beneath her ministrations, sucked in his breath audibly.

"Not yet, baby, I'll explode if you do that. Lie back for me." His hands were already assisting her, pushing her into the mattress so she lay naked and waiting for his touch. His hand stroked a caress down her body, over her breast, lingering for a moment until she shivered, over her belly, down to the thatch of curls, glided to her thighs.

He sat up, his blue eyes moving over every inch of her. She was so beautiful, moving restlessly on the bed beneath him. Wanting him. Needing him. Hungry for him alone. He loved the way the muted light skimmed lovingly over her body, touching her here and there along the curves and shadows he was familiarizing himself with.

"Dillon." It was a soft protest, that he had stopped when she was burning for him, her body heavy and throbbing with need.

"I love to look at you, Jess." His hands parted her thighs just a little wider, his fingers stroking a long caress in the damp folds between her legs. She jumped when he touched her, pushed forward against his palm, a small cry of pleasure escaping her. Dillon smiled at her, leaned down to swirl his tongue around her intriguing belly button. Those little tops she wore that didn't quite cover her flat belly were enough to drive him mad. His hair brushed her sensitive skin and he pushed his finger slowly, deep inside her tight, hot sheath. At once her muscles clenched around him, velvet soft, firm, moist, and hot. His own body throbbed and swelled in response.

Her hips pushed forward wantonly. Jessica had no inhibitions with Dillon. She wanted his body, wanted every single erotic dance with him. She had no intention of holding back; she was determined to get every last gasp of pleasure she could. She had learned the hard way that life is precarious and she wasn't going to let an opportunity slip by because of modesty, pride, or shyness. Jessica lifted her hips to meet the thrusting of his finger, the friction triggering a rippling effect deep in her hottest core.

Dillon nipped her flat belly with a string of teasing kisses, distracting her while he stretched her a little more, sinking two fingers into her soft, hot body. More than anything else, her pleasure mattered to him. He was large and thick and he could tell she was small. Her velvet folds pulsed for him, wanting, and he fed that hunger, pushing deep, retreating, entering again so that her hips followed his lead. "That's what I want, honey, just like that. I want you ready for me."

"I am ready for you," she pleaded softly, her fingers tangling in his hair.

"Not yet, you're not," he answered. His breath was warm against the curve of her hip. She felt his tongue stroke a caress in the crease along her thigh. His mouth found the triangle of fiery curls at the junction of her legs. Her breath hissed out of her as his tongue tasted her moist heat. His name was a whispered plea. He lifted his head to look at her face. Very slowly he withdrew his fingers to bring them to his mouth. She shivered, her gaze fascinated as he licked her juices from his hand. "Open your thighs wider, baby." It was a whispered enticement. "Give yourself to me."

She was lost in the pulsing hunger; the fire was racing through her body. She opened her legs wider to him, a clear invitation. She was hot and wet and slick with her passion.

Dillon pressed his palm once against her heated entrance, so that she shivered in anticipation. Then he slowly lowered his head once more.

She nearly screamed, drowning in the sensation of pure pleasure. His tongue caressed, probed deep, stabbed into hot folds, swirled and teased and sucked at her until she was mindlessly sobbing his name, writhing beneath him, her hips thrusting helplessly for the relief only he could bring her. He took her up the path several times, pushing higher each time so that her body shuddered and rippled with pleasure over and over. Until he knew she was hot and slick and needed him enough to accept him buried deep within her body.

Dillon knelt between her legs, and watched his body probe desperately for the slick entrance to hers. He wanted to see them come together, in a miracle of passion. His engorged head pushed into her. At once he felt her sheath, tight and hot, grip him, close around him. The sensation shook him so that he had to hang on to his control. "Jess." Her name burst from between his teeth. He slid in another inch, pushing his way through the tight folds. If it was possible, she grew even hotter. His hands tightened on her hips. "Tell me you're okay, baby."

"Yes, more," she gasped. He was invading her body, a thick, hard fullness, stretching her immeasurably, but at the same time, the craving for him grew and grew.

His hands tightened and he surged forward, past her barrier, and buried himself deeper. Sweat broke out on his forehead. He had never felt such a sensation of pure ecstasy. It was difficult to keep from plunging his body madly into hers. "Tell me what it feels like." He bit the words out huskily, and lowered his head to flick his tongue over her taut nipple. The action tightened her body even more around his.

"It's everything, Dillon. You're big and you're stretching me so it burns a little, but at the same time, I want more, I want all of you deep inside me," she answered honestly. "More than anything, that's what I want right now."

"Me, too," he admitted and surged forward. The sensation

shook him. Her muscles were slick and hot and velvet soft, so tight he could barely stand it. He buried himself deep, withdrew, and thrust hard again. He watched her face carefully for signs of discomfort, but her body was flushed, her eyes glazed, her breath coming in little needy pants.

Satisfied that she was feeling the same pleasure he was feeling, Dillon began to move in a gentle rhythm. Long and slow, gliding in and out of her, stretching, pushing deeper with each stroke. He tilted her hips, held her body so he could thrust even deeper, wanting her to accept every last inch of him, almost as if her body could accept his, she would see who he really was and love him anyway. He buried himself to the hilt, sliding so deep he felt her womb, felt her contractions beginning, a spiraling that began to increase in strength. "Jess, I've never felt like this. Never." He wanted her to know what she meant, how much a part of him she was.

His rhythm became faster, harder, his hips surging forward into her, his body beyond any pretense of control. Jessica cried out softly as her body fragmented, as the room rocked and the earth simply melted away. Dillon could feel how strong her muscles were, milking him, gripping him in the strength of her orgasm, taking him with her right over the edge. He pumped into her frantically, helplessly, unable to control the wildness in him, the explosion ripping through his body from his toes up to the top of his head.

Dillon didn't have enough energy to roll over, so he lay on top of her, his body still locked to hers. His heart was beating hard. He buried his face against her breast, tears burning at the back of his eyes and throat. He had never been so emotional in the old days. He had never felt like this, sated and at peace. He had never thought it possible.

Jessica wrapped her arms around Dillon, holding him close, feeling the emotions swirling so deeply in him. She knew he was struggling. Part of him wanted to remain a recluse, hidden from the past and the future, and part of him desperately wanted what she was holding out to him. It was all tied up in his music. In his perception that he had failed everyone he loved. He wanted her to love him as he saw himself, a man without anything to offer. She didn't see him that way and never could. She could only offer him what she had, her honesty, her belief in him, her trust.

She felt his tongue flick her nipple, a lazy back and forth swirl that sent shock waves through her body. Her muscles rippled with the aftershock and gripped his. He exhaled, his breath warm against her skin.

"Tell me I didn't hurt you, Jess," he asked. He lifted himself up to his elbows, his hands framing her face.

"Dillon! I was practically yelling your name shamelessly for the entire household to hear." She smiled as he leaned down to kiss her. The touch of his mouth sent a series of shocks through her body so that she once more rippled with pleasure. "I think I'm hypersensitive to you," she admitted.

His eyebrow shot up. "That appeals to me on a purely primitive level," he said as he buried his face in the valley between her breasts. "I love how you smell, especially now after we've made love." His mouth nuzzled her skin, his tongue teasing along her ribs. He allowed his sated body to slide away from hers, but his hand slipped along the path of her belly to rest in her triangle of curls. "I want to just explore every inch of you for the rest of the night. I want to know you, what brings you pleasure, what gets you hot fast and what takes a little longer. Mostly, I just want to be with you." His silky hair played over her aching breasts as he lifted his head high enough to look at her. "Do you mind?"

There was a curious vulnerability about him. Jessica stretched languidly beneath him, offering up her body to him. "I want to be with you, too."

She lay listening to the rain on the roof while his hands skimmed her body, framed every curve, touched every inch of her with tenderness. She felt as if she were drifting in a sea of pure pleasure. He made love to her a second time, a slow, leisurely joining that stole her heart along with her breath.

Jessica realized she must have fallen asleep a while ago when she woke to feel Dillon's hands gliding over her once again. She lay in the dark, smiling as he brought her body to life. His hands and mouth were skillful, teasing, tempting. He shifted to pull her closer to him, his knowledge of her body growing with every exploration.

His tongue was busy at her nipple, his mouth hot with passion, and Jessica closed her eyes, willing to give herself up to the incredible sensation. Her hands in his hair, she tried to relax, tried to ignore the shiver of awareness moving down her spine. She felt eyes on them. Watching them. Watching Dillon suckling at her breast, his fingers delving deeply into her wet core. Her eyes flew open and she looked wildly around the room, trying to see into every shadow.

Dillon felt her sudden resistance. "What is it, baby?" he asked, his mouth still busy between words. "Have I made you sore?"

"Someone is outside the door, Dillon," Jessica whispered against his ear, "listening to us." It was difficult to think when his mouth was pulling so strongly at her breast, sending white-hot streaks of lightning dancing through her bloodstream. When he pushed two fingers deep and stroked her with such expertise.

Dillon's body was hard and hot and wanting hers. His tongue flicked over the tight bud of her nipple, did a long, slow lazy swirl. He lifted his head away from the lush pleasures of her body when she tugged at his hair. His blue eyes burned over her face hungrily. "I didn't hear anything."

"I'm not kidding, Dillon," Jessica insisted, "someone is listening to us, or watching us. I can feel them." She stiffened, pushing at him, looking toward the glass balcony half expecting to see a hooded figure standing there.

Sighing with regret, Dillon left the pleasures of her body and looked around for his jeans. She had already slipped into his robe, cinching it around her slender body. Her face was pale and her red-gold hair spilled around her like a waterfall of silk. He didn't understand her. She was always a miracle of good sense, but when it came to certain things, she lost every bit of it, she was so positive that forces were conspiring to harm those she loved. He couldn't really blame her for worrying. Dillon stalked to the door and jerked it open wide to show her no one was there.

His heart nearly stopped when he came face-to-face with his bass player. They stood so close their noses were nearly touching.

Don stared for a moment at Dillon's exposed chest, then glanced past him to see Jessica huddled in Dillon's robe. Dillon stepped instantly to block Don's view of her. "What the hell are you doing, Don?" Dillon snapped, angrily.

Don flushed, glanced past him to Jessica's pale face, and half turned to leave. "Forget it, I didn't realize you were busy. I saw the light and knew you were up."

Dillon swallowed his annoyance. Don never sought him out. It was a rare chance to clear the air between them, even if it was untimely. "No, don't go, it must have been something important that brought you here this late." He raked a hand through his thick black hair, tossed Jessica a pleading smile. She responded exactly the way he knew she would, nodding slightly and drawing his robe more closely around her. "Hell, it must be close to five in the morning." He stepped back and gestured for Don to enter. "Whatever it is, let's deal with it." Don looked rumpled and Dillon smelled alcohol on his breath.

Don took a deep breath, stepped inside. "I'm sorry, Jessie." His gaze found her, then slid away. "I didn't know you were here."

She shrugged. It was far too late to hide anything that had been going on. The bed was rumpled, the pillows on the floor. Her hair was disheveled and she wore nothing under Dillon's robe. "Would you like me to leave?" She asked it politely. Don seemed terribly nervous, his apprehension adding to her own discomfort. Her stomach rolled ominously, a wave of nausea swamping her for a moment.

"I don't know if I have the courage to say to Dillon what I

need to say, let alone in front of anyone, but on the other hand, you're always a calming influence." He paced across the room several times while they waited.

"Have you been drinking?" Dillon asked, curious. "I've never seen you drink, Don, not more than one beer."

"I thought it would give me courage." Don gave him a half-hearted humorless grin. "You need to call the police and have me arrested." The words tumbled out fast, in a single rushed breath. The moment he said them, he looked for a place to collapse.

Dillon led him to one of the two chairs positioned on either side of a small reading table. "Would you like a glass of water?"

Jessica had already hurried to get a glass from the large master bathroom. "Here, Don, drink this."

He took the glass, gulped the water down, wiped his mouth with the back of his hand, and looked up at Dillon. "I swear to God I thought you knew about Vivian and me. All this time I thought you were waiting for a chance to get rid of me and replace me with Paul. I kept waiting for it to happen. I tried so hard never to give you a reason."

"Before anything else, Don, I'm a musician. I love Paul. He's my best friend. We've stood together through the best and worst of times, but he doesn't have your talent. I *wanted* you in the band. From the first time I heard you play, I knew you were right. Paul doesn't have your versatility. He helped start the band, and I had no intention of leaving him along the wayside, but once you signed on with us, you were as much a part of the band as I was." Dillon shook his head regretfully. "I'm sorry you thought differently, that I never told you how valuable you were to me."

"Great. I didn't need to hear you say that." Don heaved a sigh. "This isn't easy, Dillon. I don't deserve you to be civil to me."

"I'll admit I was shocked and upset about you and Vivian," Dillon said. He reached for Jessica, unable to help himself, needing to touch her. Needing her real and solid beside him. At once she was there, her small body fitting beneath his shoulder, her arm slipping around his waist. "It was a rotten thing to do, Don, but it hardly warrants calling the police."

"I tried to blackmail you." Don didn't look at either of them as he made the confession. He stared down at his hands, a lost expression on his face. "I saw you go into the forest that night. We all heard the yelling upstairs, and the pounding. We figured you caught Viv with one of her lovers. No one wanted to embarrass you so they all went to the studio to be out of the way, but I went to the kitchen for something to drink and I saw you go out. You had tears on your face and you were so shaken, I followed you, thinking I could offer to help. But you were more distraught than anyone I'd ever seen before and I figured, since it involved Vivian, you wouldn't want to talk to me. I walked around, undecided, and then just when I was going back, I saw you go in through the kitchen. Rita was in there and I heard you talking, telling her what happened. You were so angry, you were wrecking the place. I didn't dare approach you or Rita. I saw you start up the stairs and I headed for the studio. Then I heard the shots." As proof of his crime he pulled a plain sheet of paper from his pocket. Words cut from the headline of a newspaper were pasted on it. "This was one I was going to send you."

"Why didn't you testify to that at the trial?" Dillon's voice was very low, impossible to read. He snatched the paper from Don's hand and crumpled it without glancing at it.

"Because I was already on the basement staircase, looking out through the glass doors, and I saw you when the shots were fired. I knew you didn't do it. You had gone back outside a second time and you were heading toward the forest."

"Yet you decided blackmail was a good alternative?"

"I don't know why. I don't know why I did any of the things I've done since then," Don admitted. "All I cared about was the band. I wanted it back. You sat up here in this house with Paul, no one else could get near you. You had all that talent just going to waste, a musical genius, and you locked yourself up with Paul as the warden. He never wanted me anywhere near the place. I had this stupid idea that if you had to pay out a lot of money, you'd have to go back to work and we'd all be back on the ride."

"Why didn't you just talk to me?" Dillon asked in the same quiet voice.

"Who could talk to you?" Don demanded bitterly. "Your watchdog wouldn't let anyone near you. You have him so well trained he practically has the Great Wall of China surrounding the island." He held up his hand to prevent Dillon from speaking. "You don't have to defend him, I know he's protective and even why. I needed the band back and I felt hopeless so I sent you a stupid letter and followed it with a couple of others. Obviously you weren't very worried because you didn't respond."

"I didn't give a damn," Dillon admitted.

"There's no excuse for what I've done," Don announced, "so I'm ready to go to jail. I'll confess everything to the cops."

Dillon looked so helpless, Jessica put her arms around him. "Did you talk to my mother about this?" She couldn't see Don sneaking around her mother's car, fraying the brake lines. Nothing seemed to make sense anymore. If she felt so lost, with the ground shifting out from under her, how must Dillon feel?

"Hell no, she would have boxed my ears," Don said emphatically. "Why would I do a dumb thing like that?"

"You're drunker than you think you are, Don," Dillon said, "go sleep it off. We'll talk about this later." He had absolutely no idea what he was going to say when they talked. He almost felt like laughing hysterically.

Jessica pressed her hand to her stomach as Dillon closed the door. "I feel sick," she announced before he could speak and raced for the bathroom.

12

"Come on, Brenda, you have to come with us," Tara wheedled. "It will be fun."

"Are you certain you're feeling better? You were so sick this morning. I almost made Robert get Paul to bring in a helicopter to transport you to the hospital. And now you're jumping around like nothing happened."

Jessica looked up alertly. Everyone had gathered in the kitchen, sleeping late as usual so that it was early evening. "Tara was sick this morning? Why didn't someone come and get me?"

"*Both* the children were sick this morning and I handled it just fine, thank you very much," Brenda announced. "Some kind of stomach flu. You know, Jessie, you aren't the only one with maternal instinct. I was a miracle of comfort to them. Not to mention I was being wonderfully helpful and discreet to give you and Dillon time to . . . er . . . work things out."

Trevor made a rude noise, somewhere between a raspberry and a choking cough. "A miracle of comfort? Brenda, you were hanging out the window gagging and calling for smelling salts. Robert didn't know whether to run to you, Tara, or me. The poor guy was cleaning up the floor half the day."

"Robert, you are a true prince." Jessica flashed him a grateful smile. "Thank you for cleaning up after them."

"Just remember it was my good sense to notice him," Brenda took the credit.

Don made a face. "I thought we were working today. I want to finish the recording and see what we have. Do we have to do this now?"

"We're staying up all night working," Paul pointed out. "By the time we get up, most the day is gone and we lose the light we need hunting for the Christmas tree. I say we go now."

Don muttered softly beneath his breath, his gaze studiously avoiding Dillon's.

Jessica frowned, studying the twins. "You *both* had the stomach flu? I was feeling a bit queasy this morning myself. Did anyone else? Maybe we all ate something bad."

"Brian's pancakes," Brenda said instantly, "ghastly things designed to drive us all mad with monotony. Devoid of all nutrition and basically the worst meal on the face of the earth. And if you ask me, he's trying to poison me." She blew him a kiss, pure glee on her face. "The heinous plot won't work, genius though it might be, because I have a cast-iron stomach."

Brian leapt up out of his chair, nearly knocking it over. "I make pancakes that are works of art, Brenda," he snapped, as if goaded beyond endurance. "I don't see you slaving away in the kitchen for all of us."

"And you won't ever, darling—the very idea makes me shudder," she said complacently. "Trivial things should be left to trivial people."

"The children are fighting again," Jessica pointed out with a soft sigh, leaning into the comfort of Dillon's body. "And as usual, it isn't the twins."

"Tara, are you certain you're feeling well enough to go traipsing around in the woods? It's cold out and the wind is really blowing. There's another storm on the way. If you'd rather curl up here where it's warm, we'll go look and bring you back a tree," Dillon offered. He wrapped his arms around Jessica, uncaring that anyone saw them.

For the first time in years, he felt at peace with himself. There was hope in his life, a reason for his existence. "Jess and Trevor can stay with you, if you'd like."

"No way," Trevor objected. "I'm feeling fine. No one else can pick our tree. We know what we're looking for, don't we, Tara?"

Tara nodded solemnly, wrapping her arm around her brother's waist, her eyes on Jessica. All three smiled in perfect understanding. "We all go," she announced. "We'll know the right tree."

Dillon shrugged. "Sounds fine to me—let's do it then. Anyone who would like to find the tree with us is welcome to come. We can get the tools out of the shed and meet you on the trail." He tugged at Jessica, determined to take her with him. A few minutes alone in the shed was looking good. He hadn't had two minutes to steal a kiss from her.

"Whoa there." Trevor held up his hand. "I'm not sure how safe it is to let our Jessica go to a *shed* with you, Dad. You have a certain reputation as a Casanova type."

Dillon's eyebrow shot up. "And where would I get a rep like that?"

"Well, for one thing, look at this house. I've been meaning to talk to you about this place. You have weird carvings and things hanging off the eaves. What's that all about? This place looks like something out of an Edgar Allan Poe novel. The men in those books were always up to no good with the ladies." He wriggled his eyebrows suggestively.

"Weird carvings?" Dillon was horrified. "This house is a perfect example of early Gothic and Renaissance architecture combined. You, son, are a cretin. It's a *perfect* house. Look at the carvings on the corners: winged gargoyles scaling the south side, lions clawing their way up the east side. The detail is fantastic. And every true Gothic and Renaissance man has his secret passageways and moving walls. Where's the fun in a stately mansion? Everyone has one."

"Dad," Tara stated firmly, "it's creepy. Have you ever looked at it at night from the outside? It looks haunted and it looks as if it's staring at you. You're a little bit out there, even if you are my father."

"Treacherous children," Dillon said. "You've been spending far too much time with your aunt. She shares your opinion of my home."

Brenda rolled her eyes heavenward. "Dillon, you have things crawling up your house and watching every move one makes outside. I shudder every time I'm in the garden or walking through the grounds. I look up and there something is, staring at me."

"Technically," Brian interrupted, "they watch over the house and the people in it. If you're afraid, it's probably because you have good reason to be." He hitched closer. "Like maybe you're harboring ill will toward those inside."

Jessica crumpled a napkin and pitched it at Brian. "Back off, drummer boy, since Brenda was such a miracle of comfort to my babies, I can't very well let you spout your nonsense. I've always loved Gothic architecture, too. We used to look at all the books together and Dillon would bring home photos from Europe." She winked at Trevor. "I would think those hidden passageways would intrigue you."

Dillon captured her hand and pulled her toward the double doors leading toward the courtyard. "Dress warm you two—we'll meet you on the trail."

Jessica followed him out into the courtyard, ignoring Trevor's taunting whistle. "I don't like it that both of the kids were sick this morning, Dillon," she said. "Yesterday, Tara saw someone watching them when the landslide occurred. She couldn't tell who it was, he or she was wearing a long hooded cape. I saw the same person the night we arrived."

Dillon slowed his pace, pulling her closer to him so that she was beneath the protection of his shoulder. "What are you saying, Jess?" He was very careful to keep his tone without expression. "Do you think the landslide was rigged in some way? And the kids didn't have the flu, that someone somehow poisoned them?"

When he said the words, they did sound absurd. Oil on a staircase anyone could slip on. How could one rig a landslide and know the children would be in that exact spot? And she had been sick, too. People got the flu all the time. She sighed. How could she explain the uneasiness she felt? The continual worry that never went away? "Why wouldn't the person wearing the hooded cape help them? Clearly they were in trouble, Tara was screaming her head off."

"I don't know the answer to that, baby, but we'll find out," he assured. "Everyone certainly pitched in and helped to free Trevor. I didn't notice anyone holding back, not even Don."

"Don." Jessica shook her head. "It's hard to like that man. Even after last night, and I did feel sorry for him, I've been struggling to find something good about him."

"I did like him," Dillon answered, frowning slightly. "He was always reserved with me but he always worked hard. There was no looking around for him at the end of the night; he pulled his share of the work and then some. He was steady and I counted on him heavily at times. I had no idea he disliked me so intensely. And I sure didn't know Vivian was sleeping with him. She suggested I go hear him play, but I brought him into the band because he's so talented, not because she asked me." He sighed, raked his hand through his hair. "I don't know anymore, Jess. In the old days, it was all so easy. I never opened my eyes. I just lived my life in blissful ignorance until it all came crashing down." He looked at her, his fingers tightening around hers. "I was so arrogant, so sure that I could make it all work out. The truth is, how can I condemn Don when I've made so many mistakes myself?"

"Do you think it was a member of the band who killed Vivian and Phillip?" she asked carefully.

"No, of course not. They had five nutcases up there with them that night. All of them were mixing drugs and alcohol. For all I know, one of them brought a gun in. Someone shot Viv and Trent and maybe the others jumped the shooter, tried to wrestle the gun away, and knocked over the drinks and candles. I hope it happened that way. I hope the fire didn't start while I was beating up Trent. It was pretty wild. We knocked tables and lamps over. Maybe a candle hit the floor and no one noticed. I'll never know. The band had no idea what was going on up there. We'd just arrived."

"Why did you come upstairs?" she asked curiously.

"I wanted to check on the kids. Tara was asleep but she didn't have her blanket. I hadn't seen you in so long and I knew you must have gone looking for the thing. I was looking for you," he admitted. "I couldn't wait until morning to see you."

Pleasure rushed through her at his words. "I'm grateful you came looking for me, Dillon," she said softly.

Dillon threw open the door to the shed, flicked on a switch to flood the room with light. "So am I, honey." He couldn't look at her, knowing the fury of that moment was etched into his face. He couldn't look back and not feel it.

Jessica laughed, the sound of her joy dispelling old memories. "I would like to have known about the lights in here yesterday."

"Really." His eyebrow shot up. His voice softened into seduction. "I was just thinking it would have been smarter to keep it dark."

Jessica quirked an eyebrow at him and took a step backward. "You have that wicked look on your face like you're up to something." His expression alone sent heat coursing through her body.

"Wicked? I like that." His hand curled around the nape of her neck, drew her to him. He bent his head to claim her mouth. His lips were firm, soft, tempting. His tongue teased her lower lip, tracing the outline, probing and dancing until she opened to him.

His hand slipped under her jacket and blouse to find bare skin. Her breast pushed into his palm. He tasted the same hunger in her mouth. "Take off your jacket, Jess," he whispered as he reached once more for the light switch, plunging the shed into a murky gray. "Hurry, baby, we don't have much time."

"You can't think we're doing anything in this little shed, outdoors where anyone could find us," she said, but she was shedding her jacket, tossing it aside, wanting the searing heat of his mouth on her breast. Wanting her hands on him. It already seemed far too long.

Dillon watched her unbutton her blouse with breathless anticipation. He watched the richness of her breasts spill into his sight and he slowly let out his breath, his lungs burning for air. She did that to him with her exquisite skin and haunting eyes. "I thought about you while I showered this evening," he confided. "You should have been there with me. I thought about how you tasted and how you feel and how you sound when I'm inside of you." He bent his head to draw her breast into his mouth.

Her body rippled with instant need, with hunger. She laughed softly. "I was with you. As I recall, you did a lot of tasting."

"Are you certain? It wasn't enough, I need more." His hands slipped over her jeans, fumbled with the zipper. "Get rid of these things, you need them off." His teeth nipped at the underside of her breast, returned to the heat of her mouth, kissing her senseless. "I need them off."

"Do you think we have time?" She was already complying, wanting him so much that the stolen moments were as precious as the long all-night session of lovemaking.

"Not for all the things I want to do with you," he whispered against her ear, his tongue probing her frantic pulse. "But enough for what I have in mind. Push my jeans off my hips." The instant his body was free of the confining cloth he breathed a sigh of relief. "Much better. I'm going to lift you up. Put your arms around my neck and wrap your legs around my waist. Are you ready for me?" His fingers were already seeking his answer, probing deep, slipping into her body to find her damp with need.

He buried his face in her neck. "You are so hot, Jess. I love how you want me the same way I want you." Just feeling her dampness hardened his body even more. He took her weight as she put her arms around his neck and lifted her legs to wrap them around his waist. The engorged head of his shaft was pressed tightly to her. Very slowly he lowered her body over his. There was the familiar resistance, her body stretching to receive his fullness. The impression of sliding a sword into a tight sheath left every nerve ending raw. The sensation was building like a firestorm, spreading wilder, hotter, more explosive than ever. It roared through his body like a freight train, through his mind, a crescendo of notes and promises, of half-formed thoughts and needs.

He loved the little anxious sounds escaping her throat, the way she moved her hips to meet his, in a perfect rhythm. Jessica, the completion of his heart.

Jessica lost herself in the hard thrusts of his body into hers, in the fiery heat and sizzling passion that rose up and engulfed her entirely. She threw her head back, riding fast, tightening her muscles around him, gripping and sliding with a friction designed to drive them both up and over the edge quickly.

She couldn't believe herself, the wild wanton ride she took, there in the shed with their disheveled clothes half on and half off. But it didn't matter, nothing mattered but the burst of light and color as she broke into fragments and dissolved, her body rippling with a life of its own. She hung on tightly to Dillon as he thrust hard, repeatedly, his hoarse cry muffled by her shoulder.

They clung, their laughter coming together, a soft, pleased melding as their heart rates slowed to normal and Dillon slowly lowered her feet to the floor. The stolen moments were as precious as gold to both of them. It took a little scrambling and fumbling to adjust their clothing. Jessica couldn't find her slip-on shoes. Dillon distracted her often while she searched, kissing her neck, her fingers, swirling his tongue in her ear. She found one shoe among the pots and the other upside down on top of a bag of potting soil. She picked it up and idly picked out the seaweed caught in the sole.

"I haven't worn these shoes anywhere near the ocean bank. Where did I pick up seaweed?" She slipped the shoes back on her feet and went back into his arms again, turning up her mouth for his kiss. There was a long silence, while they simply got lost in each other. Dillon trailed kisses down her chin to her throat.

Jessica tilted her head to give him better access and caught a movement outside the small window.

"What's wrong?" Dillon asked, lifting his head reluctantly as he felt her stiffen. "Your neck is so perfect to nibble on— soft and tempting. I could stay here forever. Are you certain we have to get the Christmas tree today?"

"Something moved out there. I think someone is watching us," Jessica whispered. A shiver crept down her spine. Looking through the small window, she strained to see but couldn't spot anyone. It didn't matter. Someone watched them.

Dillon groaned. "Not again. Don had better not make another confession or I might pitch him off the cliff." He stepped past her to the small square window, looked around carefully. "I don't see anyone, baby, maybe it's the gargoyles on the roof."

Jessica could hear the amusement in his voice. Soft, gentle, teasing. She tried to respond, going into his arms, but she couldn't shake the feeling of something sinister staring at them.

"Come on, Jessie," Trevor shouted, breaking them apart immediately. "You two better not be doing anything I don't want to know about, because I'm coming in." There was the briefest of hesitations and then the door was thrust open. Trevor glared at them. "Everyone else was too chicken to come see what you were up to."

"We're looking for the axe," Jessica improvised lamely.

"Oh, really?" Trevor's eyebrow went up, in just the same way as his father's did sometimes. He fit the role of the chastising father figure perfectly. "Do you think this might help?" He flicked the switch so that light permeated every inch of the small building. He glared at his father in disapproval. "In a tool shed?"

"Trevor!" Blushing, Jessica hurried to the back of the shed

where she knew the larger tools were kept. As she reached for the axe, she knocked over the large pry bar. Muttering, she picked it up and started to replace it. The dried mud and pine needles stuck on the edge of it caught her eye. She frowned at the tool.

Trevor took up the axe. "Come on, Jessie, everyone's waiting. Stop mooning around, it's embarrassing. At least you have the good sense to fall for my dad."

"You don't mind?" Dillon asked, his eyes very serious as he studied his son's face.

"Who else would we want for Jessie?" Trevor asked matter-of-factly. "She's our family. We don't want someone else stealing her away from us."

"As if that could happen." Jessica leaned over to kiss his cheek. "Come on, we'd better hurry or the others will be looking for us." She led the way out of the shed.

"And, by the way, we had kitchen duty this afternoon," Trevor added righteously.

She turned to look at him skeptically. "*You* cleaned up or your sister did? I can't imagine you remembering."

"Well, Brenda remembered and I would have cleaned up but Tara's mothering me again because I suffered trauma yesterday." He put on his most pathetic face.

"Trauma?" Dillon interrupted. "*We* suffered the trauma, Jess, your sister, and I, not you. You ate it up. Don't think we didn't notice your sister waiting on you hand and foot. Is that a normal, everyday thing?"

"Absolutely." Trevor was grinning with unabashed glee. "And I love it, too!"

"He has no shame," Jessica pointed out to Dillon.

"Not when it comes to *domestic* chores," Trevor admitted. "Hey! I'm beginning to sound like Brenda and that's scary!" He waved to Tara and the group huddled together under the trees waiting for them. "I told you I'd get them," he called.

There was no time for anything but finding the all-important Christmas tree. Tara and Trevor had an idea where to look and they set off immediately. Paul kept pace with them, laughing, punching Trevor's arm good-naturedly and occasionally tousling Tara's hair. Brenda and Robert walked together at a much more sedate pace, whispering with their heads together. Brian and Don argued loudly over the best way to save the rain forest and the ozone layer and whether or not the taking of one small Christmas tree was going to have global effects.

Dillon walked along the trail, his hand firmly anchored in Jessica's. His life had changed dramatically. Everyone who was important to him was with him, sharing his home. He glanced down at the woman walking so close to him. Jessica had somehow changed his entire world in the blink of an eye. His children were with him, trust was slowly beginning to develop among them. He could see such potential, his mind awakening to all the possibilities of life. It was exhilarating, yet frightening.

Dillon knew his self-esteem had always been wrapped up in his music, in his ability to shoulder enormous responsibility. His childhood had been difficult, a struggle just to feel as if he counted for something. What did he have to offer them all if he could no longer play the music pounding in his head?

The fine mist began to turn into a steady drizzle as they walked along the trail. The band members pointed out tree after tree, big fir trees with full branches. The twins adamantly shook their heads, looking to Jessica for support. She agreed and followed them to the small, thin tree with gaps between the branches they had chosen the night before. The tree was growing at a strange angle out from under two larger trees at the edge of a bluff overlooking a smaller hill. The rain was making the ground slick.

"Stay away from that edge, Tara," Dillon commanded, scowling as he walked around the sad little tree. "This is your perfect Christmas tree?"

Trevor and Tara exchanged a grin. "That's the one. It wants to come home with us. We asked it," Tara said solemnly.

"I tramped through the forest in the pouring rain for that

little mongrel of a tree?" Brenda demanded. "Good heavens, look around, there are fantastic trees everywhere."

"I like it," Don said, clapping his hands on the twins' shoulders. "It hasn't a hope of surviving here—I say we take it in, show it a good time, and let it have some fun."

Jessica nodded. "It looks perfect to me." She skirted the forlorn little tree, touched one of the longer branches that reached out toward the sea. "This is the one."

Dillon raised his eyebrow at Robert, who shrugged helplessly. "Whatever makes them happy, I guess."

Brian stepped forward to take the axe out of Dillon's hands. "I like the darned thing—it needs a home and some cheering up." He sent the axe sweeping toward the narrow trunk. He was strong and the first bite cut deep.

Tara hugged her brother, her eyes shining. "This is *exactly* how I imagined it, Dad." She wrapped her other arm around her father.

Dillon stood very still while pleasure coursed through him at his daughter's affectionate gesture.

Paul laughed and began removing his jacket. "Did you imagine the rain, too, Tara? We could have done without that."

The gray drizzle was beginning to fall a little faster. Brian took another swipe at the tree trunk, sinking the blade in solidly. He repeated the action again and again with a steady rhythm that matched the drone of the rain. Robert put his arm around his wife to help protect her from the rising wind. The tree shivered, beginning to tilt.

"Hey!" Paul was shaking out his jacket, reaching across Jessica, holding it out toward Tara. "Put this on."

Tara grinned happily at him through the gray mist. "Thanks, Paul." Her fingers closed around the material just as there was an ominous crack.

The branches wavered, then rushed at them. Paul yelled a warning, stepping back in an attempt to stay out of reach. His elbow cracked into Jessica's shoulder, sending her flying backward as his feet slipped out from under him in the thick mud.

Dillon shoved Tara hard, sending her sprawling into Trevor's arms, even as he dove across the muddy ground for Jessica. To his horror, Jessica went down hard, skidding precariously close to the edge of the bluff. He saw her make a grab for the wavering tree branches but Paul's larger frame crashed into hers in a tangle of arms and legs. They both went sliding over the edge of the crumbling cliff. Paul's fingers made thick tracks in the mud as he attempted to find a purchase.

Dillon skidded in the mud, lying flat out on the ground, catching Jessica's ankle as she plummeted over the edge. He realized he was yelling hoarsely, a mind-numbing terror invading him. The Christmas tree lay beside him, inches to his left. Don threw himself across Dillon's legs, pinning him to the ground to prevent him sliding over the edge after Jessica and Robert leapt to catch Paul's wrists as he clung to the rocks. There was a moment of silence broken only by the moaning wind, the pounding sea, the sound of rain, and heavy breathing.

"Daddy?" Tara's voice was thin and frightened.

Trevor dropped into the mud beside his father, looking down over the edge at Jessica. She was upside down, straining to turn her head to look up at them. Other than her head, she was very still, aware that the only thing preventing her from falling was Dillon's fingers circling her ankle. Trevor reached out with both hands and caught her calf. Together they began to pull her up.

"It's all right, honey," Dillon soothed his daughter. "Jess is fine, aren't you, baby?" He could pretend his hands weren't shaking and his mind wasn't numb with terror. "Robert, can you hold Paul?"

"I've got him." Robert was straining back. Brenda and Tara caught his belt and pulled as hard as they could. Brian simply reached past them and added his strength to Robert's, pulling Paul straight up. He immediately turned his attention to helping Trevor and Dillon with Jessica.

All of them sat in the mud, Dillon, Tara, and Trevor holding Jessica tight. The rain poured down harder. Jessica could hear her heart thundering in her chest. Dillon's face was buried against her throbbing shoulder. Tara and Trevor clung to her, their grip so tight she thought they might break her in two. She looked at the others. Paul looked absolutely stunned, his face a mask of shock. Brenda's face was white. Robert, Don, and Brian looked frightened.

Another accident. This time Jessica was in the middle of it. She couldn't imagine that it had been anything other than an accident. Had all of the other accidents that had occurred recently really just been flukes and coincidence? Had she become paranoid after her mother's death? Certainly with Trevor's accident, she had carefully examined the ground, yet she had seen no signs that the landslide had been anything more than a natural shift in the land after a storm. But what about the hooded figure Trevor and Tara had seen yesterday and the one she'd seen the night they'd arrived on the island? Who could that be? Perhaps it was the groundskeeper and his eyesight was so poor he didn't notice anyone or anything around him. It was a poor explanation, but other than someone hiding on the island, she couldn't think of anything else.

"I saved your jacket, Paul," Tara said in a small voice, holding up the precious item for everyone to see.

Everyone burst out laughing in relief. Except Paul. He shook his head, the stunned disbelief still on his face. Jessica was certain it was on her face, too.

"Let's get back to the house," Dillon suggested. "In case no one's noticed, it's really raining out here. Are you okay, Paul?"

Paul didn't answer, his body shaking in reaction, but he allowed Brian and Dillon to help him to his feet.

Jessica mulled the idea over that she could be wrong about the accidents. Even about the brakes on her mother's car being tampered with. About her own car. All the other trivial things could be something altogether different. She swept a shaky hand through her hair. She just didn't know.

13

IT TOOK A SURPRISINGLY short time for everyone to reconvene in the kitchen, freshly showered and once more warm after the outdoor adventures. Upset by another near tragedy, Jessica kept a close eye on the twins. The string of accidents was just too much for her to believe they were all coincidences. Yet nothing ever added up.

She looked around the room at the other occupants of the house. She liked them. That was the problem. She really liked them. Some more than others, but she couldn't conceive of any of them deliberately harming the twins.

"Jessie, you aren't listening to me," Tara's voice penetrated her thoughts. "I don't know what kinds of ornaments we can make." Tara added sadly, "Mama Rita had beautiful ornaments for our trees." She stood very close to her brother, her gaze seeking reassurance from Jessica. Obviously she was as shaken by the accident as Jessica was.

"We're supposed to *make* them, Tara," Trevor pointed out. "That's the way it works, right, Jessie?"

Jessica nodded. "I have a great recipe for a dough. We can roll it out, cut out whatever shapes we want, bake them and then paint them. It will be fun." She set two mugs of chocolate in front of the twins and held up a third mug toward Paul. He shook his head and she set it down in front of her, reaching for a towel to clean the counter.

Brenda yawned. "Susie Homemaker strikes again. Do you know how to do *everything*, dear? Have you any idea how utterly tiring that can be?"

Jessica threw the wadded-up tea towel at her, hitting the

perfectly fashionable head and draping the Kelly green towel over the chic chignon. "No one believes your little heartless wench act, Brenda—you've blown it, so start thinking up ideas. And I didn't say I was going to do the mixing and baking. I'm the *supervisor.* You and the twins are the worker bees."

"Robert, are you going to let her get away with throwing things at me?" Brenda complained. She wadded the towel into a tight little ball, looking for a target. "Surely you could exact some sort of revenge for me. I'd do it myself but I've just been endangering my life, tramping through mosquito-infested waters and through alligator-ridden swamps to find the perfect Christmas tree for two ungrateful little chits. And the perfect tree turned out to be some straggly, misshapen bush!"

"There aren't alligators here," Trevor pointed out, "so technically your life wasn't really in danger. It's your duty as our aunt to do these things and *enjoy* them, isn't that right, Dad? So buck up, babe. We'll let you sing the first Christmas carol."

The tea towel hit Trevor's face dead center. "You *horrid* little boy!"

"Ouch, ouch," Trevor clutched at his chest, feigning a heart attack. "She spears me with her unkind words." He drained the mug of hot chocolate. "More?" he asked hopefully, holding up the cup.

"No, you're going to bed soon," Jessica objected. "I swear, you're becoming a bottomless pit."

"He can have mine," Tara said, pushing the mug toward her brother. "I don't want any more."

Jessica intercepted it, catching it up before Trevor could snatch it out of her reach. "What if she still has the flu, Trev? Don't drink from the same mug," she chided. "Tara, do you feel sick? You've gone so pale."

"I think I still have the flu," Tara admitted, "or maybe I'm just still scared. I didn't like seeing you and Paul falling off the cliff."

"We didn't like it much either." Jessica exchanged a small smile with Paul.

"Hey, paper chains," Don said suddenly. "When I was a kid we used to make paper chains and hang them on the tree. I think I remember how to do it."

"I remember that," Robert agreed. "We should take all those musical notations we've thrown away and use them. We all love music. Does that work, Jessie? Brenda, we made a chain one year. We didn't have a tree so we made a chain of love."

Jessica grinned at Brenda as the woman visibly winced, horrified to be found out. "A love chain, Brenda? You're really a mushy girl after all, aren't you?"

"She's all sappy like you are, Jessie." Trevor was wearing an identical grin. "Brenda, you little romantic you. A *luv* chain."

"Why, Brenda." Dillon was outright smirking. "You've truly amazed me. I had no idea you were a marshmallow under all that sophistication."

"Don't start. Robert is making it all up as you know perfectly well." Brenda looked haughty, her nose in the air.

Brian wagged his finger at her. "Robert doesn't have the imagination to make something like that up, Brenda. You did make a love chain with him."

Tara protectively flung her arms around Brenda, glaring at everyone. "Leave her alone, all of you!" She pressed a kiss against Brenda's chin. "We can make as many chains as you want. Don't let them bother you."

Jessica met Brenda's gaze across the room. Tears glistened in the depths of Brenda's eyes. She sat very still, not moving a muscle. The two women simply stared at one another, caught in the moment. Brenda nuzzled the top of Tara's head briefly, her eyes still locked with Jessica's. "Thank you," she mouthed, blinking rapidly to rid herself of unwanted emotion.

"You're welcome," Jessica mouthed back with a watery smile.

Dillon felt his throat close, his heart swelling with pride at observing the exchange. Jessica brought her light to everyone. She could so easily have turned the twins against Brenda, against him. The children loved her beyond any other. Their loyalty to Jessica was strong. A single word from Jessica would have prevented the twins from even trying to work with all the different personalities around them. Jessica had been so generous in sharing them and she had instilled her giving nature in both of them. He knew, better than most, how Brenda often appeared cold and uncaring to others. He was proud of his children, that they saw beyond the barrier she presented to the world to the real woman.

"There's always strings of popcorn," Paul pointed out. "Those are easy enough to make. We used to make those in your basement, Brian."

"We ate most of them," Dillon pointed out, laughing at the memory.

The next two hours were spent companionably, baking and coloring ornaments and stringing paper chains and popcorn. Dillon managed to lead them in Christmas carols that Paul and Brian turned into other much more ribald ballads. Brenda and Brian got into a popcorn fight until Trevor and Tara took their aunt's side and Brian was forced to cry uncle.

When Jessica could see that both Tara and Trevor were overtired and too flushed, she called a halt and took them both upstairs. She was surprised that both teenagers went without a murmur of protest.

Tara clutched her stomach. "I really don't feel very well, but I didn't want to ruin the fun," she admitted.

Little warning bells began going off in Jessica's head despite her determination not to worry. She rubbed at her temples, annoyed with herself for being so protective. Everyone got the flu, even she still felt sick.

"I wish we had played all those tricks on everyone," Trevor said suddenly to Tara. "Didn't that make you mad that they were blaming us for all those pranks while we were waiting for Jessica and Dad? It's so typical for adults to always blame kids for everything." He suddenly lunged for the bathroom.

"What do you mean they were blaming you for pranks?" Jessica tucked the blankets around Tara and smoothed back her hair. "Are you feeling any better, honey? I can get your father and we can take you to a doctor."

"I'm the one throwing my guts up," Trevor yelled from the bathroom.

"Sweetie, I'll be happy to take you to the doctor. It's just that I know you'd rather be boiled in oil than see the doc," Jessica said sympathetically.

They could hear Trevor noisily rinsing his mouth for the third time. "And it sucks that they thought we were going into their rooms. I wonder if someone's been going into Dad's room and he thinks it's us, too. Just because we're teenagers doesn't mean we don't have respect for other people's things," he said indignantly. He stumbled from the bathroom back to them, crossing the floor with an aggravated frown on his face. "I asked Brian point blank if he was in your room, Jessie, and if he'd burned incense and created one of his magic circles there, and he said no. And then he had the gall to tell me to stay out of his room."

"To stay the *hell* out of his room," Tara corrected. "He was really mad at us. I never went into his stupid room."

"Wait a minute." Jessica held up her hand. "What are you talking about? The others accused you of going into their rooms?"

Tara nodded. "Even Brenda and Robert thought we were playing pranks on them. I guess it's happened to everyone since we've been here and I don't think they believed us when we told them it was happening to us, too."

"What pranks?" Jessica wanted to know. "And where have I been?"

Trevor and Tara exchanged a slow grin. "With Dad," they said in unison.

Jessica blushed as she sat on the edge of Tara's bed. "I guess I deserved that. I'm sorry I've been in the studio working so much and that I've been going off with Dillon. I'll talk to Brian. He shouldn't have accused you. What do they think you've been doing?"

Trevor shrugged. "The usual teen-in-the-spooky-old-mansion stuff. Opening windows, leaving water running in the bathtub, moving things, writing weird leave-before-it's-too-late messages on mirrors. That sort of thing."

"Brian said no one else would be so childish." Tara was clearly offended. "Like I would want to find a stupid secret passageway and sneak into his dumb room!" Her gaze slid to her twin's face. "Well, Trevor and I did look for secret passageways, but just because it was fun. If we were going to try to convince everyone there was a ghost here, we'd have done a *much* better job," she declared. "At least Brenda and Robert said they believed us. Do you think Dad believes we're sneaking into people's rooms?" She sounded a little forlorn.

"Of course not, Tara. If your father thought you were doing such a thing, he would have spoken to you about it immediately. I'm sorry they accused you of such childish behavior. You're right, oftentimes an adult who isn't used to teenagers has a false idea of the things they do." Jessica stroked Tara's hair. "I noticed our resident ghost forgot to open the window tonight."

"Could there be a real ghost in the house?" Tara asked hopefully.

"The house isn't old enough," Trevor protested knowledgeably. He'd read a lot on the subject. "Dad had it built after the fire. The contractor finished it while he was still in the burn center." When his sister and Jessica looked at him he shrugged with a sheepish grin. "Paul told me. I ask him questions about Dad. Sometimes he doesn't mind and other times he just sort of ignores me. You don't learn anything if you don't ask questions. A house has to be really old to have a ghost."

"Or there has to have been a murder in it," Tara agreed.

A chill went down Jessica's spine at Tara's words. She remembered the sound of the gunshots, the crackle of the flames, the heat and smoke. Standing up, she walked to the window, not wanting the twins to see the expression on her face. *Murder.* The word shimmered in her mind. Both children were watching her closely. Not wanting them to know what she was thinking, she changed the subject. "Did Brenda really take care of you and Tara this morning when you were sick? That amazes me."

Trevor laughed immediately. "She tried. She was as white as a sheet. The funny thing was, Robert wanted to go get you but she said no, they could handle it. I think she really wanted to, not only to give you and Dad time to work things out, but because she wanted to be the one to help us. The crazy part was, while she was being so nice, I was thinking Robert and Brenda might have tried to poison us."

Jessica looked at him sharply. "Why would you think something like that?"

"Well, we both drank a soda in their room and then we were sick. And I found a newspaper in their wastebasket with words cut out of it like for a ransom note. I had this wild idea they were going to hold us hostage or something until you paid them money. Or kill us and collect the insurance on us." He grinned, looking sheepish.

"I was sick *before* I drank the soda, that's why I drank it so fast." Tara scowled at her brother indignantly. "Brenda and Robert weren't trying to poison us!"

"I know that *now.*" Trevor flung himself on his makeshift bed.

"You found what in Brenda's room?" Jessica tripped over Trevor's shoes and nearly fell on the bed. Don had confessed to attempting to blackmail Dillon. Why would Brenda and Robert have the remnants of a cut-up newspaper in their room? What would be the point of Don's confessing and then trying to cast blame on someone else? Jessica could feel the strange shiver of apprehension snake down her spine. Unless someone else was involved. Someone far more sinister than Don. Jessica didn't like the implications of it at all.

"It was just an old newspaper," Trevor said, shrugging it off. "Some of the words had been cut out of it, but I didn't really have time to look at it closely."

Jessica sat down on the edge of the bed. Outside the rain had started again, pounding at the window and rattling branches against the house. "What is it you two used to call me?" she asked softly. The raindrops matched the rhythm in her heart.

"Magical girl," Tara's voice was drowsy. "You're our magical girl."

Jessica leaned over her to kiss her again. "Thank you, honey, I think I need to be magical girl again. I'm going down to the studio. If you need me, come get me." She needed to go somewhere and think and it always helped when she had a guitar in her hands. Her shoulder was aching, a reminder of the day's events, as she noiselessly crept down the hall to the wide staircase. The lights were off and the house had grown silent.

Dillon would be waiting for her to come to him. If she was too long he might go looking. She didn't want to be with him while she sorted things out. He distracted her, made her lose confidence in herself. *Magical girl.* Even her mother had used that name for her because she knew things. She knew things instinctively. Things like when what appeared to be an accident was really something much more sinister. Since coming here she had been relying on Dillon. Expecting Dillon to solve the mystery, to make it all better.

Lightning zigzagged across the sky and lit up the courtyard as she paused on the landing to look out through the glass doors. She could see the fir trees as they jerked in a macabre dance like wooden marionettes. Dillon didn't believe anyone was trying to hurt the children. Jessica believed it and if she was going to find the truth, she needed to rely on herself and her own judgment.

The sound room was empty, strangely eerie with the glass and instruments in the dark. She idly picked up one of Dillon's acoustic guitars, a *Martin* he particularly loved. She ran her fingers over the strings, heard the small jarring note not quite in tune. That was what the accidents were like, a note not quite in tune. She had to sort it all out just as she so efficiently tuned the guitar. She played there in the darkness, sitting on the edge of the instrument panel, her mind compiling the data for her. She closed her eyes and allowed the music, *Dillon's* music, to soothe her as she played.

She slipped a few random notes into the melody. Notes off-key, off-kilter, like the accidents that could have happened to anyone. Anyone. The word repeated like a refrain in her head. Random accidents. Secret passageways. Blackmail. Pieces of a puzzle like musical notations written on paper. Move them around, put them together differently, and she would have a masterpiece. Or a key.

Thunder crashed all too close, the clash of cymbals, the exclamation point after the melody. She opened her eyes just as another bolt of lightning lit up the world. A figure loomed up right in front of her, a dark shadow of terror. Jessica lunged to her feet, gripping the expensive guitar like a weapon.

Brenda stumbled backward with a frightened shriek. "Jess! It's me! Brenda!"

Her heart pounding too loudly, Jessica slowly lowered the guitar. "What in the world are you doing here?"

"Looking for you. Trevor told me where to find you. You're the only one who might believe me. I don't know who else to talk to." Brenda's hand shot out, prevented Jessica from turning on the light. "Don't, I can't look at you and say this." She took a deep calming breath. "I wanted to believe the kids were behind the pranks, but I don't think so. I think it's Vivian."

A chill went down Jessica's spine. Her eyes strained in the darkness to see Brenda's face, to read her expression.

"I'm not crazy, Jessie. I feel her at times." Brenda pressed a trembling hand to her mouth. "I think the kids or Dillon, or maybe me are in danger and she's trying to warn us. Vivian wasn't a bad person, and she believed in spirits. If she could come back to help set things right, she would. I've been afraid something was wrong for a while and the minute I came to the island, I was certain of it."

"You think Vivian is opening windows and drawing magic circles on the floor? Why, why would she do that, knowing how Dillon feels?" Jessica kept her voice very even. She didn't know if Brenda was attempting to frighten her, or if she really believed what she was saying.

"To protect you. To protect me. Dillon, the children. All of us. It was the only religion she knew." Brenda leaned closer to her, pleading with her. "Do you feel it, too? Tell me I haven't completely lost my mind. I don't want to end up like Viv."

Jessica carefully leaned the guitar against the wall. She didn't know if Vivian's presence was in the house helping her or if the next flash of lightning merely illuminated her brain. Like the notes blending into harmony, the pieces clicked into place.

"Since we came here, the accidents have all been random. I was trying to mold them, fit them into my idea that someone wanted to harm Trevor and Tara. But all the accidents could have hurt any of us. Anyone in the house. Do you see it, Brenda, the pattern?"

Brenda shook her head. "No, but you're chilling me to the bone."

"And the cape. The hooded figure. The dog didn't bark."

"You've lost me. Bark when?"

"When Trevor was buried under the landslide, Tara saw a hooded figure, but the dog didn't bark. So it wasn't a stranger hiding on the island, it was someone the dog knew." Jessica knew she was on the verge of discovery. It was all there for her to see. The pattern in the discordant notes. "Why were only the three of us sick? Why Tara and Trevor and me? None of you were sick." She pressed a hand to her mouth, her eyes wide. "It's the chocolate. My God, he poisoned the chocolate. He did everything. He shot Vivian, he must have, and he covered his tracks with the fire."

"What do you mean, he poisoned the chocolate? Dillon? You think Dillon tried to poison the twins?" Brenda sounded shocked.

"Not Dillon. Of course not Dillon. You can't believe he shot Vivian! It was never Dillon." Jessica was impatient. "You'll have to call the helicopter, have them pick up the kids and

take them to the hospital and tell them to bring the police."
She had to get to the twins, hold them in her arms, make certain they were alive and well.

The next flash of lightning revealed the dark, hooded figure standing so silently in the corner. Jessica saw him clearly, saw the ugly little gun in his hand. The light faded away, but she knew he was there. Real. Solid. A sinister demented being bent on murder. Brenda gave a frightened cry and Jessica thrust the woman behind her. She felt her way along the instrument panel for the switch to turn on the recorder.

There was a moment of silence while the rain came down and the wind howled and tugged at the house. While the gargoyles watched silently from the eaves.

Jessica forced a small smile, forced a calmness she didn't feel. "I knew it was you. It's going to break his heart all over again." There was deep regret in her voice. The knowledge of such a betrayal would hurt Dillon immensely. Some part of Jessica had known all along, but she hadn't wanted to see it. For Dillon's sake.

"You didn't know," Paul denied, his face so deep inside the hood they couldn't see him. He presented a frightening image, the grim reaper. All he needed was a long-handled scythe to complete the persona of death.

"Of course it had to be you. No one but you would know that someone was trying to blackmail Dillon."

"Your mother," he spat, "was so greedy. The money he gave her to care for the children wasn't enough. I wrote the checks out to her—she had enough."

"Not my mother," Jessica snarled back. "Don was blackmailing Dillon. She came here at Dillon's request to discuss it with him."

"I don't understand," Brenda said. "Paul, what are you doing? Why are you standing in that stupid cape with a gun pointed at us? And you'd better not be naked under that thing! Everyone's being so melodramatic! What are you talking about? Why would anyone want to blackmail Dillon?"

Jessica ignored her. She didn't dare take her eyes off of Paul.

He was unstable and she had no idea what could set him off. But she knew he was perfectly capable of killing. He had done so numerous times. "You were the only one it could be, Paul. You had access to all the rooms through the passageways. You're the only one who has been here on a regular basis. Once I realized the accidents were random, directed toward everyone here, I knew they were designed to send everyone away. The landslide, the Christmas tree, the oil on the stairs. Even the chocolate. You thought if enough things happened, we'd all go away. That's what you wanted, wasn't it? You just wanted everyone to stay away from here." Her voice was soothing, the voice she had used for years on the children, a blend of sweetness and understanding.

"But you wouldn't go away," he said. "You brought them back here. *Her* children. Vivian was evil, an evil disgusting seductress who wouldn't leave us all alone."

Jessica's heart thudded. She heard it in his voice, the guilt, the seething hatred. It always came back to Vivian. She knew then. Her heart bled for Dillon. So much treachery, how did one survive it? She wanted to weep for them all. There wasn't going to be any miracle for the twins or Dillon this Christmas, only more heartache, more tragedy.

"You loved her." She said it simply, starkly, saying the words in the dark to the man who had calmly walked up the stairs, shot Vivian and her lover in cold blood and locked the other occupants in the room after ensuring the fire was raging.

"I *hated* her! I *despised* her!" Paul hissed the words. "She seduced me. I begged her to leave me alone, but she would crawl into my bed and I could never stop myself. She laughed at me, and she threatened to tell Dillon. He was the only friend, the only family I ever had. I wasn't going to let her destroy me. Or him. Phillip deserved to die, he used her to get at Dillon. He thought Dillon would pay him to leave Vivian alone."

"Where would he get an idea like that?" Brenda was far too quiet and that worried Jessica. She glanced at the other woman but couldn't see her clearly in the dark.

"What does it matter? None of it matters. He chose you. When I knocked you off the bluff and slipped myself, he saved you, not me. I couldn't believe it. He was never worth it. All these wasted years. His genius. I served his greatness, cared for him, *protected* him, *killed* for him, and he fell for another harlot." Paul shook his head so that the hooded cloak moved as if alive. "I gave him everything, and he chose you." He snarled the last words at her, like a rabid dog wanting to strike out.

Jessica forced a derisive laugh. She was inching her fingers along the wall seeking the guitar, her only weapon. "Is that how you lie to yourself at night in order to sleep, Paul? You betrayed him by sleeping with his wife. You probably brought Phillip Trent into Vivian's life. You let Dillon go through a trial, knew everyone believed he committed murder and yet you could have stopped it by telling the truth. You were responsible for the fire that burned him. You murdered my mother thinking she was blackmailing him. You left him open to blackmail and you arranged accidents that could have killed his children just to frighten them away from him. How in the world is that giving him everything? You made him a prisoner in this house and when it looked as if he might break free you started all over again to try to isolate him from the rest of the world."

"Shut up!" Pure venom dripped from Paul's voice. "Just shut up!"

"The biggest mistake you made was going after the children. Your plan backfired. You must have intercepted my letter telling him the children should be with him. You didn't want them here, did you? They were a threat to you. You wanted me to think Dillon was trying to hurt them, didn't you?" She looked at him steadily. "But, you see, I know Dillon. I knew he would *never* have killed Vivian or my mother or done harm to his children. So I brought the children here, knowing he would try to protect them."

"And delivered them right to me," Paul snarled.

"Put the gun down, Paul." Dillon's voice was weary and sad,

a melody of smoke and blues. "It's over. We have to figure out how best to handle this." Dillon moved through the doorway.

While Dillon was so calm, Jessica wanted to scream. Were the children writhing in agony upstairs, while they talked to a madman with a gun? Her fingers found the neck of the guitar, circled, and gripped hard.

"There is only one way to handle it, Dillon," Paul said just as calmly. "I'm not about to be locked up for the rest of my life. I couldn't stand being interviewed behind bars while the band makes it to the top again."

Jessica knew. She always knew before things happened, even though she had doubted herself. There in the darkness with the rain coming down, she knew the precise moment Paul shifted the gun. She knew he was finished talking and that his finger was squeezing the trigger. Without hesitation, Jessica stepped solidly in front of Dillon and swung the guitar toward Paul with every ounce of strength she possessed.

She heard the bark of the gun, the simultaneous crack of the guitar as she hit Paul hard, and Dillon's husky cry of denial even as something knocked her legs out from under her. Jessica hit her head hard on the floor. She lay still, staring up at the figure in the hooded cloak. He was bent over, twisted. She blinked to clear her vision. Everything seemed hazy, a weird phosphorescent light was seeping into the room, a mist of colors and cold. The draft was icy, so that she could see the air as a foggy vapor. It seemed to slide between Paul and the other occupants of the room.

Paul screamed, a hoarse dark cry of rage and fear. For one moment the colors shifted and moved, formed the shimmering, translucent image of a woman in a flowing gown reaching out a long thin arm beckoning toward Paul. Dillon moved then, covering Jessica's body with his own, blocking her view of the strange apparition, so that she only heard the gun as it went off a second time.

"Vivian, don't leave me again!" Brenda's cry was anguished

and she stumbled forward, her arms outstretched. Dillon caught her, dragging her down to the safety of the floor.

Jessica heard the body fall with a soft thud to the floor, and she found herself staring into Paul's wide-open eyes. She knew he was dead, with the life already drained from his body before he hit the floor. In the end, he had been determined to take Dillon with him, and she had been just as determined he would not.

Brenda's weeping was soft and brokenhearted. "Did you see her, Jessica? I told you I wasn't crazy. Did you see her?"

Dillon kicked the gun away from Paul's hand. "Call the doctor, Brenda, right now!" His voice was pure authority, snapping Brenda out of her sorrow. "Check on Tara and Trevor—make certain they're all right. And then call the police." His hands were running over Jessica's legs, searching for a wound, searching for the bullet hole that had knocked her to the floor.

There was no blood, no gaping wound, only a huge dark bruise already forming on her left thigh. The area was tender, painful, but neither Dillon nor Jessica knew who had struck her hard enough to knock her legs out from under her. Brenda had stood frozen, unable to move. They both stared at the strange mark, two circles, one inside the other, the center circle much darker. A circle of protection.

"I have to see to Paul," he said and she heard the heartbreak in his voice.

"He's beyond help, Dillon. Don't touch anything," Jessica cautioned gently. Now that it was over she began to shake almost uncontrollably. Her need to get to the children was paramount. Her need to comfort Dillon was just as great. More than anything else she was afraid for him. This time the truth had to be plain. "Wait for the police."

14

*T*HE WHITE BIRD WINGED *its way across the wet sky. Far below, waves crashed against rock, foamed and sprayed, reaching toward the heavens, toward the small white dove as it flew with a glittering object in its beak.*

"Jessie, get out of bed," Tara insisted, jarring Jessica right out of her happy dream. "It's Christmas Eve, you can't just stay in bed!"

Jessica turned over with a small groan and pulled the blanket firmly over her head. "Go away, I'm never getting up again."

She wasn't going to face Christmas Eve. She didn't want to see the disappointment on the faces of the twins. She didn't want to face Dillon. She had seen him when the police took Paul's body away, when he told the truth about what had happened. Dillon looked like a man lost, with his heart and soul torn out. Reporters had been brutal, swarming to the hospital, nearly rioting at the police station. So many pictures, so many microphones thrust at him. It had to have been a nightmare for him. It had been for her. The police had the recording Jessica had made as well as Brenda's and Jessica's statements to back up Dillon's. The crime scene people had come and gone. Paul was dead by his own hand. They all said so. By mutual consent, they kept their knowledge of the apparition to themselves. There was no need to complicate the story to the police or the newspapers. And who would ever believe them?

"Jessie, really, get up." Tara dragged at the covers.

"I'll get her up," Dillon told his daughter gently. "You go play hostess, Tara. Tell everyone your Christmas story. They all need a feel-good story tonight. And Brian's made a special Christmas Eve feast. I believe he made pancakes."

Tara giggled as her father walked her to the door. "Not his famous pancakes! What a shocker." She leaned over to kiss his forehead as she went out.

Jessica heard the door close firmly and the lock turn. There was a mysterious rustle and then the room was flooded with music. Soft, beautiful strains of music. The swelling passion of the song she and Dillon had worked on so hard. She blinked back tears and sat up as he crossed the room to sit on the edge of her bed. The light was off and the room was dark, only the sliver of moon providing them with a streak of a silvery glow.

Jessica drew up her knees, rested her chin on them. "So what now, Dillon?" She asked it quietly, facing the worst, prepared for his rejection. He hadn't talked with her, hadn't come near her in days. He'd spent most of the time on the mainland.

Dillon reached out to her, his palm cupping her chin, skin to skin. She realized then that he wasn't wearing his gloves. "It's Christmas Eve, we wait for our miracle," he told her gently. "Don't tell me after believing all this time, you've suddenly had a crisis of faith." His thumb brushed along her chin, a slow sensual movement that made her shiver with awareness of him.

Jessica swept a trembling hand through her hair as it tumbled around her face. "I don't know what I think anymore, Dillon. I feel numb right now." It wasn't altogether true. When she looked at him, every part of her came alive. Heat coursed through her body, while her heart did a somersault and a multitude of butterfly wings brushed at the pit of her stomach. "I thought, with all that has happened, that . . ." she trailed off miserably. No matter what she said, it would be hurtful to him. How could she admit she thought he would retreat from her, from Trevor and Tara?

Dillon's smile was incredibly tender. "You didn't really think I would be so incredibly stupid as to send you and the children away again, did you? I wouldn't deserve you, Jess, if I'd been thinking of doing something that thick-skulled. I don't know that I deserve you now, but you offered and I'm holding on tight with both hands." He rubbed the bridge of his nose, suddenly looking vulnerable. "I thought about things, sitting up in my room, about treachery and betrayal and about letting life pass me by. I thought about courage and what it means. Courage was Don coming to me when he didn't have to and telling me how idiotic he had been. Courage was him willing to be kicked out of the band or even prosecuted. Courage is Brenda and Robert learning how to be an aunt and uncle to two children they are secretly terrified of. Courage is Brian standing in that kitchen and telling me his beliefs."

His hands framed her face. "Courage is a woman stepping between a man and death. You fought for me, Jess, even when I wouldn't do it myself. I'm not walking away from that. I'll never play the guitar again like I did, but I still have my voice and I still can write and produce songs. I have two children you gave back to me and God willing, I hope we have more. Tell me I still have you."

She melted into him, a long slow kiss that stole her breath and took her heart, that told him everything he wanted to know.

"Everyone's waiting for you," he whispered against her mouth.

Jessica hugged him hard, leapt out of bed, rushed for the bathroom. "Ten minutes," she called over her shoulder, "I have to shower." She peeled off her pajama top and flung it toward a chair.

Dillon's breath hitched in his throat as he saw her drawstring pants slide over the tempting curve of her bottom just as she disappeared into the other room. He stood up, a slow smile softening the edge of his mouth as he tossed his own shirt aside. He padded on bare feet to the bathroom door to watch her as she stepped under the cascade of hot water. She turned her head toward him just as he slowly pushed his jeans away from his hardened body. At once her gaze was on his heavy erection. Knowing she was looking hardened him more so that the ache grew and his need was instant and urgent.

"You missed me," she greeted, her smile pure invitation. The moment he stepped into the large compartment, she wrapped her hand around his thickness, warm and tight. "I missed you."

His hands moved over every inch of her he could touch, marveling that she could want him the way she did. Dillon caught the nape of her neck and turned up her head to fasten his mouth to hers. He wasn't gentle. He didn't feel gentle. He wanted to devour her. He fed there, his hands cupping her breasts, his thumbs circling her nipples.

She was driving him crazy with her bold caresses, stroking him even as her mouth was mating with his. Hot silken kisses; the earth spinning madly. The water running over their bodies and the steam rising around them. She was soft and pliant, as her body moved against his. One leg slid up to the curve of his hip, she pressed close, as wild as he was.

Dillon bent his head to the terrible bruise on her shoulder where Paul's elbow had cracked her hard enough to send her flying toward the edge of a cliff. His tongue eased the throbbing ache, and traveled lower to trace the outline of her breast. He felt her tremble in reaction. His mouth closed over her hard nipple, his teeth teasing gently before he suckled strongly. She gasped in reaction, arcing more fully into him. His hand shaped her every curve, slid lower to push into her body. She was wet and pulsing with her own need and he wanted all the time in the world to love her. To just lie beside her and bring her so much pleasure so she would know what she meant to him.

Jessica leaned forward to catch a little drop of water that ran from his shoulder to the muscles of his chest. She wasn't fast enough. Her tongue followed the little bead of moisture as it traveled across the ridges over his heart. She couldn't quite catch up and her arms slipped around his waist as she ducked her head to lap at the droplet, racing it over his flat belly. Her hand was still wrapped proprietarily around his heavy erection. She felt him swell more, thick, and hard, as she breathed warm air over him, as her tongue lapped at the droplets on his most sensitive tip.

Dillon went rigid, his body shuddering with pleasure as she took him into the heat of her mouth. The water cascaded down, sensitizing his skin. The roar started in his brain, the fire burned in his gut, a sweet ecstasy that shook him. Strains of their music penetrated into the shower, and fired his blood even more with the driving, impassioned beat. Her hips moved against his hand, her muscles were tight and clenching around his fingers.

"Jess." He said her name. Called to her. A pleading. A promise. "I need you now, this minute." Because there was nowhere else he would rather be than in her, with her, a part of her.

Her green gaze slid over him as she straightened. Took in every inch of him, the perfection of his face, the scars on his body, his heavy, thick evidence of his need for her. And she smiled in welcome. In happiness. Deliberately she turned and placed her hands carefully on the small half bench in the corner, presenting her rounded bottom and the smooth line of her back.

His hands went to her hips as he pulsed against her. She was more than ready for him, slick and hot and as eager as he was. Even as he pushed into her tight sheath, she pushed back, so that he filled her with a single surge. Molten lava raced through her, through him. He groaned, began to move hard and fast, thrusting deeply, wildly, a frenzy of white-hot pleasure for both of them. She was meeting every stroke, demanding more, her body gripping his, clenching and building a fiery friction that shook him all the way to his soul. And then she was rippling around him, milking him of his seed, so that his own orgasm ripped through him with such intensity her name was torn from his throat.

She always managed to surprise him. His Jessica, so unafraid of life, of passion, of showing her true feelings. She cried out with her release, her body spiraling out of control, and she gave herself up to the pleasure, embraced it the way she did everything. It seemed to last forever. It seemed over far too fast. They collapsed together, holding each other, kissing each other, their hands greedy for the feel of each other's body.

Dillon caught her hair in his hand. "I can't get enough of kissing you." His mouth devoured her ravenously. "More, I need more."

"I thought you said everyone was waiting for us. It's been a lot longer than ten minutes," Jessica pointed out. "They'll send the twins."

"Promise me when you marry me, which will be very, very soon, I can spend a couple of weeks in bed with you. Just touching you. I love the way you feel." He reached past her to turn off the water.

Jessica stilled, stared up at him with the water running off her lashes. "You never mentioned marriage."

Dillon blinked down at her, managed to look boyishly vulnerable. "I'm old-fashioned, I thought you knew I meant for life." He looked around, saw his jeans carelessly discarded on the floor. "I have a ring." He said it like a bribe.

"Dillon!" Flustered, Jessica wrapped her hair in a towel, staring at him wide-eyed. "You have a ring?"

She looked so beautiful with the confusion on her face, with the water beading on her petal soft skin and her large eyes bright with happiness, Dillon wanted to start all over again. He found the ring in his pocket and caught her hand. "I want us to be forever, Jess, forever."

The diamond sparkled at her as she smiled down at it. Then he was catching her up, throwing her on the bed in a tangle of sheets and arms and legs, his tongue lapping at every bead of water on her skin.

It was considerably longer than either of them expected before they were dressed and ready to join the others. Jessica's face was slightly red from the shadow on Dillon's jaw and the insides of her thighs held matching abrasions. She went with him willingly, confidently. Together they could manage to bring off Christmas.

She stopped in the doorway of the large room where the tree had been set up. Hundreds of tiny lights were woven in and out of the branches, highlighting the ornaments they had all made.

"So this is what you've been doing all this time," Jessica whispered, joy coursing through her as she looked at the lights on the Christmas tree, at the mound of brightly wrapped presents beneath the branches. "You've been playing Santa Claus."

He grinned at her, with his boyish, mischievous grin. "I'm into the miracle business in a big way these days. I couldn't let Tara and Trevor be disappointed. They wanted their father back, didn't they?"

Jessica wrapped her arms around his neck and claimed his oh-so-beautiful mouth. Happiness blossomed inside of her. She had thought Paul's betrayal would have been the last straw, that it would have broken Dillon's spirit totally. Instead he had emerged to the other side, whole once more.

His kiss was gentle, relaxed, tasting of passion and hunger. Behind them Trevor groaned. "Are you two going to be doing that all night, because there are other rooms where you can be alone, in case you hadn't noticed."

"Don't tell them that." Brian slapped Trevor on the back. "We'll never have Christmas if you give them any ideas."

Dillon took his time, kissing Jessica. It mattered, kissing did, and he made a thorough job of it while the twins tapped their feet and the band members nudged one another. He lifted his head slowly, and smiled down into her upturned face. "I love you, Jessica, more than I can ever express, I love you."

She touched his mouth with a trembling fingertip. "Surprise! I love you right back." She would count that as her Christmas miracle. Dillon. Her other half.

"Dad!" Tara squeaked impatiently. "We all know what's going on here, so don't keep us in suspense. Are you or aren't you?"

Dillon and Jessica turned to look at the expectant faces gathered around them. "What are you talking about?" He put his arm around Jessica's shoulders, drawing her into the shelter of his body.

Trevor threw his hands up in the air. "So much for being suave. Jeeze, Dad, get a clue here. A little action on your part, you know?"

Don shook his head. "You disappoint me, Wentworth."

"Boyo." Brian slumped against the wall, a hand to his head. "You've destroyed my faith in true love."

Brenda stepped forward, caught Jessica's wrist and yanked her left hand up to their faces. "Oh, for heaven's sake, you are the most unobservant group on the face of the earth!" The ring glittered beneath the light.

"Holy cow, Dad." Trevor grinned from ear to ear. "You're amazing. I apologize. Profusely."

Jessica was kissed and hugged until Dillon rescued her, pulling her to him and waving the others off with a good-natured scowl. He turned off the overhead lights so that only the twinkling Christmas lights shone. A multitude of colors sparkled and glowed. "It's midnight. We should sing Christmas in," he announced, leaning down to steal another kiss.

Brenda settled close to Robert, resting her head on his chest. Brian sat across from the couple, on the floor, stretching out his long legs toward the tree. Don followed suit, dropping to the floor, his back against the couch, sprawling out, leaning back to look at the lights.

Dillon laced his fingers through Jessica's as he sat in the large armchair and pulled her beside him. Tara and Trevor immediately found a place on the floor close to their father and Jessica. Robert reached behind the chair where he was sitting and casually pulled out an acoustic guitar. Dillon's oldest, not expensive, but one he had carried with him for years. Robert handed it across the floor to Trevor who held it out to his father.

"Play for us tonight, Dad," Trevor said.

Jessica could feel Dillon stiffen beside her. He shook his head, took the guitar out of his son's hand and tried to give it to Jessica. "You play. I don't play anymore."

"Yes, you do," Jessica said, ignoring the instrument, "you just don't play for large crowds. We're family. All of us here together tonight. We're your family, Dillon, and it's okay to be imperfect. Just play, don't be great, just play for us."

Dillon looked into her eyes. Green eyes. Guileless. Sincere. He glanced at the others watching him while he made his decision. The lights flickered and shimmied, winking at him as if in encouragement. He didn't have to do it all himself, he didn't have to be perfect. Sometimes people did get second chances. With a small sigh, he capitulated, bringing the guitar to him, cradling it in his arms like a lost lover. His longtime companion. His childhood friend when he was lonely. A small smile curved his mouth as he felt the familiar texture, the grain of the wood, the wide neck.

His fingers found the strings; his ear listened to the sound. He made the adjustments automatically, without thinking. He lived and breathed music: the notes that took on a life in his head. He still had that, a gift beyond comparison. He had his voice. It spilled out of him, his signature, a blend of edgy smoke and husky blues. He sang of hope and joy, love found, and families together. While he sang, his fingers found the familiar chords, moved over the strings with a remembered love. He didn't have the dexterity to play the fast riffs and the intricate melodies he often heard in his mind and composed, but he could do this, play for his family, and take pleasure in the gift of love.

They sang with him, all those he loved. Jessica's voice blended with his, in a perfect melding. Brenda was slightly out of tune, but he loved her all the more for it. Tara's voice held promise and Trevor's held enthusiasm. The pleasure of sitting in his home, surrounded by his family on Christmas Eve, was incomparable. His miracle.

A slight noise at the window distracted Jessica from the music and she frowned, looking beyond the glass pane to the darkened, wild storm. There was a small fluttering of white that settled on the outside windowsill. A storm-tossed bird, perhaps lost in the dark of night and the violence of the squall.

"There's a bird at the window," Jessica said softly, afraid if she spoke too loudly the white dove would vanish before anyone else saw it. She made her way with caution across the room while the others stayed motionless. "Birds aren't out at this time of night. Did it fly into the window?"

The bird looked bedraggled—a wet, unhappy, shivering dove. Jessica carefully opened the window, crooning to the creature, not wanting to frighten it away. To her astonishment, it waited calmly on the windowsill while she struggled to push one side of the window out against the fierce wind. Almost at once, the bird hopped onto her arm. She could feel it shaking, and immediately cupped its body in the warmth of her palms. It was carrying something in its beak. She could just make out the glint of gold between her hands. There was something else: a band on its leg. Jessica felt it drop into her palm as the bird rose, flapped its wings, and launched itself into the air. It flew around the room. As the bird passed over the twins, it opened its beak and dropped something between the twins. The bird made another fast circuit of the room while the lights played over its white feathers in a prism of colors that was mesmerizing and beautiful. The dove flew out the window, back into the night, winging its way toward some other shelter.

"What is it, Tara?" Trevor leaned in close as his sister lifted a gold chain for all of them to see. "It's a locket." It was small, heart-shaped, and intricately etched on the outside.

"I think it's real gold," Trevor said, lifting it up to peer at it more closely.

"Is it for me? Did someone get this for me? Where did this come from?" Tara looked around the room at the band members who had fallen silent as she held up the necklace. "Who gave it to me?"

Dillon leaned forward to get a closer look. Brenda's hand went to her throat in a curiously vulnerable gesture. Her gaze met Dillon's across the small space and she quickly shook her head. "I didn't, Dillon, I swear I didn't."

"It opens, doesn't it?" Trevor wrapped his arm around his sister's shoulder and peered at the delicate locket. "What's inside?"

Tara pressed the tiny catch and the locket popped open. There were two smiling faces, a two-year-old girl and an identical two-year-old boy. Both children were smiling. Their black, wavy hair framing their faces.

"Dad?" Tara looked at her father. "It's us, isn't it?"

Dillon nodded solemnly. "Your mother never took that necklace off. I didn't even know the pictures were inside of it."

Tara turned to Jessica, an awkward, uncertain expression on her young face. She didn't know what to think or feel about such a gift. Everyone was stunned, and had shocked looks on their faces. She didn't know whether to hug the locket to her, or to throw it away and cry a river of tears.

Jessica immediately hugged her. "What a beautiful gift. It is a day of miracles. Every child should know their mother wanted and loved them. I remember how precious that locket was to your mother. She wore it always, even when she had much more expensive jewelry. I think the necklace is proof of what she felt for you, even when she was too ill to show you."

Brenda caught Jessica's hand and squeezed it tightly. "Vivian always wore it, Tara—I teased her about her preferring it to diamonds. She said she had her reasons." Tears glittered in her eyes. "I know why now. I would never have taken it off either."

Tara kissed her aunt. "I'm glad you're here, Aunt Brenda," she confided. "I love you." She handed her the necklace. "Will you put it on me?"

Brenda nodded, her heart overflowing. "Absolutely I will."

"It was for both of us, Trev," Tara said. "She loved both of us after all. We'll share it." She leaned over to kiss her brother on the cheek.

Jessica settled in Dillon's lap, waited until the others were crowded around the twins, and she slowly opened her hand to show him what lay in her palm. The small ring was a mother's ring with two identical birthstones in it. They looked from the ring to one another without speaking.

Jessica closed her fingers around the precious gift the dove had left behind. It was better than diamonds. The most important gift ever given. Dillon's scarred fingers settled over hers, guarding the treasure, holding it close to their hearts. Trevor and Tara were theirs. They had their Christmas miracle and it was exactly what they needed.

❧ Acknowledgments ❧

Special thanks to Dr. Mathew King for all of his help with the research needed for this book. Also to Burn Survivors online. Thank you for your courtesy and patience and all the offers of help. And of course, to Bobbi and Mark Smith of the Holy Smoke Band, who gave me their time and help with my persistent questions.

THE TWILIGHT BEFORE CHRISTMAS

🌿 Dedication 🌿

This book is dedicated to my sister Lisa, who has a special
magic all her own.

The Twilight Before Christmas
by Heather King and Rose Brungard

'Twas the twilight before Christmas and all through the lands,
Not a thing has occurred that was not of my hand.

The snowglobe they hold has a secret inside,
Where the mist rolls in place of the snow that's outside.

A chill, colder still than the air they will feel,
As I rejoice in release as I slip past the seal

A wreath of holly meant to greet,
Looks much better tossed in the street.

A town dreams of sweet thoughts while nestled in bed,
Until nightmares of me begin to dance in their heads.

The time, it was right, for a present or two,
And the fog on the sand holds a secret, a clue.

As lovers meet beneath mistletoe bright,
Terror ignites down below them this night.

And the blood runs red on the pristine white snow . . .
While around all the houses the Christmas lights glow.

A star burns hot in the dead of the night,
As the bell tolls it's now midnight.

Beneath the star, that shines so bright,
An act unfolds, to my delight.

In the stocking hung with gentle care,
A mystery, I know, is hidden there.

A candle burns with an eerie glow,
As it melts, the wax does flow,

My last gift now, is a special one,
A candy cane for a special son,

He watches and tends and knows the land,
But not enough to evade my hand.

All deeds are now done, forgiveness is mine,
As two people share a love for all time.

1

'Twas the twilight before Christmas and all through the lands,
Not a thing has occurred that was not of my hand.

"Don't say it. Don't say it. Don't say it," Danny Granite muttered the mantra under his breath as he sat in the truck watching his older brother carefully selecting hydro-organic tomatoes from Old Man Mars's fruit stand. Danny glanced at the keys, assuring himself the truck was running and all that his brother had to do was leap in and gun it. He leaned out the window, gave a halfhearted wave to the elderly man, and scowled at his brother. "Get a move on, Matt. I'm starving here."

Matt grimaced at him, then smiled with smooth charm at the old man. "Merry Christmas, Mr. Mars," he said cheerfully as he handed over several bills and lifted the bag of tomatoes. "Less than two weeks before Christmas. I'm looking forward to the pageant this year."

Danny groaned. A black scowl settled over Old Man Mars's face. His craggy brows drew together in a straight, thick line. He grunted in disgust and spat on the ground.

The smile on Matt's face widened into a boyish grin as he hurried around the bed of the pickup truck to yank open the driver-side door. Almost before settling into his seat, he cranked up the radio so that "Jingle Bells" blared loudly from the speakers.

"You'd better move it, Matt," Dan muttered nervously,

looking out the window, back toward the fruit stand. "He's arming himself. You just had to wish him a Merry Christmas, didn't you? You know he hates that pageant. And you know very well playing that music is adding insult to injury!"

The first tomato came hurtling toward the back window of the truck as Matt hit the gas and the truck leaped forward, fishtailing, tires throwing dirt into the air. The tomato landed with deadly accuracy, splattering juice, seed, and pulp across the back window. Several more missiles hit the tailgate as the truck tore out of the parking lot and raced down the street.

Danny scowled at his brother. "You just had to wish him Merry Christmas. Everyone knows he hates Christmas. He kicked the shepherd last year during the midnight pageant. Now he'll be more ornery than ever. If you'd just avoided the word, we might have gone unscathed this year, but now he'll have to retaliate."

Matt's massive shoulders shook as he laughed. "As I recall you played the shepherd last year. He didn't hurt you that bad, Danny boy. A little kick on the shin is good for you. It builds character."

"You only think it's funny because it wasn't your shin." Danny rubbed his leg as if it still hurt nearly a year later.

"You need to toughen up," Matt pointed out. He took the highway, a thin ribbon of a road, twisting and turning along the cliffs above the ocean. It was impossible to go fast on the switchbacks although Matt knew the road well. He maneuvered around a sharp curve, setting up for the next sharp turn. It ran uphill and nearly doubled back. The mountain swelled on his right, a high bank grown over with emerald green grasses and breathtaking colors from the explosion of wildflowers. On his left, a narrow ribbon of a trail meandered along the cliffs to drop away to the wide expanse of blue ocean with its whitecaps and booming waves.

"Oh, my God! That's Kate Drake," Danny said gleefully, pointing to a woman on a horse, riding along the narrow trail on the side of the road.

"That can't be her." Matt hastily rolled down his window and craned his neck, gawking unashamedly. He could only see the back of the rider, who was dressed all in white and had thick chestnut hair that flamed red in the sunshine. His heart pounded. His mouth went dry. Only Kate Drake could get away with wearing white and riding a horse so close to the side of the road. It had to be her. He slowed the truck to get a better look as he went by, turning down the radio at the same time.

"Matt! Watch where you're going," Danny yelled, bracing himself as the truck flew off the road and rolled straight into the grass-covered bank. It halted abruptly. Both men were slammed back in their seats and held prisoner by their seat belts.

"Damn!" Matt roared. He turned to his brother. "Are you all right?"

"No, I'm not all right, you big lug, you ran us off the road gawking at Kate Drake again. I hurt everywhere. I need a neck brace, and I think I might have broken my little finger." Danny held up his hand, gripping his wrist and emitting groans loudly.

"Oh shut up," Matt said rudely.

"Matthew Granite. Good heavens, are you hurt? I have a cell phone and can go out to the bluff and call for help."

Kate's voice was everything he remembered. Soft. Melodic. Meant for long nights and satin sheets. Matt turned his head to look at her. To drink her in. It had been four long years since he'd last spoken with her. She stood beside his truck, reins looped in her hand, her large green eyes anxious. He couldn't help but notice she had the most beautiful skin. Flawless. Perfect. It looked so soft, he wanted to stroke his finger down her cheek just to see if she was real.

"I'm fine, Kate." It was a miracle he found his voice. His tongue seemed to stick to the roof of his mouth. "I must have tried to take the turn a little too fast."

A snort of derision came from Danny's side of the truck.

"You were driving like a turtle. You just weren't looking where you were going."

The toe of Matt's boot landed solidly against his brother's shin, and Danny let out a hair-raising yowl.

"No wonder Old Man Mars wanted to kick you last year," Matt muttered under his breath.

"Daniel? Are you hurt?" Kate sounded anxious, but her fascinating lower lip quivered as if close to laughter.

Determined to get her away from his brother, Matt hastily shoved the door open with more force than necessary. The door thumped soundly against Kate's legs. She jumped back, the horse half reared, and Danny, damn him, laughed like the hyena he was.

Matt groaned. It never failed. He was a decorated U.S. Army Ranger, had been in the service for years, running covert missions where his life depended on his physical skills and his cool demeanor, yet he always managed to feel clumsy and rough in front of Kate. He unfolded his large frame, towering over her, feeling like a giant. Kate was always perfect. Poised. Articulate. Graceful. There she was, looking beautiful dressed all in white with her hair attractively windblown. She was the only person in the world who could make him lose his cool and raise his temperature at the same time just by smiling.

"Is Danny really hurt?" Kate asked, turning her head slightly while she tried to calm the nervous horse.

It gave Matt a great view of her figure. He drank her in, his hungry gaze drifting over her soft curves. He'd always loved watching her walk away from him. Nobody moved in the same sexy way she did. She looked so proper, yet she had that come-on walk and the bedroom eyes and glorious hair a man would want to feel sliding over his skin all night long. He just managed to stifle a groan. How had he not known, *sensed* that Kate was back in town. His radar must be failing him.

"Danny's fine, Kate," Matt assured her.

She sent him a quick smile over her shoulder, her eyes sparkling at him. "Just how many accidents have you been in,

Matt? It seems that on the rare occasions I've seen you, over the last few years, your poor vehicle has been crunched."

It was true, but it was her fault. Kate Drake acted as some sort of catalyst for strange behavior. He was good at everything. *Everything.* Unless Kate was around—then he could barely manage to speak properly.

The horse moved restlessly, demanding Kate's immediate attention, giving Matt time to realize his jeans and blue chambray work shirt were streaked with dirt, sawdust, and a powdery cement mixture in complete contrast to her immaculate white attire. He took the opportunity to slap the dust from his clothing, sending up a gray cloud that enveloped Kate as she turned back toward him. She coughed delicately, fluttering her long feathery lashes to keep the dust from stinging her eyes. Another derisive hoot came from Danny's direction.

Matt sent his brother a look that promised instant death before turning back to Kate. "I had no idea you were in town. The town gossips let me down." Inez at the grocery store had mentioned Sarah was in town, as well as Hannah and Abigail, three of her six sisters, but Inez hadn't said a word about Kate.

"Sarah came back for a visit, and you know how my family is, we get together as often as possible." She shrugged, a simple enough gesture, but on her it was damned sexy. "I've been in London doing research for my latest thriller." She laughed softly. The sound played right down his spine and did interesting things to his body. "London fog is always so perfect for a scary setting. Before that it was Borneo." Kate traveled the world, researching and writing her bestselling novels and murder mysteries. She was so beautiful it hurt to look at her, so sophisticated he felt primitive in her presence. She was so sexy he always had the desire to turn caveman and toss her over his shoulder and carry her off to his private lair. "Sarah's engaged to Damon Wilder." She tilted her head slightly and patted the horse's neck again. "Have you met him?"

"No, but everyone is talking about it. No one expected Sarah to get married."

Matt watched the way the sunlight kissed her hair, turning the silky strands into a blazing mass of temptation. His gaze followed her hand stroking the horse's neck, and he noted the absence of a ring with relief.

Danny cleared his throat. He leaned out the driver's side. "You're drooling, bro." He whispered it in an overloud voice.

Without missing a beat, Matt kicked the door closed. "Are you going to be staying very long this visit?" He held his breath waiting for her answer. To make matters worse, Danny snickered. Matt sent up a silent vow that their parents would have one less child to fuss over before the day was out.

"I've actually decided to stay and make Sea Haven my home base. I bought the old mill up on the cliffs above Sea Lion Cove. I'm planning on renovating the mill into a bookstore and coffee shop, and to modernize the house so I can live in it. I'm tired of wandering. I'm ready to come home again."

Kate smiled. She had perfect teeth to go with her perfect skin. Matt found himself staring at her while the earth shook beneath his feet. He stood there, grinning at the thought of Kate living in their hometown permanently.

A shadow swept across the sky, black threads swirling and boiling, a dark cauldron of clouds blotting out the sun. A seagull shrieked once. Then the entire flock of birds overhead took up the warning cry. Matt was so caught up in Kate's smile, he didn't realize the ground was really rolling, and it wasn't just her amazing effect on him. The horse backed dangerously close to the road, tossing its head in fright, nearly dragging Kate from her feet. Matt swiftly reached past her and gathered the reins in one hand to steady the animal. He swept his other arm around Kate's waist, anchoring her smaller body to his, to keep her from falling as a jagged crack opened several feet from them and spread rapidly along the ground, heading right for Kate's feet. Matt lifted her up and away from the gaping hole, dragging her back several feet, horse in tow, away from the spreading crack. It was only a few inches wide, but it was several inches deep, very long, and ran up the side of the embankment.

"You all right, Danny?" he called to his brother.

"Yeah, I'm fine. That was a big one."

Kate clung to Matt, her small hands clutching at his shoulders. He heard the sharp intake of her breath that belied her calm demeanor, but she didn't cry out. The ground settled, and Matt allowed her feet to touch the path but retained his hold on her. She was incredibly warm and soft and smelled of fresh flowers. He leaned over her, inhaling her fragrance, his chin brushing the top of her head. "You okay, Kate?"

Appearing as serene as ever, Kate murmured soothingly to the horse. Nothing ruffled her. Not earthquakes and certainly not Matthew Granite. "Yes, of course, it was just a little earthquake." She glanced up at the boiling clouds with a small frown of puzzlement.

"It was a fairly good one. And the ground opened damn near at your feet."

Kate continued to pat the horse's neck, seemingly unaware that Matt was still holding her, caging her body between his and the animal. He could see her hands tremble as she struggled to maintain composure, and it made him admire her all the more. She lifted her face to the wind. "I love the sea breeze. The minute I feel it on my face, I feel as if I'm home."

Matt cleared his throat. Kate had a beautiful profile. Her hair was swept up in some fancy knot, showing off her long, graceful neck. When she turned, her breasts thrust against the thin shirt, full and round and so enticing it was all he could do to keep from leaning down and putting his mouth over the clinging white fabric. He tried to move, to step away from her, but he was drawn to her. Mesmerized by her. She'd always reminded him of a ballerina, with her elegant lines and soft, feminine curves. His lungs burned for air, and there was a strange roaring in his head. It took three tries opening his mouth before a coherent word came out. "If you're really serious about renovation, Kate, it just so happens my family's in the construction business."

She turned the full power of her huge eyes on him. "I do recall all of you are builders. That's always struck me as a wonderful occupation." She reached out and took his hands. He had big hands, rough and callused, whereas her hands were soft and small. "I always loved your hands, Matthew. When I was a young girl I remember wishing I had your capable hands." Her words, as much as her touch, sent little flames licking along his skin.

Matt was certain he heard a snort and probably a snicker coming from the direction of his younger brother.

"I think you've held on to her long enough, bro," Danny called. "The ground stopped pitching a few minutes ago."

Matt was too much of a gentleman to point out to his brother that Kate was holding *his* hands. Looking down at her, he saw faint color steal under her skin. Reluctantly, he stepped away from her. The wind tugged at tendrils of her hair, but it only made her look more alluring. "Sorry, Kate. This is the first time in a while we've had an earthquake shake us up so hard." He raked his fingers through his dark hair in agitation, searching for something brilliant to say to keep her there. His mind was blank. Totally blank. Kate turned back to her horse. He began to feel desperate. He was a grown man, hardworking, some said brilliant when it came to designing, and most women quite frankly threw themselves at him, but Kate calmly gathered the reins of her horse, no weak knees, completely unaffected by his presence. He wiped the sweat suddenly beading on his forehead, leaving a smear of dirt behind.

"Kate." It came out softly.

Danny stuck his head out the window on the driver's side. "Do you want a little help with the old mill, Kate? Matt actually is fairly decent at that sort of thing. He obviously can't drive, and he can't talk, but he's hell on wheels with renovations."

Kate's eyes lit up. "I would love that, Matthew, but I really wouldn't want to presume on our friendship. It would have to be a business arrangement."

Matt hadn't realized she thought of them as friends. Kate rarely spoke to him, other than their strange, brief conversations when they'd run into one another by chance during her high school years. He liked the idea of being friends with her. Every cell in his body went on alert when she was near him, it always happened that way, even when she'd been a teenager and he'd been in his first years of college. Kate had always brought out his protective instincts, but mostly he'd felt he had to protect her from his own attraction to her. That had been distasteful to a man like Matt. He had taken his secret fantasies of her to every foreign country he'd been sent to. She had shared his days and nights in the jungles and deserts, in the worst of situations, and the memory of her had gotten him home. Now, a full-grown man who had fought wars and had more than enough life experience to give him confidence, he found he could speak easily and naturally to any other woman. Only Kate made him tongue-tied. He'd take friendship with her. At least it was a start. "Tell me when you want me to take a look, Kate, and I'll arrange my schedule accordingly. Being my own boss has its advantages."

"Then I'm going to take advantage of your generous offer and ask if you could go out there with me tomorrow afternoon. Do you think you can manage it that soon? I wouldn't ask, but I'm trying to get this project off the ground as soon as possible."

"It sounds great. I'll pick you up at the cliff house around four. You are staying there with your sisters, aren't you?"

Kate nodded and turned to watch the sheriff cruise up behind the pickup truck. Matt watched her face, mainly because he couldn't tear his gaze away from her. Her smile was gracious, friendly even, but he was aware even before he turned his head that the man getting out of the sheriff's cruiser was Jonas Harrington. It occurred to him that he knew Kate far too well, her every expression. And that meant he had spent too much time watching her. Kate was smiling, but she had stiffened just that little bit. She always did that around Jonas. All of her sisters did. For the first time he wondered why Kate reacted that way.

"Well, Kate, I see you caused another accident," Jonas said in greeting. He shook Matt's hand and clapped him on the back. "The Drake sisters have a tendency to wreak havoc everywhere they go." He winked at Matt.

Kate simply lifted an eyebrow. "You've been saying that since we were children."

Jonas leaned over to brush a casual kiss along Kate's cheek. Something black and lethal, whose existence Matt didn't want to recognize, moved inside of him like a dark shadow. He put a blatantly possessive hand on Kate's back.

Jonas ignored Matt's body language. "I'll still be making the same accusation when you're all in your eighties, Kate. Where is everyone?" He looked around as if expecting her sisters to appear galloping over the mountaintop.

"You look a little nervous, Jonas," Danny observed from the safety of the truck. "What'd you do this time? Arrest Hannah and throw her beautiful butt in jail on some trumped-up charge?"

He subsided when Kate turned the full power of her gaze on him. The wind rushed up from the sea, bringing the scent and feel of the ocean. "I had no idea you were so interested in my sister's anatomy, Danny."

"Come on, Kate, she's gorgeous; every man's interested in Hannah's anatomy," Danny pointed out, unrepentant.

"And if she doesn't want them to look, what is she doing allowing every photographer from here to hell and back to take pictures of her?" Jonas demanded. "And just for your information, I wouldn't have to trump up charges if I wanted to arrest Hannah," he added with a black scowl. "I ought to run her in for indecent exposure. That glitzy magazine in Inez's store has her on the cover . . . naked!"

"She is not naked. She's wearing a swimsuit, Jonas, with a sarong over it." Kate sounded as calm as ever, but Matt noted that her hand tightened on the reins of her horse until her knuckles turned white. He moved even closer to her, inserting himself between her and the sheriff.

"She might try a decent one-piece and maybe a robe that went down to her ankles or something. And does she have to strike that stupid pose just to make everyone stare . . ." Jonas broke off as the wind gusted again, howling this time, bringing whispers in the swirling chaos of leaves and droplets of seawater. His hat was swept from his head and carried away from the group. The wind shifted direction, rushing back to the ocean, retreating in much the same manner as a wave from the shore. The sudden breeze took the hat with it, sailing it over the cliffs and into the choppy water below.

Jonas spun around and looked toward the large house set up on the cliffs in the distance. "Damn it, Hannah. That's the third hat I've lost since you've been home." He shouted the words into the vortex of the wind.

There was a small silence. Matt cleared his throat. "Jonas. I don't think she can hear you from here."

Jonas glared at him. "She can hear me. Can't she, Kate? She knows exactly what I'm saying. You tell her this isn't funny anymore. She can stop with her little wind games."

"You believe all the things people say about the Drake sisters, don't you, Jonas?" Danny said. He imitated the opening theme of *The Twilight Zone*.

Matt stared down at Kate's hand. The reins were trembling. He covered her hand with his own, steadying the leather reins she was clenching. "I'll be happy to come look at the mill tomorrow, Kate. Would you like a leg up?"

"Thanks, Matthew. I'd appreciate it."

He didn't bother with cupping his hands together to assist her into the saddle. He simply lifted her. He was tall and strong, and it was easy to swing her onto the horse. She settled into the saddle as if born there. Elegant. Refined. As close to perfection as any dream he could conjure up and just as far out of reach. "I'll see you then. Say hello to your sisters for me."

"I'll do that, Matthew, and you give my best to your parents. It was nice to see you, Danny." Her cool gaze swept over Jonas. "I'm sure you'll be by the house, Jonas."

Jonas shrugged. "I take my job seriously, Kate."

Matt watched her ride away, waiting until a curve in the road took her out of sight before turning on the sheriff. "What the hell was that all about?"

"You know all seven of the Drake women drive me crazy half the time," Jonas said. "I've told you all the trouble they get up to. You're always grilling me about them. Well—" he grinned evilly as he indicated the truck—"Isn't this the third accident you've had with Kate in the vicinity? You should know what I mean."

Jonas had grown up with Matt Granite, had gone through school, joined the Army, the Rangers, and fought side by side with him. He knew how Matt felt about Kate. It was no secret. Matt wasn't very good at hiding his feelings from his family and friends, especially since Jonas had gotten out of the service two years before Matt and Matt had continually interrogated him about Kate's whereabouts and marital status. Matt had been home three years and he'd been waiting for Kate to come home for good, too.

Danny snickered. "You were there back in his college days, Jonas, when he drove Dad's truck into the creek bed and hung it up on a rock. Wasn't Kate about three at the time?"

Matt took a deep breath. He couldn't kill his brother in front of the sheriff, even if it was Jonas. The time he had wrecked his father's truck, driving it without permission, Kate had been about fifteen, far too young for a college man to be looking at her, and he was still embarrassed that his brothers and Jonas had known why he'd wrecked the vehicle. Of course he'd known the Drake sisters, everyone in town knew them, but he'd never *looked* at them. Not in a fascinated, physical, male way. Until he'd seen Kate standing in a creek bed picking blackberries with the sun kissing her hair and her large sea-green eyes looking back at him. The second time he'd wrecked a vehicle had been four years ago. Matt had been home on leave, and he'd been so busy looking at Kate walking on the sidewalk with her sisters, he'd failed to realize he was parked in front of a cement hump and had hung up his mother's car on it when he'd gone to pull out. Now, ignoring his brother's jibe, he moved around the truck to inspect the damage. "I think I can get the truck out without a tow."

"I see you upset old man Mars." Jonas pointed to the tomato smears on the rear window.

"You know Matt, he just had to wish the old man a Merry Christmas." Danny shoved open the door. "He likes to stir the old geezer up right before the pageant. He does it every year. The time Mom made me play the little drummer boy, Mars broke my drumsticks into ten pieces and threw them on the ground and then jumped up and down on them. All my brothers got a kick out of that, but I've been traumatized ever since. I have nightmares about being stomped by him."

Jonas laughed. "Mars is a strange old man, but he's harmless enough. And he gives away most of his produce to the people who need it. He takes it to some of the single moms in town and some of the elderly couples. And I know he feeds the Ruttermyer boy, the one with Down's syndrome who works at odd jobs for everyone. He persuaded Donna to give the boy a room right next to her gift shop. I know he helps that boy with his bills."

"Yeah, deep down he's a good man," Matt agreed. A slow grin spread over his face. "He just hates Christmas." He nodded toward the other side of the truck, and the other two men went to the front to scrape away the mud and dirt and push until they separated the bumper from the embankment. "I didn't appreciate you saying anything to Kate about her and her sisters being different, Jonas." Matt said it in a low voice, but Jonas and he had been friends since they were boys, and Jonas recognized the warning tone.

"I'm not going to pretend they're like everyone else, Matt, not even for you," Jonas snapped. "The Drakes are special. They have gifts, and they use themselves up for everyone else without a thought for themselves or their own safety. I'm going to watch out for them whether they like it or not. Sarah

Drake nearly got herself killed a few weeks ago. Hannah and Kate and Abbey were with her and also might have been killed."

Matt felt the words as a blow somewhere in the vicinity of his gut. His heart did a curious somersaulting dive in his chest. "I heard about Sarah, but I hadn't heard the others were there. What happened?"

"To make a long story short, Wilder had people trail him here. They wanted information only he could give them. He helped design our national defense system, and the government wanted him protected at all costs. With Sarah being from Sea Haven, it was natural enough for the Feds to send her in to guard him. These people had gotten their hands on him once before, killed his assistant right in front of him, and tortured him. That's why he uses a cane when he walks. They broke into the Drakes' house, armed to the teeth when he was there, and were ready to kill Wilder and the Drakes to get what they wanted." The anger in Jonas's voice deepened.

"No one said a word about Kate being in the house at the same time. I knew Sarah was guarding Damon Wilder and that he was a defense expert in some kind of trouble, but . . ." Matt trailed off as he looked back toward the house on the cliff. It was covered with Christmas lights. Beside it was a tall full Douglas fir tree, completely decorated and flashing lights even before the sun went down. When he looked toward the house he felt a sense of peace. Of rightness. The Drake sisters were the town's treasures. He looked away from the cliff toward the old mill. It was farther up the road, built over Sea Lion Cove. A strange cloud formation hung over the small inlet and spread slowly toward land. The shape captured his imagination, a yawning black mouth, jaws opening wide, heading straight for them.

"All of them were nearly murdered," Jonas said. His eyes went flat and cold. "The Drakes take on far too much, and everyone just expects them to do it without thinking of the cost to them."

"I never thought of it like that, Jonas. Now that you mention it, I've seen them all drained of energy after helping out the way they do." Matt didn't take his eyes from the sky. He watched a seagull veer frantically from the path of the slow-moving cloud, braking sharply in midair, wings flapping strongly in agitation. Wisps of fog began to rise from the sea and drift toward shore. "Maybe we all should pay more attention to what's happening with them," he murmured softly, more to himself than to the others.

2

The snowglobe they hold has a secret inside,
Where the mists rolls in place of the snow that's outside.

INHALING THE MINGLED scents of cinnamon and pine, Kate wandered into the kitchen of the cliff house. The sound of Christmas music filled the air and blended with the aroma of fresh-baked cookies and the fragrance of richly scented candles. "Is that Joley's voice?" Kate asked, leaning her hip comfortably against the heavily carved wood cabinet. "When did she make a Christmas collection?"

Hannah Drake spun around, teakettle in her hands. Her abundance of blond hair shimmered for a moment in the last rays of sunshine pouring through the bay window. "Kate, I didn't hear you get out of the shower. I think I was in my own little world. Joley sent the CD as a surprise, although she made a point of saying it was not to go out of the family."

They both laughed affectionately. "Joley and that band of hers. She can sing just about anything from gospel to blues, from rock to rap, but she's so careful not to let anyone know. I think she likes her bad girl image. Did she mention whether she's coming home for Christmas? I know she was touring."

Hannah's face lit up, her smile brilliant. "She's going to try. I can't wait to see her. We keep missing each other in our travels."

"I hope she gets here soon. Talking on the phone just isn't the same as all of us being together." Kate swept a stray tendril of hair behind her ear. "What about Mom and Dad? Has anyone heard from them? Are they coming here for Christmas?"

Hannah shook her head. "Last I heard they sent kisses and hugs and were snuggling together in their little chalet in the Swiss Alps. Libby got in a quick visit with them before she headed out to the Congo. She said she was coming home for Christmas. Mom and Dad promised next year they'd be here with us."

Kate laughed softly as she leaned over to sniff the canister of loose tea. "Mom and Dad are still such lovebirds. What are you making?"

"I was in the mood for a little lavender, but anything is fine." Hannah scrutinized Kate closely. "But let's go with chamomile. Something soothing."

Kate smiled. "You think I need a little soothing?"

Hannah nodded as she measured the tea into a small pot. "Tell me."

"I ran into Matthew Granite and his brother Danny." Kate tried to sound casual, when her entire body was trembling. Only Matt could do that to her. Only Matt moved her. She'd never understood why.

"Matthew Granite? I thought that might be him." Hannah's huge blue eyes settled on her sister with compassion and interest. "How did he seem?"

Kate shrugged her slender shoulders. "Wonderful. Helpful. He offered to look at the old mill for me and help with the renovations." She always enjoyed looking at her younger sister.

Hannah wasn't just beautiful, she was strikingly so, exotically so, with her bone structure, abundance of pale, almost platinum hair, her enormous, heavily lashed eyes, and sultry lips. Beauty radiated from her. Kate had always thought Hannah's extraordinary beauty came from the inside out. She watched the graceful movements of Hannah's hands as she went about making tea. "Matt's always so helpful." She sighed.

Hannah reached out to her, clasping Kate's hands in a gesture of solidarity. "Was it the same?"

"You mean with his brothers laughing all the time? Well, only one was with him, Danny." Color crept up under Kate's skin. "Yes, of course. Every time I get anywhere near the Granites they all laugh. I have no idea why. It isn't the same way Jonas is with you. Matthew never needles me. He's always perfectly polite, but I seem to have some humorous effect on his family. I try as hard as I can just to be polite and calm, but the brothers laugh until I want to go check a mirror to see if I have spinach in my teeth. Matthew just glares at them, but it really draws attention to all the silly things I do in front of him." She squeezed Hannah's fingers before letting her hand go. "I've showered and changed, but I came home with my clothes covered with dirt. Poor Matthew just came from work, was dusting himself off, and I had to be two steps behind him. When he tried to open his truck door, of course I managed to get too close."

"Oh, Katie, honey, I'm so sorry. What happened?" Hannah's face mirrored her sister's distress.

Kate shrugged. "The door nearly knocked me over, and he had to apologize yet again. The poor man spends every minute apologizing to me. I'll bet he wishes he never had to see me again."

"No he doesn't," Hannah said firmly. "I think he's always been sweet on you."

Kate sighed. "You and I both know Matthew Granite would never look at me twice. He's wild and rough and an adrenaline junkie. He played every sport in high school and college. He joined the Rangers. I researched what they do. Even their creed is a bit frightening. They arrive at the 'cutting edge of battle' and they never fail their comrades and give more than one hundred percent. The creed says things like fight on even if you're the lone survivor, and *surrender* is not a Ranger word." She shuddered delicately. "He's a wild man, and he does very scary wild things. He's going to look at women who climb mountains and scoff in the face of danger. Can you see me doing that?"

"Kate," Hannah said softly, "maybe he's more settled now. He went out and did his save the world thing and now he's come home and he's working the family business. He could have changed."

Kate forced a fleeting smile. "Men like Matthew don't change, Hannah. I was telling you my tale of woe. We were just at the point where Jonas drove up. You know how he has to make his little 'Drake sisters' comments. He implied every time I was around something awful happened. It just made the situation worse." She sighed again. "I tried to look as though it didn't bother me, but I think Matthew knew."

"Jonas Harrington needs to fall into the ocean and have a nice hungry shark come swimming by." Hannah dragged the whistling teakettle from the stove and splashed water into the teapot, a fine fury radiating from her at the thought of Jonas Harrington saying anything to upset Kate. The water boiled in the little china teapot, bubbles roiling and bursting with a steady fury. Steam rose.

Kate covered the top of the teapot with her palm, settling the water back down. "You were out on the captain's walk."

Hannah nodded, unrepentant. "The earthquake bothered me. I felt something rising beneath the earth. I can't explain it, Kate, but it frightened me. I was sitting here listening to Joley's Christmas music, you know how much I love Christmas, then I felt the quake. Almost on the heels of it, something else disturbed the earth. I felt it as a darkness rising upward. I knew you were out riding, so I went out to the walk to make certain you weren't in trouble."

"And you felt the wind come in off the sea," Kate said. She leaned her hip against the counter. "I felt it too." She frowned and drummed her fingers on the tiled counter. "I smelled something, Hannah, something old and bitter in the wind."

"Evil?" Hannah ventured.

Kate shook her head slowly. "It wasn't that exactly. Well," she hedged, "maybe. I don't know. What did you think?"

Hannah leaned against the brightly tiled sink, her body so graceful the casual movement seemed balletic. "I honestly don't know, Kate, but it isn't good. I've felt disturbed ever since the earthquake and when I looked at the mosaic, there was a black shadow beneath the ground. I could barely make it out because it seemed to move and not stay in one place."

Kate glanced at the floor in the house's entryway. Her grandmother, along with her grandmother's six sisters, had made the mosaic, women of power and magic, seven sisters creating a timeless floor of infinite beauty. To most people it was simply a unique floor, but the Drake sisters could read many things in the ever-changing shadows that ran within it. "How very strange that neither of us knows precisely whether the disturbance is evil." She shrugged her shoulders and drew in a deep breath filled with cinnamon and pine. "I love the fragrances of Christmas." She tapped her foot, a small smile hovering on her face.

"You're holding back on me," Hannah guessed, her voice suddenly teasing. "Something else happened, didn't it?"

"When the earthquake started, Matthew put his arm around me to steady me, and we just stood there, even after it was over." She grinned at Hannah. "He is so strong. You have no idea. That man is all muscle. It's a wonder I didn't end up in a puddle at his feet! But I managed to look cool and serene."

Hannah pretended to swoon. "I wish I could have seen it. Matthew is definitely hot, even if he is a Neanderthal. I must have come up on the captain's walk just after that, just in time to see the slimy toad of the world arrive in his little sheriff's car." She smirked. "Too bad the wind came up, and his precious little hat went sailing out to sea."

"Shame on you, Hannah," Kate scolded halfheartedly. "Jonas means well. He's just so used to everyone doing everything he says, and we always seem to be in the middle of any kind of trouble in Sea Haven. You're beginning to enjoy tormenting him."

"Why shouldn't I? He's tormented me for years."

There was so much pain in Hannah's voice that Kate slipped her arm around her sister's waist to comfort her. Jonas had known them all since they were children, and he'd never understood Hannah. She'd been an extraordinarily beautiful, very intelligent child, but she'd been so painfully shy outside of her own home, the sisters had had to work their magic just to get her to school every day. Jonas had been certain she was haughty, when in fact, she'd rarely been able to speak in public. "Well, all in all, it was a good day. You managed to lose another hat for Jonas, and I got to be up close and personal with the hottest man in Sea Haven." Kate hugged Hannah before pouring herself a cup of tea and walking into the living room with it.

Hannah followed her. "Did you get your manuscript mailed off?"

Kate nodded. "Murder and mayhem will prevail in a small coastal town. I forgot to put the tea cozy back on the pot, will you do it?"

Hannah glanced into the kitchen and lifted her arms.

When Kate looked back, the cozy was safely on the teapot. "Thanks, Hannah. I do have to say, Jonas was invaluable to me with the research."

"I know he was, but don't credit him with doing it to be nice or anything." Hannah's large blue eyes reflected her laughter. "He was trying to get on your good side so you'd persuade me to stop messing around with his precious hats."

They both swung around as the front door burst open. Abigail Drake rushed in, a small woman with dark eyes and a wealth of red-gold hair spilling down her back in a thick ponytail. Her face was flushed and her eyes over-bright. The moment she glimpsed her sisters, she burst into tears.

"Abbey!" Hannah set her teacup down on the highly polished coffee table. "What is it? You never cry."

"I humiliated myself in front of the entire Christmas pageant committee," Abigail said miserably. She threw herself into the overstuffed armchair, curled her feet under her, and covered her face with her hands. "I can never face any of them again."

Hannah and Kate rushed to her side, both putting their arms around her. "Don't cry, Abbey. What happened? Maybe we can fix it. It can't be that bad."

"It was bad," Abigail muttered from between her fingers. "I accidentally used *the voice.* I wasn't paying attention. There was the earthquake, and I was so distracted because I felt something under us, something moving just below the surface seeking a way out. I *felt* it." Of all the talents gifted to the sisters, Abigail felt hers was the worst. Her voice could be used to extract the truth from people around her. As a child, before she'd learned to control the tone and the wording of her sentences, she'd been very unpopular with her classmates. They would often blurt out the truth of some escapade to their parents or a teacher whenever they were in her presence. Abigail pulled her hands down and stared at them with her sad eyes. "It isn't an excuse. I'm not a teenager. I know I have to be alert all the time."

Hannah and Kate exchanged a long, fearful look. "We felt the shadow too, Abbey. It was very disconcerting to both of us. What happened at the meeting?"

Abbey drew her legs up tighter into her body. "We were all discussing the Christmas pageant." She rubbed her chin on the top of her knees. "I felt the rift in the earth, a blackness welling up, and the next thing I knew I was asking for the truth." She clapped her hands over her ears. "I got the truth too. Everyone did. Bruce Harper is having an affair with Mason Fredrickson's wife. They were all in the room. Bruce and Mason got in a terrible fistfight, and Letty Harper burst into tears and ran out. She's six months pregnant. Sylvia Fredrickson slapped me across the face and walked out, leaving me standing there with everyone looking at me." She burst into tears all over again.

Kate frowned as she rubbed her sister's shoulders. She could feel the waves of distress pouring off of Abigail. "It's all right now, honey. You're home, and you're safe." At once a soothing tranquillity swept into the room, a sense of peace. The wicks on the unlit candles on the mantel leapt to life with bright orange-red flames. Joley's voice poured into the room, uplifting and melodic, bringing with it a sense of home and Christmas cheer. Kate leaned into her sister. "Abigail, your talent is a tremendous gift, and you have always used it for good. This was a distortion of your talent, not something any of us could have foreseen. Let it go. Just breathe and let it go."

Abbey managed a small smile, the sobs fading at the sound of her sister's voice. Kate the peacemaker. Most thought she prevented fights and solved problems, but in truth, she had a magic about her, a tranquillity and inner peace she shared with others just by the way she spoke. "I wish I had your gift, Kate," Abbey said. She pressed her hand to her cheek. "I didn't mind everyone's finding out about Sylvia—she likes to think she can get any man—but poor little Letty, pregnant and loving her stupid unfaithful husband so much. That was heartbreaking. And at Christmas too. What possessed me to be so careless? I'm so ashamed of myself."

"What exactly did you say, Abbey?" Kate asked.

Abbey looked confused. "Everyone had put in a variety of ideas for acting out the play we do every year and someone asked if they really liked the old script and should we keep it as a tradition or should we modernize it. I think I said, now would be a good time to tell the truth if you want to make any major changes. I meant with the script, not in people's lives." She rubbed her temples. "I haven't made a mistake like that since I was a teenager. I'm so careful to avoid the word *truth*." She scrubbed her hand over her face a second time, trying to erase the sting of Sylvia's hand. "You know if I use that word everyone in the immediate vicinity tells the truth about everything."

"It worries me that we all felt the same disturbance," Kate said. "Hannah saw a dark shadow in the mosaic. You said something you would never have normally said, and a crack opened up nearly at my feet and ran all the way up the embankment."

Hannah gasped. "You didn't tell me that. Kate, it could have been an attack on you. You're the most . . ." She broke off, looking at Abbey.

Kate lifted her chin. "I'm the most what?"

Hannah shrugged. "You're the best of us. You don't have a mean bone in your body. You just don't, Katie. I'm sorry, I know you hate our saying that, but you don't even know how to dislike someone. You're just so . . ."

"*Don't* say perfect," Kate warned. "I'm not perfect. And I think that's why Matthew's brothers always laugh at me. They think I want to be perfect and fall short."

Hannah and Abbey exchanged a long, worried look. "I think we should call the others," Hannah said. "Sarah will want to know about this. She must have felt the earthquake too. We can ask her if anything strange happened to her. And we should call Joley, Libby, and Elle. Something's wrong, Kate, I just feel it. It's as if the earthquake unleashed a malicious force. I'm afraid it could be directed at you."

Kate took a long sip of tea. The taste was as soothing as the aroma. "Go ahead, it can't hurt to see what the others have to say. I'm not going to worry about it. I didn't feel a direct threat. I'm not calling Sarah though. She and Damon are probably twined around one another. You can feel the heat right through the telephone line."

"I can go to the captain's walk and signal her," Hannah said wickedly. "Their bedroom window faces us, and for some utterly mysterious reason the curtain keeps opening in that particular room."

"Hannah!" Kate tried not to laugh. "You're impossible."

Hannah did laugh. "And you are perfect whether you want to acknowledge it or not. At least to me."

"And me," Abigail said.

Kate smiled at them. "I'm not all that perfect. I'd like to give Sylvia Fredrickson a piece of mind. She had no right hitting you, Abbey. Even in high school she was nasty."

"I'll take care of Sylvia," Hannah said. "Don't worry, Abbey. She'll spend a long time thinking about how stupid it was to hit you."

"Hannah!" Kate and Abbey chorused her name in protest.

Hannah burst out laughing. "I get the message, Kate. You'll talk to Sylvia, but you don't want me casting in her direction."

Kate grinned. "I should have known you were baiting me."

"Who said I didn't mean it? Sylvia gives women a bad name."

Kate shook her head. "Hannah Drake, you're becoming a bloodthirsty little witch. I think Jonas is having a bad influence on you." She touched Abbey's cheek gently. "Even for this we can't use our gifts for anything other than good."

Hannah made a face. "It's good for Jonas to have to chase his hat. It keeps him from becoming too arrogant and bossy. And who knows what great lesson Sylvia Fredrickson would learn if I tweaked her just a little bit." Before either sister could say anything, she laughed softly. "I'm not going to do anything horrible to her, I just love to see you both get that 'there-goes-Hannah-look' on your faces."

Kate nudged Abbey, ignoring Hannah's mischievous grin. "Guess what I'll be doing tomorrow? Matthew Granite agreed to look over the mill with me tomorrow. I'm hoping none of his brothers will be around to laugh at me, and maybe he'll notice I'm a grown woman, not a gawky teenager. You'd think the fact that I've traveled all over the world and that I'm a successful author would impress him, but he just looks at me exactly the same way he did when I was in high school."

Hannah and Abbey exchanged a quick, apprehensive look. "Kate, you're going to spend the afternoon with him? Do you really want to do that?" Abigail asked.

Kate nodded. "I like to be with him. Don't ask me why, I just do."

"Kate, you haven't been home in ages. Matthew has a certain reputation," Abigail said hesitantly. "He's always been easygoing with you, and he's very charming, but he's . . ." She trailed off and looked to Hannah for direction.

"What? A ladies' man? I would presume a man his age has dated." Kate walked across the room to touch the first of the seven stockings hung in a row along the mantelpiece. It allowed her to keep her expression hidden from her sisters. "I know he's been in relationships."

"That's just it, Kate. He doesn't have relationships. At best he has one-night stands. Women find him charming and mysterious, and he finds them annoying. Seriously, Kate, don't *really* fall for him. He looks great on the outside, but he has a caveman attitude. He was in the military so long, doing all the secret Special Forces kind of stuff, and he just expects everyone to fall in line with his orders. It's probably why he isn't impressed with your world travels. Please don't fall for him," Hannah pleaded. "I couldn't bear it if he hurt you, Kate."

"You're so certain he wouldn't fall for me? A few minutes ago you were saying you thought he might be sweet on me." Kate tried to guard her voice, to keep her tone strictly neutral when there was a peculiar ache inside. "I really don't need the warning. Men like Matthew don't look at women like me." She shrugged. "It doesn't bother me. I need solitude, I always have. And I don't have a tremendous amount of time to give to a relationship."

"What do you mean, Matthew wouldn't look at a woman like you?" Abbey was outraged. "What are you talking about, Kate?"

Kate took another sip of tea and smiled at her sisters over the rim of her teacup. "Don't worry, I'm not feeling sorry for myself. I know I'm different. I was born the way I am. All of you stand out. Your looks, your personalities, even you, Hannah, with being so painfully shy, you embrace life. You all live it. You don't let your weaknesses or failings stand in your way. I'm an observer. I read about life. I research life. I find a corner in a room and melt into it. I can become invisible. It's an art, and I am a wonderful practitioner."

"You travel all over the world, Kate," Hannah pointed out.

"Yes, and my agent and my publisher smooth the way for me. I don't have to ask for a thing, it's all done for me. Matthew is like all of you. He throws himself into life and lives every moment. He's a born hero, riding to the rescue, carrying out the wounded on his back. He needs someone willing to do the same. I'm a born observer. Maybe that's why I was given the ability to see into the shadows at times. A part of me is already there."

Hannah's blue eyes filled with tears. "Don't say that, Kate. Don't ever say that." She wrapped her arms around Kate and hugged her close, uncaring that a small amount of tea splashed on her. "I didn't know you felt that way. How could I not have known?"

Kate hugged her hard. "Honey, don't be upset for me. You don't understand. I'm not distressed about it. My world is books. It always has been. I love words. I love living in my imagination. I don't want to go climb a mountain. I love to study how it's done. I love to talk to people who do it, but I don't want the experience of it, the reality of it. My imagination provides a wonderful adventure without the risk or the discomfort."

"Katie," Abbey protested.

"It's the truth. I've always been attracted to Matthew Granite, but I'm far too practical to make the mistake of believing anything could ever work between us. He runs wild. I remember him being right in the middle of every rough play in football both in high school and in college. He's done so many crazy things, from serving as a Ranger to skydiving for the fun of it." She shuddered. "I don't even scuba dive. He goes white-water rafting and rock climbing for relaxation. I read a good book. We aren't in the least compatible, but I can still think he's hot."

"Are you certain you want to spend time with him?" Abbey asked.

Kate shrugged. "What I want to do is to take a look at the

mosaic and see if I can make out the shadows in the earth the way Hannah did."

"Maybe all three of us can figure out what is going on," Hannah agreed. She followed Kate to the entryway, glancing over her shoulder at Abigail. "Doesn't Joley sound beautiful? She sent us her Christmas CD. She said she might be able to make it home for Christmas."

"I hope so," Abbey said. "Did Elle or Libby call?"

"Libby is in South America," Hannah said.

"I thought you said she was in the Congo," Kate interrupted.

Hannah laughed. "She was in the Congo, but they called her to South America. She phoned right after the quake. Some small tribe in the rain forest has some puzzling disease and they asked Libby to fly there immediately to help and of course she did. She said it will be difficult, but no matter what, she's coming home for Christmas. I think she needs to be with us. She sounded tired. Really tired. I told her we would get together and see if we could send her some energy, but she said no. She told me to conserve our strength and be very careful," Hannah reported.

Abbey and Kate stopped walking abruptly. "Are you certain Libby doesn't need us, Hannah?" Kate asked. "You know what can happen to her. She heals people in the worst of circumstances, and it thoroughly depletes her energy. Traveling those distances on top of it with little sleep won't help."

"She said no," Hannah reiterated. "I heard the weariness in her voice. She obviously needs to come home and regroup and rest, but I didn't feel as if she was in a dangerous state." She knelt on the floor at the foot of the mosaic her grandmother and her grandmother's sisters had worked so hard to make.

Relief swept through Kate. Libby always drove herself too hard, and her health suffered dramatically for it. Libby was too small, too slender, a fragile woman who pushed herself for others. Libby worked for the Centers for Disease Control and traveled all over the globe. "We'll have to watch her," Kate said softly, musing aloud.

It was one of the best-loved talents of the sisters, to be able to stay in communication with one another no matter how far apart they were physically. They could "see" one another and send energy back and forth when it was needed. Kate knelt beside Hannah in the entryway.

Kate always felt a sense of awe when she looked at the artwork on the floor. The mosaic always seemed to her to be alive with energy. Anyone looking into the mosaic felt as if they were falling into another world. The deep blue of the sea was really the ocean in the sky. Stars burst and flared into life. The moon was a shining ball of silver. Kate bent close to the mosaic to examine the greens, browns, and grays that made up mother earth.

Only Joley's voice poured into the room, then melted away on the last notes to leave the room entirely silent. The three sisters linked hands. Small bursts of electricity arced from one to the other. In the dimly lit room the energy appeared as a jagged whip of lightning dancing between the three women. Power filled the room, energy enough to move the drapes at the windows so that the material swayed and bowed.

Kate kept her eyes fixed on the darker earth tones. Something moved, down close to the edge of the mosaic, in the deeper rocks. It moved slowly, a blackened shadow, slipping from one dark area to the next. It had a serpentine, cunning way about it, shifting from the edges up toward the surface as if trying to break through. Kate let her breath out slowly, inhaled deeply to fill her lungs, and let her body go. It was the only way to walk in the shadow world that was invisible to most human eyes.

She felt the malevolence immediately, a twisted sneakiness, shrewd and determined, a being honed by rage and fueled by the need for revenge. The turmoil was overwhelming, spinning and boiling with heat and anger. It crept closer to her, awareness of her presence giving it a kind of malicious glee. She held herself still, trying to discern the dark force in the deeper shadows, but it blended too well.

"Kate!" Hannah shook her hard, catching her by the shoulders and rocking her until her head lolled back on her neck.

Abbey yanked Kate away from the mosaic and into her own body. There was a long silence while they clung to one another, breathing heavily, close to tears. The shrill ringing of the phone startled them.

"Sarah," they said simultaneously, and broke into relieved laughter.

Abbey jumped up to answer the phone. "I'm telling Sarah on you," she warned Kate, "and you're going to be in so much trouble!"

Kate gripped Hannah's hand, trying to smile at Abbey's dire prediction. "Did you feel it, Hannah?" she whispered. "Did you feel it coming after me?"

"You can't go into that world again, Kate. Not with that thing there. I couldn't read what it was, but you have to stay away from it." Hannah held Kate even tighter. "I know what it's like to be afraid all the time, Katie. I can't function in a crowd because the energy of so many people drains me. Their emotions bombard me until I can't think or breathe. You all protect me, you always have. I wish we'd done the same for you."

Kate smiled and leaned over to kiss Hannah's cheek. "I accepted my limitations a long time ago, Hannah, and I've never regretted my choice of lifestyles. I control my environment, and it works for me. I didn't have the need to do all the things you wanted to do with your life. My world is carefully built and has large walls to protect me. You're far more open to the assault. I'll be careful, Hannah. I'm not a risk taker. You don't have to worry that I'll try to find the answers without the rest of you."

"Katie!" Abbey called out. "Sarah has a few things she wants to talk to you about." She held out the phone.

Kate hugged Hannah again. "It will be all right, I promise you, honey. It's Christmas. Most everyone is coming home, and we'll have the best time ever, just like we always do when we're together."

3

A chill, colder still than the air they will feel,
As I rejoice in release as I slip past the seal

MATT STOOD BESIDE the enormous Douglas fir tree decorated with hundreds of ornaments and colorful lights. The tall
tree grew in the yard up near the cliffs in front of the house. It
was one of the most beautiful sights he'd ever seen, but it paled
in comparison to Kate. She stood on her porch, a snowglobe
in her hands, smiling at him. Her eyes were as green as the sea,
and her long, thick hair was twisted into some kind of intricate knot that made him want to pull out every pin so he
could watch it tumble free.

He walked up the porch steps and held out his hand.
"Where in the world did you get that snowglobe? The scene
inside looks exactly like your house and this Christmas tree."

She put the globe in his hands. Two of her sisters were
standing on the porch with her, watching him with serious expressions on their faces. He had been so busy staring at Kate
he hadn't even noticed them. His hands closed over the heavy
globe, his fingers brushing Kate's. A tingle of electricity
sparked its way up his arm. Almost at once the snowglobe
grew warm in his hands. "Afternoon, ladies."

"Hi, Matt," Hannah greeted. Abbey nodded to him.

Although he'd made every effort to clean up after work,
scrubbing his hands for a good half hour to get the dirt out
from under his fingernails, he noticed with dismay that he
hadn't been successful. His nails seemed to be spotlighted from

the strange glow coming from inside the glass of the globe. The lights of the tree blazed unexpectedly inside the glass, while an eerie white fog began to swirl. Fascinated, he held the globe at every angle, trying to see how he had turned it on, but he couldn't find a battery or a switch anywhere. Peering closer he noticed a strange dark shadow taking shape at the base of the tree and creeping up the path toward the steps of the house. His body reacted, going on alert as he watched the shadow move stealthily.

"This thing is spooky." He handed the snowglobe to Hannah and took Kate's elbow in a deliberate, proprietary action. Staking his claim. Declaring his intentions. His fingers settled around her slender arm, and his heart actually jumped in his chest. She was wearing some lacy white shirt that clung to the shape of her rounded breasts and left her lower arms bare. The pad of his thumb slid over her petal-soft skin just to feel the texture. She shivered, and he moved his body closer to block the breeze coming in off the ocean. They said good-bye to her sisters and headed for his car.

Kate cleared her throat. "I appreciate your coming to pick me up, Matthew. I could have met you there."

"That's silly, Kate, since we're both going to the same place, and you're on my way. I thought we might discuss the plans for the renovation over dinner when we're finished inspecting the mill." He pulled open the door to his Mustang convertible. The top was securely up. "What were you doing with the globe?"

She smiled up at him and just that easily took his breath away. "We're still putting out our decorations. Hannah just brought the globe down from the attic and was cleaning the glass. It's a Christmas tradition in our family to wish on it."

"What was that strange dark shadow moving in the globe?"

Kate abruptly turned back toward the house. Matt was standing close to her, holding the door open to the Mustang, and she bumped his chest with her nose. For a second she stood there with her eyes closed, then she inhaled deeply. He felt that breath right through his skin, all the way down to his bones. The tips of her breasts brushed his rib cage, sending fire racing through his bloodstream and pooling into a thick heat low in his belly. She smelled of cinnamon and spice. He wanted to pull her into his arms and kiss her right there. Right in front of her sisters.

"Matthew." For the first time that he could remember, Kate sounded breathless. "What are you doing?"

He realized his arms were around her. He was holding her captive against him, and his body was growing hard and making urgent demands. He cursed silently and let her go, turning away from her. "I thought you were getting into the car." His voice was rough, even to his own ears. He had never wanted a woman the way he wanted Kate. He didn't feel gentle when he wanted to be gentle. He didn't feel nice and charming when it was usually so easy for him to be charming. He felt edgy and restless and achy as hell. He had a mad desire to scoop her up and lock her in his vehicle, a primitive, out-of-character urge when she looked on the verge of flight.

"You really saw a shadow in the globe?" she asked. "What was it doing?"

It was the last thing he expected her to say, and it sent a chill skittering down his spine. "I couldn't tell what it was. The dark shadow went from the base of the tree up the path toward the porch of the house. It is your house in the globe, isn't it? There's fog or mist instead of snowflakes swirling around. It gives the globe a very eerie effect."

Kate glanced back at her sisters. Hannah set the snowglobe very carefully on the wide banister and stepped away from it. Inside the glass, heavy fog swirled. The lights from the tiny Christmas tree glowed a strange orange and red through the mist, almost as if on fire. Matt watched Kate's sister closely. He had lived in Sea Haven all of his life. He had heard strange things about the Drake sisters. Up close to them, he *felt* power and energy crackling in the air, and it emanated from them. The power filled the space around them until he breathed it. Hannah lifted her arms, and the wind swept in from the sea. With it came soft voices, whose words were impossible to distinguish, but the chant was melodious and in harmony with the things of the earth. The strange light in the snowglobe faded and diminished until it was a soft, faint glow. The voices on the wind continued until the lights behind the glass flickered and vanished, leaving the globe a perfectly ordinary Christmas ornament.

The wind swirled cool air around them. Matt tasted the salt from the sea. He looked down at his fingers curled around Kate's arm. He had pulled her protectively to him without thought or reason. He knew he should release her, but he couldn't let go. Her slender body trembled, with power or with fear, Matt wasn't certain which, but it didn't matter to him.

Kate looked up at him. "I can't explain what just happened with the snowglobe."

"I'm not asking for an explanation. I just want you to get in my car."

She smiled up at him. "Thank you, Matthew. I really appreciate it." She relaxed visibly and allowed him to help her into the warm leather seats.

Kate felt very small beside Matt. Inside the car, he appeared enormous and powerful. His shoulders were wide enough to brush against her in the confines of the Mustang. When she inhaled, she took the masculine scent of him deep into her lungs. For a moment she felt dizzy. It made her want to laugh aloud at the thought. Kate Drake dizzy from the scent of a man. None of her sisters would believe it. The car handled the tight turns along the coastal highway with precision and ease, flowing around the corners so that she relaxed a little. Being around Matt always made her feel safe. She didn't know why, but she no longer questioned it.

He glanced over at her. "Does it bother you, the way people are always talking about your family?"

"They talk in a nice way," Kate pointed out.

"I know they do. You're the town's treasures, but does it bother you?"

Kate smiled at him. "Only you would ask me that question." She sighed. "It shouldn't bother me. We are different. We can't exactly hide it, and of course people are going to talk about our strange ways. We grew up here, so everyone knows us and to some extent they protect us from outsiders, but yes, it does bother me that people are always so aware of us when we're around." She'd never voiced that aloud to anyone, not even her sisters.

"I miss you when you're gallivanting around the world, Kate. I'm glad you've decided to come home."

Her smile widened. "You're such a flirt, Matthew, even with me, and I've known you all of my life. You haven't calmed down much since your wild college days. When I was in high school, all the girls said you were legendary at Stanford."

"Well, I wasn't. I should have gone to a college far away from here instead of only a couple of hours. It might have cut down on the talk. And I don't flirt," he said firmly. He wanted to park the car and just look at her. Touch her soft skin and kiss her for hours. The moment the thoughts crept into his head his body hardened into a dull, painful ache. He couldn't get near her without it happening. He was a grown man, and his body responded to her as if he were an adolescent.

"Matthew, you flirt with everyone. And your reputation is terrible. If I wasn't already so talked about, I'd be worried."

"No one talks about me."

She laughed softly. "I can relate the story of you and Janice Carlton by heart, I've heard it so many times."

He groaned. "Is that still going around? That happened long ago. I was on leave, it must have been what? Six years ago? I did pick her up in the bar, she was drunk, Kate. I couldn't just leave her there."

"And how did her blouse get on the bushes outside the grocery store?"

Matt glanced sideways at her. "All right, I'll admit it was her blouse, but come on, Kate, I wasn't in high school. Give me a little credit for growing up. She was as drunk as a skunk and began peeling off her clothes the minute we were driving down the street. She threw her blouse out the window and would have thrown her bra but I told her I'd put her out on the sidewalk if she did. I took her straight home. And in case you want to know why my version was never told, I don't like talking about women who throw themselves at me when they're drunk. In spite of what you've heard, my mother raised me to be a gentleman. We may be a little rough around the edges, but the Granites have a code of honor."

The Mustang swung fluidly into the driveway leading to the old mill on the cliff above Sea Lion Cove. Matt drove straight up the dirt driveway to the long, wooden building and parked. He turned off the engine and slid his arm along the back of her seat. The ocean boomed below the cliffs, a timeless rhythm that seemed to echo the beat of his heart. "Most of the stories about me aren't true, Kate."

Kate stared straight ahead at the old building. Much of the wood was pitted from sea salt. The paint had long since worn away from the steady assault of the wind. She loved the look of the mill, the way it fit there on the cliff, a part of the past she wanted to bring with her into the future. She took a deep breath, composed herself, and turned to take Matt in.

Up close, Matthew Granite was a giant of a man with rippling, defined muscles and a strong, stubborn jaw. His mouth was something she spent far too much time staring at and dreaming about, and the shape of it had managed to slip into her bestselling novels on several heroes. His eyes were amazing. They should have been gray but they were more silver, a startling color that made her heart do triple time. He had the kind of thick, dark hair that made her want to run her fingers in it, and he wore it longer than most men. Kate felt a bit faint looking at his heavily muscled chest, then up into his glinting silver eyes. "Well, darn it, Matthew, all this time I thought I was in the presence of greatness." She managed to conjure up a lighthearted laugh. "It's not nice to destroy a woman's illusions."

He frowned. "I didn't say I *wasn't* the bad boy of Sea Haven."

"I thought Jonas Harrington was the bad boy of Sea Haven."

Matt looked affronted. "I never come in second place." His hand came up, unexpectedly spanning her throat.

Kate was certain her heart skipped a beat. His palm was large, and his fingers wrapped easily around her neck, his thumb tipping her head up so she was forced to meet the sudden hunger blazing in his eyes. It was the last thing Kate expected to see, and his intensity shocked her. "Matthew." She breathed his name in a small protest. It wasn't a good idea. They weren't a good idea.

He simply lowered his head and took possession of her mouth. His kiss was anything but gentle. He dragged her close, a starving man devouring her with hot, urgent kisses. The breath slammed out of her lungs, and every nerve ending in her body screamed at her. Electricity crackled between them, arcing from Matt to Kate and back again. Fire raced over her skin, melting her insides. He took the lead, kissing her hungrily, hotly, his tongue dueling with hers, demanding a response she found herself giving.

Her arms crept around his neck, her body pressing close to the heat of his. She felt so much heat, so much magic she couldn't think straight.

The blare of a horn made Kate jump away from him. Matt cursed and glanced at the highway in time to see his brothers waving, hooting, and honking as they drove by. "Damned idiots," he said, but there was a wealth of affection in his voice impossible to miss.

Kate pressed a trembling hand to her swollen mouth. Her skin felt raw and burned from the dark shadow on his jaw. She didn't dare look in the mirror, but she knew she looked thoroughly kissed. "They saved us."

"They may have saved you, but I'm in dire straits here, woman." And dammit all, he was. What was it about this woman that made him lose control whenever he was around her? Was she really a witch? He was going to have a few things to say to his brothers when he got his hands on them. He wasn't looking forward to the ribbing he was going to get after being caught necking like a teenager with Kate Drake. It didn't help matters that he saw Jonas Harrington cruising by very slowly, obviously looking for them. Damn Danny and his radio. It would be all over Sea Haven if they weren't more careful, and the last thing he wanted was for Kate to run from him because of gossip.

He touched Kate's red face. Her soft skin was raw from his whiskers. "I should have shaved, Katie, I'm sorry. I wasn't planning on kissing you." So, okay, he wanted to kiss her. He'd hoped to kiss her. He'd actually gotten down on his knees briefly last night when no one was around and asked for a Christmas miracle, but she didn't need to know how badly he wanted her.

The way he said Katie turned her heart over, sending a million butterfly wings brushing at her stomach. "I don't mind."

He caught her face in his hands. "I mind. I need to be more careful with you." Abruptly he let her go and opened the door. It was the only safe thing to do when she looked so tempting. The chill from the sea rushed in to displace the heat of their bodies inside the car.

Kate didn't wait for him to come around and open her door. She was too shaken, too shocked by her reactions to him. It was so un–Kate-like of her. Kate the practical had just made a terrible mistake, and she couldn't take it back. She could still taste him, still had his scent clinging to her body, still felt a tremendous, edgy pressure, a need as elemental as hunger and thirst. She stood in the wind and lifted her face, hoping her skin would cool and that the raging need that was always inside of her would once again find rest.

Matt took her hand and led her up the broken and uneven path to the building. She didn't resist or pull away.

"The structure's sound," she assured him as she unlocked the door. "I want to be able to incorporate as much of the original building as possible when I expand. I was thinking decks outside with some protection against the wind for the sunnier days, and indoors, a large area with chairs and small tables for reading and drinking coffee or chocolate or whatever. There's a large stone fireplace in what must have been an office, and I'd like to keep that too if possible."

Kate covered her anxiety with talk, pointing out the rustic features she wanted to save and as many of the problem areas as she knew about. She was very aware of Matt's hand holding hers securely. Twice she tried to casually disengage, but he tugged her across the room to examine a rotted section of wood near the foundation.

"Where do the stairs lead?" He opened the sagging door and peered down into the dark interior. The stairs appeared to be very steep and halfway down he was certain the walls were dirt. "Is there a light?"

"Of sorts," Kate said. "It's over the second stair down. I can't reach the chain."

"Why wouldn't it be up here?" He pulled the chain gingerly, half-expecting the light to explode. It came on, but it was a dim yellow and made a strange humming sound. "What is that?"

"I don't know, but the fire marshal assured me it was safe in here." She smiled at him. "Isn't one of your brothers an electrician?"

"It will be a while before we need him," Matt said, starting down the stairs. The staircase was solid enough, but he didn't like the look of the wall. Several cracks spread out from the center of the wall in all directions like spiderwebs. He glanced at Kate, his eyebrow raised.

She shook her head. "The earthquake must have damaged it. It wasn't like that when I came down here with the Realtor. I actually came down twice just to make certain the entire place wasn't going to sink into the ocean. I know it's in bad shape, but it's such a perfect location. If I have to, I can pull down the mill and start from scratch. If you think that's the best thing to do, I'll take your advice, but I really want to save as much of the original building as possible."

"It's going to cost more money than it might be worth, Kate," he warned.

Kate shivered as they went down the stairs to the dimly lit basement. It was far colder than she remembered. Always sensitive to energy, she felt an icy malevolence that hadn't been there before. She looked around cautiously, moving closer to Matt for protection. The atmosphere vibrated with unrestrained malicious amusement. "Matthew, let's leave." She tugged at his arm.

He looked down at her quickly. "What is it, Katie?" There was a caress to his voice, one that warmed her in spite of the icy chill in the basement. "You can wait upstairs while I look around." He felt her shiver and took the jacket she was holding from her to help her into it. "It won't take me very long." He pulled the edges of the jacket together and buttoned it up, his fingers lingering on the lapels, just holding her there, close to him.

Kate shook her head. "It feels unhealthy down here. I don't want to leave you alone. Matthew," she hesitated, searching for the right words. "This doesn't feel right to me, not the way it did before."

His silver eyes moved over her face. He suddenly winked, a quick, sexy gesture that sent her heart thudding. "I'll make it quick, I promise."

Kate trailed after him, reluctant to be too far from him in the gloomy basement. It was long and wide and had a dirt floor. "I think this was used as the smugglers' storehouse. There's a stairway leading to the cove through a narrow tunnel. Part of the tunnel collapsed some years ago, but I read in my grandmother's diary that the mill was used to store supplies and weapons and spices coming in off the boats." She pressed her lips together, determined not to distract him as he studied the walls and the floor of the basement.

"What's this?" Matt halted next to a strange covering in the dirt. It was at least two inches thick and looked almost like the lid of a coffin, except it was oval in shape. The surface was rough and covered with symbols, which were impossible to read with the dirt and grime over them. Running straight through the middle of the lid was a large crack.

Kate frowned. "I didn't notice it before. It must have been covered by the dirt. Could the earthquake have shifted that much dirt?" She moved closer to it reluctantly. The icy cold air was coming from the deep crack. "I don't like this, Matthew."

"It isn't a grave, Kate," he pointed out, crouching beside it and brushing at the dirt along the edges. "It's more like a seal of some kind."

She hunkered down beside him. A blast of cold air touched her palm as she passed it above the crumbling rock. She brushed the dirt away from the symbols, trying to decipher the old hieroglyphics. The language was an ancient one, but it was all too familiar to her. Her ancestors, generations of powerful witches, had used such symbols to communicate privately. Her mother had urged them to learn the language, and Kate knew a few of the symbols, but not all. "It says something about rage. The symbols are chipped and worn away. I can make out the words, 'sealed until the day one is born'—" She broke off in frustration, leaning closer to try to figure out the meaning of the words.

"Where did you learn those symbols? Are they Egyptian?" Matt asked.

Kate shook her head. "No, it's a family thing. We were all supposed to have learned. Do you think this is a well of some kind?"

Matt continued to dig around the edges of the thick lid. "It can't be a well, Kate. Maybe some kind of memorial?" He pushed at the heavy slab. It crumbled around the edges but slid slightly.

"No!" Kate caught Matt's arm, tugging hard. "We don't know what's inside. Something about this doesn't feel right to me. Can't you feel the malevolence pouring out of the crack?" She stumbled back, taking him with her, nearly sprawling on the ground so that he had to catch her as a noxious gas poured from the slit that had opened.

"It's just gas created from decomposed matter that's been trapped for a long time," Matt said, dragging her as far from the crevice as he could get them. He pushed her toward the stairs. "Sometimes the gases can make you sick or worse, Kate. Don't breathe it in." She looked pale, her eyes wide with horror. She stared at the lid without moving, one hand pressed to her mouth. Matt could see that her entire body was trembling.

At once he wrapped his arms around her and drew her close to him. He practically enveloped her entire body, yet she never looked away from the oddity in the basement, mesmerized by the yellow-black vapor streaming from the crack. "It's nothing, Kate, just a hole in the ground. It's probably a couple of hundred years old." He remained calm in order to reassure her, but all of his senses had gone on alert.

Matthew obviously couldn't feel the malicious triumph pouring out of the ground, a welling-up of victory, a coup of sorts. She couldn't identify it, had no idea what it was, but she was terrified they might have unleashed something dangerous. Horrified, she watched the dark, ugly vapor swirl around the room, then stream up the stairs toward freedom, leaving behind an icy cold that chilled her to her bones.

"Stop shaking, Kate. It's gas. It happens all the time in these old vents." Matt couldn't bear that she was so frightened. "We find pockets all over the place. You haven't gone into the tunnel, have you? That could have all sorts of gas pockets as well as cave-ins."

"Have you ever seen gas do that? Travel around the room?"

"We're getting some kind of wind off the ocean, Kate. Can't you feel the draft in here? It's very strong."

"I have to take a look at those symbols, Matthew. I think something was sealed beneath that lid, and the earthquake disturbed it." She knew she sounded utterly ridiculous. She probably appeared a crackpot to him, but she was certain she was right. Something had slid out of that vent, something not meant to inhabit the world.

Matt studied her serious face, the fear in her eyes. "Let me make certain it's safe, Kate." He gently set her aside and made his way across the uneven dirt floor to the crumbling rock lid.

"Be careful, Matthew." When he looked at her, she wished she'd kept her mouth shut. She was sounding more and more paranoid.

He sniffed the air cautiously. The odor was foul, but he could breathe easily without coughing. "I think it's safe enough, Kate. I'm not keeling over, and I don't feel faint. I don't know what the hell you think just happened, but if it has you so afraid, I'm going to believe it. Jonas says never to doubt any of you Drakes."

She was grateful that he was trying to understand, but she knew he couldn't. Kate ducked her head, avoiding his gaze, afraid to see the way he was looking at her. She sank down beside the lid and dusted lightly with her fingers, afraid of crumbling the old rock even more.

Matt waited silently as long as he could. There was the sound of the sea booming in the background. The echo of it pounded off the walls eerily. "Does it mean anything to you?" He tried to keep impatience from his voice when all he wanted to do was snatch Kate up and carry her out of the place.

Kate peered closer to decipher the words. Seven sisters. Seven Drake sisters. Her ancestors. They had bound something to earth, committed its spirit to the vent hole to protect something. She couldn't read it exactly as parts of the letters were smashed and worn away, but she was afraid it was the townspeople who needed to be protected. She could also make out something to do with Christmas and fire and one who would be born who could bring peace. Kate looked up at Matt. There was no way to hide the terror in her eyes, and she didn't bother to try. "I need to go home right now."

4

A wreath of holly meant to greet,
Looks much better tossed in the street.

Matt sat in his car with the heater running and his favorite CD playing low. Joley Drake's unique, sultry voice had
taken her up the charts fast. He loved this particular collection, usually finding it soothing, but it wasn't doing him any
good now. He gripped the steering wheel and stared up at the
blazing lights of the Christmas tree in front of the cliff house.
The fog was beginning to roll in off the sea, stretching white
fingers toward land and the house he was watching. There
were no electric lights in the windows, yet he could see the
flicker of candlelight and an occasional shadow as one of the
Drake sisters moved past the glass.

The passenger door jerked open, and Jonas Harrington slid
into the seat beside Matt, shutting the door against the cold.

"Dammit, Jonas, you scared the hell out of me!" Matt
snapped. He hadn't realized just how jumpy he was until Jonas
had pulled the door open.

"Sorry about that." Jonas sounded as pleasant as ever. Too
pleasant. Matt turned his head to look at his childhood friend.
"What are you doing out here? It's cold, and the fog's coming
in. You aren't stalking our Kate, are you?"

Matt studied his friend's face. He was smiling, looking ami-
cable, but his eyes were ice-cold. "Of course I'm stalking Kate.
Do you think I've lost my mind? That woman belongs with
me." He grinned to relieve the tension gathering between

them. "I just have to figure out how to convince her of that. What are you doing here? And why didn't I see the headlights of your car?" He glanced in the rearview mirror and noted Jonas had cruised silently up behind him.

"I ran without headlights, didn't want to scare you away. What happened tonight? Why are they all upset?" There was no obvious accusation in the voice, but Matt had been around Jonas his entire life, and he recognized the underlying note of suspicion.

"What the hell are you trying to say, Jonas? Spit it out and quit beating around the bush." Temper was beginning to flare. "I've had a hell of an evening, and you aren't helping."

Jonas shrugged. "I did just spit it out. They're upset. I can feel it. All of them, every single sister. Does it have something to do with you and Kate?"

"What kind of question is that? Hell, yes, I want Kate. And yes, I'd do just about anything to get her, but I sure wouldn't lay a finger on her if she didn't want me to, and I wouldn't ever hurt her. Is that what you want to know?"

Jonas nodded. "That's about what I was looking for. I'd hate to have to kick your ass, but if you hurt that girl, I'd have to do it."

"As if you could." Matt tapped his finger against the steering wheel, frowning while his temper settled. "What do you mean, you can feel they're all upset?"

"I've always been able to feel when something's wrong with the Drakes. And right now, something's very wrong." Jonas continued to look at him with cool, assessing eyes.

Matt shook his head. "It wasn't me, Jonas. Something weird happened at the old mill, and Kate was very distressed. She asked me to take her home, and I did." He raked his fingers through his hair, not once, but twice. "I didn't even have a chance to ask her out again. I was just sitting here, trying to figure out whether I should go up to the house and ask her what happened, or go back to the mill and try to figure it out."

"There they are!" Jonas muttered an ugly word beneath his

breath. "What the hell do they think they're doing going out in the middle of the night with the fog rolling in?"

Matt could just make out the three Drake sisters swirling dark, hooded cloaks around them as they hurried down the steps. The fog was heavy and thick, an invasion of white mist that hid the women effectively as they rushed down the worn pathway that wound down the hill toward the road. Matt leaped out of his car, losing sight of them in the curtain of fog. He was aware of Jonas swearing under his breath, keeping pace as they angled to cut off the Drakes before they could reach the highway.

Jonas beat him to the women, catching Hannah's arm and yanking her around to face him. "Are you out of your mind?"

Kate's expression went from startled to troubled when she caught sight of them. "Matthew, I thought you went home." She looked uneasily around her at the fog. "You shouldn't be out here. I don't think it's safe. And neither should you, Jonas."

Hannah glared at the sheriff. "Has anyone ever told you you have bad manners?"

"Has anyone ever turned you over their knee?" Jonas countered. "If you don't think it's safe out here, what are you doing running around in the dark?"

Kate indicated the heavy wall of fog. "It isn't like we're going to get very far in this stuff. We have an errand, Jonas, an important one."

"Then you should have called me," Jonas snapped impatiently. Hannah stirred as if to say something but Jonas's fingers tightened around her arm. "I'm really, really angry right now, Hannah. Don't make it worse."

"Jonas," Kate's voice was placating. "You don't understand."

"Then make me understand, Kate," he snarled.

Matt immediately stepped between Jonas and Kate. "I don't think you need to talk to her like that, Jonas. Let her explain."

Kate's fingers curled around Matt's arm. "Jonas worries about us, Matthew. We probably should have called him."

Matt didn't want her calling Jonas; he wanted her to call him when something was wrong. And something was obviously wrong. Before she could pull her hand away from his arm, he covered her fingers with his. "We're already here, Kate. Tell us what you need to do."

Her sea-green eyes moved over his face. He had the feeling she could see more deeply into him than most people, but it was always like that with Kate. He tightened his hold on her hand. "Kate. You trust Jonas. He can vouch for me."

Kate closed her eyes briefly. Matthew Granite was her dream man, and after he witnessed what really went on around the Drake sisters she wouldn't even be able to sustain the fantasy of a relationship with him. She sighed but she squared her shoulders. Some things were just more important than romantic dreams. She took a deep breath. "Something was unleashed today, something malevolent. We think." She looked at her sisters for courage before continuing. "We think the earthquake may have awakened it or at least provided it with the opportunity to rise. It was the shadow you saw in the globe, Matt, and my sisters and I saw in the mosaic. It's very real, and it feels dangerous to us." She stared up at him, clearly expecting him to laugh.

Matt kept his face completely expressionless. He knew the Drakes were different; some said they performed miracles, some said they were genuine witches. Sea Haven was a hotbed of gossip, and the Drake sisters were always at the forefront. But not Kate. Never Kate.

"So it felt dangerous to you, and the first thing you do is rush out into the night in the middle of one of the worst fogs we've ever had," Jonas snapped. "Dammit, Kate, Abbey and Hannah might rush headlong into danger, but you usually show some trace of sense." He hauled Hannah back against him when she tried to squirm away. "I'm not playing around with you, Hannah. Keep it up, and I'll lock you away for the night."

Hannah's beautiful face radiated fury, but instead of taking Jonas to task as Matt expected, she was gasping for breath.

Abbey leaped to her side. "Breathe, Hannah, very slow."

Hannah shook her head, fear filling her eyes. Abbey extracted a paper bag from her purse and handed it to her sister. "Breathe into this."

Looking alarmed, Jonas wrapped his arm around Hannah's waist to support her as she doubled over, clearly unable to breathe adequately. "What the hell is wrong with her? Should we get an ambulance?"

"Would you please stop swearing at her?" Abbey snapped. "Be very careful, Jonas, or I'll ask you questions you don't want to answer."

"Shut up, Abbey, don't you dare threaten me," Jonas growled back.

"Stop it, all of you, stop it," Kate pleaded.

Seeing the anxiety on Kate's face, Matt stepped closer to her and put his arm around her. Hannah breathed into the paper bag for a couple of minutes and lifted her head. She looked ready to cry. "Abbey, if you want to take Hannah back to the house, I'll go with Kate to do whatever it is you all think is so important." He made the offer before he could stop himself. Kate was shivering in the cold fog. She didn't need to be out on such a night. He wanted just to pick her up and take her home and lie down with her by the fireplace.

Jonas pushed back Hannah's wealth of blond hair. "Are you all right, baby doll?" His choice of words should have been insulting, but the gentle concern in his voice made them an endearment.

Hannah nodded but didn't look at any of them, still clearly fighting for air.

"Maybe that's a good idea, Hannah. I'll go with Matt and just look around a little, and you and Abbey pull out the diaries and see if you can find anything that might help us figure this out," Kate said. "Matthew, are you certain you don't mind? I want to walk around town and just get a feel for what's going on."

"I don't mind. Are you going to be warm enough?"

"Just how dangerous is this, Kate?" Jonas asked.

"I honestly don't know," she replied. "I wish I knew. We thought if we went out together, all of us might be able to pick something up, but I already feel it. I think I can track it."

Matt cleared his throat. "Track a shadow?" If they weren't all so serious, he would be thinking it was a Halloween prank. He glanced up at the house. The fog was a heavy shroud, almost obliterating the house. He could see the lights of the Christmas tree, but only as pale, orange-glowing haloes distorted by the blanket of grayish white. He went still. The fog was changing color, darkening from white to a charcoal gray. Just as the fog had done in the snowglobe when he'd picked it up to examine it.

"The fog is bad, Kate. I've never seen it like this," Jonas said. "Stay close to Matt. I'll take Hannah and Abbey back to the house."

Hannah stiffened and looked at Abbey. Abbey smiled. "We'll make it home fine, Jonas. It's just up the hill. We know the path."

"I'm coming with you, Abbey, so don't argue." Jonas turned resolutely toward the house. "Matt, if it feels wrong to you, or you think Kate's in any danger at all, get her back here and don't let her give you any nonsense."

Kate smiled at Jonas. "I never talk nonsense. You take care of my sisters because if anything happens to them . . ."

"I know, I've heard it all before." Jonas waved at her, and the fog swallowed them up, even muffling the sound of their footsteps on the path, leaving Kate alone with Matt.

She looked up at him. "You don't have to do this, you know. I'm capable of walking up and down the streets of Sea Haven."

Matthew stared down into her beautiful sea-green eyes. "But I'm not capable of leaving your side when there's even a hint of danger near you." He lowered his head slowly to hers, drawn as if by a magnet, expecting her to pull away, giving her plenty of time to think about it.

Kate watched his eyes change, go dark with desire, right before his mouth took possession of hers. It didn't matter that the air was cold, and the wind chilled them, their bodies produced a remarkable heat, their mouths fused with fire. He dragged her against his body, his muscular arms enveloping her, holding her as if she were the most precious person in the world to him. He was exquisitely rough, yet impossibly gentle, voraciously hungry, nearly devouring her mouth, yet so tender he brought tears to her eyes. She had no idea how he did it, but she wanted more.

"You're not good for me," she whispered against his mouth.

His tongue slid along the seam of her lips, teased her tongue into another brief, but heated tango. "I'm absolutely perfect for you." He tugged at her cape until her body was pressed tightly against his. "I was born to be with you, Kate. You're supposed to be some kind of a magical woman, filled with the second sight, yet you don't see what's right in front of you. Why is that?" He didn't give her the opportunity to debate, he just kissed her long and thoroughly.

Kate felt her insides melting, turning to a warm puddle and settling somewhere in her lower region as a frustrating and unrelenting ache. Her knees actually went weak. "I can't think straight when we're kissing, Matthew."

"That's a good thing, Kate, because neither can I," he answered, his lips drifting into the hollow of her neck and back up to find her ear.

Heat pulsed through her, but she forced herself to pull away from him. He wasn't for her. She knew that, and once he found out what she was really like, he'd know it too. She might seem courageous and strong, but when it came to losing him, she knew she'd be very fragile. Starting up with Matthew Granite was a decidedly ridiculous thing for her to do. "Matthew, really, I have to find this malevolent shadow and hopefully help it find some peace or get my sisters to help me seal it back up."

Matt silently cursed dark shadows and evil entities and every other thing that went bump in the night. She obviously believed they had let something harmful loose on the small town of Sea Haven. He was certain it was a pocket of gas; but if it meant walking around town with her at night, holding hands and kissing her every chance he got, well, hell, he was her man. He could do that. And he would even try to keep an open mind.

"Then let's go." He wrapped his arm around her. "I've got a flashlight in my car. This fog is really thick."

"We won't need a flashlight, Matthew. I have a couple of glow sticks. My sister Elle makes them. They work very well in the fog." She pulled several thin tubes from the inside pocket of her cape and handed him one. "Just shake it."

"I forgot about little Elle and her chemistry set. She blew up more missiles on the beach than any other kid at Sea Haven. Didn't she get a full scholarship to Columbia or MIT or some other very prestigious school? One very brave to take her on?"

Kate laughed, warmth spreading through her. "They were very brave, but fortunately they turned out a remarkable physicist able to do just about anything she wants to do. Elle is a genius and utterly fearless. She's not afraid to crawl around in caves looking at strange rock formations, and she's not afraid of taking apart a bomb when she's needed. Unlike me."

"What do you mean?" Matt tightened his fingers around hers.

"My sisters do incredible things and people expect it of us, but I wouldn't want you to think I'm capable of climbing mountains or jumping out of planes because you've heard of all of their exploits." She was feeling her way in the fog rather than following the glow stick. She lifted her face to the droplets of sea moisture, inhaling to try to catch the scent of something foul. "We have to cross the highway."

With the fog so thick there was virtually no traffic. Matt moved with her across the coastal highway and took the shortcut that led to the center of town. She was so serious all of a sudden, so distant from him, that he was actually beginning to believe she was on the trail of something evil. He could sense the stillness in her, the gathering of energy.

The survival instincts he'd honed during his years as a Ranger kicked in. His skin prickled as he went onto alert status. Adrenaline surged, and his senses grew keener. He felt the need for complete silence and wondered if he was beginning to believe in supernatural nonsense. Matt eased the glow stick inside his jacket without activating it. The fog muffled the sound of Kate's footsteps. He was aware of her breathing, of the eerie feel of the fog itself, of everything.

By mutual consent they were silent as they walked along the street. He became aware of a slight noise. A puffing. It was distant and hushed, barely audible in the murky blanket of mist. Matt found himself straining to listen. There was a rhythm to the sound, reminding him of a bull drawing air in and out of its lungs hard before a charge. Breathing. Someone was breathing, and the sound was moving, changing directions each time they changed directions.

Matt pressed his lips to her ear. "There's someone in the fog with us." He was certain someone was watching them, someone quite close.

Kate tipped her head back. "Something, not someone."

Kate turned toward the residential area. The town looked strange shrouded in the gray-white fog. Heavily decorated for Christmas, the multicolored lights on the stores and office buildings, the houses and trees gave off the peculiar glow of a fire in the strange vapor, giving the town a disturbing infernal appearance rather than a festive one. Matt wished he had brought a weapon with him. He was a good hand-to-hand fighter because he was a big man, strong, with quick reflexes and extensive training, but he had no idea what kind of adversary they faced.

Something hit him in the back, skittered down his jeans, and fell to the street. Matt whirled around to face the enemy and found nothing but fog.

"What is it?" Kate asked. Her voice was steady, but her hand, on the small of his back, was shaking.

Matt hunkered down to look at the object at his feet. "It's a

Christmas wreath, Kate. A damned Christmas wreath." He looked around carefully, trying to penetrate the fog and see what was moving in it. He could feel the presence now, real, not imagined. He could hear the strange, labored breathing, but he couldn't find the source.

As he stood, a second object came hurtling out of the fog to hit him in the chest. He heard the smash of glass and knew immediately that the wreath had been decorated with glass ornaments. "Let's get out of here, off the street at least," he said.

Kate was stubborn, shaking her head. "No, I have to face it here."

Matt pulled Kate to him, shielding her smaller body with his own as more wreaths came flying through the air, hurled with deadly accuracy at them from every direction. He wrapped his arms around her head, pressing her face against his chest. "It's kids," he muttered, brushing a kiss on top of her head to reassure her. "Always playing pranks; it's dangerous in this fog, not to mention destructive."

He hoped it was kids. It had to be an army of kids, tearing wreaths off the doors of the houses and throwing them at passersby as a prank. He heard no laughter, not even running footsteps. He heard nothing but the rough breathing. It seemed to come out of the fog itself. The nape of his neck prickled with unease.

"It isn't children playing a prank, Matt." Kate sounded close to tears. "It's much, much worse."

"Kate." He stroked a caress down the back of her head. Her hair was inside the hood of the cape, but his palm lingered anyway. "It isn't the first time a group of kids decided to play around, and it won't be the last."

The Christmas wreaths lay around them in a circle, some smashed or crushed and others in reasonably good shape. Kate lifted her face away from his chest and took a breath. "I can smell it, can't you?"

Matt inhaled deeply. He recognized the foul, noxious odor of the gases in the old mill. His heart jumped. "Dammit, Kate.

I'm beginning to believe you. Let's get the hell out of here before I decide I'm crazy."

She pulled free of his arms. "Is that what you think about me? That I'm crazy?"

"Of course not. This is all just so damned odd."

Her sea-green eyes moved over his face, a little moody, a little fey. "Well, brace yourself, it's going to get damned odder. Stay still."

The fog swirled around them, their faces, their feet, and bodies, spinning webs of charcoal gray matter. As at the cliff house, Matt got the impression of bony fingers, and this time they were trying to grab at Kate. Without thinking, he caught her up and started to run, the urge strong to get her away from the long gray tentacles, but the blanket of fog was thick around them.

Kate pressed her lips to his ear. "Stop! I have to try to stop it, Matthew; it's what I do. We can't outrun the fog, it's everywhere."

"Dammit, Kate, I don't like this." When she didn't respond, he reluctantly put her down and stayed very close to her, ready for action.

She turned in the direction of her home, her face serene, thoughtful, yet determined. She radiated beauty, an inner fire and strength. She whispered, a soft, melodic chant that became part of the night, of the air surrounding them. She wasn't speaking English but a language he didn't recognize. Her voice was soothing, tranquil, a soft invitation to a place of peace and harmony with the earth.

The fog itself breathed harder, in and out, a burst of air sounding like a predatory animal with teeth and claws. The mist seemed to vibrate with anger, roiling and spinning and growing darker. Gray fog whirled around the Christmas wreaths at Matt's feet, spinning fast enough to lift them into the air. Bright green wreaths withered and blackened as if all the life was being sucked out of them. The objects reminded Matt of the garlands at funerals rather than the cheery decorations for a holiday, and each of them seemed to be aimed straight toward Kate.

His breath caught in his throat, and his heart pounded. Kate looked small and fragile under the onslaught of the vicious gray-black vapor. He moved, a fluid glide that took him into the path of the blackened garlands so that they smashed into his larger frame. Kate ignored the fog and the wreaths, concentrating on something inside of herself. She stared toward the house on the cliffs and abruptly lifted her arms straight up into the air. The wind rushed in from the ocean with wild force. It carried the crisp scent of the sea, the taste and feel of the waves, and a spray of salt. It also carried voices, soft and melodious and very feminine. The wind swept through the fogbank, the voices swelling in strength, Kate's voice joining theirs until they were in perfect harmony, in total command.

The spinning Christmas wreaths dropped to the road. The fog receded, heading inland, blanketing the residential homes; but the wind was persistent, shifting directions and herding the fog back toward the ocean. Kate looked translucent, her skin pale and beaded with moisture, wisps of hair clinging to her face, but she didn't falter. Her voice brought a sense of peace, of tranquillity, of something beautiful and satisfying. It filled Matt with longing for a home and a family of his own. It filled him with a deep sense of pride and respect for Kate Drake.

He watched the fog reluctantly retreat until it was far out over the ocean, dissipated by the force of the wind. There was a silence left behind in the vacuum of the tempest. Kate dropped her arms as if they were leaden. She staggered. He leaped forward to catch her before she collapsed, swinging her into his arms and cradling her against his chest.

"It's growing in strength. I couldn't have sent it away if my sisters hadn't helped." Kate looked up at him with frightened eyes.

Matt kissed her. It was the only thing he could think to do. She seemed weightless in his arms. He kissed her eyes and the tip of her nose and settled his mouth, feather-light, over hers. "It's all right now, Kate. Rest. You sent it away. Tell me what you need." He could see that every drop of her strength had been used up in fighting the unseen enemy in the fog. She'd made a believer out of him. He was a man of action, having spent several years in the service training to protect his countrymen, yet there had been nothing he could do to stop the evil shadow in the mist. "What is it?"

She rubbed her face tiredly against his jacket. "I don't know, Matthew, I honestly don't know."

"How did you know what to say to it? What language it would understand?"

"I didn't know. I was using a healing chant my family has passed down from generation to generation. I was attempting to heal its spirit."

He stared at her, trying not to look shocked. The dark shadow seemed beyond any sort of redemption to him, something dark and dangerous, looking for a chance to strike out at anything or anyone around it.

Kate looked at the wreaths strewn all over the road. "Strange that he would choose to attack us with the wreaths."

"Strange that it could use them at all. Do you think it's a he?"

She shrugged. "It felt male to me."

The adrenaline was beginning to subside, but he continued to eye the cliffs warily. "I'm never going to look at fog again in the same way."

"A wreath is a continuous circle, Matthew, and it symbolizes real love, unconditional, true affection that never ceases." Her voice was thoughtful.

"I didn't feel love flowing out of the fog," he answered. He began walking back in the direction of her house, Kate in his arms.

"But he tore the Christmas wreaths off every door on the street and threw them."

"At *us*," he said grimly. "I'm used to looking my enemy in the eye, Katie, fighting him with weapons or my bare hands. I couldn't exactly grab the fog and throttle it, although I wanted to."

"Put me down, Matthew, I'm too heavy for you to carry all that way."

"I was a Ranger for ten years, Katie, I think I can pack your weight with no problem."

She wasn't going to argue, she was just too drained. "Ten years. That's right, you joined right out of college. I've been wandering around so much, and I knew you didn't live here, but your family always made it seem as if you were here."

"I spent my leave here, every chance I could. I picked up my life here again immediately after I got out of the service because the family business was waiting for me. My father and brothers kept me a part of it, even though they did all the work."

"Why did you join the Rangers, Matthew? As soon as I heard, I researched what they were all about. It was very—" she hesitated, searching for the right word—"intense. And frightening. Why would you want to do something like that?"

"I've always needed to push myself to find out my limits. And I believe in my country, so it seemed a perfect fit for me. The Rangers embody everything I believe in. Move farther and faster and fight harder than any other soldier. Never surrender, never leave a fallen comrade, survive and carry out the mission under any conditions."

Kate sighed heavily and turned her face into his shoulder, hiding her expression from him. Something about that sigh gave Matt a sick feeling in the pit of his stomach. He wanted to ask her about it, but by the time he reached the path leading to the house, Kate was asleep.

5

A town dreams of sweet thoughts while nestled in bed,
Until nightmares of me begin to dance in their heads.

"KATE. KATIE. WAKE up, hon." The soft voice beckoned Kate from layers of sleep. "You need to eat now, wake up."

Kate opened her eyes and stretched, blinking drowsily up at her sister. "Sarah. What are you doing here?" She pushed at the heavy fall of hair tumbling around her face. She always braided her hair before she went to bed, yet it was everywhere. She turned her head and went still. Matthew Granite was sprawled in a chair beside her bed, his silver gaze trained intently on her face. Her stomach did a funny little flip.

A slow smile softened his tough features, lit his gray eyes, and stole her heart. "You're finally awake. I was getting worried."

"You slept in the chair?" Kate couldn't imagine his large body finding a relaxing position in her bedroom chair.

"Well, I did want to share your bed, but I was worried about your sisters giving me the evil eye." His smile widened into a teasing grin. "Jonas slunk out of here a couple of hours ago afraid even to drink a cup of coffee. He warned me one of you might slip an eye of newt into my coffee, so I thought it best to stay in everyone's good graces."

"You like coffee that much, do you? Enough to stay in our good graces?" She couldn't stop looking at him. There was a blue-black shadow along his jaw, and his clothes were rumpled, but it didn't make him any less attractive to her. "Just so I'm not the one slipping the eye of newt to you, why are you sleeping in my room?" She glared at Sarah rather than at Matt.

Sarah held her hands up, palm out. "We all tried to get him to leave last night, Kate, but he wouldn't go. Granite might be his last name, but it's also what he's made of. No one could budge him. Jonas tried scaring him off, but that didn't work either."

Kate tried not to be pleased. She tried to frown at Matt, to pretend displeasure, but there was no way she could carry it off, so she gave up. He just winked at her anyway, looking sexier than ever with the dark stubble shadowing his jaw.

Sarah sat on the edge of the bed. "I hate interrupting, but you have to eat. You expended far too much energy last night. Even Joley called and was feeling drained." She waved a hand toward the drapes, and, to Matt's astonishment, the curtain slid open to allow the morning light to pour in. "I know you don't feel hungry, you never do afterward, but you have to eat for all of us."

Neither Kate nor Sarah seemed to think anything was unusual. Matt blinked several times to test his eyesight.

"How's Hannah?" Kate sat up, thankful she was still wearing her clothes. Matt and her sisters must have removed her cape and her shoes and socks before putting her in her bed, but at least she was safely clad in her slacks and blouse. "I couldn't believe with all of us working on her, she still had an attack. That's the first time I can remember that our joining together failed her."

Sarah glanced at Matt and hesitated. He raised his hands. "If you need to be alone with Kate, I'll go on down to the kitchen and see what kind of trouble I can get into." He stretched out his hand to Kate, resting it palm down on the bed.

"It's just that Hannah is such a private person, Matthew." Kate placed her hand over his. "She was embarrassed that it happened in front of you and Jonas. Especially Jonas."

"It? You mean her asthma attack?" He turned his hand to circle hers with his fingers, knowing she was trusting him with something private. "It was an asthma attack, wasn't it?"

"Not exactly." Kate sighed. "I wish Jonas would let up on her a little bit."

"She seems to be able to dish it right back to him." Matt leaned over to brush strands of hair from her face. "I don't quite get your relationship with Jonas, but I served with him in the Rangers. Jonas, me, and Jackson Deveau. Jonas is a good man."

"Jackson Deveau is the deputy who scares the hell out of everyone," Sarah informed Kate when she frowned. "You must have seen him a few times. He doesn't ever say much, but he looks lethal. He came to Sea Haven with Jonas when he returned from the Army."

"Jackson's a good man too," Matt said.

Kate hadn't met the deputy because she hadn't been back long, and she tended to wrap herself up in the cocoon of her own world. "I take it Jackson isn't from here originally."

"No, but he often came to Sea Haven on leave with us. He had no family and nowhere else to go when he left the service, so we asked him to come back with us. This town is friendly and tolerant, and Jackson needs tolerance. He's family to us. As for Jonas, you have to understand him. I saw him go in under heavy fire to drag a wounded man out of a battle zone. He carried that man for miles on his back. And Jackson . . ." He broke off, shaking his head. "I know Jonas watches over you all."

"Like a hawk," Sarah interjected dryly.

Matt shrugged. "Maybe it's because he really cares about all of you."

"Don't worry about our relationship with Jonas," Kate said. "We all love him dearly, even when we want to conjure up a spell to turn him into a toad."

Matt cleared his throat, rubbed the bridge of his nose, and sat back in his chair. "Can you really do that?"

Kate exchanged a mischievous grin with Sarah. "You never know about the Drake sisters. Really, Matthew, Jonas is intertwined deeply with our family. He always seems to know when something is wrong. He's sensitive to things not seen with the human eye."

Sarah leaned toward Matt. "You felt it last night, didn't you, when you were in the fog with Kate, and we joined with her? You knew something was wrong."

Matt sighed. "I don't know what happened last night, but I sure as hell don't want Kate facing anything like that again." His gray eyes smoldered with something dangerous as he looked at Kate. "I didn't like the way the fog seemed to be attacking you."

Sarah gasped. "What do you mean attacking her?"

"Nothing came at me," Kate denied hastily. "Really, Sarah, it was just throwing Christmas decorations around and Matthew was actually hit a few times. I was never touched."

Sarah looked at Matt steadily. "Why did you think it was after Kate?"

"I stepped in front of her to protect her. The wreaths were thrown, but not very hard in the beginning, yet when Katie began to talk to it, whatever it is, the Christmas wreaths were thrown much more forcefully and with greater accuracy."

"Were you hurt?" Kate looked suddenly anxious, coming up on her knees on the bed to look at him. "Libby's the best at healing, but Sarah. . . ."

"I'm fine," Matt said, but wished he didn't have to admit it. She looked incredibly beautiful leaning toward him with her hair tousled and her eyes enormous with concern for him.

"Kate—" Abbey stuck her head in the room—"Gina over at the preschool says something's wrong, and she needs you. I could hear the children crying in the background. I told her you weren't well, but she said it was an emergency. She said she needed your help. I'll go if I absolutely have to go."

Abbey was clearly apprehensive about going in Kate's place. Matt looked at Sarah. "What does Kate have to do with the preschool?"

"Haven't you noticed Kate has a gift for calming people with her voice? She's able to bring peace to even the most distressed person or situation," Sarah answered.

"Is that what your lives are like? People need you, and it doesn't matter if you're tired or not, you just go to them."

"We were born with certain gifts, Matt," Kate said. "We've always known we were meant to serve others. Yes, it isn't always easy, and all of us have to have ways of protecting ourselves but when we can help, we have to go."

"How do they know to call you?"

Sarah smiled. "You were older than us, Matthew, ahead of us in school, so you really weren't around when our talents began to develop. I'm sure you've heard the rumors, but you didn't witness what we could do the way other people in town did. Jonas has always connected with us in some way, so it was easy enough for him to believe."

"Kate?" Abbey prompted.

"I'll go. Give me a few minutes to shower and have a cup of tea."

Matt followed her to the bathroom door. "I don't like this, Kate. You look fragile to me. I think Sarah's right. You need to stay home."

Sarah's eyebrow shot up. "Did I say that?"

Kate rubbed a caress along Matt's stubbly jaw right in front of her sisters, then closed the bathroom door on his startled expression. When he turned around, Sarah and Abbey were grinning at him. "She doesn't listen, does she?" he asked.

"Not very well," Sarah agreed. "Kate may be quiet about it, but she goes her own way and does what she thinks is right."

"Do you have another bathroom so I can clean up really fast?"

Sarah grinned at him. "I even have an extra toothbrush. You've got that look in your eye when you look at her."

He followed her down the hall. "What look?"

"You look at her like you can't wait to kiss her," Sarah said. "A toothbrush is definitely in order."

"Does she have something against the Rangers?" Matt asked, remembering the small sigh from the night before. It had haunted him most of the night.

Sarah pushed open a door to a powder blue bathroom. "Of course not. Why would you think that?"

"No reason. Thanks, Sarah." Matt didn't want to think

about that strange little sigh of Kate's. She wasn't the type of woman to react that way unless she had a reason. He'd ask her about it later. He hurried through his shower wanting to get back to her.

Kate was still in the bathroom when he returned to her room. He rested his palm on the door, the exact level as her head. "Come out of there, Katie, you're beautiful enough without working at it."

From behind the door she laughed. "How do you know? You took a terrible chance staying. You could have woken up and my mask could have slipped off in the middle of the night."

"I didn't go to sleep. I watched over you."

There was a small shocked silence. Kate jerked the door open and stared up at him. "You must be exhausted. Go home and go to bed."

"I'd rather go with you." He reached out and pulled her to him. Her body fit perfectly against his, as if made to be there.

"Matthew." There was hesitation in Kate's voice.

He kissed her. He didn't want her to voice her reservations. Kissing her was a much better and far more enjoyable idea. It was magic, if there was such a thing, and he was beginning to believe there was. He meant for it to be a brief, good morning kiss, a gentle shut-up-and-just-kiss-me kiss, but she caught fire, or he did, and they both just went up in flames. He wanted more than to kiss her, he wanted to touch her, to claim her soft body, to feel her moving beneath him, her hands clinging . . .

"Stop!"

Matt and Kate drew apart, their hearts racing, and blinked at each other, then looked around in surprise to see Sarah, Hannah, and Abbey in the doorway glaring at them.

"Kate," Sarah said, taking a deep breath. "You know we're all connected in some way. You can't be in such close proximity to us and carry on like that. We're all in overdrive, thank you very much."

Unrepentant, Matt grinned at them as he pulled Kate tight against him. "Sorry about that. We're off to see some preschoolers." Kate hid her face in his shoulder, trying not to laugh. He did the gentlemanly thing and got her out of there quickly, waving at Damon, Sarah's fiancé, as they hurried past him.

"The man should thank us," he whispered, and pretended to wince when Kate smacked his arm.

Kate stared out the window of the Mustang at the white-capped ocean as they drove along the highway toward the exit to the street where the preschool was located. "The fogbank is very thick out over the ocean," she said, a note of apprehension in her voice. "See how dark it is, more gray than white, and it seems to be churning." She turned her gaze on Matt. "I should have been more careful. Somewhere in the diaries there has to be something about this strange phenomenon."

"What diaries? You've mentioned the diaries before. How can they help?"

"My family keeps a history, books handed down generation to generation. Somewhere this event had to be recorded. The problem is, all of us were supposed to learn the earlier languages used, but we gave it a halfhearted attempt. All of us know a little, but Elle really can read it. We have to decipher the books."

Matt turned the car onto the exit. "You think this thing is coming back."

"I know it is. Can't you feel it on the wind?"

He could only feel how close he was to her. How just out of his reach she always seemed to be. Matt parked the car in the lot at the preschool, and they sat for a moment, absorbing the unnatural silence. There were no children playing in the small yard.

Kate squared her shoulders. "Do you want to wait out here?"

For an answer, he got out of the car and went around to open her door. He wasn't about to miss his opportunity to see more clearly what Kate's life was all about.

Gina Farley greeted them with obvious relief as they entered. Many of the children were sobbing and sniffling as if they'd been crying a long time. Some of the children stared silently at Kate and Matt with large, frightened eyes. Others hid their faces. In the room were several adults, many of whom Matt recognized and nodded to.

There was tension and fear in the room, but Kate smiled at everyone and went directly to the children. "Hello, everyone. I'm Kate Drake." She sat down in the circle and looked at the little ones in invitation.

Matt stood back and watched her. She looked utterly serene, a center of calm in the midst of a violent storm. Immediately the children were drawn to her, pushing and shoving to sit as close to her as they could get. She began talking to them, and a hush fell over the room so that only Kate's magical voice could be heard, bringing a sense of peace and contentment.

"So most of you had a bad dream last night?" Kate's smile was a starburst, radiating light and warmth. "Dreams can be very frightening. All of us have had them. Haley, would you tell us about your dream?" she asked the little girl who had been sobbing the hardest. "Dreams are like stories we make up in our imaginations. I make up stories and write them down for people to read. My stories can be very frightening sometimes. Was your dream scary, Haley?"

It wasn't so much her actual words that were magic as it was her voice. It became apparent to Matt that somehow Kate drew the intensity of the children's emotions out of them. As the room grew calm, and the children quieter, the tension dropped dramatically. It was only Matt who could see the effect on Kate. How draining it was to accept the backlash of emotion not only from the children but their parents as well.

Haley revealed her dream in halting sentences. A skeleton-like man in a long coat and old hat with glowing eyes and bony fingers came out of the fog. He burned the Christmas tree and stole the gifts, and he did something awful to the shepherd in the Christmas pageant. Matt stood up straight when the shepherd was mentioned. His brother, Danny, always played the shepherd in the Christmas pageant. His alarm grew as child after child revealed they'd had a similar dream.

Kate didn't seem the least bit alarmed. Her smile never wavered, and her voice continued to dispel the trauma the nightmares had caused. She told several Christmas stories and soon had the children laughing. As she stood up to leave, Matt saw her sway with weariness. Without a word, Matt waded through the children and slipped his arm around her. She leaned heavily into him as they spent the next ten minutes trying to leave gracefully.

"You look a bit on the fierce and forbidding side," she said once they were back in the car. "I've never quite seen that expression before."

"I was contemplating picking you up and carting you out of there."

Kate laughed softly. "That would have given everyone something to talk about, wouldn't it?" She pressed her fingers to her temples. "Where are you taking me?"

"To the Salt Bar and Grill. You need to eat. Danny's been dating the waitress there, Trudy Garret, so we've spent quite a bit of time sampling the food. It's not bad." He glanced at her and noted that her hands were shaking. "You were using some sort of magic, weren't you? With your voice, and it drained your strength."

"There's always a cost to everything, Matthew." She shrugged without looking at him, closing her eyes and leaning back against the leather seat. "I'm not certain I'll be able to eat, but I'll try."

"You're already too thin, Katie."

She laughed. "A woman can never be too thin, Matthew, don't you know that?"

"That's what women like to think, but men think differently." He parked the car. "I don't mind carrying you."

She opened her eyes then. "Don't you have work to do?"

"I am working. I'm courting you the old-fashioned way. Showing you what a great guy I am and impressing you." He opened the car door for Kate and helped her out, happy to see her laughing. Some of the shadows had disappeared from her eyes.

"You think you're impressing me?"

"I know I'm impressing you."

"Only when you kiss me. I'm really impressed when you kiss me," she admitted, deliberately tempting him. She needed the comfort of his arms more than she needed anything else.

Matt didn't need a second invitation. He pulled Kate's slender body into the shelter of his and lowered his mouth to hers. He brushed her lips gently, back and forth, giving her teasing little kisses meant to prolong the moment. Then his mouth settled over hers, and he kissed her hungrily, like a man starving for more.

Kate's slender arms circled his neck, and her body pressed tightly against his. He knew she couldn't help but feel his body's stark reaction to her, but she didn't seem to mind, burrowing even closer to him so that he felt the warmth of her breasts and the cradle of her hips beckoning with heat.

Tendrils of fog floated in from the sea, ghostly gray strands drifting past them as they stood together on the steps of the restaurant. Kate stiffened, her fingers gripping Matt's shoulders. "Did you hear the weather report? Did they say there would be fog?"

Matt scowled at the mist floating lazily into the parking lot. "We get fog all the time here in Sea Haven, Kate." But it didn't make the hair on his arms rise or his reflexes leap into survivor mode as it had the night before. "I don't smell that noxious odor, do you?"

She shook her head. "But the sun should have burned this fog off. The sky isn't that overcast, Matthew."

"Let's go inside." He held the door open for her to precede him. At once they could hear the wailing of a child in terror. The tension in the restaurant was tangible.

"Oh, Kate! I'm so glad you're here." Trudy Garret beckoned to them from behind the counter, her expression anxious. She was tall and pretty even with the apron she was wearing. Her youthful face was lined with worry.

Danny Granite stood behind her, his arm wrapped around her. He looked relieved to see them. There were a few people in the Salt Bar and Grill, but they were obviously tense and upset over the continual unrestrained sobs coming from somewhere in the back.

"Danny, why aren't you at work?" Matt asked. "Is everything all right at home?"

"Trudy's son had a bad nightmare last night. She can't seem to calm him down, so I offered to come over and see what I could do for him. He's only four years old, a cute little tyke, and I could hear him crying when I called her. I couldn't stand it."

"We haven't been able to calm him down," Trudy said. She was wringing her hands and looking imploringly at Kate. "I'm so glad you came in. Would you talk to him, Kate? Please?"

The cook stuck his head out of the kitchen. "Kate, thank heaven you're here!"

A few of the local patrons broke into applause.

Matt looked at Kate. Her face was pale, her eyes too big for her face, and there were shadows under her eyes. He stirred protectively but didn't speak when Kate put a light, restraining hand on his forearm. She smiled at Trudy. "Of course, I'll be happy to talk to him, Trudy. He isn't alone, many of the children at the preschool had nightmares last night."

Matt slid his hand down her arm, circling her wrist with his fingers. Her pulse was very fast, her skin cool. "While Kate talks to your son, Trudy, maybe you can heat a bowl of soup for her."

"Of course, be happy to," Trudy said. "Right this way, Kate, he's in the back."

Matt followed Kate behind the counter to the back room. The wails grew louder as they approached the small room. Kate opened the door. Matt winced at the high-pitched shrieks, but he stepped inside with her. It was the same scenario as at the preschool. Little Davy Garret sat in Kate's lap, telling her the details of a skeleton in a long coat and old hat in between gulping and tears, finally listening to the sound of her magical voice. Kate replaced the boy's memory of the terrifying nightmare with several funny Christmas stories. She rocked him while she talked, using her talent, her gift, to bring him peace, to soothe him, and make him feel that his world was right again.

After Kate spent twenty minutes sitting on the floor with the boy, Matt reached down and took the child from her arms and set him aside to play happily with his toys. "Danny can take over, Kate. Come eat the soup, then I'll take you home. You're exhausted." He pulled her gently to her feet.

Kate nodded. "I am tired. I wish I knew what was going on, though. I've never seen anything like this. How could all these children have the same dream? At the preschool, at first I thought maybe Haley told her dream to the others, and they all became upset because she was; but the parents said, no, the children had woken up that way. And Davy certainly didn't have contact with any of them. I don't like it at all." She slipped into a booth near the window and peered out. "The fog seems to be rolling in again, Matthew." She couldn't keep the apprehension she felt out of her voice.

"I noticed," he said grimly. The bright, blinking Christmas lights and cheerful music couldn't quite dispel the tension in the air. "Tell me more about the diaries."

Kate sipped at the hot tea Trudy brought her and stared out the window, avoiding his gaze. "Each generation in our family records our activities in journals, or diaries as we sometimes call them. They're considered the history of the Drake family. The earlier journals were recorded using a language or code of symbols like the ones we saw in the mill. I could read part of what was written on the seal. Someone in my family sealed that malevolent force in there. If it was that dangerous that they decided to seal it without laying it to rest, it was because they couldn't give it peace. And that's very frightening."

"And Elle's the only one who can read the language?"

"Sarah knows a little, just as I do. The others have some working knowledge as well, but there's a lot of history to go through when you don't have a good understanding of the language. We need Elle, but I'm certain Sarah and the others will keep trying to find the proper entry and hopefully decipher it."

The wind whirled through the room as the door to the restaurant was thrust open and Jonas strode in, coming directly to them, his face etched with deep lines. Without asking, he slid into the booth beside Kate. "It's Jackson, Kate. I've never seen him like this. I need you to come and talk to him."

A chill went down Matt's spine. "What's wrong with him?"

At Matt's tone, Kate looked up quickly and caught an expression passing between the two men. "What is it? Why are you both so worried?"

There was a small, uncomfortable silence. "You know how you said Hannah was a private person and wouldn't want people to find out what happened the other night? Jackson is the same way," Matt said.

Jonas sat up straight. "What doesn't Hannah want talked about?"

"We're talking about Jackson," Kate reminded him. "What's wrong with him, and why are you both so worried?"

The two men exchanged another long look. Jonas sighed and shrugged in resignation. "I need your help or I wouldn't be telling you this, Kate. I expect you to keep it confidential."

She nodded because he had actually waited for her answer.

"Jackson is—was—is a specialist for the Rangers."

There was another silence. Kate watched their eyes. They looked grave, more than a little worried. When neither was more forthcoming she took a guess. "He's trained in things I don't want to know about, and you don't want to talk about. Right now he's in a bad way and both of you are concerned for his mental well-being. And what do you mean by is—was—is?"

"That about sums it up, Kate. Let's go," Jonas said.

"Once a Ranger always a Ranger," Matt added. "And she needs to eat her soup. Give her a few minutes."

"Do you have any idea what's going on, Kate?" Jonas asked.

"Your sisters are all upset, and whatever happened last night to you and Matt sounds bizarre. You were so drained, even I could feel it."

She shook her head. "My sisters are still looking in the old family diaries for an explanation, but I don't have any answers, Jonas. I wish I did."

The time, it was right, for a present or two,
And the fog on the sand holds a secret, a clue.

JACKSON DEVEAU PACED back and forth in complete silence. That was the first thing Kate noticed, how very silent he was. His clothes didn't rustle, and the soles of his shoes didn't make any noise. His eyes were as cold as ice, as bleak and as dead as she had ever seen in a human being. She sat down in the one good armchair and tried to repress a shiver. If the man had any gentleness in him, she couldn't detect it.

"I told you I didn't need a damned psychiatrist, Jonas," Jackson snapped, without looking at her. "Get her out of here. You think I want anyone to see me like this?" Sweat beaded on his forehead, dampened his dark, unruly hair.

"I'm not a psychiatrist, Mr. Deveau," Kate said. "I'm simply a friend of both Jonas and Matthew. I have a gift, and they thought it might help you in some way. Neither meant to upset you."

"Stop growling like a Neanderthal, Jackson, and let her

talk," Matthew said. "You'd think you didn't have a civilized bone in your body."

"How strange that you would choose that particular description when my sisters said the same thing about you, Matthew," Kate replied. "Did you have a particularly disturbing dream, Mr. Deveau?"

Jackson whirled around and stalked toward her from across the room, his body moving like a large predatory cat's. "What'd they tell you about me? That I'm crazy? That I have nightmares and can't sleep? What the hell do you want me to say?"

Kate noted both Jonas and Matt were close to her, ready to defend her if necessary. In spite of the shiver of fear, she calmly looked up at the deputy. "They didn't say anything. They've told me next to nothing about you. Most of the children in town seem to have had a collective nightmare. So far, none of the adults have admitted to it, but everywhere we've been today, there's unexpected tension. I thought maybe you would be able to tell me about it. I'm getting garbled accounts from the children, and so far no adult has been courageous enough to admit they had the dream too."

Jackson raked both hands through his dark hair, the muscles rippling under his thin, tight tee shirt. He looked from Jonas to Matthew as if expecting a trap. "Kids have been having nightmares?"

Kate nodded. "Last night, after the fog rolled in, something bizarre happened. This morning, children from all over town were distressed and in tears, some traumatized by a dream they all seem to have shared."

"About what?" For the first time since she'd entered the room, Jackson sat down, his hands still gripping his head as if he had a violent headache.

"They described a skeleton man in a long coat and old hat."

Jackson hesitated, clearly reluctant to discuss his problem with her. He looked from Jonas to Matt and finally capitulated. "The coat and hat were old-fashioned, a heavy wool, maybe. There was no real face, just white-gray bones. There was a woman and a baby and a shepherd, or at least someone with a shepherd's staff." He scrubbed his hand over his face. "I go after real people, real threats, but this thing, this was from a place I can't get to, and I sense that everyone is in danger." He looked at Kate. "More than the actual dream, it was the feeling the dream left me with that's disturbing. The danger was real. I know it sounds crazy, but dammit, it was real!"

Matt stiffened. Jackson Deveau had never feared very much, certainly not his own mortality, yet he was deeply shaken by the nightmare.

"Then you felt it too. That the threat is real," Kate said, leaning toward Jackson.

Jackson drew back. Matt had forgotten to tell Kate the deputy didn't like physical contact. "I know it is." He looked at Jonas and Matt. "You two probably think I've finally gone around the bend, but I swear, whatever that thing was in my dream, he's looking for a way to walk among us."

"He uses the fog," Kate explained. He was no child to be soothed with Christmas stories and loving smiles. He was a grown man, a warrior, and what he needed was the naked truth. It was the only thing he would accept. He needed facts to assure him he was not losing his mind. "Whatever he or it is, he's growing stronger. I think the earthquake cracked a seal locking him deep in the earth, and he managed to escape. Matthew and I found a broken lid in the basement of the old mill. Something came out of a crack in the form of a noxious vapor. I've smelled the same odor in the fog." She met Jackson's gaze steadily. "If you're losing your mind, so am I. So is Matthew. And so are all the children of Sea Haven."

Matthew heard it then, that magical note that brought absolute peace to a troubled mind. He had become attuned to it, aware of the surge of energy in the room, going from Kate to the person she was speaking with. He was also aware of her absorbing the negative energy, taking it in and holding it away from its victim.

"That's a relief. I thought this time I was really losing my mind. I have nightmares, and I can deal with them, but this was something out of a horror film." Jackson shook his head. "I'm not going into an institution."

"You're the only one who ever thinks that way," Jonas said quietly. "So do your sisters have any ideas, Kate? This is more your field than ours." He nodded toward the other two Rangers. "We can be your soldiers, but you're going to have to give us a direction."

Kate leaned back in the chair, fatigue in every line of her body. "We're working on it. Abbey and Sarah and Damon were going through the diaries this morning. We'll find the reference and at least have a starting point."

"I notice you didn't mention Hannah," Jonas observed. There was a challenge in his voice. "Is she ill? Is that what's wrong with her?" When Kate didn't answer, Jonas swore. "Dammit, Kate, if she's ill, you owe it to me to tell me. Something's wrong with her."

"Something's always been wrong with her, Jonas, you just never noticed before." Kate folded her arms. "I'm not going to be bullied into telling you something that is Hannah's private business. Ask her."

Jonas swore again and stormed out. Kate rolled her eyes. "His temper hasn't improved much with age."

"Come on, Kate, I'm taking you to dinner at my house. I'm a great cook." Matt reached down and drew her up from the chair. "I think it's the only sanctuary left to us."

"I should go home and help the others."

Jackson stood up too. "You made me feel better. How did you do it?"

Kate smiled at him and offered her hand. "It was a pleasure finally to meet you, Mr. Deveau. Jonas and Matthew speak so highly of you."

He hesitated but took her hand. "Please call me Jackson."

Kate felt the jolt of his heavy burden go up her arm. It was difficult to maintain her smile when she felt the brooding darkness in the man. She wasn't Libby. She couldn't heal the sick, and in any case, she didn't sense that Jackson Deveau was physically ill so much as spiritually so. "I wish you peace, Jackson," she murmured softly, and allowed Matthew to draw her from the house out into the cool air.

"He didn't have a Christmas tree up, or any decorations at all," she said sadly. "If anyone needs Christmas, it's that man."

"He'll work it out, Kate," Matthew assured her. "He has his demons, but the bottom line is, honor and integrity rule his life. He would never do any of the things he's afraid he will, and, just like Jonas, he would protect this town and the people in it with his last breath."

"I'm glad you brought him to Sea Haven. You were right about this place. There's just something about the way the people are here—they're welcoming to outsiders." The interior of his car was warm after the chilling wind blowing in off the ocean.

"Did your sisters really call me a Neanderthal?"

She burst out laughing. "Well, yes, but in a good way. I think they could easily picture you beating your chest and tossing your woman over your shoulder to carry her off to somewhere private."

He nodded. "I can understand that. I do have those urges. Often." He looked at her, his hand still around the key. "I really want to take you back to my house, Kate." He waited a heartbeat before starting the engine.

"Are your brothers going to be there? Because, honestly, I think I'm too tired to have them all laughing at me today. I'd probably burst into tears."

He pressed a hand to his heart. "Don't even say that. I think I'd rather take a bullet than see you cry. And my brothers don't laugh at you." He glanced at her to see if she was serious.

"They *always* laugh at me," she said. "I'm always doing these idiotic things whenever I'm around you. Like the other day when you had that accident and you tried to get out of the truck and I was standing too close." She looked down at her hands. "Danny just about fell out of the truck laughing."

"At *me*, Katie, never at you. My entire family knows how I feel about you, and they think it's a riot that I can make such a complete fool of myself every time you're near."

Kate sat very still, her gaze fixed on his face. "How do you feel about me?"

"I've made that pretty damn clear, Kate."

"Have you? I know you're attracted to me physically."

He gave a small snort of derision. "Is that what you call it? I haven't had a good night's sleep since I looked at you when you were fifteen years old. I hate admitting that. I shouldn't have been looking at you, but I did, and I just knew. I've had more dreams about you, more fantasies, than any man should admit to having." He pulled the car into the driveway of his yard and turned off the engine before facing her. "Hell, Kate, if you didn't know, you're the only person in this town who didn't. Jonas asked me last night if I was stalking you."

"He wouldn't do that. You're his friend. He must have been kidding."

"With his hand on his gun. Afraid not, and here you are, at my house, all alone with me. Are you coming in?"

"Am I supposed to be afraid now?"

"I thought my fantasies might scare you off."

"Did you?" Kate slid out of the car. The wind whipped her hair around and tugged at her clothes. "Actually I'm intrigued."

His entire body reacted to her sultry tone. Maybe she didn't mean it the way it sounded, but he was going to take her words as an invitation to love her every way a man could love a woman.

Kate smiled to herself as she went up the stairs to his home. It was situated on the bluff above the ocean, his deck wrapping around the house providing a view from every direction. The house itself was obviously built for a man of Matt's size. The ceilings were vaulted, there were few walls, so the space seemed enormous, one room running directly into the next. His furniture suited the house, casual, yet overstuffed to go with the dimensions of the house.

"It's so beautiful, Matthew. I love all the bay windows and the alcoves and the way everything is so spacious. Did you design it?"

He felt a little glow of pleasure. "Yes, I wanted a home I was comfortable living in day in and day out. I need space. Even the doorways are wider and taller than normal, so I don't always feel as if I might have to duck."

"I love the open beams and the rock fireplace. This is what I had in mind for my house, or at least something very similar. I love the beams and the natural-looking fireplace in the mill." She turned to smile at him. "We do have very similar taste."

His heart did a curious somersault in his chest. He gripped the edge of the door. "I think so. It should be easy to come up with a design you'll really fall in love with." He said the words deliberately.

Kate stilled and turned her head to look at him. The movement was graceful and elegant. So Kate. He ached, just looking at her. Color swept her face. She glanced from him to the tall Christmas tree in his front room. It was a silver tip, beautiful and decorated with lights and a few ornaments. "Did you put up your tree?"

"I brought in the tree and hung the lights. Mom insisted I get ornaments. She said I was supposed to have a theme, but I just picked up ones I liked."

Kate wandered around the tree. One of the ornaments was a wooden house carved by a local artist. She was surprised and pleased to see it was her cliff house. She didn't comment on the ornament, but she hoped it meant he'd been thinking of her when he'd bought the miniature replica of her home.

"This is my favorite room. I spend a lot of time in here. My office is straight ahead, and I have a large library. I call it a library; Danny and Jonas call it my den." He grinned at her. "They talked me into a pool table."

She laughed. "Of course they did. I'll bet they had to twist your arm."

Matt hastily gathered up a few shirts he'd tossed aside earlier in the week. There was an old pizza box on the coffee table along with an empty doughnut box overturned beside a half-full coffee cup.

Kate grinned at him. "I see you're into health food."

"I actually like to cook. I used to cook all the time for the men in my unit." He opened a door, tossed his shirts inside without looking where they landed, and hastily closed the door to gather up the dirty boxes and coffee cup. "I haven't been home much. Dad's running a big job, and all of us have been working to bring it in on time."

"Matthew." Kate put her hand lightly on his arm. "Are you nervous?"

He stood there looking down at her upturned face. Her enormous soft eyes. Her tempting mouth. Could she be any more beautiful? "Hell, yes, I'm nervous. I don't even know what a woman like you would be doing in the same house with a man like me."

"A woman like me?" She looked genuinely puzzled.

Matt groaned. "Come on, Kate. Are you telling me you haven't known I've been wild about you for years? I can't even have a good time with another woman. I've tried dating numerous women. We have one date, and I know it isn't going to work."

"You're wild about me?" she echoed.

He tossed the boxes on the couch and pulled her into his arms. Hard. Possessive. Commanding Ranger style. "I can't even think straight around you."

There was no way to think when his mouth took hers, hot and hungry and devouring her. Her body melted into his, her arms sliding around his neck, her fingers brushing the nape of his neck intimately, creeping into his hair while she met his ravenous hunger with her own.

He couldn't kiss her and not touch her soft, tempting skin. Without conscious thought, he slid his hand beneath her blouse to move up the soft expanse of skin. Just that slight contact brought him such deep pleasure it bordered on pain.

He trembled, his hand actually shaking as he brushed the pads of his fingers over her rib cage, and up to cup the soft weight of her breast in his palm. His body went into overdrive, his heart slamming in his chest and his jeans growing uncomfortably tight.

"Aren't you going to stop me, Kate? One of us should know what we're doing." He wanted to be fair with her. She was exhausted and obviously not thinking straight, arching into his hand, pushing closer, rubbing her body against his. Soft little moans came from her throat, driving him right over the edge. He found himself kissing her again and again, long hot kisses that pushed their temperatures even higher.

Her lips smiled under the assault of his. "I know exactly what I'm doing, Matthew, you're the one who's unclear." Her hands dropped to the buttons of her blouse.

There was a strange roaring in his ears. He had waited years for this moment. Kate Drake in his home. In his arms. Kate's body open to his exploration. It would take a lifetime to satisfy him. More than that. Much more. Her blouse fell open, exposing the creamy swell of her breasts. White lace cupped her skin lovingly.

Matt stared down at her body, mesmerized by the sight of his large hand holding her, his thumb brushing her nipple through the white lace. For one moment, it occurred to him he was making the entire thing up. Kate Drake. His Christmas present. He bent his head to her breast, his mouth closing around soft flesh and lace. His tongue teased and danced over her nipple while his arms enfolded her closer.

The pounding on the front door was abrupt, loud, and unexpected. Kate cried out, and he felt her heart beneath her skin jump with fear.

Matt lifted his head, his gray eyes appearing silver as they smoldered with a mixture of anger and desire. "Don't worry, Katie." He pulled the edges of her blouse together. Why couldn't the world leave them alone for one damned hour? Was that too much to ask?

Kate buttoned her blouse and tried to finger comb her hair. He caught her wrist and brought her hand to his mouth. "You look beautiful. Whoever it is can just go away."

She waited in the middle of his living room while he yanked the door open. The sheriff stood there, his fist poised for another assault. "Jonas, I'm beginning to think our friendship is going to suffer," Matt greeted with a scowl.

Jonas pushed right past him. "Come on out here and take a look at this." His voice was grim. He stalked through the house to the ocean side, pushing open the double doors leading to the deck overlooking the sea. "What the hell is going on, Kate?"

The fog whirled around the house as if alive. Dark and gray and gloomy, the mist was thick, almost oily. It crept up the walls and swirled around the chimney. Jonas glared at the fog. "No one can drive anywhere. Car accidents are happening all over town. Your sister Elle called. She's in the islands and yet she had *the exact same dream as Jackson and the children.* How could she have the same dream? She said to tell you the symbols meant something. When I asked her what they meant she said you would know."

Both men looked at Kate. She hesitated, trying to remember, but there was nothing that seemed to be of great significance. "There were symbols on the seal, but the only thing of importance I could read was that a locking spell had been placed on the lid to hold something in the ground. I'll call Elle and ask her to give me details. Is she on her way home? She was going to try to make it back for Christmas."

"She said she'd be catching a late flight." Jonas stared at the thick gray blanket of mist, frowning as he did so. "The worst of the fog seems to be centered here. It's much heavier around your house, Matt. People are going to start dying if we don't figure out what's going on. We've been lucky, most people pulled their cars over to wait it out and the accidents that have occurred have been minor. But it would be very easy to drive off the cliff in this dense fog. We've asked the radio stations to alert everyone to the driving hazards."

"I'm guessing you called the weather station and the meteorologists there told you this fog is unnatural," Matt said with a small sigh. The supernatural wasn't his realm of expertise, but he had the feeling he was going to have to learn more about it very fast. A part of him had hoped it would all go away. Instead, the fog was wrapped tightly around his house. He glanced at Kate. She stood very still, her hand to her throat, staring out into the dark gray mist. There was fear on her face.

Anger began to smolder in the pit of his belly, not hot and fiery, but ice-cold and clear, dangerous and deadly, an emotion he recognized from his combat days. Matthew took Kate by the shoulders and pulled her back, away from the deck and into the safety of the house. "Did Sarah say whether or not they found anything in the diaries, Jonas? They were all looking, hoping to find an explanation."

Jonas shook his head. "Sarah said she doesn't have a clue as to what's going on, but she thought with all the sisters concentrating, they might be able to drive this fog back to sea to give us more time to figure it out."

Matt's hands tightened on Kate's shoulders. "I don't want you to do it again, Katie. I think you're making it angry, and it's striking back at you. Why else would it have followed us to my house and stayed here?" He couldn't articulate the emotions the fog gave off, but there was something dark and ugly about it that reeked of pitiless hostility. He didn't want Kate anywhere near it.

"We can't take chances, Matthew," Kate said, her voice trembling. She pressed her lips together. Instinctively she moved back toward Matt as if for protection. "Jonas said there have already been traffic accidents."

Matt could feel her reluctance. Whatever was in the fog had grown in strength and intensity. The previous night it had been an eerie annoyance; now it seemed darker . . . more aggressive and dangerous.

"The fog swept through town, Kate, right after the two of you left Jackson's house," Jonas explained. "People came out of their houses to stand there and watch it. The sheriff's office logged well over a hundred calls. When it receded, it left behind a mess. All over town gifts left outside, everything from bicycles and ATVs to garden furniture, were smashed and covered with sea trash—sand, kelp, driftwood, smashed seashells, you name it. Even crabs crawling around." Jonas pushed back his hat and rested his gaze on Kate's face. "The worst damage was done to the town square. The three wise men statues were all but destroyed, and the gifts they carried were ground into the lawn. The statues had kelp wrapped around their necks and wrists and ankles. It was bizarre and ugly and it scared everyone enough that the folks on the committee are concerned about the safety of the men playing the parts of the wise men in the pageant. Do you think it was a warning?"

Kate rubbed at her throbbing temples. She was already so tired. She felt drained and just wanted to lie down for a few hours. "I honestly don't know, Jonas, but the entity is accelerating its destructive behavior."

"Dammit, Kate, what the hell could be alive in the fog?" Matt burst out, wanting to throttle the thing. "I don't want you anywhere near this stuff. Why do you have to be the one to face it?"

"My voice. The others can channel through me. And Hannah can call up the wind to drive it back to sea."

He wasn't touching that. It sounded like witches and spells and things he saw in movies, not in real life.

Matt began a slow massage at the nape of Kate's neck to help ease the tension out of her. "Katie, why would this thing smash gifts? If it's capable of destroying things and moving objects as it did with the wreaths on the doors, why such a silly, almost petty display? Why do the gifts bother it? What would be the significance?"

Jonas followed them back to the sliding glass door. "That's a good question. Is that all it can do? When the calls started coming in I thought it was kids and childish pranks. Smashing gifts and outdoor ornaments and leaving behind dead fish are relatively harmless acts of vandalism a kid might do. Well, at least I thought a kid might be the culprit until I saw the three kings smashed to pieces. Jackson came out to the square to take a look at the damage, and he said the scene was reminiscent of his nightmare."

Kate shook her head. "I think it's growing stronger, testing its abilities. It doesn't feel childish to me. It used wreaths, a symbol often associated with Christmas, and now gifts. Elle said the symbols matter. Gifts obviously are another symbol of Christmas." She sighed and rubbed at her temples. "Obviously this thing does not like Christmas at all. Any guesses as to why?"

"I have no idea," Matt said. He used his body to gently shepherd her farther back into the room, wanting to close the doors against the fog.

She turned in his arms and pressed her body close to his for strength and comfort. "My sisters are waiting. Even Libby. It isn't easy to sustain a channeling for any great length of time."

Matt tightened his arms around her, holding her captive, holding her safe. He buried his face against her neck. "I hate this, Kate. You have no idea how much. I want to pack you up and take you far away from this place. I know you're in danger."

"If I don't do this, Matthew, one of my sisters will try, and they don't have my voice." She hugged him hard and slowly pulled away from him.

Matt allowed her to slip from his arms, taut with fear for her when she stepped onto the deck. He stepped beside her. Close. Protective. Daring the thing to come through him to get to her. Jonas took up a position on her other side. Kate closed her eyes and raised her face to the sky.

A breeze from the sea fluttered against her face. She felt the cooling touch. She felt the joining of her sisters. All seven, together yet apart. Strength flowed into her, through her. She lifted her arms and knew Hannah stood on the battlement of their ancestral home and simultaneously did the same.

Matt heard the moaning of the wind. Out on the ocean, the caps on the waves reached high and foamed white. The fog became frenzied, whirling and spinning madly, winding around Kate so that for a moment it obscured Matt's vision of her. He reached out blindly, instinctively, and yanked her into the protection of his body. "This is bullshit, Kate." He pressed her face against his chest and wrapped his arms around her head to keep the fog from getting at her.

Kate didn't struggle. She didn't act in any way as if she noticed. Her voice was soft, barely above a whisper, yet the wind carried it into the bank of mist, and it vibrated through the vapor, taking on a life of its own. Kate remained against him, her eyes closed but her chanting continuing, a gift of harmony and peace, of contentment and solidarity. She called on the elements of the earth. Matt heard that clearly.

Voices rose on the wind. Seawater leaped in response to the chant, waves rising high, bursting through the fogbank and breaking it into tendrils out over the ocean. The wind howled, gathering strength, rushing at them, bringing the taste of salt and droplets of water to brush over their faces. Thunder crashed, shaking the deck. Still the voices continued, and the tempest built.

"Hannah." Jonas said her name softly, slightly awed by the raw power forged and controlled between the sisters.

Kate took a deep breath and let go. Let go of her sisters and her body and the physical world she lived in to enter the shadow world. Far off, she heard the echo of Hannah's frightened cry. The world wasn't silent as one would expect. She never got used to that. There were noises, moans and cries, not quite human, unidentifiable. Static, the sound of a radio not tuned properly. And the terrible howl of the wind endlessly blowing. It was cold and bleak and barren. A world of darkness and despair. She looked around carefully, trying to find the one she was seeking.

She wasn't alone. She could feel others watching her. Some were merely curious, others hostile. None were friendly. She was a living being, and they were long gone. Something slithered close to her feet. She felt the touch of something slimy against her arm. Kate took another breath and called out softly. At once she saw it. A terrifying sight. Tall, bare white bones, the skull ghastly with a gaping mouth and empty sockets for eyes. It wasn't fully formed. A great hole was in the chest cavity. The ribs were missing. It came striding toward her, and she noticed that the skeleton wore old-fashioned boots stuck at the end of the sticklike bones of its legs. She might have laughed had it not been so frightening. The bones rattled as it rushed toward her, deadly purpose in every bone.

"Kate!" Abigail's cry echoed Hannah's and Sarah's.

Kate held up her hand to ward the thing off as it reached her.

Matt felt Kate's energy crackling in the air around them, a fierce force never wavering, yet her slender body shook with the effort, or maybe with fear, crumbling beneath the strain. Without warning he felt every hair on his body stand up. Kate went sickly pale. Afraid for her, he swept her up into his arms and held her tight against his chest, the only thing he could do to shelter her from the onslaught of the wind and the menace of the fog.

Kate wrenched herself from the shadow world, opened her eyes, expecting to see Matt. Empty sockets stared back at her. The skull's mouth gaped wide, the jaw loose, bony fingers wrapping around her throat. She screamed and pulled away, trying to run when there was nowhere to go. The pressure on her throat increased. She choked.

The wind rose to a howl. Feminine voices became commanding. The bony fingers slid from Kate's throat. She fell to the ground and stared in horror as the voices of the Drake women forced the skeleton away from her one dragging step at a time. Those pitiless empty eye sockets stared at her with malice. Kate tried to scoot crablike in the opposite direction, feeling sick as the entity clacked white bones together in a dark, ugly promise of retaliation.

The wind blew sand into the air, obscuring Kate's vision.

She squeezed her eyes closed tightly against the new assault. At once she felt Matt's body pressed close to hers. Afraid to look, she lifted her lashes, hands out in front of her for protection. Matt's reassuring face was there, the planes and angles familiar to her. She buried her face against his throat, felt the warmth of his body leeching some of the icy cold from hers.

The fog crept back toward the ocean slowly, almost grudgingly, retreating from around the house and deck to the beach, with obvious reluctance. With Kate safely in his arms, Matt stared in horror at the wet sand. Distinct footprints were left behind, as if someone had backed toward the ocean with short, dragging steps, a man's boots with run-down heels. A cold chill swept down his spine. His gaze went from the prints in the sand to Jonas. "What the hell are we dealing with here?"

7

As lovers meet beneath mistletoe bright,
Terror ignites down below them this night.

Matt STARED DOWN at Kate's face. She lay in his bed, sound asleep, the signs of exhaustion present even as she slept. She looked more fragile than ever, as if fighting back the entity in the fog had taken most of her spirit and drained all of her strength. The curtains over his sliding glass door were pulled back to allow him a clear view of the ocean. He had always enjoyed the sight and sound of the waves pounding, but now he searched the horizon for signs of the fog. Kate was worn out.

He worried that if the entity returned, she wouldn't have the strength to fight it, even though she'd slept for hours. The day had disappeared, and night had fallen.

He rubbed his hands over his face to wipe away his own exhaustion. He hadn't slept the night before, standing watch at Kate's bedside, and he was feeling the effects. He had stripped her of her clothes and wrapped her in one of his shirts. It was far too big for her and covered every curve. He'd tucked her in his bed and all the while she lay passively, making little effort to do anything but close her eyes. He had the feeling she'd faced something far worse than the fog, but she hadn't been ready to talk about it with him. Recognizing the signs of exhaustion, he hadn't pushed her.

Matt removed his shirt and shoes and socks and stretched out beside her. He had built his home in the hopes of finding a wife when he returned from serving his country, but no matter how many women he had dated, there had been only one woman for him. Kate had been in his dreams from the moment he'd first laid eyes on her. He would never forget that moment, driving his father's truck, his rowdy brothers cranking up the music and laughing happily. He had glanced casually to his right, not realizing that his life was about to change forever. Kate was standing in the creek bed with her six sisters, her head thrown back, laughing, her eyes dancing, totally oblivious to his gaze. A jolt of electricity had sizzled through his entire body. In that one moment, Kate Drake had managed to burn her brand into his very bones, and no other woman would do for him.

"Matthew?" Her voice was drowsy. Sexy. It poured into his body with the force of a bolt of lightning, heating his blood and bringing every nerve ending alive.

"I'm here, Katie," he answered, wrapping his body around hers as he slipped his arm around her waist.

"Didn't Sea Haven always seem like home to you? When you were far away, in another country, in danger, didn't you dream of this place?"

"I dreamed of you. You were home to me, Kate." There in the darkness with the ocean pounding outside his bedroom he could admit the truth to her. "You got me through the gunfire, and the ugliness, and it was the thought of you that brought me back to Sea Haven. My family always kept track of you for me."

Kate turned her face into his shoulder, snuggling closer to him. "I heard you were doing things that seemed so scary to me. I have such an imagination, and I would wake up in the middle of the night picturing you rising up out of the desert sand in your camouflage fatigues with your rifle and enemies all around you. Sometimes the dreams were so vivid I'd actually get sick. I've never told that to anyone, not even my sisters. They saw the differences in us and knew we weren't right for each other."

"Kate." He said her name tenderly. With an aching need in it. "How can you say that? Or even think it? I was made for you. To be with you. I feel it so strongly, the rightness of it. You feel it too. I know you do." He held her possessively, his arms locking her to him. Matt buried his face in the soft warmth of her neck. "Katie, you can't hand a man his dream, then take it away. Especially not a man like me. I stood back and gave you all the room in the world when you were too young for me. Later, when you were grown, you were busy and happy with your life, traveling around the world doing what you do. I never once made a move on you. I knew you needed your freedom to pursue your writing. But now you're home, telling me you're ready to settle down, and I can't just step back and pretend we don't feel anything for one another. Every time you looked at me, you had to know we belonged. You should never have kissed me if you weren't willing to give a relationship between us a try."

Kate closed her eyes, feeling tears welling up. His lips moved over her neck, drifted lower to nudge the collar of the shirt aside. Her pulse pounded frantically. Her heart went into overdrive. "I'm not brave the way you are, Matthew," she admitted in a small voice. "I can't be like you. I'm not at all a person of action.

In a few months when you realize that, you'll be so disappointed in me, and you'll have too much honor to tell me."

Matt lifted his head and looked down at her. Tears shimmered in her eyes, and his heart nearly stopped beating in his chest. "What the hell are you talking about, Kate?" He bent his head to kiss the tears away. He tasted grief. Fear. An aching longing. "Dammit." He muttered the words in sheer frustration, then kissed her hard, his mouth claiming hers. A ravenous hunger burst through him, over him. There was a strange roaring in his head. His chest was tight, his heart pounding with the force of thunder. He had faced enemy fire without flinching, but he couldn't bear the idea of Kate walking away from him.

He poured everything he felt into his kiss. Everything he was. His hands framed her face, held her to him while he ravaged her mouth. Heat spread like a wildfire, through him, through her, catching them both on fire until he thought he might ignite. She melted into him, her arms sliding around him, nearly as possessive as he was. He lifted his head to look at her, memorizing every beloved line and angle of her face. He was gentle, his fingertips stroking caresses and tracing her cheekbones, the shape of her eyes, the curve of her eyebrows. The pad of his thumb slid back and forth over the softness of her lips. He loved her mouth, loved everything about her. "Kate." He kissed her gently. Once. Twice. "How could you think I don't know you? We've lived in the same town practically all our lives. I've watched you. I've listened to you. Do you know how many times I've dreamed of you?"

"Dreams aren't the same as reality, Matt," Kate said sadly.

Her gaze moved over his face, examining every inch of his features. Matt waited, holding his breath. He was rough and she was elegant. He was a man who protected the ones he loved. And he loved Kate Drake.

"Matthew . . ." There was that catch in her voice again. Need. Caution.

Matt couldn't imagine why Kate would fear a relationship

with him, a life with him, but the thought that she might pull away had him bending his head. His teeth tugged at her delicate ear. His tongue made a foray along the small shape. She shivered in reaction. He grew harder. Thicker. His body was heavy and painful, straining against the confines of his jeans. "Katie, unzip my jeans." He breathed the words into her ear, his lips drifting lower to find her neck. Her soft, sensitive neck.

Kate closed her eyes as his teeth nipped her chin, her throat, as his lips found her collarbone, his chin nudging aside the shirt collar again. She ached with wanting him, her body hot and sensitive. Her breasts felt swollen, begging for his attention. What was so wrong with reaching for something, just this one time? He was everything she'd ever wanted, yet was always out of her reach. Matthew Granite was a fighter, larger-than-life. He'd done things she would never comprehend, never experience. He felt like a hero from one of her novels, not quite real and too good to be true. She knew she'd thought of him when she'd written each and every one of her books. She'd used him as her role model because, to her, he was everything a man should be. Why would he ever choose to be with a woman who looked at life, wrote about life, but refused to participate in it?

Kate was certain she was going to leap from the bed and run, but her body had a mind of its own. She was already working on the button at the waistband of his jeans, finding the zipper and dragging it down. The air left his lungs in a rush when her hand shaped the thick, heavy bulge, caressed and stroked with loving fingers. "You're wearing too many clothes, Matthew," she pointed out, determined to have her time with him, even if it couldn't be forever.

"So are you." His hands dropped to the buttons of her shirt, sliding them open so that the edges gaped apart. He raised his upper body in order to stare down at her, to drink in the sight of Kate Drake in his bed. She shrugged out of the shirt and allowed it to fall to the floor before lying back. His mouth went dry.

Outside, the continual booming of the sea seemed to match

the pounding of his heart. In the soft light, her skin was flaw-less, inviting. Her breasts were full and round, her nipples taut inviting peaks. Kate's long hair spilled around the pillows, just as he'd always fantasized. For a moment he was caught and held by the sight of her, unable to believe she was real. "There was more than one night out in the desert when I was lying half-buried in the sand, surrounded by the enemy. It was im-portant to get in and out without being seen. The enemy showed up and set up camp virtually on top of us. It was the fantasy of you lying just like this in my bed, waiting for me at home, that got me through it."

"Then I'm very glad, Matthew." She tugged on the loop at the waistband of his jeans. "Get rid of those things."

He didn't wait for a second invitation. "I've always loved you, Kate. Always." She would never know how often he thought of her, in the hot arid desert and the freezing nights, in the painful sandstorms. Lying in a field with the enemy not ten feet from him. He had been all over the world, performing high-risk covert missions in places no American leader would ever admit to sending troops, and Kate had gone with him every single time.

He stroked his hand down her leg, more to ensure she was real than for any other reason. He felt her shiver in response. Her lips parted slightly. Her sea-green eyes watched his every move. Matt knelt on the bed, tugging on her ankles, a silent command to open her legs. She complied, parting her thighs wide enough to allow him to slide between her legs.

Matt was a big man. At once Kate felt vulnerable, the cool night air teasing the tiny curls at the junction of her legs. His hands, sliding up her thighs, were gentle, removing her anxiety as fast as it rose. She loved the way he looked at her, almost wor-shiping her skin, her body, his hot gaze exploring in the same thorough way as his hands. A wave of heat rushed through her, of anticipation. Matt took his time caressing every curve along her slender leg, even the back of her knee as if memorizing the texture of every inch of her was terribly important.

His touch sent darts of fire racing over her skin, penetrating every nerve ending until she could hardly lie still beneath his touch. Her breath was coming in a gasp, and heat coiled deep inside her, a terrible pressure beginning to build.

Matt couldn't contain himself another moment. She lay there like a beautiful offering. He bent over her, kissed her enticing navel, his tongue swirling in the small, sexy dip, his hands continuing their foray lower. He felt her reaction, a warm, moist welcoming against his palm as he pushed against her. He kissed his way up her smooth body to the underside of her breast. Kate gasped and arched her body, her hips moving restlessly. She flushed, her luminous skin taking on a faint peach-colored glow.

He groaned. His body reacted with another swelling surge. Fire raced through his veins. His tongue flicked her nipple, once, twice, and his mouth settled over her breast. Kate cried out, her hands grasping handfuls of his hair, tugging him closer to her. She was magic. He could think of no other word to describe her. His body pressed into the softness of hers, while he lavished attention on her breasts. He'd dreamed of her skin, of the feel and shape of her every curve, and his imagination hadn't come close to the real thing. He cupped her other breast, teasing her nipple, feeling the response in Kate. She was very sensitive to his touch, to his mouth, to every caressing stroke. And she showed him she loved his touch.

Her soft moans heightened Matt's pleasure. He hungered for the sounds and responses Kate showed him. He needed them. She was generous in her reception, her hands moving over him, her body restless with the same hunger. He flicked her nipple one more time with his tongue and took possession of her lips, swallowing her moan, robbing her of breath.

Matt kissed her mouth over and over because no amount of kissing Kate would ever be enough. He trailed kisses down her throat, in the valley between her breasts. Her fingers dug into his hips, urging a union, but he took his time. He rained kisses across her stomach, pausing to dip again into her fascinating belly button.

"Matthew, really, I don't think I'm going to live through this." Her breath came in a series of ragged gasps.

"I waited a long time, Kate. I'm not rushing things." He ducked his head, his tongue sliding wickedly over her wet, hot sheath. She nearly jumped out of her skin. He grinned at her. "I may only have this one chance to prove my worth to you. I'm not about to blow my chances by charging the battlefield." He bent his head and blew softly against her sensitive body. He caught her hips more firmly, dragged her closer to him, and bent his head to taste her.

Kate screamed and nearly rose off the bed. He held her hips firmly, locking her to him while he feasted. She was hotter than he had ever imagined, a well of passion, and he had just begun to tap into it. He felt the first strong ripple of her muscles rushing to overtake her, and his body swelled even larger in response.

"I think you're ready for me, Kate." He didn't bother to hide the satisfaction in his voice. It was still a miracle to him that she chose to be with him. He pushed her thighs a little wider to accommodate his hips, pressing against her so that the sensitive tip of his penis slipped into her hot, welcoming body. The breath slammed out of his lungs. He pushed deeper so that she swallowed the tip, her tight muscles gripping with soft relentless pressure that sent violent waves of pleasure shooting through his body.

Kate gasped and clutched at the bedsheets. Matt froze, understanding dawning. He bit back a string of swear words, took a deep breath, and let it out. "Relax, honey, just relax. I swear, we fit together perfectly."

She smiled at him. "I'm not afraid, you idiot, I've never felt this before, and it's amazing. I want more, Matthew, all of you. Stop being so careful." If he didn't quit moving so slowly, she was going to spontaneously combust. She wanted to push her body over his. It was difficult to hold back when every instinct demanded she lift her body to receive his.

"Dammit, Kate, you're not experienced." He was sweating

now. It was impossible to hold back. She was squirming, her hips pushing hard into his, and he was inching his way deeper into the hot core of her. Pleasure was building at such a ferocious rate he was losing all control just when he needed it the most. She was so damned tight, squeezing and gripping him, the friction like a hot velvet fist pumping him dry. Matt thrust deeper because he had no other choice. It was that or risk death. He was certain of it. She took him in, gasping with pleasure, when he'd been so worried.

Matt let go of his fears and took the ride, thrusting deep, tilting her body until she could take all of him. He moved the way he wanted, the way he needed, hard and fast and deep, joining them together in a rush of heat. The ocean pounded the shore just outside the glass door. Matt was unaware of it, unaware of anything but Kate and her body and the way she gave herself so completely to him. She came over and over, crying out, clutching his arms, lifting up to meet him as eagerly as he surged into her. The explosion started somewhere near his toes and blew through his entire body. His voice was hoarse, a roar of joy, as he emptied himself into her.

He sank on top of her, completely spent, completely sated, his lungs burning for air and his heart pounding out of his chest. And it was a perfect moment in time. Her body was soft and welcoming beneath his. He turned his head to capture her breast in his mouth, to lie there in contentment, to have her with him. He had been in hell many times in his life. But he had never been in paradise until now. His arms tightened around her possessively. "Dammit, Katie, don't ask me to give you up." He said the words around her tantalizing breast.

Kate combed her fingers through his hair, lying back with her eyes closed, savoring every aftershock while his mouth pulled strongly at her breast, and his tongue did delicious things to cause fiery sparks zinging in her deepest core. "Silly man," she murmured, clearly amused by his reaction. "I'm right here. Did you think I was going to grab my clothes and go slinking off?" The smile faded from her mind. There was a small part of her that wanted to do just that, run while she still had the chance. Self-preservation was strong in her. Everything about Matthew appealed to her. His lovemaking dazzled her, but she wasn't so far gone that she couldn't look ahead to the future and realize they couldn't spend every moment in bed.

Matt shifted position enough to take most of his weight off of her smaller body, but his arms held her in place and he turned her so he could keep access to the temptation of her breasts. His tongue flicked her nipple. "I want you forever, Kate. I want to grow old and have you here in my arms. I want children. I've wanted you for so long. I don't think that's about to change." He noticed that when he drew her breast into his mouth her hips moved restlessly. It was a wonderful find and one he intended to spend time exploring. He stroked her stomach and moved his hand between her thighs to cup her heat. She jumped but pushed against his hand. His thumb caressed her, his finger pushed deep to find the one spot that could give her another release.

Kate was Kate. She didn't try to pull away or pretend she wasn't ready for another orgasm, she rode his hand, gasping with pleasure, her fingers digging into his shoulder with one hand and the other curled in his hair directing his mouth. He wanted this every damn day of his life. Not just a Christmas present. He wanted to go to sleep with her breast in his mouth. He wanted to wake up with his body buried deep in hers. He wanted to be the man to bring her pleasure in every way possible.

"Marry me, Kate. Stay with me."

She heard him through a haze of piercing fulfillment, so sated with contentment, with the throbbing fire spreading through her like a storm, she could only lay there dazed by the gift he was holding out to her. The temptation.

Matt lifted his head to look at her, his fingers still buried deep inside of her. "Kate. I'm serious. Marry me. I'll make you happy."

"I am happy, Matthew," she said. "I lead a relatively quiet life. I work hard, meet my deadlines, and I'm looking forward to renovating the old mill."

Sensing her withdrawal, he turned to lie over the top of her, his head resting on her stomach. He pressed a series of kisses along her sensitive skin and flicked her enticing navel with his tongue. "We can renovate the old mill together, Katie."

"You're moving a little too fast for me, Matthew."

His Kate was becoming cautious again. He should have known she would. He nibbled his way down her body to her thigh. "We don't have to move fast. We don't have to go for the wedding and children and the entire package if that's too much for you right now." His teeth nipped as his fingers moved deep inside of her. He wasn't above a little persuasion. "We can keep it to great sex. Incredible sex."

She heard the note of pain in his voice, and it upset her. "Matthew, I'm not normal. I'll never be normal. You think you know me, but you don't. You can't. My sisters and I inherited a legacy that we have no choice but to use. It comes with a price. Sarah has phenomenal athletic abilities, and she can sense things before they happen. Abigail can demand the truth. I can bring peace to people in need. Libby heals people. Joley has incredible powers, and so does Hannah. Both command the wind and the sea. And our Elle." Kate shook her head. "Elle's legacy is tremendous and important and very frightening. She has it all, along with the responsibility to bring the next generation into the world. We each have gifts, but when we're together, we are very powerful. We try to lead our own lives, but we keep the cliff house so we always can be together."

He lifted his head, his silver eyes darkening to smoldering charcoal. "You think I can't understand honor and commitment? You live by a code the same as I do. I understand codes. You have a way of life that's important to you. Why would you think it would be any less important to me? I don't mind sharing you with your sisters, Kate."

She sighed. "I'm sorry. I didn't mean to upset you, Matthew.

I just want you to know what we do isn't going to go away, even if we wanted it to. And it isn't only sharing me with my sisters, but with a lot of other people as well." But it was more than that. She wasn't like her sisters, embracing life in the way they did. In the way he did.

"I know a lot of ways to be happy with you," he promised, dipping his head to her breasts, not wanting her to see his face. "We'll take it slow if that's what you need, Katie. Just don't shut me out because you're afraid."

She tried not to react to his words. Of course she was afraid. She was afraid of everything, and that was exactly why she couldn't agree to marry him.

He kissed her ribs, her belly button. The phone rang, startling them both. He ignored it, dropping kisses over her stomach. The shrill ringing of the telephone persisted. Matthew sighed heavily and reached lazily across her small body, deliberately brushing across her bare breasts. "Hello." It was the middle of the night. He didn't have to be polite. He didn't want to waste a single moment of his time with Kate, especially when she needed persuasion to stay with him.

"This is Elle Drake. I need to speak with Kate." It was Kate's youngest sister, reputed to be traveling home for Christmas. There was anxiety in her voice. Without a word, Matt passed the phone to Kate.

She sat up, dragging the sheet over her breasts. "Elle? What's wrong, hon?"

"Something's there, Kate. Something's where you are. Below you. It's dangerous, and it's below you."

"Are you certain?" Kate leaned over the bed to examine the floor. Matt could clearly hear the terrified voice on the other end of the phone. "Calm down, Elle, I'm fine. We're both fine."

"Kate, I'm really afraid for you. What's going on? I saw you clearly. You were kissing Matthew Granite. There was mistletoe very close to you, but not directly over your head. And then something bright burst out from under you, a flash and flames, and it was truly frightening. What is it?"

"I don't know, but we'll find out."

Matt was already out of the bed, pulling on his jeans, his eyes searching every inch of the floor. Moonlight pouring through the sliding glass door provided enough light for him to search every corner of the room. With his training ingrained in him, Matt chose not to turn on the light and give their position away to the enemy. He might have dismissed the phone call as hysteria or a nightmare, but he had been around the Drake sisters long enough now to see the strange things Jonas sometimes spoke of and to know to take them seriously.

"I'll call you later, Elle," Kate said, her eyes mirroring her fright. "Thank you for the warning." She placed the receiver in its cradle and looked up at Matt. "She's never wrong, Matthew. Do you have a basement? Maybe whatever it is has found a way to get in through the basement."

He shook his head. "There is no actual basement. I did take the space beneath the deck and create storage rooms and a lab to develop photographs." Their eyes met in sudden silence.

Kate slid out of bed and caught up his shirt, the nearest article of clothing she could wrap herself in. "Do you have mistletoe in the house, Matthew?"

"No, but it grows in several of the trees outside near the deck. I've stood on my deck to knock it out of the branches a few times."

Quickly buttoning the shirt, she followed him on bare feet. He didn't like her exposed to danger, but at least he could keep an eye on her if she were with him. He reached back to take her hand. She looked small and vulnerable in his too-large shirt with her hair tousled from their lovemaking. He bent his head and kissed her, a brief hard kiss of reassurance. Kate's public image was always neat and elegant. He liked that Kate very much. He loved the one with him now. His sexy, passionate, private Kate, with her hair mussed and her delicate skin red from his five o'clock shadow. Nothing was going to harm her. *Nothing.*

Kate felt her heart beating wildly in her chest. She tightened her fingers around Matt's hand. Matt slid open the glass door leading outside. The wind rushed in, bringing a cold chill and the scent of the salty air. The roar of the ocean was loud, whereas before the walls of the house had muffled it. She glanced nervously out toward the open sea, afraid of seeing the gray fog, but the ocean's surface was clear.

"Kate." Matt said her name as a warning.

Kate froze and dropped her gaze to the sand below them. It was wet from the continual pounding of the waves, rolling up onto the beach and receding according to the tide. There was a clear trail of boot prints, coming out of the ocean, and marks alongside them that indicated something heavy had been dragged. Kelp lay in tangles along the path toward the stairs leading up to Matthew's home. There was a heavy dark stain, much like oil in several spots in the sand. Kate wanted a closer look and stepped out onto the deck.

Matt pulled her back and thrust her behind him. "It doesn't feel right to me." He had long ago learned to rely on his survival instincts when something wasn't right. "Stay in the house, Kate."

"The fog isn't out there anymore," she pointed out, but she stayed behind him, holding tight to his hand. "Should we call Jonas?"

Matt sighed. "I imagine Elle called him. Don't all your sisters call him when something supernatural happens? I don't think the poor man's had a night's sleep since Sarah came home."

"Supernatural? I never thought of it like that. We've always had certain gifts. We were born with them, and using them seems as natural as breathing. Some people call us witches, and others just think we're able to use magic, but it's different. More. And less. I wish I could explain it." Kate frowned up at him. "It's natural to us."

Matt pushed her hair from her face, his fingers lingering in the silky strands. He tucked her hair behind her ear, the gesture tender. "You don't have to explain it. I'm a believer, Kate."

He paused and drew in a deep breath. "Something's wrong. We're not going out on the deck. Come through the house with me." Matt silently slid the glass door closed, lifting his gaze to the night sky, where patches of dark, ominous clouds floated lazily.

Deliberately he didn't turn on any lights as he led her through the house. He paused long enough to slip a leather sheath around his calf. Kate's eyes widened as he shoved a long knife down into it. "Do you think that's necessary?"

"I believe in being safe. You're with me, Kate. Nothing's going to take you away from me. I don't care if it's a monster in the fog or something crawling out of the ocean." He pushed open the door to his house and stepped outside. His eyes searched the terrain restlessly, never stopping. "Do you smell something burning?"

The breeze shifted again, but Kate caught the peculiar pungent odor. "Oily rags?"

Matt hurried over the stepping-stones leading around to the back of the house. He had a good ocean view on three sides, but the bedroom was to the back. The dark stains led from the beach to the stairs and straight to the small photography laboratory he had built. The door was closed and appeared locked, but there were oily smudges all over the door, the same oily smudges they'd seen on the beach.

Kate's heart began to pound. She felt the danger swamping her. Glancing up, she could see the branches of the tree spread over the top of the deck, reaching over the bedroom where she and Matt had been kissing. In the branches were nests of mistletoe and the base of the tree was covered in the oily substance. "Matthew, let's wait for Jonas."

"I have photo-developing chemicals in there, Kate. I'm not losing my house to this thing." He set her away from him. "You stay back. I mean it, Kate. If I have to run, I'll need the way clear. Drag the hose over here for me, but don't get too close."

Matt felt the door. It wasn't hot to the touch. He opened it cautiously. The stench was overpowering, smelling of the sea, dead fish, and heavy oil. Black smoke seeped from a pile of photo paper and rags piled with smashed glass and a mixture of what he knew was lethal chemicals. He dragged some of the papers from the pile, trying to stop the inevitable. Tiny flames licked up the sides of the pile. There was a flash of white and a popping sound.

Kate thrust the hose into his hands. The water was running full out. He turned it on the greedy flames. "Get out of here, Kate," he ordered.

Kate stifled a scream when Jonas emerged out of nowhere and pulled her back, away from the deck. "Call the fire department," he snapped. "Use my car radio and stay out of the house." He pointed to the driveway, where he'd pulled in and left the door on the driver's side open. "I have a jacket in the car, put it on, you aren't wearing very much."

Kate heard the wail of a siren and saw the deputy's car tear up the driveway. She ran to Jackson as he stepped out of his car. "Jonas says to call the fire department."

He made the call from his radio, pointing silently to the car, as if that was enough to make her stay, then he quickly joined Jonas and Matt. Kate dragged on Jonas's jacket, nearly sagging with relief. There was something utterly reassuring about the three men being together. They exuded complete confidence and worked as a team, almost as if each knew what the others were thinking. They had the fire out before the fire trucks even arrived. It took longer to go through the mess in the photo lab, searching for evidence. She was grateful to be able to return to the house where it was warm. Kate curled up in a chair and waited for Matt to return to her.

8

And the blood runs red on the pristine white snow . . .
While around all the houses the Christmas lights glow.

MATT STARED OUT the large bay window of his kitchen at
the pounding sea. He frowned at the foaming waves, peering
toward the darkness far out in the distance, almost at the horizon where a mass seemed to be congealing. Dark clouds had
spread across the entire sky by the time the three men had sifted
through the mess in his photography lab. Matt had taken calls
from his parents and his brothers making certain he was alive
and well and the house was still standing. Kate had received
calls from her sisters.

Kate, fresh from her shower and wrapped in his robe, sat in
the chair nearest him. "It's out there, isn't it?" she asked quietly. "I'm sorry about all your equipment."

He spun around to look at her. "Do you think I blame you
for this?"

She hesitated. "I don't think he would have come here if I
hadn't been here. I don't know why I draw him," she said,
shaking her head. "Maybe he got my scent in the old mill, or
maybe he perceives me as a threat."

"So it's definitely a he. I think it's taking shape, gaining a
form," Matt said.

"I need to go home and help find the appropriate entry in
the diaries. There are quite a few written in the symbols, and
my sisters will need help. I don't think we have a lot of time to
figure this out, Matthew. It's only a few days until Christmas,

and I think this thing means to stop the town from having a Christmas." It sounded melodramatic even to her own ears. How could she expect to have any kind of a relationship with Matthew Granite and still be who and what she was?

"Time enough, Kate. We'll go right after we take care of things here. I promise."

She lifted an eyebrow. "What things? I thought you and Jonas and Jackson took care of everything."

Matt padded over to her on his bare feet and simply lifted her in his arms. "It takes some getting used to."

Kate clasped her fingers at the nape of his neck. "I'll admit I've never faced anything like this before." She wanted him. Suited or not, for just this space of time, Matthew belonged to her.

"I wasn't referring to our foggy fiend. I was referring to you. Having you in my house. Having you right here where I can look at you or touch you." He set her on the tiled counter and slid his hand inside the warmth of the robe.

He loved her instant response, the way she pushed into his hand. Welcoming him. "Remind me to thank your sister for the warning." Matt leaned forward to take her offering into the warmth of his mouth.

"I think you're a breast man," she teased.

"Mmmm, maybe," he agreed, his hands sliding down her waist and over her hips inside the robe. "But you also have a beautiful butt, Kate. I absolutely love the way you walk. I used to get behind you just to breathe a little life into my fantasies."

He was wedging himself between her legs, and Kate opened her thighs wider to accommodate him. "You've had fantasies about my rear end?"

"More than you'll ever know." He leaned in to capture her mouth. To spread heat and fire. Her fingers tangled in his hair. His fingers tangled in hers. Their mouths welded together so that they breathed for one another. He pulled her bottom closer to the edge of the counter and yanked her robe all the way open. "I've had fantasies about every separate part of you." Very gently he slid her legs apart.

"Matthew." There was a gasp in her voice. Kate stared at the long bank of windows, her hands still in his hair. "What are you doing?"

"Having you for breakfast. I've always wanted you for breakfast."

If Kate had thought to protest, it was far too late. He was already devouring her, and she was too far gone to care where they were. It was a deliciously decadent moment, and she reveled in it as wave after wave of pleasure crashed over her and rushed through her. The room spun dizzily, and colors mixed together, while his tongue and his fingers worked magic on her body. Her hands grabbed the edge of the smooth-tiled counter to keep herself anchored when she was flying so high, but then he was lifting her and laying her on the table, his body buried deep inside of hers, and there was no room for thought. No room for anything but feeling. The sound of his body joining with hers, their pounding hearts and heavy breathing, was a kind of music accompanying the strong orgasms as they broke over her and through her. His heat was so deep inside of her, she felt as though she were melting from the inside out.

She stared up into his face, the hard angles and planes, the rough shadow on his jaw. His eyes held secrets, things he had seen that should never have been witnessed. She realized how alone he seemed, even in the midst of his family. Like Jonas. Or Jackson. A man apart, not by choice, but by experiences. Kate framed his face with her palms, her thumb sliding in a caress over his faint whiskers. "You're a very wonderful man, Matthew Granite. I hope you know how special you are."

He gathered her to him as if she were the most precious being on the face of the earth, carrying her tenderly to the bathroom so they could shower. He said little, but he watched her all the time, would reach out and touch her body, her face, his fingers lingering against her skin, almost as if he couldn't believe she was real.

"My clothes are dirty," she said, pulling them on. At least she managed to tame her hair, braiding the long length and swirling the braid around the back of her head in an intricate knot.

He smiled at her. "Your clothes are never dirty, you just think they are." He dragged out a fresh pair of jeans from his drawer. "How can we find out what this thing is, Katie? I need to know what we're facing."

"My sisters are poring over the diaries, and I think Damon is helping them. I can try as well, and Elle's on her way home. We should be able to find some clue."

"What's your gut telling you?"

She pressed her lips together to keep from smiling. There was something raw about the way Matt talked, something that always intrigued her. "I think it has to do with the history of our town, possibly an event that happened around Christmas, maybe the pageant itself. I think whatever is in the fog is gaining strength and becoming more destructive, but I'm not entirely certain why. The tree beside the deck with the mistletoe in it is a fir tree, and you had lights strung in it. You didn't have them on, but the dark stain, which seemed to be oil of some kind, was all around the bottom of the tree and going partially up the trunk."

"I noticed that," he agreed. "But there was nothing to ignite it."

"If Elle hadn't called and warned us, we never would have gone outside, Matthew. We would have been above the room when the fire took off, and it might have exploded. I think the fire would have raced to the tree, and he was hoping it would go up in flames as well."

"Strange way to kill us."

"Maybe not just us. Maybe it was the fir tree." She sat on the edge of the bed to watch him dress. He moved with such power, so fluidly, with a masculine grace he didn't seem aware of having. "Each symbol attacked so far has been attached to the Christian belief. There were ancient beliefs far before Christianity ever celebrated Christmas. It's widely believed the birth of Christ was in April, not December."

He paused in the act of buttoning his shirt. "I didn't know that."

She nodded. "I'm not Elle, or the others who sometimes are able to see things clearly, but I *feel* it's connected in some way."

"I get feelings when there's danger near." He suddenly grinned, transforming his face from man to boy. "Unless I'm otherwise occupied."

Kate couldn't help smiling back. In spite of everything, he looked more relaxed than she'd ever seen him. She always thought of him as a great tiger prowling through town. "We can forgive you that." She stood up. "The fir tree's needles rise toward the sky, and the fir tree stays green all year round."

"And that means something?"

"Everlasting hope, and, of course, the raised needles are re-puted to represent man's thoughts turning toward heaven. If I were right, why would he want to destroy those symbols? He's not attacking Santa Claus. He isn't someone thinking Christmas is too commercial, he's actually destroying the symbols themselves." She looked up at him, rubbed her temple, and smiled a bit tiredly. "Or not. I could be way off base."

"I doubt it, Katie. I think your guess is as close as we can get right now." Matt looked across the room at her, still astonished that she was in his bedroom. "Let's go shopping for groceries. We can take them to your house and spend the day going over those diaries until we find something."

"Sounds good. I want to get home and put some decent clothes on."

She wandered out of the room while he pulled on his socks and boots. The house was so open, it beckoned her to walk the length of it. Entering the kitchen, she found herself smiling. In her wildest dreams she had never considered making love on a tabletop. A character in one of her novels might do such a thing, but not Kate Drake, with her every hair in place and her need for order. She'd never be able to look at a kitchen counter or table in quite the same way again.

Matt listened to Kate moving around his home. He liked

the scent of her, the soft footfalls, the way her breath would catch when she looked at something she liked.

"Matthew?" Kate called out to him. "You have a very interesting kitchen. I wanted to put the cups in the dishwasher, and it seems to be a bread bin."

There was a small silence. Matt cleared his throat. "I've never actually used the dishwasher, Kate. I just do dishes by hand."

"I see. I guess that makes sense. But why would you put all the fruit in the microwave?"

He hurried into the kitchen. "It's convenient. What are you looking for?"

She grinned at him. "You don't really cook much, do you?"

He rubbed the bridge of his nose. "I do a mean barbecue."

"I'll just bet you do. Are you ready?"

Matt took her hand and drew her close to him as they went out into the morning air. She fit with him, belonged with him. She didn't believe it. He could see the reservations in her eyes, but he was determined to change her mind.

All the regulars considered the grocery store the center of town. Inez Nelson had a way with people. She didn't know the meaning of the word *stranger* and nearly everyone shopped at the local market, more to catch up on all the news and see Inez than for any other reason. She had known every one of the Drake sisters since their births and considered them akin to family.

Matt parked his car in front of the town square just to the left of Inez's store. "The Christmas pageant is growing, so many people want to participate that I think we're going to have to get a larger town square. The actors can barely get through the crowd as they walk up the street to the manger."

"I love the fact that everyone participates. It's so fun for the children afterward, when Santa shows up with his reindeer and gives out candy canes." Kate took the hand Matt held out to her. They stood together looking at the nativity scene in the town square, astonished that the statues, minus the wise men, had already been cleaned and the scene put back together. It would be reenacted with humans Christmas Eve, but a local sculptor had created the beautiful statues and several artists had done woodwork for the manger and life-size stable, and others had painted the entire backdrop. This year, Inez had managed to find a powdery substance that looked exactly like snow and had sprinkled it on the roof of the stable and on the surrounding ground, to the townspeople's delight and amusement. Snow was rarely seen in their coastal town.

"How many kids do you think have snuck into the square for a snowball fight?" Matt lowered his voice and looked around, half-expecting Inez to hear him even though she was a safe distance away inside the store.

Kate turned her laughing gaze on him. "You would have, wouldn't you?"

Fast-moving shadows slid across the ground, blocking out the sun's rays. "Damn right. Jonas and I would have made a snow fort and pelted everyone within throwing distance." His smile faded even as he finished his sentence. His hand gripped her arm to draw her attention. He nodded toward the sky. Seagulls filled the air overhead, winging their way fast inland. The birds were eerily silent, their great wings flapping as they hurried away from the ocean.

Kate shook her head and looked out toward the sea. The gray fog was rolling in fast. It roiled and churned, a turbulent mass, displaying raw energy. Lightning arced, chains of red-orange flashing within the center of the gray mist.

Matt swore and tugged her toward the store. "Let's get inside."

"It's growing stronger," Kate said.

Matt could feel her trembling against him. He pulled her closer to him. "We knew he would get stronger, Kate. You'd think the damned thing would take a vacation and give us a break. We'll figure this out."

"I know." She walked with him to the store. The entity was growing stronger and she felt stretched and tired and breakable.

She couldn't very well tell Matt. He was already worried about her. She could read it in his eyes. How had she never managed to see the stark loneliness in him before? The aching desire? It was deep and intense and swamped her sometimes when he looked at her. Yet still, as he walked beside her, a tall, formidable man with wide shoulders and a thick chest and eyes that were never still, she could barely take in that he loved her.

Matt slid his arm around Kate's shoulders as they entered the building. As always, the small store had more than its share of customers. Inez greeted them loudly, gazing at them speculatively with bright eyes and a cheerful smile. "Kate, how lovely to see you, dear. And with Matt. I swear you grow taller every day, Matt."

Her comments effectively turned him into a boy again. Only Inez could manage to do that. "I feel a little taller today, Inez." He winked at Kate.

"Are you two coming to the pageant practice?" Inez asked. "I organized another one after the big fiasco the other night. No one blames Abbey, Kate. It certainly wasn't her fault that rat Bruce Harper is having an affair with little miss hot pants Sylvia Fredrickson."

"Abbey felt terrible, Inez," Kate said. "I'm sure it must have caused problems."

"Well, Bruce's wife left him. You know she's due to give birth any day now. They all dropped out of the production, and I had to find replacements." Inez glared at Matt. "Danny was in a fine snit saying he wasn't certain he could work with *amateur* actors. I told him he was an amateur actor."

"Inez," Kate protested. "You probably broke his heart."

For a moment Inez pursed her lips, looking repentant. "Well, he deserves it. I've got enough trouble without that boy complaining about his part. The three wise men are nervous, and I'm afraid they're fixing to drop out. I don't want to cancel the pageant. It's been put on every year since this town was founded."

"Danny won't drop out. He likes to herd those sheep around," Matt said.

Inez scowled. "He likes to chase them toward the kids and get a huge reaction."

"That is the truth." Matt grinned at her, but his eyes were on the wisps of gray-white fog slipping into town. He moved away from the women toward the plate-glass window, where he studied the fog. The enemy. It was strange to think of the fog, a nearly everyday occurrence on the coast, as the enemy.

The dark tendrils stretched toward houses, reached with long, spiny arms and bony fingers. The image was so strong Matt took a step closer to the window, narrowing his eyes to peer into the fog. "Katie, come here for a minute," he said softly, and held out his hand without taking his eyes from the fog. Something was moving inside of it.

Kate immediately put her hand into his and stepped up beside him. "What is it?"

"Look into the fog and tell me what you see."

Kate studied the rapidly moving vapor. It was darkening and spinning, almost boiling with turbulence. She shivered as long streaks stretched across the highway and began to surround the residences. It made her think of a predator hunting something, sniffing for the right scent. She thought something moved in the middle of the thick fogbank, something shaped vaguely like a tall man in a long, flowing coat and an old hat. She glimpsed a form, then it disappeared in the seething mass, only to reappear moments later, fading into the edges of the whirling mists. It was tall with bare white bones, pitiless eyes, and a wide, gaping mouth. She stepped back, gasping. The skeleton had more than taken shape. This time the entire chest was intact, and small pieces of flesh hung on the body, making it more grotesque than ever.

Kate put a hand protectively to her throat to stifle the scream welling up as she backed completely away from the window. She realized the store was eerily silent. Inez and the patrons stared out the window fearfully.

"It's taking shape, isn't it?" Matt asked.

Jonas and Jackson stalked into the store, Jonas's expression grim. "Kate, get out there and get rid of this before we start having fatalities," Jonas snapped without preamble, ignoring everyone else. "No one can see to drive the highway. I issued a warning on the radio, but we're going to have people not only driving over cliffs but also walking over them. Unfortunately, not everyone listens to the radio."

"Go to hell, Jonas." Matt was furious. *Furious.* At the thing in the fog. At Jonas, and at his own inability to stop the entity. "You're not sending Kate out there to battle that damned thing alone again. She's scared and tired, and I'll be damned if you bully her into thinking she's responsible for taking this thing on by herself. You want someone to fight it, be my guest."

"Dammit, Matt, don't start with me. You know I would if I had a chance in hell, but I don't. This is the Drakes' territory, not mine," Jonas bristled.

Kate put a restraining hand on both men's arms. "The last thing we need is to fight among ourselves. Jonas, I can't manage it alone. I really can't. I need Hannah." She leaned her head against Matt's chest. "I don't bring the wind, Hannah does. She's exhausted with fighting this thing. My sisters have been working with me the entire time. Without Hannah, we can't do anything."

Matt glanced down at her face, saw the lines of weariness there, the look of far too much energy expended, and for the first time, uncertainty. He wrapped his arms more tightly around her, and addressed Jonas. "How bad is it out there? Can they pass on this one and get some rest?"

"I'm getting damned sick of this secrecy where Hannah's concerned," Jonas said, obviously trying to get his temper under control. He felt every bit as impotent against the entity as Matt did, and it was clearly wearing on him. "We may have a running battle going; but if she's ill, it matters to me, Kate. You've been my family for as long as I can remember."

Kate felt Matt stirring, a fine tremor of anger rippling through his body at the tone Jonas used with her. She rubbed her head against his chest. "I know that, Jonas. Hannah is aware you're angry too. You know we all have a difficult time after we use our gifts. Hannah has to expend a tremendous amount of energy controlling something as capricious as the wind. Using our gifts is very draining. And whatever is in the fog has been growing in strength and resisting us, so we're having to expend more effort to contain it."

"Can you get rid of it, Kate?" Inez asked.

Everyone in the store seemed to hold their breath, waiting for her answer. Kate could feel the hope. The fear. All eyes were on her. "I honestly don't know." But she had to try. She could already hear the feminine voices whispering in the soft breeze heading inland from the sea. She felt her sisters calling to her to join with them. Hannah was already on the battlement, drooping with weariness, but facing the fog, waiting for Kate. Sarah and Abbey stood with her, and Joley had arrived. She'd been traveling for two days, yet she stood shoulder to shoulder with her sisters, waiting for Kate.

Kate closed her eyes and drew in a deep breath in an effort to summon her strength. Her courage. A paralyzing fear was beginning to grip her, one she recognized and was familiar with. Like Hannah, she suffered from severe panic attacks. Unlike Hannah, she was not a public figure. As a writer, her name might be known, but not her face. She could blend into the background easily, yet now everyone was watching. Waiting. Expecting Kate to work some kind of magic when she didn't even know what she was dealing with.

Matt felt the fine tremors that ran through Kate's body and turned her away from everyone in the store, his larger body shielding her. "You don't have to do this, Katie." He whispered the words, his forehead pressed against hers.

"Yes, I do," she whispered back.

Jonas instinctively stepped in front of her to protect her from prying eyes. Jackson spoke. His voice was utterly low, so soft one felt one had to strain to hear his words, yet his voice carried complete authority. "Inez, move everyone to the center of the store away from the windows, and let's give Kate some room to work. We have no idea what's going to happen, and we don't want to take chances with injuries."

Kate was grateful to the three men. She took another breath and pulled away from Matt, deliberately yanking open the door and slipping outside before her courage failed her. At once she felt the malevolence, a bitter, twisted emotion beating at her. The dark fog wrapped around her body, and twice she actually felt the brush of something alive sliding over her skin. She pressed her teeth together to keep them from chattering. Strength was already flowing into her—her sisters, reaching out from a distance, calling to her with encouraging words.

Matt joined her outside, slipping behind her, circling her waist with his arms, drawing her back against his hard, comforting body so that she had an anchor. Jonas took up a position on her right side, and Jackson was at her left. Three big men, all seasoned warriors, all ready to defend her with their lives. It was impossible not to find the courage and the strength she needed when it was pouring into her from every direction.

Kate faced the dark, boiling fog, lifting her arms to signal to Hannah, to signal to bring in the wind. She began to speak softly, calmly, using the gift of her soothing voice in an attempt to bring peace to the swelling malevolence in the fog. She spoke of peace, of love, of redemption and forgiveness. Gathering every vestige of courage she possessed, Kate made no attempt to drive it away. Rather she summoned it to her, trying to find a way to pierce the veil between reality and the shadow world where she could see into the soul of what was left behind and, hopefully, find a way to heal the broken spirit.

The fog spun and roiled in a terrible frenzy, a reaction to the sound of her voice. Her sisters protested for a moment, frightened by what she was trying, but joining with her when they recognized her determination. Jonas made a small sound of dissent and moved closer to her, ready to jerk her back into reality.

Moans assaulted her ears. The shadow world was vague and gray, a bleak hazy place where nothing was what it seemed.

She chanted softly, her voice spreading through the world with little effort, stilling the moans and alerting whatever lived there to her presence. Kate felt the impact when the entity realized she'd once again joined him in his world. She could feel his blazing rage, the fierce anger, and the intensity of his guilt and sorrow. The thing turned toward her, a tall skeleton of a man, blurred so that he was nearly indistinct in the gray vapors surrounding him. He wore a long coat and shapeless hat, and he shook his head and pressed his bony hands over his ears to stop the enchantment of her voice. Flesh sagged from the bones, a loose fit in some places, stretched tight in others.

Kate whispered softly to him, calling, beckoning, trying to coax him to reveal the pain he suffered, the torment of his existence. She used her voice shamelessly, cajoling him to find peace. The shadowy figure took a few steps toward her. Kate held out her hand to him, a gesture of camaraderie. *There is peace. Let yourself feel it surround you.*

The being took another cautious step toward her. Her heart pounded. Her mouth was dry, but she kept whispering. Speaking to him. Promising him rest. He was only a few feet from her, his arm stretching out toward her hand. The bony fingers were close. Inches away from her flesh. She remembered the feel of the finger bones closing around her throat, but she stood her ground and kept enticing him.

Something slithered around his boots. Snakelike vines wrapped around bony ankles. Out of the barren rocks bounded a huge creature with matted fur and yellow eyes. In the cold of the shadow world, she could see the creature's vaporous breath mingling with the fog. The eyes fixed on her, an intruder in their world.

The tips of her fingers touched the bony ends of the skeleton as it reached toward her. The creature howled, sending a shiver of fear down Kate's spine. Her sisters held their collective breath. Jonas stiffened, communicating his apprehension to Matt and Jackson.

Kate continued to whisper of peace, of aid, of a place to

rest. The being took more shape, the pitiless eyes swimming with tears, extending its hand as far as the snakelike vines allowed. Abruptly the skeleton threw back its head and roared, rejecting her. Rejecting the idea of redemption and forgiveness. She glimpsed a raging hatred of self, of everything symbolizing Christmas, of peace itself. There can be no peace. She caught that as the being began to whirl around, furious, using the vortex of its wild spinning to hurl objects at her. The moans rose to shrieks. The huge creature bounded toward Kate, breathing as loudly as any bull. Kate made one last grab for the hand of the skeleton, but it had turned on her completely, rushing at her along with the beast.

"Get her out of there!" Jonas shouted, catching the collective fear that ran through the Drake family. He gripped Kate's arm hard, shaking her. "Matt, pull her back to us!"

"Kate," her sisters cried out, "leave him, leave him there."

"Hannah!" Jonas cried the name desperately. "The wind, Hannah, bring in the wind."

Kate stared at the terrible figure coming straight at her, fury in its every line. The eyes glowed red through the dark fog; the face was made of bones, not flesh. The mouth gaped open in a silent scream. She was trapped there in the world of shadows, real, yet not, unable to find her way back. The worst of it was, she caught sight of a second insubstantial figure coming at her from the left.

"Kate." Matt whispered her name, lifted her into his arms. Her body was an empty shell, her mind caught somewhere else.

"Kate, darling, go with the other one, he'll lead you out." Elle's soft voice pushed everything else away.

The dark demon was almost upon her. Kate felt a hand on her arm. She looked down and saw Jackson's fingers circling her wrist like a vise. She didn't have time to go voluntarily; he yanked her out of the shadows, back into the light. She heard a roar of rage, shuddered when she felt bones brush against her skin. Matt was real and solid, and she gripped him hard, needing to feel grounded. She felt physically ill, her stomach a churning knot. She closed her eyes, sliding into a dead faint.

The wind swept in from the sea, a strong tempest of retaliation. Hannah's fear added to the strength of the storm. Rain burst down on them. The dark fog swirled and fought, not wanting to give ground. For a brief moment there was a confrontation between the entity and the Drake sisters, sticks and debris flying in the wind. The three men could hear the desperate cries of seagulls. And then it was over, the fog retreating to the sea, leaving behind silence and the rushing wind and rain. Matt stood there on the sidewalk, Kate, safe in his arms, staring in shock at the mess left behind.

Clouds overhead obscured the sun, the day overcast and gloomy. Christmas lights twinkled on and off where they hung over the buildings in rows of vivid colors, a terrible contrast to the scene left behind in the town square. Feathers were everywhere and in the pristine white snow by the manger there was a bright red pool of blood.

A star burns hot in the dead of the night,
As the bell tolls it's now midnight.

"NEVER AGAIN. NEVER again." Matt shoved both hands through his hair and glared at the Drake sisters. "I swear, Kate, you are never doing that again." He paced restlessly back and forth across the living room floor.

Sarah, Kate's older sister, rested her head against her fiancé's knee, and watched Matt in silence. Abbey sat on the couch,

Joley's head resting in her lap. Joley lay stretched out, her eyes closed, appearing to be asleep in spite of his tirade. Hannah lay on the couch closest to the window, lines of exhaustion visible on her young face.

"It doesn't do any good to get upset," Jonas said. "They do whatever they want to do without a thought for the consequences."

Sarah sighed loudly. "Don't start, Jonas. That's not true, and you know it. If you were the one trying to get rid of this thing, you wouldn't worry about your own safety, and you know it. You'd just do whatever had to be done."

"That's different, Sarah," Jonas snarled back. "Dammit anyway. Look at Hannah. She can't even move. I think she needs a doctor. Where the hell is Libby when we need her?"

"Are you ever going to stop swearing at us?" Sarah asked. She rubbed her face against Damon's knee. "Hannah needs rest and maybe some tea."

"I'll make tea," Damon offered. "I think all of you could use it."

"Damon, you are a darling," Sarah said. "The kettle's boiling."

Matt glanced into the kitchen, and, sure enough, the kettle was steaming. He knew very well it hadn't even been turned on minutes earlier.

Damon leaned down to brush a kiss across Sarah's temple before making his way into the kitchen. "This feels like old times," he called out, reaching for the tea kept for just such occasions.

"We could use a little more festive atmosphere," Abigail decided. She stared at the row of candles on the mantel until they spluttered to life, flames leaping and flickering for a moment, then taking hold. At once the aroma of cinnamon and spice scented the air.

"Good idea," Sarah agreed and focused on the CD player. Instantly Joley's voice filled the room with a popular Christmas carol.

"Not that one," Joley protested. "Something else."

"Are you all insane?" Jonas demanded. "Kate could have been killed. Are we going to pretend it didn't happen and have a little Christmas get-together?"

"Jonas, it does no good yelling at them. What do you want them to do?" Damon returned, carrying a tray with several cups of tea on it. He distributed them among the Drake sisters.

"And you were the one asking me, no, telling me to get out there and stop the fog," Kate pointed out.

Jonas muttered something ugly under his breath and reached down for Hannah's limp wrist to take her pulse. As he did a breeze swirled around the room, and his hat sailed from the chair where he'd placed it and landed in the middle of the room. Jonas straightened and glared down at Hannah, who didn't stir.

"Jonas, we didn't know the entity was going to try to hurt Kate," Abbey pointed out. "We have to know what his motivation is."

Sarah shoved a heavy book across the floor. "Trying to read this thing without Elle is impossible. She's the only one that can read the language our ancestors used. The writing is in that strange hieroglyphic language we were all supposed to study back when we were teens. Mom told us to learn it, but we kept putting it off, wondering why we needed to delve that far back into the past. With the little bit we know, it's impossible to find a single entry in all of this."

Matt stopped pacing, coming to a halt beside Kate, his hand resting on the nape of her neck. "Elle's on the way home, isn't she? It shouldn't be long. How come she learned the language when the rest of you only know a little?"

Abbey blew on her tea. "She learned it in order to teach the next generation, just as our mother did."

"Speaking of Elle, how did she connect with you, Jackson? How did she know you were able to go into the shadows and bring Kate out?" Sarah asked.

There was a sudden silence, and all eyes turned to regard the man sitting in absolute stillness just to the side of the window.

His cool dark eyes moved over their faces, a brooding perusal. "I don't know what you're talking about. I don't even know Elle."

Abbey sat up straighter. "That's not the truth, Jackson."

Jonas sucked in his breath sharply. "Don't, Abbey!" His warning came a heartbeat too late. She'd already said it, her voice pitched perfectly to turn people inside out, to reach into their darkest depths and pull the truth from them.

Jackson stood up slowly, his eyes hard steel. He walked across the floor without a single sound. Joley sat up and blinked at him. Matt moved in on one side of Abbey, Jonas on the other. Ignoring the two men, Jackson bent down until he was eye level with Abbey. "You don't ever want to ask me for the truth, Abbey. Not about me and not about Elle." He hadn't raised his voice, but Abbey shivered. Joley put her arm around her sister.

"I'll be outside," Jackson said.

"He's never met Elle," Sarah said, after the door closed behind the deputy. "Jonas, he hasn't, has he?"

Jonas shook his head. "Not to my knowledge. And he's never mentioned her. They both had the same nightmare, but so did half the kids in Sea Haven."

"He scares me," Abbey said. "I don't want Elle near him. She's so tiny and fragile and so sweet. And he's . . ."

"My friend," Jonas said. "He saved my life twice, Abbey."

"And mine too," Matt added. "You shouldn't have done that."

Abbey looked down. "I know. I don't know why I did. It's just that he's so frightening, and the thought that Elle was out there in the shadow world too . . ."

"But she wasn't," Kate interrupted. "She wasn't there. I heard her voice, but she wasn't in the world, she was in my head." Her voice trailed off in sudden speculation. The sisters exchanged a long look. "Jonas, is Jackson telepathic?"

"How the hell would I know?" Jonas asked.

"Well, because you are. Sort of." The sisters looked at one another again and burst out laughing. Their bright laughter dispelled the air of gloom in the room.

Jonas made a face at Matt. "See what I have to put up with?" He stomped across the room to reach down and retrieve his hat. Before his fingers could close around the rim, the flames on the candles flared from a sudden gust of wind, and the hat leaped away from him to land dangerously close to the fireplace. Jonas straightened slowly, his hands on his hips, glancing suspiciously around the room at the Drake sisters. They all wore innocent expressions. "You are not going to get me to believe that the wind is in the house without a little help."

Unexpectedly the logs in the fireplace burst into flame. Jonas took a step toward his hat. It went up on the rim and rolled a few inches toward the burning logs. "My hat had better not go into that fire," Jonas warned.

"Really, Jonas." Joley didn't open her eyes. "You're becoming paranoid. Hannah's already asleep."

He continued to study their faces and finally crossed to the couch where Hannah lay asleep, looking almost like a child. "I'm taking the baby doll to bed. It's the only safe thing to do." He simply lifted her in one quick movement and, before anyone could protest, started out of the room.

"The tower," Sarah called after him.

"What a surprise there. I can see Hannah as the princess in her tower," Jonas called back.

The sisters looked at one another and burst out laughing. Matt shook his head. "You all are downright scary."

Joley leaned her head back and grinned at him. "I'd like to know what's going on with my sister and you all alone up in that house of yours. I was going to help Hannah whip up a little love potion and stick it in your drink the next time I saw you, but they tell me you've been playing fast and loose with her already."

Kate turned a particularly fetching shade of crimson. "Joley Drake, that will certainly be the last we hear on that subject."

Joley didn't look impressed with the stern tone. "In case anyone is interested, I took a good look at Kate's neck, and she has a particularly impressive love bite."

Kate clapped her hand over her neck and shook her head. "I most certainly do not. Drink your tea."

"What's even more impressive," Joley continued, "is that Matt seems to be sporting one of his own."

A collective gasp went up. "We want to see, Matt," Abigail pleaded.

"Only if I get to make a wish on the snowglobe," he bargained.

There was instant silence. Sarah sat up straighter. "Matt," she paused and glanced at Kate. "Wishing on our snowglobe is not like making a silly, frivolous wish. It's very serious business. You have to know what you want and really mean it. You have to have weighed your decision very carefully."

"I can assure you I have. If you want to see the love bite, you can produce the snowglobe." Matt folded his arms across his chest.

"Matt," Kate cautioned, "if you're thinking about wishing for anything we already discussed—don't. It wouldn't work."

Joley lifted her head off the back of the couch and eyed them both. "This sounds very interesting. Does anyone else want Christmas snacks to go with the tea, because I really could go for those little decorated sugar cookies." She waggled her fingers in the direction of the kitchen. "Tell us more, Matt. The snowglobe is right over there by the fireplace. Please do step on Jonas's hat. It always livens things up when he does his sheriff he-man routine." She turned her head to glance at the stairs. "He's been up there a long time. You don't suppose he's taking advantage while Hannah is asleep, do you?"

Sarah nudged Joley with her foot. "You're terrible, Joley."

Matt skirted around Jonas's hat and reached for the snowglobe. It felt solid in his hands. He glanced at Kate. She shook her head, looking fearful. The globe warmed in his hands. He stared at the scene, the snowflakes whirling around the house until they all blended together to become fog. The lights on the tree sprang to life.

"You activated it," Sarah said. "That's nearly impossible."

"Not unless he's . . ."

"Joley!" Kate interrupted her sister sharply. "Matt, really, it isn't something to play with."

"I've never been more serious. Tell me what to do." He looked at Sarah.

She glanced at Kate, then shrugged. "It's relatively easy, Matt, but be sure. You look into the fog and picture what you want most in the world and wish for it. If you meet the criteria, the globe will grant your wish."

"And it works?"

"According to tradition. Family is allowed one wish a year, no more. And you can't wish for harm to anyone."

"That's why we don't allow Jonas access to it," Joley said.

Matt inhaled the fragrance of the candles and fresh-baked cookies wafting from the kitchen. He didn't question who made the cookies. He wasn't even surprised by the fact that there were cookies. He stared into the fog inside the snowglobe and conjured up the exact image of Kate. With everything in him, body, soul, heart, and mind, he made his wish. The fog was still for a moment, then swirled faster, dissipating until the globe was once more clear and the lights on the tree dimmed. He placed the globe back on the shelf carefully and grinned at Kate.

"Let's hope you know what you're doing," Joley said.

Suddenly in a much better mood, Matt flashed her a smile. "At the risk of sounding like an adoring fan, I love your collection of blues. You have the perfect voice for blues." He grinned at her. "Or Christmas music."

Joley winced. "I just sent that to my family for fun."

"It's beautiful," Abbey said. "Are you having fun on your tour?"

Joley frowned. "Yes, it's tiring, and there are always the freaks out there, but there's nothing quite like the energy of forty thousand people at a concert."

"What freaks?" Jonas demanded, walking back into the room. "Hannah didn't even wake up, not even when I called her Barbie doll. Are you certain she's okay, Sarah?"

Sarah paused for a moment, seeking inside herself, reaching

out to her sister. "She's exhausted, Jonas, and needs sleep. We'll have to find a way to get some food into her soon."

Jonas rolled his eyes. "We can't have Miss Anorexic gaining an ounce. She's probably worried the camera won't love her, and she won't be able to parade around half-naked on the cover of a magazine for the entire world to see."

Kate tossed her napkin at Jonas. "Go away, you're annoying me. We have to have clear heads to decide how to handle this, and you just stir everyone up."

Jonas shrugged, in no way perturbed. "I have to go back to work anyway. But I want to hear about these freaks of yours, Joley. You haven't been getting any nutcases stalking you, have you?"

Joley took a sip of tea and looked up at Jonas. "I don't know. I hired a couple of bodyguards, bouncers really, just to protect the stage. Each concert hall has a security force, of course, but I thought if these two traveled with us, we'd have a little extra protection. Stalkers come with the territory, you know that. The more famous you get, the more crazies you attract."

Matt sat down beside Kate. "Do writers have that kind of problem?"

Before Kate had a chance to deny it, Jonas answered. "Of course they do. Anyone in the public eye does, Matt. Writers, musicians, politicians, and—" he glanced toward the stairs— "supermodels."

Joley laughed. "You worry so much, Jonas, you ought to go into law enforcement. It's right up your alley."

"Ha-ha, very funny. I'll call you later to see if anything new has happened." Jonas glanced out the window. "I never thought I'd dread nightfall."

Matthew looked out the window to the pounding sea. "Is Elle expected tonight?"

"She said around midnight. She's flying into San Francisco and renting a car to drive here. I offered to pick her up," Abbey said, "but she didn't want any of us on the road with the fog. She promised she'd check the weather station before she came into Sea Haven."

Jonas scooped up his hat. "I'll keep an eye out for her. You all rest and stay out of trouble." He left, banging the door behind him.

At Sarah's urging, Damon nodded toward the kitchen and Matt obliged.

Abbey waited until the men were out of the room. "I didn't mean to challenge Jackson like that." She pressed her hand to her mouth, her eyes enormous. "That's twice now. And the house should have protected me. How could that happen in our home?"

"You were relaxed," Sarah said. "You let your guard down."

Abbey shook her head. "I haven't let my guard down since I caused such a problem during the committee meeting. Poor Inez called me this afternoon and told me no one realized it was me, but Sylvia knew."

"She went to school with us," Joley pointed out.

Hannah walked back into the room. Tall and blond and beautiful, she looked so fragile she could have been made of porcelain. "Don't worry about Sylvia. I'm certain she's very sorry she hit Abbey."

Joley held out her arms. "Come here, baby, sit by me. You look done in. You were very bad teasing poor Jonas that way and making him think you were sleeping." Joley kissed Hannah. "You really should be in bed."

"I couldn't sleep," Hannah admitted. "I needed to be with all of you."

Joley stroked back her hair. "You didn't do anything awful to Sylvia, did you?"

Hannah's eyes widened in a semblance of innocence. "You all think I'm so bent on revenge all the time."

Sarah paused in the doorway to the kitchen. "That's not an answer, you bloodthirsty little witch. Exactly what did you do to Sylvia?"

Hannah leaned against Joley. "I'm glad you're home. You don't give me that stern face like Sarah does."

"Hannah Drake, what did you do to Sylvia?"

Hannah shrugged. "I *heard* from a reliable source . . ."

"Inez at the grocery store," Abbey supplied.

"Well, she's reliable," Hannah pointed out. "I heard Sylvia developed a bright red rash on the left side of her face. It appears to be in the shape of a hand. I couldn't help but think it was fitting."

Sarah rubbed her hand over her face, trying to stare down her younger sister without smiling. "You know very well you can't use our gifts for anything other than good, Hannah. You're risking reprisal."

Hannah stretched her legs out in front of her and gave Sarah a sweet smile. "You never know what a humbling experience can do for someone's character."

"I'm getting your tea for you, but I hope this is a big joke, and I won't hear about it later at the store." Sarah turned away quickly to keep Hannah from seeing her laughter.

Abbey squeezed Hannah's hand. "You didn't really do anything to Sylvia, did you?" There was a hopeful note in her voice she couldn't quite hide.

"Drink your tea," Sarah said. "And eat some cookies. You're too pale. Matt and Damon are making us dinner tonight."

"Did I miss anything important while I was making Jonas carry my deadweight up those long and winding stairs?"

"Only Matt wishing on the snowglobe," Joley said. "And we're all fairly certain what he wished for."

"You're so brave, Kate," Hannah said. "I could never be with a man so absolutely frightening. They have those cold eyes and those scary voices, and I just want to curl up and fade away." For a moment tears shimmered in her eyes. She looked over the rim of her teacup at Kate. "You thought I was so brave to go out into the world and be seen, while you chose to stay out of sight and share your wonderful stories with the world, but you're willing to try with a man to have a real life with him."

"I haven't made up my mind yet," Kate admitted. "I'm afraid he'll wake up one day and realize what a coward I am. You'll find someone though, Hannah."

Hannah shook her head. "No, I won't. I don't want some man snarling at me because I forgot to put the dishes in the dishwasher, or angry because I had to fly to Egypt to do a photo shoot. And I could never live with a man who always seemed on the edge of violence, or even capable of violence. I'd be so afraid I'd be paralyzed."

Kate laid her hand on Hannah's knee. "Matt isn't capable of violence against a woman. He's protective, there's a difference."

"That's how everyone describes Jonas, as protective, but he's really a bully. He'll order his wife around day and night."

"If Jonas ever falls in love with a woman, I think he would move heaven and earth to make her happy," Kate said. "He looks after all of us, and we're sometimes very aggravating. He has a job to do, and he works hard at it. We often make his job much more difficult. And it must be very disconcerting to be so connected emotionally to us. He senses when we're in trouble or hurt, and unfortunately we're in trouble quite often."

Hannah sighed. "I know. He's just so annoying all the time. I closed the window in the entryway; too much fog was drifting in, and it scared me." She forced an uneasy laugh. "I never thought I'd be afraid of the fog."

Kate stood up and looked around the house. "What do you mean too much fog was drifting in?" She stared out the window toward the sea. "You saw it? You weren't dreaming? What did it look like?"

Sarah stood up too and began to move uneasily about the room, checking the windows.

"It looked like fog," Hannah said. "I came down the stairs and, to be honest, was a little unsteady, so I sat on the floor in the entryway for a couple of minutes. I could see fog drifting in through the open window. It appeared to be normal fog, a long wisp of it, but the fact that I could see it in the house upset me. So I closed the window."

"Nothing can get into the house, Sarah," Abbey said. "It's protected. You know that the house has always protected us."

Sarah shook her head. "Mom told us we needed to know the ancient language of the Drake sisters, and we all shrugged it off with the exception of Elle. She also told us we needed to renew our safeguards every single time we came home, but did we do that? No, of course not—we've become complacent. Mom has precog, we all know it. It was a foreshadowing, but we didn't take her instructions seriously."

Abbey put a hand to her throat. "Do you think the entity was influencing me to use my voice on Jackson as well as at the committee meeting?"

Sarah nodded. "There's a good chance of it. We have to be very careful. None of us are handling this very well. We've never faced such a thing before."

"And I never want to again," Kate said fervently.

"Dinner," Matt called from the kitchen. "Come eat. And bring Hannah with you. Jonas said she had to eat something."

Hannah rolled her eyes. "There's my point exactly, Kate. Men always try bossing women around. It's their nature, they can't help themselves. We know the thing in the fog is a male, and I'll bet he's seriously upset with a woman."

They all started into the kitchen. Sarah and Kate helped steady Hannah. "Actually, I felt guilt and sorrow and rage coming from him," Kate said. "I could feel the connection, but he tossed it away because he feels he doesn't deserve forgiveness. Something terrible happened, and he believes he's to blame for it."

"Why is he causing terrible things to happen now?" Hannah asked.

"I don't know," Kate admitted. "But it has something to do with Christmas. Sarah's right. We have to really pay attention to every detail now. He can't get any stronger, or we won't be able to stop him."

Matt spent the rest of the day poring over the entries in the diaries and listening to the easy teasing back and forth between the sisters. The women slept on and off throughout the day. Damon and Sarah spent a lot of time kissing every chance they could steal away, and he was a bit jealous that he didn't have the right to be as openly demonstrative with Kate. As the hours slipped by, all he could think about was Kate and being alone with her.

He slipped his arm around her shoulders. "It's late, let's go back to my house."

"Elle's driving in tonight. I'd like to wait for her. She's supposed to be here any minute, and we slept most of the day after that horrible encounter this morning," Kate replied.

"The fog is coming in," Matt announced. He opened the door and wandered out to the wide, wraparound veranda to stare out over the ocean.

"Elle should be here any minute; she told us midnight," Kate said, studying the wisps of fog as they drifted toward land. "She'll make it before the fog hits the highway."

"Who decorated your Christmas tree?" Matt indicated the huge tree covered in lights and adorned with a variety of ornaments.

Kate went down the porch stairs to stand in front of the tree. She touched a small wooden elf. "Isn't it beautiful? Frank, one of the local artists, did this carving. Many of these ornaments have been handed down from generation to generation."

"Don't you worry about them out in the weather?" The tree was inside the yard, and two large dogs protected the area. Sarah's dogs. No one would sneak in and steal the ornaments, even the more precious ones, but the sea air and the continual rain could ruin the decorations.

"We never worry about weather," Kate said simply. "The Drakes have always decorated a tree outside and, hopefully, we always will."

The fog burst over them in a rolling swirl, wrapped around

the tree, and filled the yard, streaming in from the ocean as if pushed by an unseen hand.

"I think our old nemesis is attacking another Christmas symbol," Matt said, pointing to the top of the huge Christmas tree in the front yard. "What does the star stand for? There has to be a meaning."

The fog tangled around the branches, amplifying the glow of the lights through the vapor. Kate looked up at the star as it shorted out, sparks raining down through the fog. It brightened momentarily, then faded completely. She was looking up and saw through the wisps of clouds a hot, bright star streaking across the sky, plunging toward Earth. She went still, the color draining from her face. "Elle." She whispered her sister's name. "He's coming for Elle. That's what he was doing in the house. He's after Elle." The fog was choking the road, making it impossible to see.

"What the hell do you mean, it was in the house?" Matt raced back inside the house just as her sisters hurried outside to join Kate. He caught up the phone and called Jonas. He had no idea what Jonas could do. No one could see in the fog. They didn't know exactly where Elle was, only that she was close. She had said she'd arrive sometime around midnight. It was close to that now. She might be on the worst section of narrow, twisting highway leading to Sea Haven.

Kate whirled around, facing toward the town as a bell began to ring loudly. The sound reverberated through the night. "The bell is the symbol for guidance, for return. She's here now. She's coming up the highway now, returning to us. Returning to the fold. Sarah—" she caught her sister by the hand—"she's nearing the cliffs right now. Even if Hannah had the strength to bring in the wind, it's too late. He's warning us, telling us what he's going to do. Why would he do that?"

Kate reached for her youngest sister, mind to mind. She wasn't the most telepathic of her siblings, but Elle was a strong telepathic. Kate heard music, Joley's voice filling the car with her rich, warm tones. Elle's voice joining in. Elle drove slowly, crawling through the thick fog, knowing she was only a mile from her home. It was impossible to see in front of the car; she had no choice but to pull off the road and park until the fog lifted.

Elle peered at the side of the road, trying to see where the shoulder was wide enough to get her car off the highway in case another vehicle came along. She steered slowly over, aware the cliff was high above the pounding sea. Joley's voice was comforting, a sultry heat that kept the chilling cold from entering the car. Elle turned off the engine and pushed open the door, needing to get her bearings. If she could see the lights from any direction, she would know where she was. She knew she had to be close to her home. The fog surrounded her, a thick, congealed mass that was utterly cold.

Kate drew in her breath, tried to touch Elle, tried to warn her of the impending danger. Elle kept her hand on the car. *What is it, Kate?* 🌿

Kate cursed the fact that she couldn't form an answer and send it to her sister. She could only send the impression of danger very close. They all knew when their siblings were in danger, or tired or upset. But Kate didn't have the ability to actually tell Elle something was in the fog, something that was taking enough of a form that it could cause bodily harm. She didn't even know whether to tell her to stay in the car or to get away from it. She could only hope that Elle was sufficiently tapped in to all of her sisters and would know what was transpiring. Elle turned in the direction of their home and began to walk along the narrow path.

Matt rushed past Kate, heading toward the highway. The fog swallowed him immediately. "Try to clear it out, Kate," he called back. His voice sounded muffled in the thick mist, even to his own ears. He knew the trail; he'd walked it enough times over the years and was certain Elle would do the same.

Jonas and Jackson were converging from their locations as well, all of them running to Elle's aid from three different directions, but Matt had no idea if any of them would be in time. He only knew that his heart was in his throat, and he had such an overwhelming sense of imminent danger, he wanted to run flat out instead of carefully jogging his way along the steep, uneven path.

10

Beneath the star, that shines so bright,
An act unfolds, to my delight.

MATT HEARD VOICES, the rise and fall of feminine voices. He knew Kate and her sisters were doing their best to fight against the wall of fog crouched so malevolently on the high-way. He picked his way as fast and as carefully as he could. The ocean pounded and roared beneath him, waves slapping against the cliff and leaping high so that every now and then, as he jogged, he could feel the spray on his face. Rocks and the uneven ground impeded his progress. The wind picked up, blowing fiercely against the fog, taking chunks out over the roiling sea.

"Matt!" Jackson's disembodied voice called to him from deep inside the fog, somewhere ahead of him. "She's gone over the cliff. She's not in the water, but she's not going to be able to last much longer. Search along the edges." The voice was muffled and distorted by the fog.

"Watch yourself, Jackson, the cliff is crumbling in places," Matt cautioned. He didn't ask how Jackson knew Elle had gone over. Hell, he was beginning to believe he was the only person in the world without some kind of psychic talent. "Dammit, dammit, dammit." He couldn't return to Kate and tell her Elle was dead, that they'd been too late. He'd never be able to face her sorrow.

Matt inched toward the cliff, testing the ground every step of the way, making certain it would hold his weight. "Elle!" He shouted her name, heard Jackson, then Jonas echo his call. The ocean answered with another greedy roar, lifting higher, seeking prey. "Dammit, Elle, answer me." He felt desperation. Rage. Fear for Elle was beginning to swirl in the pit of his stomach. He detested inaction. He was a man who took charge, got the job done. He could have endless patience when needed, but he had to know what he was doing.

It seemed a hundred years until Jackson called out. "Found! I'll keep calling out so you both can get a direction. She's not going to be able to hang on, so I'm going down after her. I've tied off a safety rope."

Even with the fog distorting the voice, Matt got a sense of Jackson's direction and moved toward him. Jackson's voice was far more distant the second time he called out, and Matt knew he'd gone over the side of the cliff to try to get to Elle before she plunged into the sea. He'd been in combat with Jackson, had served on many covert missions with him. He wasn't a man to rush headlong into anything. If he was already going over the cliff to get to Elle, she needed the help. He was counting on Jonas and Matt to rescue them both. He knew they'd come for him.

Matt felt the crushed grass with his hand and flattened his body, belly down, reaching along the crumbling edge of the cliff until he found the rope. Jackson had tied off the end, using an old fence post. Matt sucked in his breath. The fence post was rotted and already coming out of the ground. "I'm tying off again, Jackson, give me a minute," Matt called down to him. He peered over the cliff.

Jackson was climbing down almost blind, feeling with his hands and toes for a grip. Elle lay sprawled out on a small ledge, clinging to a flimsy tree. He caught only glimpses of her as the fog was pushed out toward the sea. The heavy mist crawled down below the cliff line, hovering stubbornly in the more protected pocket to obscure the vision of the rescuers.

"Pass the rope back to me," Jonas said, coming up behind Matt.

Matt did so immediately, not taking his eyes from the scene unfolding below him. The fog was thick and churning, but the wind kept attacking it, driving it out in feathery clumps. It was the only thing that provided him with glimpses of the action. Jackson made his way, with painstaking care, down the sheer side of the cliff. Jonas tied off the rope to a much more secure anchor behind them, where Matt couldn't see.

"We're ready up here, Jackson, say the word," Matt called when Jonas signaled him the rope was safe to use. "Elle, I'm not hearing anything from you." He hadn't. Not a moan, not a call for help. It was alarming. He thought he could see her actively holding on to the small tree growing out of the side of the cliff, but the more he tried to pierce the veil of the fog, the more he was certain Elle wasn't moving.

As Jackson reached her, Matt held his breath, waiting. Afraid to hear, afraid not to hear. His heart beat loudly over the sound of the sea.

"She's alive," Jackson called up. "She has a nasty bump on the head, and she's bruised from head to toe, but she's alive."

Matt leaned farther over the cliff to hear the conversation below him. Jackson's voice drifted up to him. "Lie still, let me examine you for broken bones. I'm Jackson Deveau, the deputy sheriff."

"This ledge is crumbling." Elle's voice trembled. "Someone pushed me. I didn't hear them, but they pushed me."

"It's all right. Don't move. You're safe now." Jackson's voice was soothing. "Do you remember me? We met once a long time ago."

Matt recognized instantly the calming quality to Jackson's voice. He was talking to keep her from being agitated. "Jonas,

I think Elle's injured. I can tell by the way Jackson's acting."
Keeping his voice low, he gave the news to the sheriff, aware
that Jonas was anxious to know Elle's condition.

"I heard your voice, in a dream," Elle said. Her words
blurred around the edges, sending Matt's heart tripping. "You
were in pain. Terrible pain. Someone was torturing you. You
were in a small closet of a room. I remember."

Matt went still. Jonas froze behind him, obviously hearing
Elle's response.

"Then you know you're safe with me. You helped me when
I needed it. I'll get you out of this. That's the way the buddy
system works."

It was the most Matt had ever heard Jackson say to anyone.
He glanced back to look at Jonas's face. The fog along the
highway was clearing. The wind gusted, careening off the cliff
face in order to push the heavy mist away from Elle and Jackson. Jackson never talked about being captured. Never talked
about the treatment he'd endured. He never spoke of the escape that followed or how difficult it had been as he led a
small ragtag group of prisoners back through enemy lines to
join their forces.

That a Drake sister might be aware of details Matt and
Jonas weren't privy to no longer surprised either of them.

"Can you hold on to me as I climb up?" Jackson asked. "I
can send you up by the rope. Matthew Granite and Jonas Harrington are up top waiting for you. You're bound to accumu-
late a few more bruises being hauled up that way."

"I'd feel safer going up with you, but I seem to keep fading
in and out. Things sort of drift away," Elle answered.

Matt felt the tug of the rope, knew Jackson was tying the
safety line around Elle.

"Then we'll go up together," Jackson said. "I'm not going to
let anything happen to you."

"I know you won't." Elle circled his neck with her arms and
crawled carefully onto his back. Matt felt more tugs with the
rope and knew Jackson was tying her body to his.

"Your arm is broken. Can you hold on?"

"I don't exactly like the alternative, and Libby is blocking the pain for me."

Matt shook his head. Libby Drake, the doctor. A woman reputed to have a gift for healing the impossible. "Did you know Libby was anywhere near here?" he asked Jonas.

Jonas shook his head. "I knew she was coming home for Christmas, but not that she was on the way. But that isn't unusual for the Drakes. They're all connected somehow, and they tend to do things together."

Jackson's voice drifted up to them. "Good. I'm going to start climbing, Elle. It's going to hurt."

Elle pressed her face against Jackson's broad back. Matt watched Jackson start up the cliff, testing each finger- and toehold carefully before committing to the climb. Matt and Jonas kept the rope just taut enough to allow him to scale the vertical rock face. When Jackson was halfway to the top, the fog simply gave up, retreating before the onslaught of the wind. Matt leaned down to grasp Elle, as Jackson gained the top of the cliff.

Matt untied the rope and gently laid Elle on the ground. "I'll get to a car and radio for an ambulance," Jonas said.

Elle shook her head. "Libby's on her way. She'll fix me up." She turned her head to look at Jackson. "Thank you for coming for me. I didn't think anyone would find me." She touched the bump on her forehead. "I know the fall knocked me out."

Jackson shrugged and glanced at Matt and Jonas, shook his head, and remained silent. A car pulled up beside them and Libby Drake leaped out, dragging a black leather case with her. "How bad is she hurt, Jonas?"

"I'm fine, Libby," Elle protested.

Libby ignored her, looking to Jonas for the truth as she knelt beside her sister. Jackson answered her. "I think her left arm is broken. She definitely has a concussion, and she's either bruised her ribs or possibly fractured them. She's very tender on the left side. There's one laceration on her left leg that looks as if it could use a few stitches. Other than that, she's a mass of bruises."

"I don't want to go to the hospital, Libby," Elle protested.

"Too bad, baby, I think we're going to go and check you out."

Libby's word was obviously law. Elle protested repeatedly, but no one paid any attention to her. Matthew found himself holding Kate's hand in the waiting room while Libby went through all the required tests with Elle and finally settled her in a hospital bed for the remainder of the night.

Kate leaned into Matt's hard frame, looking up at him. "Thank you. I don't know what we would have done if you, Jonas, and Jackson hadn't found her. She looks all cut up." There was a little catch in her voice.

Matt immediately put his arms around her. "I'm taking you home. To my home, where you can get some rest, Kate. Elle's in good hands, you've kissed her ten times, and Libby's going to stay overnight with her. She can't be safer than that. Jackson brought her car to your house and left it for her, so everything's taken care of. Come home with me, Katie. Let me take care of you."

"You need a shave," she observed, her hungry gaze drinking him in.

They walked together to his car, their steps in perfect harmony. Matt smiled because he loved being with her more than anything else. He rubbed his jaw. "You're right, I do. You're not only going to have whisker burn on your face, but if I'm not more careful, you'll have it other places too."

She blushed beautifully. "I already do."

He opened the door for her, caught her chin before she could slide in. "Seriously?" Just the idea of it made his body hard.

Kate nodded. "It's nice to have a constant reminder." It was more than nice. Just the thought of how the marks had gotten there made her hot with need.

Matt dragged her close to him, his mouth taking command of hers. It seemed far too long since he'd been able to kiss her.

To have her all to himself. "I want to get you home where I can put you into my bed. I still have such a hard time believing you're with me."

She laughed. "Imagine how I feel."

Kate leaned her head back against the seat of his car and looked at him, the smile fading from her face. "Matt, you shouldn't have wished on the snowglobe. It isn't an ordinary Christmas globe."

He glanced at her, then back at the road, his expression settling into serious lines. "Nothing about you or your family is ordinary, Katie. I knew what I was doing."

She opened her mouth to speak, shook her head, and stared out the window into the night.

Matt searched for something to say to reassure her. Or maybe it was he that needed the reassurance. Kate was still resistant to the idea of a long-term relationship, and he wasn't certain he could change her mind. He couldn't begin to explain the sense of rightness he felt when he drove up to his house with Kate beside him. He sat in his car, looking up at the house with its bank of windows for the view, and the wide, inviting decks going in every direction. "I built this house for you. I even put in a library and two offices, just in case you wanted your own office. I asked Sarah a few years ago, when I first came back, if you had a preference where you wrote, and she said you preferred a room with a view and soft music. I added a fireplace just in case you needed the ambience."

Kate blinked back tears, leaned over, and kissed him. What could she say? Everyone in town knew Sarah. Sarah was magic. She could scale cliff walls and she knew things before they happened. She could leap out of airplanes and climb tall buildings. Sarah lived her life. She didn't dream the way Kate did or live in her imagination.

Matt took her hand and pulled her out of the car. "I soundproofed your office so the noise wouldn't bother you."

"What noise?" She knew better than to ask, but she couldn't stop herself.

"Our kids. You do want kids, don't you? I'm afraid the Granites tend to throw males. I don't have a single female cousin. You do like boys, don't you?"

Kate looked away from him, out to the booming sea. Sarah would have children. All of her sisters would have them. She'd probably tell them all stories. Maybe she should have been the one to wish on the snowglobe. Maybe she should have wished for the courage to do the right thing.

"Katie, if you don't want children, I'll be happy with it being just the two of us. You know that, don't you?" He unlocked the door to the house and stepped back to let her in. "Children would be wonderful, but not necessary. If we can have them. Sometime in the future, after I've spent endless time making love to you all over the house."

Kate went straight to the Christmas tree. She wanted him. She wanted him for as long as she could have him. She swallowed her tears and lifted her chin, smiling at him. "I like that idea. Making love to you all over the house. Would you turn on the Christmas lights? I love miniature lights like these."

Matt plugged in the lights for her. His house was dark and quiet and a bit on the cool side. He'd never bothered with heavy curtains in the living room because he had no close neighbors, and the bank of windows faced the sea. Kate dropped her purse on the nearest chair and kicked off her shoes. "It's nice to come home. Just for tonight, I want to think about Christmas and not some awful thing coming out of the fog to hurt everyone." She looked up at him, her large eyes sad. "Do you think we'll manage to get one night together, Matthew?"

"I don't know, Katie. I hope so. I'm going to check the house and downstairs, and I'll be right back." He didn't think he could sleep, not even holding her in his arms, until he checked the sand outside for any peculiar footprints.

"That's a good idea. I'll make us up a bed. You don't mind if we sleep out here by the tree, do you?"

Matt looked around the huge, spacious living room. The

miniature lights winked on and off, colors flickering along the walls and the high ceiling. "I'd like that, Kate."

He circled the house, checked the rooms beneath the deck and the beach for any signs of intrusion. He had the feeling the enemy was as fatigued as they were. He glanced out to sea. "How about giving us a break, buddy," he murmured softly. "Whatever has you all upset, Kate had nothing to do with it."

Above his head the skies opened up and poured down rain. Matt grinned wryly and hurried back to the house. Back to Kate. The gas fireplace was lit, the "logs" burning cheerfully. On the mantel were several lighted candles. The scent of berry permeated the air. In the flickering lights, he saw Kate, lying naked on the sheets, her body beautiful, sprawled lazily on the covers while she watched the lights of the Christmas tree. His breath rushed from his lungs, so that he burned for air, just standing there in the doorway staring in surprise at the most incredible Christmas present he could imagine. That was how he thought of her. His Christmas present. He would love this time of year forever.

"Matthew." She turned over, smiled at him. "Come lie down with me."

He could see the real Kate Drake. On the outside, she seemed flawless, perfect, out of reach, yet she was really vulnerable, and as fragile as she was courageous. Kate needed a shield and he was more than happy to be that shield, for her. He could stand between her and the rest of the world. "Give me a minute, Kate."

Kate turned back to the tree, watching the lights blinking on and off, so many colors flickering across the wall. It was heaven just to lie down and rest. To relax. More than anything she loved to feel Matt's heated gaze on her. He made her feel beautiful and incredibly special. He was a large man, and the feel of his hands on her body, the way his body came alive at the sight of her, was a gift. A treasure.

Kate lay with the sheets cool on her skin and the lights playing over her body. She imagined his hands on her. His eyes on her. Thinking about him made her grow hot with need. A small sound alerted her, and she looked up to see him towering over her. For a moment she couldn't breathe. She drank him in. His strong legs and muscular thighs. His amazing erection. His flat stomach and heavily muscled chest. Finally, his eyes. His eyes had turned smoky, seductive, and now they smoldered with intensity and heat. "You take my breath away." It was a silly thing to say, but it was true. She patted the blanket beside her. She wanted to touch him, to know he was real. To feel him solid and strong beneath her fingertips.

"I'm supposed to say that to you." He stretched out beside her, gathered her into his arms to hold her to him. "I want to lie here with you for a very long time."

She rested her head on his shoulder, fitting her body more closely to his. "I wouldn't mind staying here for the rest of the winter, locked away in our own private world." She stretched languidly, pleased to be able to relax. To have him holding her with such gentleness.

Matt knew she was tired, and it was enough to hold her in his arms, even with his body raging at him and her body so soft and inviting and open to his. His mouth drifted down the side of her neck. She snuggled closer, turning her head toward the Christmas tree, giving him even better access.

"I love the way you smell," he said. Because he couldn't resist, he slid his palm over her skin. He'd never felt anything so soft. He traced her ribs, a gentle exploration, not in the least demanding, simply wanting to touch her. Her soft belly called to him, a mystery for a breast man, but he loved the way she reacted each time he caressed her there.

Kate smiled. "I love the feel of your hands."

"I've always hated my hands. Workingman hands, rough and big and meant for manual labor."

"Meant to bring pleasure to a woman, you mean," she contradicted, and caught his hand to bring it to her lips. She kissed the pads of his fingers, nibbled on the tips, and drew one into her mouth.

He caught his breath, aching with love, burning up with need. "Everything about you is so damned feminine, Kate. Sometimes I'm afraid if I touch you, I'm going to break you." He measured her wrist loosely by circling it with his thumb and index finger.

She laughed and rubbed her body against his affectionately, almost like a contented cat. "I doubt you have to worry about breaking me. This thing with the fog is draining, but I recover quickly." She frowned, even as she ran her fingertips along the hard column of his thigh. "I am a little worried about Hannah though, and now Elle."

He was very much aware of her fingers so close to his throbbing erection. She was tapping out a little rhythm on his upper thigh. His stomach constricted, and his blood thickened. The lights on the Christmas tree blinked on and off in harmony with the drumming of her fingers. Every tap brought a surge of heat through his body. "The doctors said Elle was going to be fine. She'll have a whale of a headache, though, and Jackson was right about her ribs and arm, but she'll heal fast with Libby around."

Matt cupped her breast in his hands, his thumbs teasing her nipples into taut pebbles. He felt her response, the swift intake of breath. The flush that covered her body. "It seems such a miracle to me to be able to touch you like this. I wonder if every other man knows what a miracle a woman's body is."

"And all this time, I thought the miracle was a man's body." Kate ran her fingernails lightly along his belly.

"Maybe the miracle is just that I finally managed to stop you from hiding from me," Matt decided. He bent his head, flickered her nipple with his tongue, made a lazy foray around the areola. She moved slightly, turning to give him better access.

"I've been thinking about the fog. Something isn't quite right."

"Quite right?" He lifted his head to look at her, arching his eyebrow. The Christmas lights were playing red and green and blue over her stomach. A bright red light glowed across the small triangle of curls at the junction of her legs. It was distracting and made it hard to concentrate on conversation. He slipped his hand in the middle of the flashing light, watched his fingers stroke the nest of curls, felt Kate shiver, and pushed his fingers deep into her warm wet sheath. She pushed back against him, a soft moan escaping. He dipped his head to find her breast, suckling strongly. "What are you thinking, Kate?" His tongue swirled over her nipple, and he pushed deeper inside her until her hips began a helpless ride.

"He isn't going after Hannah. Why attack me? Or Elle? Or even Abbey? He should go after Hannah. She summons the wind to drive him out to sea. She stops him." Her words came in little short bursts. She gasped as she pushed against his hand, as her body tightened with alarming pressure, with the pure magic of passion shared with Matthew.

"Take the pins out of your hair," he whispered, his voice raw. "I love your hair down. You look very sexy with your hair down."

"You think I look sexy no matter what," she pointed out.

His teeth teased her nipple, nibbled over her breast. "True, but I love the hair."

"You won't love it when it's falling all over you." But she was lifting her arms, pulling out pins and scattering them in every direction while he shifted her, lowering his body into the cradle of her hips, thrusting deep inside her.

She cried out when he surged forward. Whips of lightning danced through her blood. "Matthew." There was a plea for mercy, and he hadn't even gotten started.

"We have all the time in the world, Katie," he whispered, his lips sliding over her throat, her chin, and up to her mouth. His strong hips paused, waiting. She held her breath. He thrust hard, a long stroke surging deep to bury himself completely within her. A coming home. She was velvet soft and tight and fiery hot. He wanted a long slow night with her. His hands shaped her body, stroking and caressing every inch of her.

"I don't feel like we have all the time in the world." She protested, breathless, arching her hips to meet the impact of his. "I feel like I'm going to go up in flames."

"Then do it," he encouraged. "Come for me a hundred times. Over and over. Scream for me, Kate. I love you so much. I love watching you come for me. And I love your body, every square inch of it. I want to spend the night worshiping you."

Kate wanted the same thing. She did scream, clutching at the bedcovers for an anchor as her body fragmented, and she went spinning off into space. She couldn't tell if the whirling colors were behind her eyes or from the Christmas tree lights. She found it didn't matter when he caught her hips firmly, held her still, and began surging into her once more with his slow, deep strokes.

11

In the stocking hung with gentle care,
A mystery, I know, is hidden there.

MATT WOKE ALREADY aroused. He was thick and aching, so tight he thought he'd burst through his own skin. The blankets had fallen onto the floor as if he had spent a long, restless night. His body was stark naked and mercilessly aroused. He looked down at Kate. She smiled up at him, her sea-green eyes sultry, her hands moving gently over his flat stomach. Her long hair spilled over his hips and thighs, teasing every nerve ending. He knotted a long strand around his fist. "I dreamed of you, Kate."

Her smile was that of a temptress. "I hope it was a good dream." She bent her head to her task, lovingly stroking her tongue over the thick inviting length of him, sliding the velvet knob into the heated tightness of her mouth.

Matt gasped as the pleasure/pain of it rocked him. "How could it not be?" he asked when he got his breath back. Her tongue made a teasing foray along the rigid length and stroked over him before she once again slid her mouth around him.

He closed his eyes, his hips surging forward, wanting more, needing more, as waves of heat spread through his body, as every muscle clenched and tightened. Kate's fist wrapped him up while her mouth performed miracles. "I don't know if I'll survive this, Kate."

Her answer was muffled, her breath warm and enticing, her mouth hot and tight. He was certain he felt her laughter vibrate through his entire body. There was joy in Kate. That was her secret, he decided. Joy in everything she did with him. She didn't pretend not to enjoy his body, she reveled in exploring him, teasing him, driving him to the very edge of his control.

Kate kissed her way up his belly and over his chest. She mounted him, the way an accomplished horseback rider smoothly slides aboard a horse, settling her body over his with exquisite slowness. She put up her hands and he took them so she could use leverage as her body rose and fell, stroking his. Her hair spilled around her, adding to her allure as her full breasts bounced and beckoned with every movement. She threw her head back, arched back, moving differently, tightening muscles until he was certain he would explode.

"Kate." Her name was a husky, almost hoarse sound, escaping from his constricted throat. His lungs burned. A fire spread through his belly, centered in his groin, and gathered into a wild conflagration. He couldn't take his gaze from her. There was a sheen to her skin, a flush over her body. She moved with a woman's sensuous grace and mystery. "The feel of your hair on my legs and belly makes me crazy." It should have tickled his skin, but the silky fall brushed over sensitive nerve endings and added to the heat and fire building in the deep within him. He felt as if every part of his body was being pulled in that direction.

Kate moved with exquisite slowness, undulating her body, sending him right out of his mind. The erotic visual only increased his raging hunger for her. In the soft morning sunlight, her hair flashed red streaks, and her pale skin seemed made of dewy petals. Most of all, the expression on her face, deeply absorbed in the ride of lust and love and passion, shook his entire being. He could read the way her body began to build pressure, her muscles clenching tightly, gripping him strongly. He could see it on her face, the rapture, the passion, the intensity of the orgasm as it overtook her. He watched her ride it out, watched the excitement and pleasure on her face, in her body. Seeing her like that heightened his own pleasure, and he wanted more, wanted her flushed body to feel it again and again and bring his body to his own explosive orgasm.

He caught her hips in his hands, taking control, guiding her ride, thrusting upward hard as she slid down over him, encasing him in a fist of hot velvet. He shuddered with pleasure, feeling the pressure building relentlessly. He could feel her body preparing for a second shock, the muscles tightening around him, adding to the intensity of his explosion. It shook him, a volcano going off, detonating from the inside out, taking everything in its path. He caught her to him, fighting for air, fighting to regain some sense of where he was, of a time and place, not fantasyland, where his every dream came true. It seemed impossible to be lying on his living room floor, his heart raging at him, his body in ecstasy, and the love of his life in his arms. His world had been guns and sand and jungles and an enemy fighting to kill him. Women like Kate were not real and they didn't wind their arms around his neck and rain kisses all over his face and tell him he was too sexy to be alive.

They lay together just holding one another, trying to get

their heart rates back to normal and to push air through their lungs. Kate lay stretched out on top of Matt, pressing her soft body tightly against his. Beneath her, he suddenly stiffened.

"What the hell is that?" he growled, hearing a noise outside the house.

Kate gasped and rolled off of him, landing on the pile of blankets. "We have company, Matthew," she whispered, gathering the sheets around her.

He sat up abruptly, his breath hissing through his teeth. He'd asked for a night with Kate, he should have asked for the entire damned week. He was never going to get enough of her, never be sated. "I thought I'd at least get you for a few more hours," he groused as he padded naked across the floor. He suddenly halted halfway to the door and uttered a string of curses. "It's my parents."

Kate's eyes widened. She clutched the sheet to her naked breasts. "What?"

"My parents," he announced. He reached down to help her up. "Why is it that even when you're grown, parents can make you feel like a teenager caught in the act?"

Kate wrapped the sheet around her and hurried toward his bedroom while Matt scooped up the blankets and followed her. "Did you get caught in the act often?"

"Are you laughing at me?" he asked, a dangerous glint in his silver eyes.

"Only because I'm disappearing into the bathroom to leave you to face the music alone. You might get dressed." She grinned mischievously at him as she gathered up her clothes and retreated behind a securely locked door.

Matt caught sight of the wisp of peach-colored lace that lay on the floor and found a wicked smile stealing over his face. He stooped down and picked it up, bunching it into his hand before shoving it into the pocket of his jacket, which was lying on the back of a chair. He dragged on clothes as fast as he could, combing his hair with his fingers just as the polite knock on his door came.

He could hear Kate laughing, and it was contagious. He couldn't wipe the grin off his face as he opened the front door. Victoria Granite threw her arms around her son and hugged him hard. "You frightened us, Matt! We called and called and you never answered. First there was a fire here and Danny told us about that horrible incident at the store and then a call went out and . . ."

"Victoria, take a breath," Harold Granite advised. He smiled lovingly at his wife, used to her run-on sentences. "We heard the fog came in last night, and Elle Drake went over the cliff. Victoria was worried."

Matt's mother made a face. "Really, Harold, I knew he was perfectly fine; you were the one who spent the entire morning trying to call him and pacing back and forth like a wild tiger. I was fine!"

Matt met his father's gaze over the top of his mother's head. They both stifled a knowing grin. "I'm sorry, Dad. I should have remembered after all these years, how you worry."

Victoria smiled and patted Harold's arm. "There, dear, you see there was nothing at all to worry about. All that pacing." She shook her head, stopping in midsentence as she looked up at the mantel and the candles that had burned down to the holders. "Oh my goodness." She looked around carefully. "Matthew Granite, you had a woman here last night, didn't you?"

"Mom, once I turned thirty, I thought we agreed I didn't have to talk about women with you."

From the bedroom came the sound of a door closing. His parents exchanged a long, satisfied look. Victoria arched her eyebrow at her son. "She's still here?"

"As a matter of fact, yes. And don't start on her, Mom. I don't want her scared off. This is the one."

There was another startled silence. "Kate's here?" Harold asked, clearly astonished. "Kate Drake?"

"Of course it's Kate," Victoria said.

Kate came out of the bedroom with a bright smile and desperation in her eyes. She was wearing one of his shirts over her thin white blouse. Matthew was instantly mortified. He thought he would tease her, and at the same time, he'd have the added pleasure of knowing she was sitting beside him in the warmth of his car without a bra. He'd planned to slip his hand inside the white silk of her blouse and caress her soft creamy skin. The idea alone had made him as hard as a rock. It hadn't occurred to him that her blouse was sheer enough that her darker nipples would show so alluringly.

Kate always presented a near flawless appearance to the world, and he realized immediately when he saw the desperation in her eyes that it was her armor. She wore her clothes and hair and makeup to keep people from seeing the real Kate. The vulnerable Kate. The Kate she shared only with her sisters, and now with him.

"Hello Mrs. Granite, Mr. Granite," she greeted.

Matthew drew the edges of his shirt together around her, sliding several buttons in place. He bent to kiss her, shielding her from his parents' scrutiny for a brief moment. When he was certain she was sufficiently covered, he circled her waist with his arms and held her in front of him. He could feel her soft unbound breasts pushing against his arms. Instantly his body reacted, thickening, hardening, an ache pounding through his blood. He held her close to him, covering the painful bulge stretching the material of his jeans. Kate was without mercy, slowly and sensuously rubbing her round bottom over the hard ridge. "I would very much like to visit, but Elle's in the hospital, and we have to go by Kate's house before we go to see her." Was that his voice? It sounded thick and husky to his ears. He was even afraid color burned in his face. His palms itched to cup Kate's breasts in his hands. The soft weight on his arms was driving him crazy. His mouth had actually gone dry. And if she didn't stop the way she was rubbing against him, he was going to shock everyone right then and there. "Let's have dinner tonight," he suggested, in desperation making eye contact with his father.

Harold, taking the cue, caught Victoria's elbow firmly.

"Danny will be spending the evening with Trudy Garret and her little boy at the Grange. Santa Claus is stuffing stockings and delivering presents around seven. We were going to watch," Victoria said. "Can we plan for another night?"

"Tomorrow is the pageant rehearsal," Matt said. "You all are in that. Maybe we can grab dinner afterward."

"There's never time." Harold shook his head, but headed across the living room to the front door. "The pageant rehearsal never runs smoothly, and we're always there until midnight."

"Good point," Matt agreed. "Don't worry, Mom, we'll have dinner together soon." He walked them to the door. "Who's playing Santa Claus this year?"

Harold grinned. "No one's supposed to know, Matt." He went out into the light drizzle and paused. "Jeff Burley broke his leg a couple of weeks ago. He's done it every year, and we had a bit of trouble finding a replacement. Everyone's afraid of the fog. Some of the townspeople think it's some kind of alien invasion."

Victoria put up her umbrella and made a little face. "People are so silly sometimes."

"I hope you're not trying to ask me to be Santa Claus this year, I'm more afraid of the kids than I am of aliens." Matt sounded as stern as he dared with his mother.

Kate made a move to retreat back into the house, but Matt held her firmly as if she were his only refuge. The cold air hardened Kate's nipples into tight buds, and she was acutely aware she wore no bra beneath Matt's shirt. The drizzle was penetrating straight through the material and turning the silk blouse beneath it transparent. She crossed her arms over her chest and kept her smile firmly in place.

"There aren't any aliens," Victoria said, exasperated. "And no, you don't have to play Santa. I know better than to ask any of you boys. You'd frighten the children with your nonsense."

"Not Dad!" Matt suddenly sounded authoritative, and Kate looked up. "Dad, the doctor told you not to overdo."

"Playing Santa Claus wouldn't overdo anything." Harold was clearly annoyed. "And no, it isn't me. We had someone come forward, but he wishes to remain anonymous. It would ruin all of his fun if I revealed his identity."

Matt followed his parents to their car, taking Kate with him. "I'm not going to tell anyone."

"The last man you'd ever expect," Victoria said primly.

"The last man I'd ever expect to play Santa would be Old Man Mars." Matt laughed. "Can't you see Danny's face? He'd run from Santa."

Victoria and Harold looked at one another and burst out laughing. Victoria waved gaily at Kate. Matt stared after them. "You don't think they meant that mean old man is going to play Santa."

"I can't imagine it. I think they were teasing you. Do you have the car keys? I'm getting cold, and I have to stop by my house to pick up some clothes before we go to the hospital."

"I've got them. Come on. Let's get you out of the rain." Matt drew her bra from his jacket pocket and held it out to her. "I'm sorry, Katie. I couldn't stop thinking about playing out my little fantasy of being able to touch you when I was taking you home. It was childish of me."

Kate merely looked at the peach-colored bra in his outstretched hand, but made no move to take it. "And you wanted to be able to touch me how?" She walked past him to the car. There was a distinct sway to her beautiful rear, one he couldn't resist. Kate settled into his car, slowly unbuttoned the wet overshirt, and allowed the edges to gape open to reveal the transparent silk blouse underneath. She leaned back against the seat.

Matt drove slowly along the coastal highway, fighting for air when there was none in the car. The shape of her breasts was not only outlined beneath the see-through material, but highlighted. "Kate, you're an incredible woman."

"I'm a lucky woman. I rather like your fantasies. By all means, tell me whenever you get one."

He couldn't resist. Matt slipped his hand inside her blouse, cupped the soft, creamy flesh in his palm. His knuckle rubbed gently over her breast, the pads of his fingers possessive as he caressed her body. Right at that moment he could think of a hundred fantasies. He turned the car onto the drive leading to the bluff overlooking the sea. The moment he parked, he caught the back of her head and held her still while he devoured her mouth.

They spent an hour in the car, laughing like children, necking like teenagers, wildly happy as they held hands, touched and kissed and whispered of dreams and hopes and erotic fantasies.

When they arrived at the Drake house, no one was home; the sisters were all at the hospital. There was a note for Kate telling her Elle was doing much better and instructing her to join them when she could. Kate took the time to shower. Matt joined her and spent a long while leisurely lathering soap over her and rinsing her off. He made love to her under the spray of water, then dried her off with large towels. He couldn't take his eyes off of her while she dressed. "I've never been happier, Kate," he admitted, as she pinned the thick length of hair on top of her head into her "perfect Kate" style.

"Me either," she answered, and leaned over to kiss him.

Matt caught her hand and dragged her through the house into the living room. "Kate, do you love me? You know I love you. I tell you. I show you. I want to spend my life with you, and I've made no secret about that. Do you love me?"

Kate nearly stopped breathing. She touched his face. "How could you not know, Matthew? I love you so much I ache with it sometimes."

"Then why won't you agree to marry me? I don't think your family objects to me, and obviously my family would welcome it."

She let her breath out slowly. "I have some things to work out, Matt. I want to marry you. I do. But I have to be certain it's right for you. That I'm right for you."

"Katie. Honey. I know you're right for me." He looked

around the room. "Where's that damned snowglobe anyway?" He retrieved it from the shelf.

Kate took it out of his hands. "You only get one wish, Matt, and you've had yours." She went to place the globe back on the shelf, but it came alive in her hands, the fog swirling. Waiting. Kate closed her eyes and made her wish. She couldn't stop herself. She wanted Matthew Granite more than she'd ever wanted anything in her life.

Matt said nothing, asking her no questions. He simply took her hand in a gesture of solidarity.

Kate and Matt spent most of the afternoon in the hospital with Kate's sisters in Elle's room. Matt and Damon played a game of chess while the seven sisters caught up on news. Joley helped Damon, and when Matt expressed disapproval, Abbey immediately took Matt's side. They did their best to entertain Elle, who looked bruised and very young. Her bright red hair tumbled around her white face and heightened her pale skin and deepened the purple in the bruises. She was in good spirits but weak and still had a headache.

Matt and Kate left the hospital in the evening to meet the Granites at the Grange, where most of the townspeople were bringing their children for photos with Santa and a small party.

The Grange hall was packed with parents and children. "Jingle Bells" blared through the building, mistletoe was hung in every conceivable place, and holly decorated the tables laden with cookies and punch. A fake mantel went along the entire length of one wall with holly, candles, and tiny sleighs filled with candy canes adorning the top. Rows of stockings hung on gleaming hooks. The silver-tipped fir tree nearly reached the ceiling and was covered in lights, ornaments, and a multitude of white angels with silver wings.

"The ladies at the arts and crafts shop have been busy," Matt whispered.

Kate shushed him, but her eyes were laughing. Several elves hurried past them, bells tinkling from their hats and ankles. Kate and Matt followed the elves through the crowd to the back of the building, where Santa Claus sat in a high-backed chair surrounded by more elves and a reindeer that looked suspiciously like a dog with plastic antlers attached to his head. The line to visit Santa was long, small children clutching parents' hands and staring with large round eyes at the jolly old man. The Santa suit fit perfectly, and the white beard and mustache seemed natural, both bushy enough to hide the face successfully. Matt tried to get close enough to get a good look at the Santa. Several preteenagers rushed past him laughing loudly, tossing popcorn at each other.

"Do you think it's Old Man Mars?" Matt whispered.

"How could it be?" Kate asked. "He hates Christmas."

"Right height. I could tell if he were talking loud or maybe even by the way he walks." Matt weaved his way through the small children.

"Hey!" a young boy with red hair protested. "No cutting in."

"I just wanted to ask Santa if he'd give me Kate for Christmas," Matt explained.

Unimpressed, the boy wrinkled his nose, and all of his friends made faces. "Well, you got to stand in line like everyone else."

Kate laughed and dragged Matt away from Santa Claus. He spotted Inez and pulled Kate toward her. "If anyone knows who Santa Claus is, it'll be Inez. She knows everything."

"Doesn't that come under the heading of gossip?"

"News, Katie. How can you even use the word *gossip*?" Matt stopped moving abruptly and brought her up short, staring out the window. He bit out a string of curses. "The damned fog is rolling in, Kate. It's coming right this way."

Kate looked at him, then looked around at the children. "I don't want people to panic and run for their cars to get away from here. No one would be able to drive in the fog. I'll find a way to distract the kids." She hurried toward Santa Claus, whispering softly to the children so that the throng parted like the Red Sea to give her access to the jolly old man sitting with a child on his lap. She leaned in and spoke to him.

From a distance, Matt watched Santa stiffen, listen some

more, and nod. Kate straightened up and directed the children into a large circle. Santa gave out candy canes, patting heads and laughing as he did so. Several mothers began distributing cookies and punch while Kate started an enthralling Christmas story. Matt had never seen anyone hold an entire room in her hand, but there was no sound other than the faint background of Christmas music and Kate's spellbinding voice. He found himself caught up in the sheer beauty of the magical tone, even when the fog began to seep through the cracks of the doors and windows.

There was no way to keep the fog out. It was only the magic of Kate's voice, the anonymous Santa Claus's cheerful punctuation of ho, ho, ho woven cleverly into the storyline, and the Granite reputation in the community that kept panic from spreading as the gray-white vapor filled the room, bringing with it the scent and feel of the sea. Kate smoothly incorporated the fog into the storyline, having the children hold hands and interact with Santa's ho, ho, ho. The children did so with enthusiasm, laughing wildly at the antics of Kate's characters in the fog. Matt realized she was creating the illusion that the fog was deliberate, a part of the story she was telling, used for effect. He could see parents relaxing, thinking Kate had found a way to keep the children from fearing the incoming fog, a part of life for anyone who lived on the coast.

It seemed hours to Matt, watching the fog churning, swirling in deeper shades of gray, spinning when there was no breeze to create the effect, yet it was only a few minutes before the fog began a hasty retreat . . . almost as if it couldn't take the sound of Kate's voice. It was a silly notion. Fog had no ears to listen, but it also shouldn't have been able to leave footprints in sand or do damage to property. He made his way closer to Kate, knowing she would pay a steep price using her energy to keep such a large crowd under the spell of her voice. As he moved toward her, he felt something in the fog, something tangible brush against his arm.

Matt whirled toward it, hands going up in a fighter's defensive position, but there were only coils of vapor surrounding him. He heard a sound, a growling voice muttering a warning.

A chill went down his spine. He felt the touch of death on him, bony fingers reaching for him, or someone who belonged to him. The hair on his body stood up in reaction to the half moan, half growl that could have been wind, but there was no wind to generate the sound. Matt knew it was a warning, but the words made no sense.

Anger was impotent against fog. He couldn't fight it, couldn't wrestle it; he couldn't even shoot it. How could he protect Kate when he couldn't see or get his hands on the culprit? He stood very still as the vapor simply rolled from the building, leaving behind the soft Christmas music and the laughter of the children. He looked around the room, at the sunny faces, at the tree and decorations. Why had the fog come, only to recede without incident?

He made his way to Kate's side, slipping his arm around her waist to lend her strength. She sent the children to the tables of food, a smile on her face, shadows in her eyes. Laughter picked up as if the fog had never been; but Matt continued to survey the room, inch by inch, concerned there had to be more, something they were all missing.

Kate leaned into him as they looked out the window. "It's heading out to sea on its own. Why would it do that? Why would it come here and leave?"

Matt watched the children eating. Santa Claus was eating. "Could it have poisoned the food some way?" he asked, his heart in his throat at the thought. His parents were seated at a table with Danny, Trudy Garret, and her young son.

"I doubt it, Matthew, how could it?"

"How could he do any of the things he's been doing?" His hands tightened on her shoulders. "Santa Claus is a symbol of Christmas, right? What does he represent?"

"You don't think he came to attack the man playing the part of Santa, then decided against it, do you?" Her anxious gaze followed the burly man in the red-and-white suit.

Matt shook his head. "I feel danger, Katie. When I feel it this strong, it's here, close by. Tell me what Santa represents."

She rubbed her throbbing temples. "Goodwill, I suppose. He represents goodwill and generosity. He gives presents, stuffs stockings, eats the children's milk and cookies."

"He spreads goodwill among the people and is generous, teaching by example to be generous." Matt tugged on her hand, moved toward the tree where Santa's pack lay. He peered inside. There were a few netted candy cane stockings holding small toys, candy, and various small personal items the town always generously donated for the event. Santa had slipped most of the candy cane net stockings into the children's stockings hanging from the fake mantel earlier when he'd first arrived, so that each child would have something to take home after the party.

Matt went to the brightly colored stockings, each with a child's name stitched in bold letters across the top. Kate's fingers tightened around his. She already knew, just as he did. They peered inside. She drew back, stifling a cry, looking at him with fear. Inside each stocking, the fog had added to Santa's generous gift. A mass of sand and sea bugs writhed in hideous black balls in the toes of the stockings. All were damp with seawater and smelled faintly of the noxious odor the fog seemed to leave behind. Crushed shells and spiny sea anemones, kelp and small crabs were mixed with the wiggling insects.

Santa Claus joined them, staring at the mess while all around them children ate and laughed and played. "We have to get rid of these. Some of these creatures are venomous."

Matt glanced quickly at the man, recognizing the voice. Old Man Mars was indeed playing Santa. "You're right. I'll get a couple of the men, and we'll get the stockings out of here before the children start trying to collect them. Kate." He pulled out a chair for her. "Sit down before you fall down. I'll take you home when we're through here."

"To my house," she said in a weary voice. "I need to go to my house."

He nodded, his gut knotting tightly.

12

A candle burns with an eerie glow,
As it melts, the wax does flow,

"THE THING IN the fog spoke to me." Matt made the announcement after the Drake sisters had settled Elle firmly in the living room. It was late afternoon before the doctors let her go home, and her family had been so anxious, Matt had steered clear of the subject of the danger in the fog. He and Kate had gone to the mill earlier in the morning to reexamine the seal and see if she could find anything new about the spirit. He hadn't wanted to bring up the subject at the very source of the trouble.

There was a sudden silence. He had their attention immediately. Kate set down her teacup. "You didn't say anything to me about it."

"You were exhausted and worried about Elle last night, Katie, and again this morning. I didn't want to bring it up. Now that she's home and safe, I thought it was a good time to discuss it." En masse, the Drake sisters were difficult to contend with. He could feel every eye on him. There was power in the room, intangible, feminine, but a steady flow of it. An energy he couldn't begin to explain, but he knew it moved from sister to sister.

"What did it say?" Sarah asked. Her voice was gentle, nonjudgmental. Practical, magical Sarah. She was the oldest and the most influential.

"It made no sense. It was a moan and a growl mixed together. The syntax was old-fashioned, but from what I got, it was a warning to keep my loved ones away from the one with the staff."

"The staff? He used the word *staff*?" Kate asked.

Matt nodded. "I've thought a lot about it, and maybe it all ties up with Christianity and the staff of life or something. Anything to do with the Christian beliefs of Christmas is under attack?" He made it a question.

Elle lifted the old journal Sarah handed to her. "I'll do my best to try to find a reference to a staff in here," she said. "I don't think I thanked you for coming to my rescue the other night, Matt. One minute I was making my way home, and the next I felt something shove me over the side of the cliff. I broke every fingernail on the way down, grabbing at dirt and rocks. I have no idea how Jackson climbed down to get me. I couldn't even call out with a strong enough voice for help, and I was afraid to move. The ledge was literally crumbling under me."

"I know it was frightening, Elle, but we have you, you're safe now," Joley soothed.

"Kate said something the other evening about how the entity didn't go after Hannah. It's strange because Hannah's the one providing the wind to drive him out to sea and away from the town," Matt said. "Do any of you have any idea why he's chosen not to try to harm her?"

Sarah frowned. "It really only went after Elle."

Kate shook her head. "It definitely tried for me, Sarah. And I think it tried to use Sylvia and her amorous ways to get to Abbey, then made a second attempt here in the house, pitting her against Jackson. Jackson's a mercurial man, and Sylvia's unpredictable. I think it wanted Abbey out of the way too. Of all of us, wouldn't Hannah be its main obstacle?"

"What do you all have in common?" Matt asked. He watched as Sarah moved through the living room lighting tall, thick candles at each entranceway. The candles each had three wicks and sat in wrought-iron holders. She murmured something he couldn't hear as she lit each candle. He realized the windows had arrangements of colorful flowers and herbs tied in bundles on either side of the sills and above the window frames. The bundles of dried arrangements hadn't been there before. The fragrance was a blend of outdoors and strong scents of rosemary, jasmine, and something else he couldn't quite identify. The lights of the candles flickered on the walls, dancing and leaping with every movement of the sisters, as if tuned to them.

"Abbey, Kate, and Joley all have special gifts involving their voices," Sarah answered, bending over a tall cranberry candle near the bay window. She glanced over at her youngest sister before lighting the round candle. "Elle has many talents, but she doesn't share their voice. She is, however, a strong telepath, and she can share the shadow world with Kate. Neither Joley nor Abbey has that ability."

"But nothing happened to Joley," Matt said. He sighed. "So much for my great detective work."

Joley made a small dissenting sound. "That's not exactly true." Immediately, she had the attention of all of her sisters.

"Something happened that you didn't tell us," Kate asked.

"I didn't want to worry anyone," Joley admitted. "I get all kinds of silly threats on the road, and in light of the threat to Kate, I didn't want to worry anyone."

Joley stretched, a sensuous flow of feminine muscle. Everything Joley did, every way she moved or even spoke was sultry. It was as natural to her as breathing. Matt found he could appreciate her looks and voice, yet not react in the least. It was a further revelation to him just how deeply in love he was with Kate. He sank onto the floor in front of Kate and leaned against her knees. At once her fingers tunneled into his thick hair, a connection between them.

"What happened, Joley?" Sarah prompted.

"I went up to my room after we all talked the other day. Hannah said she closed the window because the fog was slipping into the house, and it made her uncomfortable. I was so tired I just crashed on the bed, and I didn't think to pay attention to the feel of the room. I woke up choking, strangling really. At first I thought I'd wrapped a scarf around my neck in my sleep and somehow pulled it tight. But the fog was everywhere, layers of it. I could barely see. I pulled the scarf away from my throat and turned on the fan. My throat hurt and . . ." She hesitated, sighed softly, and dragged the turtleneck sweater away from her throat. Distinct round bruises marred her skin.

"And you didn't think it was important to tell us?" Sarah turned on her younger sister. "That we shouldn't know this thing has advanced to such a sophisticated level of violence? Joley! You weren't thinking."

"I know." Joley rubbed her palm over her thigh. "At first I was terrified, and I went through the house and began to gather the herbs and flowers for the windows, but the entire time I wondered why it just didn't kill me. If it could partially strangle me, why didn't it just do it all the way?"

"Maybe he isn't strong enough," Abbey ventured.

Sarah glanced toward the sea. "He's strong enough. He managed to take shape and, from what Matt says, even find a voice."

"Are you saying he didn't try to kill Joley? He certainly tried to kill Elle," Abbey argued. "Maybe he wasn't prepared for how hard she fought."

"*I'm* saying it didn't try to kill me," Joley said.

"Then what was it doing?" Sarah asked.

"I think it was trying to silence my voice."

Kate put a protective hand to her throat. "In the shadow world, he went for my throat as well."

Something deep inside of Matt went very still. Kate had an incredible voice. "If he wants to still the voices capable of enthrallment, Joley, Abbey, and Kate are definitely on the hit list." He looked at Elle. "But why you?"

She smiled, her green eyes bright. "Maybe he doesn't like redheads."

"I think he doesn't want to be saved," Kate announced.

"When I touched him, I felt rage, yes, but it wasn't his primary emotion." She leaned towards Elle. "Didn't you feel sorrow and guilt? You were there, you had to have felt it."

Elle looked down at the journal, her expression sorrowful. "I felt it," she said in a small voice.

Matt raised his head sharply. "Elle shares emotions, doesn't she? You connected with Jackson when he was taken prisoner."

Elle refused to meet his eyes. "Yes."

"But he was halfway around the world," Matt protested.

Libby put her hand out to her youngest sister, and Elle took it immediately. "It's very difficult sometimes, Matthew," Libby explained. "We're different. We look the same and try to act the same, but we're not normal and sometimes the overload is . . ." She searched for the right word, looking helplessly at her sisters.

"Dangerous," Sarah supplied. "Using our talents is very draining. Each of us has to overcome by-products of her gift."

"I've seen it in Kate," Matt agreed. "Is there any way to minimize it?"

The seven women looked at one another. As usual, it was Sarah who answered. "We all handle it in different ways. Most of us find our own space and live there, as shielded as we can manage to be." She smiled at Matt. "I know it will help Kate to have you. Damon helps me."

"So far I haven't managed to keep her from wearing herself out. Every time I think we're going to get a little respite, the fog comes in again," Matt pointed out. He was extraordinarily happy that Sarah had accepted his relationship with Kate.

"You've helped enormously," Kate acknowledged.

Elle leafed through the journal. "You said there were symbols on the seal, Kate? Could you read it at all?"

"The first Drake settlers must have been the ones to seal the restless spirit, Elle. It was definitely formed around the time the town was settled. From what I could read, it was something about rage and sealing until one is born who could do something. I went back to take another look, but most of the seal was crushed and the actual writing lost," Kate admitted.

"Until one is born who can do something," Sarah repeated aloud. "Something to do with a voice."

"Here it is," Elle said triumphantly. "'He who will not receive forgiveness shall remain sealed until one is born who can give him peace.'"

There was a long silence. Matt stared at the cranberry candle as the three flames leaped and burned. Hot wax poured over the side like a lava flow, forming a thick pool around the holder. It was a fascinating sight, deep purple wax flowing almost like dark blood. "Why would he need peace?"

Elle pushed a pair of glasses on her nose and studied the faded writing. "One of the sisters who helped to seal the spirit must have had precognition the way Mom does. If that's the case, it means we should be able to find a way to allow him to rest."

"Unless the earthquake opened the crack in the ground and allowed him to escape before his time," Matt said.

"I doubt it," Sarah said seriously. "Things usually happen the way they're supposed to happen, Matthew. It's obviously our time. We have no choice but to figure this out. It's our destiny."

Matt wiped his hand over his mouth. He wasn't certain he believed in destiny. He felt Kate's hand in his hair and changed his mind. "Hannah, are you feeling any better?" She didn't look better. Without her, he wasn't positive they could have managed to get Elle back up the cliff in the midst of the thick fog or drive the entity out to sea and away from the townspeople time after time.

"I've been resting. Libby's helped."

Libby Drake. Matt looked at her. She was legendary in the small town. She was the only Drake with midnight black hair and pale, almost translucent skin. She was a natural-born healer, the real thing. He smiled at her. "It's good to see you again, Libby. Maybe you better hide out while you're home. If word gets out you're back, you'll have everyone in town lining up for a cure."

"I do want to visit Irene's son while I'm home. My sisters went to see him and did what they could to make him comfortable, but I promised I'd go see him."

"Libby—" Matt shook his head—"you know he has terminal cancer. Even you can't get rid of that." He waited. When no one said anything he looked at her. "Can you?" The idea was unsettling.

"I won't know until I visit him," Libby admitted.

"What would be the price?" Matt couldn't imagine what it would cost Libby to actually cure someone sent home to die.

Libby smiled at him. "I can see why Kate loves you so much, Matt. You're very discerning. It's a trade-off. I might save one person, but while I'm recovering, I might lose a hundred others."

"That bad?" He reached his hand for Kate. The thought of what the women had to go through on a daily basis moved him. In their own way, they were warriors, and he had a deep respect for them.

"Does anyone want more tea? I'm getting another cup," Hannah volunteered.

"I can get it," Matt offered. He felt a little useless.

Hannah paused just a few feet from the entrance to the kitchen. "I'm already up, but thank you," she said, and took two steps, halting abruptly, staring at the flickering candle in the bay window facing the sea. "Sarah, you need to come look at this."

Matt got to his feet, pulled Kate up beside him. Apprehensively, he glanced out the large window to the sea. He already knew what he would see. Anytime anything strange happened, the fog was back, settling over the town like a smoky monster crouched and waiting.

"What is it, Sarah?" Elle asked from her position on the couch. She had pillows piled around her, a comforter over her, and strict orders to remain where she was.

"The wax is forming something as it runs down the sides," Sarah explained. "It looks like a hook to me."

"Or a candy cane." Matt was more pragmatic.

"It's a staff," Hannah corrected. "A long staff, or maybe a cane. Something used to walk with."

"This is getting more bizarre by the minute," Abbey said, rubbing her hands up and down her arms. "And while we're on the subject of bizarre, Joley, I'm sorry, but there was no excuse for your not telling the rest of us what happened. You take shielding all of us way too far."

Sarah's smile at Joley was gentle. "She's right, hon. You should have told us what happened. Do you have any other bad news you don't want to worry us with?"

Joley hesitated for a brief moment, then shrugged. "I'm sorry, I should have mentioned the strangling fog. Do you have any idea how ridiculous that sounds?" She burst out laughing.

Kate joined her. "I have to admit, it threw Christmas wreaths at me."

"And no one is going to believe the fog *pushed* me over the cliff," Elle said with a small grin. "This one will go into our journal and nowhere else!"

"I plan on telling our children," Matt announced. "It's a great story for around the campfire, and they aren't going to believe us anyway. They'll think I'm a brilliant storyteller."

"Children?" Joley raised her eyebrow. "I love the idea of Kate having children. Don't the Granites produce boys? Very large hungry boys?" Her sisters erupted into laughter while Kate covered her face and groaned.

"You aren't helping, Joley," Matt said, putting his arms protectively around Kate so she could hide her face against his shoulder. "She hasn't even agreed to marry me yet. Don't be scaring her off with the idea of little boys running around."

Sarah continued to study the wax flow over the sides of the candle. "Do you see anything else that could be helpful in that book, Elle?"

Elle rubbed at the bump on her head and frowned at the thin pages. "There was no single predominant religion in the town at the time people first settled here. A faction celebrated the birthday of a pagan god. This is very interesting." Elle looked up at her sisters. "Many of the settlers here came together to celebrate their differences, unable to live anywhere else. The founding fathers wanted a safe haven by the sea, a place they envisioned would one day have a port for supplies. It actually says a lot about the town's founders and perhaps gives us insight to why the people here are so tolerant of others."

"And it explains why our own people settled here."

Kate nuzzled Matt's throat. "If I remember my grandmother and her history lessons correctly, she said Christmas was slow to catch on in America, that the colonists didn't celebrate it, and in some instances actually banned it."

"That's right." Joley snapped her fingers. "It was considered a pagan ritual in some places. But that was a long while before this town was settled, wasn't it?" She swept Elle's hair away from her face and fashioned it into a ponytail. "Does that have anything to do with all of this?"

"Thanks, Joley," Elle said. She smoothed the worn pages. "The townspeople wanted to celebrate the Christmas season and settled on a pageant. They asked everyone to participate regardless of their beliefs, just for the fun of it. They treated it more as a play, a production that included all town members, meant to be fun rather than religious." She looked up with a small smile. "Libby, our however-many-greats-grandmother has your very interesting handwriting. Aside from the language, I have to decipher the worst handwriting on the face of the earth."

"I do not have the worst handwriting on the face of the earth." Libby tossed a small pillow at her sister, missing by a great distance.

"There's something else in the wax," Sarah said. "All of you, look at this! Tell me what you see."

The sisters crowded around the cranberry candle. Kate tilted her head, studying it from every angle. "Where did you get this candle, Sarah? Is this one Mom made?"

"Yes, but I didn't know it would do this."

"Is a candle a symbol of Christmas?" Matt asked.

"Yes; some people say the light of the candle relieves the unrelenting darkness," Kate answered. "My mother makes incredible candles."

"I can imagine. Do they all do this?" Matt indicated the flowing wax.

"It's a face, I think," Sarah said. "Look, Abbey, don't you think it's a face?"

"That wouldn't surprise me." Matt peered at the thick pool of wax. "The spirit found feet, a coat and hat, and bones, why not get himself a face, even if it's made of wax. Does it have eyes? Maybe he wants to get a good look at us."

"Ugh." Kate made a face. "That's a horrible idea. It could never use one of Mom's candles for that. Mom instills a healing, soothing magic in each of them. We were the ones who forgot to guard our home. She insisted we make certain every time, but we just got complacent. I'm not forgetting this lesson for a very long time."

"Me either," Joley agreed.

"I think I found it now," Elle said in excitement. "Most everyone wanted to participate with the exception of a small group of believers in the gods of the earth. They considered the pageant a Christian holiday celebration and felt it was wrong to participate. One of the most outspoken said the pageant was evil and those participating would be punished. His brother-in-law, Abram Lynchman, went against his advice and allowed his wife and child to take part. Because he stood up to Johann, the rest of the group also decided to join the town in the pageant."

"Is this Johann angry because his flock was out of his control?" Joley asked.

Elle held up her hand for silence. Her hand went to her throat. Matt noticed that her hand was trembling. "Everyone helped with the production, bringing homemade candles and lanterns. The shepherd herded several sheep with his staff, and the sheep got away and ran through the crowd."

None of the sisters laughed. They were watching Elle's face intently. Matt glanced out the window to see the fog solidly in place. For some reason, his heart began to pound. The strange radar that always told him danger was near was shrieking at him, even there in the warmth and safety of the Drakes' home.

"The people were having fun, laughing as the sheep rushed through the crowd with the shepherd running after them. The sheep panicked and ran straight into the small shelter the town had erected to use as the stable for the play. The shelter crumpled, knocking several candles into the dry straw. Fire spread along the ground and across the wooden planks used to make the shelter. Several participants were trapped under the debris, including Abram's wife and child." Elle had a sob in her voice. She shook her head. "I can't read this. I can't read the words. Anastasia, the one writing the journal, was there, she saw the entire thing, heard the cries, saw them die. Her emotions are trapped in the book. I can't read it, Sarah." She sounded as if she were pleading.

Matt wanted to comfort her. The feeling was so strong he actually stepped toward her before he realized he was feeling the emotions of Elle's sisters. They rushed to her side, Sarah pulling the book from her hands, Kate putting her arms around Elle. The others touched her, helping to absorb the long ago, very strong emotions still clinging to the pages of the journal.

"I'm sorry, honey," Sarah said gently, "I should have thought of that. You've been through so much already. Kate, do you think you can get an idea of what happened next? I wouldn't ask, but it's important." She held the book out to Kate.

Matt wanted to yank the book out of her hands and throw it. "Kate's been through enough with this thing, Sarah. You can't ask her to do any more." He was furious. Enough was enough. "Elle almost died out there. Without Jackson, she would have. You have no idea what a miracle it was that she didn't end up at the bottom of the ocean."

Kate put a restraining hand on his arm. Sarah simply nodded. "I do realize what I'm asking, Matthew, and I don't blame you for being angry. I don't want Kate to touch the journal, but the truth is, if we don't know why this spirit is doing the things he's doing, someone very well could die. We have to know."

Kate took the book from Sarah's hand. Matt muttered a string of curses and turned away from them, feeling impotent. All of his training, his every survival skill, seemed utterly useless in the unfamiliar situation. Not wanting to look at Kate, not wanting to witness the strain and weariness on her face, he stared hard at the cranberry candle and the eerie flow of wax. He stared and stared, his heart suddenly in his throat. He took a step closer, stared down in a kind of terror. "Katie." He whispered her name because she was his world, his talisman. Because he needed her.

Kate put her arm around him, held him. He couldn't take his eyes from the face in the wax, praying he was wrong. Knowing he was right. She looked down and gasped. "Danny. It's Danny."

13

My last gift now, is a special one,
A candy cane for a special son,

He watches and tends and knows the land,
But not enough to evade my hand.

MATT TOOK KATE by the shoulders and set her aside. She made a grab for him, but he was already moving swiftly for the front door.

"Danny's at the pageant rehearsal," Kate reminded him. She ran after him, tossing the journal onto the floor, trying to keep up with him. Hannah grabbed Kate's coat and hurried after both of them.

The fog obstructed Matt's vision, but he could hear the women. "Go back, stay in the house, Kate. It's too dangerous." His voice was grim. Authoritative. It made Kate shiver. He didn't sound at all like her Matthew.

"I'm coming with you. Stay to the left. The path leads down the hill to the highway. If we cross right beside the three redwood trees, like we did the other night, we'll end up quite close to the shortcut to town." Kate followed the sound of his voice. Hannah took her hand and held on tightly.

"Kate, dammit, this one time, listen to me. I have to find Danny, and I don't want to have to worry about what's happening to you."

Kate wished he sounded angry, but Matt's tone was chillingly cold. Ice-cold. She tightened her fingers around Hannah's hand but continued hurrying along the narrow path. "Hannah's with me, Matthew, and you're going to need us." She kept her voice very calm, very even. She ached for him and shared his rising alarm for the safety of his brother. The features in the wax had definitely been Daniel Granite. She had a strong feeling of impending doom.

Hannah pressed closer to her. "It's going to happen tonight, Katie." Her voice shook. "Should we try to clear the fog now?"

Matt loomed up in front of them, startling both of them, catching Kate by the shoulders. "It has never gone after me. Only you. Go with your sisters and work your magic. Clear the fog out of town, and this time get rid of it. I'll do what I can to keep Danny alive. I'm safe, Kate." His gray eyes had turned to steel. "I need to know you're as safe as possible in this mess."

She clung to him for just one moment, then nodded. "We'll be up on the captain's walk, where we can better bring in the wind."

Matt dropped a hard kiss on her upturned mouth, turned, and hurried down the narrow, well-worn trail. His mind was racing, working out the route the actors in the pageant used. Had they noticed the fog rolling in and taken shelter in one of the businesses along the parade route, or had they gone ahead with the rehearsal plans? Matt made it to the highway and stood listening for a moment in silence. He couldn't hear a car, but the fog seemed capable of muffling every sound. Still, he didn't want to wait. He felt a terrible sense of urgency, of his brother in acute danger. He cursed as he ran, nearly blind in the fog. It was only his training that kept him from being completely disoriented. He moved more from instinct than from sight, making his way toward the town square. Most of the committee meetings were held at the chamber of commerce building near the grocery store. The players were supposed to be rehearsing, though, and he doubted whether Inez would let a heavy fog and some entity she couldn't see change her plans.

He heard a shrill scream, the sounds of panic, and his heart stuttered. "Danny!" He called his brother's name, using the sheer volume of his voice to penetrate the cries coming out of the fog. He followed the sound of the voices, not toward the square, but away from it, back toward the park on the edge of town, where the river roared down through a canyon to meet the sea. The wall along the river was only about three feet high, made of stone and mortar. He nearly ran into it in his haste to reach Danny. At the last moment he sensed the obstruction and veered away, running parallel with it toward the cries.

He was getting closer to the sounds of the screams and calls. He heard Inez trying to calm everyone. He heard someone shout for a rope. The river, rushing over the rocks, added to the chaos in the heavy fog. "Danny!" Matt called again, trying to beat down his fear for his brother. Danny would have heard him, would have answered.

Right in front of him, Donna, the owner of the local gift shop, suddenly appeared. Her face was white and strained. He caught her shoulders. "What happened, Donna? Tell me!"

She grabbed both of his arms to steady herself. "The wall gave way. A group of the men were sitting on it. Your brother, the young Granger boy, Jeff's son, I don't know, more maybe. They just disappeared down the embankment, and all the rocks followed like a miniavalanche. We can't see to help them. There were some groans, and we heard cries for help, but we can't see them at all. We tried to form a human chain, but the bank is too steep. Jackson went over the side by himself. He was crawling. I heard a terrible crack, now he's silent. I was going to try to find a telephone to call for help. The cell phones just won't work here."

"What was Jackson doing here?" He knew the deputy never participated in the town pageant. "Is Jonas here?" As he talked he was moving along the wall, feeling with his hands for breaks, taking Donna with him.

"Jackson happened to be driving by when the fog thickened. He was worried about us, I think, so he stayed. I haven't seen Jonas."

"Don't wander around in this fog. Hopefully, Kate and her sisters will move it out of here for us." He patted her arm in reassurance and left her, continuing the search for the break in the wall with an outstretched hand. When he found it, he swore softly. He knew the section of wall was over a steep drop and the river below had a fast-moving current running over several submerged boulders. The bank was littered with rocks of every size, with little to hold them in place should something start them rolling.

"Danny! Jackson!" His call was met with eerie silence. He began to crawl down the bank, distributing his weight, on his belly, searching with his hands before sliding forward. It was painstakingly slow. He didn't want to displace any more of the rocks in case his brother or any of the others were still alive and in the path of an avalanche.

Matt's fingertips encountered a leg. He forced himself to remain calm and used his hands to identify the man. Jackson was unconscious, and there was blood seeping from his head. In the near-blind conditions, it was impossible to assess how badly he was injured, but his breathing seemed shallow to Matt.

Something moved an arm's length below Jackson. Matt followed the outstretched arm and found another body. The Granger boy. Matt knew him to be sixteen or seventeen. A good kid. The boy moved again, and Matt cautioned him to stay still, afraid he would disturb the rocks.

"You okay, kid?" he asked.

"My arm's broken, and I feel like I've been run over by a truck, but I'm all right. The deputy told me not to move, and the next thing I knew he was somersaulting and smashed hard into the rock right there. He hasn't moved. Is he dead?"

"No, he's alive. What about the others? What about Danny?" He crawled around Jackson to get to the boy, to take his pulse and run his hands over him to examine him for other injuries.

"Tommy Dockins fell too. Danny tried to push him clear when the slide started. We didn't really have any time. I didn't see either of them, but Tommy's yelled for help a couple of times. I couldn't tell from which direction though."

The kid sounded tinny and distorted in the fog, and his voice shook, but he lay quietly and didn't panic. "Your name's Pete, right? Pete Granger?" Matt asked.

"Yes, sir."

"Well, I'm going to slide on around you and see if I can locate Danny and Tommy. Don't move. The fog will be gone soon, and Jonas is on the way with the rescue squad. If you move, you'll send the rest of those rocks right down on top of the others and me. Got it?"

"Yes, sir."

"I'll be back as quick as I can." Matt glanced in the direction of the cliff house, where the Drake family had lived for over a hundred years. He needed the modern-day women to work their magic, to remove the fog so he had a semblance of a chance to save his brother and Tommy and to get Jackson and Pete to safety.

"Come on, baby," he whispered, hoping the swirling clouds would take his voice to her. "Do this for me. Clear this mess out of here."

As if they could hear his words, the seven Drake sisters moved together out onto the battlement and faced the sea. Libby and Sarah both had their arms wrapped around Elle to aid her as they stood in the midst of the swirling fog.

Sarah looked up at the sky, to the roiling clouds gathered over Sea Haven and back to her sisters. "This troubled spirit is in terrible pain and does not believe there can be forgiveness for his mistake. He cannot forgive himself for what he believes to be bad judgment. I am certain his motive was to save others his sorrow. He believes that by halting the pageant, history will not repeat itself. He has lived this unbelievable nightmare repeatedly and needs to be able to forgive himself and go to his rest." She looked at Kate. "Your gift has always been your voice, Kate. I think the journal is referring to you. One born who can bring peace."

Kate could think only of Matt, somewhere out in the fog. She didn't want to be up on the captain's walk facing another struggle, she wanted to be with him. It was the first time in her life she had ever felt so divided around her sisters. She knew at that moment that she belonged with Matthew Granite. It didn't matter that she was an observer and he was a doer, she loved him, and she belonged with him.

As if reading her mind, Hannah took her hand, squeezed it tightly. "He's counting on you to do this, Kate. He's counting on all of us."

Kate took a steadying breath and nodded. She stepped away from Hannah, knowing Hannah would need room. Facing the small town invaded with the fog, Kate began to chant softly. An inquiry, no more, a soft plea to be heard. Her voice was carried on the smallest of breezes as Hannah faced the sea and lifted her arms, directing the wind as she might an orchestra.

Behind Kate, Joley and Abbey began to sing, a soft melody of love and peace, harmonizing with Kate's incredible voice so they produced a symphony of hope. Power began to build in the wind itself, in the sky overhead. Lightning forked in the spinning clouds. Kate spoke of forgiveness, of unconditional love. Of a love of family that transcended time. She beckoned and cajoled. She pleaded for a hearing.

"You've touched him," Elle reported. "He's fighting the call. He's determined to keep the accident from happening. There is no past life or future life as he understands it, only watching his wife and child die a horrible death over and over, year after year." She staggered under the burden of the man's guilt, of his loss.

Kate didn't falter. Matt was out there somewhere in the fog, and she felt him reaching for her, counting on her. And she knew he was in danger. She talked of the townspeople coming together with every belief represented. Of the elderly and the young given the same respect. She spoke of a place that was a true haven for tolerance. And she spoke of forgiveness. Of letting go.

Power spread with the building wind. The ocean leaped in response. A pod of whales surfaced, flipping their tails, almost in unison, as if creating a giant fan. Joley's voice, a sultry purity that couldn't be ignored, swelled in volume, taking over the lead, while Abbey's voice joined in perfect harmony.

Hannah's voice called on the elements she knew and loved. Earth. Wind. Fire. Rain. Lightning flashed. The wind blew. Rain poured from the clouds. And still the power continued to build. Her hands moved in a graceful pattern as if conducting a symphony of magic.

Kate lured the spirit to her with promises of peace. Rest. A family waiting with open arms, holding him dear, not placing blame. An accident, not the hand of an ancient god angry that he had allowed his loved ones to participate in something different. Simply an unfortunate accident. Joley sang of Christmas, past, present, and future. Of a town committed to all the members celebrating together in a variety of ways. Of festivals for ancient gods and a gala for those who didn't believe. The two voices blended, one in song, one in storytelling, weaving a seamless creation to draw the lost soul back home.

Abbey lifted her voice finally, a call for those lost to welcome loved ones. As she could draw truth, so did she speak truth. She added her voice to the tapestry, promising peace and rest and final sleep in the arms of those he loved most.

"He's coming. He's beginning to believe, to want to take the chance," Elle said. "He's hesitant, but he's so utterly weary, and the idea of seeing his wife and child and resting in their arms is irresistible."

Libby raised her arms with Hannah, sending the promise of healing, not the body, but mind and soul. She added her power to the force of the wind, added her healing energy to Kate's soothing peace.

The wind increased in strength, blowing with the force of a small gale, tearing through Sea Haven, herding the fog, guiding it toward the sea. Toward the house on the cliff and the seven women who stood on the battlement, hand in hand. The feminine voices carried unbelievable power throughout the air, land, and sea. Rising on the wind. Calling. Promising. Leading.

And the fog answered. The thick gray vapor turned toward the sea, drifting reluctantly at first, tendrils feeling the way, hesitant and fearful. The voices swelled in strength. The wind blew through the fog.

Elle reached for Kate. "Now, Kate. Go to him now."

Kate never stopped talking in her beguiling voice, but she closed her eyes and deliberately entered the world of shadows. He was there. A tall, gaunt man with sorrow weighing him down. He looked at her and shook his head sadly. She held out her hand to him. Beside her, Elle stiffened as a beastly creature with glowing eyes and fur stared down at Kate with hate. As the snakelike vines slithered and coiled and hissed as if alive, wanting to get to her sister. Elle moved them, holding them back with the sheer force of her power, giving Kate the necessary time to lure the spirit of Abram to her.

Kate told a story of the love of a man for his wife and children. A man who made a courageous decision to go against what others said was right and allowed his family to participate in a production designed to bring people together. She spoke of laughter and fun and his pride in his family as he watched them. And the horror of a terrible accident. The candles and dry straw, the heavy planks coming down on so many. The man watching his loved ones die. The guilt and horror. The need to blame someone . . . to blame himself.

Joley and Abbey sang softly, the voice of a woman and child calling for the one they loved to join them. Kate used the purity of her voice, silver tones to draw him closer. The woman and child waited. Loved. Longed for him. His only job was to go to them, to forgive himself. There was no one to save but himself.

Kate kept her hand extended and pointed behind him. Clouds of dark gray fog drifted aside. He turned to see the shadows there. A woman. A child. Far off in the distance waiting.

There was a sharp cry like that of a seagull. The waves crashed against the cliff, rose high and frothed white. Lightning veined the clouds, forked into the very center of the fog. The flash lit up the shadows, throwing Kate out of that world and back into the reality of her own. She landed heavily on the wet surface of the captain's walk, in the middle of her sisters. Libby held her close.

"You're all right. It's all right now. You did it, Kate. You gave him peace," Sarah said.

"We did it," Kate corrected with a wan smile.

They sat together, too weary to move, the rain lashing down at them. Sarah turned her head to calculate the distance to the door. "Damon will be here with tea, but I don't think he can carry us back inside."

Elle draped herself over Abbey. "Who cares about going inside? I want to just lie here and look up at the sky."

"I want to know Matt's safe and that he was able to get to Danny," Kate said. "When Damon comes up, please have him call Jonas."

• • •

Matt scooted carefully down the steep bank, skirting rocks until it became impossible to go farther. He had no choice but to go over them.

"I'm Tommy, not Kate," a voice called weakly from his right side.

Matt didn't realize until that moment that he was whispering her name over and over like a prayer. He glanced up at the sky, felt the wind in his face, the first few drops of real rain. He felt power and energy crackling in the air around him. "Thank you, Katie, you are unbelievable." He said it fervently, meaning it. Already the fog was beginning to thin so that he could make out the boy lying a few feet from him. "Are you hurt?"

"I don't think so. I don't know what happened though. One minute I was falling off the fence and rolling, and the next Danny shoved me. I woke up a few minutes ago and when I tried to move, I dislodged several rocks. I didn't know where anyone was, so I thought I'd better just wait until help came."

Matt remained lying flat, searching carefully for Danny. The wind drove down through the canyon and shifted abruptly, coming back off the river. He caught sight of his brother a few yards away. Danny was lying facedown on the cliff over the water's edge, partially buried under debris. He wasn't moving. The pulse pounded in Matt's temples. He forced himself to go to the boy and examine him first. "You'll be fine. Just stay down until we can get help to you. I'm checking on Danny."

He took a deep breath and called toward the top. "Donna? Is Jonas here yet?"

"He's on his way along with the rescue squad," she yelled back.

"I'm working my way down to Danny. Everyone else is alive. Jackson looks the worst. Could be a concussion. The entire mountainside is unstable. Tell them to be careful moving around up there until I can get Danny out of the avalanche zone."

Matt patted the teenage boy and proceeded to make painfully slow progress through the rocks. The smallest trickle of pebbles could bring down a tremendous storm of boulders on his brother. He inched his way through the rubble until he reached Danny's side.

Danny was precariously balanced at the edge of the bank. It was actually the rocks that saved his life, holding him pinned in the dirt. Matt was very gentle as he examined his brother. He couldn't find a single broken bone, but there were several lacerations, particularly on Danny's hands. His face was pushed hard into the dirt. He carefully turned Danny's head, scooping dirt from his mouth. Danny coughed, and the rocks slid. Some dislodged and one fell to the river below. "Don't move, Danny, don't even cough if you can help it," Matt instructed.

"Tell us what you need, Matt," Jonas shouted down to him.

"I've got to move Danny. When I do, everything above him is going to slide. You'll have to get Pete out of there and Jackson. When you move them, Jonas, don't disturb the rocks. If I take Danny now, there's a chance we'll lose those two. I'll shield my brother, just work fast."

Matt knew Jonas wouldn't bother to argue with him. There was no way Matt would leave his younger brother hanging out over the edge of the fast-moving river with an avalanche of boulders poised to slide. The Drake sisters had managed a miracle removing the fog, but there was still dangerous work to be done.

"Don't forget about me," Tommy called.

"We'll get you," Jonas promised.

"You're going to be just fine, Danny boy," Matt said, brushing more dirt from the lacerated face.

"Get out of here, Matt," Danny barely mouthed the words. "Breathing moves the rocks. If they're working up above, the boulders will smash us both."

"Have a little faith, bro, that's Jonas up there. Are you hurt?"

"What does it look like?"

Matt heard the ominous rumble above him. "Incoming," Jonas yelled from above them. Matt shifted so his upper body protected Danny's head. He put his arms over his own head and tried to shrink as rocks bounced down, knocking a few more loose. The rocks rained down and splashed into the river below. One glanced off his calf and rolled away, dislodging more rocks before it hit the water.

"Dammit, be careful." Matt could hear Jonas snarling at the rescue team. "If you can't move them without setting off a landslide, get the hell back up here and let someone else do that! You all right down there, Matt?"

"We're fine. Just be careful," he called back.

"You weigh more than the rocks do," Danny complained.

"You deserve it, scaring the hell out of me like this. Anything broken?"

"Naw. I'm a Granite. We're tough."

Matt rubbed his brother's head in a rough, affectionate gesture. He glanced up. "They've got Jackson and the boys out, and they're on the way to us. When we move you, Danny, the entire side of the bank is going to come down. I won't be able to be very gentle, but I'm not going to let anything happen to you."

"Just get me the hell out of here."

It was not an easy task. The rescuers inched their way down and worked out a coordinated plan to move Danny, knowing once they pulled him from under the pile of rocks it would set off an avalanche. Matt stayed beside his brother, joking, keeping Danny's spirits up. The men cleared as many of the rocks from Danny as they could without triggering the landslide. It was only the soft damp dirt that saved Danny from terrible injury or death. His body was pressed deep into the muck. They dug around him with painstaking slowness, careful not to disturb the precarious balance of boulders poised over their heads.

"Ready, Danny boy?" It was Matt who locked arms with his brother.

"More than ready." There was fear in Danny's eyes, but he winked at his older brother and managed a weak smile.

Matt didn't wait. They had cleared as much of the ground as possible out of the way of the landslide path so that Matt had a clear trail on the steep embankment to drag Danny quickly out of harm's way. He exerted his great strength, pulling his brother out from under the rocks, moving as fast as humanly possible. The rocks immediately crashed into the river, starting the avalanche. The boulders above, with nothing to hold them, rolled down, taking most of the embankment with it. Matt covered Danny's body a second time, waiting until the debris had cleared.

Danny tried to stand, but his brother held him down. "You made me come down here and play mud-cakes with you, you can just get on the stretcher and let the medics carry your butt to the hospital and check you out."

"I'm fine," Danny protested, as they strapped him into a litter. "I feel like an idiot," he said.

"That's good, Danny. You are an idiot." Matt took up a position at the head of the stretcher to help carry him up the steep bank. They were still cautious, worried about the unstable conditions, but managed to get him to the top without incident.

Danny protested more when they put him in the ambulance, but no one paid him any attention. Matt jumped in beside him, keeping one hand on his brother's shoulder. It wasn't until the doctors pronounced Danny bruised, but fine that Matt left him to go check on Jackson and the teens.

By the time he returned to the cliff house, he was tired and only wanting to hold Kate to him. The Drake sisters were sprawled in every chair of the living room, pale and drawn, all greeting him with their brilliant smiles.

Matt gathered Kate to him, holding her close. All he wanted to do was take her home with him where she belonged. She looked exhausted and in need of a hot meal and two or three days of sleep. Kate clung to him, turning her face up for his kiss, burrowing against him.

"I heard there was an accident on the river wall," she greeted.

"Everyone's fine. Shook up, but fine. Did Jonas stop by?"

She shook her head. "Inez called to make certain we were all right. She knew we must have cleared out the fog and that we would be exhausted. She told us what happened. Jackson's in the hospital, but the two boys were treated and released. She said Jackson's going to be fine." Her smile was slow coming but bright. "I have a feeling he'll make a terrible patient."

"Somehow I think you're right. Danny was treated and released also. He's bruised from head to toe, but he didn't have a single major injury." There was elation in Matt's voice. "He's hoping Inez will upgrade his part next year in the pageant due to his, quote, 'heroism.' It was pretty dicey, Kate. Thanks for all you did."

"We all did it. I could never have managed without my sisters. I'm so glad your brother is fine. The pageant just wouldn't be the same without him in his annual role as the shepherd. Speaking of the pageant—" She broke off as her sisters burst out laughing.

Matt's head went up suspiciously. He was beginning to know the Drake sisters, and their laughter heralded trouble for him. He was certain of it.

"Inez sent over a costume she made for the third wise man. A king," Kate said brightly. "She asked if you would be willing to fill the role at the last minute and of course, with Inez being so distressed, we said we were certain you'd want to help out."

He stiffened. "I'd rather be boiled in oil."

"Acting runs in your family," she pointed out.

He held up his hand. "You can't look at me with those eyes while you're weak and tired, it's unfair tactics."

"I know, Matthew," she said. "I'm trying not to, but Inez is such a good friend, and I couldn't bear her being so upset. The pageant is important to the town after all the near accidents. We need to get our confidence back."

"And I have to be in the pageant in order for our town to do that?" He raised one eyebrow skeptically.

"All you have to do is walk through the town. No lines, nothing awful. You don't mind, do you?"

"Does wanting to be boiled in oil instead sound like I want to do this?"

She turned her face into his chest. Pressed her lips against his skin.

He growled, deep in his throat. The growl turned into a groan. "I can see what my life's going to be like. I'll do it. This one time. Never again."

"Thank you." She kissed him again. "I just want to go home with you and sleep in your arms," she said, uncaring that her family could hear her. "Let's go home, Matthew."

Matt kissed her gently, her lips, her throat, bringing her hand to his mouth as elation swept through him. She had said, "Let's go home." He lifted her with ease. "I'll take good care of her," he promised her family.

Sarah nodded. "We have every confidence that you will, Matt."

14

All deeds are now done, forgiveness is mine,
As two people share a love for all time.

"WE'RE GOING TO be late," Kate said, evading Matt's outstretched hand. "We promised the committee you'd be on time. We didn't make rehearsals, and everyone's worried you're going to mess up their play."

"I wasn't the one who agreed to wear that silly-looking robe Inez made. *You* agreed I'd wear it! Is it my fault they lost a couple of their stars to a scandalous affair?" He stalked her through the house, one slow step at a time.

Kate laughed and dodged around the table, putting a chair between them. "You theater people are always involved in scandals."

He moved the chair out of the way and proceeded to back her into a corner. "I'd be more than willing to cause a scandal. Just let me get my hands on you."

"I don't think so. Inez is probably watching her clock and tapping her foot. I'm not about to get a lecture about the benefits of being on time. Put on your costume!"

"I am in my costume. What king travels by starlight from one country to another and wears a satin bathrobe with cheesy lightning bolts sewn all over it? And I doubt very much if he sat on that camel naked under the robe."

Kate held her stomach, laughing so hard she could barely manage to squeak through a small opening he'd left beside the counter. "Somehow I think Inez might object to the idea that you were running around naked in her kingly robes. I, however, am rather intrigued by the idea." She backed down the hallway, holding her hand palm out. "Seriously, Matthew, she'll reprimand you in front of the entire town if you're late."

She was nearing the entrance to the bedroom. His silver eyes gleamed with anticipation. "If you think that's more humiliating than wearing this damned robe, which, by the way, is two sizes too small, you're sadly mistaken. I think Bruce had the affair with Sylvia just to get out of wearing it."

She pressed her hand to her mouth to keep an undignified giggle from emerging. "I think it looks dashing on you." He was right; the robe looked utterly ridiculous on him. His huge muscles strained the material so that it stretched tight over his wide shoulders and back. Instead of reaching the ground, it was halfway up his calves, and the front gaped open to reveal . . . She laughed. "I think it has interesting possibilities."

He spread his arms wide and rushed her, using an old football tackle. She screamed and turned to run, but he caught her up and carried her across the floor to the bed, where he unceremoniously dropped her. The kingly robe made its way to the floor. "I'm the king, and I demand my rights."

Kate pushed one hand against his chest to fend him off. "You have no rights. Inez has you under contract, and you're supposed to be *on time*. Do you want the entire town waiting for you?"

"I wouldn't mind in the least." He caught her legs, pinning her to the bed, stopping her from scooting away from him. "I think everyone should wait on me. I have this tremendous need to see your breasts. Why don't you unbutton your blouse for me?"

"It doesn't have buttons, oh mighty King."

"Who the hell cares," he growled. "Get rid of the shirt."

"I think that robe went to your head." Excitement raced through her, curled heat in her deepest core. She drew the blouse obediently over her head so that her full breasts spilled over the fine white cups of her bra. "Is this what you're looking for?" She slid her hand over her skin, drawing his attention to the taut peaks.

Matt reached to draw the zipper of her jeans down. "Exactly like that." There was a husky catch to his voice, the playfulness slipping away as he tugged the material from her body. He left her sexy little thong. "Every time I see that thing, I want to take it off with my teeth," he admitted, and bent to the task.

Kate enjoyed the feel of his hands on her body. Big hands. Capable. Nearly covering her buttocks as he lifted her hips and teased her skin with his teeth. Just that fast she was swamped with heat, her body flushed and alive and in desperate need. The thought of the Christmas pageant went out of her head, and much more erotic thoughts took its place. His mouth was everywhere, his tongue teasing and dancing, his teeth pulling at the only barrier between him and his goal.

She felt the sudden release as the material parted, the cool air mingling with her own heat, then the plunging of his tongue going deep while she nearly came off the bed, air bursting from her lungs in a wild rush. It was only his hands holding her down that kept her open to him while he made certain she not only was prepared for him, but that she hungered for him. Laughing, he slid his body over hers, settling over her soft form, gripping her hips to pull her to meet the hard thrust as he joined them together.

"I think that kingly robe works just fine," Kate managed to say, in between gasps of pleasure.

"Maybe I'll keep it if it gets this kind of results," he teased. He began to move, a slow assault on her senses, driving deep, needing her body, needing to feel the way she welcomed him. The heat and fire. Flames licking over his skin. "I love watching you when we make love," he admitted. She was so completely abandoned in the way she gave herself to him.

Kate loved the way he watched her. There was desire etched into the lines of his face. There was hunger in the depths of his eyes. There was steel in his body and a fine hot heat that made her flame, catch fire, and burn with passion. "I love making love with you," she told him, sliding her arms around his neck to draw his head down to hers.

"That's a good thing, Katie." His teeth nibbled at her chin, her full bottom lip. "Because I think we're going to be spending a lot of time doing just that."

Kate gave herself up to the sheer glory of his body driving so deeply into hers. The pressure built and built, and she dug her fingers into his shoulders, holding on as they soared together in perfect unison.

He lay over her, fighting for his breath, trying to slow his heart rate.

"You're laughing," she observed. "I told you, your entire family laughs at me."

"I can't help it, Kate. And I'm laughing at me. I feel like one of those sappy men who run around with a big grin on his face all the time. I feel like grinning all the time around you, and it's so idiotic."

Kate's answering smile was slow. She rubbed her face against his chest. "I'm just beginning to realize how much I mean to you, Matthew."

He kissed her tenderly, his hands framing her face. "I adore you. Why else would I ever put that horrible robe on in front of the entire town?"

Kate looked smug. "And you know what I'll be thinking about when you come walking down the street looking sexy and kingly."

"I'll tell you what you'd better be thinking, Katie." He took a deep breath. "You'd better be thinking, 'here comes the man I intend to marry.'" He feathered kisses along the corners of her mouth. "Marry me, Kate. Spend your life with me."

She looked up at his beloved face. Her fingers slid through his hair in a loving caress. "I don't climb mountains or swim seas, Matthew. I sit in the corner and read books. I'm not at all brave. You have to be very sure that it's me you want."

"More than anything in the world, Kate. You. With you I have everything."

"Well, I guess that kingly robe is lucky after all." She kissed his throat, his chin. Found his mouth with hers and poured heat and fire and promises into her kiss.

He responded just the way she knew he would, his arms wrapping her close, his body coming alive, growing hard and thick deep inside her. He made love to her slowly, leisurely, as if they had all the time in the world and the entire town wasn't waiting on them. He made a thorough job of it. Kate felt like the most important person in the world. And the happiest.

They lay on the bed in a tangle of arms and legs, fighting to breathe. She turned her head to look at him. "I'm thinking you should wear that robe more often, Matthew."

He snorted his derision and glanced at his watch. "Kate! We're late."

"I told you we were late."

"Not this late, we're holding up the parade." He hastily leaped off her, looking around for his clothes. Kate laughed at him through the entire drive to the park where the members of the production were assembling. He caught Kate by the hand and ran across the lawn to the pavilion.

"Where have you been?" Inez demanded, gesturing toward the huge crowd assembled along the streets. "We've all been waiting for you."

"*And,*" Danny added, "you didn't answer your cell phone." He shook his head, hands on his hips, clucking like an old hen. "You aren't even in that lovely costume Inez made for you. What have you been doing?" He wiggled his eyebrows at Kate.

"Are you feeling all right, Danny," Kate asked.

He tugged her hair affectionately. "I'm fine, but don't tell Trudy, she's babying me. And Mom's worse."

Inez all but stamped her foot. "Why are you late?"

"Kate made me late," Matt told Inez, and the interested group of actors crushed together to see the fireworks when Inez told Matt off. Matt exchanged a long, slow smile with Kate while he listened to Inez politely.

"I believe him," Jonas said. "You know how the Drake sisters are. Barbie doll alone takes three hours to get ready for anything. Put them all together, it could take days."

Kate glared at both former Rangers and took Hannah's hand. "Why aren't you participating this year, Jonas?" she asked sweetly. "Inez, didn't he promise you last year? I could have sworn Sarah told me Jonas really wanted to play a major role."

"He likes to stand out," Hannah added, smiling at Inez. "If you don't offer him a lead, he won't cooperate. You know Jonas. He has to be the star."

Inez turned to the sheriff. "Why didn't you sign up this year?"

"I didn't sign up," Matt pointed out.

"We don't have time for this argument," Jonas said, glaring at Kate. "Traffic is going to be backed up from here to hell and back. Get this show on the road, Inez, or we'll have to shut it down."

Inez began barking orders like a drill sergeant. Hannah nudged Jonas. "Don't look so smug. I'm putting your name in for the role of donkey next year. I'm certain Inez will come up with a suitable costume."

Deliberately the sheriff leaned into her, so close her body was pressed up against his. "That's great, baby doll, as long as you're the one riding me." He breathed the words against her ear, then stalked away from her.

The wind rushed over him and sent his hat sailing toward the river. He glanced back, his grin wide. "You have such a bad temper, Hannah. Merry Christmas."

Matt tried to cling to Kate but was dragged firmly away and forced into his satin costume. He did his best not to notice the other actors hiding their smiles behind their hands as they looked at him, or that Inez and Donna looked horrified. The streets were lined with townspeople, from the oldest to the youngest. Even Sylvia had turned up, with one side of her face covered in a red rash.

The parade began, and Matt was forced to endure trudging through the streets where everyone could see Inez's bizarre creation. The other two wise men went before him. He thought they looked somewhat ridiculous in their robes of velvet, but if he squinted enough, he could use the word *regal.* Cursing the fact that his costume looked more like a woman's bathrobe than a king's robe, Matt thought it took an eternity to get through town, with everyone singing slightly off-key, and to finally catch sight of the town square. Worse, he couldn't prevent the silly grin from breaking out on his face. It just wouldn't go away, and he knew it had to look like he was enjoying parading through town in a woman's bathrobe. He knew Kate and her sisters had grabbed a spot near the makeshift stables to wait for him, and he kept a sharp eye out for them. He let out a sigh of relief when he finally spotted them.

"You look really good in that satin robe, bro," Danny declared, nudging his brother with the hooked end of his staff.

"Shut up, Danny, or I'm going to kick your butt," Matt threatened out of the side of his mouth. He kept his eyes straight ahead, trudging like a man doomed, carrying his gift of frankincense on a white satin pillow out in front of him. He'd argued the wise men hadn't had white satin pillows to use carrying the foul-smelling stuff, but not a single person had listened, and his protests had earned him a black scowl from Inez. He kept his eyes straight ahead, not looking at the waving townspeople as he marched stoically onward to the town square with his silly grin on his face.

Danny whistled at him. "That robe manages to show your butt off nicely, Matt." He tapped the offending part of Matt's anatomy with the staff again. "Sorry, little accident, couldn't help myself."

"I hope you have life insurance," Matt said in his most menacing voice. He made the mistake of looking up to judge the distance to the square. He had to know the exact amount of time he would have to suffer further humiliation. Kate stood there with her sisters. Every last one of them had a huge smile on her face. Matt entertained the idea of throwing the frankincense at their feet and hauling Kate over his shoulder like the Neanderthal they all thought he was. He'd keep the robe, it might come in handy.

Danny poked him with the staff again. "Get along there little dogie," he teased.

Matt's furious gaze settled on Old Man Mars. He stood slightly apart, watching the pageant with a peculiar look on his face, somewhere between mortification and shock. It was obvious he shared Matt's view of the idiotic robes. The old man caught his eye, read the pain on Matt's face, and stepped closer to commiserate. He walked alongside Matt.

"She made you do this, didn't she?" Mars asked.

"Damn right. Otherwise, I wouldn't be caught dead in this getup," Matt replied, hope beginning to stir.

Mars nodded as if he understood Matt's total misery and stepped back away from him with his arms folded. Behind him, Danny began the mantra. "Don't say it. Don't say it. Don't say it." He glanced nervously at the old man as he approached him.

"Merry Christmas." Matt turned back with a cheerful grin. "Merry Christmas, Mr. Mars," he said happily.

A black scowl settled over Old Man Mars's face. His craggy brows drew together in a straight thick line. He made a single sound of disgust and spat on the ground. The old man delivered his yearly kick right to Danny's shin and shuffled off, muttering something about tomatoes. Danny howled and jumped around, holding his injured shin. The staff swung around in a wide circle so that the participants had to break ranks and run for safety. Matt kept walking straight past Inez and the outraged look on her face. Kate met him at the stable, lifting her face for his kiss, while Inez followed Danny, giving him her annual Christmas lecture on behavior.

"All in all, Katie," Matt said, holding her close, "I'd say this was a very satisfactory pageant."

EPILOGUE

"So, DID YOUR wish come true?" Sarah asked.

Matt reached out to take the snowglobe from her, turning it over and over in his hands. He looked across the room at Kate. His Kate. The flames leaped and danced in the fireplace. The Drake sisters were decorating a live tree they'd brought in for Christmas Day. The next day they would plant it on their property near the many other trees that marked the passing of the years.

The house smelled of cedar and pine and cinnamon and spice. Berry candles adorned the mantel and the aroma of fresh-baked cookies drifted from the kitchen. Jonas appeared in the doorway of the kitchen. Red and green frosting smeared his face and fingers, and an apron covered his clothes. "No one asked me if my wish came true," he complained.

"You're such a baby, Jonas," Joley informed him with a little sniff. She caught the apron strings and dragged him backward. "You were the one who said there was nothing to baking cookies, and we should try our hand at doing it the old-fashioned way."

Jonas escaped and raced back into the living room. "*You!* *You!*" he protested. "*Women* bake cookies. That's what they do. They sit around the house looking pretty and hand their man a plate of cookies and a drink when he comes home."

Jonas grinned at the women tauntingly. Matt groaned and covered his face with his hands, looking between his fingers. He already felt power moving in the air. Curtains swayed. Hair stood up. Crackles of electricity snapped and sizzled. The flames on the candles and in the fireplace leaped and danced. Jonas watched the sisters, clearly expecting reprisal. It came from behind him. The small fish tank lifted into the air and tilted part of the contents over Jonas's head. Water rushed over his head. He stiffened, but he didn't turn around, nor did he attempt to wipe it off.

"I just want to point out that this is Christmas Day," he said. "And you all just came back from church."

Joley sat down at the upright, perfectly tuned piano. "And we're all feeling full of love and goodwill, Jonas. Which is why you aren't swimming in the sea with the sharks right now. Shall I play something cheerful?"

"Oh, please do, Joley," Hannah entreated wickedly. "I'm feeling *very* cheerful."

"You would be," Jonas muttered. He took the towel Libby handed him and wiped off his face and hair.

Hannah blew him a kiss.

"Matt didn't answer my question," Sarah persisted.

"The globe only works for family," Abbey said.

Music swelled in volume, filling every corner of the house with joy. Matt heard the sound of feminine laughter, felt his heart respond. Kate walked around the tree, an ornament in her hand. She moved with grace and elegance, his perfect Kate. Feeling the weight of his gaze, she looked across the room at him and smiled.

"Yes, that's true, Abbey," Sarah said. "It only works for family. Matt? Did the globe grant your wish?"

He cleared his throat. "Yes." The affirmation came out on a husky note.

Joley's fingers stilled on the piano. She turned to look at him. Libby put her hand out to Hannah. Abbey put her arm around Elle. All of the Drakes looked at Matt. Kate's sisters. The magical witches of Sea Haven. He thought he fit in rather nicely.

"What did you wish for, Matthew?" Sarah asked. She sat down in Damon's lap, wrapping her arms around his neck.

"I wished for Katie, of course," he answered honestly.

Kate walked over to him, leaning down to kiss him. "I wished for you," she whispered aloud.

"So that little jewelry box in your jacket pocket means something?" Elle asked.

"It means Kate said yes," Matt said. He believed his grin was a permanent fixture on his face.

Jonas shook his head, still mopping up the water. "You got her to say yes just by wishing on that snowglobe?"

"That's what it took," Matt said. "But they say it only works for family. I guess it acknowledged that Katie belonged with me."

"Really? It can reason all that out, can it?" Jonas stared at the snowglobe sitting so innocently on the shelf. "Family, huh? Well, I've been family for about as long as I can remember."

A collective gasp went up from the seven Drake sisters as Jonas reached for the snowglobe.

"No! Jonas, don't touch that." Hannah sounded frightened.

"You can't, Jonas," Sarah said.

His hand hovered over it. Matt could swear he heard hearts beating loudly in the sudden silence. Jonas picked up the globe. Almost at once it sprang to life, the tiny lights on the tree glowing, the fog beginning to swirl.

"Jonas, put it down right now and step away from it," Joley warned.

"You can't play with things in this house," Elle added. "They can be dangerous."

"Jonas," Abbey said, "it isn't funny."

Jonas turned toward the women, his hands absently cradling the globe. "Aren't you all supposed to be cooking dinner for us? Jackson's going to be here any minute, expecting the full Christmas fare, and all he's going to get is some cookies I made." As he spoke, he kept his gaze on Hannah. All the while his palm rubbed the globe as if he could conjure up a genie.

"Don't you *dare* wish on that globe, Jonas Harrington," Hannah hissed. She actually backed a step away from him. "I'm sorry about the fish tank. And the silly hat thing as well. Just put the globe down and keep your mind blank. We'll call it even."

"Are you watching this, Matt?" Jonas asked, clearly taunting Hannah. "This is called power."

"Not for long," Kate said. She held out her hand for the globe. "Hand it over and stop tormenting Hannah. We're liable to serve you up dragon's liver for dinner."

"All right," Jonas agreed. He looked into the glass. "It's certainly beautiful." Instead of giving it to her, he stared into it for a long moment. The fog swirled into a frenzy, obliterating the house until only the lights on the tree blazed, then it slowly subsided, leaving the glass clear and the lights fading away. Only then did he hand it over to Kate.

There was a long silence. Jonas grinned at them. "I'm teasing. You all take things so seriously." He nudged Matt. "I'm not a dreamer like my friend here. I wouldn't let a snowglobe decide my fate. Come on, let's get that turkey carved."

Kate accepted Matt's kiss and watched him go into the kitchen with Damon and Jonas. She joined her sisters as she did each year in surrounding the tree, hands connecting them in a continuous circle. The overhead lights went off, leaving them in the shadows with the flickering candles and Christmas lights. She felt the familiar power running up and down her arms. Running through her. Tiny sparks leaped into the air like little fireflies. Electricity crackled around them. She could feel the minuscule threads in the tapestry of power that wove them together. Energy sprang from one to the other.

Matt stood in the doorway with Damon and Jonas and Jackson, who had come in through the kitchen, and watched the seven women as they stood hand in hand circling the Christmas tree. The women looked beautiful and fey, with their heads thrown back and the sparks leaping around them like miniature fireworks.

Jonas nudged him. "Welcome to the world of the Drake sisters, Matt. And Merry Christmas."

Matt couldn't imagine a better one.

🌿 Acknowledgments 🌿

Thank you to Heather King and Rose Brungard for the wonderful chilling Christmas poem they so graciously provided to me to use for this book!

ROCKY
MOUNTAIN
MIRACLE

❧ Dedication ❧

This book is dedicated to Sheila Clover,
a woman I admire very much.

1

Cole Steele could hear the screams coming from the room down the hall. He knew those nightmares intimately, because the demons also visited him every time he closed his own eyes. He was a grown man, hard and disciplined and well able to drink his way through the night if necessary, but Jase was just a young teenager. Guilt edged his anger as he made his way through the dark to the boy's room. He should have done something, to spare his half brother the horrendous legacy of his own past.

In truth, he hadn't been in touch with his father for years. It hadn't occurred to him that his father would remarry a much younger woman and produce another child, but he should have considered the possibility, not just dropped off the face of the earth. Cole shoved open the bedroom door. Jase was already fully awake, his eyes wide with the terror of his memories. Something twisted hard and painfully in Cole's chest.

"I'm here, Jase," he announced unnecessarily. He wasn't good at soothing the boy. He had been born and bred in roughness and still had a difficult time being gentle. Worse, Jase barely knew him. He was asking the teenager to trust him in spite of his reputation and the rumors of attempted murder flying freely through the town. It was no wonder the boy regarded him with some suspicion.

"I hate Christmas. Can't we just make it go away?" Jase asked. He threw back the covers and paced across the room, the same edgy tension in his teenage body that Cole had in abundance as a grown man. Jase was tall and gangly, like a young colt, all arms and legs, looking a bit like a scarecrow in flannel pajamas. He had Cole's dark hair, but his eyes must have been his mother's, as they were a deep, rich brown. Right now, his eyes were wide with terror, and he turned away to hide his trembling.

Cole felt as if he were looking at himself as a youngster, only Jase had poured himself into books and Cole had become a hellion. Cole knew what it was like to hide the bruises and the terror from the rest of the world. He had grown up living in isolation and hiding, and he still lived that way, but he would be damned if this boy would endure the same.

"Did he shoot your dog for Christmas?" Cole asked bluntly. "That's what he did for me the last time I wanted to celebrate the holiday like my friends. I haven't ever wanted a Christmas since. He also beat the holy hell out of me, but that was insignificant next to the dog."

Jase faced him slowly. The horror was still all too stark in his eyes. "I had a cat."

"I'll bet he said you weren't tough enough and that only sissies needed pets and Christmas. He wanted you to toughen up and be a man. Not get attached to anything."

Jase nodded, swallowing an obvious lump in his throat. "He did a lot of things."

"You have burn marks? Scars from cuts? He liked to whip me with a coat hanger. And when I didn't cry, he took to using other things."

"I cried," Jase admitted.

"I did too, at first. He was a mean son of a bitch, Jase. I'm glad he's dead. He can't touch you anymore. I'm not going to lie to you and tell you the nightmares go away because I still have them. We both lived in hell and he had too much money for anyone to want to believe us." Cole rubbed his hands through his thick black hair. "He was sick, Jase. I got out, changed my name thinking he'd never find me, and stayed as far from him as I could possibly get. That's no excuse. I should have kept tabs on him. Maybe I could have gotten you away from him."

Jase shook his head. "He never would have let me go."

"You know what they're all saying, don't you? They think I had something to do with his death."

Jase nodded, his eyes suddenly wary. "I've heard. Why did you come back?"

"I was named your guardian in his will. It was the first I'd heard of you. I didn't know you existed until five months ago. I knew he must have done the same thing to you and your mother that he did to me and mine. I thought I could protect you, at least until you're old enough to live on your own. I figured I would be a better guardian than anyone else the court might appoint or that our father had named if I didn't accept."

Dawn was creeping in through the huge plate-glass window. Cole watched the sun come up. It was cold, and the ground outside was covered with several feet of snow, turning the hills into a carpet of sparkling crystals. "You hungry?"

"Are you cooking?"

Cole managed a lazy shrug even though he really wanted to smash something. It was always there, that volcano inside him, waiting to erupt. The thought of his father, the time of year, it wasn't all that difficult to bring rage to the surface. "I thought we'd go into town and give them all something more to gossip about."

Jase met Cole's eyes squarely. "They say you killed the old man and that you're planning to kill me next. Sixty-four million dollars is a lot of money, twice as much as thirty-two."

"They do say that, don't they?" Cole said. "And don't forget the ranch. It's worth twice that easily, maybe more with the oil and gas deposits. I haven't actually checked into how much yet." His eyes had gone ice-cold, a piercing blue stare that impaled the boy. "What do you say, Jase? Because in the end, you're the only one that counts as far as I'm concerned."

Jase was silent a long time. "I say I'm glad you came back.

But I don't understand why he left us the money and the ranch when he hated us both so much. It doesn't make any sense." He looked around the enormous room, frowning. "I keep expecting him to show up in the middle of the night. I'm afraid to open my eyes because I know he's standing over the bed, just waiting."

"With that smile." Cole's voice was grim.

Jase nodded, a small shudder betraying the fact that he wasn't as calm as he tried to seem. "With that smile." He looked at Cole. "What do you do when the nightmares come?" He punched his fist into his pillow. Once. Twice. "I hate this time of year."

Cole felt a sharp pain in his chest and the familiar churning in his gut. His own hand balled into a fist, but he tamped down the smoldering anger and hung on to control for the boy's sake. "I drink. I'm your guardian, so I have to say that's not allowed for you. At least not until you're a hell of a lot older."

"Does it work?"

"No," Cole said grimly. Honestly. "But it gets me through the night. Sometimes I go to the workout room or the barn. I hung a heavy bag in both places, and I beat on them until my hands hurt. Other times I take the wildest horse we have and go out into the mountains. I run the hills, using the deer trails, anything to make me so tired I can't think anymore."

"None of that works either, does it?" Jase had tried physical activity as well, but he was finding that talking quietly with his half brother was helpful. More helpful than anything else he'd tried. At least one person believed him. And one person had gone through the same torment. It created a bond in spite of the ugly rumors that surrounded his tough, harder-than-nails half brother.

Cole shook his head. "No, none of it works, but it gets you through the night. One night at a time. He's dead, Jase, and that's all that matters."

Jase took a deep breath. "Did you kill him?"

"No, but I wish I had. I used to lie awake at night and plan how I'd do it. That was before Mom died. Then I just wanted to get out." Cole studied the boy's face. "Did you kill him?" He concentrated his gaze on the boy. Every nuance. Every expression, the way he breathed. The flick of his eyes. The trembling of his hands.

Jase shook his head. "I was too afraid of him."

Cole let his breath out slowly. He had stayed alive using his ability to read others, and he was fairly certain that Jase was telling the truth. Jase had been in the house when someone had shot Brett Steele right there in his own office. He wanted to believe that the boy wasn't involved in Brett Steele's death. Cole wasn't certain how he would have handled it if Jase had admitted he'd done it, and for a man in Cole's profession, that wasn't a good thing.

"Cole, did he kill your mother?" For the first time, Jase sounded like a child rather than a fourteen-year-old trying to be a man. He sank down onto the bed, his thin shoulders shaking. "I think he killed my mother. They said she was drinking and drove off the bridge, but she never drank. Never. She was afraid to drink. She wanted to know what was happening all the time. You know what he was like, he'd be nice one minute and come after you the next."

Brett Steele had been a sadistic man. It was Cole's belief that he had killed for the sheer rush of having the power of life and death over anything, human or animal. He'd enjoyed inflicting pain, and he had tortured his wives and children and every one of his employees. The ranch was huge, a long way from help, and once he had control over those living on his lands, he never relinquished it. Cole knew he'd been lucky to escape.

"It's possible. I think the old man was capable of paying everyone off from coroners to police officers. He had too much money and power for anyone to cross him. It would be easy enough for a medical examiner to look the other way if there was enough money in bribes. And if that didn't work, there were always threats. We both know the old man didn't make idle threats; he'd carry them out."

Jase met his brother's stare directly. "He killed your mother, didn't he?"

"Maybe. Probably." Cole needed a drink. "Let's go into town and get breakfast."

"Okay." Jase pulled a pair of jeans from the closet. They were neatly hung and immaculately clean, just like everything else in the room. "Who do you think killed him? If it wasn't either of us, someone else had to have done it."

"He made a lot of enemies. He destroyed businesses and seduced as many of his friends' wives as possible. And if he killed anyone else, as I suspect he must have, someone could have known and retaliated. He liked to hurt people, Jase. It was inevitable that he would die a violent death."

"Were you surprised he left you the money and guardianship over me?"

"Yes, at first. But later I thought maybe it made sense. He wanted us to be like him. He had me investigated and found I spent time in jail. I think he believed I was exactly like him. And the only other choice of a guardian he had was your uncle, and you know how much they despised one another."

Jase sighed. "Uncle Mike is just as crazy as Dad was. All he talks about is sin and redemption. He thinks I need to be exorcised."

Cole swore, a long string of curses. "That's a load of crap, Jase. There's nothing wrong with you." He needed to move, to ride something hard, it didn't matter what it was. A horse, a motorcycle, a woman, anything at all to take away the knots gathering in his stomach. "Let's get out of here."

He turned away from the boy, a cold anger lodged in his gut. He detested Christmas, detested everything about it. No matter how much he didn't want the season to start, it always came. He woke up drenched in sweat, vicious laughter ringing in his ears. He could fight the demons most of the year, but not when Christmas songs played on the radio and in every store he entered. Not when every building and street displayed decorations and people continually wished each other "Merry

Christmas." He didn't want that for Jase. He had to find a way to give the boy back his life.

Counseling hadn't helped either of them. When no one believed a word you said, or worse, was bought off, you learned to stop trusting people. If Cole never did another thing right in his life, he was going to be the one person Jase would know he could always trust. And he was going to make certain the boy didn't turn out the way he had. Or the way their father had.

The brothers walked through the sprawling ranch house. The floors were all gleaming wood, the ceilings open-beamed and high. Brett Steele had demanded the best of everything, and he got it. Cole couldn't fault him on his taste.

"Cole," Jase asked, "why were you in jail?"

Cole didn't break stride as he hurried through the spacious house. At times he wanted to burn the thing down. There was no warmth in it, and as hard as he'd tried to turn the show-piece into a home for Jase, it remained cold and barren.

Outdoors it was biting cold. The frost turned the hills and meadows into a world of sparkling crystal, dazzling the eyes, but Cole simply ignored it, shoving his sunglasses onto his face. He went past the huge garage that housed dozens of cars—all toys Brett Steele had owned and rarely ever used—to go to his own pickup.

"I shouldn't have asked you," Jase muttered, slamming the door with unnecessary force. "I hate questions."

Cole paused, the key in the ignition. He glanced at the boy's flushed face. "It isn't that, Jase. I don't mind you asking me anything. I made up my mind I'd never lie to you about anything, and I'm not quite certain how to explain the jail time. Give me a minute."

Jase nodded. "I don't mind that you've been in jail, but it worries me because Uncle Mike says he's going to take you to court and get custody of me. If I lived with him, I'd spend all my life on my knees, praying for my soul. I'd rather run away."

"He can't get you away from me," Cole promised, his voice

grim. There was a hard edge to the set of his mouth. He turned his piercing blue gaze directly on his young half brother. "The one thing I can promise is I'll fight for you until they kill me, Jase." He was implacable, the deadly ruthless stamp of determination clear on his face. "No one is going to take you away from me. You got that?"

Jase visibly relaxed. He nodded, a short jerky gesture as he tried to keep his emotions under control. Cole wasn't certain if that was good or bad. Maybe the boy needed to cry his eyes out. Cole never had. He would never give his father the satisfaction, even when the bastard had nearly killed him.

It was a long way to the nearest town. There had been numerous guards at the ranch when his father was alive, supposedly for security, but Cole knew better. Brett had needed his own private world, a realm he could rule with an iron fist. The first thing Cole had done was to fire all of the ranch hands, the security force, and the housekeeper. If he could have had them prosecuted for their participation in Brett's sadistic depravities, he would have. Jase needed to feel safe. And Cole needed to feel as if he could provide the right atmosphere for the boy. They had interviewed the new ranch hands together, and they were still looking for a housekeeper.

"You know, Jase, you never picked out one of the horses to use," Cole said.

Jase leaned forward to fiddle with the radio. The cab was flooded with a country Christmas tune. Jase hastily went through the stations, but all he could find was Christmas music and he finally gave up in exasperation. "I don't care which one I ride," Jase said, and turned his head to stare out the window at the passing scenery. His voice was deliberately careless.

"You must have a preference," Cole persisted. "I've seen you bring the big bay, Celtic High, a carrot every now and then." The boy had spent a little time each day brushing the horse and whispering to it, but he never rode the bay.

Jase's expression closed down instantly, his eyes wary. "I don't care about any of them," he repeated.

Cole frowned as he slipped a CD into the player. "You know what the old man was all about, don't you, Jase? He didn't want his sons to feel affection or loyalty to anything or anyone. Not our mothers, not friends, and not animals. He killed the animals in front of us to teach us a lesson. He destroyed our friendships to accomplish the same thing. He got rid of our mothers to isolate us, to make us wholly dependent on him. He didn't want you ever to feel emotion, especially affection or love for anything or anyone else. If he succeeded in doing that to you, he won. You can't let him win. Choose a horse and let yourself care for it. We'll get a dog if you want a dog, or another cat. Any kind of pet you want, but let yourself feel something, and when our father visits you in your nightmares, tell him to go to hell."

"You didn't do that," Jase pointed out. "You don't have a dog. You haven't had a dog in all the years you've been away. And you never got married. I'll bet you never lived with a woman. You have one-night stands and that's about it because you won't let anyone into your life." It was a shrewd guess.

Cole counted silently to ten. He was psychoanalyzing Jase, but he damned well didn't want the boy to turn the spotlight back on him. "It's a hell of a way to live, Jase. You don't want to use me as a role model. I know all the things you shouldn't do and not many you should. But cutting yourself off from every living thing takes its toll. Don't let him do that to you. Start small if you want. Just choose one of the horses, and we'll go riding together in the mornings."

Jase was silent, his face averted, but Cole knew he was weighing the matter carefully. It meant trusting Cole further than perhaps Jase was willing to go. Cole was a big question mark to everyone, Jase especially. Cole couldn't blame the boy. He knew what he was like. Tough and ruthless with no backup in him. His reputation was that of a vicious, merciless fighter, a man born and bred in violence. It wasn't like he knew how to make all the soft, kind gestures that the kid needed, but he could protect Jase.

"Just think about it," he said to close the subject. Time was on his side. If he could give Jase back his life, he would forgive himself for not bringing the old man down as he should have done years ago. Jase had had his mother, a woman with love and laughter in her heart. More than likely Brett had killed her because he couldn't turn Jase away from her. Jase's mother must have left some legacy of love behind.

Cole had no one. His mother had been just the opposite of Jase's. His mother had had a child because Brett demanded she have one, but she went back to her model-thin figure and cocaine as soon as possible, leaving her son in the hands of her brutal husband. In the end, she'd died of an overdose. Cole had always suspected his father had had something to do with her death. It was interesting that Jase suspected the same thing of his own mother's death.

A few snowflakes drifted down from the sky, adding to the atmosphere of the season they both were trying so hard to avoid. Jase kicked at the floorboard of the truck, a small sign of aggression, then glanced apologetically at Cole.

"Maybe we should have opted for a workout instead," Cole said.

"I'm always hungry," Jase admitted. "We can work out after we eat. Who came up with the idea of Christmas anyway? It's a dumb idea, giving presents out when it isn't your birthday. And it can't be good for the environment to cut down all the trees."

Cole stayed silent, letting the boy talk, grateful Jase was finally comfortable enough to talk to him at all.

"Mom loved Christmas. She used to sneak me little gifts. She'd hide them in my room. He always had spies, though, and they'd tell him. He always punished her, but she'd do it anyway. I knew she'd be punished, and she knew it too, but she'd still sneak me presents." Jase rolled down the window, letting the crisp, cold air into the truck. "She sang me Christmas songs. And once, when he was away on a trip, we baked cookies together. She loved it. We both knew the housekeeper would tell him, but at the time, we didn't care."

Cole cleared his throat. The idea of trying to celebrate Christmas made him ill, but the kid wanted it. Maybe even needed it, but had no clue that was what his nervous chatter was all about. Cole hoped he could pull it off. There were no happy memories from his childhood to offset the things his father had done.

"We tried to get away from him, but he always found us," Jase continued.

"He's dead, Jase," Cole repeated. He took a deep breath and took the plunge, feeling as if he was leaping off a steep cliff. "If we want to bring a giant tree into his home and decorate it, we can. There's not a damn thing he can do about it."

"He might have let her go if she hadn't wanted to take me with her."

Cole heard the tears in the boy's voice, but the kid didn't shed them. Silently he cursed, wishing for inspiration, for all the right things to say. "Your mother was an extraordinary woman, Jase, and there aren't that many in the world. She cared about you, not the money or the prestige of being Mrs. Brett Steele. She fought for you, and she tried to give you a life in spite of the old man. I wish I'd had the chance to meet her."

Jase didn't reply, but closed his eyes, resting his head back against the seat. He could still remember the sound of his mother's voice. The way she smelled. Her smile. He rubbed his head. Mostly he remembered the sound of her screams when his father punished her.

"I'll think about the Christmas thing, Cole. I kind of like the idea of decorating the house when he always forbade it."

Cole didn't reply. It had been a very long few weeks, but the Christmas season was almost over. A couple more weeks, and he would have made it through another December. If doing the Christmas thing could give the kid back his life, Cole would find a way to get through it.

The town was fairly big and offered a variety of late-night and early-morning dining. Cole chose a diner he was familiar with and parked the truck in the parking lot. To his dismay, it was already filled with cars. Unfolding his large frame, he slid from the truck, waiting for Jase to get out.

"You forgot your jacket," he said.

"No, I didn't. I hate the thing," Jase said.

Cole didn't bother to ask him why. He already knew the answer and vowed to buy the kid a whole new wardrobe immediately. He pushed open the door to the diner, stepping back to allow Jase to enter first. Jase took two steps into the entryway and stopped abruptly behind the high wall of fake ivy. "They're talking about you, Cole," he whispered. "Let's get out of here."

The voices were loud enough to carry across the small restaurant. Cole stood still, his hand on the boy's shoulder to steady him. Jase would have to learn to live with gossip, just as he'd learned to survive the nightmare he'd been born into.

"You're wrong, Randy. Cole Steele murdered his father, and he's going to murder that boy. He wants the money. He never came around here to see that boy until his daddy died."

"He was in jail, Jim, he couldn't very well go visiting his relatives," a second male voice pointed out with a laugh.

Cole recognized Randy Smythe from the local agriculture store. Before he could decide whether to get Jase out of there or show the boy just how hypocritical the local storeowners could be, a third voice chimed in.

"You are so full of it, Jim Begley," a female voice interrupted the argument between the two men. "You come in here every morning grousing about Cole Steele. He was cleared as a suspect a long time ago and given guardianship of his half brother, as he should have been. You're angry because your bar buddies lost their cushy jobs, so you're helping to spread the malicious gossip they started. The entire lot of you sound like a bunch of sour old biddies."

The woman never raised her voice. In fact, it was soft and low and harmonious. Cole felt the tone strumming inside of him, vibrating and spreading heat. There was something magical in the voice, more magical than the fact that she was sticking up for him. His fingers tightened involuntarily on Jase's shoulder. It was the first time he could ever remember anyone sticking up for him.

"He was in jail, Maia," Jim Begley reiterated, his voice almost placating.

"So were a lot of people who didn't belong there, Jim. And a lot of people who should have been in jail never were. That doesn't mean anything. You're jealous of the man's money and the fact that he has the reputation of being able to get just about any woman he wants, and you can't."

A roar of laughter went up. Cole expected Begley to get angry with the woman, but surprisingly, he didn't. "Aw, Maia, don't go getting all mad at me. You aren't going to do anything, are you? You wouldn't put a hex on my . . . on me, would you?"

The laughter rose and this time the woman joined in. The sound of her voice was like music. Cole had never had such a reaction to any woman, and he hadn't even seen her.

"You just never know about me, now do you, Jim?" she teased, obviously not angry with the man. "It's Christmas, the best time of the year. Do you think you could stop spreading rumors and just wait for the facts? Give the man a chance. You all want his money. You all agree the town needs him, yet you're so quick to condemn him. Isn't that the littlest bit hypocritical?"

Cole was shocked that the woman could wield so much power, driving her point home without ever raising her voice. And strangely, they were all listening to her. Who was she, and why were these usually rough men hanging on her every word, trying to please her? He found himself very curious about a total stranger—a woman at that.

"Okay, okay," Jim said. "I surrender, Maia. I'll never mention Cole Steele again if that will make you happy. Just don't get mad at me."

Maia laughed again. The carefree sound teased all of Cole's senses, made him very aware of his body and its needs. "I'll see you all later. I have work to do."

Cole felt his body tense. She was coming around the ivy to

the entrance. Cole's breath caught in his throat. She was on the shorter side, but curvy, filling out her jeans nicely. A sweater molded her breasts into a tempting invitation. She had a wealth of dark, very straight hair, as shiny as a raven's wing, pulled into a careless ponytail. Her face was exotic, the bone structure delicate, reminding him of a pixie.

She swung her head back, her wide smile fading as she saw them standing there. She stopped short, raising her eyes to Cole's. He actually hunched a little, feeling the impact in his belly. Little hammers began to trip in his head, and his body reacted with an urgent and very elemental demand. A man could drown in her eyes, get lost, or just plain lose every demon he had. Her eyes were large, heavily lashed, and some color other than blue, turquoise maybe, a mixture of blue and green that was vivid and alive and so darned beautiful he ached inside just looking at her.

Jase nudged him in the ribs.

Cole reacted immediately. "Sorry, ma'am." But he didn't move. "I'm Cole Steele. This is my brother, Jase."

Jase jerked under his hand, reacting to being acknowledged as a brother.

The woman nodded at Cole and flashed a smile at Jase as she stepped around them to push open the door.

"Holy cow," Jase murmured. "Did you see that smile?" He glanced up at Cole. "Yeah, you saw it all right."

"Was I staring?" Cole asked.

"You looked like you might have her for breakfast," Jase answered. "You can look really intimidating, Cole. Scary."

Cole almost followed the woman, but at the boy's comment he turned back. "Am I scary to you, Jase?"

The boy shrugged. "Sometimes. I'm getting used to you. I've never seen you smile. Ever."

Cole raised his eyebrow. "I can't remember actually smiling. Maybe I'll have to practice. You can work with me."

"Don't you smile at women?"

"I don't have to."

2

COLE STEELE WAS back *again*. The bar was jammed, bodies welded together as they moved to the rhythmic beat of the music Maia Armstrong provided on the drums. The band was hot tonight, she could feel the music pounding inside of her exactly the way it needed to be to keep the house rocking. She tried not to see him, tried not to notice his body stretched out in a chair in a sexy, lazy sprawl. The music was usually all that mattered, all she thought about when she played. She could lose herself in the primal beats, the familiar feel of her hands on the sticks, whirling them in her fingers and finding that perfect pocket of sound.

Music took her far away from the terrible things she saw every day. The things that kept her on the move, town after town, knowing she could never really settle anywhere. Music was her solace. Cole Steele changed all that. What was he doing there? Had he already gone through all the women in the more upscale bars in town?

He was stinking rich and so sinfully sensual he should be locked up. He wasn't just the local bad boy; he was a hard, dangerous man, one that wielded absolute power. He knew it too. It was in the arrogance stamped into his very bones. He sat there watching her through hooded eyes, intent, focused, his hand absently stroking the long neck of his beer bottle. He looked so sexual to her. It wasn't a charade, he was really that way, his body hard and hot and . . . Maia groaned inwardly. She was not falling for a bad boy. She had too much sense and too much self-respect. And he had far too much money and drama for her even to consider such a folly.

She wasn't going to look at him, wasn't going to let him get to her. A man like Cole Steele left fingerprints on a woman, took away her soul, and never returned it to her. Once he left burn marks—and he would—they would never fade. She refused to allow her gaze to stray his way, although she could feel the weight of his heavy, brooding stare. Instead, she picked a table near the front and flashed a high-wattage smile at the nearest man, wanting to focus anywhere but on the dark devil watching her.

Cole shifted his legs into a more comfortable position in an attempt to ease the relentless ache in his body. His fingers tightened around the neck of the beer bottle, nearly crushing it. Maia didn't need to be smiling at any other man in the room, not when she should be smiling at him. She didn't want the others, wasn't interested in them, but he could see her heightened awareness of him. She wasn't adept at hiding it.

Cole knew he was going to have to change his strategy completely. He might even have to eat his words and actually learn to smile at a woman. He'd wasted nine nights coming down to the El Dorado Saloon after hearing that Maia Armstrong, the traveling veterinarian, often sat in jamming on the drums in the evening. He was either losing his touch or his mind. There were a dozen women who'd made it plain they were willing to go to bed with him, so why was he so damned fixated on the one who refused to give in to him? With a series of storms coming, most likely bringing severe blizzard conditions, this was going to be his last chance to persuade her for a long while.

She'd noticed him all right. He'd made it abundantly clear he was interested. He'd managed half a dozen conversations with her. She was always polite, but she kept a distance firmly between them. He tapped his finger on the small round table as he watched her. Why was he so fascinated by her? Her smile could light up the entire room, and her laugh was contagious. He shouldn't have noticed, but it was nearly impossible not to. Especially when she was turning that smile on another man.

He dreamt of her. Ever since he'd seen her in the diner the

nightmares that always plagued him during the Christmas season had been replaced with highly erotic dreams of her. Even Jase was beginning to tease him about her, knowing Cole only left the ranch in the evenings to see her. Cole absently stroked the neck of the beer bottle, wishing it were her skin beneath his fingers. He'd made up his mind he was going to have to be aggressive with her tonight. Subtle wasn't working at all. He'd had plenty of time to study her. It was his business to read people. Maia Armstrong was no pushover with men, but she detested public scenes. She wouldn't fight it if he didn't push beyond her limit.

A woman leaned close, blocking his vision, deliberately bending over him to give him a better view of her ample cleavage. He stared up at her with hard eyes and a distinct scowl. "You're blocking the view."

The woman flushed, but slid into the chair at his table. "You like this band?"

He glanced at her. Once. A curt dismissal. He stared at her until she got up and stomped away. His rude behavior would only add to his carefully cultivated reputation of being a complete bastard. What did it matter? His reputation had been blackened a long time ago. Maybe he really had become a complete bastard, but the truth was, he rarely found anything he wanted, and he wasn't going to tolerate anyone's interfering with his getting it. His gaze returned to the woman playing the drums.

Maia Armstrong intrigued him. It was as simple as that. He'd investigated her, of course. He investigated anyone and everyone who touched his life, or Jase's. She was the new veterinarian and played in a band in the evenings. She never took a permanent position in any town, but traveled, often filling in for other vets. She had taken the place of the local elderly vet who, because of failing health, had been forced to give up his practice before he could find someone to buy him out. Already, she was popular and very well thought of by everyone who had worked with her.

There were rumors about her. Some said she possessed magic. The majority said mysterious things happened when she was around animals. She managed to save the hopeless and was fast earning a reputation with the ranchers for being able to handle the wildest stock. The rumor persisted that she was able to cast spells, on both animals and men, and Cole was beginning to think there might be some truth to it. He was obsessed with her.

He took a long, slow pull of his beer, never taking his gaze from her. The band was finishing their set. He knew their music now, knew Maia's habits. He also knew she was very aware of his reputation, both as a lady's man and as a dangerous felon. She didn't like gossip, probably because so many people gossiped about her, and he was fairly certain she wouldn't make a scene when he made his move on her. He calculated the odds, just like he calculated everything in his life.

The drum built to a crashing crescendo, and Maia set her sticks aside and swept back stray tendrils of hair that had escaped from her intricate braid. Her skin was damp, glowing, her smile satisfied. She'd liked the way the music sounded, and it showed in her expression. Maia was never closed off to the world the way he was, and Cole found even that intriguing. He had positioned himself perfectly, making it impossible for her to get to the bar without walking past his table.

Cole caught her wrist as she swept by him, pretending, as she did each night, not to notice him. He shifted in his chair so that she was suddenly wedged between his outstretched legs, imprisoning her. "Have a drink with me."

Maia could hear her own heart thundering in her ears. Up close he was overpowering. He looked all male, his blue eyes dark with a desire he didn't try to hide from her. In fact, he wore his sensuality easily, with complete confidence, a devil in blue jeans and sin in his heated gaze. She knew the rumors. She knew what the town suspected Cole of doing. Murder. He'd been in jail. There was a tattoo on his upper arm, which he'd obviously gotten in jail and didn't bother to try to hide.

His body was hard and fit; but sometimes, when he didn't think anyone was watching, she saw something sad and tragic in his unguarded expression. And that was truly dangerous.

The last thing she wanted to do was to add to the rumors flying around him. She couldn't imagine how difficult it was to be the favorite subject of the town's most malicious gossips. He couldn't possibly have done a third of the evil deeds attributed to him. Maia patted his dark head, a deliberate show of camaraderie for the patrons in the bar. At the same time, she wanted to let him know, very politely, that she wasn't playing his game. She leaned close to him, put her lips against his ear. "The lady sitting on the barstool to your right is devouring you with her eyes. You have an easy score right there to take care of any urgent . . . er . . . needs you may have."

Cole felt her warm breath against his ear, the whisper of her lips against his skin. When she leaned into him he inhaled the scent of her. Peaches and rain could be very intoxicating. His fingers around her wrist kept her connected to him. "I want you to have a drink with me." His voice was huskier than he intended, and her close proximity had more of an effect on him than he'd anticipated. His heart pounded, and he could feel his blood surging hotly through his veins.

Maia sucked in her breath sharply. Cole Steele was used to giving orders, used to having them obeyed, and he certainly knew his effect on women. His voice was almost mesmerizing. She could feel the hard column of his thighs pressing against her legs, as his thumb stroked over her bare skin where he held her arm.

Maia tugged a little on her wrist, not making it obvious to the curious onlookers. "I don't think that's a good idea." She smiled to take the sting out of her refusal.

"You never told me your name."

"You know my name." Mentally she kicked herself. She was engaging with him when it was the last thing she should be doing. How in the world did the man manage to be so potent? He was the most sensual man she'd ever encountered. Her hor-

mones were already in overdrive, just as they'd been for the last
few days. And, of course, it had to be for the resident bad boy.

"What is it going to hurt to sit at my table and have a beer
with me?"

"Because that isn't what you want from me. Let go." She
stood waiting, looking down into his brilliant eyes. Cold eyes.
Eyes that had seen things no one should ever witness. Maia
sighed, trying desperately not to see those things, not to see or
feel or react to the pain swirling so deep in their vivid blue
depths. "Please."

Cole removed his hand instantly. Maia made herself walk
when she wanted to run. Her heart was beating too fast. He
was frightening in his intensity, and she was very susceptible to
the man he hid behind his remote mask. She knew a hurt creature when she saw one. Man or animal, her entire being reacted to them. Cole Steele was one of those creatures, and he
was just too darned dangerous for her to get involved with.

"Sounded great tonight," Ed Logan, the bartender, said in
greeting. He pushed a frosted glass toward her and leaned close,
lowering his voice. "Keep away from him, Maia. He's bad news."

She tilted the glass, savoring the ice-cold water as it went
down her throat. Her gaze strayed toward Cole Steele. His
gaze was on her. Hot. Intense. Drifting over her body possessively. She turned her back on him, leaning against the bar.
Immediately she was all too aware that her movement left
Cole staring at her bottom, encased in tight jeans. It was all
she could do not to shift positions immediately. "I have no
idea what you're going on about, Ed."

"He's got a look about him. He's on the hunt for a woman,
and it's rather obvious he has his sights set on you. You don't
play with a man like that and win."

"You're such a sweetheart, Ed. I'd marry you myself if you
weren't already taken. You can stop worrying. Cole Steele is so
far out of my league that I don't even want to play. He'll settle
his sights elsewhere fast enough. He'll get bored and move on
to greener pastures."

"Just so you know to be careful. People are saying bad things about him. Most probably aren't true, but I know men, and he's dangerous."

"At least to women," she agreed. "Seriously, Ed, I can look after myself."

"He made a whole lot of enemies in this town when he came in five months ago and fired the crew that was working out at the ranch. Times are hard and in the winter everyone needs work. No one knows why he did it, and he isn't saying, but there's hard feelings."

"A man doesn't fire everyone without a reason, Ed," Maia pointed out. "Especially not a rancher with a spread the size of his. He needs them. Maybe a few head of cattle were missing. It happens all the time."

Ed shrugged his shoulders and picked up an empty whiskey glass, dismissing the subject of Cole Steele. "Loretta said to tell you to drop by anytime. And if you don't have plans for Christmas dinner, you're invited to that as well."

"You tell her thank you. Lucky you to have her."

Ed nodded. "I can't get over you managing to save that dog of hers. She loves that mutt, and I was certain there was no hope after the car hit it, but you pulled it off."

Maia patted his hand. It hadn't been Loretta who fell apart when the little Jack Russell terrier had darted out in front of a car. Big Ed had been sobbing so hard he couldn't speak when he and Loretta had brought the dog to her.

She turned away and immediately felt the impact of Cole Steele's piercing gaze. It should have made her cold, but she felt heat spreading dangerously to every part of her body. She braced herself to get past him a second time. The jukebox was playing, and a few couples were swaying on the dance floor to a sultry love song. It might be more prudent to cut across the dance floor, but doing so would brand her a coward in her own eyes. Or maybe she was feeling reckless.

He stood up, a lithe, male movement of grace and sheer power, blocking her path. Cole towered over her. With his wide shoulders and muscular body, he made her feel intensely feminine. His hands found her wrists, his grip firm, but not hurting her as he drew her arms around his neck, fitting her body tightly against his hard, masculine frame. His arms caged hers, his thighs pressing against her until she was forced to walk backward to the dance floor. Immediately she was engulfed in flames, a wrenching desire spreading through her body and making her weak with need. His heavy erection was pressed tightly, unashamedly, against her stomach, spreading flames over her skin.

She said nothing. She refused to cause a scene by fighting him publicly, and in any case, she'd definitely wanted this. She wasn't a child who lied to herself. She'd deliberately chosen to walk past him to give him another opportunity to claim her. She closed her eyes and drifted with him on a tide of sexual awareness, on arousal, on heat and flames and lust all mixed together. It was a unique experience for her. Maia felt her body melting into his.

Cole bent his head to the invitation of her bare neck. With her hair braided, it left her vulnerable to the brush of his mouth against her pulse. She fit perfectly in his arms, as if she'd been made for him. He felt the urgent demands of his body, but more than that, there was an unfamiliar longing that rose and lodged deep where he knew he wasn't going to be able to remove it easily. Maia Armstrong left her brand on him, and he hadn't even made love to her. Or maybe he was; he'd never actually made love to a woman before, and maybe that was what he was doing.

She stole his breath. Took his animal hunger and turned it into something altogether different. Cole's arms tightened around Maia, urging her body even closer to his, wanting to imprint her into his bones. He had come to her to rid himself of demons for a night or two, but with her body fitting into his, something was softening inside of him, and for the first time since his childhood, Cole was terrified. He wanted to let her go and walk away, to be safe in his isolated world; but he couldn't let go of her warmth or the promise of magic in the curves of her body pressed so tightly to him.

Cole became aware that the last notes of the song were fading away. He was completely confident when it came to women. He was a highly sensual man and knew how to make a woman need him. It always came easy to him. "I want to go home with you," he said shamelessly.

Maia pulled out of his arms, refusing the stark hunger and dark intensity that drew other women to him so easily. She flashed her powerful smile, the one he felt all the way down to his stone-cold heart.

"Pheromones are nasty little devils, aren't they?" Maia asked. "They strike at the most inopportune times."

He couldn't let her go. He saw it in her eyes that she was just going to turn and walk away from him. "Then come to the ranch with me." Was that really bad boy Cole Steele acting desperate? What the hell was wrong with him? He should go straight to the woman at the end of the bar who was devouring him with her eyes and walk out with her. It would serve Maia right. He knew she wanted him. She couldn't hide her reaction to him.

"You're afraid of me," he taunted her.

"Do I look stupid to you?" She stepped back cautiously, making certain she could walk without trembling. "Any woman with half a brain would be afraid of you. You have trouble stamped on your forehead and packaged not so subtly there in the front."

"Nice of you to notice, since you're the one causing the trouble." He made it a challenge.

"Nice to know I can," she replied, in no way perturbed by the accusation. "Go away, Mr. Steele. You're way out of my league."

The jukebox music shifted into another moody, sensual song, and Cole reached out to pull her back into his arms. "What puts me out of your league?"

She tilted her head to look up at him, which was a major

mistake. His eyes were such a deep blue, almost metallic, and he looked at her with dark desire. With hunger. With possession and determination. There was a ruthless edge to his mouth and a need in the depths of his gaze she couldn't avoid. Her breath left her lungs in a rush. "Everything. Money. Experience. Life. I don't want to get singed, let alone burned. You come with far too high a price tag."

His eyes were locked on hers, and she couldn't break away, held captive in spite of her resolve. It was the fleeting glimpse of the hurt animal, the shadows of pain and betrayal he hid behind his cool, icy demeanor that kept her from walking off the dance floor. She slipped her arms around his neck and allowed her body to sink into the heat of his.

His chin rubbed the top of her head. "All this time I was thinking you were the one with the high price tag."

"You probably think all women come with price tags," she muttered against his chest. She turned her head to lay her ear over his heart.

"Don't they?" he asked. "Usually it isn't all that difficult, but you, lady, present a problem."

Maia listened to the steady rhythm of his heart. "I refuse to be a problem for you. You're the one insisting on dancing with me. I told you no."

"I didn't hear you say no."

"Really?" She smiled against his shirt. "I could have sworn the entire room heard me. I thought I was very emphatic about it."

"No, you definitely didn't say no."

"Well, I should have. My guard must have been down." She laughed softly, and the sound played right through his body.

"You're dangerous."

"Funny. That's what everyone says about you," Maia said.

Cole bent his head once more to the temptation of her bare neck. She was warm satin. He tasted her, teased her earlobe with his teeth. Before she could protest his action he lifted his head to distract her. "Why did you stick up for me in the diner the other day?" he asked. "Everyone believes I killed the old man. Why don't you?"

Maia shivered, tried to pull her suddenly scattered defenses back around her. His mouth had sent small flames licking over her skin. "You were cleared as a suspect. It's all they talk about sometimes, and it gets annoying. You were a thousand miles away when your father was murdered, but they want to believe you did it." She burrowed closer to the warmth of his heart without realizing she was doing it. "You inherited all that money and the ranch after you left home and turned your back on your father. And then you dared to fire everyone. It's human nature I guess. They want you to be guilty. And it gives them someone to talk about."

"I still might have had it done," he pointed out. His hands traced the contours of her back, slid down to her waist and over her hips.

"It was wrong of them. I felt bad for the boy. What is he? About fourteen, fifteen? He just lost his father, and they want to spread gossip about his guardian. It's malicious, and it makes me angry."

"He's fourteen, and he hated the old man." Cole heard the contemptuous words come out of his mouth. He never revealed anything private to anyone, least of all a complete stranger or a woman he had sex with. What the hell had gotten into him?

They weren't even dancing anymore, just holding one another and swaying, their bodies moving in a perfect rhythm. His arms tightened around her, and he drew her hips closer to him. The rest of the room seemed to have fallen away, leaving them wrapped in a world of two. Maia looked up at his face. Something fluttered in her stomach. His head began to descend toward hers, inch by slow inch. She could see lines etched into his face, the shadow on his jaw, his long eyelashes and the intent in his hungry eyes.

"Don't you dare."

"I have to."

"I said no. Very decisively." Maia pulled her head back to keep his lips from touching hers. She'd be lost if he kissed her with his sinful mouth. She was taking no chances.

"You are a such a coward. You're running."

"Like a rabbit," she confirmed.

"You haven't asked me why I was in jail. Is that the reason you won't take me home with you?"

His hands were making slow circles along her spine. His erection was pressed tightly against her stomach. She ached in places she didn't know could ache. "I haven't asked why because it isn't my business," she said, breathing a sigh of relief when the song ended. "I have to play."

Cole let her slip out of his arms because if he held her any longer, he was going to throw her over his shoulder and take her out of there to any place he could have her to himself for a long, long time. He managed to make it back to his seat without breaking anything. He took a long pull on the beer. It was warm and did nothing to cool the fire racing through his veins.

Cole watched her through half-closed eyes, already staking his claim on her, making certain the other men in the bar knew she belonged to him. No woman had ever gotten to him before. She seemed lost in her music, unaware of him when he was burning for her.

His cell phone beeped, and, scowling, he glanced down to identify the caller. "What is it, Jase?" Cole demanded, his eyes on Maia. If she smiled one more time at the lunkhead in the front row, he was going to have to smash his beer bottle right over the man's head.

For a moment there was silence, then a harsh, tearing sob. "I trusted you. You knew I cared about him. You knew Celtic High mattered to me."

Cole went still. "What are you talking about, Jase? Calm down and tell me what's going on."

"The bay. He's all torn up. What'd you do to him?"

"I didn't do a damned thing to him," Cole bit the words out

in anger before he could stop them. "I'll have the vet there in an hour." It was over an hour's drive to the ranch, but he could shave off minutes. He couldn't blame Jase for accusing him. The kid had been taught not to trust anyone, but it still hurt. Much worse than that, Cole couldn't help his own suspicions. He'd investigated the kid's past, looking for red flags, cruelty to animals, anything that might indicate the old man had passed on his sick genes, but he'd found nothing. Still, the doubt crept in.

"He's in too much pain," Jase said. "He'll have to be put down. I can't do it. I tried, but I can't do it." He was sobbing openly. "He went through a fence and he's really torn up. There's wood sticking in his chest and stomach, splinters buried in his belly and legs. Some of the cuts are down to the bone. I can't put him down, Cole."

"Listen to me, Jase. I'll be there in an hour with the vet. Get Al and the other hands to help you. Take Celtic High to the big barn where all the equipment is. The vet will need light to work on him, and that's the most sterile environment we have. Tell Al to keep that horse alive."

"But, Cole," now Jase sounded like a young child seeking reassurance, "he's suffering."

"I didn't do this, Jase. I wasn't even there."

"I found your work glove in the snow by the fence." Jase sounded apologetic. "I don't know what I was thinking. I knew you went to town."

"I'll be there in an hour," Cole repeated. "Get Al and stick close to him until I figure out what's going on."

Maia watched Cole's face as he talked on the phone. He gave very little away with his expression, but something was wrong. She saw the way his hand tightened around the neck of the beer bottle. He'd been absently stroking it, almost seductively, and now he gripped it as if he wanted to throttle something. Cole abruptly broke the connection and shoved the cell phone into his pocket, stood up and looked directly at her.

At once her heart began to accelerate, pounding in her

chest. His gaze was cold, hard, and very direct. He began to walk toward her with long strides, a ruthless stamp on his features and purpose in every step. For the first time, she faltered in her playing, losing the rhythm that was so much a part of her. The band ground to a halt. There was a sudden silence in the bar.

"Come on. I need you out at the ranch. Let's go." Cole's voice brooked no argument.

Maia studied his harsh expression. He reached out and caught her arm, nearly pulling her off her stool. "I said now."

A murmur of protest went around the room. It didn't deter Cole in the least. He crowded closer to her.

Maia glanced around the bar, a quick appraisal of the situation, then her gaze was back on his face. Implacable resolve. He didn't care that others might come to her rescue. He was perfectly prepared to fight, and worse, he might win.

His fingers tightened around her arm. "You don't want me to carry you out," he warned.

"You don't want me to slap your face either," Maia said, her gaze flicking coolly over his face. "Let's go."

3

"DON'T EVER DO that again," Maia warned. She paused just outside of the bar to take a deep, calming breath of the night air. "I know something upset you, and believe me, that's the only reason I'm out here with you right now. I am not the kind of woman you can order around."

Cole looked down at her, at the smoldering anger he saw in

her eyes. It was snowing large flakes, falling softly and mutely between them. He reached out, his fingers curling around the nape of her neck, and pulled her toward him, his mouth taking possession of hers before she could protest.

She expected his kiss to be as wild and dominating as he was, but it was just the opposite. His mouth was incredibly gentle on hers, soft but firm, a whisper of fire, his lips brushing at hers with a disarming tenderness. He lifted his head, his blue eyes nearly dazzling her.

Cole could feel his heart thudding hard, too hard. There was a curious melting sensation in the region of his stomach, and his body reacted instantly to the close proximity of hers. He knew immediately he had made a big mistake. Maia Armstrong was no ordinary woman, and he was going to get burned if he didn't regain some control, and fast. His fingers massaged the nape of her neck, brushing caresses in her soft hair. He was renowned for his control, yet she seemed to turn him inside out. His careful defenses didn't work with her.

Maia managed to pull away from him. "If this emergency is some sham to get me to your ranch for more of *that* . . ." She glared at him and wiped her mouth with the back of her hand, desperate to remove his taste. His kiss had felt like a brand, making fire race from his lips and tongue to her belly, lower still, so that she'd felt her body go liquid with desire for him. *And he'd barely touched her.*

"*That* was an apology. And stop trying to wipe it off." He caught her wrist, pulling her hand away from her mouth, satisfaction mixing with something else in his eyes, something that could have been alarm. He led her across the parking lot. "I'm used to giving orders and getting things done. We have to get to the ranch immediately and telling you to come seemed like the fastest way to accomplish that."

Maia bit down hard on her lower lip. She should have stopped him, slapped him, done anything besides participate. She touched her mouth. It was still burning. She'd definitely participated. Where was her pride? Her outrage? The man was more dangerous to her than she'd realized. With an effort, Maia found her voice again. "You might want to give me the particulars." She sounded a little husky. "What type of animal, and what's the injury?"

"A horse. Jase's favorite horse Celtic High, although he won't admit it. Unfortunately, there's a blizzard coming, a bad series of storms that could hang you up for days. I can't trailer the horse out during the storm, so I'll need you to come with me now. I can only promise that if it's at all possible, I'll have the roads cleared for you to return."

Maia glanced upward at the rapidly falling snow. "I thought the storm wasn't supposed to hit for several hours."

"It's early. We've got to move fast to stay ahead of it."

"I'll need my rig. I can follow you out," Maia said, switching directions, the professional taking over. "I have the drugs and everything I need in the sterile packs. I have to call the service and let them know and get Dr. Stacy to take over while I'm gone. He's able to work on an emergency basis. If we're lucky, we'll beat the storm."

"I'll drive. We keep the road to the ranch plowed, but it can get rough in spots," Cole said, easily keeping pace with her. "And there's no way to plow during a blizzard. Jase said the bay went through a fence and that it has multiple injuries, gashes down to the bone and splinters of wood embedded in it. He said he thought the horse was suffering and should be put down, but he couldn't do it."

"And you want me to save the horse even if it can't ever be ridden again?" Many ranchers put down a horse that was no longer a working animal.

"Absolutely. Whatever it takes, as long as the horse isn't suffering," Cole said. "We've got a big ranch. He can live out his days there."

Maia nodded. "Okay then. And maybe we'll be lucky, and it won't be as bad as it looks. Horses can sustain heavy injuries, and if you keep them from getting an infection, can come back quite sound." She glanced back toward his truck, white from the fall of snow. "I'm used to driving in the snow. You don't want to leave your truck here."

"I have plenty of vehicles at the ranch, including a helicopter. And no one's going to touch my truck." His gaze met hers squarely.

Maia couldn't prevent the small shiver that went down her spine. Cole was right. Maia knew most of the townspeople feared him. There was always that dangerous edge to him he couldn't hide, and he didn't bother to try. Recognizing there was little use in arguing, she pulled out her cell phone and made the call to her service. The snow fell into her hair and down the neckline of her shirt while she gave the necessary instructions.

As she pushed the small phone back into her pocket, she reached for the driver's door just as Cole did. Maia pulled her hand back to avoid contact. "My rig," she said.

"But I'm driving. I know the road, and the storm is coming in far faster than we thought. It'll be safer with me driving because I know every rut and curve in that road." Cole swept the snow from her hair, sheltering her with his body from the worst of the flurries. "We don't have much time. Give me the keys."

Maia paused, her hand gripping the keys. "Why were you in jail?" She didn't want it to matter, but it did. She wasn't about to become another victim because she was too stupid even to ask.

Cole yanked open the door on the driver's side, swift impatience crossing his face. "Not rape, if that's what you think. I don't abuse women." He slid behind the wheel and slammed the door with unnecessary force.

"Oh, really?" She hurried around the vehicle to slide in beside him, handing him the keys. "All those poor women you take to bed must feel pretty abused when you never call them again." The moment she closed the door she felt trapped. He was potent up close, intensely male. His shoulders were wide, and his chest thick and well muscled. She could smell the faint scent of his aftershave. And his kiss lingered on her lips.

His gaze dwelt on her face for a long moment as he turned

the engine on. Immediately "White Christmas" blared out of the speakers, filling the Toyota Land Cruiser with music. Cole winced and turned it off.

"We need to get one thing straight right now, Maia," he said. "When I take a woman to bed, she *never* feels abused. And I detest Christmas music."

"That's two things," she pointed out, furious at herself because she was tantalized by the very thought of going to bed with him. He was far too arrogant and sure of himself for her liking. *And he was a bad boy. Trouble. The kind of man a smart woman stayed away from.* "And I love Christmas music."

"You would."

"What does that mean?" He'd dragged her off before she could grab her jacket, and the temperature had dipped sharply, leaving her cold and shivering. Maia switched the heater to full power and rubbed her arms for warmth.

"It means you're one of those sappy women who get all gooey around little kids and animals and you love the holidays. You probably give the garbageman a present." With something close to impatience, Cole tossed her his jacket. "Put it on until it gets warm in here. And you do, don't you?"

"There's absolutely nothing wrong with giving the garbageman a present. He works hard." She took the jacket only because she was freezing. "Why?" she asked.

"Why what?" He kept his eyes on the road, picking up speed and heading out of town, pushing the speed limit as well as the margin of safety.

"Why do you detest Christmas music?" Maia watched him closely. His expression didn't change, but the tension in the Land Cruiser went up a notch.

"Doesn't everyone detest Christmas music?" he countered.

"No, most people love it. It's a happy time of year."

"Is it?" His voice was grim. "Maybe to you. To me, it's a damned nightmare."

"I take it you don't buy gifts for your lady friends," she teased.

He glanced at her then, his gaze ice-cold as it moved deliberately over her body. "I might be willing to come up with a gift or two for you if that's what it takes."

Maia locked her fingers together to keep from smacking him and turned her face away to stare out the window at the white world around her. If not for the injured horse and the thought of the boy waiting for them, she would have told Cole Steele to go to hell, pushed him out of her truck and driven back to town.

Cole felt the silence cut between them like a knife. He preferred quiet. He was never uncomfortable with it. Yet with Maia, he found himself wanting to reach out to her, to bridge the gap he was creating between them. He was fighting for the life he was familiar with, the one he knew and could survive in. He didn't trust things like laughter and warmth, had never thought about having them for himself until he'd pulled her into his arms and held her against his body. His body had demanded hers, and that should have been enough. No-entanglements sex was all he ever wanted, yet he didn't think it would be enough with Maia. She touched him in ways that were unexpected, intriguing, and frightening all at the same time.

He turned off the main highway onto the private road that led to the ranch. The snow was heavier than he'd counted on, but he knew every twist and turn. The snowplow had cleared the road before he left for town, but already, the surface was covered with a thick white blanket. He peered out at the snowflakes bursting at the windshield. Maia suddenly tensed and pulled back, making herself smaller in the seat, throwing up a hand to shield her face. A huge owl nearly slammed into the window, wings outstretched and flapping, head back, talons extended as if going in for the kill. It had come at them swiftly and silently, an apparition swooping out of the blinding snow.

The wicked talons reached straight toward Cole's eyes with only the glass separating them. Beside him, Maia gasped. He swerved, nearly losing traction, a string of curses erupting from him until he felt the tires grip and hold. The owl just cleared the top of the vehicle, and Cole breathed a sigh of relief. The bird had been so close he had been able to see individual feathers on its body.

Maia huddled inside Cole's jacket, closing her eyes, trying to calm her pounding heart. The owl had shrieked a warning to her, risked its life to caution her to go back. She glanced at Cole's face, the lines etched deeply there. The owl had flooded her mind with quick, flashing images of violence. It happened so fast, Maia hadn't gotten a clear glimpse of the animal's projection. Only the ominous warning. She took a deep breath and let it out slowly, trying to sort out what the bird was striving to communicate. Darkness. Horses moving. Men. Flashes of lights that could have been rifle fire. None of it made sense.

"That's never happened to me before," Cole said. "Maybe it was confused by the storm. Owls see and hear so well, I imagine accidents would rarely happen."

"He was in hunting mode."

Her voice was so low, Cole barely heard her. He flicked a quick glance her way. She looked pale, her eyes clouded with fear.

"I'm a good driver, Maia. I'll get us there."

She didn't answer. Cole sighed. She was doing him a favor, coming out to the ranch in the middle of what was rapidly becoming a mean blizzard. He should have been more polite. She'd probably worked all day, and she had a long, cold night ahead of her, trying to save the horse for Jase.

"I shouldn't have said that about buying you." Cole glanced at her. It was always so easy with women. He looked at them, they fell into his arms. They had sex, they went home, and he didn't think about them again. That was how it was supposed to work, but Maia seemed to blow his carefully constructed barricades all to hell.

For a moment he thought she wouldn't respond. She didn't turn her head to look at him, but stared out the window at the flurry of snowflakes. "Why did you?"

"You get under my skin, and I don't like it," he answered truthfully. "I've never met a woman like you."

"You've met a million women like me. It's just that none of them ever stood up to you before." Her voice was low and half-muffled by his thick jacket, but it found its way into his body, past his skin and muscle to his very bones.

She turned back toward him, and his breath left his lungs in a rush. He wasn't used to anyone having that kind of effect on him, and it shook his usual calm. He kept his expression carefully blank, his warning system shrieking at him that he was in trouble. "You're an interesting woman. Anyone else would have jumped on the fact that I admitted you get to me, but not you. You have to be different."

"It wouldn't serve any purpose to discuss it. I'm not going to sleep with you. I don't do one-night stands. I'm not at all into casual sex." She managed a small smile. "But I'll admit you're a terrible temptation."

He glanced at her, felt the wheels slide in a particularly heavy drift of snow, catch, and propel them forward. She flung out her hand to grab the dashboard, but she didn't tell him to slow down.

"I always get what I want, Maia." He said it with complete confidence. He didn't know if it was her cool refusal, the warmth in her small smile, or the stark intensity of his desire for her, but he was determined she wouldn't elude him. Even when he knew he was risking more than he should.

"Well, want something else. I don't have a lot of energy to put into fighting with you. You're the kind of man who normally sets my teeth on edge."

"And that would be why?"

"You're arrogant, bossy, too rich for your own good. Sexy as hell, but you know it, so you don't even bother to be polite. There are a lot of willing women out there, Steele, go after one of them. I told you, straight up, I'm not a one-night-stand kind of woman. That should be enough for you."

"It should be, shouldn't it?" His gaze slid sideways toward

her for a brief moment. Her hands were twisted together to keep them from trembling. The vehicle slid several times, but he kept it on the road. "I'm a good driver, Maia," he reiterated. "Relax. I won't let anything happen to you."

She tensed again, pushing back into the seat and bracing one hand on the dashboard. He tapped the brakes, slowing the Land Cruiser just as several deer leapt in front of them. The snow nearly coated them, giving them a ghostly appearance, eyes shining, tails flicking in alarm. Cole swerved again, barely missing the high embankment. The deer were gone as silently as they appeared. Maia's breath was audible in the close confines of the car.

"I don't know what the hell is going on tonight. Usually the deer are bedded down and under cover during a storm."

Maia huddled inside the jacket. The images were more vivid this time, but still jumbled. Fists pounding into flesh. Blood on the grass. On the rocks. Her mouth was too dry to speak. She could feel a bead of sweat trickling down the valley between her breasts, but she shivered with cold . . . with fear.

Cole slowed the Land Cruiser, anxiety creeping into him. "Maia, are you all right?" He couldn't really take his eyes from the road, just small glances at her, but she was definitely frightened. "I know it looks bad out here, but I know the road. This is a good rig. The drifts are so high on the embankments, we can't possibly get lost, even with the road covered. You must be used to animals rushing out in front of the truck with all the driving you do." What he wanted to do was stop the truck and pull her into his arms.

Maia felt suffocated by the snowy white world enclosing them. "Maybe we should turn around." The panic in her voice made her wince.

"We're closer to the ranch than to town. I can't leave Jase out there alone, not with a wounded horse. I hope he listened to me and got Al to help him. By now, the ranch hands will have gone home to avoid getting caught in this blizzard." He reached out to comfort her, but she shrank away from him, and he gripped the steering wheel, angry at himself for the gesture. "Is that what you really want? To turn around?"

Maia made an effort to pull herself together. What could she say in her defense? That animals were warning her away from the ranch? He'd have her thrown in a padded cell. "No, of course not. I take it that this horse is very special to Jase."

"He won't admit it, but yes," Cole answered. "If it's at all possible, save the horse for him. The cost doesn't matter. And if you could make Jase a part of it in some way, maybe have him assist you in treating the bay and caring for it afterward, that would be great."

There was something elusive there. Maia heard it, but couldn't grasp it. "Have you always been close to Jase?"

"We met when I was given guardianship over him. We had different mothers, and I didn't know he existed until I was contacted by the private investigators the lawyers hired to find me."

"How could you not know you had a brother?"

Cole shrugged. "I checked out of that life a long time ago. When the lawyers told me about Jase, I was shocked." He frowned. "The snow's really coming down. I left Jase out there with Al, my foreman, to watch over him."

"Weren't you afraid you'd get caught in town?"

"I knew the storm was coming, but I thought I had a couple of more hours before it really hit. I'd never allow Jase to spend the night alone there, so one way or another, I would have gotten back to the ranch."

Maia heard the note of honesty, of absolute determination in his voice, and she believed him. Cole was such a deceptive mixture. He'd come to the bar hunting for sex. He made no apologies for it and cared little what others thought of him. He exuded complete confidence, even a coldness, yet there were terrible shadows in his eyes. And there was Jase. He barely knew the teenager, yet he looked out for him with a fierce protectiveness she would never have credited him with having. She believed Cole would have tried to walk back to the ranch rather than leave the boy alone with just the foreman. Things didn't add up.

"Do you have children of your own?" she asked.

"What do you think?"

"I think you'd never let anyone get that close to you. You must have been terrified when you were named guardian to this boy. Why did you say you'd do it?"

"What is it they all say? So I can murder him and get all the money instead of sharing it with a kid."

"You don't even change expression when you hand out your nonsense. Don't worry, Steele, I don't want to know your deep dark secrets."

"You think I have secrets? I thought my life was an open book. Haven't the gossips given you the scoop on me?" The snow was nearly blinding him as he maneuvered on the road. At the rate it was coming down, he wasn't certain they would make it to the ranch before the road became impassable. Even if he could call Al to bring out the snowplow, he wasn't all that certain it would do any good. They were no longer in front of the storm but in the thick of it.

"Don't you have secrets? Doesn't everyone?" Maia wanted to keep talking. She would have chosen to sit it out rather than continue driving. It was becoming difficult to see more than a foot in front of the truck.

"Even you, Doc? Do you have secrets as well? You're always laughing and seem so carefree, yet you move from place to place, no home, nothing permanent in your life. No boyfriend who'll get upset when you move on."

"Who said I don't have a boyfriend? And I usually fill in for the same vets, so I make a lot of friends along the way."

"You don't have a boyfriend, or you wouldn't have let me get away with putting my hands on you while we were dancing. You aren't that kind of woman."

Shocked, she turned toward him, but he was staring out the window into the driving snow. "A compliment. Who would have thought?" Maia burrowed deeper into his jacket. The inside of the car was warm enough, but his jacket gave her a sense of security. She could smell his scent, masculine and outdoorsy, the spice of his aftershave. He drove with the same confidence he did everything, and it helped ease her anxiety a bit, but they seemed to be enfolded in a white, silent world. She wished he'd play music just to keep her nerves from jangling. She had nothing else to hang on to but their conversation. And he wasn't comfortable with making small talk.

"Why don't you have your own practice?" Cole asked, flicking a quick glance her way.

Maia stiffened. Her eyes held a wariness that hadn't been there before.

"Maia, it was an idle question to keep the conversation going. You don't have to answer. I detest people prying into my private life."

He heard her swift, indrawn breath, and saw her turn toward the passenger-side window. Cole was ready instantly for trouble, peering through the windshield to try to see what might be coming at him beyond the heavy shroud of snow. He spotted dark shapes running alongside them, slipping in and out of his field of vision. "What the hell is that?"

"Wolves."

He didn't dare take his eyes off the road to look at her. Cole concentrated on driving, alert for the moment the wolves would run out in front of the Land Cruiser. He didn't doubt it was wolves. Jase and he owned several thousand acres, and their ranch backed up to the national forest where wolves had been relocated.

"The wolves have always stayed away from my ranch and well back into the forest. What's bringing them out?" He glanced at her. Somehow she knew. "You've known the animals were there each time before we saw them, before they jumped out in front of us."

"How could I?"

He didn't listen to the words so much as her voice. It was strained and trembling. She was lying to him. She knew, but he couldn't figure out how. "I don't know, but you reacted, bracing yourself."

"I must have seen them."

A mournful howl rose, sending a shiver down Maia's spine. A second, then a third wolf joined in. A chorus followed them, long, drawn-out notes of warning. She bit down on her knuckles to keep her teeth from chattering.

"What are they doing?" Cole asked. "Why are they running alongside the truck in hunting mode? And the owl, it was coming in as if hunting, head back, talons extended, coming right at me." Even to him, it sounded completely ridiculous. Had he not been trapped in the middle of a snowstorm, he wouldn't have ever said such a bizarre thing, yet it felt right, not strange.

"I have a certain affinity with animals," Maia admitted. She sent up a silent prayer that he wouldn't ask what it meant. She didn't know what it meant. "Stop! Don't hit it." She flung out her hand to brace herself on the dashboard as he fought the Land Cruiser to a halt without even seeing what was in the road.

Before he could stop her, Maia was out of the vehicle, dragging a bag with her, disappearing into the swirling white flakes. Cole slammed his fist against the steering wheel, pulled a gun from where it was holstered in concealment on his calf, and checked the load before he shoved open his own door.

The snow swirled around him immediately, engulfing him in a white, silent world, and as fast shifted with the wind to allow him glimpses of the animals and Maia. He heard the chuffing of the wolves as they surrounded the vehicle. Maia crooned to something in the distance. He began to move toward her, watching the wild creatures warily. Immediately the chuffing turned to warning growls. He froze, trying to peer through the heavy fall of snow. The wind blasted through the canyon, and he saw her crouched over something on the ground.

"Maia? I didn't hit it, did I?"

"No, it was injured earlier. I'll just be a minute. Get back in the Cruiser. The wolves are getting agitated."

"I'll stay here and watch your back."

She hissed her displeasure. Actually hissed. He heard it. "I can't protect you while I'm working. Get in the car and wait for me." It was a definite order.

The wind blew a blanket of snow between them again, and when it lifted, he could see the darker shapes slinking around them. He stayed where he was, afraid of disturbing the precarious balance Maia seemed to have. The next blast of chilling wind revealed her straightening and backing away from the shape on the ground, clutching her bag in her hand. She walked quickly toward the Cruiser as the wolf jumped to its feet, shook itself, and hurried off.

The moment he slid in beside her, her gaze went to the gun in his hand. "Good grief. I thought you couldn't carry a gun once you'd been in jail."

"Ranchers need guns." He shoved it back into his leg holster and glared at her. "The next time you decide to take a stroll with a bunch of wolves in a blizzard, let me know ahead of time." He wanted to shake her although she was already shivering uncontrollably and covered in white and that instantly made him feel protective of her.

"I'll do that." She didn't sound as tough as she would have liked with her teeth chattering. "Is that heater putting out any heat?"

"Yes, you should warm up again in a minute." He was cautious as he began maneuvering along the road, alert for any more animals. "Are you going to explain what just happened?"

Maia pushed the alarming warnings out of her mind and shook her head. "I don't think there is an explanation. Do you want to tell me how you get away with carrying a gun?"

"I hide it."

"I'm not buying that. You wouldn't risk losing Jase over it. You're not even on parole are you? Is all the gossip untrue? Have you ever been in prison?"

He sighed. "Maia, I have a job. I'm good at what I do, and I'm good because I don't answer questions. Most people I just tell to go to hell, or look at them and they shut up. Why don't you believe what everyone else wants to believe and make it easy on me?"

She leaned back against the seat, for the first time relaxing. "Because it's all made up, and I prefer to hear the real story. What kind of job do you have?"

Exasperated, he glared at her. "It isn't going to happen."

She thought it was progress that he didn't tell her to go to hell.

4

"I'M GOING TO pull your rig into the barn. You'll need all your equipment, right?" Cole asked.

Maia nodded as she climbed into the backseat. "Keep looking straight ahead while I change into my scrubs. I don't have a lot of clothes with me and I don't want to get everything filthy."

"I do have a washing machine."

"Since I only have what I'm wearing and my scrubs, I'm not taking any chances," she said.

He glanced at her in the rearview mirror. She was shocked to see humor creeping into his eyes. It wasn't much, and it faded fast, but it was there. "I managed to keep this thing on the road through animals running out in front of me and a blizzard, but now you're asking just a little too much. I'm not exactly a saint."

Maia wiggled out of her jeans and dragged her familiar soft cotton, drawstring pants over her hips. "You will get us into an accident if you don't watch what you're doing." She tossed her shirt aside and pulled her loose top over her head, showing the minimum amount of skin. "And I'll bet no one has ever accused you of being a saint." She whistled as Cole honked the horn in front of a large building. "Nice setup."

The doors swung open to allow him to drive inside. The barn was huge and very clean, obviously used as a hospital for the animals on the ranch when needed.

Jase Steele waited anxiously as they parked the Cruiser in the huge barn. Maia saw his face, puffy and swollen from shedding tears he thought no one would see. The boy was unable to hide his relief as Cole unfolded his large frame from the Land Cruiser. "It's bad, Cole," he greeted.

"Let the vet take a look, Jase," Cole advised. For one moment he thought about hugging the kid, but he couldn't quite find a way to do it. Instead, he handed the teenager one of the packs. "We'll need your help."

"I would have put the horse down, Mr. Steele," Al Benton said, "but the boy refused to let me."

"Were you able to tell how this happened?" Cole asked, choosing his words carefully.

Al scowled. "Someone had to have run him into the fence, Mr. Steele. His rump had a couple of welts on it."

"Who was around?"

"All the hands were already gone when Jase called me."

Cole let his breath out slowly. Al hadn't been with Jase. That didn't sit well with him. Doubt tickled at his brain, even though he didn't want to think the boy could have done such a thing. It made him feel like a monster even to entertain such a notion. He ticked suspects off in his mind. Al, the ranch hands, Jase. The ranch hands were working away from the main house and shouldn't have been there. He shook his head to rid himself of the persistent doubt about his younger brother. If he was lucky, it was a legitimate accident. Maia was already walking briskly toward the horse, and he trailed after her, grateful for the distraction.

"The wounds are down to the bone, Mr. Steele. The horse isn't going to be any good for work," Al said.

Maia flashed a brief smile in the foreman's general direction.

"Let's not draw any hasty conclusions. I haven't had a chance to assess the damage yet." She glanced at Jase. "You did great getting him in out of the snow and putting him in the stocks so he can't move."

"Al helped me," Jase said. "He's been quiet." He patted the horse's neck, his hand trembling. "He didn't give us any trouble at all."

"What's his name?"

"His official name is Celtic High, but I call him Wally." His gaze shifted toward Cole, then away.

"Let me see what I can do for him." Maia put her hand on the horse's neck as she moved around to look into its eyes. Her stomach somersaulted. Images crowded in fast and ugly. Brutal, mean memories of an animal watching helplessly as a boy was beaten and taunted and cruelly punished for nonexistent crimes. The images were harsh and jumbled together. The animal's sorrow and pain, both physical and emotional, beat at her.

She saw through the horse's eyes, memories of young Jase hiding repeatedly in his stall, only to be dragged out again and again while the animal could do nothing to help him. She felt the familiar lurching in her stomach, the sweat beading on her body and the strange dizziness that always accompanied revelations the animals passed to her. It was her greatest gift, and a terrible curse. She could do nothing to help the children and animals she saw coming through her practice. She could only remain silent, just as the animal was forced to do, and move on, move away.

"Maia?" Cole's hand went to her back to steady her. "Put your head down."

She kept her hands firmly against the horse, forcing herself to see what the animal was willing to share. Something stinging his rump. The shadow of a big man in the snow, raising his arm and slamming it down with purpose. Repeated lashings across the hind legs and rump until the horse ran without thought into the fence in a desperate effort to escape the terrible blows. Too big to be Al or Jase. Wide enough shoulders to be Cole, but the horse displayed no nervousness near him.

"Maia." Cole gripped her hard. "You're as white as a sheet." She was sweating too, and her gaze was filled with a kind of horror. It had nothing to do with the gaping wounds or the blood. He knew it was something else, something entirely different.

Maia shook her head, letting go of the horse's neck and stepping back. "I'm all right." She couldn't look at him. Couldn't look at Jase. Who had done such things to the boy? Who had kicked him? Broken bones? Killed pets in front of him? *He's fourteen, and he hated the old man.* She remembered the icy cold of Cole's voice when he'd made the statement. But Brett Steele was dead. Who had cruelly tormented the horse until it had rushed headlong into a strong fence, nearly killing itself?

Maia forced herself to appear normal. "I'm not the best traveler." She used her stethoscope to check the horse's heart, lungs, and bowel sounds, which gave her some time to compose herself before she faced the Steele brothers.

"If you don't need me, Mr. Steele," Al said, "I'll be heading back to the house before it gets so bad I can't make it. My wife's called a hundred times already, worried."

"Yes, by all means, Al." Cole's gaze was on Maia's pale face. He didn't take his hand from her back. He could feel the small tremors running through her body. "Be careful. This storm looks bad. I take it all the animals are bedded down in sheltered areas?" His tone implied they'd better be.

"Yes, sir. It was all taken care of before I let the hands go home." Al turned back. "I know this isn't the best time, but Fred, my wife's brother, came by again looking to get his job back. He's a good hand, Mr. Steele. He's got a couple of kids. It's not like there's a lot of work this time of year."

Jase whipped his head around, his face still and white. The horse suddenly moved, reacting to the boy's sudden tension. The movement flooded the animal with pain, but the bay rubbed its head against Jase in an attempt to comfort him. The gesture immediately brought the teenager's attention back to the animal.

Cole's fingers, on Maia's back, pressed deeper into her skin. There was heat there, a touch of anger. "I told you no, Al. No one who worked for Brett Steele will ever work for me or for Jase. I know he visits you, but I don't even like the man to set foot on this property. I've looked the other way because I know family's important to you and your wife, but I don't want to see him and I don't want him to go anywhere on the ranch other than to your home. Is that understood?" His voice was ice-cold and carried a whip.

"Yes, sir."

"And I don't want you to bring this matter up again." It was a distinct threat. Even Maia recognized it as such. She glanced at Jase, who was stroking the bay's neck. She touched Cole's wrist. Gently. Reminding him he wasn't alone. Lines etched his face, and he looked quite capable of anything. Even murder. If she could see the buried rage rising up to swirl so close to the surface, so could Jase.

Cole let his breath out slowly, trying to relieve the anger boiling up in him. Al kept hammering away at getting his brother-in-law a job, but one look at Jase's pale face told him the man had been present during one or more beatings. He felt like smashing something, preferably Al's face, for bringing up the subject yet again and putting that look back on the boy's face.

"Yes, Mr. Steele," Al said and turned and walked away.

Cole looked at Maia. "You ready to do this?" What he wanted to do was thank her, but the words stuck in his throat. Jase looked as if he couldn't take much more.

"Al wanted to put him down," Jase said. "He kept telling me it was best. I knew the horse was suffering, Cole, but I couldn't let him go."

"I told you to hang on," Cole said. "Let's see what the Doc has to say."

Maia took the horse's head in her hands a second time and looked into his eyes, acknowledging pain and memories, giving brief reassurance. She didn't care if the Steele brothers thought she was a nutcase, the horse deserved some comfort before she went to work. When she was certain the animal understood what she was going to do, she began her inspection, her face carefully blank as she evaluated the damage. "Left hock has a three-inch laceration with bone exposed. Right hock, most wounds are superficial abrasions. We have a left front dorsal forearm laceration through the muscle down to the bone, approximately five inches long. We have major splintering from the fence around the laceration, one piece fairly large." It looked like a stake to her, but she was very matter-of-fact, aware of Jase watching her every expression. She put her hand on his shoulder. "We can deal with this if you're willing to help out. First I need to give him painkillers and start him on antibiotics, then we'll get to work."

Jase watched her preparing syringes, his eyes wide. "What are you giving him?"

"Four different types of painkillers. All of them do something a little different. We don't want him to feel anything while I work on him, but he has to stand, so we can't exactly knock him out. He'll be sedated though, Jase." Maia gave the shots deftly, using her fist to strike and numb the muscle before jamming the needle in. "The last two shots are for tetanus and a good dose of penicillin."

Jase crooned to the horse as she administered the rest of the shots. "He's been so good. He hardly moves, and it must hurt so bad."

"The shots will numb everything for him," Maia assured. "Our next step is to get the wound sites as sterile as possible. That's imperative. We're going to flush the site, and remove the debris and splinters, including the large one. Horses can lose a lot of blood, Jase, and still be fine." She worked quickly as she explained, mixing a liter of saline with Betadine. Without giving Jase any time to think about it, Maia grasped the small stake with both hands and pulled the large piece of wood from the horse's chest.

"The barn's well lit, great in fact," Maia said, to keep the boy focused on her and not on the blood. She filled a syringe with the mixture of saline and Betadine. "I need you to begin flushing, Jase. You have to squirt this all over the wound sites. We'll flush all three sites, and I'll clean them, then suture them. This one here"—she indicated the hole where the stake had been—"we might leave open to drain."

Jase took the syringe from her and aimed it at the gaping wound on the horse's foreleg and chest. The flood of saline and Betadine removed dirt, debris, and even splinters. "Is this right?"

Maia noted his hand was much steadier. "That's exactly what I need. We want the area really, really clean." She soaked gauze in Betadine and washed the area thoroughly, making certain to rid the wounds of all foreign objects. "What I'm doing is clipping the skin so we can suture the clean edges. I've flushed it again with Betadine and deadened the area with lidocaine, so really, Jase, he isn't feeling any of this."

Cole watched her hands, fingers deft and sure, as she used stents to keep the skin loose as she sutured the wound. She worked with obvious skill. It took a long time to close the five-inch gash to her satisfaction.

"This is a drain. I don't want to close off that hole in him. It's too big and we want to encourage it to drain. We'll have to really watch that area for infection." Maia spoke patiently to Jase. Her voice was very calm and her hands steady. "I'm also putting a second drain in the gash as well. The stents will keep the skin loose, and I think it will heal nicely, but I'll want you to check this area several times a day for any signs of infection."

Jase nodded, looking very solemn. "I'll do it, Doctor."

"I'm Maia Armstrong, Jase."

He nodded again, ducking his head a little to avoid her gaze. "I can sleep out here with him and sort of keep watch."

"It's too cold," Cole said abruptly.

Maia glanced at Cole from under long lashes. He felt her reprimand all the way to his toes. The woman knew how to give a look. She turned her high-wattage smile on Jase.

"That won't be necessary, Jase, although it's so good of you to offer. He'll be fine out here, and I want him to stay quiet."

Every now and then she spoke softly to the horse and to Jase, instructing him to flush the wound on the hock a second time before she worked on it. When he was finished she used gauze soaked in Betadine to clean it again, removing the last of the dirt and splinters.

"Is he going to be all right?" Jase asked.

"We'll see. We have a long way to go." She crouched beside the horse, working close, without fear or hesitation, as she closed the second gash. She didn't seem to be aware of time passing or the temperature in the barn dropping.

"I'm going to put antibiotic paste on him, Jase. You can't let this stuff touch your skin, so we use tongue depressors to smear it on. Primitive, but it works." She straightened, stretching a little as if her muscles were cramped from crouching so long beside the horse. "We'll have to take his temperature every day, and he'll need antibiotics injected into the muscle twice daily. Have you given shots before?"

Jase nodded. "A couple of times. Cole's been teaching me. Before, I didn't really go near the animals."

She smeared the paste on liberally. "Don't worry, soon you'll be an expert in giving horses shots. You're a natural."

"Do you really think so? I thought about working with animals a long time ago. I like being around them." Jase glanced at Cole, clearly nervous by the admission.

Maia ignored the significant rise in tension and continued applying the antibiotic paste. "I think you're good with animals. You have to read them, their body language, the look in their eyes. I think you have a real affinity for that."

"What do I have an affinity for?" Cole asked.

Maia laughed, the sound unexpected in the large barn. White vapor drifted around them from the simple act of breathing. She sent a mischievous smirk in Jase's direction, winking at him. "Trouble, Mr. Steele. I think you're a magnet."

Jase made a strangled sound, trying to suppress his laughter. Cole turned away from them. It was the first real laugh he'd heard from the boy, and the sound flooded him with warmth.

Maia had a way of bringing Jase out of his shell, and Cole was grateful to her, even though he wished he'd been the one to make Jase laugh.

"You got that right, Doc," Jase agreed.

Maia crouched once again beside the horse. "What I'm doing now is putting pressure wraps on three of his legs to help prevent swelling. I considered putting a stack wrap on his left front, but we'll see how he does. I think he'd just rub it off. I want to keep a careful record, Jase. I'll put this chart out here, so if you happen to take his temp or administer his penicillin when I'm gone, we'll have a record of everything."

"I'll do it," Jase promised.

"I think we're just about finished. We'll let him rest." Maia stretched, yawning as she did so. "I hope you have some extra clothes you're willing to share, Jase. I didn't bring much with me, and I have a feeling you may be stuck with me a while. I'll need to wash my scrubs, and I'd really love something to sleep in."

"Sure, Doc," Jase said, eager to find a way to repay her. "I'll find you something. And you won't have to worry about getting lost in the snow between the house and barn. All the walkways are covered and enclosed."

She smiled at him. "That's handy. I really think he'll be fine. If we weren't in the middle of a full-blown blizzard, I'd trailer him into the clinic, but I have all my equipment with me. I think we're prepared to handle anything that comes along."

"Will I be able to ride him eventually?"

"Let's make it past the infection stage and see how everything heals," Maia hedged. "He had some nasty injuries." She patted the horse's side. "He wants to get better, and that's more than half the battle right there."

"Did he tell you that, Doc?" Cole asked, his eyebrow raised.

"Well, of course. And he's rather fond of Jase as well. I'm surprised a man as sensitive as you didn't catch all that." She grinned at him and blew on her hands to warm her aching fingers.

His heart lurched uncomfortably. He couldn't help tucking

stray strands of hair behind her ear. She looked tired. "Jase, you need to shower and hit the sack. I don't want you staying up all night." Cole took her hands and began to rub them between his own.

Jase glanced at his watch. "I haven't eaten, Cole. I need food. Sustenance. Something like pizza."

The moment he said the word, both brothers reacted, expressions shutting down, wariness creeping into their eyes. They had already compared experiences of their father's reaction when as a boy Cole had stayed after school to have pizza with his friends. Jase had done the same thing. Brett Steele believed in absolute control and his punishments had been vicious.

"I know how to make pizza," Maia said into the silence. "If you have the ingredients, I can make it." Deliberately she pulled her hands away from Cole and clapped Jase on the shoulder. "You do have flannel pajamas, don't you?"

"You're bribing him," Cole pointed out, taking direction from her. Maia seemed to know naturally what to say and do with the boy, where he was still floundering, feeling his way, knowing he was out of his depth. "Jase, don't give up your flannels. I think she's hungry enough to make pizza for us anyway."

"Well, I am, but I had planned on making *you* cook," Maia said.

Jase snorted. "Don't even go there, Doc. Cole's cooking is downright ugly."

"Hey, traitor." Cole managed to ruffle the boy's hair. His affectionate gesture startled both of them. He dropped his hand quickly and Jase suppressed a small grin. "A beautiful woman comes along, and you side with her."

"I show good sense, you mean," Jase bantered back. "She can cook."

Maia's smile widened. "I'm an awesome cook. And I love flannel, so I can be bribed."

"I have a flannel shirt," Cole said. "If we have to pay for our four-in-the-morning supper, I'll contribute to the cause." He took Maia's arm. "You're falling down you're so tired. And if you continue to shiver from the cold any longer, you're going to rattle your teeth loose. Let's get up to the house."

Jase patted the horse good night and hurried after them. "Thanks, Doc. I know it wasn't easy doing all that work."

"I like being a veterinarian. I really think you should give it some thought, Jase. School's hard, and you have to be at the top of your class to get in, but I'll bet you have the brains for it."

"He's a great student," Cole acknowledged immediately.

"I had tutors most of the time," Jase admitted. "My father didn't want me to go away to school."

She'd bet he didn't. The wrong person might see his bruises. And a man like Brett Steele wouldn't want to lose control of his prized possessions. His own sons. She stole a quick glance at Cole's darkly etched features. He'd managed to escape his father's world, but now he was trapped all over again. What had that done to him? He was removed from everyone, keeping a distance from the rest of the world, yet trying desperately to keep the same thing from happening to Jase.

She sensed that Cole had to let Jase inside of him. Into his heart. His mind. He had to allow himself to love Jase, to care about him. Obviously he felt affection and a need to protect the boy. And that made him vulnerable. Brett Steele had effectively tied Cole to him, to this place so haunted with his chilling ghost. The elder Steele was certain that his money and his influence would enable him to reach his sons from beyond the grave. Cole was trying to find a way to fight back, to give Jase a life. He just didn't seem to understand that he and his brother would have to save themselves together, that it was a package deal.

"Do you go to a regular school now?" Maia shivered as Cole flicked a switch and the barn went dark. He waved her through the open door to the covered walkway. The floor was constructed to drain the water away from the center as the heating coils embedded in the concrete path melted the snow. Drifts of snow were piled high on either side, cutting the wind.

"Cole wants me to go to a private school, but I don't mix

too well with other kids." Again Jase glanced nervously at his brother as if he feared he was revealing too much and would be reprimanded.

"You might like it if you try it," Cole said with no inflection. "You wouldn't have any trouble academically. You're really smart, Jase, and you know it."

"That doesn't make me socially acceptable," Jase muttered.

"Is anyone ever socially acceptable?" Maia asked.

Cole made a snorting sound of derision. "I'll bet you were the most popular girl in school. Prom queen. Cheerleader."

Maia winked at Jase. "What do you think?"

"I think you should have been if you weren't," Jase said honestly.

"You don't have to find me flannel pajamas, and I'll still make you a pizza," Maia declared. "That was a nice thing to say."

"I said it first." Cole crowded closer to her, keeping his body between her and the elements as best he could. She was wearing only the thin scrubs and couldn't control her continuous shivering. "You're making me crazy, Doc." He put his arm around her and pulled her closer to the heat of his body.

"I'm a mess," she said, drawing away. "I'll need that washing machine."

He pulled her back to him, slipping his arm around her waist so that she fit even closer. "I don't think you know how cold you are, Doc. You're turning blue. You look good blue, but it clashes with your spunky attitude."

"I'm not spunky." This time she stayed near the intense heat pouring off his body. Warming her. It felt good, and she was chilled to the bone. He smelled masculine. She'd never smelled a man before, but inhaled deeply, taking him into her lungs and trying not to rub her head against his chest like a cat. It wasn't just the way he felt and smelled, it was the way he made her feel. "No one says 'spunky' anymore."

She'd never been so physically close to a man before. She moved around too much to form really close relationships with people. She'd certainly never experienced such tremendous

physical attraction before. Cole Steele made her feel ultrafemi-
nine, completely aware of herself as a woman—and him as a
man. "The word 'spunky' is definitely out," she affirmed.

As the walked, her body moved against his in a perfect
rhythm reminiscent of dancing. She could feel her color rising,
or maybe it was her blood pressure, as she remembered the feel
of his body pressed so tightly against hers when they'd danced
together. The last thing she needed was to be trapped for any
length of time on his ranch with him. She had no idea if her
self-control was that strong.

Cole raised an eyebrow at his younger brother. Jase grinned
at him, genuine amusement on his face. "I'd have to agree with
Cole on this one, Doc. You are one spunky woman."

Feeling deeply unsettled by her attraction for the larger-than-
life man walking so close to her, Maia was grateful when Cole
opened a side door to the main house, and they were in the snow
room. Jackets were hung on the walls, and boots lined the floor.
Both men removed their shoes, and Maia did the same. It was
cool in the room, but far warmer than outside.

The inside of the house was so warm she felt the blast of
heat on her cold skin. The entryway was tiled, but warm on
their feet. She looked up at the archways and high ceilings, her
breath catching. "Good grief. You live here? This is a modern-
day miracle."

Cole and Jase exchanged a long look. Jase cleared his throat.
"I'll find you some warm clothes." He hurried off while Cole
pulled a blanket from the back of one of the deep, oversized
couches and wrapped it around her. "How about I make you
something hot to drink, and I'll cook tonight." He glanced out
the series of glass windows making up the front of the house.
The snow was steady with no letup. "I think you're going to be
here a few days, and you'll get the chance to make Jase your famous pizza another time. Right now you need to warm up."

Maia couldn't argue with him. She was shivering uncontrollably. "I'd love a hot shower." Just the idea sounded like ecstasy.

The thought of Maia naked in the shower was enough to

give Cole heart failure. "Sure." His voice was husky and she
gave him a sharp glance. He put his hand over his heart.
"You're killing me."

"Good. It's about time someone did. All those women come
way too easy for you. It isn't good for you, you know."

"What? Women? You make me sound like a gigolo. There
haven't been all that many." Why was he defending himself? It
was her smile, the way it lit her eyes, the way her soft mouth
curved. Inwardly he groaned. His mouth tightened. His jaw
hardened. Why did he have to be so intrigued by everything
she said and did?

Maia pinned him with her gaze, a small smirk escaping over
his reaction. "There were that many women. Point me toward
the shower and the bathroom had better have a really good
lock on the door. I did mention I'm proficient in several forms
of martial arts, didn't I?"

"I knew we were compatible. So am I."

She heaved an exaggerated sigh. "Of course you are. What
was I thinking?"

5

MAIA THREW OFF the goose-down quilt and sat up. It was
impossible to go to sleep. She was so tired she wanted to scream
in frustration, but the house seemed to whisper to her. Evil,
haunting whispers she couldn't ignore. The pain in the house ran
deep, was soaked into the walls and floors and ceilings. She
pressed her hands over her ears, trying to drown out the whispers, and finally gave up, leaping from the bed. It wasn't because

she was psychic that she could feel the pain radiating out off the walls, it was because it was so intense *anyone* would have felt it.

The blizzard had to stop soon, or she would be going out of her mind in this place. Maia wandered through the spacious hall and down the curving staircase. The front of the house was mainly glass, and the snow reflected light from every source, illuminating the interior of the house with soft silver light. The house was beautiful, but it was a cold beauty, almost cruel. It gave her the creeps. Shivering, she made her way toward the kitchen. Something to warm her up might help her sleep. If it weren't so cold, she would go out to her Land Cruiser and sleep there.

"What are you doing up?"

Maia whirled around, her heart in her throat. Cole Steele was sprawled out on the overlarge couch, long legs stretched out in front of him and a bottle of Jack Daniel's on the table. Her gaze jumped from the bottle to his face. In that one, unguarded moment, she caught a glimpse of a man ravaged by pain, by unspeakable horror, and she knew the truth. Jase had not been the only one to be abused. Cole had suffered the same torment as Jase, and it explained a lot about the man he had become. Wary. Dangerous. Solitary. It was a miracle that he had come back to take care of his half brother.

Cole wrapped his hand around the neck of the bottle, his gaze all at once hot as it drifted with too much interest over her body. "I asked why you were still up." There was a dark sensuality that called to everything feminine in her.

"Ghosts live in this house, but you already know that, don't you?"

His fingers tightened around the bottle. Without taking his eyes off her, he lifted it to his mouth and took a drink. His shirt was open, leaving the heavy muscles of his chest bare. There was rage in his eyes. Too many memories and none of them good. "Yes," he answered abruptly, studying her over the rim of the bottle. "When they get to be too much, I drown them. Do you want to join me?"

Maia shook her head, resisting the need in him. So much darkness and intensity, and Cole was very tempting. She healed hurt animals, and right now, he was far too close to being one. His way of forgetting was to drink, to have sex with a woman . . . any woman. "Hot chocolate for me. I presume you must keep a supply of chocolate on hand with Jase around."

He nodded and turned away from her, setting the bottle carefully on the table and staring out the huge glass panel to the pristine snow endlessly coming down. He looked utterly alone, and her heart stilled. Maia glanced around the enormous room, with its cathedral ceilings, and the curving stairway that went off in two directions. The house should have been alive with joy and music and Christmas decorations. There should have been logs in the fireplace and the fragrance of cinnamon and pine wafting through the air. Instead there was a boy alone in his room struggling to find a way to survive and a man drowning his demons in alcohol.

She shook her head. The pain and suffering in the house was overwhelming for someone as empathic as she was. And it made her angry on a level she'd never experienced before. Cole and Jase Steele existed, yet they weren't really living. The ghost lived, and he ruled with an iron fist in the house.

Maia thought it over as she made the chocolate. The house itself was the most beautiful thing she'd ever seen, yet it was bleak and as empty as the life Cole Steele seemed to live. Earlier, in the kitchen, Jase had laughed with her, teasing her about his pajamas being too big when she rolled up the cuffs and generally acting like a happy boy. Her heart had gone out to him as he worked so hard at being normal when the very walls of the house shrieked and wept for his suffering.

Cole had said little, never smiled, his blue gazed focused and direct, watching her watch Jase. Sitting in the kitchen chair, in his own home, he should have been relaxed, but instead, he had been on edge, wary, aware of everything around him. Now she knew why. She could have sat in that chef's dream of a kitchen and wept for both of them. Two men struggling to learn to come together as a family. Wary. Secretive. Ready to push everything and everyone away—including each other. Everything, healer and woman and compassionate human being responded to the intense pain in both of the Steeles, but a part of her, her instinct for self-preservation, wanted to run away and hide. She had no idea what to do to help either of them.

With a small sigh of resignation, knowing she couldn't just ignore it all, Maia added marshmallows to the chocolate and, picking up the mug, went to lean in the doorway to the living room. Cole's head was in his hands, his body tense, hair damp as if he'd just woken from a night terror—or still remained locked within it. She dug her fingers into the doorframe to keep from going to him. He wouldn't accept comfort, unless she offered sex—and she wasn't about to offer herself up as a sacrificial lamb.

"Go to bed, Maia," he muttered without looking up. "It isn't safe when I'm like this."

She took a cautious sip of the hot chocolate. Waiting in silence. Cole turned his head and looked at her, and her heart jumped, nearly melted. "Why are you doing this to yourself?"

The careful, expressionless mask was back in place, but he couldn't hide the pain revealed in his eyes. It remained there. Alive and ugly and so ingrained she wanted to comfort him. *Needed* to comfort him.

"You think I do this to myself?" There was controlled violence in his voice.

A shiver of fear went down her spine, but Maia persisted. She gestured around the house. "You keep this house a monument to the pain and suffering he caused. You live inside his world, and you expect somehow that you and Jase can overcome it. He's all around you, alive, here in this house, and you don't do anything to get him out of here."

"Who do you mean by *he*?" he asked suspiciously. He stood up, tall and lethal, a man who worked hard to stay in shape, to train himself to be the weapon he'd become. A man who despised pity and refused sympathy, preferring to remain alone rather than risk trusting anyone. Few knew about his past, he'd come clean with a soft version for his superiors at work, but never a woman. He didn't need a bleeding heart trying to stake a claim on him.

Maia's heart began a frantic pounding. She was very aware she was isolated from help, possibly for days. Cole looked capable of anything. She forced a shrug, trying to look nonchalant. "The ghost, of course. You admitted you have one."

He shook his head as he took an aggressive step toward her, bare feet making no sound in the thick pile of carpet. "Don't dodge the truth. Someone's been talking to you. What did they say?"

She took another sip of chocolate. The cup was shaking so she steadied it with her other hand. "I know something happened to Jase, yes. It's not all that difficult to figure out. And"—she indicated the bottle with her chin—"that says it happened to you as well."

He spat out a string of ugly imprecations, taking a second step toward her. "You don't know anything about us. Big deal, I'm having a drink. Don't feel sorry for me, Doc, I don't need it."

Despite her fear—or maybe because of it—Maia burst out laughing. "I definitely am feeling sorry for *me*, not you. Everyone has to live with demons, Steele. Some are worse than others, but we all have them. It's your choice how you deal with them. Drink yourself silly if that's what floats your boat. Personally, I'd drive the ghost out of my home. Reclaim it from him. Exorcise him, if you will." She looked around the house. "It's beautiful here and you've allowed it to become a mausoleum, cold and ugly with something cruel living in it. I can feel it. You can too. And so can Jase. I don't know why you want to keep it alive, but, hey"—she shrugged—"it's nothing to do with me."

Her heart hurt for him. Ached for Jase. But Cole Steele was never going to accept compassion from her. It would seem too much like pity to him. And if she had sex with him, which he so obviously wanted, it might get him through the night, but he'd still have to face his nightmares again and again.

"You're damned right it's nothing to do with you." Cole crossed the room, to stand in front of her. The top two buttons of his jeans were carelessly unbuttoned as if he'd pulled them on hastily and exited his bedroom as fast as he could.

Maia refused to be intimidated. She knew he was being blatantly sexual on purpose, hoping to scare her away or get her into his bed. The knowledge gave her the confidence to walk right past him and she set her mug on the coffee table.

Using her most casual voice, as if they were conversing over a trivial matter rather than one that cut so deep, she said, "It doesn't matter, Cole. We just believe in handling things differently. It doesn't mean I'm right, and you're wrong, it just means I wouldn't do things your way, and you wouldn't do them my way."

His cool blue gaze drifted over her. "What would you do if you lived here with ghosts?"

It sounded taunting, like a challenge.

She raised an eyebrow, turned to look around the spacious room. "I wouldn't let him drive me out or ruin my life. I'm mean like that. If I could actually have a home, no one would take it from me."

Maia wanted a home, but for some reason wouldn't stay too long in any one place. Cole filed the information away for future use. "Give me an example. Jase hates Christmas. It wasn't a nice time of year for him. He doesn't even like to hear the music, it brings on nightmares. If I cranked up 'Jingle Bells,' I'd just be making things worse for him." And for himself. He'd looked death in the eye a thousand times, courted it, spit at it, and he'd never so much as broken a sweat. But the thought of hearing Christmas music, seeing decorations, reliving nightmares every moment scared the hell out of him.

Maia nodded. Cole might be telling the truth about Jase, but in the scenario he was describing his and his brother's names were interchangeable. She took a deep breath and let it out. She wasn't a psychiatrist, and she didn't have anything but her instincts to go on, but she knew someone had to reach out to Cole Steele before it was too late. He shut out the world, preferred to live in isolation, but Jase had provided him with a small window of opportunity to get his life back. What Cole would not do for himself, he might be willing to do for Jase, and heal them both in the process.

"Everyone is different in how they handle these things, but the truth is, Christmas comes every year. Jase is going to have to face it year after year. And the season seems to come earlier every year. What happens if he wants to get married and have children? It doesn't mean he can't have a great family life without celebrating Christmas; but if he falls in love with someone like me, someone who loves Christmas, it might be difficult."

Someone like me. Cole's heart did a funny somersault. Maia did love Christmas, and he could see with her sunny, outgoing, giving personality, she would. She was happy and cheerful, and she wanted a home. Families celebrated things like Christmas. He nodded, feeling more alone than ever. "I've considered that. I just don't know how to go about getting him to enjoy the season. If we go into town, and he looks at all the decorations, that's enough to trigger the nightmares."

"It started here, didn't it? With his father?" She asked it carefully, not looking at him, not taking a chance he'd see the knowledge in her eyes. She was treading on very dangerous ground. Cole would be lethal under the right circumstances, and she didn't want him to feel as if he had to defend himself.

"Yes." He bit the word between his teeth. It wasn't talked about. Jase wouldn't be happy she knew he'd been abused, any more than Cole wanted her to know. There was a sense of shame in being a victim, even if you were a child and couldn't stop it.

"Jase has to feel his father's presence here all the time, especially if you both leave everything the way it was. I feel the man's presence. How could you not? If I was making the decisions, and I was going to keep the ranch, I'd change every single room. I'd redecorate, even use rooms for different things. I take it Christmas was never celebrated here?"

"God, no," Cole said. "The old man hated Christmas."

"Do you know why?"

Cole shrugged. "I'm guessing his old man hated it, but whatever his reasons, he used it to hurt everyone. He was at his most dangerous then. He seduced women, even brought them home in front of his wives. If anyone made the mistake of turning on the radio where he could hear a Christmas song played, and I'm talking the housekeeper or one of the ranch hands, he'd play it over and over and beat the hell out of Jase or his wife."

Or Cole and his mother. Maia sat down in the wide, cushioned chair. She deliberately chose a single chair rather than the couch to keep a safe distance between them. Cole made her feel vulnerable. There was too much pain and suffering, and she was a healer. When she felt pain, she responded. She forced herself to remain calm, to breathe in and out when she wanted to scream with anger at the destructive monster who had caused so much suffering in his own children. "So in effect, that man is still dictating what goes on in this house."

Cole passed his hand over his face, as if to wipe away the memories crowding in. "I fired everyone. The ranch hands, the housekeeper, anyone that was here and had to have known what was happening to him, but it didn't help much. I keep Jase with me when we interview people, and I listen to his input. He has a say in whom we hire and whom we pass on. I want him to feel safe here."

"How can he when that man is still in this house? Brett Steele is everywhere, in every room. And he's still the boss. He forbade you to enjoy such a simple thing as a Christmas season, and you don't. So he wins. Even from the grave, he wins."

Cole swore savagely, making Maia wince. She stared out the window to the heavy snowflakes, waiting for him to regain control of his temper.

"I'm sorry, Steele. You asked, and I gave my opinion. I'm no professional, and I'm sure you must have sought counseling for Jase. I shouldn't have said anything when I don't have any experience."

He waved a dismissing hand. "I wanted your opinion, or I wouldn't have asked. I've considered what you're saying myself. I guess I just wanted you to say there was another, easier way. I've taken Jase to counselors; he doesn't trust anyone. He refuses to talk to them."

"There has to be a really good professional who could help him."

"Maybe, but I haven't found the person. I can't blame Jase. He tried to get help when his father was alive, and no one listened. In all fairness, they didn't dare listen. Money talks, and the old man had a lot of power. He could destroy a business easily and did if his son befriended someone or talked out of turn. Jase's trust is a fragile thing right now. I'm not going to force him to see anyone until he knows he can count on me."

"And can he?" Maia asked quietly.

"If I never do another thing right in my life, I'll do this. Yes, he can count on me. He's coming first in my life. I've put my job on hold until he's squared away."

Maia's gaze met his. "What job?"

Cole sprawled out in the chair across from her. "Does it matter?"

"Sure it does. Do you like what you do? Do you miss working?"

"I like the isolation of it. It's comforting. I know the world and the rules, and nothing is ever a surprise." Cole was astonished the words slipped out. Maybe he'd had more to drink than he'd realized. He pushed the bottle away with the tips of his fingers.

"I guess I feel the same way about my job," Maia said.

Cole regarded her through half-closed eyes. She was always surprising him. There was something soothing and right about having her in his house. He could never imagine anyone else ever being there, but somehow Maia just fit. "Why do you travel so much? You should have a home."

She flashed him her smile. The one that could knock a man off his feet even from a distance. He'd wanted that smile turned on him; yet alone in his house, with demons surrounding him and alcohol buzzing in his veins, it was all too dangerous. She was so beautiful, curled up in the chair, her bare feet tucked under her. And the question had to be asked, what was under those thin, flannel pajamas? He'd never considered flannel sexy before, but he was looking at it in an entirely new way.

"What? Stop looking at me as if you're the big bad wolf." She shook her head. "I guess you can't help yourself, you're always in hunting mode."

Instantly his expression closed down. His gaze was watchful, shrewd. "I don't like games, Maia. What the hell are you talking about?"

He was thinking conspiracy theory. She sat across from him, weariness plain on her face, no makeup, no guile, and he was actually considering the possibility that she had somehow set up the injury to the horse and was out to get him, using Jase. Had he gone over the edge? To be paranoid of the veterinarian? *She traveled all the time. Was a stranger in town, but was able to gain the trust of those around her fast.* Nonetheless, the little voice that was always asking questions and compiling data persisted.

Maia saw the wariness in his eyes. The sudden alertness. There was danger, but she couldn't figure out what button she'd pressed. Talking with Cole Steele was like walking through a minefield. It was no wonder he preferred one-night stands. No talking, just get down to business and he was safe. "I'm sorry, I didn't mean to upset you. I was referring to your penchant for hunting for women in bars. I was just about to say when you're not treating women like sex toys, you're really an okay human being, but I've changed my mind. You're a very difficult human being."

His eyes went cold and hard. "What the hell does that mean? I don't treat women like sex toys."

"Of course you do. It's *exactly* what you do. You troll the bars for women willing to get you through the night, no strings attached. Hopefully you're also a safety boy."

"Safety boy?" he repeated, unable to believe what she said.

"I hope you at least protect all those women; otherwise, there's no hope for you at all." She turned away from him, shrugging her shoulders carelessly when she didn't feel careless at all. She was beginning to be pulled into the drama in the Steele home, and it frightened her. She didn't want to care about them, or worry about them. She couldn't afford to get involved with someone like Cole Steele.

"I'm not about to pick up a disease or get someone pregnant, if that's what you mean. And I don't give a damn what you think about me."

His voice was as cold as ice, but he was smoldering with anger. She could tell.

Maia stared out the glass window, watching the snow coming down relentlessly. It was much safer looking at the snow than looking at him or around at the ice-cold beauty of the house. "I was stating a fact, not making a judgment; but you obviously have an entirely different set of values, so of course you wouldn't see it that way."

Cole could feel his temper rise. No one managed to get under his skin the way she did, although he couldn't deny her accusation. He had gone into the bar several nights running with the sole intention of sleeping with her in the hopes of getting through the Christmas season. Looking at himself through her eyes wasn't a pretty sight, and the revelation was difficult to take.

"How do you know how I'd see anything?"

Maia turned her attention back to him, her too-cool gaze sweeping his face. "I don't, Cole. And I don't want to know anything. Whatever your suspicions of me are, I'm not looking for a husband, a lover, money, or anything else. I do my job, and I get out of town."

Cole could feel his stomach churning. She'd given him an out. He should go the hell to bed, walk away and leave her alone. But something held him to the chair. Held him under her gaze. He wished it were sex. Wished it were the intense physical attraction he felt for her. He didn't want it or need it to be anything else. He scrubbed his hand over his face, trying to rid himself of the demons that refused to let go.

"The first lesson I can ever remember learning was never to trust anyone at all. Not my mother, certainly not my father, not the housekeeper or any of the hands. It didn't matter how nice or friendly they seemed. They would report everything to him. They would stand there watching when he killed something I made the mistake of caring for. They stood in silence when he beat me with his fists or a whip or a hanger or whatever else happened to be handy." He waved his hand to encompass the ranch. "This was a prison. There was no way to get away from him. He had his security force, who watched our every moment."

He was half-angry with himself the moment he revealed one of his darkest secrets. He'd told her by way of apology for his paranoid conspiracy theories. Or maybe to prove to himself he wasn't as far gone a human being as he believed he was. Whatever the reason, he couldn't take it back no matter how much he wished he could.

Maia was silent, careful to keep her expression from reflecting the horror and compassion in her mind. She couldn't blow the moment by speaking, by saying or doing the wrong thing. Cole Steele was telling her something she doubted he'd ever admitted to anyone. He might have glossed over a difficult childhood, but he'd never spoken the details aloud to another human being. She picked up the mug of chocolate, now cool, wrapping both hands around it.

"Don't think I'm telling you this for sympathy," Cole said harshly. "It's important for you to know what Jase has had to deal with. I don't want him to become like me. I want him to be normal. This is about Jase. You understand? Just Jase."

Maia managed to nod, blinking rapidly to keep tears at bay. Cole Steele was a lost man fighting desperately for his younger half brother. She swallowed the lump threatening to choke her. Who was going to save Cole?

"He responded to you. You're the first person I've ever seen him do that with. He has that distance between him and everyone else, but he laughed with you. Actually laughed. Jase needs something I can't seem to give him."

"You're giving him exactly what he needs right now, Cole. Stability and a sense of family. After so many years, you said he's, what? Fourteen?" At Cole's nod, she continued. "Jase is afraid to trust anyone completely. He wants to, but it's ingrained in him not to. Time will take care of that. As long as you don't let him down, he'll count on you and learn to rely on your relationship."

"Men like Al's brother-in-law, they wanted to pretend what went on here at the ranch was all right, just something they had to put up with to keep their families going, but they were part of it, holding Jase here, watching what the old man did to him. I don't want them anywhere near Jase, with their smirks and patronizing bullshit."

Maia heard the suppressed rage in Cole's voice. The men he'd fired were luckier than they knew. Cole was capable of extreme violence. "Jase isn't ever going to get over this completely, Cole. It doesn't work that way. The things we've experienced become part of who we are. It can make him a stronger, better person, but he won't ever forget it or be able to get away from the consequences, the impact on his personality."

Cole leaned back in his chair, allowing his breath to leave his lungs. "Who are you, Doc? Where do you come from?"

"I'm no big mystery, Steele. I grew up in a small town. My parents were killed in a car accident when I was about sixteen, and I went to live with my only relative, my grandmother. She was an awesome woman, and I hope I learned a lot from her. I loved animals, got decent grades, and decided I'd be a veterinarian. I was about halfway through school when my grandmother died, and I discovered she had a bit of money put away. It enabled me to buy my own equipment, and the rest is history."

"Your entire life in a few short sentences." He saluted her. Maia smiled at him. "I told you it wasn't a big deal. Now, *you* are different. You're surrounded by mystery and intrigue."

"It's what women find appealing."

"Really? I thought it was your brooding loner image. I guess it ties in though, I can see that. Are you going to give tips to Jase on dealing with women?"

Cole shook his head. "Jase is going to find a really nice woman someday and have a family. He'll have two kids and come home every night to someone who loves him." He sighed. "He's not excited about going to a regular school. I was hoping he'd go to a private one or even the public school, but he's always had tutors, and he isn't comfortable with anything else."

"He isn't comfortable not being with you. In effect, this ranch has been the only place he's ever been. Didn't you say your father kept him prisoner here? Or close to it? He's staying in his comfort zone. We all do that. We stay with what we know."

Cole tried not to wince. She was lashing him, and she wasn't even aware of it. If anyone stayed in his comfort zone, it was he. Cole didn't duck the issue. He was an adrenaline junkie, and he kept the rest of the world at a distance. She was just sitting there, looking beautiful, pointing out his every flaw, and through it all he had the most incredible urge to kiss her until neither of them could think anymore. "Isn't it about time you tried to get some sleep?"

Maia glanced at her watch, deliberately ignoring the flare of desire in his eyes. "You're right. It's already morning. It doesn't look like we're going to get much of a break from this storm."

Cole stood up, waited until she'd rinsed out her mug and climbed the stairs to the long sweep of a landing. "Good night, Doc, thanks for everything you've done."

Maia smiled at him over her shoulder. "Anytime, Steele."

6

"Jase," Cole said casually, "the doc's out with the horse right now, so there's no rush. Before you go out to check on him I want to run something by you. I need a little advice."

Jase sat down at the kitchen table across from his older brother. "What is it?" They'd slept in late, and he was anxious to make certain his horse had gotten through the night without a problem.

"The doc." Cole pushed his hands through his hair, leaving it spiked and disheveled. "I checked the weather, and it looks like we'll be socked in for at least a week."

"She'll have to stay here?" Jase couldn't prevent the grin from spreading across his face. "I don't mind. I think the doc's all right."

"She loves Christmas, Jase, and she'll be stuck here with us probably through the twenty-fifth. She'll miss it." Cole didn't look at the boy, but stood up and paced across the room in a restless, edgy movement. "She came out here doing us a favor, she's stuck working; in fact she's already out with Celtic High"—he glanced briefly at Jase, assessing his expression—"I mean Wally. I don't know, what do you think we should do?"

Jase rubbed his hand over his face, subconsciously copying his older brother's gestures. "Anything to eat around here?" He looked around the room, anywhere but at his brother. "I'm starving, and it smells good in here."

"You're always starving. She made breakfast burritos for us. You just scoop up the eggs and wrap them in the tortilla. The tortillas are still warm."

Jase made his burrito, took a healthy bite, and sat there chewing, contemplating. "I don't know, Cole. What do you think? She's really nice. Maybe we could put up a tree or something."

Cole had his back to the boy, and he closed his eyes, his gut kicking up a protest. His ear was finely trained, tuned to catch the slightest nuances, and he could hear the combination of hesitancy and hope. "We've never done that before, either one of us. It might be interesting. The old man would turn over in his grave."

"As long as he stays in it," Jase said.

Cole turned back to face him. "I saw the body, Jase. He's dead." Cole didn't admit he had insisted on seeing the body. He wouldn't have believed anything or anyone would ever manage to kill Brett Steele. The man had seemed invincible, a monster with such power he could live forever. *Jase had been in the house when the old man had bought it.* Cole tried to push the thought away. *Jase wasn't capable of murder—not even of a monster like their father, was he?* That niggling doubt persisted no matter how hard Cole worked at keeping it at bay.

"Who do you think killed him, Cole?"

"It could have been anyone. He had a lot of enemies," Cole answered honestly, feeling relieved that there were other suspects. "I think the question we need answered is why someone killed him. Did it have anything to do with us? The ranch? The money? Anything that could affect us."

"I didn't think of that. Why would it have something to do with us?"

Cole shrugged. "I don't know, but it bothers me that all these rumors are so persistent, the ones about me trying to do you in. Al mentioned you were helping him feed horses the other day, and you leaned against the fence in the corner and it gave way. If he hadn't grabbed you, you would have gone over that small cliff. You often lean up against that section when you watch the horses run. I've seen you do it."

Cole had personally gone out to inspect the fence. Someone had deliberately loosened the post from the cement. The fall wouldn't have killed Jase, but it might have broken a bone or two. What had been the point? Any of the new hands could have done it. Cole had hired them out of Jackson Hole, but that didn't mean they might not be friends with the former crew. Al had even mentioned that his brother-in-law, Fred, had been around that day.

"Al said the fence was old and needed repairing."

"Maybe. But now there's this incident with Wally. Don't you think it's strange my glove was found by the fence? I haven't been out there in a week, and my work gloves are always in my truck. I don't believe in coincidence. The old man was murdered, and, even though these incidents seem unrelated, I'm not so certain they are."

Jase sagged in his chair. "I was thinking the same thing." He looked at Cole, fear in his eyes. "But I was thinking maybe it was him. I know it's crazy, Cole, but what if he found a way to come back? I read a couple of books on the subject, and some people believe a spirit can linger after death, especially if the death was violent."

"That's a load of crap, Jase. He's dead and gone."

"Then why does it feel as if he's still here? I swear I'm afraid to do anything. I even look up when I go into all the rooms, looking for the cameras he had to watch us all the time." Jase looked about to cry.

"I destroyed the cameras and all the tapes, Jase. I did it right in front of you. We cleaned him out of here." Cole cleared his throat. "Maybe we should try a Christmas tree and a few decorations. Let's take the house back completely. He can't dictate to us what we can or can't do. If you're still feeling him here, it's because we haven't made the house ours." He tried not to wince as he repeated Maia's logic. "So it's really up to you if you want to try to celebrate Christmas this year. I'm game if you are."

Jase shrugged, trying to look casual. "Well, maybe we should do it for the doc. I'd hate for her to be out here looking after Wally and missing something she loves."

Cole kept his expression carefully blank. He wasn't about to take away the boy's courage by letting on that the very thought of trying to celebrate the holiday scared the hell out of him.

He knew what he was getting himself into. Brett Steele had been particularly cruel at Christmas, and the number of Cole's nightmares increased in direct proportion to days of celebration. "Since I've never actually had a Christmas, we might need a little help in figuring out what we're supposed to do."

"You know how pathetic that makes us, Cole?" Jase asked. "I can't go to school with a bunch of other kids and pretend my life is okay. I know you think I should, but I'm never going to be like them. I don't want to have to pretend anymore."

Jase took every occasion to remind Cole he objected strenuously to going into a classroom. Cole sighed. "I want you to have friends, Jase. You don't want to end up being a loner. If you don't get out there and mix it up with your peers, you'll never be able to."

"Is that what happened to you?" Jase asked, belligerence creeping into his tone.

"As a matter of fact, yes. I grew up the same way you did, remember? You aren't alone in this. I wasn't allowed friends either. I had tutors right here on the ranch. If I liked one of the hands too much, he was sent packing. I don't have friends, and I don't make them. It's a hell of a way to live."

"I don't want to go to school," Jase said stubbornly.

Cole was happy the boy was at least telling him how he felt. That said he had grown comfortable enough with Cole to do so. In the first few weeks they'd been together, the boy had rarely offered an opinion on anything. "Let's do this, Jase. We'll start with this Christmas thing for the doc. If we can manage to get through it without the two of us going nuts, maybe we can move forward from there."

Jase nodded. "I don't mind trying for the doc, but I'm not promising about school." He scooped up more eggs and rolled them in a tortilla. "She's a pretty good cook, isn't she?"

"I thought so."

"You like her don't you, Cole?"

Cole went very still inside. He tried a casual shrug. "What's not to like?"

Jase pushed his fork around the table. "Have you gone into the old man's office since he died?"

Cole's head went up alertly at the boy's tone. "A couple of times, not recently."

"He has a couple of maps of the ranch that I wanted. I was going to put them in my room, but they're gone. They were in his desk drawer."

"What do you mean, 'gone'? No one's here but the two of us. I didn't touch the maps, didn't even know they were there."

Cole felt a twinge of alarm. It was a silly thing, a missing map meant nothing at all, so alarms shouldn't be going off, but he'd long ago learned to pay attention when a small detail was out of place. "Jase, are you certain the maps were still there after Brett was killed? Someone could have borrowed them."

Jase nodded. "I looked at them a week or so after he died."

Cole drummed his fingers on the table. "That was before I fired Justine and Ben Briggs. It didn't occur to me they might take anything. I wouldn't know it if they did. They worked here for years, so they'd know more about what was in the house than either of us. They could have robbed us blind, and we wouldn't know." But why would they take maps and not the Ming vase or the artwork worth thousands? Or any of the other priceless objects decorating every room of the house. "You're certain of the time line?"

"Cole, I was terrified to go into his office. I waited a week after he died, then when I pulled the maps out, I couldn't make myself take them to my room. I folded them carefully and put them back in the drawer in his desk."

Cole decided the kid looked scared. "Jase." His voice was very gentle. "Brett Steele is dead, and his ghost can't do a damned thing to us. It certainly didn't remove maps from his office. You have to stop reading those books."

"I didn't think about Justine or Ben taking anything," Jase admitted with a small sigh of relief. "That makes more sense."

"Why were you interested in the maps, Jase?"

Jase pushed the last bite of burrito around on his plate with his fork. "The ranch is so big, and I hated that all the workers knew every canyon and peak and I had no idea what they were talking about. They'd be talking about the cattle being in some canyon; I'd ask where it was, and they'd laugh at me. I hated that. I hated feeling so small and stupid all the time. I was the boss's son, and they knew more than I did."

Cole swore savagely under his breath, his back to the boy. Every little hurt added more to Jase's feelings of inadequacy. The old man had purposely made him look small in front of the ranch hands, belittling him and correcting him, even publicly humiliating and punishing him every chance he got. Cole knew without Jase's telling him, because he'd received the same treatment.

"I'll find you maps of the ranch, Jase," he promised gruffly. "Even if I have to draw them myself."

"Thanks, Cole." Jase stood up and carried his plate to the sink. "Has the doc been up a long time?"

Cole inhaled the scent of fresh coffee. "Yeah, she's been up a while. She's out there with that horse of yours. Go on, I'll take care of cleanup this morning." Cole waved the boy out, not wanting to face Maia yet. She'd disarmed him without even trying, filling the house with the fragrance of breakfast, giving him an unfamiliar sense of warmth and home. He sat there for a moment contemplating that. He'd never felt as if he'd had a home before.

When he woke up that morning he'd been instantly aware that Maia Armstrong was in his house. Not just any woman, but Maia Armstrong. He never let a woman spend the night with him, and he always left their houses immediately after sex. With Maia, everything seemed different, but he couldn't put his finger on why. It wasn't the fact that he'd awakened with a hell of a hard-on from the erotic dream he'd had about her, instead of waking from the usual nightmare, tangled in his sheets with a gun in his hand. It was because she'd brought a sense of home to the monstrosity of a house he occupied.

He had awakened looking forward to the day and he hadn't

experienced that feeling very often. He had lain there, staring at the ceiling, his heart pounding and his mouth dry, terrified that Maia Armstrong could do that to him. Make him happy by just being in his house. By making a building seem like a home just with her presence. By removing the endless nightmares and replacing them with dreams of her. Her smile. She had a killer smile. Her eyes went soft, almost mesmerizing. The sound of her laughter. It seemed to vibrate through his body, wrap around him until it squeezed his heart and lungs.

He swore out loud, jumping up fast enough to knock over his chair and turning around in the huge kitchen without a real purpose. She was getting under his skin. He should have found a way to seduce her last night and get it over with; instead, he'd revealed intimate, private details he never should have admitted. She had ammunition to use against him, and he'd given it to her. "Oh, you're good, lady," he said. "What are you after?" He picked up the chair, slamming it against the table.

Immediately he was ashamed of himself. What was he thinking she wanted? Him? She'd made it clear she had no intention of sleeping with him. His money? That would entail some kind of a relationship with him. He threw a plate into the soapy water, avoiding the dishwasher. Suds and water splashed over the edge of the sink. He needed a damned housekeeper, not a girlfriend.

"Cole!" Jase burst through the kitchen door, slamming it back on its frame so hard it nearly bounced. "Come quick. The doc fell and hit her head."

Cole rushed past him, his heart in his throat. "How the hell did that happen?"

"I don't know, I found her on the walkway. There's ice all around her."

"Ice?" Cole sprinted along the covered walkway. There was snow piled high on either side and more flakes were coming down rapidly. The walkways had been specifically constructed with a wide overhang to keep any water from running down onto the surface for the very purpose of keeping ice from forming. The latticework and snow, piled so high on either side, kept the wind and drafts at bay, forming a warmer tunnel for them to use in going back and forth between the various buildings.

Maia lay sprawled on the ground, one hand at the back of her head. Cole could see the bright red blood staining the white snow underneath her. He crouched beside her, catching her hand gently and drawing it away from the wound. "Let me see."

She looked up at him, her wide eyes dazed and slightly unfocused. "I just slipped. It wasn't icy when I came out here, and I didn't notice the surface."

Cole felt the lump on her head through the mass of thick dark hair. It was sticky with blood. He studied the walkway. There was no dripping water that could have caused the snow to ice over the way it had. The surface was slick with a layer of ice, almost as if someone had sprayed water over it. He studied the latticework. A few drops of ice clung to the wood just about level with his waist. "Don't move, Doc, just lie still while I take a look at you." *Jase was the only person around.* He swore silently. He didn't want to think the boy could in any way be like their father, but his own past and his job gave him a suspicious nature. He had to eliminate Jase as a suspect. There were ranch hands— even Al—living on the ranch and even in a blizzard one of them could have arranged the "accident."

He glanced once more at Jase. The boy looked so anxious, every instinct Cole possessed told him he couldn't possibly have sprayed the water on the walkway to make it icy.

"The fall just stunned me for a minute."

"Did you get knocked out? Jase, was she out for any length of time?"

"She swore a lot," Jase reported.

"Did she now? I wasn't sure you knew how to swear," Cole said, looking down into Maia's eyes. It was a big mistake. A man could lose himself there. He couldn't look away from her. He bent his head and brushed a kiss across her mouth to break the spell.

Her eyelashes fluttered, and she managed to glare at him. "I work with animals, believe me, I know how to swear. And was that another apology?"

"Sheer desperation."

"You do look a bit desperate," Maia conceded, struggling to sit up. "And I didn't lose consciousness. I think I knocked the wind out of myself, and my head hurts pretty bad, but if you'll help me up, I'll be fine."

"I'm going to lift you, Doc. Just put your arms around my neck. Jase, watch your step, the surface is icy, and we don't need another accident."

"I've never seen the walkway ice over before," Jase said. "Maybe there was rain or slush coming down with the snow."

"Maybe," Cole conceded, but the temperature was far too cold for rain or slush, and they both knew it. "Just stay close until I can take a look around, Jase." He lifted Maia into his arms, holding her against his chest. Her skin was cool after being outdoors for so long. She was heavier than he expected, her muscles solid and firm. He felt the tension in her the moment he cradled her close. The same faint fragrance of peaches and rain he'd noticed the night before clung to her skin and hair.

"I can walk," she protested. She tried to hold herself rigidly away from him. "I'm ruining your shirt." Maia felt silly being carried by Cole Steele. If her head hadn't been throbbing with enough intensity to make her teeth ache she would have insisted on walking.

"Relax, Doc, I have a lot of shirts, and there's only one of you. I don't give a damn about the shirt."

"That's a good thing, because it's a mess already." She tried to move her head to keep the blood from dripping onto his shirt.

Cole made a single sound of impatience and she subsided, trying to relax against him in spite of her embarrassment. Jase skirted around the ice and hurried ahead to open the door. "I'll get blankets," he called over his shoulder.

Cole carried her to the oversized couch, placing her with care in the middle of the cushions. "When you went to the barn this morning, you're positive there was no ice on the walkway?"

Maia looked up at the concern on his face. His voice was low, obviously to keep Jase from overhearing. "It was easy to get to the barn. I remember thinking everyone should have a walkway like that. Most ranches in the outlying areas use rope or cable as a guideline when it's snowing."

"We've got cable up in places," Cole said. He took the ice pack and washcloth from Jase as the boy hurried up to them. "Thanks, Jase. The doc's going to be fine. She just looks a little pale. Women do that to give men heart attacks."

Maia laughed. Cole should have known she would in spite of her injuries, but he wasn't at all prepared for the sound filling the space around them. His space. It was always there, between him and everyone else, but she didn't seem to see it, and she put things there like her laughter. She was definitely getting under his skin, and it made him edgier than usual.

"Well, I don't think you should, Doc," Jase chastised, his hand over his heart, "because I was really scared."

"I'm sorry, Jase. I didn't see the ice. I guess I wasn't looking. And just for your information . . . Ow!" Maia pulled her head away and glared at Cole as he dabbed at the cut on her head. "That hurts."

"Stop being such a baby." Cole was extraordinarily gentle as he wiped away the blood. There was an unfamiliar lump in his throat. All the while he was turning over possibilities in his mind. Had someone sprayed the walkway with water in order to cause Maia harm? Who could have done such a thing? He needed to take a closer look at Al and his wife. Find out if anyone had been visiting. Perhaps Fred had stayed with them instead of going home to his family.

"Does it really hurt, Doc?" Jase asked, frowning at Cole.

"I'm fine," Maia assured. "He's being gentle. I feel a little stupid falling on my head." She wasn't going to mention the bruises all over her backside. Cole's face was very close to hers, and she could see his long lashes, the bluish shadowing along his jaw, the tiny lines etched into his weathered features. His gaze met hers and her heartbeat accelerated instantly. "You're lethal." She didn't mean to say it aloud. She had to blame the bump on her head. It knocked out her good sense.

"Yes I am," Cole warned. "Don't forget it."

Maia looked up at Jase and burst out laughing a second time. "At least I'm not the only one saying dumb things. Your horse, by the way, is doing great, Jase. No temp, the drains are working, and I gave him his antibiotic shots, so he's fine for the time being. I didn't feed him, so you'll have to do that. And I want to move him to a small enclosure where he can get around without hurting himself. The trick is to get him to walk enough to keep the swelling down, but not so much that he pulls out the sutures or does more damage."

"I still have to feed the other horses this morning," Jase said. "I told Al I'd do it so he wouldn't have to risk driving in the storm. We knew the storm would be bad, so I'll take care of the stables, then let Wally into the small round pen inside the big barn. I can feed him there, unless you just want him to exercise a couple of times a day."

"I'll feed the horses, Jase," Cole said. "Give me a few minutes with the doc here to get her settled, and I'll go make the rounds."

"I don't mind, Cole," Jase objected. "I can do the job."

Cole scowled and opened his mouth to make it a command, but Maia deterred him, touching his wrist with her fingertips. When he glanced at her she shook her head slightly and turned her head to smile up at Jase. "Actually, I was hoping you'd stay with me for a little while so we could come up with a plan for Wally." Her smile widened until it lit her eyes. "I think the name suits him. He likes it."

"Did he tell you that?" Cole asked, his voice edged with sarcasm.

"As a matter of fact, he did. What do you say, Jase? Let the grouch feed the horses this morning, and we'll map out a plan of action for Wally."

"You may as well plan Christmas for us too." Cole made the

suggestion to forestall Jase's protest that the horse wasn't anything special to him. His heart jumped, slamming hard against the wall of his chest in protest. He would have taken the proposal back, but the boy suddenly looked hopeful.

Maia's fingers tightened on his wrist. He hoped to hell she had no idea what the turn in the conversation cost him. Cole refused to meet her eyes, instead busying himself with getting the matted blood from her hair so he could see the wound.

"You sure you didn't try ice-skating," he said gruffly as he looked at the laceration.

A faint smile softened the lines around her mouth. "I've always wanted to learn, but it wasn't my intention."

"I can take her ice-skating if she wants to go," Jase volunteered. "There's a pond that freezes over every winter. It's great for ice-skating."

Cole glanced at the boy's face. He was staring at Maia as if she were a goddess. He sighed and leaned down, his mouth against her ear, his lips brushing her skin. "Tone it down before the boy asks you to marry him." The faint scent of peaches in her hair triggered a heat flash that seemed to spread through his veins straight to his belly and centered in his groin.

She turned her head so that her mouth was brushing against his cheek. "Really? I didn't realize I had such an impact."

Her voice vibrated down his spine. He could have sworn her finger stroked his wrist but when he looked down, her hand was lying there motionless. Innocent. Her lips were feather-light, soft and full. Cole felt the burn right through his skin. He jerked away from her. She was reducing him to a smitten teenager. Jase could fall under her spell, but he was damned if he would. It was supposed to work the other way around. He certainly wasn't mesmerizing her. And she sure wasn't falling into his bed. Maia looked up at him, her eyes wide and beautiful, and the breath left his lungs in a rush.

Cole backed away from the couch. "I think you'll be fine. Jase, get the doc an aspirin and stay with her while I get the chores done."

"And you're really fine with decorating the house, or maybe even getting a Christmas tree?" There was a note of fear in Jase's voice.

Cole felt the echo of fear in his gut. "Sure. Sounds like a plan." He turned away from them. A woman who appeared soft and gentle but had a core of steel. A boy, lost in his past and trying desperately to find security and a home. Cole shook his head. How the hell had he gotten into such a mess? He needed familiar ground. He was never afraid. He had nothing to lose, and when a man had nothing to lose, he didn't experience fear. He was letting some little slip of a woman scare the holy hell out of him.

Outside, he examined the ice-coated walkway. Someone had poured water over the snow to form the icy surface. The hose was buried in the large snowbank on the outside of the walkway, but he could see the hose had been stuck in one of the latticework holes and sprayed onto the surface. Small droplets of water had frozen on the lattice.

Was it Jase? It didn't feel right to him. Jase seemed to be genuine. A nice kid who needed a family. Could he be as sick and disturbed as their father? They were in the middle of a particularly harsh blizzard. No one else was in the house or around the ranch that Cole was aware of. He studied the ground near the hose. The boot impressions in the snow were large—too large to be Jase's—and led back toward a door that opened into the barn. Someone had opened that door and spied on Maia while she worked on the horse. Jase hadn't been wet or covered in snow when he'd come running in.

If Maia had gone out early to tend the horse and the walkway had been fine, then only Jase had gone after her. It was possible Jase had shot the old man. He'd never been ruled out as a suspect. He didn't want Jase to be guilty, but the evidence wasn't stacking up in the boy's favor.

Brett Steele had been found in his office, dead from a single bullet smack in the middle of his forehead. Cole shook his head. Jase had found the injured horse. He could have easily driven the horse into the fence and then gone to get Al, making a show of being upset and blaming Cole. Jase claimed he found Cole's glove in the fence.

Cole straightened and took a cautious look around. His alarms were shrieking at him. Something was terribly wrong, and he knew he was in danger. Maia Armstrong could very well be too. And Jase.

He shook his head, vowing to find out who was sneaking around the ranch and why as he trudged through the snow to the stables to feed the horses.

He patted an outstretched neck as one of the horses greeted him, then tossed a flake of hay into the last feeding bin.

He ran his hand along one of the horses' backs, bent closer, and noticed a girth mark near the horse's belly. It could only mean the horse had been ridden recently, within the last couple of days. Cole leaned down to pick up a foot, examining the hoof. Dirt and debris were caked in the shoe. Very slowly he lowered the hoof to the stable floor, a slight frown on his face. Al hadn't said anything about taking the horses out.

Cole closed the door to the stall and went to examine the saddles and bridles. A large saddle was set to one side, slightly off kilter, but it didn't mean anything. A rifle scabbard was hooked to the saddle, and it had a mud pattern splattered across it.

A muffled footfall alerted him. Cole eased back into the shadows of the tack room and drew the gun from the holster strapped to his calf. Only the munching of the horses as they chewed hay and the sound of their continual restless movements in the stalls broke the silence. Cole didn't make the mistake of moving. He had endless patience when needed. A shadow stretched across the wall, a man holding a pitchfork out in front of him. Cole stepped out into the open, his gun rock steady, an extension of his arm.

Every vestige of color drained from Jase's face. He dropped the pitchfork and backed against the stall. "Don't shoot me."

Cole swore savagely. "What the hell is the matter with you?

I *could have* shot you. What were you thinking?" He shoved the gun out of sight.

"I came out to help you," Jase defended, his face tight with fear and growing anger. "What are you doing with a gun?"

"None of your damned business," Cole snapped. Jase turned and ran out of the stable, disappearing from Cole's line of vision.

Cole crushed down the need to throw something. He should have identified the intruder before coming out of hiding with his gun. He knew better than to let his highly tuned instincts take over completely. Dammit. He was going to have to explain the gun. How did you tell a teenager your entire world was made up of conspiracies, and you siphoned through them one at a time to get to the truth?

7

COLE ENTERED THE living room to find Jase pacing furiously back and forth across the room. The boy cast a dark, furious look at his brother. Maia looked up and met Cole's gaze, lifting her hands palm up in inquiry. Jase stopped pacing abruptly and stood breathing heavily, his hands on his hips.

"You could have killed me! Maybe you want to kill me just like everyone says," Jase burst out. He glared at Cole. "Maybe you tried to kill the doc just so she wouldn't find out about you."

"Jase!" Maia said firmly. "That's enough. You're afraid and angry, but don't say things you can't take back."

"He didn't put a gun in your face. He's been in jail. Everyone knows he's been there," Jase continued, breathing hard, his young face twisted with fear and hurt.

"Come sit down over here." Maia patted the couch beside her. "I can tell you whatever Cole may have done or not done in his life, he wouldn't do anything to hurt you. Someone is trying to drive a wedge between the two of you." She didn't look at Cole. She couldn't bear to see the hurt in his eyes she knew would be there. He stood motionless, a man apart, isolated, hurt beyond reason and unwilling to risk himself further.

Jase flung himself onto the couch beside Maia, tears glittering in his eyes. "I hate this. I hate my life." He included Maia in his glare. "I hate that you stick up for him. You don't even know him. You don't know whether he killed our father, or whether he hurt Wally and tried to hurt me. You don't even know whether or not he covered that walkway with ice in order to hurt you. Everyone says he's after my share of the money, and maybe he is." A sob escaped, and his chest heaved as he tried to hold the emotion in.

"That's enough." Cole's tone was low, but it was a whiplash.

"That doesn't even make sense, Jase," Maia said softly. "I knew about the gun. If you went into the stable and startled Cole, of course he pulled the gun. Someone hurt your horse. Naturally Cole would be worried about all of our safety."

Jase rubbed at his eyes with his knuckles, looking four instead of fourteen. Cole let out his breath slowly as his younger brother's expression became somewhat mollified.

"Cole, you need to talk to Jase. I can leave the room if you want me to, but he needs you to share your life with him. You're helping whoever is persisting in these rumors about you trying to kill Jase. You're enabling whoever is attempting to keep you from trusting one another by remaining silent about your past. If you want this to work between you, you have to trust one another, and the only way to do that is to get to know each other." Maia held her breath, waiting for Cole to tell her to go to hell.

There was a long silence. She stole a quick glance at his face.

His rugged features were very still, expressionless. He stared over her head at the wall behind them. A muscle jerked in his jaw, the only sign that he'd heard her. She could feel Jase trembling, could feel the tension in his body winding tighter and tighter. With a small sigh, she twisted her fingers together. What could she say to convince them?

"I saw the shadow of a man holding a pitchfork and thought someone was stalking me. I didn't know it was you. I yelled at you because I was afraid I could have hurt you accidentally. I didn't hurt the horse, and I sure don't want your money."

Jase looked a little embarrassed. "Maybe I didn't mean everything I said. It just reminded me of . . . things."

"I know what you mean," Cole said. "He shoved a gun in my face more than once too. I'm sorry I scared you."

"That's all right." Some of the tension began to drain from the boy's body.

"I was in jail, Jase." Cole took a deep breath, let it out. His fingers curled involuntarily into a fist. "I work for the DEA. I went into prison undercover to stop a very large drug ring involving guards, inmates, and the supply trucks. I've worked undercover most of my life. It's an isolating job and makes you very distrustful of everything and everyone around you." He made the confession in a rush, wanting to get it over with, half-horrified that he was letting them both into his life. "I don't tell people what I do. It's habit, and it's kept me alive over the years."

Maia kept her lips firmly pressed together, astonished, not by what he'd said, but that he'd admitted it. Cole Steele was not a man who'd easily reveal the details of his life. She wanted to console him, put her arms around him and hold him close, but neither Jase nor Cole could allow a show of compassion. Beside her, Jase was trembling, uncertain how to react to his brother's revelation. Tension coiled around Cole, his face a mask without expression. Only his eyes were alive, turbulent and raw with pain.

"You're some kind of a cop?" Jase asked. His voice cracked, making him sound younger and even less sure of himself.

Cole nodded. "I have a small apartment in San Francisco that I rarely use. Most of the time I'm on the road, sent undercover to various countries. Sometimes it's here in the U.S. We carefully cultivated my reputation and network in the drug world. When the old man was investigating me, the P.I. raised a red flag, and we fed him the details of my life just the way we do everyone who investigates me. I was using a different name, and the private investigators just assumed I'd covered my tracks to be rid of the old man. They bought my undercover role and took it at face value. So now Cole Steele has the same background as my persona at work."

"And you didn't want me to know?"

Cole flinched inwardly at the hurt in the boy's voice. "I wanted to wait until we knew each other better, Jase. Things have been so bad for you. I'm not used to being around anyone for an extended period of time. I had to know if I could be someone you could count on."

"But you let all those people say that you were here to kill me."

Cole nodded. "And I'll continue to let them say it. I don't care what people say or think about me. I'm only concerned with what you say and think."

"I tried not to think they might be right, but I found your glove by the fence. And sometimes, when you look really mean, you look a little bit . . ." Jase trailed off.

The knot in his gut tightened. Cole refused to look at Maia. "I've seen the resemblance. I always carry a gun, Jase."

"I guess I'm not supposed to tell anyone."

"I'd rather you didn't," Cole said.

"Are you going to go away again?"

Maia felt the boy beside her, stiff and awkward. She could feel fear rolling off him and immediately locked her gaze with Cole's. Pleading with him. Hurting for him. Did he realize how important that single question was? The relationship between the two brothers was so fragile.

Cole felt the impact of Maia's eyes. He swallowed his first

careful answer. He had promised himself he would change the boy's life. He couldn't very well do it from a distance. His leave of absence might turn out to be far longer than he'd anticipated. "I'll stay as long as you need me, Jase. Or want me. It's up to you."

Jase jumped to his feet. "All right then. I won't say anything." His voice was gruff, covering his emotions. "I'm sorry I believed those people, even for a minute."

"I think you were smart to be careful, Jase. After what we've been through, we need to build our relationship on solid ground."

Jase nodded and practically ran from the room.

Maia guessed he was close to tears. "I'm sorry," she said. "I didn't mean to intrude on such a personal moment with Jase. I couldn't figure out a way to leave gracefully in the middle of it all. I won't say anything about your life to anyone."

"I never thought you would." And he hadn't. That was the strange part. It never once occurred to him she might reveal the truth about what he did. And did that mean he trusted her? Cole turned away from her to stare out the window at the driving snow. "We have a problem here, Doc. More than one, and I'm going to need your help."

"You don't think the ice got there naturally, do you?" Maia said shrewdly.

"No I don't. And I don't think a ghost is running around the ranch turning on hoses and arranging accidents with the horses."

She studied his face. He wore an expressionless mask, but there was something frightening about the expression in his eyes. "It's Jase, isn't it? You're worried about him."

Cole glanced toward the door. "Yeah, I'm worried."

Maia sighed. "It was definitely a human driving Wally through the fence."

He spun around, his gaze sharp as it raked her face. "What makes you so sure?"

She pulled the ice pack away from her head. "If I told you, you'd want me locked up in a little cell. Suffice to say, I just know."

He stalked across the room and crouched down in front of her, his face inches from hers. "Not good enough. Tell me."

Maia pushed at the wall of his chest. "Stop invading my space. I don't know you well enough to tell you. I don't know anyone that well." She couldn't think straight with him so close. He was the most sensual man she'd ever met. His eyes were just so intense, his features etched with need.

"I told you about the DEA."

"You told Jase, not me. I just happened to be in the same room."

"I told *you*. You know damn well I was telling you." He pulled away from her, a flash of irritation on his face. "I don't even know why I wanted you to know, but if I'm going to come unraveled around you, the least you could do is open up a little."

"You aren't asking for a little. You had me investigated before you ever made your big move on me, didn't you?"

"Hell yes. I'd investigate the pope if his life touched Jase's life." He stood up and put the length of the room between them, his eyes alive with the suppressed rage that was always swirling so close when he confronted his own demons.

She stared up at him for a long moment. "You investigated Jase too, didn't you?"

"I'm not about to apologize for it either, Doc. You have no idea what our lives were like." He stopped abruptly, going very still, watching her expression. "Or do you? How do you know things?"

Maia hesitated. She was going to ruin her chances of ever being a permanent veterinarian anywhere if she told him.

"It's important. Do you really know things? Would you know if Jase drove that horse into the fence? Or if I did it?" How could she know?

Maia caught a glimpse of the fear in him, and it all fell into place. He suspected Jase of being like their father. It made sense. "It wasn't Jase. The man was too big." She didn't want to continue, but she couldn't let him think such a monstrous thing.

"How do you know?"

"The animals."

The room went totally silent. Maia shifted deeper into the cushions, trying to avoid seeing the look she knew would be in his eyes. She pressed her fingers into her eyes in an effort to relieve the headache that continued to pound.

Cole studied her face for a long time. "You mean they really do talk to you?" he asked, trying hard to keep skepticism from his voice. She was being serious and waiting for him to scoff at her. Maia Armstrong had secrets; it was there in her eyes, in the way she avoided looking at him, and he intended to find out what they were.

"Not exactly," she hedged. "Look, do we have to do this? Is it really necessary?"

"You know things about me no one else knows. Hell, you know more about the Steele family than most people do. What are you afraid of?"

"I'm a veterinarian, Steele. You think people are going to want some nutcase treating their animals? And that's what they'll call me." She didn't have to tell him anything. She could stare him down, tell him to go to hell, be stubbornly silent. Maia was capable of all of those things. So why was she sitting there like some sacrifice, waiting for the axe to fall?

"No one is here but the two of us." Cole was back in front of her, crouching down, his hand on her knee. His piercing blue eyes caught and held her gaze as if to give her courage. "How do the animals talk to you?" Could it really be possible? There was no getting around the fact that several animals had run out in front of his vehicle as he drove through the blizzard to get to the ranch, and each time she had known they were there before they could actually see them.

Maia shook her head, but couldn't look away from him. There was no escaping Cole Steele and his brother, or their pain, shrieking at her from the depths of their being.

"Telling you the truth about working for the DEA wasn't so bad once I did it. It was actually a relief to tell you the truth. I don't talk about the old man and my childhood, but now you know, and I don't have to worry that somehow I'll slip up and you'll find out things that I've kept hidden away."

"It isn't the same thing, Cole."

"Just say it, Maia. You know I'm going to badger you until you do."

It was the way he said her name. A caress. A silky, satin tone that brushed over her skin and slipped inside of her. Disarmed her. He always called her "Doc" and somehow by using her first name it created an intimacy between them. A trust. "I see their memories. I don't know how, but I've always been able to see things they've seen. The memories come to me in images, very vivid and, most of the time, very distressing."

He caught her chin in his hand, forcing her to look at him. "Why would you be afraid to tell me?"

Maia pulled away from him, shrinking back against the thickly upholstered couch. "Most people would just think I was crazy." She shook her head, her gaze avoiding his. "I know it sounds crazy." Why had she even admitted it? What was wrong with her? She knew better than to say anything. Cole Steele of all people. What was she thinking?

"Tell me what Wally saw."

Maia's gaze jumped to his. Held there. "A young boy dragged from the stable, kicked, beaten around the head and shoulders. Something thin and long hitting the child over and over. The boy screaming. The man was about your height, but thinner. Once he dragged the boy out by his hair. He slapped him repeatedly in the face." She swallowed, rubbed her hand over her face as if to clear away the memories. "The boy was Jase and the abuse didn't just happen once." She pressed her fingertips against her eyelids again as if she could shut out the vision. "I hate that I know these things because there's never anything I can do about it."

Cole's palm curved around the nape of her neck, his fingers massaging the tension out of her. "It never occurred to me that animals would be witnessing crimes."

"Just because they can't talk doesn't mean they don't see things."

Cole turned over her revelation in his mind, over and over. It was a fascinating premise. Could it be true? He had his hand on her, could feel the tension running through her body. She was waiting for him to scoff at her, yet the idea that she could really "see" memories of an animal was bizarre. She could easily have guessed the things that had happened to Jase.

"What about the attack on the horse? Who drove him into the fence?"

"A large man, tall with wide shoulders. It couldn't have been Jase. He's small and thin, and Wally likes him."

"Tall like me, you mean," Cole said, his voice cool.

"Yes, but Wally likes you too." It sounded so stupid. Utterly ridiculous. Maia shook her head, her face flaming. "I know it sounds weird. Go ahead, tell me I belong in a mental institution."

The pad of his thumb absently stroked her pulse. Each brush sent small tongues of fire licking over her skin. Electricity seemed to leap from his skin to hers. She forced air through her lungs, waiting for him to react. Waiting for his condemnation.

"Who told you that you were crazy?" he asked quietly.

She flinched. She tried not to, but she couldn't prevent her reaction. "Does it matter? It does sound crazy."

"I think so."

She lifted her chin, her turquoise eyes blazing into his. "A man I dated. Another vet. I thought we were close, and he asked me how I managed to figure out what was wrong all the time with wild animals, and I was dumb enough to answer him."

"And he said you were crazy?"

"I don't blame him. Unfortunately, he told everyone at the

clinic, including the pet owners, and I was out of work. That I did blame him for."

Cole leaned in close and brushed his lips, feather-light, over hers. Her heart somersaulted. "He was the idiot, Maia." He pulled back slightly, blinking so that her attention was drawn from his mouth to his lashes. He was so masculine, but for those incredible eyelashes. She wanted to touch his face, to feel his skin. Cole Steele was totally mesmerizing, and she could see why women fell so easily under his spell.

"You're way out of my league, Steele. Sit over there somewhere and stop touching me." She pointed to a chair across the room.

"Am I getting to you?" A ghost of a smile flickered over his mouth for the briefest of moments.

Maia's heart stuttered in reaction. She'd never seen him smile, and she couldn't actually call the curve to his lips a smile, it hadn't lit his blue eyes, but it was enough for her to know if he ever did, she would melt. "Yes."

Cole didn't move, his gaze going hot as it moved over her face, focusing on her mouth. "It's about time."

"Stop that." His mouth was only a scant few inches from hers. She could feel the warmth of his breath. His body leaned into hers, his chest bumped against her knees. His palm was still curled around the nape of her neck, and his thumb swept over her jaw. Her stomach tightened. "You're dangerous." Her voice came out in a whisper. An ache.

"I thought I was, but I've changed my mind." His lips brushed a second time over hers. Teasing. A caress that wasn't quite a caress. "I've decided you're the dangerous one. I tell myself to stay away from you, but I just can't seem to do it." His lips tempted hers again. Firming. Coaxing. His tongue stroked across the seam of her mouth. His teeth tugged on her lower lip.

Maia gasped and let him in. Let him stake his claim. His mouth pressed firmly against her, hot and moist and all too expert. Somehow he wedged his body between her legs, pulling her close, his arms strong as they wrapped around her. Her body went boneless, the heat leaping like a wildfire between them.

His fingers snagged in her hair and she yelped. They pulled apart, staring at one another, Maia gulping for air. His fingertips moved gently over her scalp. "I'm sorry, I got carried away."

"I'll say you did!" Jase's voice was stern.

Cole turned to find the boy leaning his hip against the doorway, his arms across his chest, a frown on his face.

"Would either of you like to tell me what's going on?" Jase asked straight-faced, effectively reducing his older brother to a teenager caught necking.

"I'd rather not," Maia said, trying not to laugh.

"I have absolutely no idea what's going on," Cole admitted. "But, whatever it is, it's her fault." He couldn't stop looking at her, mesmerized by the warm laughter in her eyes, the curve of her mouth. She hadn't lived a perfect life, he had felt the sadness, the wariness in her when she talked about the strange ability she had of reading images in the minds of animals, yet she still found joy in life. She made him want to laugh with her. He wasn't certain he was capable of laughter, but he felt himself wanting to be.

"Hey now, don't you go blaming anything on me," Maia objected. "Honestly, Jase. He started it." She rubbed her mouth. "At least I think he did, I can't remember now. But he's such a flirt."

"He said he doesn't have to smile at women," Jase reported. He was trying desperately to make up for the accusations he'd leveled at his brother earlier. Unsure of himself, he followed Maia's lead, teasing Cole.

Maia's eyebrow shot up. Cole sank back on his knees, groaning aloud. "Jase. That was a brotherly confidence you weren't supposed to share." He looked at Maia. "We're still trying to get the hang of being brothers. Neither of us knows a lot about it yet, but I'm certain that was confidential."

"Brotherly advice?" Maia asked.

"Something like that," Cole admitted.

Maia shook her head. "Don't listen to him, Jase. Women like men to smile once in a while. They can only take brooding hunks for so long, then they get bored."

"You didn't look bored to me," Jase pointed out, abruptly switching sides.

Maia laughed again, and the sound wound itself around Cole's heart and warmed his insides.

"*And,*" Jase added, "it's rather sickening to hear my brother referred to as a hunk."

"She did call me that, didn't she?" Cole said with evident satisfaction.

"No one said you weren't a hunk." Maia's blue-green eyes darkened as her gaze drifted over him with deliberate inspection. "But just because I noticed that you were hot doesn't mean I liked you kissing me."

Jase snorted. "She liked it."

Cole nodded. "Yeah, I know."

"So did you." Jase grinned at him mischievously.

"Way too much. The doc is one of those dangerous women your elders are always going to be warning you about."

Maia shoved at Cole with her foot. "I love the way you manage to turn the tables on me. I'm injured here. You're supposed to be soothing me, not stirring things up."

Cole raised his eyebrow at her, his eyes going dark. "I don't think I'll touch that." He went back up on his knees to examine the back of her head. "The ice seems to have done its job and stopped the bleeding and the swelling."

"Well, good thing, since you weren't paying attention," Maia scolded.

"I had better things to do." Ignoring her wince, he pushed the matted hair from the cut. "I don't think it needs stitches."

Maia jerked her head away. "Since I'm the only one capable of stitching anything, I should say not."

"I can stitch a wound if I have to. I sewed up my arm once," Cole said.

Jase and Maia exchanged a long frown. Maia wrinkled her nose. "Don't tell us anything else. I'm going to have night-mares."

"I ran into a guard down in Colombia. He had a big knife. He wasn't supposed to be there, and I got careless."

Maia reached out and pushed up the sleeve of Cole's shirt to reveal a jagged scar about three inches long. "You aren't mak-ing it up."

"I don't make things up." Cole got to his feet with a sigh of regret. It was time for all of them to return to the real world. "Jase, did you and Al go riding the other day? The day Wally was injured?"

Jase shook his head. "No, the hands took care of the cattle, and Al stayed with me working around the ranch house. We saw the fence over by the corrals leaning and we repaired that. I nearly fell actually, but Al caught me before I went down the hill. The post was rotten or something and gave way. I discov-ered Wally a couple of hours later when I came back to the ranch house to put away the tools. I called Al, and he came right away."

Cole sighed. Someone had taken the horse out earlier. Ei-ther Jase was lying to him or something he didn't understand was going on. "I didn't like the look of the walkway this morn-ing, Jase. It's too much of a coincidence to have the horse in-jured and the walkway iced and the fence post give way when you leaned against it. I don't like any of it."

"What are you saying?" Jase asked.

Maia could see the fear creeping back into the boy's eyes and it saddened her. For a few minutes, he had been a normal teenager, teasing an older brother.

"I'm just saying we're stuck here until this series of storms passes, and I want you to be careful," Cole said. "We should stick together when we go outside."

"Cole, who else is on the ranch? You told me no one was here other than the three of us," Maia said. "Is it possible you're being . . ." She broke off when his gaze swept over her face. The dark hunger was gone. His eyes were back to ice-cold, piercing blue.

"Paranoid? Maybe. But it's how I stay alive. I don't know what's happening, and until I do I just want to err on the side of caution." He stood beside Jase, clapping a hand briefly on his shoulder. "That doesn't mean we can't have fun, or do the Christmas thing, it just means we stick closer together if we go outside. We can share the work and keep an eye on the doc when she's looking at the horse for us."

"I came down here to tell the doc that my mother's things are in the attic," Jase said. "There's a chest up there that might have a few Christmas ornaments in it."

Cole glanced at Maia's face, trying to get something from her. He wasn't certain what it was. Reassurance maybe. Courage. The thought of decorating the house turned his stomach.

"I'd love to see some of your mother's things, Jase," Maia said with her usual warmth. Her gaze was on Cole, watching his face closely, reading too much.

He presented a stone carving to the world, a man invincible, one who had no fear, yet she seemed to see through the barrier between him and the rest of the world. The one woman he wanted to impress. The only woman who got under his skin and threatened to turn his carefully ordered world upside down was the one who saw him vulnerable.

Maia sighed. "Jase, you ever notice Cole can look scary?"

"I told him he did," Jase said, with a triumphant grin toward Cole. "Just last week I told him that."

"He does it when he's losing a battle."

Cole raised an eyebrow. "I don't lose battles. Don't be telling the boy a thing like that." A part of Cole stood off to the side, observing the banter, the way Maia seemed to be able to bring them all together when there was always such a distance between him and everyone else. A distance between Jase and everyone else. He wished he knew how she did it.

No one had ever teased him before. Even his coworkers refrained from venturing into personal territory with him, but

Maia had no problem giving him a bad time. He reached out, tucked a stray strand of hair behind her ear before he could stop himself. He wanted to touch her, to feel her skin. He ached for her. Cole pulled himself up short. He was beginning to want more than her body. He found himself looking for her smile, listening for her laughter, watching the expressions chase across her face.

Jase's rude snort of derision dragged him from his thoughts. "You've got it bad, Cole. You're a goner."

Cole couldn't take exception when he heard the laughter in the boy's voice. It was genuine and even affectionate. Maia had managed to put it there somehow. He turned away from both of them, a lump in his throat. "I'm denying everything," he managed to get out. His voice was husky, and he knew if he looked at her, Maia would have a small knowing smile on her face.

"What are we going to do with the doc?" Jase asked.

"She can just sit there holding the ice pack, and we'll go up to the attic and get this box you want. I finished feeding the horses before I came in. Al's got the cattle under shelter with plenty of feed, so we're good for a few hours. We may as well start figuring out what we're supposed to do about Christmas."

Maia's laughter came again. "You sound like a man about to be hung. Christmas is *fun*, Steele, not a funeral. Jase, the man has such an Eeyore attitude."

Cole swung around. "*Eeyore*? You just called me *Eeyore*."

Jase burst out laughing, joining Maia. The sound drifted through the ranch house, dispelling the cold, barren feeling and replacing it with a warmth that had never been there before.

8

COLE DUSTED OFF the box before he brought it down to Maia. Jase had obviously managed to remove things he'd treasured and conceal them before his father could throw them out. It said a lot about the boy's courage. He'd only been ten when his mother had been killed. He must have been terrified to defy his father and gather her things. The housekeeper would have reported it had she seen him, and there were the cameras to avoid, yet the boy had managed to keep a few precious items. As Cole placed the box carefully in front of Maia, he realized his genuine affection for the boy was growing. And that was frightening.

He couldn't warn Maia how much the contents of the box meant to Jase because the teenager was right beside him, anxiously watching his every move. He could only hope she would notice as she seemed so aware of every little nuance involving the boy.

"This is wonderful, Jase," Maia said, warmth and enthusiasm spilling over into the room. "Like discovering a treasure box. How ever did you know it was up there?"

Cole let his breath out. "He managed to put it up there when he was ten, right after he lost his mother."

Maia looked up at the gruff note in Cole's voice. "I'll be very careful going through it, Jase, don't worry." She slipped off the couch and sat tailor fashion on the floor beside the box. "Do you remember what you put in here?"

Jase sank down beside her. "Yeah. I never went up to the attic, although I thought about it a lot, but I was afraid the old man would catch me and throw it all out." He glanced at Cole fearfully as if he might be revealing too much.

"That was smart," Cole said. "If he caught you, there would have been hell to pay. While you're looking over what we have, why don't I fix us something to eat. How's the head feeling, Doc?" He needed her to look at him. He had to know Jase was safe with her, but he had to get out of the room before that box was opened.

His blue gaze met and clung to hers. Maia sat very still, letting the heat in his eyes wash through her. She saw into a part of him he tried so hard to hide. Ravaged. Damaged. A man struggling to overcome his own past in order to save a boy. She didn't want to see it because it only drew her deeper into the lives of the Steeles and she didn't want that. She'd disclosed too much to him already. Kissed him when she should have resisted. She ached for the boy he'd been and the man he'd become. "A bit of a headache, nothing serious," she answered.

Jase watched Cole leave the room. "He says it's okay to celebrate Christmas; I don't think he really wants to."

"Maybe he needs to celebrate it, Jase," Maia said. "He's a grown man, and he's quite capable of deciding what he does and doesn't want to do. If he's given you the go-ahead, then he must want to celebrate the holiday as well. And isn't it about time? Christmas is a special time of year. I love the way it brings everyone together. It's a time for family. Cole never really had a chance to have a family before, but now he has you." Carefully, she began to open the box.

"Do you have a family waiting for you to get home?"

"Not anymore. I was an only child. My parents died when I was sixteen, and I went to live with my grandmother. I lost her a few years ago. No cousins, no aunts or uncles. I'm pretty much it."

"That must be awful for you not to have someone to be with when you love it so much."

Maia smiled at him. "I would prefer to have a huge family, but since I don't, I find ways to celebrate."

"My father hated Christmas," Jase began in a rush. "He was really mean around Christmas, and he forbade us to ever have a tree or presents or decorations. If Mom gave me a present, he threw it away and he . . ." Jase trailed off. "Mom was like you."

"She loved Christmas?" Maia pulled open the flaps of the box, nearly holding her breath, careful not to look at Jase.

"Yeah. She used to sneak me presents, and when we were alone she'd show me the decorations her mother had given her. They'd been in her family a long time. She loved the ornaments and always wanted them on a tree. She used to tell me we'd put them on a tree together someday, but we never did. If she'd tried to do that, my father would have smashed them . . . and her."

Maia took a deep breath and let it out slowly, praying she could come up with the right words for Jase. The pain and horror and guilt of a young boy being the cause of his adored mother being "smashed" by his abusive father were in Jase's voice. Despair and helplessness, love and regret were in his eyes. She was determined to find a way to heal the pain in the boy she was growing so fond of.

"We can do it for her, Jase. This was her house too, wasn't it? We can give it back to her. If you tell me the things she loved, we can redecorate and make it your mother's home the way she wanted it. The way it should have been." Maia leaned toward him. "You asked me how I celebrate. Well, I always do something fun, but I want to do something for someone. Let's do it for your mother."

"But she's dead."

"You think about her every day, don't you?"

Jase nodded.

"Then she'll never be dead. It doesn't matter whether you believe in another life after this one, Jase, only that she's alive through you. She wanted to celebrate Christmas and we can give her this. If you want to do it. As long as you're comfortable with it." Without waiting for an answer, Maia looked into the box. Everything was carefully wrapped in paper. She could tell the tissue was old and that Jase's mother had been the one to preserve many of the items originally. Jase had simply done what his mother had taught him. Several tissue-wrapped items lay on a folded quilt. She lifted the first one out of the box, brought it to her lap, and gently began to unwrap it.

Beside Maia, Jase audibly drew in his breath, his body tensing as she slowly drew back the tissue paper to reveal the treasure it protected. The ornament was beautiful, a shimmering star, platinum and covered with glass sparkles that reflected light from every angle so that it seemed to shine on its own right there in her hand. She held it up.

"I remember that star," Jase said. "She took it out and held it up just like you're doing. She said when she was young her mother always put it near the top of the tree closest to the lights so it would shine all the time."

"Where are we going to get a tree? We might have to improvise," Maia said.

Cole had been listening just outside the entryway, unable to stay away. He sighed, knowing she was drawing him deeper into unknown territory. He moved back into the room to stand in front of her. "We'll manage a tree, Doc. There's bound to be a break or two in between storms."

"You'll really get a tree, Cole? Bring it in the house?" Jase asked.

"Sure. We can put it in front of the window. I doubt if you have enough decorations for a big one, but we can improvise."

Maia put the star carefully to one side and reached for a second ornament. "We'll have fun making ornaments. And I checked out the kitchen. You're certainly not short on food supplies. We can bake all kinds of things and probably cook a traditional Christmas dinner as well."

"I like the sound of that," Jase said. "I'm hungry all the time."

"He's a bottomless pit," Cole confirmed. "We bring in more groceries than we do feed for the stock."

Jase was thin, even for a teenager. Maia could imagine that he was just beginning to trust enough and be confident enough in his relationship with Cole to regain his appetite. She leaned back against the couch as she held up the second ornament. It was an alligator with a red knitted scarf circling the neck. The jaws of the alligator opened and closed when she turned the tip of the tail.

"Why would someone have an alligator hanging on the tree?" Cole asked, taking it from her to examine it closely. "I thought you always had Santa Claus and things like that. This is pretty cool."

"Mom was from Louisiana," Jase reminded. "She used to pretend the alligator was going to bite my finger. She said it was to remind her of home."

"What else is in there?" Cole asked, curious. He had never really looked at any Christmas ornaments before, avoiding the decorated trees in the stores wherever he happened to be when the holiday rolled around. For most of his life he'd told himself it was stupid, hanging things on trees, but the little alligator evoking the memories of Jase's mother seemed different.

Maia handed him the next ornament, a crystal crescent moon with a small baby lying inside the curve of the moon and a little silver star hanging off the tip. It was dated fourteen years earlier. Cole turned it over and over. He looked at Jase. "This is commemorating when you were born. I wish I'd had the chance to meet your mother, Jase."

"Too bad we can't get to town," Maia said, struggling to keep tears from flooding her eyes. She might have lost her family, but when she had one, it had been wonderful. She'd been raised to feel secure and loved by her parents and grandmother. "This will be the first Christmas you're spending together as a family. We could have picked up an ornament celebrating that."

"I would have liked that," Jase said, taking the small crystal moon from Cole.

"The great thing about not having a tradition is, you get to start your own," Maia pointed out.

"We don't need to go to a store," Cole said gruffly. "I can carve an ornament for us. What do you think it should be?"

"Cole's a great wood-carver," Jase said. "You should see

some of the things he's done. Something to do with a horse, Cole. Can you do that?"

"I can come up with something."

"Carve the date into it," Maia advised.

"Dinner's ready if you two want to eat something," Cole said to hide how uncomfortable he was with the way the conversation was going. Have someone take a few shots at him with a gun, and he was on familiar ground, but he was feeling his way with Jase, trying to give his brother a sense of security and home. He couldn't believe he'd opened his mouth and offered to carve a Christmas ornament.

He shoved his hands through his hair in sudden agitation. He didn't even know what a home was. Who was he kidding? He was beginning to sweat just thinking about night coming. They'd arisen late after staying up taking care of the horse, and now the afternoon was waning. He glanced out the window. The snow was coming down endlessly, large flakes that held them prisoner at the ranch. He hated the place. How could bringing in a tree and hanging a few ornaments change that?

Maia set the ornaments back in the box. "After dinner we should build a fire," she said, indicating the huge stone fireplace that was a showpiece along the center of one wall.

Jase drew in his breath audibly, his shoulders stiffening and his face paling.

Cole stood up. "I don't think there's ever been a fire in the fireplace." He reached down and with his casual strength, pulled her up. He drew her body close to his, bending over her to examine the back of her head. "You have quite a bump there."

"And a headache, but it will go away." She knew better than to look up at him with his face so close to hers, but the temptation was too much. Her gaze met his. His eyes had once again darkened. She put her hand on his chest to keep a few inches between her and the heat of his body. Just for protection. If she knew any incantations for self-defense, she would have been chanting them. "What's the use of having a fireplace if you never light a fire?"

Cole exchanged a long look with Jase, even as his hand came up to capture Maia's. To press her palm tighter against his heart. "Good question."

"You think we should try to light a fire?" Jase was breathing too fast, almost gasping for air. He actually looked scared, searching the living room as if someone might have heard them talking.

"Calm down," Cole said gently. "You're starting to wheeze. He's dead, Jase. Keep telling yourself that. This is our house now, and we can have a damned fire in the fireplace if we want to have one." He allowed Maia to escape him. "You're right. We have a ghost in the house, and I want him gone."

Jase slowed his breathing, following Cole's direction until the wheezing was gone. "All right, we'll light the fire."

Maia followed them into the kitchen. Cole swept his arm briefly around Jase's shoulders. It was momentary, but he'd done it obviously without thinking about it and that pleased her. "I'm sorry if I'm stepping on everyone here," she said. "I'm not trying to push anything on the two of you. You're both obviously uncomfortable with having a fire. We don't need one. Please don't change everything for me. It's your home, do whatever makes you comfortable."

"Our father liked to brand things," Cole said. "Including people."

Maia winced at the grim tone. She stared in horror first at Cole, then Jase. "No way." She felt sick, actually sick.

The brothers nodded.

How did anyone survive such a childhood? Who was she to tell them how to get over it? Horrified at the things she'd said to Cole, she gripped the back of a chair, her knuckles white. "Please don't feel like you have to celebrate Christmas for me. Is that what you're doing?"

Jase shook his head adamantly. "No, I want to celebrate it for my mother. I thought a lot about what you said. She loved this house. He wouldn't let her have any of the things she wanted in it, but she would tell me what she'd put in spots if she had her way. She wanted cream-colored drapes in the library. She said they'd look great with the wood."

"Cream-colored drapes? I guess we're going to change the drapes." Cole raised his eyebrows at Maia. "You know anything about drapes?"

She laughed just like he knew she would. "Don't panic. We're grown-up. We can figure out how to fit drapes." Maia didn't feel like laughing, but Cole was trying to bring back levity for Jase's sake, and she was more than willing to help him.

Cole knew he could get used to the way the house felt with her in it. Jase set the table, and Cole pulled a chair around for Maia. "Sit down. You're looking a little pale. I'll see to the horse tonight. Maybe you should have let me put a couple of stitches in that cut on your head."

"I don't think so." She glared at him. "You come near me with a needle, and you'll find out how mean I can be."

Jase snorted. "You're a baby, Doc."

"Oh, like you'd let him sew up your head! I'd wind up looking like Frankenstein's mother."

Jase grinned at Cole. "She'd make a great monster, don't you think?"

"Great, just like *The Nightmare Before Christmas*. I'm Sally."

Jase and Cole exchanged a puzzled look. Both shrugged, nearly at exactly the same moment.

Maia groaned. "Don't tell me you're both so deprived you never saw that movie? Good grief. Live a little. Rent it. I'll even spring for it."

"Yeah, she says that now with the snow coming down, but once the roads are clear, she's going to renege," Cole said. "Eat your steak."

"I don't eat meat, but the salad's wonderful," Maia said politely.

Jase took one look at Cole's face and burst out laughing. "I wish I had a camera."

"And why don't you eat meat?"

Maia made a face at him. "I told you why."

"I guess I could understand if animals talk to you all the time," Cole teased.

The tone was gruff, but Maia was pleased he'd actually managed to say something to kid her. She tried to keep a stern face, but she knew her eyes gave her away every time. When she wanted to laugh, it always showed.

"You wouldn't want to eat your clients," Jase added.

"Oh you two are a laugh a minute," Maia said. "You should take your little comedy act out on the road."

"She's getting grouchy. Must be the headache. Women, by the way"—Cole leaned across the table toward Jase, to impart his wisdom in a conspirator's overloud whisper—"get headaches a lot."

Jase's grin widened.

Maia lifted an eyebrow. "Really? I wouldn't have thought you'd get that reaction, Steele, but now that I've spent time with you, I can see it."

Jase nearly fell off his chair laughing, so much so that Cole rolled up a newspaper and smacked him over the head.

"It's not that funny, little bro."

"If I'm little, what's Maia? I'm taller than she is."

"Everything is taller than Maia."

Maia managed an indignant glare. "I'm not short. I happen to be the perfect height. Sheesh, not everyone has to be a moose."

"Now she's calling you a moose," Jase said. He was laughing so hard he was beginning to wheeze.

Cole reached out and put a calming hand on his shoulder. "She's going to kick off an asthma attack if you're not careful, and she'll be chasing you around the house with that needle she uses on the horse. Take a breath, Jase. Use your inhaler if you have to."

Although he was automatically breathing slow, deep breaths to aid his younger brother, Cole was watching Maia as well. She was clearly becoming distracted, trying to stay in the conversation, but bothered by something he couldn't hear or see.

"What is it, Doc?"

The smile faded from her face, and she turned her head toward the kitchen door. "Do you have a patio out there, a shelter?"

"Of course. Everything is connected by walkways to the house," Cole said. "That way, when it snows, there's no way to get lost."

Maia stood up, pushing back her chair. "I'll be right back."

Jase was startled out of his wheezing when she left the room. "What's she up to, Cole?"

"Lord only knows," Cole said, but he glanced toward the kitchen door. The sound of the wind and tree branches hitting the house could be heard, but nothing else.

"I like having her here," Jase confided.

"So do I." Cole realized it was true. He never spent so much time in anyone's company. Jase had been the first real commitment he'd made outside of his job. Maia brightened the house, brought warmth and laughter and a sense of home. His heart lurched at the idea. "Do you think any woman would make this place feel the way she makes it, or just the doc?" He kept his voice very neutral but found his stomach was tied up in knots. The kid mattered to him, even his opinion mattered, and that realization was almost as shocking.

Jase shook his head. "It's definitely the doc. I like her a lot, Cole."

Cole crumpled his napkin and threw it on the table. "Yeah, I do too."

Jase frowned. "You don't sound too happy about it."

"Would you be? Hell, look at us, Jase. We're about as dysfunctional as two men could get. You think the doc is going to be looking at me. I can't even make up my mind if I want her to." He shoved his chair back.

"She kissed you," Jase pointed out. "Do you think she kisses everyone?"

Cole's entire body tensed, every muscle contracting. The

knots in his belly hardened into lethal lumps. "She'd better not be kissing everyone," Cole said. There was enough of an edge to his voice that Jase looked wary.

"Are you angry, Cole?"

"I just don't trust anything I don't understand, Jase. I don't altogether understand the doc or how she makes me feel." Telling the kid the truth wasn't as easy as he thought it would be when he'd first made the promise to himself. He hadn't counted on meeting Maia Armstrong and feeling so intensely about her.

"Well, talk nice to her," Jase advised. "Otherwise, you'll scare her off."

"Scare whom off?" Maia asked as she came back into the room carrying her small bag. She was dressed in a thick coat and mittens. "If you're talking about me, Jase, your brother doesn't scare me. He's all growl and no bite."

"Where the hell do you think you're going?"

Jase groaned and shook his head, covering his face with his hands. "Do you ever listen? Even I know you can't talk to women like that."

"Thank you, Jase," Maia said. "You know, Cole, if you took a few lessons from your younger brother, you might develop a certain charm."

"Just answer me."

Maia sighed, color washing into her face. "I have to make a call."

"A call? What the hell?"

"You already said that. Didn't he say that, Jase? Yes, a call. I heard an animal, and I'm going to go see what's wrong."

"I didn't hear anything," Jase said, frowning slightly.

Cole ignored his younger brother, his gaze holding Maia to him. "Didn't you pay any attention to me saying I wanted everyone to stick together when we went outside?"

Maia winced a little at his sharp tone. "Yes, of course I did." Truthfully the moment she heard the call of an animal in distress she hadn't thought of anything else. "I'm just going out onto the patio. You can come if you want, but you'll have to stay quiet."

His blue eyes slashed her as she gave the order, but she didn't look away, staring right back at him, refusing to be intimidated.

Jase jumped up with determination. "I'm coming too."

"You just don't want to do the dishes," Cole said.

The two grabbed jackets and gloves from the rack just outside the door in the small mudroom as they followed Maia out. Cole hung back watching as she stood on the large covered patio looking out into the snow. She didn't call out, and he heard nothing, but she suddenly turned her head toward the north and stepped off the patio into the snow. He moved quickly, catching her arm.

"Maia, call whatever it is to you. You can't go out into this. Jase and I will hang back out of the way, but you stay under cover."

The storm had let up some, but it had dropped several feet of snow, and with the next serious storm approaching fast, he didn't want to take any chances.

"I'm not sure it will come to me with the two of you so close," she said.

"At least try."

She hesitated a moment, glanced at Jase, then complied, whistling softly as if calling a dog. The sound of the wind answered her. Snowflakes fell in a continuous soft drift, muffling sounds of the night.

"I'm going to have to go out to it," she persisted.

Cole retained possession of her arm. Something was moving just outside his range of vision, the fall of snow nearly obscuring it. "Stay here. I want you where I can see you at all times." He whispered it, straining to see beyond the veil of white.

Beneath his fingers, Maia suddenly tensed and stepped away from him, moving to the very edge of the patio. "She's coming in."

Cole felt the hairs on his body raise. He moved closer to Jase, shifting his body to place himself between the unknown and his brother. What he wanted to do was drag Maia back into the safety of the house. While the snow was white and seemed to sparkle everywhere, the clouds were dark and ominous with the continuing threat of the blizzard. He didn't know if that was what triggered his protective instincts or whether it was sheer self-preservation, but his warning radar was shrieking.

The mountain lion emerged out of the snowdrift, covered in flakes, ears flat, eyes alert and watchful. The yellow-green gaze settled not on Maia, but on the Steele brothers.

"Maia." Cole reached out and caught the back of her coat, giving it a small tug to try to bring her to him. "Jase, back into the house. Come on, Maia. This is dangerous."

"No," Maia kept her tone low and almost crooning. "She's coming to us. She's feeling threatened, and any movement on your part will have her running away. Just stay calm and don't move." As she spoke, Maia knelt and patted the patio beside her.

Nearly belly to the ground, the cat inched its way to her, using a freeze-frame stalking motion, never taking its gaze from the men. The cat crouched rather than stretched out, presenting its left side to the veterinarian, but obviously ready to spring away quickly should there be need. Maia put her hand on the cat's back, fingers sliding into the rich fur.

Cole pressed one hand to his heart and slid the other down to his calf, where his gun was stashed.

Maia allowed the images from the mountain lion to crowd into her mind. Something moving through the air, nearly over the top of her. A loud noise that had the cat snarling. Men and horses. The scent of man invading her territory. The sting in her side that spread pain through her body and slowed her down, accompanied by the sound of the rifle.

"She's been shot," she said quietly.

9

MAIA TOOK A deep slow breath. "It isn't as if I can keep her from going against her natural instincts. If you are going to watch this, please don't turn your back on her and don't stare directly into her eyes. I sometimes look them in the eyes, but I have some strange affinity for wild animals." She kept her voice crooning, as if talking to the cat.

"The wound is in her shoulder which is a good thing. I'm going to give her both Rompom and Ketamine to knock her out. Jase, it's always much harder with exotics, particularly large cats. Normally you have to dart them, and the problem is, they are very hard to dart down because there is no set dosage even if they're the same age and height, the normal criteria for dosing an animal or even a human. It's different with them because their adrenaline is pumping very fast. It's rare to take a large cat down with one dart." As she spoke she was preparing the shot.

"Maia." Cole didn't like her in such close proximity, yet she was moving with confidence.

"Please don't talk. This is very hard on her. She trusts me, but not you. You have to look at the body language of a cat to know what's going on inside of them." She set the dose of Ketamine aside and withdrew a second syringe. "This is yohimbe, Jase. You *always* have it ready when you're working with exotics. The danger is, they'll fight the drug until they finally drop, but then, as they relax, they can go into cardiac arrest. I think she'll be fine, she isn't fighting it, but we have to be ready. Yohimbe reverses the Ketamine. I'm giving the injection in the muscle and it will sting, so expect a reaction and don't move. Once she's out, you can get close to her."

Cole kept the gun hidden along his thigh. His heart was pounding in fear, and his mouth was dry, not for himself, or even Jase, but because the sight of Maia so close to the wild animal was terrifying.

Maia caught the head of the cat in her hands and leaned forward nose to nose, her face inches from the cat's teeth. She seemed to exchange breath with the animal, obviously communicating in some way, but Cole's fingers tightened around the gun. It took a tremendous effort to keep from aiming it at the animal. Maia put her hand on the cat's heart as if matching her own heartbeat with the mountain lion.

Maia pulled back to pick up the syringe. The cat yowled as she administered it. "I know, baby," she said softly, "it stings, doesn't it? Just go with it and get sleepy for me." She glanced over her shoulder. "I need to work fast, this won't keep her under for long."

"Can we help?" Cole asked, shoving the gun back into his holster.

"Remember how I mixed the Betadine and saline? You can do that while I give her fluid. It's going to balloon up at the site, Jase, but the lump will dissipate as the fluid is absorbed in the cat's body. I'm giving her a sub queue of lactated Ringer's solution for dehydration. It's hard to find a vein on the big cats, but they absorb liquid under the skin. I'm putting in the fluids right here in this area."

"Do you want me to put this in a syringe like we did for the horse?" Jase asked. He crouched quite close to Maia, almost nudging her out of the way.

"Yes. Use it to flush the wound site. The wound is on the trapezoid muscle, but it looks like the bullet just sliced it rather than penetrated." Maia turned her head toward Jase.

Cole could see they were nearly nose to nose. For some reason it put a lump in his throat. Something deep inside him shifted. Moved. Melted. He saw his young half brother, so starved for love and attention, turning to Maia. She seemed so willing to give the boy the things he needed. It came naturally to her. She imparted knowledge casually, and Jase soaked it up.

"You lavage it, and I'll debride the area. We want it sterile, just like with Wally."

"She's so big," Jase observed. "I've never seen a mountain lion other than in pictures before." There was awe in Jase's voice. Unable to help himself, just as curious as Jase, Cole crowded closer to see what they were doing.

"They're solitary animals, Jase," Maia explained. "The females are smaller than the males. This one probably weighs in around ninety-five pounds and most are somewhere between seventy-five to one hundred and twenty-five pounds, so she's average and healthy. A female will keep her cubs with her about a year to a year and a half. This one is still young, maybe two years old."

"Can I touch her?" Jase was already reaching out, his expression lit up with excitement. Cole had never seen him as fascinated or intrigued with anything. The boy moved even closer, actually bending over Maia to peer at what she was doing. She didn't seem to mind in the least, showing him what she was doing next.

"Sure, it's safe. She's out. Her eyes are open, but she's out." Maia squeezed ointment into the cat's eyes to prevent them from drying out. "She can't blink like this, so we have to do it for her."

"I've heard them scream before," Jase said. "It was like something out of a scary movie."

"Mountain lions purr, rather than roar like the other big cats do, and yes, they have a phenomenal scream," Maia said, guiding Jase's hand along the cat's back.

Cole watched the way her hands moved through the mountain lion's fur. He tasted envy in his mouth. Need. How did he become a part of such a thing?

Maia glanced at Cole over her shoulder. "You don't hunt them on this ranch, do you?"

"It's legal here in Wyoming," he said. His voice was strangling around the lump in his throat. "But since I've been here we certainly don't hunt them, and we wouldn't unless they went after our horses or cattle. Most stay in the high country." Forcing his mind to concentrate on details, he studied the cat, trying to determine, from the lacerated muscle, the angle the shooter had shot from. "How old is that wound?"

"It's fresh. Maybe twenty-four hours, a little longer, but not by much. Damn hunters. It makes me so mad, they wound an animal and leave it to suffer."

"You're saying she was shot on this ranch yesterday or the day before?" Cole's body touched hers, as he bent over her to get a closer look at the wound.

Maia glanced at him, recognizing the edge in his voice, the sudden alert interest. "She definitely was shot somewhere on the ranch."

"There was no one here but Al and me," Jase said. "I didn't hear a shot."

"It was probably miles from the ranch house," Cole said.

"I'm going to give her an injection of antibiotics, then we'll put them in her food and try to keep her here over the next few days," Maia deliberately changed the subject when she realized Jase was becoming agitated. She sent Cole a warning glance.

Cole shook his head. "Maia, this is a working ranch. You have any idea how dangerous that is? If you feed her, and you'll have to, she might want to come around here. And then we're going to have to shoot her anyway."

"I'll make certain she knows to stay in the high country."

He stepped even closer. "Fine. If I have to have it here, I want to pet it too." He felt stupid asking, but it was the chance of a lifetime. There was breathtaking beauty in the animal and a sense of raw power. The moment his fingers sank into the fur, he felt connected to it, and in some strange way, the mountain lion solidified his connection to Jase and Maia. He dropped his other hand on Maia's shoulder, needing to touch her as he took the unique opportunity to get close to a live mountain lion. Jase beamed at him. They exchanged a small grin. Maia was magic and mystery, and it was becoming difficult for Cole to focus his mind on anything else.

Maia's hand covered Cole's as he petted the cat's deep fur.

"Amazing. I've never had an experience like this." There was wonder in his voice, a boyish excitement, much like Jase's, yet there was that underlying dark sensuality he couldn't suppress. Seeing Maia with the cat, getting so close with Jase, just being herself seemed to bring it out in him.

Reluctantly, Maia pulled her hand away to reach for the needle. She had to avoid looking at Cole. Sharing the experience with him was a fantasy she'd always kept secret, sharing her love of exotic cats with a man she . . . Abruptly she pulled her mind away from the thought. "I'm suturing the wound, Jase," Maia continued. "If it were any older, there would be too much bacteria in it, but I'll leave a drain and use dissolving sutures. Hopefully we can keep as much air getting to it as possible."

"How'd you learn all this?" Jase asked eagerly. "This is what I want to do."

"I specialized in exotics as well as smaller animals. I actually interned in both Africa and Indochina," Maia said. "I may go back to specializing, but for the time being, the mobile clinic works for me."

Jase looked up at his brother, a grin on his face. "I know I could do this, Cole."

"I know you could too, Jase," Cole encouraged. Because Jase was so excited, the boy didn't even notice he was shaking with cold.

"Large cats can't be treated lightly, Jase," Maia said as she worked. "You always have to be aware that they are wild creatures, even the 'domesticated exotics.' You have to pay attention to body language all the time. And you have to be aware of what 'zone' they're in. I have a five-zone gauge I use to determine the risks of working with a wild animal. Things like bad weather, such as we have now, high winds, tornadoes, and such will drop them into the zone, and we're very much at risk. As she comes out from under the ketamine she'll be at her most dangerous because she'll be dopey and fearful. We don't want to be around for that."

"Where do you want to put her, Doc?" Cole asked, trying to be practical, trying to find a way to help, to be a part of what she was.

"Somewhere she'll be safe out of the storm and fairly warm, where I can easily check on her and feed her."

"We have the toolshed," Jase said. "It has heating coils in the floor although we never use them. We could lock her in there."

"You two get it ready while I finish up here. I wish I had a Fentanyl patch for pain, that would be the best, but I don't carry that with me. I'll have to use a combination of morphine and Valium instead. Hurry, she's going to start waking up, and she won't be a happy kitty."

Cole frowned. "I don't like you carrying any of those drugs around with you. It's too dangerous." He couldn't resist petting the cat a second time.

Jase and Maia exchanged a quick grin behind Cole's back, Maia rolling her eyes at his warning. She made no comment, knowing it was useless to argue with his protective bristling. She was a vet and needed the drugs. "Any ideas on how we're going to move her?" she asked.

"I can carry her," Cole said. "But she'd better not wake up and bite my face off."

"She won't. Let's go then. Is it far?"

"No. We'll use the main walkway, then have to use the cable to get to the shed, but it's only a few feet." Cole hesitated as he crouched beside the big mountain lion. "You're sure she's under?"

Maia took one last listen to the cat's heart and lungs. "Yes, let's go."

Cole would be lifting a deadweight and trudging a distance,

part of it in deep snow. Maia didn't have to like it, but she couldn't think of any other way to transport the animal.

Using the covered walkway was easy enough, but Cole struggled a bit in the deep snow. Jase hurried ahead to get the shed ready and to kick on the heating coils. He snagged a couple of blankets from the barn and came running back with them as Cole staggered through the door.

"I feel her moving," he announced.

"Lay her down," Maia instructed, "and back off. We'll just let her be. You have something for water for her?"

"I have this old bucket," Jase said, and held it up.

"Good, we'll use that then. Come on, she's definitely coming around." Maia backed out and closed the door, leaving the mountain lion to wake up on its own.

She stretched tiredly. "I'm suddenly freezing."

"So is Jase," Cole said. "Let's get back to the house."

Cole stayed behind Maia, crowding her close as she followed Jase through the snow and the walkway back to the patio, where she collected her equipment. They entered the mudroom to remove jackets, mittens, and shoes. "I don't know about encouraging these wild animals to come around. What if that cougar decides Wally's an easy meal?"

"She won't," Maia said, trying to keep her teeth from chattering.

"That's the coolest thing I've ever seen," Jase said.

"I'd prefer you didn't mention it to anyone," Maia said.

"There sure is a lot of cool stuff I can't tell anyone," Jase groused.

She was shivering so much Cole pulled her against the warmth of his body and began to run his hands up and down her arms. "What are we going to feed her?"

"*I'm* going to need ten to fifteen pounds of beef or chicken for her daily. They eat bones and all, and they're *always* hungry. Jase, don't you go near her. She's a wild animal and injured, so she's unpredictable. I'll put her antibiotics in her food."

"What do you know about mountain lions, Cole?" Jase asked. "Do we have a lot of them around here?"

"We have our share, but honestly, I don't know that much about them at all."

"They are the second largest cat in the Western Hemisphere," Maia said, "and they're also the fastest. Unfortunately, they tire easily because their hearts don't match their size. They lose stamina in a long run and generally miss their kill nine out of ten times, which means a lot of hunting for them."

Cole stooped to pull off her boots. "I couldn't believe how powerful the animal felt to me. Just being in its presence was intense."

"Big cats are at the top of the food chain, so they have an 'arrogance' and mantle of power they wear like a second skin." Maia grinned at Cole. "Those of us who are drawn to them are often accused of being the same way."

"Great, are you saying I'm a predator? Or that you are?"

"Maybe parts of you are. You definitely have power, and you know it." Her smile widened. "I know I do."

"I was drawn to it too," Jase reminded, tossing his boots aside. "And I don't have any power at all."

"Sure you do. And there are people who believe animals come to you to give you messages. A mountain lion crossing your path is a sign you have power, and maybe it's time you should learn about yourself, strengthen and sharpen your own powers. That could be the message to you." Maia tried to get across to the boy that if he knew and could read the mountain lion, he could understand Cole and maybe himself a little better.

"Do you believe in that?" Cole asked.

Maia shrugged. "Cats fascinate and repel and inspire fear all at the same time in most people. Because of that, exotics are often labeled as magic or mystical."

"Don't you think people are fearful because they're in the presence of a predator, a natural killer?" Cole asked.

"Sure, subconsciously I'm sure they are, but it's that very energy that attracts people to the cats and gives them the mystique."

Cole opened the door to the kitchen and waved them through. "Does this kind of thing happen to you everywhere you go? Wild animals appearing out of nowhere?"

"Just about," Maia admitted with a small secret smile. She had turned a corner in the restaurant and run right into the Steele brothers. To her, they weren't that much different from the mountain lion. She rubbed at her arms in an effort to get warm. "I think my blood has turned to ice."

"Come on, let's get that fire built," Cole said, pulling her into the living room.

"Jase, would you get the doc a blanket? She's freezing."

Jase hesitated only a moment, clearly not wanting to miss anything, before he hurried off, taking the stairs two at a time.

"Cole." Maia waited until he turned to face her. He knelt in front of the massive fireplace, a log in his hand, his hair spilling across his forehead, and her stomach gave a curious flutter. "You don't have to do that."

"Actually I do. You're right, you know. It's silly not to use a fireplace just because the old man could be cruel. I'm hoping it gives the room a completely different atmosphere. Mostly I'm hoping Jase will like it."

"Someone should have done something about that man." Her voice was tight. She couldn't imagine how Brett Steele had gotten away with his vicious behavior for so long. How could the ranch hands and housekeeper look the other way?

"Someone did." Cole turned back to building a fire.

Maia studied him in silence, rubbing her chin on her knee as she watched him. His movements were all efficient, graceful. There were sharp edges to Cole's personality but none to his physical movements. He reminded her of the mountain lion, moving with fluid, sure strength. She loved just looking at him.

Jase hurried in with a down comforter she recognized from

her bed. He tucked it around her, flicking a quick glance at the fireplace. Flames crackled brightly, casting shadows on the wall and window. Outside the glass, the light flickered across the snow so that flames leapt and sparkled in a strange, beautiful illusion. "Wow. Did you know it did that?"

Cole sat back staring out the glass at the phenomenon. "No. The architect must have designed it that way." He scooted back until his back was pressed against the couch, close to Maia's legs. "It is amazing."

"Breathtaking," Maia agreed. "You know, we could easily cut some branches and make a wreath for the fireplace and door. That would bring in the smell of Christmas. I looked in the freezer, and there is a turkey. If we take it out now, we could thaw it in the refrigerator and cook it."

"You're planning on cooking it, right?" Jase said. "Because the thought of Cole cooking a turkey is scary."

"What exactly do you do in the kitchen, Steele?" Maia asked.

"He set off the smoke alarms three times already," Jase said. "And the food . . ."

Cole moved so fast he seemed a blur, dragging Jase to the floor in a wrestling move. Jase stiffened, letting out a squeak of terror in spite of the fact that Cole cushioned his fall. Cole froze. Maia launched herself from the couch, blanket and all, landing on Cole's back. "Jase, pin him! Pin him! You've got to get him in a headlock!"

"No fair double-teaming me," Cole protested, reaching up to hook Maia around the waist. "You're on time-out with that scalp wound."

"You're just afraid," Maia taunted. "You don't want to get beat up by a woman."

Cole rolled her in the comforter, careful not to flip Jase off him when the teenager did his best to put him in a headlock and hang on as Cole wrestled with Maia. She was like an eel and believed in using her skills, even in playing. She had no intention of surrendering easily, and what had started out as aid to Jase in learning to play turned into a challenge. She called out instructions to the boy, and he readily threw himself into the game, trying to get a lock on Cole's legs to prevent him from getting leverage.

Maia laughed so hard she couldn't get a good grip on Cole and found herself lying on her back, staring up into his blue eyes. Jase slipped off Cole's back to land beside her, laughing with her. Cole stretched across the two of them. "Consider yourselves officially pinned."

"You cheated," Maia accused. She turned her head to laugh with Jase. "He tickled me. In wrestling, there's no tickling."

"I had to end it fast. You shouldn't be playing around with your head banged up." Cole tried to use his toughest voice, but Jase and Maia only laughed harder, shoving at him, their eyes bright with fun. He found himself lying in a heap on the floor, his arms around the two of them with something hard deep inside of him slowly melting away. It had started when he saw Maia and Jase together with the mountain lion and now, playing in the living room with them, a dam seemed to be bursting inside of him. It was a frightening feeling, one he wasn't ready for.

"My head's just fine. It was just a little cut."

"Still, it's better for you to take it easy for a few days." His voice was gruff.

Maia's fingers tangled in his hair, and he felt a surge of electricity rushing from her to him. His body reacted, and he immediately slid away from the two of them. What had possessed him to start a game of wrestling with Jase? He sat back, eyeing Maia as if she were some kind of sorceress. He knew he was looking wild and crazy but he couldn't help it. She destroyed his control.

"What is it, Cole?" She sat up too, pushing her tumbling hair out of her eyes and looking up at him with concern. "Did I hurt you?"

"Not yet," he said before he could censor himself.

Jase sat up slowly, looking from his older brother to Maia, his smile widening as he did so.

Cole glared at him. "Don't say a word."

Jase held up both hands. "I wasn't going to say a word." He exchanged a slow smile with Maia before turning his attention to his mother's treasures.

For the next hour they examined the contents of the box, putting the ornaments aside and unfolding the obviously old quilt.

Maia took a shower and washed her hair, coming down once more dressed in Jase's clothes. They checked the horses together in the evening, and Maia frowned a bit over Wally, concerned he might be getting an infection. When she went to feed and water the mountain lion, Cole insisted on standing by with a gun. He had long since sent Jase to bed and stood guard over her by himself.

As they walked back to the house he shook his head. "This is crazy, Maia, you know that don't you? Having a mountain lion locked up in the toolshed on a horse and cattle ranch. We'll have to watch Jase every minute. He's likely to try to sneak another peek at that animal."

"She's trying to be good. She wants to leave," Maia admitted, "but she'll stay a couple of days. I'd like a good seven days with her before she takes off, but I'm not going to get it."

"They really talk to you?" He pushed open the door for her and waited while she hung up her jacket and pulled off her boots. "Because after watching you with that animal, I think I'm ready to believe anything."

"It's not actually talking. More like images."

"You're frowning."

"It's just that I'm very concerned about what the animals keep showing me." Maia was reluctant to admit it for obvious reasons. "I feel silly telling you, but if I don't, and something happens, I'd blame myself." She sighed and moved away from him to go into the kitchen. The making of tea was a soothing ritual, and in any case, she needed to take the turkey from the freezer. "You already know I pick up images from animals, so there's no reason to pretend it isn't happening."

Cole followed, aware it was difficult for her. "I'd like to know."

"It's just that there's always violence involved. Wally and the deer are the only animals that revealed to me the violence toward Jase. The rest of the animals are showing me things that are happening away from the ranch house."

He toed a chair around and straddled it in the middle of the kitchen, watching as she filled the teakettle and set it on the stove. "What kinds of things?"

"Something flying above their heads. Men and horses moving on the ground. Rifle flashes in the night. I get bits and pieces, nothing concrete, but I think some men may have had a fight and someone was killed here on the ranch." She pulled open the freezer to remove the turkey, setting it in the refrigerator without looking at him. "I could be way off base, but something traumatic happened here some time ago, and I think something happened here again very recently."

Silence stretched out between them.

She didn't want to see his face, to know he thought she was crazy. Why had she said anything? Would she ever learn? She was falling in love with him, and it was far too soon. Love wasn't supposed to happen so fast, rushing at her like an avalanche. She knew better. She spooned loose-leaf tea into the teapot, thankful the kitchen was a chef's delight and so well stocked with everything. Once again she was blowing her chances with a man she could care about because she admitted her affinity with animals.

Maia spun around. "You know what? I don't care if you believe me or not. This is who I am, and I'm not going to apologize for it." She pushed her hand through her hair in agitation. "I like animals better than people anyway."

His eyebrow shot up. "You don't like them better than you like me."

"Yes I do. I don't know what I was thinking." She glared at

him, angry at herself for being so vulnerable to whatever he might think of her.

"You were thinking the animals might be warning us about something, and it was important." He tried his hand at teasing her. "Has anyone ever called you Dr. Doolittle?"

"No! And they'd better never do it either."

His blue eyes moved over her face with cool amusement. "You have a temper." Obviously he wasn't that good at teasing, but he liked her reaction.

"No, I don't. Well," she hedged. "Okay, maybe I do. But the fact is, I don't care whether you believe me or not." She couldn't tell if he was making fun of her or whether he really meant what he said—that he was worried the animals were warning them. It didn't seem possible that he could believe her.

"Yes you do."

His voice was low, a seduction of her senses that she felt all the way through her body. "I hate that you're so good at flirting, Steele. You've been a playboy for so long, you don't know when to stop."

He stood up, an act of aggression, and she recognized it as such, stepping back until she was pressed tightly against the sink, one hand up to stop him. "I'm tired of you calling me insulting names, Maia."

"I wasn't insulting you, I was stating a fact. You're too experienced, and you know it and you use it, and I just want to kick you for it," she defended.

He walked right up to her, his chest pressing into her palm until it was the only thing between them. She could feel his muscles beneath the thin shirt, the rise and fall of his breath, the steady beat of his heart. His skin radiated heat. "Back off, Steele."

"I'm about to apologize again. I seem to do that a lot nowadays."

There was genuine amusement in his voice. Real laughter even if his mouth didn't curve into a smile. It was in his eyes, in his voice. She felt it in his chest. She had given him that gift, and she knew it. There was seduction in the knowledge.

She stared, fascinated at the warmth that replaced the ice in his eyes. He lowered his head until his lips were inches from hers. Until his breath was warm against her mouth.

He kissed her hard, taking her breath, devouring her rather than coaxing her. His arms swept around her, pulled her to him, fitting her body into his.

Maia melted into him, her body going pliant, her mouth answering with a ravenous hunger of her own. Her arms slipped around his neck, fingers tangled in his hair, and she gave herself up to his kiss. His hand slid up her back inside her shirt, fingers splayed wide to take in as much bare skin as possible. Heat spread, heat and hunger and need. His kiss deepened, and his hand closed possessively over her breast.

Maia gasped and arched into his palm. His mouth left hers, blazed across her chin, down her neck to nuzzle at her breast until she moaned a soft protest, her arms cradling his head to her. "Stop. We have to stop."

"Actually, I'd rather not." He kissed his way back up to her mouth, settled there with long, persuading kisses.

Maia kissed him right back but kept a hand wedged between them. "I'm not quite ready for this."

He groaned and rested his forehead against hers. "I am."

"Yes, well now I'm the one apologizing," Maia said. "I have to be certain of what I'm doing and what I'm getting into. I'm sorry, Cole. I'm just made that way."

"I like the way you're made, Maia, but dammit all, I want you in my bed."

"I do rather like the way you apologize," Maia said, touching her fingertips to her mouth, a faint smile appearing as he swore. She could still feel him burning on her lips. Could still feel his hands on her skin. She ached, her body tight and full and edged with need. She had to go upstairs, right away, or she was going to take her clothes off right there in the kitchen and give him more than he ever bargained for.

"Good. I have the feeling I'm going to have to spend a lot of time apologizing to you."

"You're probably right." She removed the teakettle from the heat. "I'm going to bed now. Alone. It's the only safe thing to do."

"You're certain I can't change your mind?"

"No, that's why I'm leaving now before it's too late." She slipped past him and hurried away, leaving him standing in the kitchen with a rueful expression on his face. She was fairly certain it was a good thing he couldn't read her mind.

10

"COME ON, JASE, Doc, bundle up, and let's go looking for a tree. We have a couple hours of break in the storm, and this might be the best opportunity we have."

"What did the weather report say?" Maia asked.

Cole gave her a sharp glance. "Don't think you're escaping when you've got a mountain lion penned up in my shed and a horse in the barn and a teenage boy looking for a huge meal. I don't have the time to clear the road and let you out even if I were so inclined, which I'm not."

"You'll do anything to get out of cooking, won't you?" Maia said, her grin as contagious as always. She slipped into her jacket and pulled on gloves. "I'm definitely going with you. I'm very particular about trees."

Jase and Cole exchanged a long, amused look, then groaned in unison. "You would be," Cole said. "We'll take the snowmobiles and head out toward the upper ridge. The fir trees are thick there, and we can top one of them."

"Why are we just taking the top of the tree?" Jase asked.

"We don't want to kill the tree," Cole said. "I like our trees. You can never have enough trees."

Jase looked out the window toward the tree-covered mountain. "Guess not. We'd have such a shortage if we took the whole tree." He exchanged a grin with Maia.

"I did notice the trees on the ranch were getting thin from all the Christmas celebrations going on around here," Maia teased.

Cole opened the door to the mudroom and waved them through. "I can't believe how funny the two of you are. I let you spend a little time together taking care of that horse, and you develop a comedy routine."

Maia leaned in close to Jase, her arm slipping around his shoulders. "He's grouchy this morning."

"Yeah, it's the one cup of coffee syndrome. I've seen it before," Jase replied. "No one talks to him before the first cup of coffee, or he bites off their head. After the first cup of coffee he growls at everyone, but there's no biting."

Cole caught Maia around the waist, bringing her to a halt, his teeth scraping back and forth at the nape of her neck. "I bite after the first cup of coffee if you deserve it," he warned. His teeth nipped a little harder, sending chills down her back. His tongue swirled over the sting right before he pressed a kiss against it.

"Bite Jase if you're going to bite someone," Maia admonished, shoving at him.

"Ugg. That's sick, Doc," Jase protested. "Totally sick. Cole, don't you even try biting my neck."

A mischievous grin curved Cole's mouth very slowly, giving him a young, boyish look. Maia's breath caught in her throat. Jase backed away from him, laughing, holding out a hand to stop his older brother's purposeful advance.

"Back off!" He dashed out into the snow.

Deliberately, Cole pelted his brother with several snowballs, packing the white flakes into round balls and heaving the missiles on the run. Maia sided with Jase, just as Cole knew she would, throwing snowballs with good aim, scoring several hits. She threw hard and accurate so he was forced to turn away from his intended victim to protect himself. To his astonishment, Jase tackled him from behind, throwing him into the snow and leaping off, running, his laughter carried away by the wind.

The sound stirred some long-forgotten emotion in Cole. He had to fight back a lump in his throat and blink to clear what had to be tears from his burning eyes. He got up slowly, keeping his back to the two of them, shaking with the tidal wave of intense feelings Jase and Maia roused in him. A dam really had burst somewhere deep inside of him, blown open by the happiness spilling over from a simple snowball war.

Or maybe it was so much more than that. Maybe it was all the things in his life he had now that he'd never had, never trusted, and never thought he wanted.

He watched Maia chase Jase through the snow. Her cheeks were red and her eyes filled with merriment, with happiness. He had all but forgotten those things until he found her. The boy was throwing missiles as fast as he could, but Maia clearly had him on the run. Cole could only stare at her, flooded with the knowledge that the intensity of the emotions she brought to him was the very thing he had feared from her. He loved her. It was too fast and too insane for someone like him to even consider, but he knew he needed her. And Jase needed her too.

Jase turned and streaked past Cole, skidding to a halt behind him so that a snowball landed with a splat on Cole's chest. The snow was dazzling white, nearly blinding him. He pushed sunglasses on his nose and settled them in place just as Maia plowed into him. Catching her in his arms, he fell backward, Maia landing on top of him. He rolled, pinning her beneath him.

Time seemed to stop, and he felt his heart somersault, his stomach tighten. She was so damned beautiful lying beneath him with her eyes so full of life.

Cole bent his head and kissed her. Hard. Hungry. Hot. Meaning it.

Maia stared up at him a long moment, the only sound their mingled breathing. She felt her heart stuttering hard in her chest. Little butterflies fluttered in her stomach. She was falling hard. Fast. She didn't even know if Cole was capable of loving her. It was frightening to think how much she cared when she didn't have the slightest idea of his real feelings. Needing space, she scooped up a handful of snow and plastered it against the side of his head. "Cool off, Slick, we're hunting for a tree."

Cole studied her face, the way she suddenly withdrew from him. He had to let her go, with Jase standing over them, but he didn't want to. He wanted to hold her to him. Instead, he made himself wipe at the wet snow trickling down his face. He raised his eyebrow. "You take all the fun out of things."

"I do my best." She shoved at his chest. "And we're getting that tree today. All the kisses in the world aren't going to change my mind."

Cole got to his feet, pulling Maia up with him. Jase sat in the snow staring at them as if they'd both grown new heads. "You going to sit there all day?" Cole asked.

"I just might," Jase said, and took the hand Cole extended to help him up. He was grinning from ear to ear, and Cole resisted the urge to drop him back in the snow.

Jase moved ahead of them, bounding like a frisky colt through the snow to the garage housing the snowmobiles. Cole paused just outside the door, staring up at the second garage looming taller right alongside the first building.

"What is it?" Maia asked.

"I don't know exactly." But he suddenly wished he were alone, able to conduct an investigation.

"What's in there?"

"The helicopter and a small plane."

"Really? You have your own helicopter? Do you fly it?"

"Yes. I can fly both the plane and the helicopter. I was in the service for a while. It was the best way to get away from the ranch and have enough money to live. The old man could have destroyed or bought any company I chose to work for, but he couldn't exactly make the Air Force disappear."

"The things I'm learning about you are fascinating." She took a step toward the larger garage but stopped when Cole put a hand on her shoulder. He was looking around the countryside, his eyes flat and hard and ice-cold. She froze, taking her cue from him.

Cole caught the brief glint of light reflected from a ridge up above the house. He didn't make the mistake of staring into it, but a chill went down his back. It could have been a scope, but more likely it was binoculars. Deliberately he glanced up at the sky. "We'd better find that tree before the next storm hits."

Jase eagerly shoved open the garage doors to reveal several snowmobiles. "Come on, Doc, I'll race you!"

Maia felt Cole's hand on her shoulder guiding her toward the snowmobiles so she went with him. "What is it?"

Cole was grateful she was always so alert and kept her voice low. She never seemed to panic. "I don't know yet. All these strange things the animals have been showing you, the things you've described to me, do you believe they're trying to convey something to you?"

"Absolutely," Maia said firmly.

"Keep Jase occupied for a few minutes."

"Don't do anything crazy."

Cole slipped into the shadows of the building, encouraging Jase and Maia to follow him inside. If someone were lying up along the ridge with a scope or binoculars, they wouldn't be able to see him go through the door of the covered walkway leading back to the house.

"I forgot something, Jase. We need a couple of tools. You check out the snowmobiles, make certain we have plenty of gas and they're running fine, while I go back and get what we need."

"Sure," Jase agreed.

Maia was silent, watching him with fear in her eyes. He

couldn't help brushing a brief, reassuring kiss over her mouth as he passed by her. "Keep him in the garage," he whispered as he moved into the walkway.

He sprinted along the covered path, forced to take a round-about route to keep from exposing himself to the ridge, but he made it back to the house certain he hadn't been spotted. Up in his room, he retrieved a rifle with a scope and binoculars. With the white sheet wrapped around him, he scooted on his belly onto the balcony, rolling into position.

He raised the binoculars to his eyes, scanning the ridge for activity, keeping his own movement to a minimum. It took a moment to spot his quarry. Fred Johanston, Al's brother-in-law, lay on the ridge, watching the activity in the garage through a pair of binoculars. Cole lowered his glasses and scooted back into the house, carefully sliding the balcony door closed, not wanting to give away his position.

Fred Johanston was up to something, but what? There was no way he'd inherit the ranch should both Jase and Cole die. He had no hope of being Jase's guardian. What was he up to? Cole didn't have much time. He didn't want to tip off Fred that he was on to him. Hurrying through the house, back outside, he took even more care to keep out of sight of the ridge, but he took several weapons with him.

He'd already committed to taking Jase and Maia on a hunt for a Christmas tree, and if he abruptly changed plans it could alert Fred that Cole was on to him. Better to act as if nothing were wrong and figure things out the way he always did, methodically, slowly, putting the pieces of the puzzle together until they fit perfectly. Now that he knew they were under surveillance, he could take the appropriate steps to keep them safe.

Maia looked up as he hurried in through the side door, his weapons stashed safely in a small toolbox. "Everything all right?"

"The snowmobiles are gassed up and ready to go," Jase said.

"Well, put on your gloves and pull down your hat over your face. The doc and I are going to race you."

"No we're not," Maia said.

"Awesome," Jase said. "I'm the king on a snowmobile."

"The rules are, we go out the door full throttle, head for Moose Creek, and you have to zigzag through every open field or you're disqualified."

"Piece of cake," Jase said. "You'll never catch me."

"Don't be so cocky, kid." Cole reached over to zip the boy's jacket to his neck. "You're also disqualified if you take a spill."

"*Hello*! I don't suppose you heard me say no way," Maia said, tugging at Cole's arm. "We are *not* racing."

"I can't believe you'd be afraid of a little speed, Maia," Cole said. A mischievous almost grin slid over his face.

Maia glared at him with suspicion. "If I thought you could do that on purpose . . ."

"What?" He sank down onto the snowmobile and patted the seat behind him. "Climb aboard, and let's go get that tree."

Maia slid behind him and wrapped her arms around his waist. "You aren't going to tell me what's going on, are you?"

"I don't know yet," he said truthfully, "but we're going to be very careful."

The ride through the snow was wild and exhilarating. The two snowmobiles flew over the snow. A few flakes fell from the clouds, reminding them they didn't have much time, but they still played, Jase and Cole racing across the pristine fields toward Moose Creek. Maia's laughter rang in Cole's ears and found its way into his heart. She rested her head against his back and urged him on when Jase was inching ahead of them.

All the while, Cole made every effort to keep trees and slopes between them and the ridge. He encouraged Jase to play, deliberately forcing the boy to zigzag through every open field so it would be nearly impossible to get off an accurate shot should Fred have the desire. Cole hadn't seen a rifle, but he'd seen the saddle and blanket and the scabbard, and he was certain it had been Fred who'd taken the horse out. And it must have been Fred who shot the mountain lion the same day he'd run Wally into the fence. But why? What possible reason could he have? He certainly couldn't expect to get his job back that way. Revenge? Could it be that simple?

Jase brought his snowmobile to a halt in front of a particularly tall fir tree, pointing. The branches were full and the tree's needles were thick. "This one's a beaut! What do you think, Doc?"

"He would ask you," Cole said, helping her off the machine. In the thick of the trees they were well protected. Snow was beginning to fall again, and the wind was picking up. He glanced up at the sky. "I think this one's going to have to be it, Jase. We've just about run out of time. The storm's coming in fast."

There was a lot of laughter and just as much argument as Cole and Jase decided what was the best way to top the tree. Maia stood back watching, laughing at them, but all the while she could see that Cole was extremely alert, his eyes restless, constantly moving. He was wary, extremely so, and he exuded a powerful aura of danger. He was hunting, she knew, but had no idea what he was looking for.

The tree was tied to a sled and secured behind Jase's machine. That told Maia Cole wanted to be mobile or he would never have risked allowing Jase to pull the tree. They made their way back at a much more cautious and sedate pace. It was far colder with the snow flying at their faces in spite of their warm coats. The snow fell steadily, a sign that they were in for another long storm.

Maia was happy to see the inside of the house. It was warm and felt welcoming with the fire in the fireplace and Jase's mother's quilt along the back of the couch. She'd put cider on the stove to simmer, and the fragrance wafted through the rooms. "Much better," she said and smiled at the teenager.

He was too busy struggling to get the tree inside the house, maneuvering it with Cole giving orders and both staggering and tripping until Maia nearly fell over laughing. "I wish I had a camera. You two are not very good at this."

Cole glared at her. "I don't see you helping, and this was your idea."

"I'm suffering the effects of my scalp wound from yesterday," Maia said.

"You were able to wrestle yesterday." He walked his end of the tree around, keeping away from the windows, always conscious of the watcher on the ridge. He glanced outside. The snow was relentless, falling steadily in a soft, silent monotonous way that packed on feet rather than inches. Cole seriously doubted if anyone could be out in the whiteout. The tension immediately drained from his body.

"Fine," Maia said. She took the toolbox Cole had insisted on carrying along with the tree. "I'll find the perfect position for you. The two of you just hold on to it while I study the situation."

"Study the situation?" Jase yelped in protest. "This is *heavy*."

"Yes, well." Maia waved a dismissing hand and settled herself on the couch, the toolbox at her feet while she examined every angle of the room.

"Oh, for God's sake," Cole said, exasperated. He shoved on his end until Jase went with him, standing the tree dead center in front of the window. "Right here. The damned thing is going right here, and we're *not* moving it."

In the end they moved it four times, Maia going from one end of the room to the other to study the positioning from every angle. Jase threw himself on the floor twice, laughing at his older brother's expression and pointing to him until Cole threatened to throw him out in the storm.

"That's perfect. Now we need wire and those pincher cutter things," Maia said. "We'll make a wreath."

"I thought we were going to eat, woman," Cole objected. "You have to feed men if you want them cooperative."

"You just ate," Maia protested.

"That was hours ago," Jase said. "Sorry, Doc, but I'm with Cole on this. I'm on empty."

"You two are bottomless pits! Fine, I need to make popcorn anyway."

"I love popcorn. Make the buttery kind," Jase said.

"*Not* to eat." Maia put her hands on her hips. "We string it and make a garland to wrap around the tree."

Jase and Cole exchanged a long look. "I think that knock on the head did more damage than we suspected," Cole told his younger brother. "We're not wasting the popcorn on the tree, Doc."

Jase shook his head. "What part of *starving* don't you understand?"

"Oh for heaven's sake. We'll make sandwiches, and you can eat them and leave the decorations alone," Maia said.

"I like the part about the sandwiches," Jase said, and took off for the kitchen.

As soon as she and Cole were alone, Maia caught Cole's arm. "What is going on? I know something is, so don't pretend you don't know what I mean."

"I'm not sure what's going on, other than I want us all to stick together," Cole said. "When I figure it out, I promise, you'll be the first to know."

"Is there something I can do to help?"

He framed her face. "You're doing enough already. There's no way to make it up to you, the things you're doing for Jase."

Her heart did a silly flutter as the pad of his thumb slid back and forth over her lower lip. She was beginning to think of various ways he could repay her if he really insisted on it. Maia knew she was incredibly susceptible to him. Jase was her savior, whether he was aware of it or not. She would never be able to hold out against Cole if the boy wasn't with them almost constantly, and once she gave herself to him, she knew it would be forever. It was a terrible realization that she'd fallen so deeply for a man she had known for only a few days.

She couldn't look into his eyes. There was need there and hunger and something so compelling she would never be able to resist. He was doing all the things he knew would cause him nightmares in order to give his younger brother a chance at a normal life. She was hurting him. She ached inside knowing she was the cause. Yet because he was a willing participant, she was falling deeper and deeper in love with him.

"I'm enjoying myself, Cole. This has been fun." Her voice was so husky with her awareness of him she was embarrassed. If his thumb touched her lower lip another minute, she was going to bite him.

"Maia." He bent his head.

She groaned, knew she was lost as she moved into the heat of his body. Her arms stole around his neck, and she instantly became a part of him. Skin to skin. Breath to breath. His hair felt like silk between her fingertips. And his mouth was a haven of fire and hunger that matched her own. She sank into him, his kiss sweeping her away just as she knew it would. She was just as demanding as he, matching fire for fire, hungry, almost greedy in her response.

His arms tightened around her, and his kiss was possessive, a man starved, claiming her, and she claimed him right back, pushing so close they didn't need the clothes separating them.

"Get a hotel room," Jase said. "Geez, this place is getting to be X-rated." He leaned against the wall, a cold piece of pizza in his hand, chewing as he regarded them with feigned disgust. His eyes were bright with happiness, and neither could fail to recognize the hope on his face.

Maia pulled her mouth away from Cole's, pressing her forehead against his chest, trying to find a way to breathe when her lungs felt starved for air. "He's getting hard to resist, Jase. I think we need to put some kind of warning label on him."

"You're just tired, Doc," Cole said, catching her chin, forcing her to look at him.

A woman could definitely get trapped in his blue eyes. She sighed. "That must be it, but just in case, kiss me again."

He didn't wait for a second invitation. He lowered his head to hers, his hand sliding around her neck, holding her still for his kiss.

"I could kiss you forever," she murmured.

Jase rolled his eyes. "Well, don't. Think food instead."

Maia blushed, shocked she'd admitted it aloud. "He mesmerized me, Jase, it isn't my fault."

"That's not how it looked to me," Jase said. "You were definitely doing the kissing."

Maia pulled out of Cole's arms. "I'm going to go check the horse and the cat in that order."

"You're running," Cole informed her.

That intriguing trace of amusement flashed momentarily in his eyes. She had to look away from temptation. "Yes, I am, but don't go thinking it's because of your studly self. I'm running from having to cook. I'll make the popcorn, but the two of you are bottomless pits, and if I'm the one putting together Christmas dinner and baking . . ."

"Cookies," Jase interrupted. "Lots of cookies. And pies." He poked his brother. "She just zapped you, bro, put you right in your place."

"I thought you wanted to let that cat rest. Stop avoiding me and come into the kitchen. I'll do the cooking, and you do your strange thing with the popcorn." Cole took her hand and drew her into the kitchen. "I started on the wood carving by the way. I've actually found a couple of pieces of wood that might be perfect for a couple of them."

"I've never seen anyone carve before. Will you teach me?"

His gaze moved over her face. Dark. Brooding. Sexy. Maia backed into the table. "Maybe not." She waved at him. "Get started on your cooking."

"I'm making progress."

"You *were* making progress, but I've come to my senses again." She turned her back on him, rummaging through cupboards to find the popcorn. "Jase, find me a needle and thread please."

"Did you really go to Africa and Indochina, Doc?" Jase asked, stuffing potato chips into his mouth.

"Yes. It was beautiful. I loved it, but you have to be prepared for a lot of bugs."

"I'm going to do that someday," Jase said. "What you did

for Wally was so great, but I couldn't believe how it felt to touch that mountain lion." He leaned both elbows on the table, chin in hand, and studied her with his bright eyes. "I *have* to do that again."

"There's something incredible about a wild cat. Tigers and lions and leopards, all the exotics. You look them in the eye, and you just know we need to find a way to share our space with them. They're incredible."

"Do you want to go back there?" Cole asked, his voice tight.

There was a sudden silence in the room. Maia knew the Steele brothers were watching her closely. She turned her head, meeting Cole's gaze. Her stomach did a crazy flip. It wasn't often she could read his expression, but he was tense, expecting a blow. She forced a casual shrug. "If I want to work with exotics again, most likely I'd find a zoo somewhere. I'm a fill-in vet, so I can make enough money to start my own practice."

"Why don't you take over the one here?" Jase asked.

"Money, honey. I've got some saved, but not enough."

Popcorn began to sound off, a rapid gunfire of miniexplosions.

"Smells good," Jase said.

"I think you'd eat anything if it didn't move," Maia observed, laughing at him. "Leave my popcorn alone. And I'm putting you to work stringing it while Cole makes dinner." She tossed him the small sewing kit containing needles and thread. "Come on, help out, shark tooth."

11

THREE A.M. THE small alarm clock beside Maia's bed bla-
zoned the time in bright glowing numbers. It seemed she was
always awake at 3:00 a.m. in this house. She wasn't used to the
creaks and strange noises, although, she had to admit with a
great deal of satisfaction, the aura of the house was undergoing
a change.

She shifted restlessly in the bed, sighed, giving up on sleep,
and threw back the covers. Cole had participated in decorating
the tree, but he'd been thinking of something else. She'd
watched him closely. He had made a dozen excuses to go outside. He'd checked the windows and doors in the house, and
for the first time since she'd been there, he'd turned on a security alarm, after first changing the code. And that told her
something. Cole was worried about an intruder other than the
ghost of his father.

She was falling madly in love with him. She hadn't expected
it, and the depth of the emotion was terrifying. She needed to
get off the ranch. To go far away. She couldn't stop thinking
about Cole. She dreamt of him. Longed to touch him, to take
away the shadows always present in his eyes. She'd known
from the first moment she'd laid eyes on him that she wouldn't
walk away unscathed, but she hadn't counted on the intense
attraction she felt for him. He never said a word to her about
his real feelings. He never said a word about love or indicated
that when she left he wouldn't be happy or even that he might
want to see her again.

A sound penetrated through the walls, echoed down the
hall. A cry of despair. A tortured protest. Maia stood for a mo-

ment, her hand to her throat, hearing the tormented groan of despair. If she went to him, she knew she would never be able to resist giving him what he needed, yet making love to him would only make leaving more difficult for her. She heard a string of curses. Unable to resist his terrible need, she hurried out of her room.

Cole's door was closed, but she pushed it open to see him raking his hands through his hair. His body still shuddered with the aftereffects of his nightmare. As she entered, he swept a gun from under the pillow, pointing it straight at her heart.

"Damn, Maia." He pushed the gun out of sight, struggling to slow his heart rate. "I told you it was dangerous to come downstairs when I'm like this. You think it's any safer in my bedroom?" Cole sat up. The sheets were tangled around his legs and hips, covering part of him but leaving his thigh bare. He knew it looked as if he'd fought a battle and lost.

"I don't care." She crossed the room to his side, pushing the hair from his forehead, her fingertips lingering on his face, tracing a path to his mouth. "I don't want you to be alone tonight, Cole." She knelt on the bed, the light from the snow spilling through the window to bathe her in silver.

Cole's breath caught in his throat, his lungs burned, and he could only stare as her hands went to the buttons of the soft flannel shirt covering her body. She slid each one open. Slowly. One by one. He caught brief glimpses of her body. A soft expanse of skin he ached to touch.

His fingers curled into two tight fists. "Not like this, Maia. You don't have to come to me feeling sorry for me because I had a damned nightmare." What the hell was he saying? He wanted her. Ached for her. His body was so damned hard, he was afraid he might shatter. "I don't want you like this." It was a total lie. He wanted her any way he could have her.

Maia flashed her killer smile, the one that sent his body into overdrive and caused him to turn into a jealous idiot if any other man was within several hundred feet of her. His breath left his lungs in a rush when she allowed the flannel shirt to slide from her shoulders to the mattress. The silvery light played over her body, caressing it lovingly. She looked like a temptress there, kneeling on his bed, her hair tumbling around her face, her eyes enormous and sexy and looking at him with hunger. Her body's feminine curves invited his touch.

"You're killing me."

She leaned forward, her tongue swirling over his chest. "I hope so."

The action exposed the enticing curve of her hip and buttocks. His hands trembled as he reached to cup her bottom, sliding his palms over her smooth skin. She did that to him, made him ache and tremble with the intensity of his hunger for her. He burned from the inside out, a rush of fire that engulfed his body and heightened his senses until he was afraid of losing his control.

Her tongue licking so delicately at his body nearly drove him out of his mind. She pushed the sheets away from him, exposing him to the cool air, but it only hardened his body more so that he was thick and bulging with his desire for her. Maia murmured something against his chest, her tongue tracing a path to his belly. Every muscle in his body contracted. His heart shuddered in anticipation.

"Maia, what the hell do you think you're doing?" His voice was strangled as his lungs labored for air.

"Exactly what I want to do," she said, and wrapped her fingers around his erection.

A groan exploded from his throat. He'd had too many erotic dreams of Maia in his bed, his hands on her satin skin. "You'd better know this is what you really want," he warned. Because he wanted her more than he wanted the sun to come up in the morning.

"I always know what I want." Her breath was warm and moist, and his heart stopped beating for one moment, then began to slam with alarming force in his chest. She did the same delicate licking that had driven him wild. Now it was beyond his imagination. He was going to implode if she didn't stop. Just when he was certain he couldn't take it anymore, her mouth closed over him, tight and hot and moist, drawing the relentless ache to a fever pitch.

His hands fisted in her hair, his hips coming off the sheets, thrusting in a rhythmic slide. He swore, the words tumbling out in an animalistic growl. His control was nearly shattered. His muscles clenched so tight he thought his jaw would break.

Maia lifted her head and smiled at him, satisfaction evident. "Are you thinking of me yet? Of my body? Because I want you to know who's in bed with you."

"I know damned well who I'm with, Maia." He pushed her backward until she tumbled onto the bed, her legs sprawled, her body open to him. "I know *exactly* who you are. I feel like I've waited a lifetime for you."

His hands pressed into her hips, locking her there, pushing her thighs wider apart for him. "Every time I look at you, I think about what I'd really like to be doing. I want to feel you coming apart for me, Maia."

Before she could respond, he lowered his head as he brought her hips to him. His tongue slid over her heated center, teased and tasted before probing deeply. Maia writhed beneath his hungry mouth, bunching the sheet in her fists, sounds she couldn't prevent escaping, which only fed his voracious need to show her she belonged with him. He didn't have the words, so he used his body to prove it to her. His tongue stroked and thrust and cleverly pulsed until she was consumed with wave after wave of orgasm rippling through her. He sank his fingers deep, and she exploded again, crying out his name.

Cole lifted his head, kissed his way up her body to the underside of her breasts. The cool air was nearly Maia's undoing after his hot mouth. She ached, and still the pressure was relentless in spite of her orgasms.

"What are you doing?" she demanded.

"Making sure you know who you're in bed with. I don't want you ever to be satisfied with any other man." His teeth scraped back and forth on the sensitive flesh. Tiny little bites that drove her insane. "I want you to belong to me. All of you, Maia, not just your body." His mouth closed over her breast, tongue flicking her nipple, teeth teasing until she couldn't tell if the pleasure was so great it was painful.

He rose over her, pushing against her entrance, so that her body, so slick and hot, reacted with a slow giving of way for his penetration. He paused for one slight moment, their mingled breathing the only sound, and then he thrust hard, driving the full length of him as deep into her as he could go. He discovered he loved her cries as much as her laugh. He thrust again, over and over, hard and fast, long, deep strokes, driving her higher and higher until she was clutching at his forearms, crying his name.

Sensation after sensation rocked her body, heat seared her until she thought she would have to scream for him to relieve the terrible ache. More. She wanted more. Everything he had, everything he was. She gave herself up to him, surrendering completely, her hips rising to meet the brutal thrust of his, every bit as hard, desperate for him to fill up every empty space.

"Maia, you're so damned tight." Cole's voice was husky, the words torn from his rigid throat. "Hot and tight and dammit all, you belong to me. Like this, baby, just like this." He plunged into her again and again, groaning with pleasure as her muscles pulsed and throbbed around him even more. Until her control was shattered and she burst into fragments, her body convulsing around his, tightening and squeezing and milking him dry so that he called her name aloud, his voice rough with sensuality.

Maia stared up into his face. The harsh lines were gone, the horror of his nightmares replaced with satisfaction. He looked like a well-sated lover, his body relaxed and his piercing blue eyes soft with contentment.

Cole propped himself up on his elbows, looking down into her face, still trying to get his breathing under control. He could feel her body still rippling with aftershocks around his. "You're so beautiful you take my breath away."

Her laughter was soft, musical, tightening his body all over again. "That's not what took your breath away. And you lie so wonderfully. I'm ordinary-looking, but I don't mind if you want to delude yourself." Her hands slid over his body, traced his sculpted buttocks and hips. She could see a brand burned into his flesh on the back of his thigh. Her fingertips smoothed over the ridges with a small caress.

"I probably should sneak back to my room," she added.

He stiffened. "This is not a one-night stand, Maia. I told you that."

"You did not. I forget your exact words, but . . ."

He caught her hands, stretched them above her head, pinning her wrists to the mattress so he could bend his head and take possession of her lips. He sank his tongue into the velvet darkness of her mouth, his tongue tangling with hers, exploring, commanding a response. He bit lightly at her lower lip, her chin, blazed a path of fire from her throat to her breasts.

For a moment he breathed in the sight of her bathed in the silvery light as it spilled across her breasts. Her nipples were peaked and hard, already roused. Her soft mounds were rising and falling with every breath she took, jutting upward toward his mouth. His body stirred to life, deep inside of hers, hardening impossibly. He bent to the offering, flicking her nipple with his tongue, feeling her response, the way her hips thrust upward and her body convulsed around his. He drew her breast into his hot mouth, suckling strongly, his tongue teasing her nipple, teeth scraping gently.

Maia gasped and moaned, her body tensing, her breasts swelling with the attention. His body began to move, long slow strokes that left her moaning and lifting her hips in an attempt to control the rhythm. Cole held her beneath him, pressing kisses between her breasts, nibbling at her chin and lower lip, using his mouth to bring her to another climax while his body kept a slow, lazy tempo.

"Cole." It was a protest. A plea.

He smiled. A genuine smile. He felt it welling up out of

nowhere. Cole could make her want him, plead with him, make her body come apart. She didn't try to hide the way she felt such an urgent need of him, and that was more of an aphrodisiac than anything else ever could have been.

"Cole what?" he whispered against her mouth. Her muscles were already suckling at him, so tight and hot he wasn't certain he could keep the slow, languid pace he was setting. "What do you want, Maia?" The pleasure kept building and building inside of him, starting somewhere in the region of his toes, becoming an excruciating pleasure/pain in his groin and belly. There was fire in her tight sheath, her skin soft and inviting, her breasts thrusting up toward him with her arms stretched out above her head. An offering to him. Maia gave herself to him completely, and there was so much seduction in that knowledge.

"Hurry up. Now *you're* killing *me*." She lifted her hips again, deliberately tightening her muscles around him.

With a groan, Cole gave in, plunging deep and hard, unable to resist the hot furnace of her body. He couldn't resist kissing her, sucking on her lower lip. How often had he found himself staring, enthralled by the soft curve of her mouth? His tongue plunged into her mouth with the same urgency his hips drove into her. It could never be enough with Maia and he knew he never wanted it to be.

Stretched out under him as she was, helpless under the pounding force of his body, she still tried to reach him, to lift herself to meet him. Cole felt her body stretching to accommodate him as with each thrust he seemed to grow thicker and harder, nearly bursting with the pleasure she brought him. He held them there, on the edge of a great precipice for what seemed forever, then both went over, climaxing together, the force of it leaving them shuddering and limp, a fine sheen glossing their bodies.

Cole groaned softly and rolled his weight off of her when he could, but he kept his hand on her ribs, just under her breast, wanting to keep her in his room. "Just stay," he ordered softly. "I need you to stay."

It took Maia longer to catch her breath, to gather her scattered thoughts. "I've never felt that way before, Cole."

He turned his head to look at her. "That's a damned good thing, Maia. I'm looking to be number one in your life. Being a fantastic lover is one of the requirements."

She laughed, just like he knew she would. "Is it? I had no idea. Well, you definitely passed that test." She glanced at the door. "I hope I didn't scream. Please tell me I didn't."

"Unless Jase has a nightmare, he sleeps deeply, and his room is way down at the other end of the floor. We wanted to give one another a lot of space when we first moved in together."

"He's a good kid."

"Yeah, he is. All along I've been so worried that Jase might have killed the old man. I wouldn't have blamed him for it, but I didn't want him to have done it. I couldn't find a way to prove him innocent and even in some of our conversations, little things he said made me wonder."

"How awful for you both," Maia sympathized. She reached for his hand, twining her fingers through his. "Jase isn't naturally violent, Cole. If he killed his father, he would have done it in self-defense. And to be honest, I don't think he could have. He was too afraid of him. And it isn't in him to kill anyone."

"No, it isn't." Cole turned over, his arm sliding around her waist. "But it is in me, isn't it?"

The sadness in his voice shook her. Sadness. Distaste. A note of fear. Maia framed his face with her hands, shifting so she could rise above him to look directly into his eyes. "You're *nothing* like that man, Cole. You're strong and yes, you could be violent if the circumstances called for it, but you're nothing at all like him."

"You don't know that, Maia."

"Yes I do. I saw your face when you touched the mountain lion, when I worked on the horse. I watch you with Jase, how careful you are. Even when you're trying to get him to play, you protect his falls. There's nothing in you that is cruel. Your father reveled in being cruel. It isn't in your nature, or in Jase's nature. You like to be the boss, but you're not out to control everyone. You encourage Jase to speak his mind and make decisions. That's not wanting control."

Cole slid his hands up her rib cage, cupped her breasts in his palms and leaned forward to rest his head against her soft flesh. Maia immediately cradled his head to her. "I read people, just as I read animals, Cole. I would never have allowed myself to become involved with you and Jase if for one moment I thought either of you was cruel to humans or animals. I have too much respect for myself." She smiled. "I have a little bit of violence in me as well, and a great deal of self-preservation."

His arms tightened around her. "I see him in myself sometimes, Maia."

"He had strength of will, Cole, and he passed that to you. He must have had a way with women, and you have that attraction as well. Not everything about him was bad. Some of his traits are useful and, hopefully, both you and Jase have them."

He lifted his head, his blue eyes moving over her face, studying her features inch by inch. "You're a damned miracle, you know that?"

"Of course I do. Temper and all." She laughed, the sound happy and warm, filling the large bedroom.

Cole felt her laughter all the way to his bones. She had the power to shake him with that simple lighthearted sound. Her body was soft and warm and welcoming, but she was so much more to him. *She would always be so much more to him.* The revelation was no longer a shock. Maia seemed as much a part of him as breathing. She was the joy that had been missing from his heart. When he woke in darkness, she brought light to him. She brought out things in him he hadn't known were a part of him.

How could he tell her these things when they'd only been together so short a time? She wouldn't believe him. How could she? His arms tightened until she stirred in protest.

"You're going to break me in half, Cole," Maia said. "What's wrong?"

He forced himself to let his arms slide away from her, to lie back and lace his fingers behind his head. "I know you've told me about the images the animals have shown you several times, but would you go over it again in detail. Everything you can remember."

"Why?"

"You ought to be over being uncomfortable about it with me," Cole said. There was a soft growl in his voice, a deep note that seemed to vibrate right through her skin. "I'm just thinking about all the images the animals have been conveying to you, and I'm trying to put it together. Maybe the answer to the mystery of what's going on at this ranch is in those images."

Maia sat back, her hand on his chest, right over his heart. She knew he hadn't told her what had put the shadows back in his eyes, but if he wasn't ready to tell her, she wasn't going to force a confidence. "I'm going to let you get away with that just because I know you're worried about something happening on the ranch, and I want to be filled in, but I know that's not what you were worried about."

Maia waited, but Cole didn't respond. "Fine. The owl was very vague. Impressions of dangers, something flying overhead. Flashes of light. Horses moving. I couldn't get a very good take on it because the images seemed faded and far away." She shrugged. "I know that sounds dumb."

"The deer then."

"Blood on the grass and rocks. Fists hitting flesh. More impressions of danger."

"Were the images as vague?"

"Distant. And the wolves were even more so. Something overhead. Blood on the ground. The one I treated was injured some time ago."

"Someone shot it?"

"No, I think it was kicked by a horse or trampled. The bone was out of the socket, but I'm not certain how the injury actually occurred or how long ago. The poor thing had really suffered."

"All this time I thought my father's death had something to do with his fortune or the ranch or Jase. I couldn't figure out why he was murdered and how anyone other than my uncle would profit and only if he was named guardian, which he wouldn't be. Besides, he wouldn't want the responsibility."

"So if your father wasn't murdered for the inheritance, what was the reason?"

He shrugged, a small sigh escaping. "I'm not actually certain, but I think your animals were trying to tell you something. I'm working on a time line. Tell me how preposterous this sounds. I think your cat, the owl, and the wolves were showing you something that happened a while ago."

"*Maybe*. It was vague."

"Exactly. The memory wasn't fresh."

Excitement flared. "You're right. When Wally showed me the images of Jase as a boy being beaten, the memories weren't nearly as vivid as when he showed me how he was driven into the fence. I had a very difficult time making out the images from the owl and the wolves, but the mountain lion's images were much clearer."

"You're certain she was shot the day Wally was injured?"

"The wound would have been infected if more time had gone by. Yes, it was definitely fresh."

"Could she have been shot from someone in a helicopter?"

Maia shook her head. "No, she was above the shooter, at least that's the way the angle of the wound appeared to me."

Satisfaction edged his expression. "That's what I thought too. So the event in which the helicopter was flying overhead could have taken place when my father was still alive."

"Well, of course there's no way of knowing for certain, but it's a realistic possibility," Maia said. "I'm lost, Cole. You obviously have an idea where all of this is leading, but I haven't a clue."

He kissed her, a brief hard kiss, his eyes alive with excitement. "That's because you don't think like a criminal."

"I suppose that's a compliment. You have such a sweet tongue on you."

He showed her he did, kissing her again and making a thorough job of it.

Maia caught his shoulders and pushed him back down to the bed. "Talk. Explain."

"I think my father brought something onto the ranch, most likely something illegal. Some of the ranch hands were probably involved. They would have had to be. Most people didn't know it, but the old man could fly a helicopter. He employed a full-time pilot, but only because he liked to feel superior to everyone and give orders. He thought flying was a menial task."

Maia reached for his hand again. Cole didn't seem to realize how agitated he became when he talked about his father. It wasn't overt, but more a subtle tension rising, building and building until she felt he might explode with the force of a volcano. "I'm not certain I understand."

"Suppose he brought in something worth a fortune, and some of the hands were in on it and expected to get a share. The old man goes out with his pilot and moves it from wherever it was originally stashed."

"You're thinking of a shipment of drugs."

"I always think in terms of drugs or weapons. It's my job. But yes, suppose the old man was running drugs out here. He has a few thousand acres. The ranch backs up to a national forest. Parts of our ranch are on the border. He could bring in drugs, and no one would be the wiser. Or diamonds. Anything. An illegal shipment worth a fortune."

"The horses and packs. The helicopter overhead. Maybe. It's a stretch."

"Not that big a stretch if you knew him. He would revel in working outside the law. He thought he was smarter and more cunning than anyone. I could easily see it. And if some of the hands were in on it and knew he had the shipment and he suddenly announced he was cutting them out, it would be a damned good reason for someone to kill him."

"Why would he do that?"

"Because he could. You would have had to know him. He liked the power of it all. Suppose he went with his pilot and moved the shipment somewhere the hands wouldn't know about it, and then he killed the pilot and left him behind with the stash."

Maia shook her head. "It doesn't make sense."

"You said someone was killed. I checked, Maia. The pilot went missing a few weeks before the old man was murdered. He was actually considered a suspect. No one's heard from him. The rumor was, he and the old man had a falling out, and he quit."

"So your father killed the pilot, but why?"

"Because the old man moved his stash, and the pilot knew where, so he had to die. Then he told the ranch hands he was cutting them out of the deal. He knew they couldn't go to the police, and they wouldn't want to lose their jobs, so he felt very safe. But one or more of them decided they didn't want to take orders from him. So they killed him in his office and went out to pick up the stash, only it wasn't there anymore."

"Because he'd moved it before he cut them out of the deal."

"I think that's what's going on, Maia. They didn't care who was named guardian because we didn't know about the stash. They could look around the ranch for it, and we'd never know."

"Until you fired them."

"That's right. I fired them, and I'd be very suspicious if they began hanging around the ranch. Jase told me some maps disappeared from the office. I didn't really give it all that much thought, but it makes sense. They're looking for whatever the old man hid."

"So they wanted you out of here at least long enough to do a thorough search of the ranch. That's why the rumors, to get you to take Jase and leave."

"And that's why the accidents. They knew the storm was coming. Jase was supposed to go into town with me that day, but he decided he wanted to hang out with Al. So they tried to injure him just enough so Al would have to drive him into town, and they could poke around. That didn't work, so they drove Wally into the fence thinking Al would trailer the horse into town. The storm was breaking too fast, and I opted to bring you home with me."

"Why push it? Why didn't they just wait?"

"Maybe they have a buyer, or they're getting anxious. Whatever it is, one of my horses was ridden the day Wally was hurt. I think while Al and Jase were tied up looking after him, Fred took the horse and went looking. That's probably when he shot the mountain lion."

"This is all speculation."

"Yes," Cole admitted. "But Fred was watching us when we went to get the tree yesterday. And I've got this gut feeling. I've never been wrong when I've had that feeling before."

"So why the ice on the walkway?"

"To get us out of here. If you or Jase or even I were injured, we'd have to go into town to the hospital, and they'd be able to search without interruption."

"In a blizzard?"

"Four separate storms, Maia. It wasn't supposed to be this bad. And if we were trapped on the other side, the road wouldn't be cleared, and we'd have a hard time getting home."

"So how do you prove it?"

"I'm working on it." He reached out to cup her breasts again, thumbs caressing her nipples into hard peaks. "I'll think better in the morning. Right now, I want to spend the rest of the night getting to know every inch of your body intimately."

She felt her body respond immediately. "Sounds like a good plan to me."

12

"Tomorrow's Christmas Eve, Cole, and I haven't had a nightmare since we ran into Maia in the restaurant." Jase shoveled scrambled eggs onto his plate and scooped up bacon to go along with it. "If the doc is a vegetarian, why is she all gung ho to cook us a turkey?"

"You'll have to ask her that."

"Have you had nightmares since we met Maia?"

Cole nodded. "Yeah. But they don't last long."

Jase paused in his frantic eating to look up at his brother. "If the tree really bothers you, Cole, I'll help you take it down. The doc will understand."

"No, the tree stays up. I can get through the night, Jase. I like the tree."

"I do too," the boy said, relieved. "I kind of like the whole Christmas thing. The doc makes it feel different. I'm not sure why, but she makes everything so fun."

"On Christmases past, I always felt an outsider looking in," Cole said.

Jase blinked and swallowed quickly. "That's it! That's how I always felt. Sometimes you're smart, Cole."

"Thanks, Jase." A trace of humor showed in Cole's eyes.

"You're welcome." Jase leaned his chin into his palm as he thoughtfully chewed a mouthful of food. "I've been giving a lot of thought to this, Cole. I think we should keep her. We need to keep the doc."

Cole's mouth twitched in an odd approximation of a smile. "Keep her? As in lock her up? I don't know that she'd be too happy with that, Jase."

Jase flashed an exasperated frown. "Do I have to spell it out for you? You need a wife. You really do. And I need a mom, and the doc is perfect for us, so ask her to marry you."

"You've been thinking about this for all of what? Five minutes? What exactly are we offering her, Jase?"

"Money. We've got lots of money. She likes the house, and she really likes kissing you, so maybe you should step up that part of it. I think she'll go for it."

Cole shook his head. "You need to do a little more thinking, Jase. You know we can't just buy her. Maia isn't like that. And I don't have all that much to offer her, but I'm working on it."

Jase's face brightened. "You are? I really want her to stay with us, Cole. She makes us feel like we belong."

"We do belong. Whether or not I can get her to stay, we're always going to be family."

"Good morning!" Maia entered the kitchen, her smile wide as she took in the sight of the two brothers eating breakfast. "You're up before me this morning."

Cole was not going to allow her to get away with putting distance between them. He'd made it damn clear last night he was making love to her, not having sex. And this wasn't going to be a one-night stand. Jase might have had the right idea. He needed to step things up.

Cole snagged her around the waist and pulled her into his arms, settling his mouth over hers firmly. Staking a claim as blatantly as he could. His hand curved around the nape of her neck, held her still while his teeth tugged at her lower lip and his tongue teased at the seam until she opened for him. Her body softened, seemed to melt right into his as he kissed her thoroughly. At once he pulled her tight against him, losing himself in her heat, in the rising tide of intense desire she brought with her.

Jase cleared his throat. "See? I told you she likes kissing you. Are you two going to be doing that all the time, because it's okay with me if you are, just not in the kitchen."

"Yes," Cole said decisively.

"No," Maia assured at the same time. They exchanged a long look. She laughed and rubbed Cole's jaw. "You're looking all serious and stubborn this morning, Steele. I was planning on making gingerbread for a gingerbread house and using the gumdrops in the cupboard for trees. No one can be serious when we bake for Christmas."

"Hey! Those are *my* gumdrops! I made Cole buy them for me, and I'm not giving them up."

"We need them for the gingerbread house. It's part of decorating for Christmas," Maia explained patiently. "We have to use whatever is available and gumdrops work."

Jase held up his hand. "We're not going to eat the gingerbread?"

"No, I'm going to make a really cute house and decorate it with frosting and whatever else I can find."

He shook his head. "She's crazy, Cole. You can't bake bread and not expect us to eat it. You're going too far, Doc. I can do without the cute house, but the stomach demands food and baked goods."

"You aren't getting into the spirit of the season, Jase," Maia pointed out.

"Yeah, and I'm not going to either if you deny me food." He stuffed more toast into his mouth. "And stay away from my gumdrops."

"Don't talk with your mouth full."

Cole poured Maia tea from the teapot he had steeping under a small towel. "Before you start baking gingerbread for houses, would you mind going out to the stable and checking out the horses. See if any of them pass on any memories to you."

Her heart gave a curious flutter. He'd made her tea the exact way she liked it, even adding a small amount of milk. "What are you planning?" She set the teacup on the counter, a slight frown on her face.

There was anxiety in her turquoise eyes. Cole caught her hand, holding it against his side. "It's no big deal if you can't find out any more details," he assured her. "I'm going to shake things up a little regardless and see what happens. I checked, and we've got a short window of opportunity. The weather should clear for Christmas Eve."

"I don't like the sound of that," Maia said. "Opportunity for what? And what are you shaking up?" She tightened her fingers around his. "You aren't going to do anything crazy, are you?"

She looked so afraid for him he bent down to brush the top of her head with a kiss. It was an amazing feeling to have someone worry about him. "I just want you to see if you can give us a little clearer picture, that's all."

"Clearer picture of what?" Jase asked, his eyes bright with curiosity.

Maia expected Cole to hedge, but he didn't. He let go of Maia, to sit across the table from the boy. She picked up her tea and followed.

"I'm beginning to think all these accidents, with the horse, with you, Maia and the ice, even the old man's murder, are all connected. We promised one another we'd be honest. You're not a baby, and I don't intend to hide anything from you. I may be completely off base, but if I'm not, we have a problem on our hands."

Jase went very still. "You think it's Al?"

Cole drummed his fingers on the tabletop. "I don't know about Al. I hope not. He pulled you away from the fence that was giving way, and he's done a good job with the crew and given his best to the ranch."

"He's helped me a lot," Jase said, his voice tight. "No one ever took the time to work with me. I've learned about the horses and cattle, the hay, even repairing fences. He always answers my questions, and he never makes me feel stupid."

"I like the man too, Jase," Cole said. "I honestly don't know one way or the other, but if I'm right about all this, I don't think he could be in on it. If I'm right, his brother-in-law is the perp, and he tried to get you and Al off the ranch."

"I never liked Fred." Jase ducked his head. "I was sometimes afraid it was you, Cole." He confessed it in a soft rush of words. "I'm sorry. I tried not ever to think it, but I can't seem to trust anyone very much."

Cole's smile held no humor. "If anyone can understand, Jase, it's definitely me. I was having the same problem worrying about you. We'll make it through this and whatever else is thrown at us. Together. Maia's right. We can make our own traditions and become a family right here. We've come a long way just by taking back the house."

Jase nodded. "That's true. And it looks great. The doc threw a bunch of pillows on all the furniture in the living room, and it looks completely different. With the tree and Mom's quilt, I feel like the house is really ours."

Maia set her teacup on the table and stood up. "I'm glad you like it, Jase. I'd better get to work if you want me to check the horses in the stable too. I'll see to Wally first, check the horses, then feed the mountain lion. I don't want her scent on me when I'm around the horses."

"I didn't think about that," Jase said.

"You've always got to remember what you're doing around exotics, Jase. You can never become complacent. You can't ever turn your back on them. People have no business owning them and trying to turn them into pets. I've heard of a tiger being kept in an apartment building. It was rescued, but then what do you do with it? Zoos have little funding, and the rescue sanctuaries are full. It leaves euthanasia as the only choice. It makes me angry."

Her gaze met Cole's piercing blue eyes, and she shrugged. "I told you I have a bad temper. Anything to do with the mistreatment of animals brings out the worst in me. It takes so much to run the rescue sanctuaries, and half the time they don't have the funding they need to feed and shelter and provide veterinarian care for exotics."

"Why is it so much, Doc?" Jase asked. "You'd think people would pay to see the animals, and that would provide the money for their care."

"It would be nice if it were that simple, but it isn't. You need licensed people who know what they're doing, an enormous area, and all exotics have special needs. You can't return them to the wild like a lot of people mistakenly want you to do." Maia realized her voice was rising, and she blushed, holding up her hands in surrender. "I'll stop, it's the only safe thing to do."

Cole leaned over to brush her mouth with his. "I like you all fired up. I can see we aren't going to have any hunting on this property anytime soon."

She looked flustered, indignant, a little wary. Maia pulled away from him, glancing at Jase, who was grinning. "Is the weather really going to give us a break tomorrow?"

Immediately the smile left the boy's face. "Not that much of a break, right, Cole? Not enough to get into town."

Cole's expression shut down completely. His shoulders tightened. He drummed his fingers on the table, watching Maia closely. "We could probably get you out if you really wanted to leave before Christmas, Maia. I don't want you to go, and neither does Jase, but if you have somewhere important to go, we'll do our best to get you there."

Jase shook his head hard, his lips pressed tightly together. Maia caught the glitter of tears in his eyes as he turned away from her. The room was suddenly filled with terrible tension.

"Somehow I can't see the two of you taking care of the mountain lion without me." She tried to keep her voice teasing to lighten the situation. Her heart was breaking for them both. A man and boy struggling to be normal when they didn't even know what normal was. She didn't need the pretense from them, and she didn't want it. Deliberately she poked Jase in the ribs. "You'd get eaten, although if Cole doesn't feed you every five minutes, the cat might be in danger."

"It would depend on how hungry I am," Jase said.

"Are you saying you would eat a cat?" Cole lifted his eyebrow, but inside he could feel the tight knots in his stomach beginning to loosen. She wasn't going to leave them. He had a reprieve.

"Ugg, you're a sick, sick man, bro. I wouldn't really."

Maia stood up, pushing back her chair. "I'm off to work; you both behave while I'm gone."

"Actually, we're coming with you," Cole said decisively.

Maia shrugged and picked up her bag. Frankly, she'd feel far better if they did come with her. If Cole was right, and his father had hidden something on the ranch that people felt was worth killing for, she didn't want to run into someone looking for it.

Wally looked much better, and there was no sign of infection. His temperature was normal, and he was moving around the enclosure much more comfortably. Maia fed him his antibiotics with his grain and hay while Jase talked to him at great length.

"He's a natural with animals," she told Cole, seeing the pride on his face as he watched his brother. "If he wants to be a veterinarian, he'll be a good one."

"He's a great kid," Cole agreed, leaning one hand against the wall near her head, effectively caging her between the wall and his body. "And he's smart, Maia. The old man was a complete bastard, but he had brains. Jase is serious about hitting the books. He hasn't gone to a regular school, but he's had the best of tutors. Brett Steele didn't want idiots for sons, and he made certain we were well educated."

"You don't have to convince me, Cole, I can see Jase is smart." She was fairly certain Cole had no idea how proud of his brother he sounded.

"I wanted to thank you, for saying you'll stay through Christmas. He really needs you here." Cole hesitated a moment. He could hear his own heartbeat. "I do too." Had he really said it aloud? Damn, he sounded pathetic. He stood there, blocking her way so she couldn't walk away from him, terrified of losing her when he didn't really have her. When had his feelings changed from wanting to go to bed with her to needing her in his life? How had she wrapped herself inside of him?

Maia stroked a hand down his chest. There were shadows in his eyes, a set to his mouth she didn't quite understand, and she was trained and always alert to read subtleties. More and more he reminded her of the mountain lion, wary, dangerous, in need but ready to strike out if threatened. "I want to stay," she admitted softly.

Desire mingled with relief flared in his eyes. It hit her then. Cole Steele, the invincible, the man always aloof and uncaring, the man with supreme confidence, had very little where she was concerned. She went up on her toes and pressed a kiss onto his chin. "I really wanted to stay and not just because of the cat."

"Or Jase. You're very fond of Jase," he prompted, needing to hear her admission.

She laughed, her eyes warming into a brilliant blue-green. It was all he could do not to sweep her up into his arms and carry her off. Who would have thought one person could impact his life this way, make something he thought he lacked come alive deep inside of him and thrive and grow into such intense emotions.

"You're such a baby. I'm *very* fond of Jase."

He waited. When she didn't continue he stepped closer until her soft breasts pushed against his chest and his hips aligned perfectly with her, pressing against her body. "That's not very nice."

There was a growl to his voice, a sensuality that sent fire zinging through her veins. It was impossible to resist him and she didn't even try. She moved her hips suggestively, a slight feminine enticement, her body soft and welcoming. "I wanted to stay to be with you."

"Was that so hard?" He lowered his lips to hers mostly because he had to, because if he didn't he might really lose his mind and carry her off. The shape of her mouth was incredibly sexy, especially when she flashed her dynamite smile. He was drowning in lust, but more terrifying than that, he could feel love and it was overwhelming. So much so that he dared not examine the emotion too closely.

Maia's arms encircled his neck, her fingers tangling in his hair. "You know it was," she murmured into his hot mouth.

She loved kissing him. Loved touching him. She had no idea where it would lead, if anywhere. Her job kept her traveling constantly and Cole Steele wasn't exactly the settling-down type. She had left herself open for a tremendous amount of pain, and worse, she'd known it before she'd ever gone to his bedroom. It had been her choice. She'd made it willingly, hoping she would think her time with him had been worth it when she had to go.

For a moment she leaned against him, into him, wanting to cling to his strength. All the while he was kissing her, making it impossible to think straight. And she didn't really want to, she wanted the fire flashing through her veins and over her skin. And she wanted the warmth in her heart, filling her until she ached with it.

Jase banged Wally's stall gate closed with a little extra force to remind them he was still in the barn. Maia glanced at him to find him grinning from ear to ear. He shook his head at her.

"I know. He's just irresistible, but we won't mention it because he's already so arrogant we can't take it."

"Speak for yourself, Doc," Jase protested. "He doesn't do a thing for me."

"Come on, you two," Cole said. "I'm letting you clean out the stalls while I feed the horses just for that, Jase," he added.

Jase put his hand on his back and began groaning loudly as he followed them along the covered walkway to the stable.

Cole and Jase fed and watered the horses while Maia wandered around the stable, taking her time, trying to get a feel of the place. It was a beautiful structure, well lit and functional. The horse stalls were roomy, and each led to the wide ring in the center of the building where the horses could be exercised and worked in any kind of weather. Like everything else, the builders had spared no expense, and the setup was as good as it could get.

Maia leaned against the gate of a stall and talked softly to the occupant, waiting for the horse to come to her. She loved horses, loved the way they moved and the way they pressed

their velvet noses into her palm when she murmured to them.
They were always responsive. Most of the horses had memories of packing bundles along a mountain pathway to one of
the larger buildings on the ranch. Two had memories of a
young boy being beaten. The horse in the corner stall had
vivid memories of being ridden hard, quartering the ground
back and forth up in a mountainous area. A shudder ran
through the horse when it recalled the sight of a mountain lion
perched on a branch a distance away, the rifle burst, and the
cat leaping to the ground and disappearing into heavy foliage.

"Are you picking up anything?" Cole asked curiously.

Maia nodded. "But I'm not certain what you're looking for."

"Landmarks, something I can use to identify the area they
were in, rock formations, the type of trees, a mountainous area
versus a valley or a meadow. We have a couple of thousand
acres, and if we include the state and federal lands, we're looking for a needle in a haystack."

"I'll try again, but I can't direct them. I'm sort of a receiver."
She felt she was failing him. The information was obviously
important.

Cole's hand curled around the nape of her neck, his thumb
sliding along her jaw. "Whatever you give me is more than I
had to start with."

"Give me a little more time with this one." She indicated
the horse in the corner stall.

Cole watched as she brushed the animal and spoke softly to
it, spending another fifteen minutes lavishing attention on it.
He waited to ask her about the images until after she had fed
the mountain lion and checked it over thoroughly. She was
mostly worried about infection. The cat stared at Cole and
Jase the entire time, and they kept a good distance away at
Maia's insistence, but behind her back, Cole had a weapon out
and ready if the animal made one wrong move toward Maia.

"I'm telling her," Jase whispered, a grin on his face.

Cole shrugged. "She can learn to live with it," he said, his
jaw set in a stubborn line. "Someone has to look out for her."

Maia stroked a hand through the cat's fur before leaving it to rest, backing out of the shed. "The two of you look as if you're up to some deep dark conspiracy." The truth was, the lines etched so deep in Cole's face were softening, and every once in a while a faint smile would appear. There were times he actually appeared at peace. Even Jase seemed more relaxed and laughed often.

Her heart gave a funny little lurch. She felt a part of them, as if they were all connected in some strange way. As if she belonged. Maia had to look away, tears burning in her eyes. It was ridiculous to be so involved so fast. She could only put it down to the intensity of the Steele brothers' needs. The thought of leaving them was breaking her heart, so she just couldn't think about it. She would have Christmas with them, and that would have to be enough.

"Whatever you're thinking about, stop," Cole instructed, his arm curving around her waist to draw her beneath his shoulder. "You looked so sad." He put his other arm around Jase's shoulders, pulling him closer as well. "I want you to help Maia inside with her baking. I'm expecting you to look after her, Jase."

Maia glanced up at his face quickly. He was moving them both back toward the house at a brisk pace. A small spurt of fear burst through her. "What are you going to be doing?"

"Just looking around a little more. I need for you to tell me if you have any other details for me." He reached past her to open the door to the mudroom.

Maia waited until they were back in the kitchen and she had control of her frantically beating heart. He wasn't going to go looking around a little; he was going to bait a trap for a killer. She feared he was the bait.

"You're shaking your head." His tone was very gentle. "Does that mean you don't have anything for me?"

"No, it means I don't want you to do this. Go to the police."

"I am the police."

Maia sank into a chair. "I know, but you don't have anyone to help you."

"Maia, I would never go into a situation without backup. I'm good at what I do. I trusted you with the mountain lion and the wolves. You'll have to trust me with this."

She flashed him a faint smile. "Should I stand out in the yard with a gun?"

"No, you can stay in here and have faith that I'm really not a nice guy at all." He sat down across from her. "What did you see that could help me?" He glanced at his brother, who was leaning against the counter, his face pale. "I'll need you to listen to her, Jase, and help me figure this out."

The boy took a deep breath and nodded, dropping into the chair next to Maia.

Beneath the table, Maia slipped her hand into the teenager's. "I didn't get much that made sense to me, but I can describe the area fairly well. It's definitely up in the mountains, where there are lots of trees. There are huge rocks and a formation that looks as if it's a fortress. I had the impression of a series of caves."

"Yeah, I've been there," Jase said. "I went one time when the old man was gone on a business trip. I snuck away from the men watching me and got lost. I found a trail off of the streambed, just past where the waterfall is. I followed it because the trail was a little wider than a deer trail and my horse had almost automatically turned on it, as if he'd been there before. I was pretty certain I could find my way back, and eventually I did."

"I remember those old caves. You didn't go into them, did you?"

"No, I was only about nine at the time and pretty scared of all the stories the hands told about bears and mountain lions."

"Which are true," Cole pointed out. He stood up and pushed back his chair. "I'm going to take the snowmobile out while the weather is holding." He glanced at his watch. "I've got about an hour and a half before the next storm breaks."

"I don't like you going out alone," Maia objected, shaking her head adamantly. "Let's just call the police and let them investigate."

"I agree, Cole," Jase said, trying to sound adult and firm. "I don't want anything to happen to you."

"I'm just going to take a look around," Cole said. "Nothing's going to happen to me. You both have to remember, the old man owned this town. The police, the school officials, even the counselors were afraid of him. They needed his money, and he had too much political clout to fight him. I don't know who at the police department I can trust. And if he was smuggling something, especially drugs, he's been doing it for years and getting away with it. That means corruption somewhere."

Maia put her arm around Jase. "An hour and a half, Cole. Give me a number to call, someone you trust, if you don't come back."

He studied her face, set in a determined expression, for a moment before scribbling a number on a tablet beside the phone. "Give me two hours, Maia. I'll be back, I promise."

"You'd better be," she answered.

13

THE SNOW HAD been falling for hours. Maia stared out at the white, silent world. It had seemed so beautiful, a sparkling crystal world, and now it appeared hostile and suffocating. The world outside her window was so white; even though it was nighttime, it appeared light. Through the swirl of flakes she could see the trees and shrubbery encased in ice. Long icicles hung from the overhang of the walkways and decorated the outbuildings. The corrals had layers of snow topping each rail. There was no movement, the world was silent and still as if locked in a frozen time frame.

Cole had come back from his snowmobile ride on time, but his entire demeanor had changed. He hadn't discussed anything with either Jase or her. He'd glanced at their baking project, an elaborate gingerbread house, nodded without really listening to them, and disappeared into an office to spend the rest of the evening on the phone. He was distant and almost frightening, his features expressionless, his eyes hard. He seemed so remote from her, almost as if he were a different person.

"Maia?"

She whirled around, her heart pounding, her hand going protectively to her throat. There'd been no sound to give him away, but Cole stood in the middle of her bedroom wearing only a soft pair of jeans. His face was in the shadows, and he looked intimidating, a man possessing raw power, filling the room with his muscular build and the force of his personality.

"You aren't afraid of me, are you?"

Maia took a deep breath and let it out slowly. She knew wild animals, had been around them in various environments, and she was well aware that Cole's instincts were those of a trapped animal. She could almost smell the danger emanating from him.

"You've put on your DEA persona, the one you use to stay alive," she stated, her gaze meeting his steadily. "Poor Jase was frightened, and, yes, so was I. You become a different person, one neither of us is familiar with."

"Dammit, Maia."

She sent him a faint smile. "If it keeps you alive, Cole, it's all right with both of us. Whatever it takes to do your job, just do it and don't worry about us being a little uncomfortable with it. Jase told me you were this way when he first met you. I don't blame him for being intimidated."

"What do I do?"

"You put distance between yourself and everyone else, and you shut down your emotions."

"I work undercover, Maia. I can't be showing my emotions to the world, and if I discuss anything with anyone, someone might overhear me or be an enemy. That's the world I live in."

"It's the world you've always lived in. As an adult, you simply went out and found the environment most comfortable for you, the one you were familiar with, where you knew all the rules."

He pushed a hand through his hair, his only sign of agitation. "Am I going to lose you because you finally figured out who I really am?"

She smiled, her lips curving into a soft, amused smile that lit up her face. "I've always known who you are, Cole. I knew there was this side of you. It comes out at unexpected times, and it's disconcerting and intimidating, but it isn't anything I can't handle." She shrugged. "You don't know me very well. Most things don't throw me all that easily. I was raised to be my own person, to think for myself and follow my instincts. I can be afraid *for* you and not be afraid *of* you."

"Come here to me."

"You need to talk to Jase. He's too young to understand why you need to withdraw from him." She crossed the distance because she couldn't resist the dark sensuality of his voice. There was something in him she couldn't help but respond to, and tonight he wore that dark intensity she found so compelling.

"I will, Maia," he promised, drawing her into his arms. "I didn't like not having you in my bed."

"I've only been in your bed once, Cole," she pointed out.

"You were there all night. I've never wanted anyone in bed with me all night. I can't sleep because I'm always on edge and feel I have to be alert just in case. I didn't feel that way with you. I wrapped my arms around you and fell asleep. It felt right."

"You didn't do much sleeping."

His hand cupped her face, his thumb sliding over her soft skin. "I'm planning on not sleeping much tonight either."

"Oh really?" She slid her arms around his neck and pressed her body against his. "That's a good thing. Are you going to tell me what you're up to with the snowmobile and phone calls?"

"Later. I'll tell you later." His teeth tugged gently at her ear. "Much later." He slid his hands under the hem of the soft flannel shirt she wore to find bare skin. His hands cupped her bottom, and lifted her to bring her more in line with his own body, holding her there for a moment, savoring the way she fit against him. Her soft body stilled the pounding in his head and tamed the roaring of his nightmares, the terrible memories he could never quite push into oblivion.

Her hands skimmed over his chest, her lips sliding over his neck, his jaw, her teeth nibbling on his lip until he was kissing her, losing himself in her heat. He drank her in, devoured her, needing to be closer to her to keep the demons at bay. "I have too many clothes on," he whispered into her hot mouth.

"Yes you do," she agreed, her hands dropping to the waistband of his jeans.

He felt the brush of her knuckles against his belly, over his hard arousal. Every thought went out of his head but his need to feel her body surrounding his. Heat and flame danced over his skin and invaded his veins, spread through his muscles. Whatever roaring beasts had threatened to consume him with rage and hatred fell quiet under the caress of her stroking fingers, under the assault of her hot mouth gliding over his chest. He was harder than he'd ever been in his life, more in need, his mind crowded with erotic images, with hunger and need that left no room for nightmares.

His hands slid over the curves of her hips, along her thighs, his fingers dipping into the moist heat of her body. He loved the way she responded to him, the way she gave herself so generously to him. She made it clear she wanted to touch him, needed to feel and taste him with the same urgency he felt for her. He slid the flannel shirt from her body and dropped it onto the floor before catching her up in his arms and carrying her to the bed.

"I'm not going to let you go, Maia," he warned, wanting to

be honest, hating to be so damned vulnerable. "I can't let you just walk away from me."

Her fingers skimmed his face, caressed his shoulders, and moved down his back. "Who said anything about going anywhere, Cole? A little action would be appreciated."

"You want action?" His eyebrow shot up, his face darkly sensual.

Maia arched up to press her aching breasts against his chest, to rub the tips of her nipples across his skin while her teeth nipped at his chin. "I'm on fire here."

He felt it then, a wild rush of excitement coursing hotly through his body. She tightened every muscle, brought every nerve ending alive. He wanted to pound into her, drive so deep she could never get him out. Brand her. At once he stiffened. Pulled away from her, sitting up on the bed and wiping his face.

Maia sat up, her arms sliding around his waist. "What is it?"

He shook his head. "You shouldn't be here with me. The things I think about are wrong. There's too much violence in me. I don't want you to get hurt, Maia, not you."

"Do I look fragile to you? I want you just the way you are, Cole. I know what you are and who you are. You just have to figure out I'm quite capable of handling anything you can throw my way. You think you're rough with me, but you're not. You're strong, and the way your body is so frantic for mine only makes me want you more."

"Do you think I don't see the bruises on your skin from my gripping you too tight? Dammit, Maia, I thought I could find some way to be normal with you."

She laughed. "That's just silly. I have bruises every day from the work I do. I'd rather you put them there when you're giving me so much pleasure you're driving me out of my mind."

He should have known she would laugh. He turned his head and met her eyes. Desire, hot and intense and filled with some emotion he shied away from trying to identify. He couldn't stop himself from having her, not when she was so hungry for him. Cole spread her across the bed, coming down on top of her, his hands sliding over silken skin as his mouth settled over hers.

Her thighs tightened and she shifted her hips, aligning her body more perfectly to rub against him in temptation, a siren's call. His palm stroked over her breast, captured it to roll her nipple between his thumb and finger. Her breath caught in her throat, and she arched back, open to him, wanting him. His mouth left hers at the invitation, and he kissed his way over the creamy mound to settle there, fingers stroking and massaging while she cried out, unable to prevent the sound of pleasure from escaping.

"I need you, Maia," he whispered softly.

Maia trembled, shuddering with arousal, lifting herself almost desperately into his mouth. "I need you too." Her hands skimmed over his back, caught at his hips to guide him into her.

His knee nudged her thighs wider apart so that he could easily settle there, pushing into her slowly, penetrating with a deep, long stroke that pushed through velvet-soft petals, forcing her tight muscles to open for him. Immediately he was bathed in tight, hot-silken heat. The breath left his body in a rush, and fire streaked from his toes to the top of his head. She did that. Maia. She did things with her body he still couldn't comprehend.

His hands pinned her hips, holding her firmly, giving him the ability to set the pace and control the ride. He needed that, needed to allow his own driving violence to well up slowly, to mingle with the passion and emotion he felt for her. He began to move harder, deeper, until he was plunging into her over and over as her breathless cries urged him on. Her fingers biting into his buttocks nearly drove him wild. He held on to his sanity as long as he could, pushing her higher and higher, holding off her release until she was writhing beneath him, every bit as desperate as he felt.

When it came, their release was shattering, her body gripping his so tight he thought he'd explode as they came together. They stared into one another's eyes for a long time, then he was kissing her over and over, greedy for the taste of her, needing her sweetness, afraid of saying or not saying the right words to her.

He held her to him, his hand stroking through her hair, aching to say something, anything to make her feel what he was feeling. "Maia?" His heart pounded in a kind of terror. His mouth went dry.

She turned her head and smiled at him. "I'm here."

Her smile always affected him. He dreamt of her smile now. Just as he dreamt of her body open and soft for him, a haven, a refuge he never wanted to give up.

He tried to say the words women needed. He wanted to tell her to stay forever. What did he have to offer her? He was consumed with rage at times. At those times he needed the rush of working undercover. He was driven to find and arrest men who thought themselves above the law, more clever and superior to all others. There were parts of him he was afraid of. A violence he sometimes dealt with by beating a boxing bag for hours, or racing a horse over a mountain trail. So many things he held in little compartments in his mind, deep where no one saw.

Until Maia. She looked through the emptiness in his eyes, somewhere beyond the shadows, and she seemed just to accept him. It was terrifying to think he could be wrong. And if he asked her and she turned away from him, he'd be lost.

Cole sighed. "I found the old man's stash," he confessed. He turned on his side, rising above her to prop himself up on his elbow. He could hear the regret in his voice and knew she would think it was because of his father. "I didn't want to know anything more about him. And I didn't want to have to tell Jase."

"Jase has you now, Cole," Maia said, placing her palm over his heart to comfort him. If anyone needed comfort it was Cole. He just didn't recognize it.

"It wasn't all that hard to find it. When I was a kid I used to go up to that large rock formation, and there was a series of caves. One of them was very small, but when you accessed it, if you crawled to the back, there was a larger chamber. I couldn't find it and I knew immediately the old man had covered it up. I knew approximately where it was, so it didn't take long."

"It was a shipment of drugs?"

"A large shipment. The remains of the pilot were propped up in the back against the wall of the cave like some macabre pirate skeleton left to guard the bundles. I should have known having oil wells, natural gas reserves, and a thriving cattle business wouldn't be enough for the old man. He needed to feel superior. He needed the rush of pitting his brains against law enforcement."

"Maybe you did know what he was doing, or suspected on some level as a child, Cole. You became a DEA agent. Subconsciously you may have been trying to find a way to separate and define yourself."

He bent his head to kiss her. "You say the nicest things, Maia. I don't know how you always think of exactly the right thing to say to make me feel better when I'm feeling low, but you manage it."

She nibbled her way across his jaw to tease at his mouth with her teeth. "I say what I think, which isn't always a good thing, Cole."

"I have to go, honey. I checked with the weather service, and I've only got a few hours to pull this off. Follow me down to the kitchen. I want to show you how to set the alarm." He brushed back her hair, kissing her again and again as if he might not stop, then pulled abruptly away.

Maia followed him to his room and sat on his bed. She sat up, watched him dress, clutching the sheet to her as if that might protect her from the sudden fear she was trying to suppress. He was dragging weapons out of every conceivable hiding place and shoving them into holsters, taping them to his back until she could only stare in horror.

He tossed her his own flannel shirt wishing he could stick around and enjoy her in it. "Come on, Maia. I have to go now." He couldn't look at her much longer and not feel the choking fear of losing her. Facing gunfire and possible death was nothing compared to the terror of being so vulnerable to another human being.

Maia followed him down the stairs, buttoning buttons as she went, trying to look casual and calm, wondering if Cole had felt the same way when she had attended to the mountain lion. She listened dutifully to all his instructions, but when he turned away from her she caught his hand and tugged him back, reluctant to let him go.

"You're coming back."

"Of course." Cole kissed Maia hard. "Turn on the security alarm the moment I leave. All the doors and windows will lock automatically. You know where the safety rooms are. One upstairs and one down. Use them if you have to."

She clutched his fingers, holding him to her. "Don't do anything stupid."

"I'm never stupid, Maia, and I never forget details. Take care of Jase. There's paperwork in the top desk drawer in case of emergencies. My boss has copies. I faxed them to him last night."

"Don't tell me that. Tell me you're going to come back to me all in one piece."

Cole leaned down to kiss her again. "Stay out of trouble and keep Jase occupied. I don't want either one of you to get any ideas about being a hero. When I'm out there, I'm going to treat everyone as the enemy. I can't be worried that you or Jase will get it in your heads to try to help. I might end up shooting one of you."

"I'm not stupid, Cole," Maia assured him. "I'll take care of Jase, but he's not going to like that you snuck out so early."

"He'd want to come, and I don't have a lot of time to spend arguing with him." He glanced at his watch. "The weather will be closing in faster than anticipated. I have maybe three or four hours at the most, then the storm will break again."

"You mean you don't have a lot of time to spend reassuring him," Maia corrected. She let him go because she had no choice. Cole Steele couldn't be anything other than who he was, any more than she could be. "Then I'll see you in three or four hours."

He slipped out the kitchen door into the mudroom to pull on the clothes he'd prepared and slung his pack and rifle over his shoulder before going outside. He wanted to be seen, but look like he was being cautious, wary of anyone who might be watching. He was a man with something to hide. The minute he set foot outside of the mudroom, he became that person, walking with deliberate stealthy intent, casting glances back toward the house as if someone might catch him leaving. He moved in stops and starts, hurrying across open space, stopping in the shadows and behind buildings and trees to look around. It wasn't until he was by the garage housing the snowmobiles that he was certain he was being watched.

The air was cold and dry, the wind coming at him in gusts. He pulled his knitted cap over his face to keep from being burned or frostbitten as he burst out of the garage, the snowmobile swaying wildly, then catching traction to skim over the snow. Maia was right, he realized, as he flew over the snow toward the trail leading into the higher mountains. He should have talked to Jase. If something did happen, this could look bad. He was deliberately setting it up to make others think he was taking the drugs for himself and selling the shipment to the highest bidder.

He shook his head, a frown on his face. That was straight from Maia's mind to his. She was even making him think like her. He had never thought to let anyone into his life to such an extent, but there was no keeping Maia out. She had managed to twist herself deep inside of him until he didn't want her out. She brought him alive in a way he'd never been before.

Cole scanned the surrounding areas, openly using binoculars, wanting those watching him to be aware he was leery. He was a man doing something illegal, and he knew it. He felt an itch between his shoulder blades and sent up a silent prayer it wasn't the scope of a rifle trained on him. He was counting on the fact that Fred and his people had murdered Brett Steele *before* they realized he'd moved the shipment, and they wanted Cole to lead them to it.

He'd never had so much to lose before, and the thought of the danger didn't give him quite the same rush it always had.

He glanced at the sky before setting off again. The clouds were heavy and dark, but the weather was holding. He could have moved the stuff closer to the house, but it might have endangered Maia and Jase. This way, if anyone wanted to take the shipment from him, they had to follow him away from the ranch house, but with the weather so dicey, it was touch-and-go whether he was going to pull the entire thing off and make it back before the next storm hit.

He was able to maneuver the snowmobile up the trail through the rock formation because the snow was so deep. It enabled him to move the sled he was dragging into position at the front of the cave before rolling back the rocks blocking the entrance. He had to use a pry bar as leverage to remove the boulders before crawling inside. This was the most dangerous part. While loading the snowmobile, he would be vulnerable. He was inside the cave and would have to crawl in places to drag out the bundles to stack onto the snowmobile. He wouldn't be able to see or hear an approaching enemy.

Cole worked steadily, sweating as he did so, aware of the least little noise, every moment feeling as though it might be his last. They didn't need him to bring out the shipment, only to lead them to it. He tried to keep his exposure down, keeping as much of the bare foliage between him and open spaces when he came out of the cave to add to the burden on the sled.

When they came, they came like wolves, slinking out of the forest to surround him, guns drawn, Fred leading the pack. He grinned at Cole. "Like father, like son. But I'm afraid that's my dope you're trying to steal."

"It belongs to you?" Cole asked, straightening slowly as he tied off the last bundle. "I don't think so. I don't see your name on it anywhere."

Fred held up his gun. "This is my claim, Steele. Keep your hands where I can see them."

"How'd you know about it?" Cole said, sounding disgusted.

"I helped bring it in before your old man got greedy and moved it. We did it all the time. I have the connections, Steele, you don't. I've got everything in place; you'd just lose it all. You should thank me." He laughed and cocked his gun, pointing it straight at Cole's heart. "You can go join your daddy in hell."

"Hold it, Fred!" The voice came from above them. Al lay stretched out in the snow, the rifle trained on his brother-in-law. "I'm not going to let you kill him, Fred. I don't know what this is all about; but I saw you watching him, sneaking after him, and you're not going to kill him."

"What are you going to do, Al?" Fred snarled. "Choose your almighty boss over your own family? Has he promised you a share if you side with him?"

Cole looked anxiously toward Al. He knew a couple of Fred's buddies were circling around trying to get position on him. The last thing he wanted was his foreman to get killed. "What are you planning, Fred? We can make a deal."

"I had a deal with your old man. He double-crossed us. He sat there in his stinking office surrounded by enough money for a hundred men, but he was so damned greedy. He laughed at me, laughed at all of us. He dared us to go to the police."

"So you put a bullet in his brain."

"You should have seen his face when I pulled the trigger. He was good at killing, but he didn't want to die. I should know, I did enough of it for him."

"But you did it too soon, didn't you, Fred? You didn't know he'd moved the shipment."

Fred shrugged, glanced up toward Al, obviously waiting for his men to pick off his brother-in-law. He scowled, angry they were taking so long and Al still had the rifle rock steady on him. "I thought I'd have time to find it, but you fired us all."

Cole smiled at him. "Smart of me, wasn't it? How long were you killing and running drugs for the old man? You the one who killed Jase's mother?"

"She kept trying to take the kid. He wasn't going to let her do that. She should have known better."

"So you arranged the accident? How'd you manage all this time to get away with it?" Cole made a small movement toward the snowmobile.

Fred brought his gun up. "Don't be stupid, Steele."

"Don't you be stupid, Fred," Al said.

"I've been getting away with things a long time. You just need a few key people in your pocket," Fred bragged. "Put the rifle down, Al, or my sister is going to be a widow. Do it now."

"You're under arrest. All of you. Put your guns down," Cole said. "Right now you're surrounded by federal marksmen with rifles trained on every one of you. Drop your weapons now." Cole sent Fred a grim smile. "I'm with drug enforcement."

"What the hell are you talking about?" Fred whipped his head around wildly, looking for his crew. He caught a glimpse of several of his men down on the ground, others clothed in all white standing over them and holding rifles to the backs of their necks. "You've been in jail. What are you, a snitch?"

Cole walked across the scant feet of snow separating them and removed the gun from Fred's hand. "You bought a cover story, Fred." He pushed the man toward one of the officers. Flakes of snow were already drifting from the skies.

Al stood up slowly, rifle at his side. "This is going to kill my wife. I'm sorry, Mr. Steele. I had no idea what he was up to."

"He wanted you to think I drove that horse into the fence. It was to get you and Jase off the ranch so he could search it."

"I figured that out. He was watching you all the time. I didn't ever consider drugs might be a part of it. I just thought he was mad over losing his job."

"Thanks for coming after me."

Jase sat white-faced at the table as Cole told him about the drug shipment, the murder of the pilot and the boy's mother. The teenager went very still, tension and anger radiating from him. Abruptly he rose and without a word, ran out of the kitchen into the mudroom. They could hear him stamping into his boots.

Cole sighed and stood up. "I'd better follow him."

He looked tired and strained. Maia went to him, put her arms around him. "At least you both know what really happened to Brett. You don't have to wonder about it anymore. And neither of you has to worry about the other's having been involved in that violent act."

His hand slipped over her silky hair, but Cole didn't answer. There was no way to tell her how deep rage could go. How it could consume one and eat away every good thing until there were only nightmares and demons left in the world. Jase had to fight it the same way he did.

Maia watched him go before sinking down into the chair Jase had vacated, hands over her face, weeping for both of them. She cried for a long while, and, when they didn't return, she washed her face and went after them. It was instinct more than anything else that led her in the right direction. Before she reached the barn she could hear the rhythmic pounding of flesh against something solid.

"Jase!" Maia stopped in the doorway of the barn staring at him with horror. "What are you doing to yourself?"

Jase slammed his bloodied hands into the heavy bag repeatedly. "I hate him. He's taken everything from me. *Everything*!"

"Jase." There was a wealth of warning in Cole's voice.

Maia glanced at Cole, saw the misery and despair in his eyes as he crouched against the wall, watching his little brother rage at things neither of them could control.

"Stop it right this minute!" She used her most authoritative voice. It startled both men so that Jase dropped his arms to his sides and stood breathing heavily, small droplets of blood trickling down his knuckles to the floor. She moved into the barn, marched straight over to Jase, and took his hands in hers to prevent further action.

"He took your mother, and he took your childhood, Jase. You have a right to be angry about that," she said, turning his bloodied, swollen hands over to examine them much more closely. "But doing this to yourself is just plain stupid."

"Yeah, well, you don't have a father who murdered and ran drugs and abused animals and every other thing he could get his hands on," Jase snapped, snatching his hands away. "He didn't beat you and brand you and humiliate you, and he didn't kill your mother."

Cole stood up, a flow of strength and power, instantly protective of Maia.

She didn't look at him as she stepped closer to them. "Jase," she kept her voice low and even. "You persist in thinking Brett Steele was normal. He was ill. I don't know if something made him that way, or whether he just deteriorated into his sickness. Power can corrupt. He was a genius. You both know that, and you inherited his brains and his strengths. He wasn't all bad. There were good traits in him. He can only destroy your life if you let him."

"What if I'm like him? I could be like him," Jase said.

Of course he would have the same fears as Cole. She glanced at the older man, and he immediately put his hand on Jase's shoulder.

"I thought the same thing, Jase," Cole admitted. "About me, about you. Hell, we share the same genetics. But you're nothing like him, even less so than I am. Look how good you are with animals. And you hit the books instead of turning out to be the resident bad boy. I'd put your sanity and your character ahead of those of anyone I know."

"What he did is no reflection whatsoever on you as a human being, Jase. You have your own life and your own responsibility to live your life in the best way that you can. Of course your childhood will impact your adult life, but you're aware of it and can take steps to counter any demons that arise. You're strong and you're smart and you can handle anything that comes your way."

Jase shook his head, tears glittering in his eyes, spilling over to run down his cheeks. His chest heaved, and his shoulders shook. "I don't think I can ever be okay again, Maia."

She gathered him into her arms, pressing his face into her

shoulder while she held him. The teenager sobbed as if his heart was breaking. She looked desperately up at Cole.

Cole swept his arms around both of them. "We're going to make it, Jase," he reassured, rubbing the boy's neck, crowding close so Jase would feel his determination and strength. "We're going to be all right together."

14

"IT'S MIDNIGHT, OFFICIALLY Christmas," Maia announced. She rubbed the top of Jase's head as she set a tall glass of cider on the coffee table in front of him. "Merry Christmas."

Jase was much calmer, sitting in the living room and staring at the tall tree. His mother's ornaments adorned the tree, and he stared at the alligator. Maia twisted the tail and watched the jaws open and close around a strand of popcorn. She was rewarded with a faint smile from Jase.

"When do we get to open gifts?" he asked. His voice was gruff, husky with leftover tears, but he had his emotions back under control.

"Usually Christmas morning," Maia answered, curling up on the couch beside Cole. "Although some people open them on Christmas Eve." She leaned over to check the ice packs she'd placed on his hands. "Keep those there. It's a wonder you didn't break all your bones."

"I can't exactly drink my cider if I've got this stuff wrapped around my hands," Jase pointed out. There was a flash of a smile in the look he exchanged with Cole.

"Then you can just stare at the cider," Maia said, "but you keep your hands in those wraps. You're lucky I didn't chase you around the house with a needle to give you a tetanus shot at the very least."

"You did," Jase reminded her. "Cole had to save me. You threatened to numb my knuckles too or something equally scary." He looked at his older brother. "Do you do that a lot? Go undercover and have guns pointed at you?"

"Yes." Cole refused to lie or gloss over his job to Jase.

"Have you ever been shot?"

"Twice, and I was stabbed a couple of times. Just like when Maia works with the animals, she has to watch herself, never forget even for a moment what she's doing; my job is the same. I can never get careless."

"How did you get all those agents here?"

"It wasn't easy. I couldn't go to the local police because I didn't know who was dirty or who could be trusted. I called my boss, and we set the trap fast."

"You took a big risk," Maia said. Cole had been away from them for the four hours he'd indicated he would be, and the agents had spent several more hours trying to get the prisoners and the shipment of drugs off the ranch. The storm had moved in slowly, and with Al and Cole working together, they'd finally managed to get everyone out safely. Maia had spent hours wanting to be alone with Cole, needing to touch him, to reassure herself that he was unharmed, but then Jase had broken down completely, and they had spent the remainder of the time consoling him.

"The weather was closing in, and it worried me that Fred was getting anxious. I didn't want either of you caught in the middle. And remember, I didn't know whose side Al was on. I'm glad it was ours."

"Are you going to go away, Cole?" Jase finally voiced the question that was preying on his mind.

For the first time, Cole hesitated. Maia and Jase regarded him with wide, fearful eyes. Cole leaned over the table toward his brother, avoiding looking at Maia. "Jase, I want to tell you I'm always going to be here, but that would be a lie. I have to work sometimes. I won't be working as much, but every now and then, I need to work." It was the adrenaline rush. It was the rage that swirled too close to the surface that was never going to go completely away. He hoped he wouldn't need it as much, but he knew he'd never be utterly free of his demons, and if Maia was going to agree to be in his life, he needed both Jase and her to know he would have times he couldn't help but leave them.

"You have money. You can have my money," Jase burst out.

"That's not what he means," Maia said gently. "He means when things are really bad for him, working undercover is a way of sorting it out."

Jase just stared at her, hurt and fear mingling together in his eyes.

"Like you pounding the bag," she added. "He goes undercover and becomes someone else for a while. Does that make sense?"

Cole wanted to protest, but she was right. It was a world he was familiar with. Lies and deceit and never getting too close. A world of violence, where explosive rage often had a legitimate target. He was going to lose here. He could see the handwriting on the wall, and it was killing him.

Jase subsided, shrinking back into the chair, making himself very small as he turned to Cole. "Are you planning on putting me in a boarding school so you can go back to the drug enforcement work?"

"No! Absolutely not. Why would you think that, Jase? I want you to attend a regular school, but not a boarding school." Cole shoved both hands through his hair. "This is crazy. My work has nothing to do with you going to school. If I have to leave on an assignment, I'll have someone who you trust stay here with you. Someone I trust that we're both comfortable with. I'm not going anywhere until that happens."

Jase took the ice packs off his hands and grabbed a handful of cookies. "Well, I'm not going to worry about it then. It's not like we have anyone else."

"I told you, we're getting a housekeeper. I just haven't found one yet." There was a warning note in Cole's voice.

Jase shrugged. "You scare everyone, Cole. I don't have to worry about anyone coming here to work in the house unless she's after your money."

Maia hastily covered her mouth with her hand and looked away from them. They sounded more and more like brothers every day.

"Don't encourage him, Maia," Cole said.

She didn't even wince at the hard edge to his voice. Her smothered laughter rang out from behind her hand before she could stop it. "I'm sorry, really I am, but you so deserved that one. You need to practice smiling in the mirror, Cole. It will help you win over the ladies."

"He doesn't have to smile at women," Jase reminded with a wicked grin.

"Put the ice packs back on your hands and stop eating so many cookies," Cole said. He reached under the coffee table and pulled out a small object. "Here's your Christmas present." His voice turned gruff and it embarrassed him, but he persisted with a dogged determination. "I don't know exactly how this is done, and I didn't wrap it, but I made this for you, Jase." His fingers remained wrapped around it, concealing the object. "You know I'll get you something nice from town once we can get out of here, but I wanted you to have something on Christmas morning."

"Let me see it," Jase said eagerly, holding out his swollen hand.

Cole placed the wood carving in his brother's hand. A snarling mountain lion was crouched protectively over a small alligator. The carving was intricate, each curve and line smooth and etched deep so that the figures seemed to be alive. Jase turned it over and saw the date carved into the bottom.

"It's the two of you, isn't it?" Maia asked, taking the carving out of Jase's hand to stroke her finger down the cat's back. "You and Jase. That's what it represents."

"It's all of us," Jase corrected. "You, me, my mom, and Cole."

Maia handed the carving back to him. "It's beautiful, Cole. You're an unbelievable artist. I had no idea."

"It looks so real," Jase said. "Thanks, Cole."

Cole let his breath out slowly, a small smile somewhere inside of him. Jase understood what he was trying to say with the carving, and more than anything else, that mattered.

"I have something for you too, Jase," Maia said. "It's not nearly as nice as what Cole made for you, but you might be able to use it." She pulled a book out from under the cushions of the couch. "It's a book on animal behavior. I learned a lot from it, and as you can see, it's been well used, but I thought if you were really interested in becoming a vet, you'd enjoy it."

Cole put his arms around Maia. He'd never heard her sound quite so vulnerable, her words spilling out too fast. The book had to have meant a great deal to her, and she wanted Jase to feel the same way.

Jase opened it, read what she had written, and smiled. "We did share a journey, didn't we, Maia? Look at this, Cole. Maia's mother gave this to her."

"I was about ten," she admitted. "All I could think about were animals. My poor parents had to put up with me constantly bringing home hurt things."

"You still do that," Cole said, "or maybe they just gravitate to you."

"Thanks, Maia." Jase nudged his brother.

"Jase and I have a present for you," Cole said. He pulled an envelope from his pocket and held it out to her.

Maia opened the seal slowly and took out the card. She blinked several times trying to make sense of the lettering. "I don't understand." Her heart was pounding out of control. She swallowed several times, before raising her gaze to Cole's.

"You own the clinic," Jase said eagerly. "It belongs to you. You don't have to go away now."

Cole gazed at her steadily, not blinking or looking away, compelling her toward the unknown. Maia blinked rapidly to break the spell. He was so deep inside of her she could hardly breathe without him. The feeling was too strong, too fast, and she didn't entirely trust it.

"But I can't take this. I can't possibly accept this." Maia shoved the card back into Cole's hand. "You know I won't, Cole."

"You have to accept it," Jase said. "If you don't, you'll ruin the rest of it."

"The rest of what? There can't possibly be anything more. Are you two crazy? You can't go buying a clinic for me. I love you both dearly for the gesture, but I'm not going to accept it."

Cole sat there, staring into her eyes, his face hard and etched with lines of suffering. "The part where we ask you to stay. The part where I ask you to marry me."

Her heart sounded like thunder in her ears. For a moment she thought she might actually faint. He looked so alone, so prepared for her refusal of him that she ached with a need to give herself to him. She didn't dare look at Jase, but she knew he would have a similar expression of need on his face.

"Why, Cole?" She moistened dry lips with the tip of her tongue. "So when you need to go away you'll have someone you trust here with Jase?" It didn't matter that she loved him so much. She couldn't live with him knowing he didn't return her feelings. She knew she could love Jase always, be a good mother or sister and friend to him, but she didn't want to be a convenience. She had far more respect for herself than that.

Cole groaned inwardly. He should have known it would look like that to her. Maybe it was part of it, maybe it was all wrapped up in needs and hunger and longing for a home and a family. He took her hand, his rough fingers sliding over her soft skin, his thumb caressing her ring finger. "I don't want to be without you."

"How can you possibly know whether you do or you don't, Cole?" Maia was going to cry. She hated crying, and her reaction was generally to strike out at whoever managed to cause the tears.

Cole felt her trembling. "I know because I know the difference between living in hell, and being alive in paradise. I don't want to lose what you've given me. I *feel* all the time when I'm with you. The entire range of emotions. Happiness, sadness, exasperation, even anger. All of it. I've never had that before. I want you to be happy, Maia. I watch every single expression that crosses your face. I watch you with Jase, with the animals. I think about you day and night. I want to go to bed at night with you beside me, and I want to wake up with you in my arms. I've never felt that way about anything or anyone before."

"You can't leave us, Maia," Jase burst out.

"Jase needs you almost as much as I do," Cole added, feeling on the verge of desperation. She was blinking back tears, and he had the feeling she was going to pull away from him at any moment. He slid a ring from his pocket, a circle of brilliant diamonds to slide on her ring finger. "Jase found the perfect Christmas present for me, and gave it to me ahead of time. I want to give it to you."

"Cole," she warned, shaking her head, looking down at the ring. She'd never seen anything like it, and it had to be worth a fortune. "Where in the world did you get this, Jase?"

"It was in the box with my mother's things," Jase said in a low voice.

"Oh, my God, you cannot give this to me. You have to keep it for the woman you marry," Maia said, turning her head to look at him.

It was a mistake. The boy had tears in his eyes. He immediately reached out, putting his hand over hers and Cole's. "I gave it to Cole because it was all I had to give him. He needs you. He's different around you. Relaxed and happy, and he smiles. I'd never seen him smile until you came to be with us. And I need you too. Don't leave us, Maia."

She took a deep breath. It was overwhelming to be caught between the two of them, their dark secrets and their dawning hope. "There's more to being married and relationships than need. If I stayed, and it wasn't right, eventually it would all fall apart. You both know that." She wanted love. She deserved love. As much as she loved them both, she would not be cheated.

"Maia." Cole caught her chin and forced her to look at him.

"I'll be the first to admit I don't have a lot of pretty words to make this right. I don't know the first thing about how to tell a woman she's my entire world, but that's what you are to me. You're not someone I want as a housekeeper for Jase, but if I could choose a woman to be a mother figure, a sister, a friend for him, then it would be you."

"What do you want for yourself?"

"I want a woman who loves me in spite of all my failings. A woman who understands when I have nightmares and do things she might be afraid of. I want you, Maia. I don't even know when I fell in love with you. I just know that I am in love with you."

For a moment she could hardly believe he'd said the words. She'd wanted to hear them so badly, she was afraid it was a trick of her imagination. The wild pounding in her heart began to subside and she could feel peace stealing into her. "Funny thing, Steele," she said, "I feel *exactly* the same way about you."

Cole sat in shocked silence, afraid to move or speak. Afraid of breaking the spell. Someone, a long time ago, told him miracles happened on Christmas. He was terrified of believing it.

"I'm very much in love with you."

Jase hissed out a breath between his teeth. "You two are making me want to pull out my hair! Cole, you should have told her you loved her right away. Maia just say yes, so I can breathe again. I'm having an asthma attack and trying not to die while you two figure it out."

"Yes," Maia said.

Cole dragged her into his arms and kissed her. She fit there, fit him. Understood him. He had no idea how it had happened, but the how and why didn't matter, only that she loved him.

A noise drew his attention and he turned to find Jase waving his arms, wheezing, desperate to breathe.

"You weren't joking," Cole said. "Where's your inhaler?" He searched through the pockets of Jase's shirt. Jase pointed frantically toward the kitchen, and Cole sprinted away.

"Calm down, Jase," Maia added, taking his hand. "It's going to be all right. We're all going to be fine."

Cole was back, handing the boy the inhaler and watching with a slight frown on his face as Jase used it. "Next time, don't be fixing my problems until you're safe, Jase. I should have been watching you more carefully."

Jase took a deep breath and smiled at his brother. "Someone has to look after you and Maia. You're really not all that good with the women, Cole. I know more than you do about romance. And you'd better smile at her *a lot*."

Maia laughed. The sound filled Cole with joy. He looked around the house. His home. It belonged to them now. Maia, Jase, and Cole. It was their home. The fire burned brightly and filled the room with warmth and comfort. The Christmas tree filled it with fragrance.

"You know, Jase," Cole said. "I think Christmas is going to be our favorite holiday."

"I think you're right," Jase said with complete satisfaction.

The two brothers looked at Maia, and she threw her arms around them. "I knew you'd see it my way," she said happily.

EPILOGUE

FOUR YEARS LATER

COLE SAT IN his parked truck watching the people hurry along the streets, carrying brightly wrapped packages and waving cheerfully to one another. The stores were heavily decorated, as were the streetlights and even one or two of the trees in front of the shops. The tall fir in front of the veterinarian clinic was a masterpiece, with lights and ornaments and a blazing star on the top, courtesy of Maia.

He could hear music blaring out of the clinic, a wild rendition of "Jingle Bells." That was so like Maia. The clinic was closed, but people were going in and out carrying boxes of food and presents to cars. As always, she headed up the drive to take dinners and gifts to the less fortunate, and she'd managed to rally quite a crew to help her.

He couldn't wait to see her, to watch the way her eyes lit up when she first saw him, to see her smile blossom and hear her laughter. He ached to hold her, to feel her skin against his and he could already taste her kiss. Sometimes, when he was away from her, he woke up with the taste of her in his mouth. He'd been gone two months this time. It was the longest they'd ever been apart, and he'd felt every second of the separation. He'd never stay away that long again. He needed his family far more than he needed the outlet of his undercover work. He would still continue it, but he would not take a job where he would be separated from them for so long. He'd learned, in his long absence, that they were his balance and sanity.

A part of him was afraid of his welcome. Afraid that smile, the light in Maia's eyes wouldn't be there for him this time. His hands gripped the steering wheel, thinking about losing her, losing what he had because he could never quite rid himself of the demons that plagued him his entire life.

He heard laughter and turned his head to see the two little girls running up the street, clutching at Jase's hands, dragging him toward the clinic. Their dark hair, so like his, was shiny and bobbed as they ran. His three-year-old twin daughters had Maia's deep blue-green eyes and her smile. He loved the sound of their laughter. He still couldn't believe he had daughters. Beautiful twins who climbed all over him and kissed him every chance they got. Maia had given him that gift.

Observing Jase with his daughters brought a lump to his throat. His brother had grown into everything he'd hoped. He was tall and strong, his gangly frame filled out. He carried himself with confidence. The shadows that had always been present in his eyes were replaced with contentment. He had friends and did extraordinarily well in school. Maia had managed that as well. She'd had him working daily in the clinic with her, taking him on ranch calls and teaching him her craft, encouraging him in school and, more importantly, bringing him a sense of family.

Cole slid from the truck, knowing he was going to have to go in and face his fate. Unlike Jase, he knew he would never be rid of the past. He would awaken in a cold sweat, Maia in his arms, her voice soothing, her body soft and inviting, always ready to take away the nightmares. He loved her so much he ached with it, yet he couldn't always stay. No matter how hard he tried to hide it, Maia always saw the demons growing in him.

It was always Maia who put her arms around him and told him to go. "It's okay," she would whisper, kissing her way up his back to the nape of his neck. "Do what you have to do and come back to us." She never cried, and she never chastised him or made him feel guilty. She was Maia, offering him freedom with love in her eyes. And he always returned because he couldn't live without her.

But as he opened the door to the clinic, his heart pounded with fear. If she rejected him, his life was over. He knew that, knew he needed her more than most men needed their wife and lover. She gave him acceptance and understanding when he didn't have it himself. She taught her daughters that same acceptance and understanding of his shortcomings, and she'd taught it to Jase.

The music greeted him as the door swung open. Someone bumped into him, laughed, and called out a merry Christmas. He just kept walking through the outer office, down the decorated hall to the back room, where the operation of filling boxes was taking place. Dread was growing, a dark ugly feeling he couldn't stop. All around him were the signs of Christmas, of happiness overflowing. He walked with confidence, but deep inside, where no one saw, he was screaming inside.

"Daddy!" Ashley screamed his name and rushed him, a

small dynamo, throwing her arms around one leg, effectively stopping him.

Mary cried out and followed her twin, twining her arms around the other leg.

Cole reached down for them, his heart nearly bursting as he picked the girls up and settled them on his hips, kissing them over and over, but all the time his attention was on her. On Maia. He heard Jase's greeting. Felt the boy clap him on the back, and he returned the awkward hug. But it was Maia he watched. Maia he waited for.

She turned slowly, as if she were afraid to believe it was true. Her gaze settled on his face. He held his breath. There it was. That slow smile of joy that lit up her eyes, brightened her face. Tears shimmered. The tears that were never there when he left but always there when he returned.

"You're home."

He handed the twins to Jase. "I'm home." He gathered her into his arms and found her mouth with his. She fit close to him, her arms winding tightly around his neck, her mouth every bit as demanding as his. He tasted her sweetness. He tasted acceptance. Desire. Most of all he tasted love. He felt weak with joy, with relief. Maia was his rock, his foundation. His very life.

"Get a room." Jase and the twins chimed in together, something they did often around Maia and Cole.

Maia laughed, resting her head on Cole's chest. "You made it home for Christmas."

"I'd never miss Christmas. Did you put up the tree already?" He held his breath again. It was silly to want to choose the tree, not when there were only three days left.

"We never break tradition," Jase answered. "It wouldn't be the same without you."

Maia just burrowed closer to him, her arms sliding around his waist. Cole looked at his brother over her head, and they smiled. They had a home. A family. And they had love. If that wasn't a Christmas miracle, nothing was.

❧ Acknowledgments ❧

I have to thank Dr. Lisa Takesue of Main St. Veterinarian Clinic for her unfailing patience when I asked veterinarian questions and, most especially, Tory Canzonetta, a federally licensed trainer at Destiny Big Cat Sanctuary, a last-stop haven for exotic cats. Visit the website at www.destinybigcats.com and see the beautiful tigers and other cats! Tory rescues exotic cats and keeps them safe and healthy. She gave me so much information and opened her heart and sanctuary to me for research.

I love to hear from readers. Please feel free to visit my website, www.christinefeehan.com, and join my members-only private e-mail list to receive free screen savers, view teasers, and receive new-release announcements of my books.

Christine Feehan

recently took time from her busy writing schedule to talk to us. Here are the highlights of that conversation.

What inspired you to write *The Twilight Before Christmas,* a novella about a family of witches during the holiday season?

I loved growing up in my family. I have ten sisters. And yes, they are all biological. We had an amazing childhood. Our friendships with one another were, and remain, very strong. Christmas was my favorite time of the year. My uncle was in a wheelchair, and he lived with us. He made Christmas an exciting and special holiday. We collected ornaments from around the world, and to this day I keep that tradition, as do my children. I think loving my sisters and feeling that when we are together there is a special magic, first brought the idea of writing about a family of very magical sisters into my head. All of us have different talents as well as different trials, and we're strong women . . . but when we're together, we're at our strongest. We see one another through every difficult time and every joyous occasion. And we all love to come together at Christmas!

Kate Drake, the heroine of *The Twilight Before Christmas,* is a bestselling author. Readers can't help but wonder how much you modeled her after yourself. Any similarities?

Maybe a few. Kate does things she doesn't think she can do and she doesn't consider herself courageous. I think I started out the same way, believing I couldn't do things, although martial arts definitely changed that in me. But Kate Drake and I share a love of books. My all-time favorite thing to do is curl up in a chair and read a book by my favorite author, or to read a great new find. I'm a reader, and I read everything. I love the written word, and if I could sit in the old mill coffee shop or down on the beach and read, I'd be very content. Kate is more of a composite of two of my sisters and a wonderful, bestselling author, Jayne Ann Krentz, who I thought of often as I wrote this story. I even pictured her in the role of Kate. I've often curled up with Jayne's book and escaped into another world, and it was easy to imagine her as Kate writing her wonderful books for me to read.

Your martial art expertise is fascinating. Can you tell us how old you were when you started training, why you started training, and the level of your ability today?

I started training when most women didn't do martial arts, so in the early years I trained mostly with men. I had always been interested in karate as an art form, the beautiful and powerful katas and, of course, I wanted the benefits of gaining more confidence in myself. I loved the discipline and philosophy of the various arts and studied many of them. I was lucky enough to train under a wonderful man in the Korean art of Tang Soo Do and I hold a third degree black belt in that art. I also hold rank in several other disciplines as well. I taught self-defense to women and martial arts to both men and women and helped with battered women seminars and various other projects to empower women. Martial arts became a way of life for me, one I believe in and highly recommend. I had to retire due to my health a few years ago, but the training I received has enabled me to write realistic action scenes and to develop real characters in difficult situations. My training allowed me to spend a great deal of time around a certain type of alpha male so I developed an understanding of how they act and react when they are attacked or encounter physical danger. And no, it is not always the way our society would prefer them to do so!

No doubt there's a touch of magic in the Feehan household during the holiday season. Are the Feehan family's celebrations anything at all like the Drake sisters' holiday festivities?

Yes, very much so. Christmas is one of the biggest events of the year for my family. Everyone comes home. It's a time we look forward to throughout the year. Our Christmas celebration is huge. My mother has a very large two-story house (and it is needed!) and we all gather there on Christmas Eve. My brothers and sisters are married and have children of their own. My parents have seventy-two grandchildren. The house has high ceilings, and the top of the tree touches the ceiling. My sisters have a traditional party just before Christmas to decorate, and the ornaments are blown glass from all over the world! You can imagine the number of gifts beneath the tree. There's always music and laughter, and my mom loves candles, so the scent is wonderful! Several sisters love to bake, so we have tons of wonderful desserts. Everyone brings an enormous amount of food. Wineglasses have been handed down from generation to generation and the glasses are brought out and we toast the coming seasons and any new babies in the family! Usually at some point a cat runs up the tree. Dogs mill around. We play Ping-Pong and cards and other games. We tell stories and open gifts. And we often attend midnight mass together.

Do you have a favorite holiday tradition you perform every year?

Yes, we always decorate a live Christmas tree. The children love decorating the tree, as I've collected ornaments over the years. I get teased about my ornaments because the children think I have too many! And my husband says I have too many lights to go with my too many ornaments. We spend hours decorating the tree. There's a lot of laughter, but mostly at my expense! The children spend hours playing "I spy" with the ornaments. When Christmas is over, we plant the tree in the yard. My family thinks I have a tree fetish as well as an ornament fetish. We always watch my husband's favorite Christmas film, *It's a Wonderful Life,* together as well. Then the children all tease him instead of me!

What is your favorite holiday tune?

"I'm Dreaming of a White Christmas."

Okay, this is a "revealing" interview, so would you please tell us whether you and your family open presents on Christmas Eve or Christmas Day?

My father is a retired fireman and usually worked Christmas Day, so it became a tradition to always open the gifts Christmas Eve. We've continued that, going to my parents' house and spending Christmas Eve with them, and then opening gifts at the Feehan house very early the morning of Christmas Day. The floor is covered with paper, and there's a lot of laughter and teasing!

And who cooks Christmas dinner?

My husband Richard is a fabulous cook and he always cooks Christmas dinner. Some of the grown children bring side dishes, but for the most part, he plans, shops, and cooks the entire thing!

Getting back to your professional life, what prompted you to become a writer?

I believe I was born a writer. I honestly can't remember a time in my life when I didn't write. I used to make up stories as a child, and my sisters would have to listen. Once I could write my brilliant masterpieces down on paper (and they were truly awful) my sisters would read them all dutifully. Writing is a part of me, just like breathing. I can't imagine not writing. When the day comes that I am no longer published, I will still be writing!

Critics and reviewers hail you as one of the most imaginative authors writing today. Where do you get your ideas? And why do you choose to write stories with Gothic elements and paranormal characters?

I love action and very edge-of-the-seat creepy suspense, both in movies and in books. I wanted to be able to combine that with my love of romance and happy-ever-after endings. I also am very intrigued with the paranormal and with myths and legends that have persisted throughout the history of the world, in every country. What better way than to combine them all and write what I love to read? As for my ideas and where I get them—everywhere! Everything I see, or hear, newspaper articles on some strange happenings. It can be something small like the way a woman turns her head, or more intense, such as a freak fog moving into a town that never has fog! My imagination doesn't need much help to take flight.

What was the biggest challenge in writing *The Twilight Before Christmas*?

In all honesty, it was finding the time. I had the town, the characters, and the legacy of the Drake sisters already firmly in my mind. I did research on symbols and settlers and even the history of Christmas, but I had wanted this story, all the Drake stories, to be incredibly magical. To do that, I had to find the time. I stayed in a wonderful little house on the coast and wandered up and down the coastal highway to really get the right feel before I began writing the actual story.

You strongly evoke the atmosphere of a California coastal town in *Twilight*. Have you ever lived in a town like the fictional Sea Haven?

I grew up in a small town very close to the California coast and have lived much of my life in or near a small coastal town. I love the atmosphere and have so many pleasant memories of my mom and my sisters and me walking along the wooden sidewalks and enjoying the year-round flowers growing wild. Herds of wild elk populate the area, and the beaches are wonderful. Seals are in the water, and you can whale watch during certain times of the year. I love the fishing villages and have favorite restaurants I enjoy.

Will readers see more of the Drake sisters in the future?

I certainly hope so! I love the Drake family. In fact I really enjoy all the characters in Sea Haven. Yes, I have plans to give each sister her own unique story.

Finally, is there one special wish you would like to have come true this Christmas?

It sounds sappy to say Peace on Earth, but it sure would be wonderful.

And this interview wouldn't be complete if I didn't ask: How *do* Carpathians celebrate Christmas?

The Carpathians have their own traditions, but as for Christmas, they only began celebrating that holiday recently. Raven Dubrinsky, lifemate to the Prince, was an American and loved Christmas very much. She invited her family and friends to the Dubrinsky home this year. Antoinetta Justicano agreed to make the trip with Byron to play the piano for everyone so they could all sing time-honored carols. Raven had fun insisting that Mikhail decorate the tree using human methods and he ended up wrapping the Christmas lights around the tree, around himself, and around the furniture. Each Carpathian made an ornament to adorn the first Carpathian Christmas tree and mark the occasion. They came from all over to sing and celebrate and join in the festivities. If they had one wish to make on the Drakes' snowglobe, it would be that their women could bring babies safely into the world to live and thrive!

Merry Christmas from the Feehans, the Drakes, and all the Carpathians!

Christine Feehan